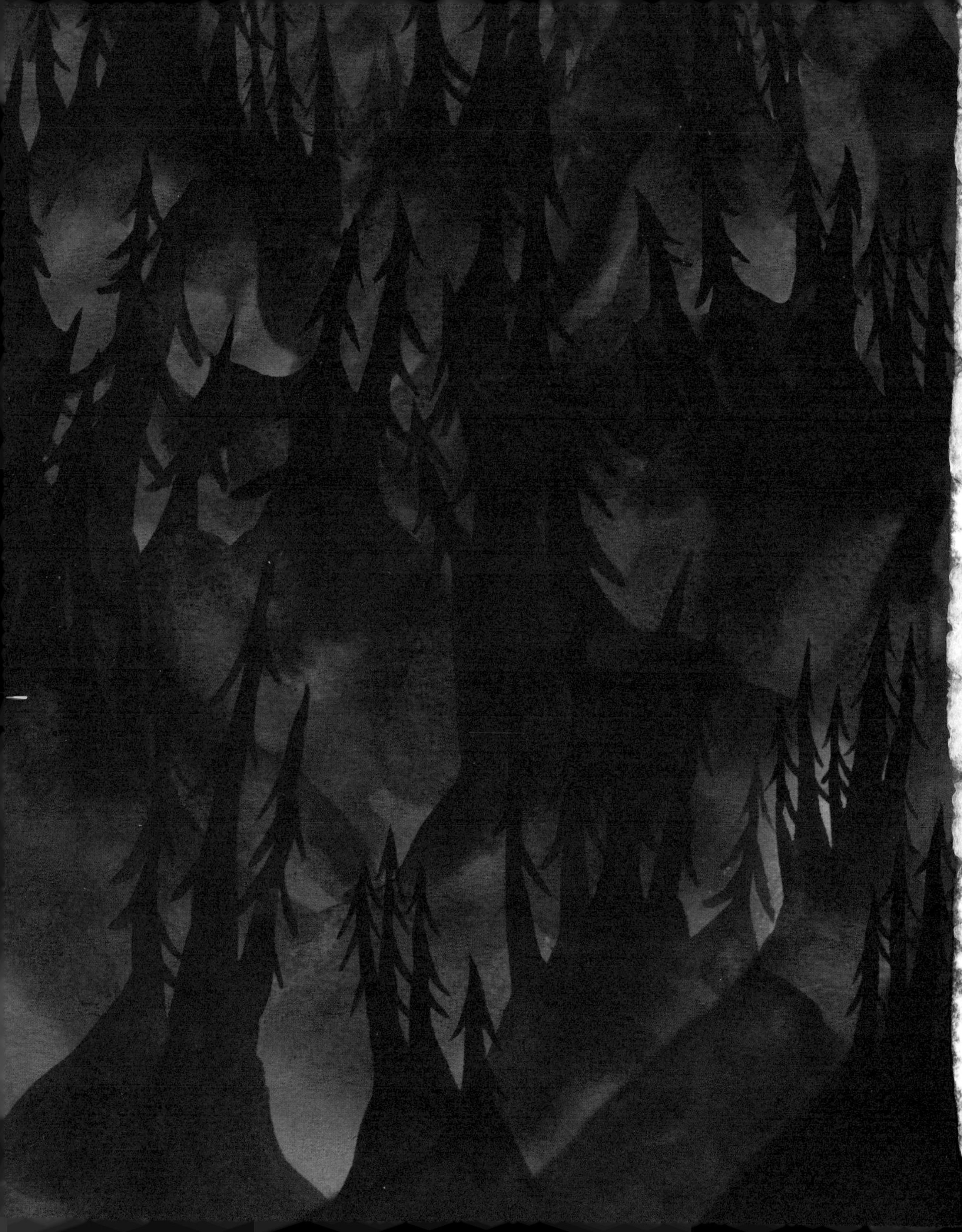

WHERE WAS THE BEAR BORN
WHERE DELIVERED?
BY THE MOON, NEXT TO THE SUN
AMONG THE STARS OF THE PLOUGH
SENT TO EARTH
IN A GOLDEN CRADLE
WITH SILVERY CHAINS.

~ SONG OF THE ~
BIRTH OF THE BEAR

OKSI

This is an Em Querido book
Published by Levine Querido

www.levinequerido.com • info@levinequerido.com
Levine Querido is distributed by Chronicle Books LLC
Story and art copyright © 2021 by Mari Ahokoivu
Translation © 2021 by Silja-Maaria Aronpuro
Originally published in Finland by Asema Kustannus
All rights reserved
Library of Congress Control Number: 2021932073
Hardcover ISBN - 978-1-64614-113-5
Printed and bound in China

FSC
www.fsc.org

MIX
Paper from
responsible sources
FSC™ C104723

Published September 2021
First printing

The author would like to thank the following establishments for their support:
FILI / Finnish Literature Exchange
The Finnish Cultural Foundation, The North Ostrobothnia Regional Fund
Arts Promotion Centre Finland, comics and illustration
WSOY Literature foundation

MARI AHOKOIVU
OKSI

LEVINE QUERIDO
MONTCLAIR AMSTERDAM HOBOKEN

PROLOGUE

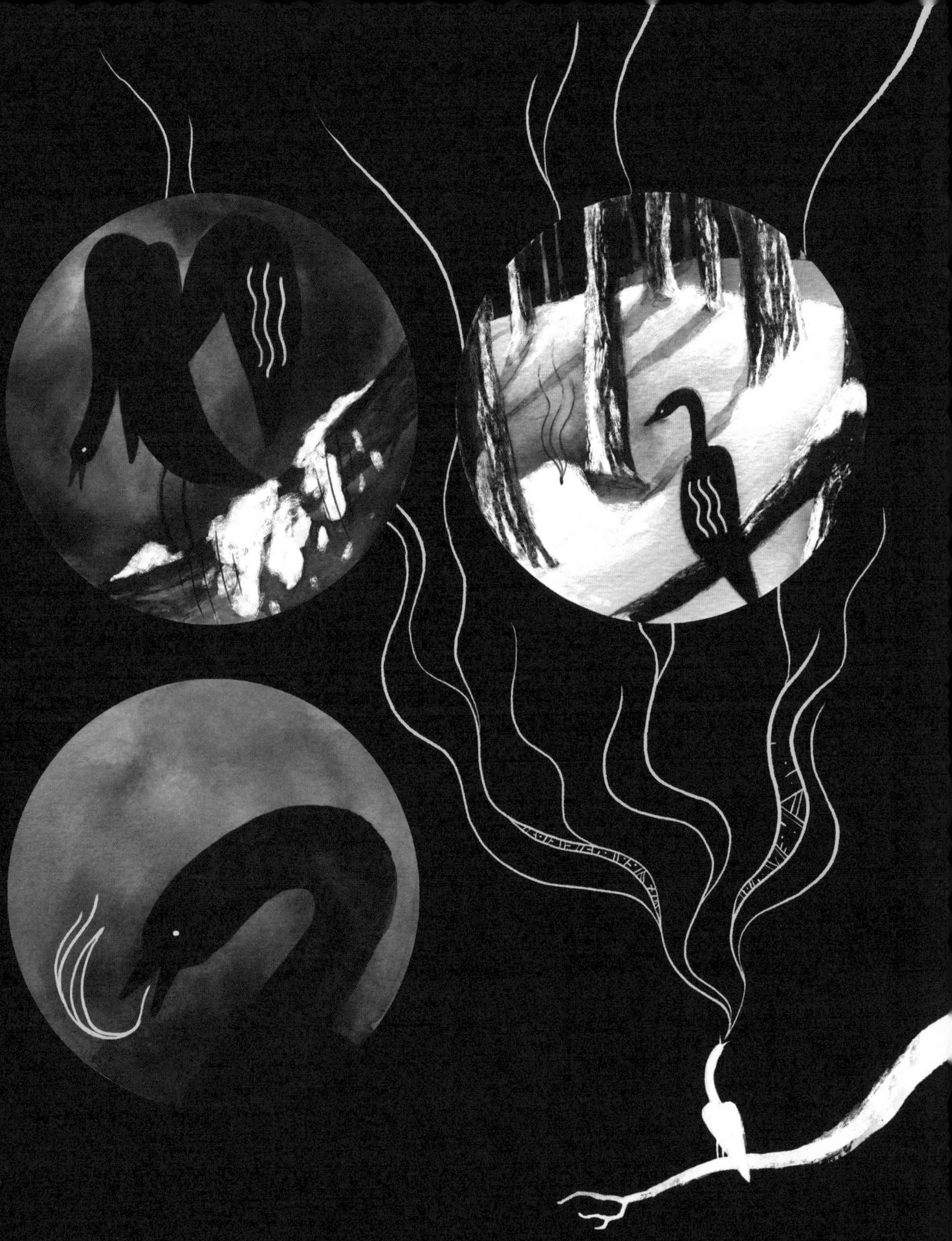

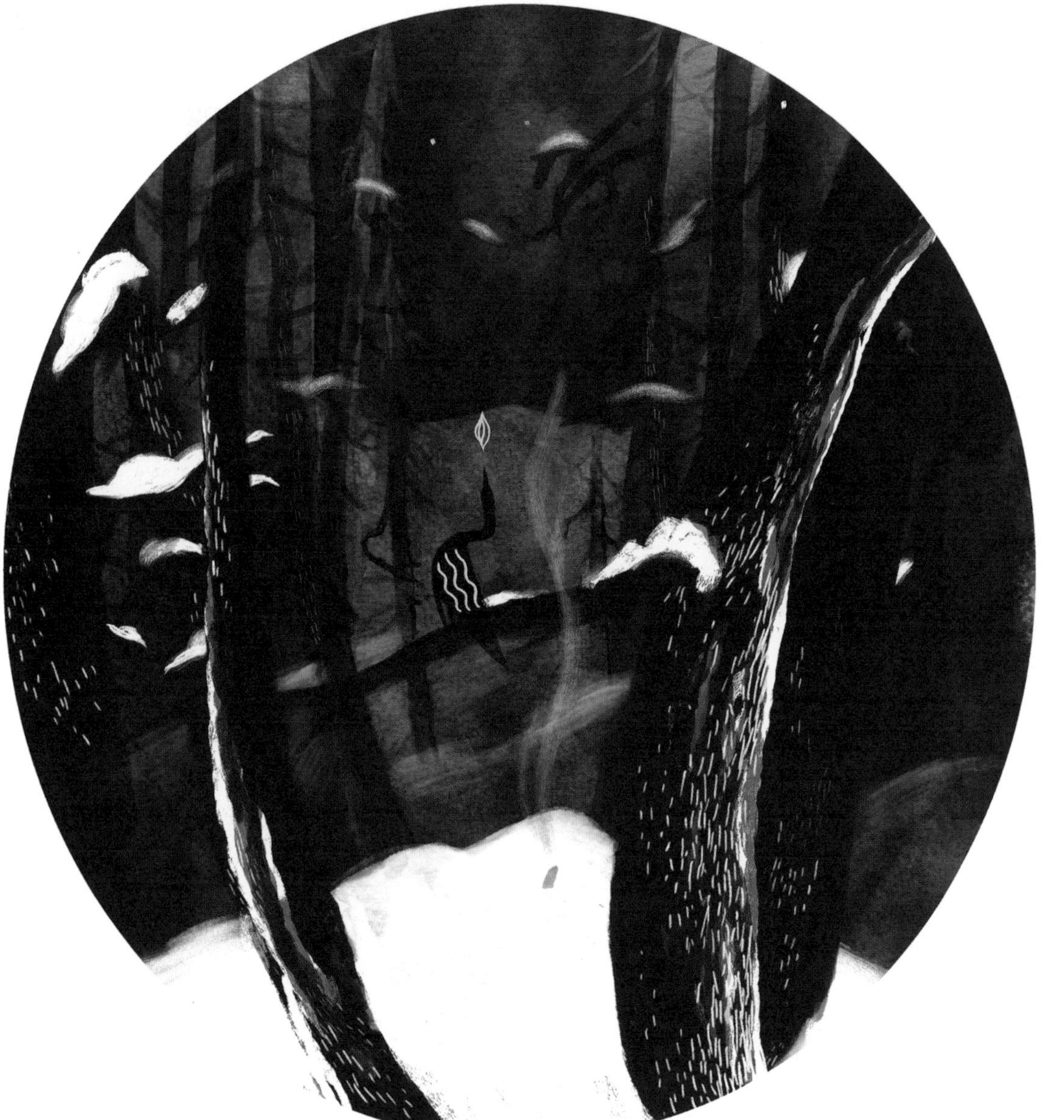

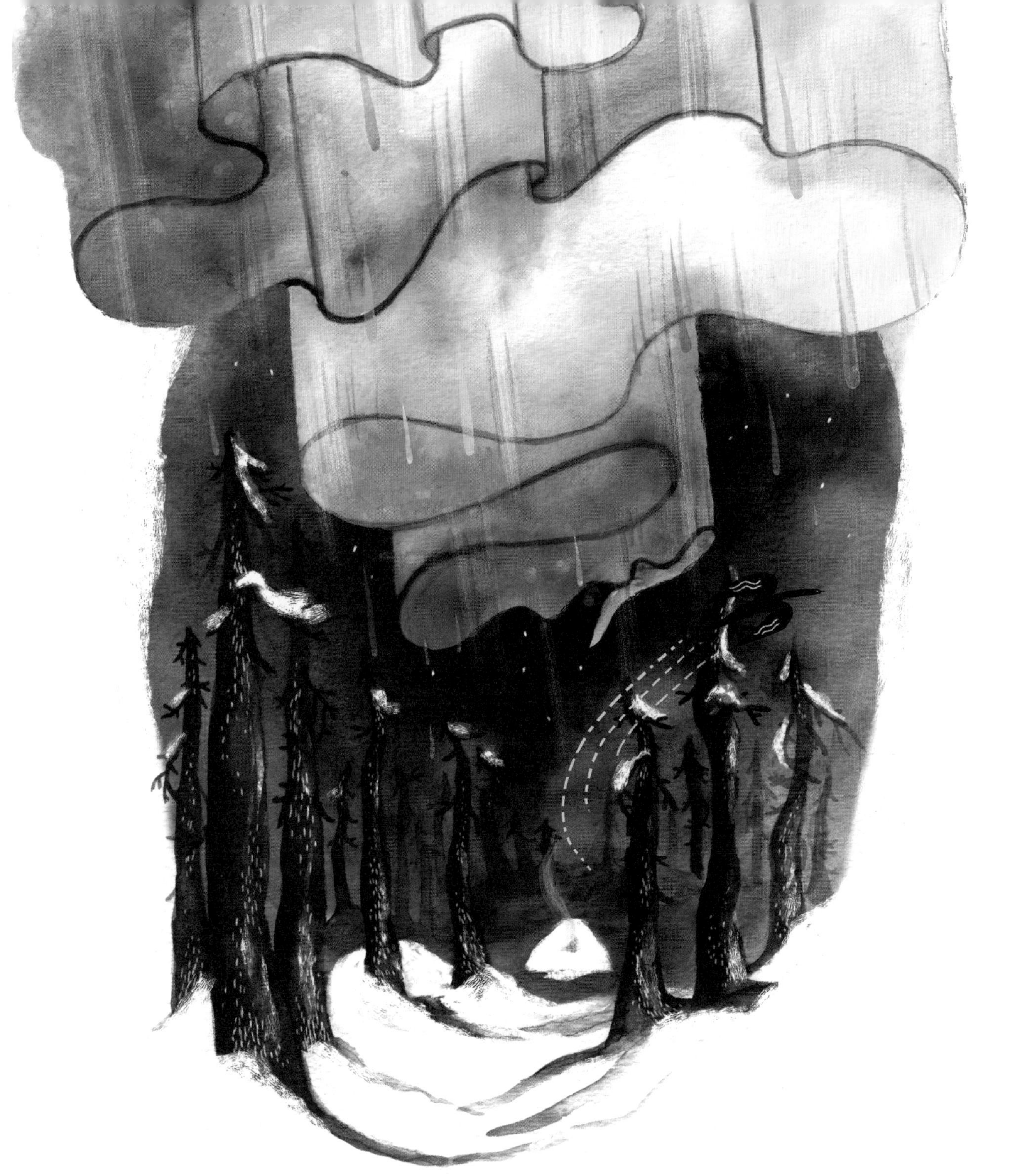

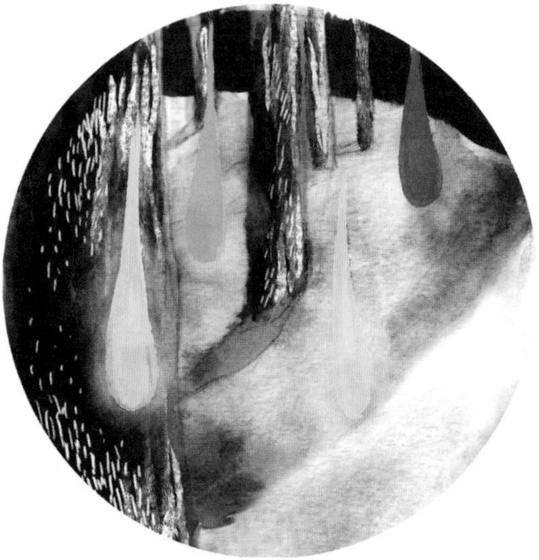
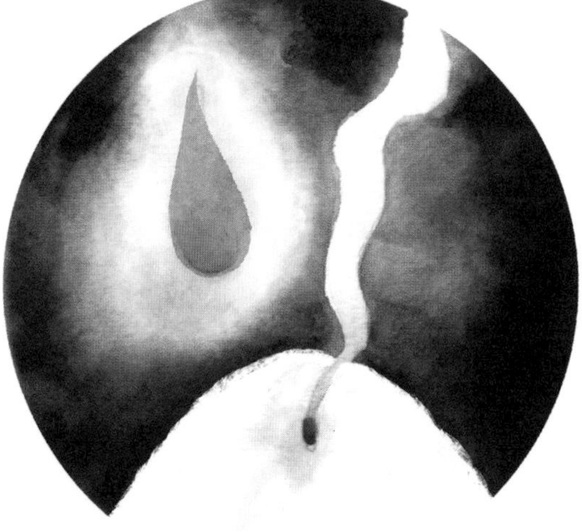
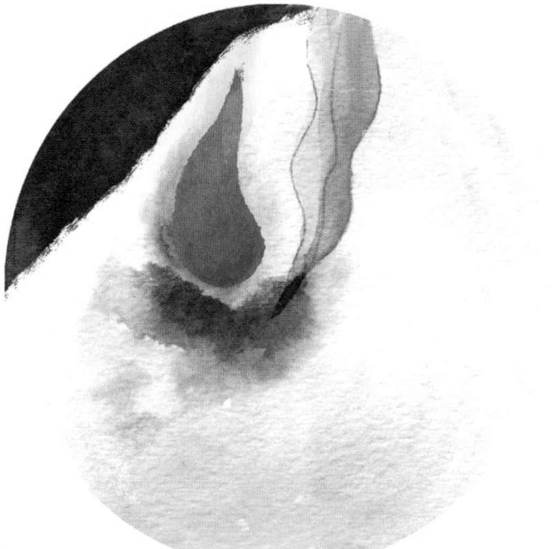
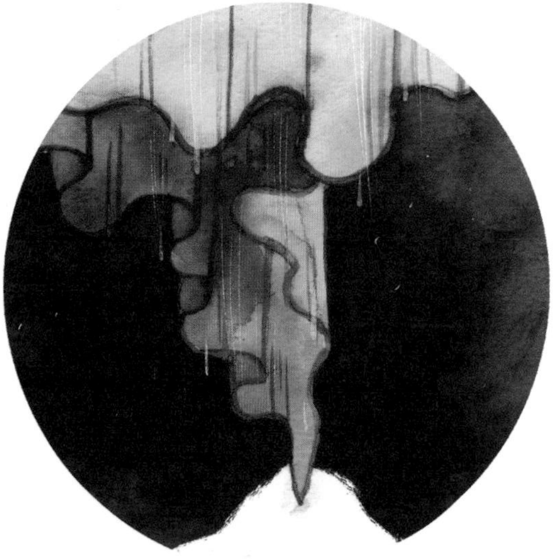

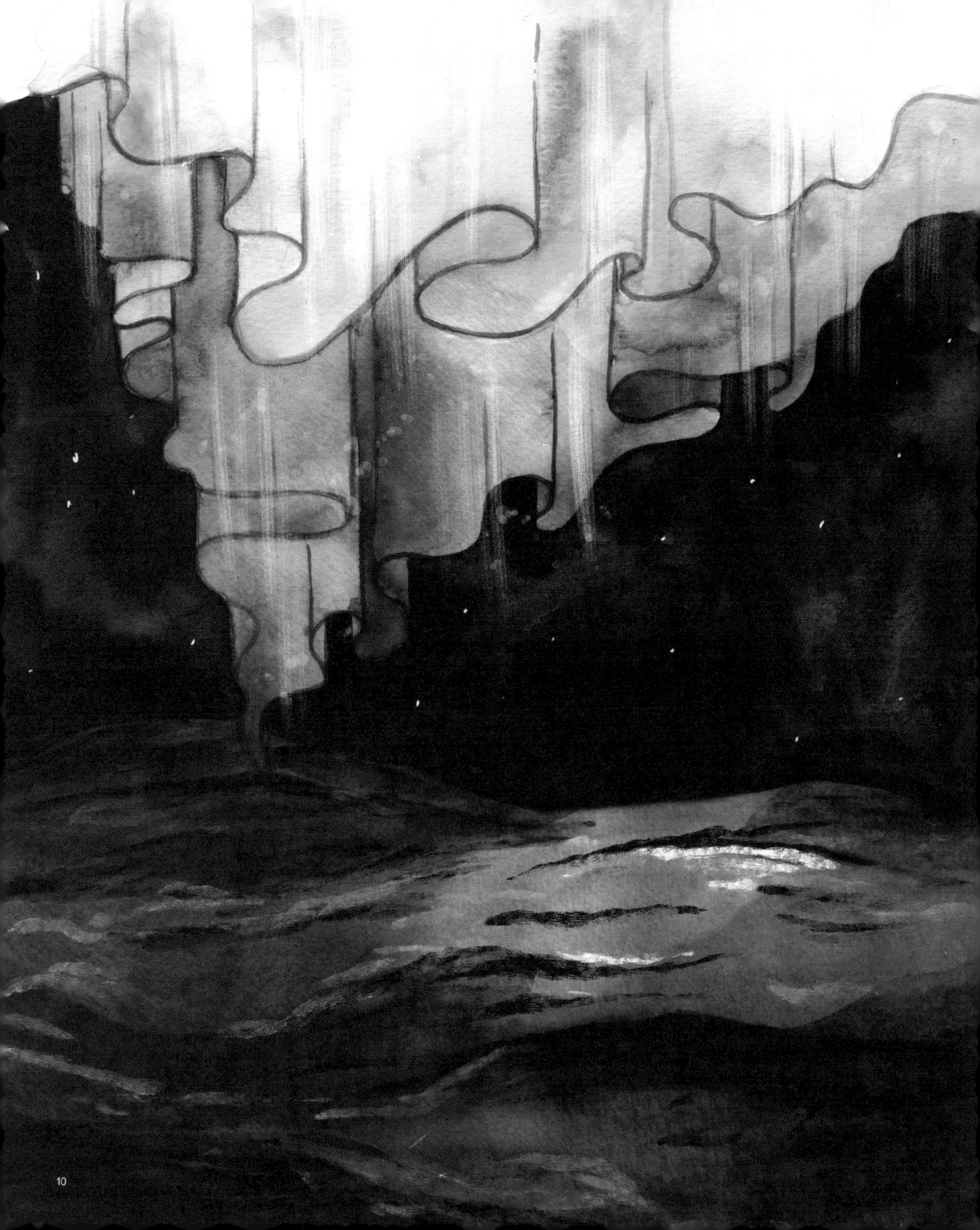

I

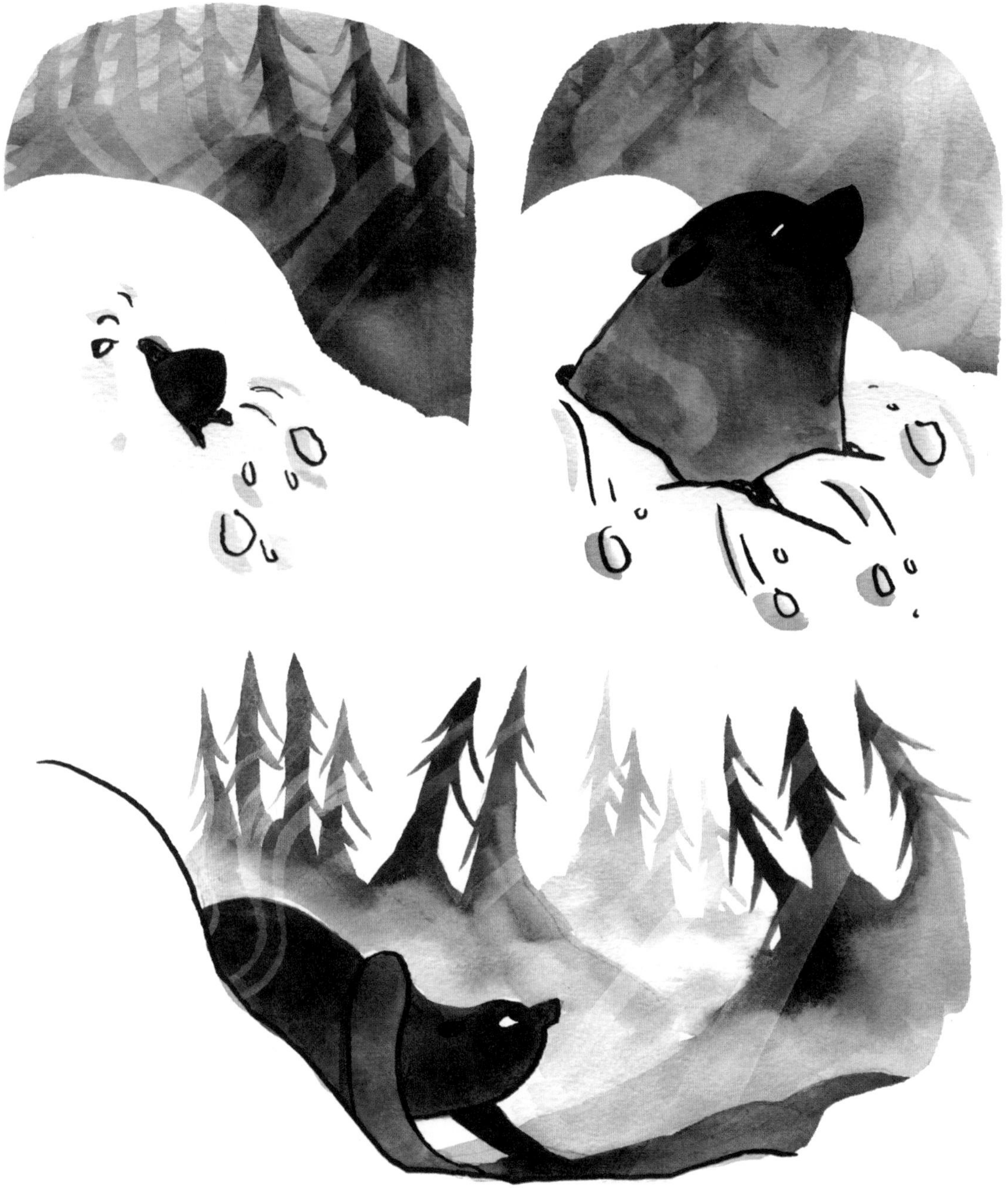

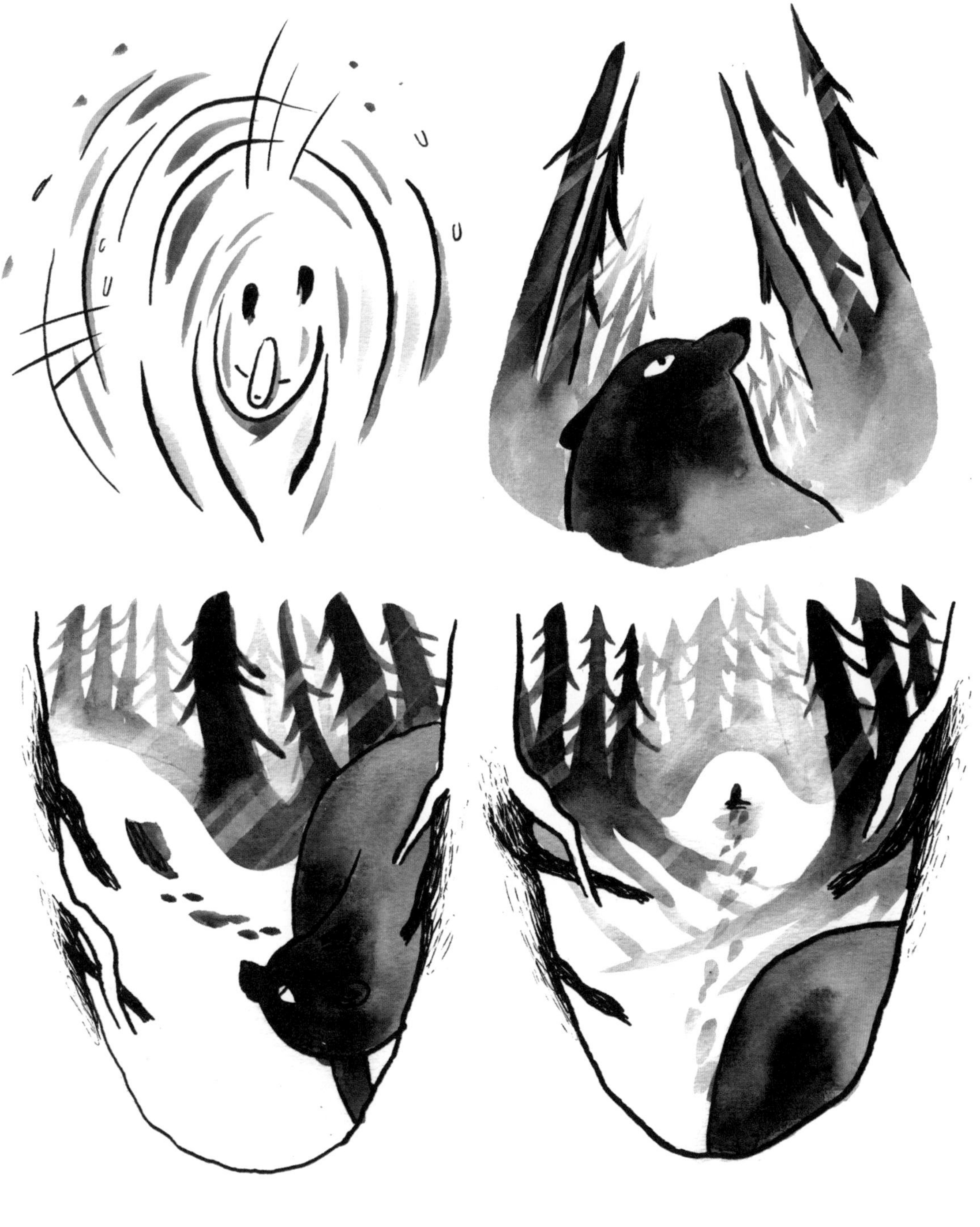

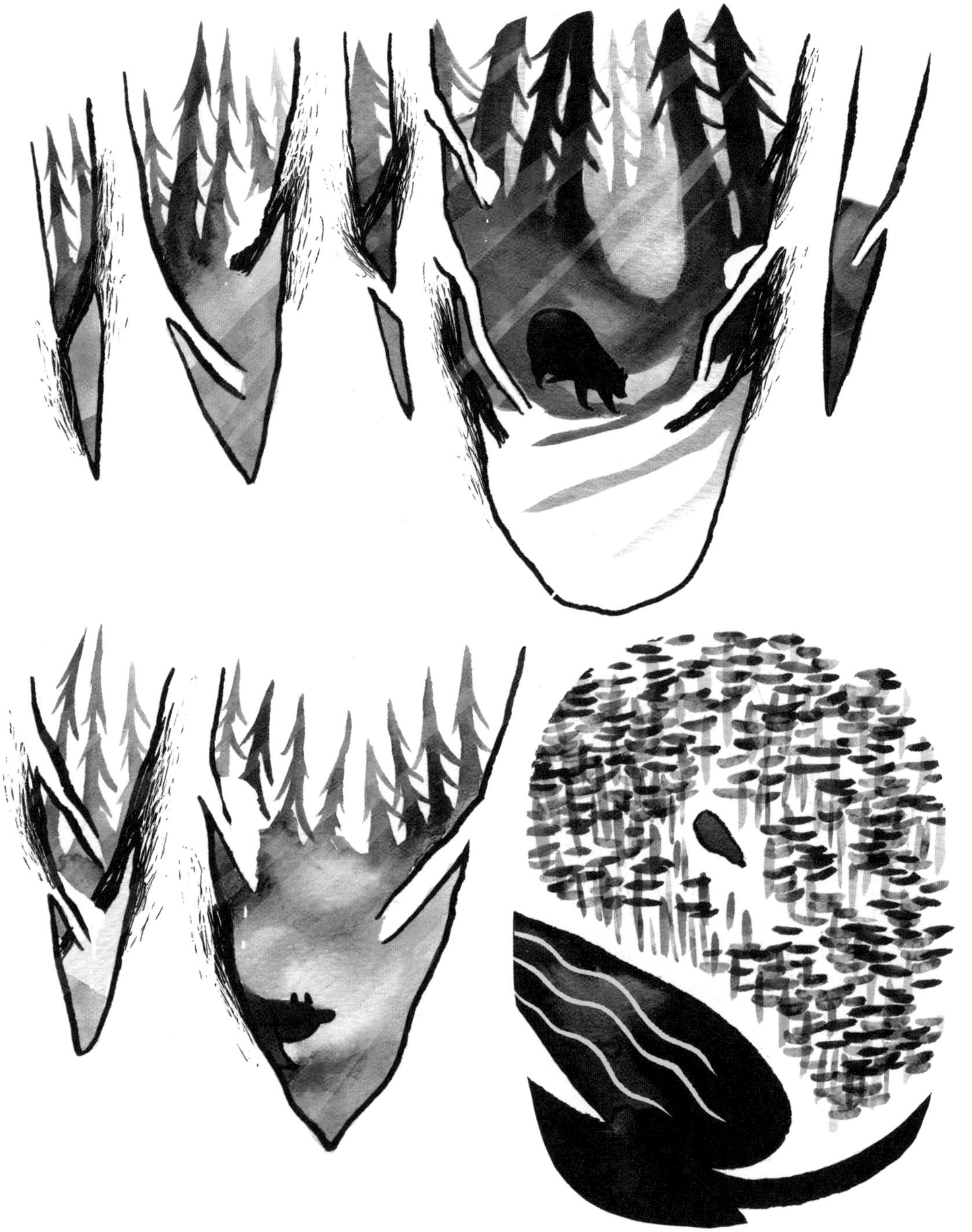

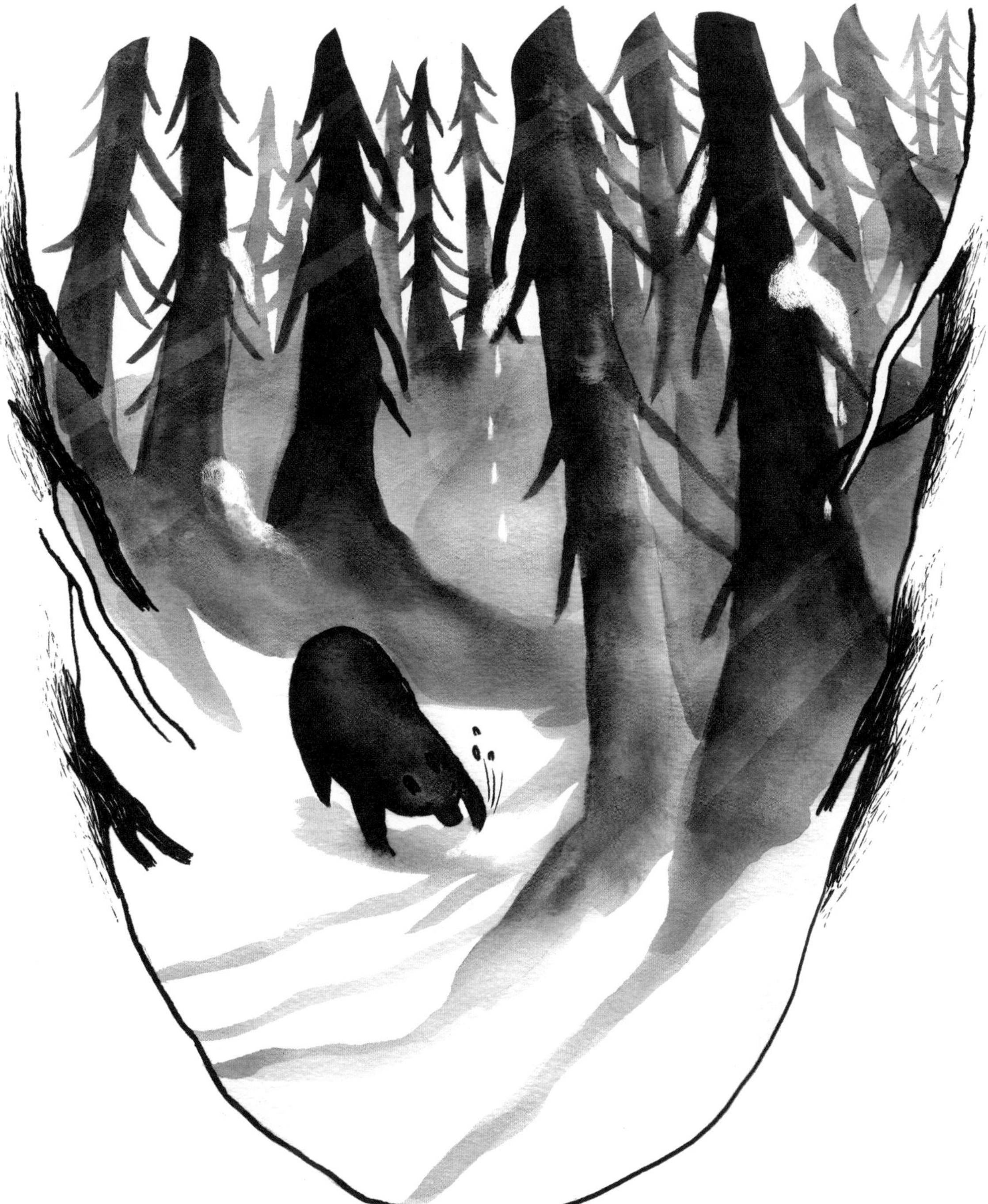

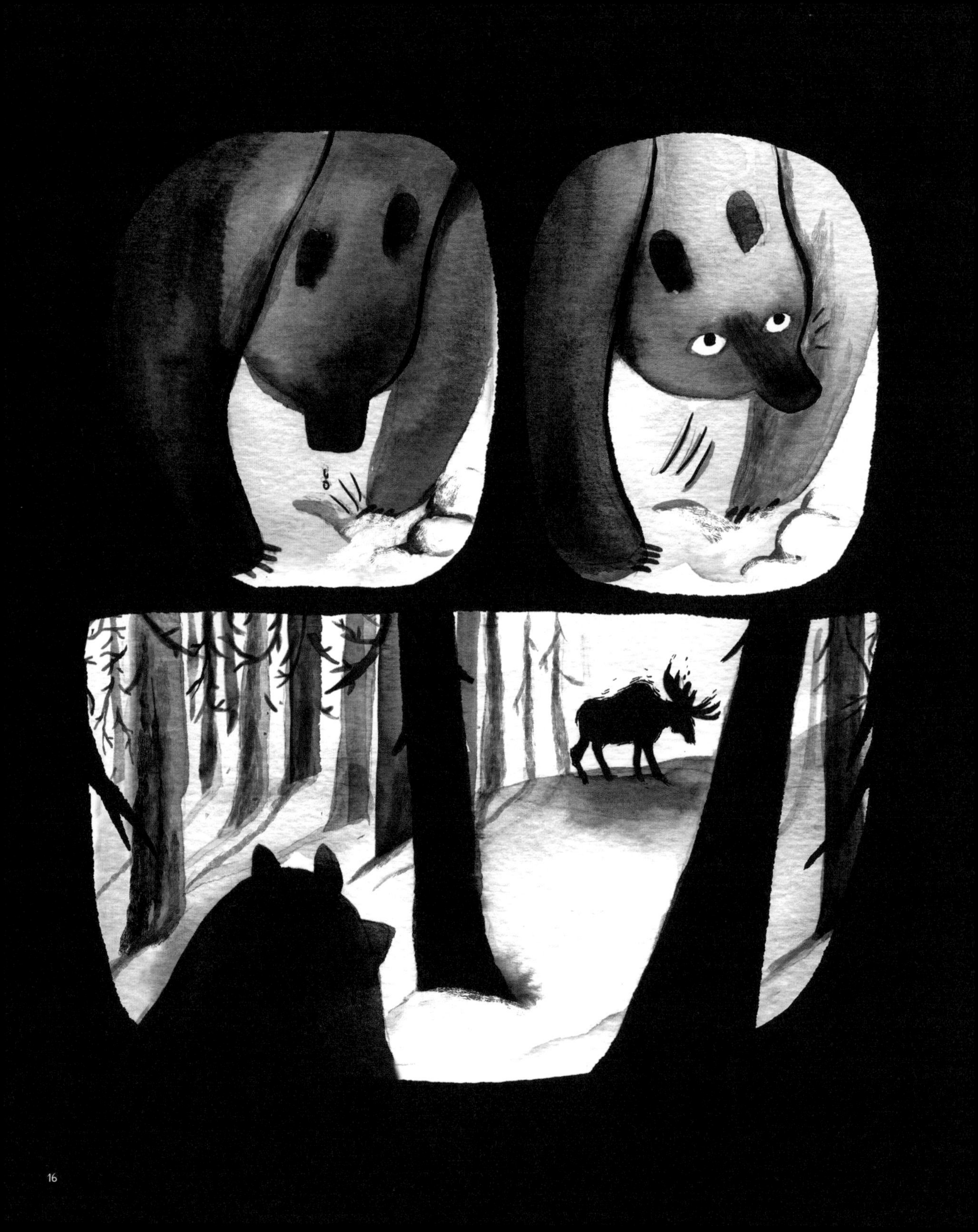

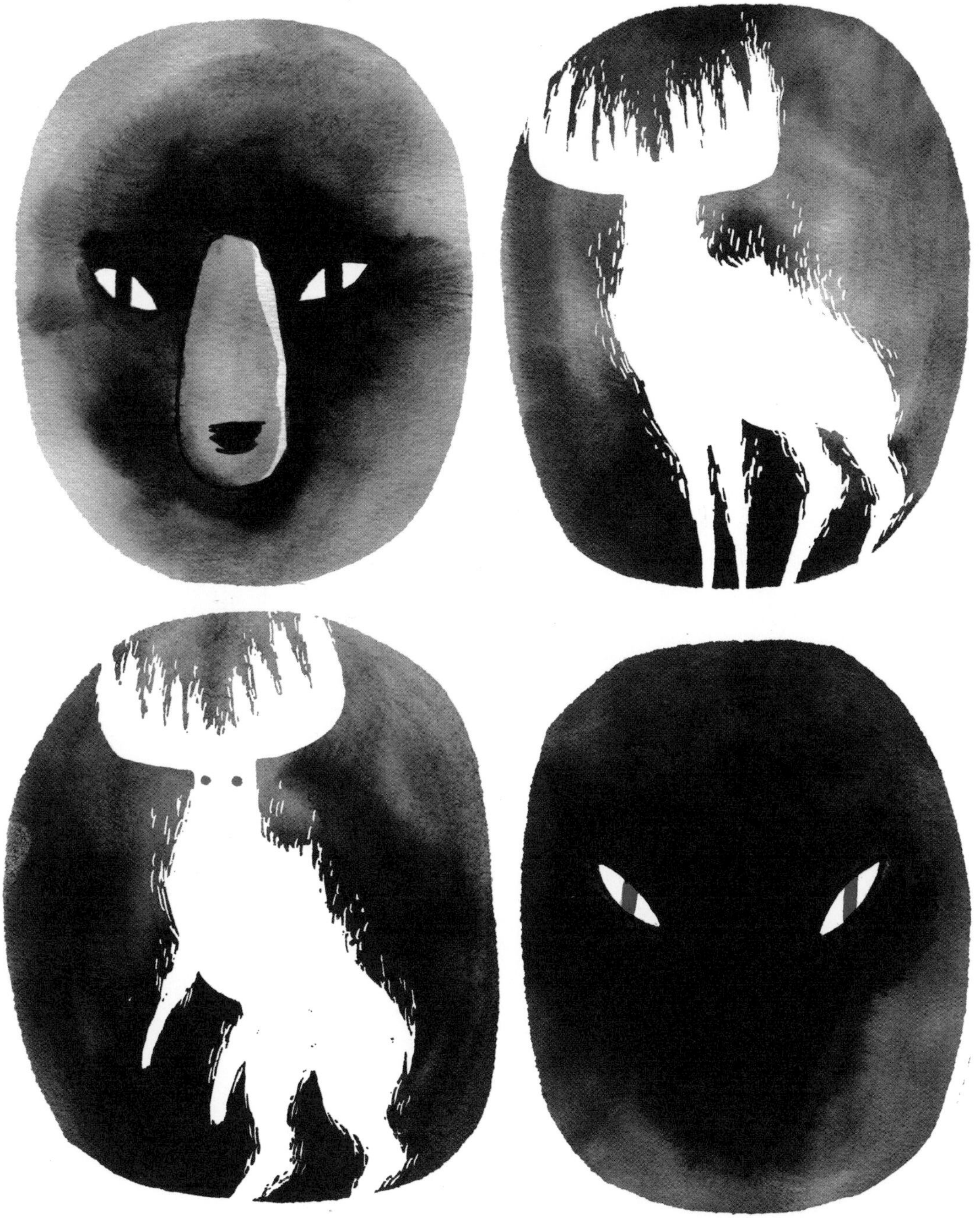

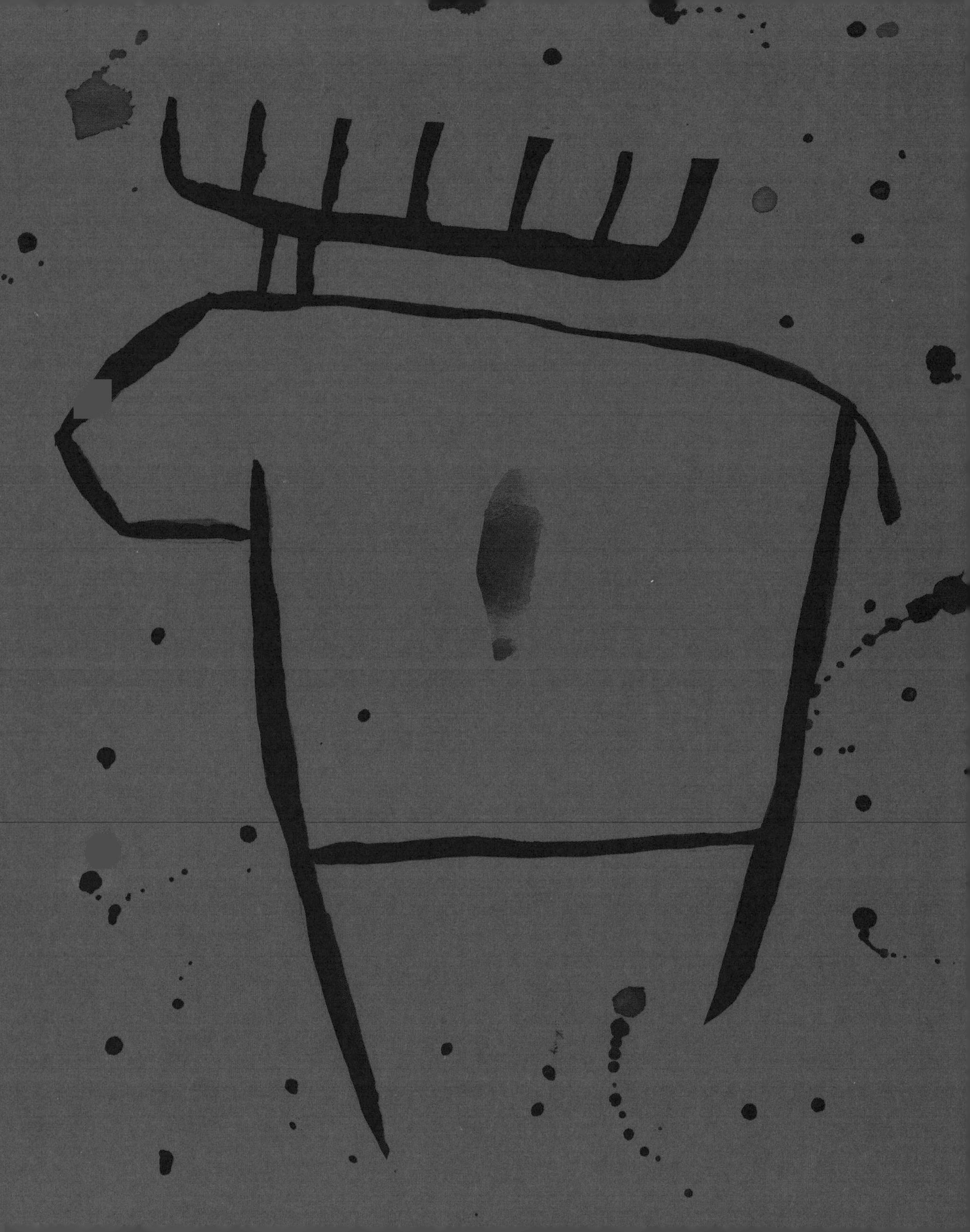

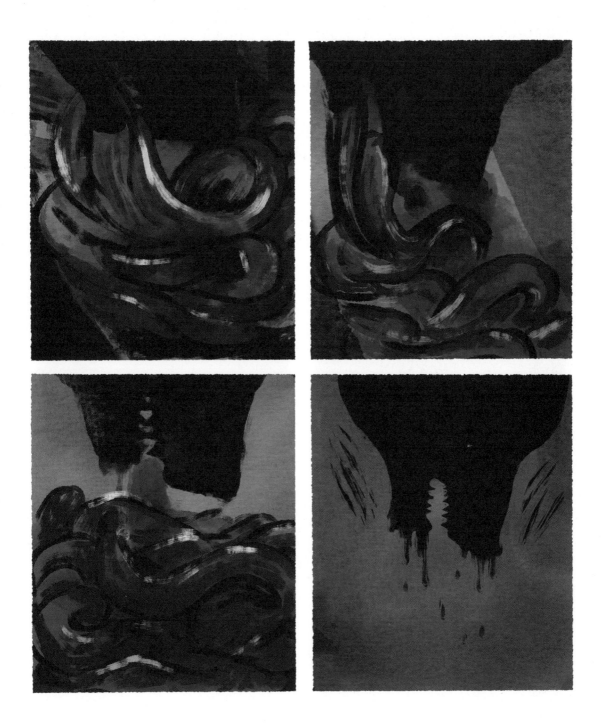

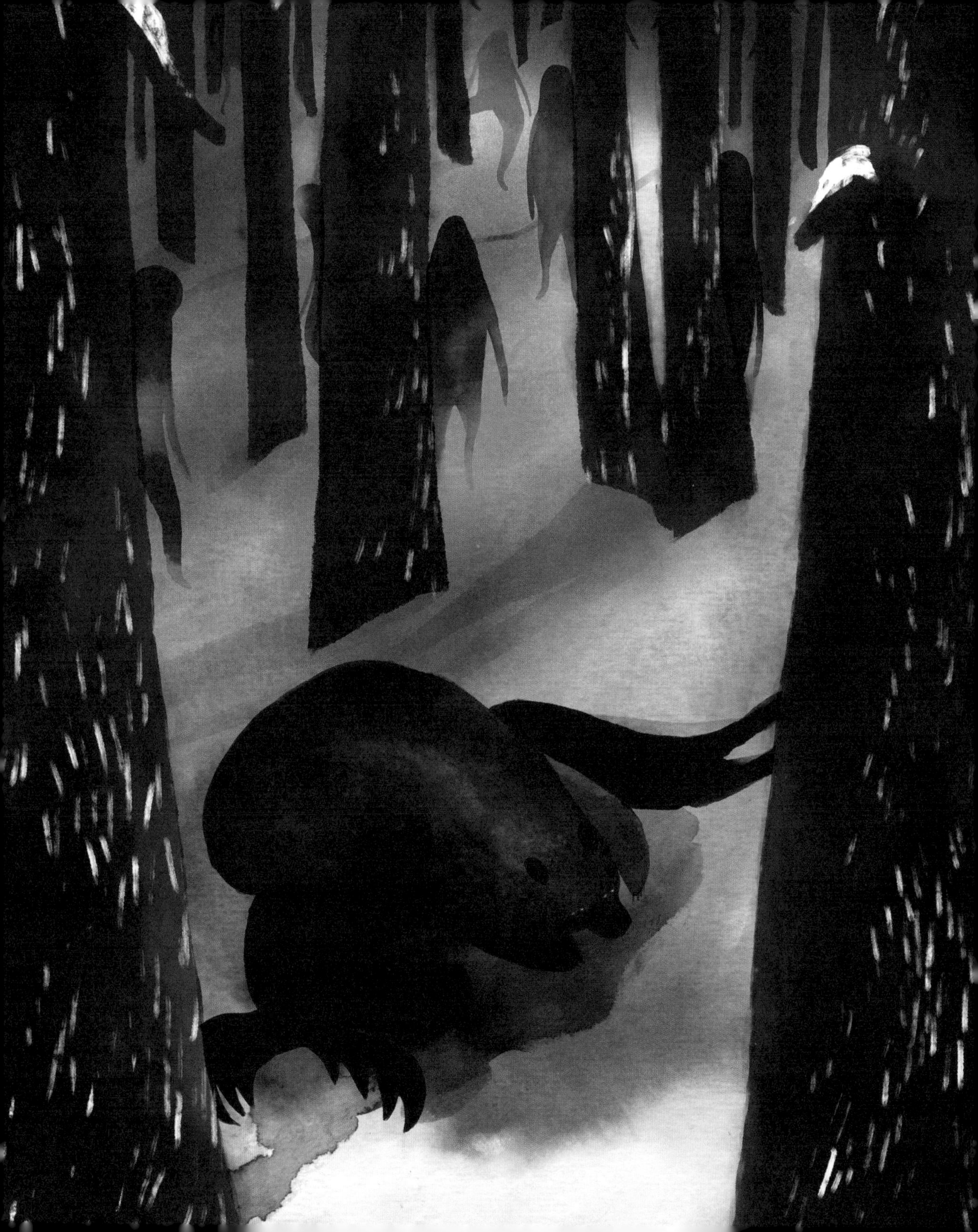

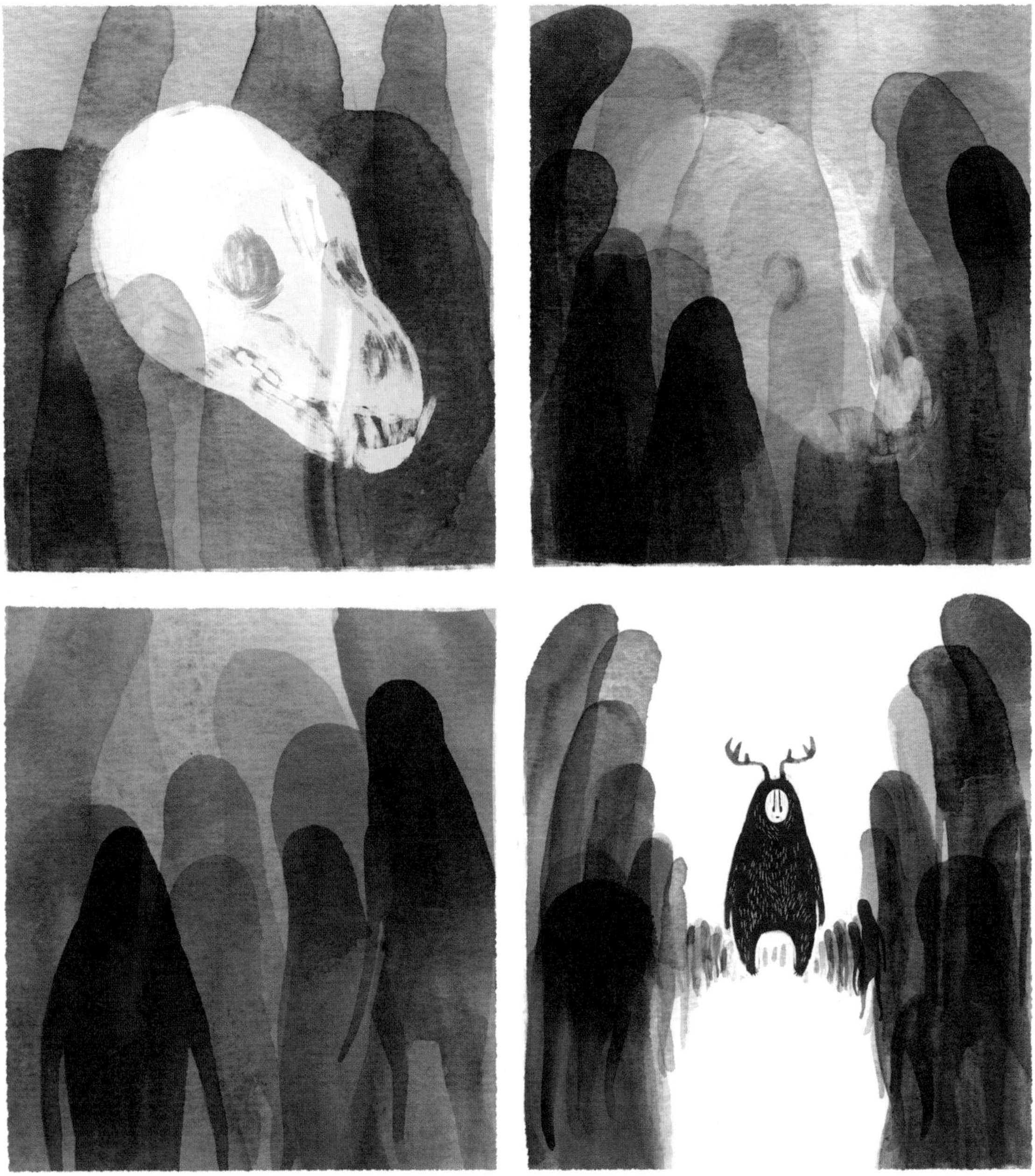

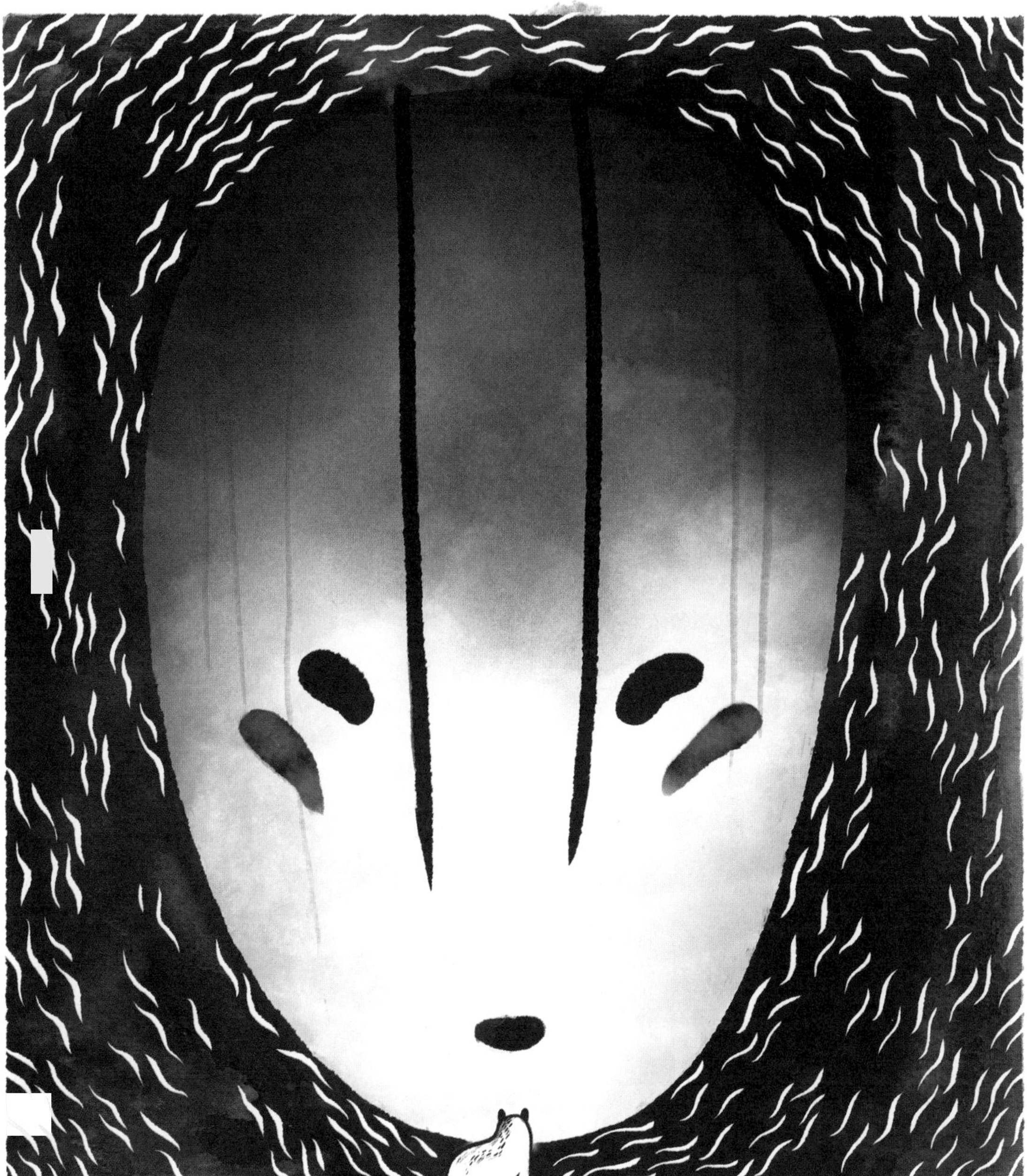

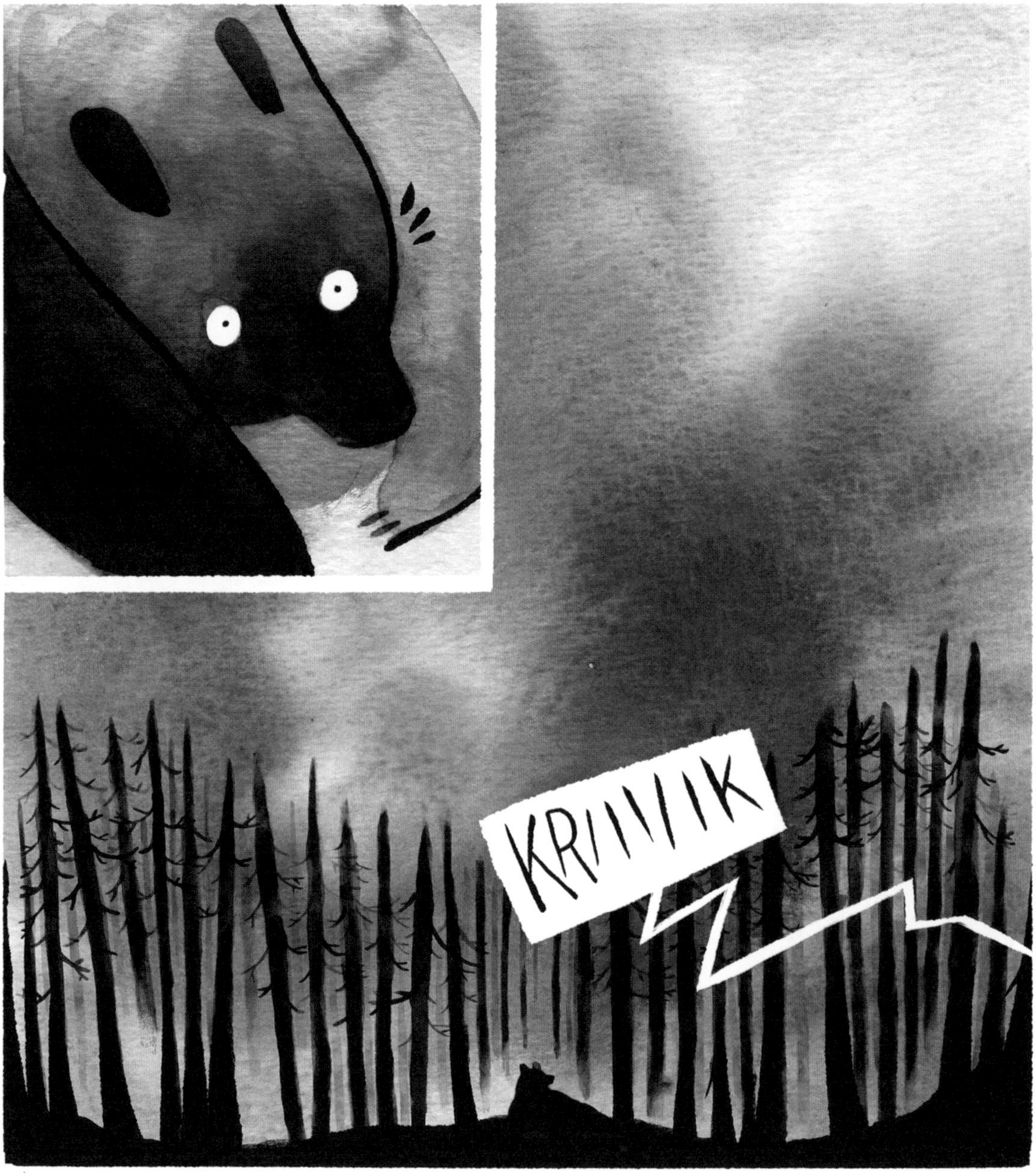
KRIIIIIK

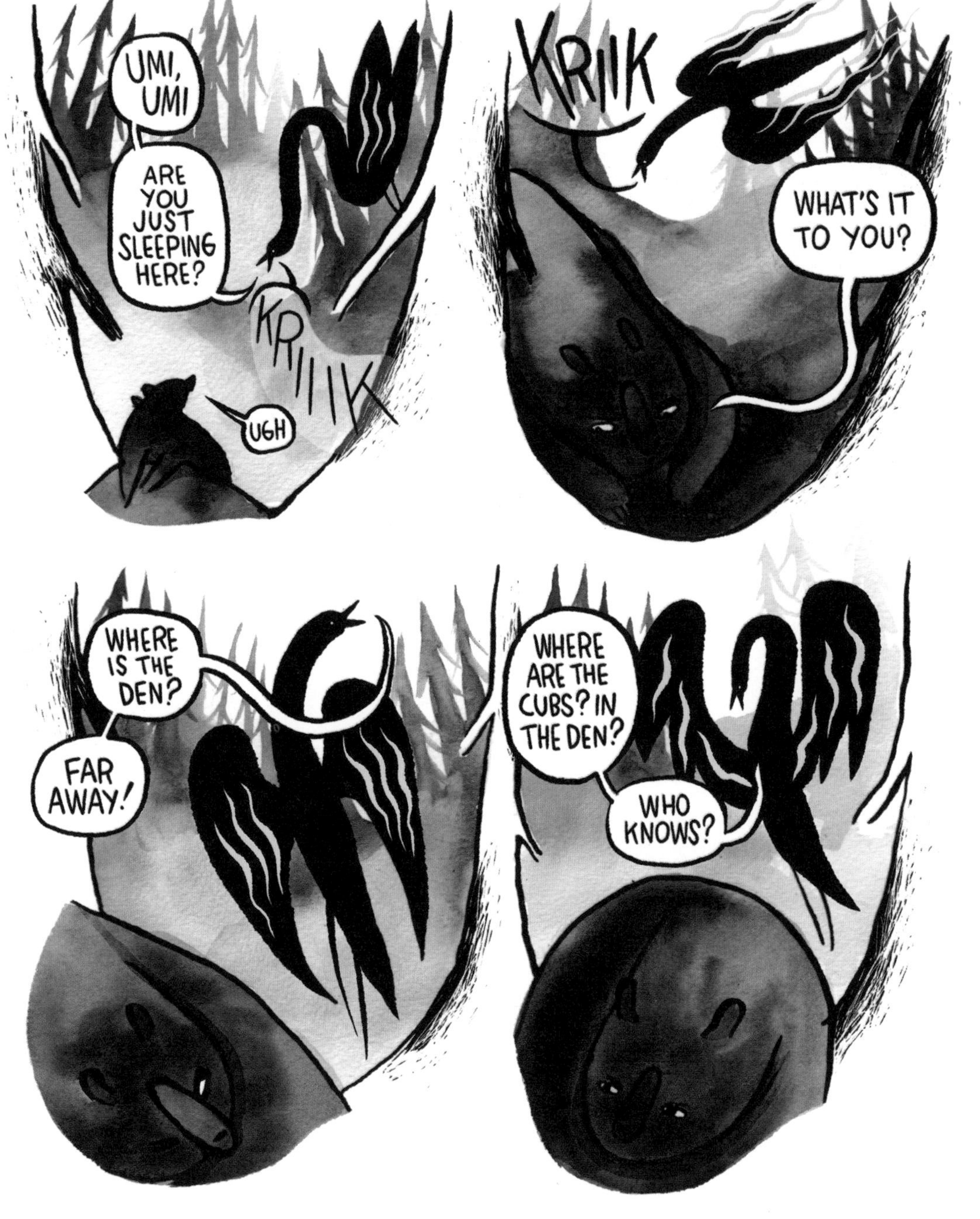
UMI, UMI
ARE YOU JUST SLEEPING HERE?
KRIIIK
UGH
KRIIK
WHAT'S IT TO YOU?
WHERE IS THE DEN?
FAR AWAY!
WHERE ARE THE CUBS? IN THE DEN?
WHO KNOWS?

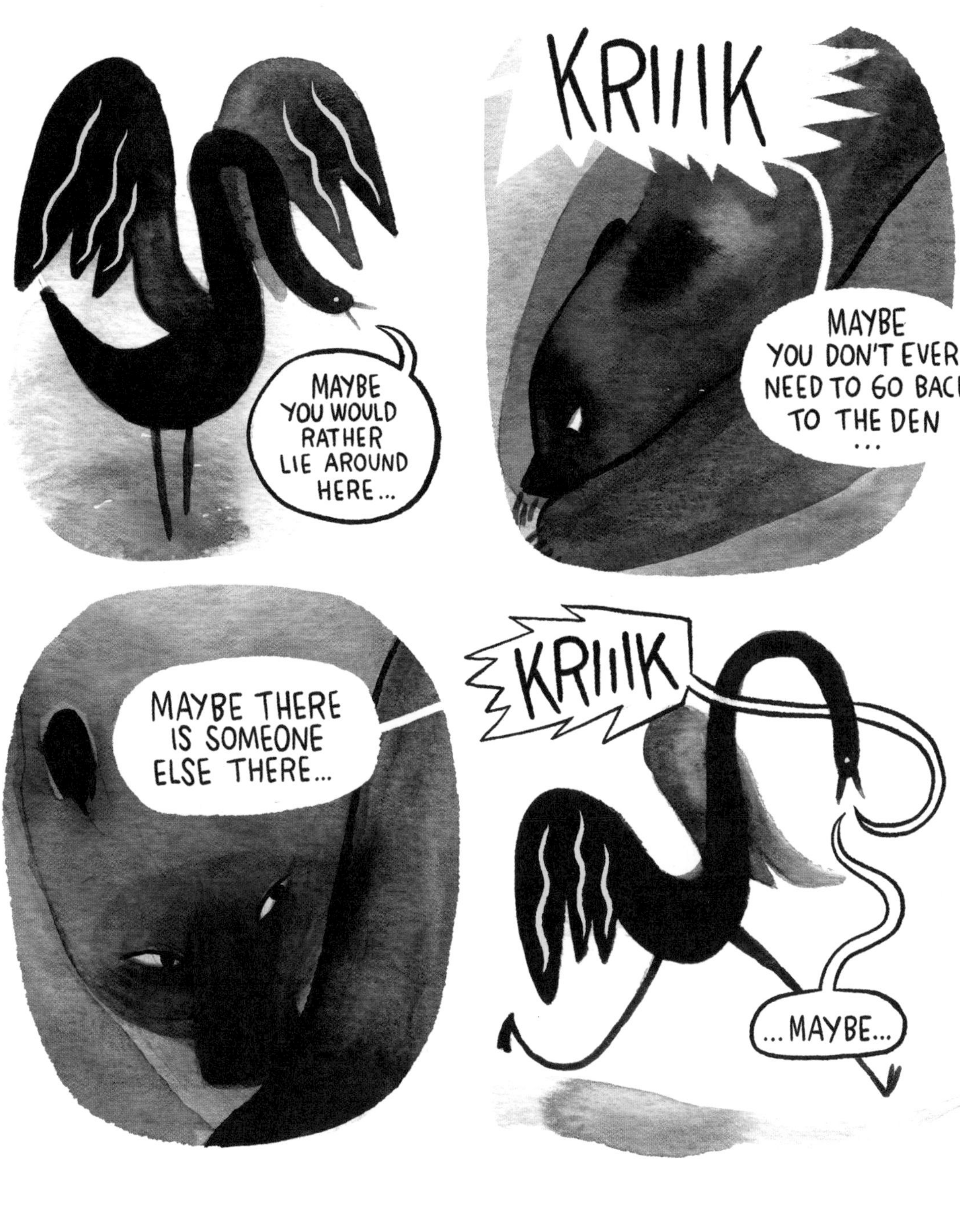
MAYBE YOU WOULD RATHER LIE AROUND HERE...
KRIIIK
MAYBE YOU DON'T EVER NEED TO GO BACK TO THE DEN ...
MAYBE THERE IS SOMEONE ELSE THERE...
KRIIIK
...MAYBE...

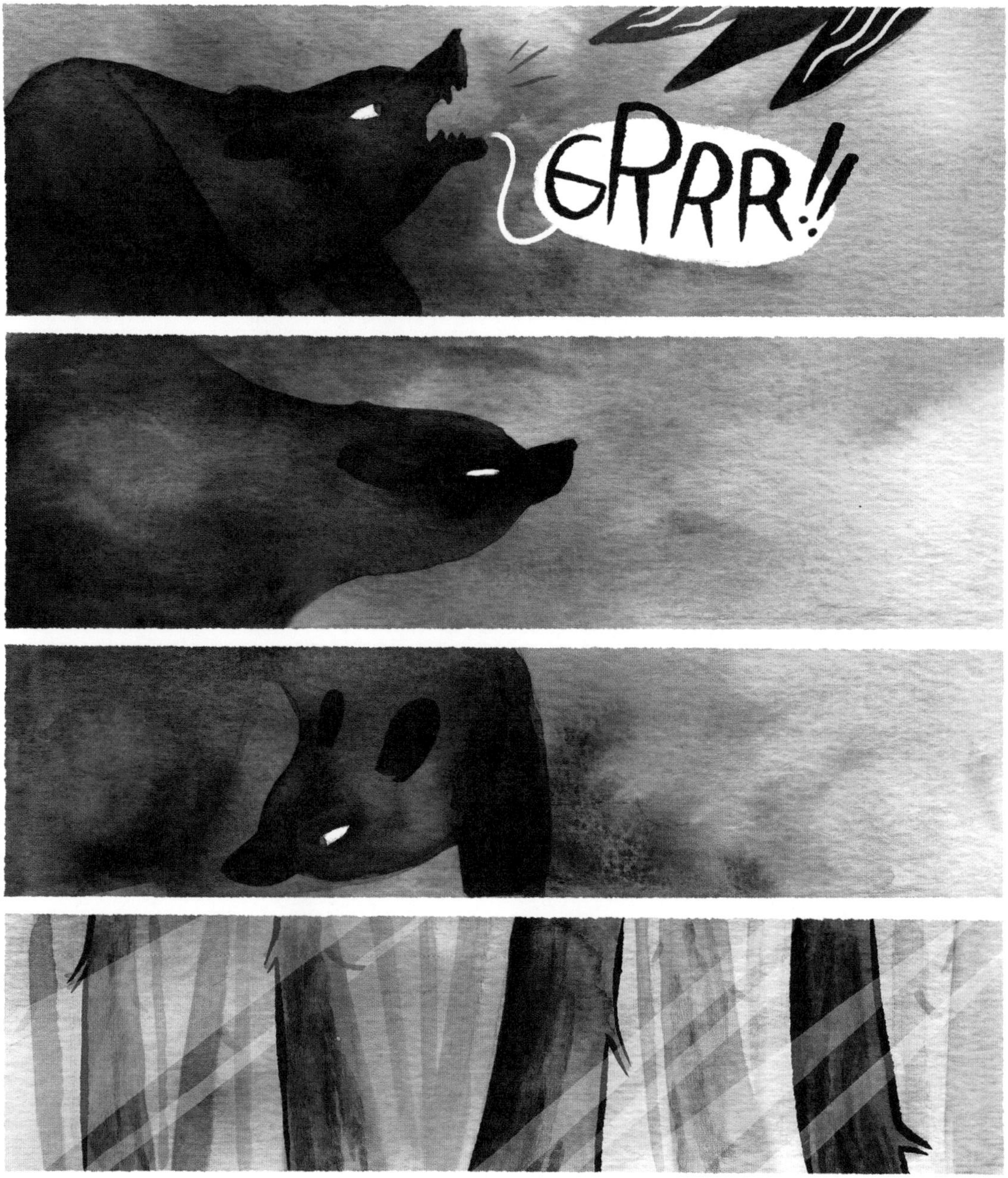
GRRR!!

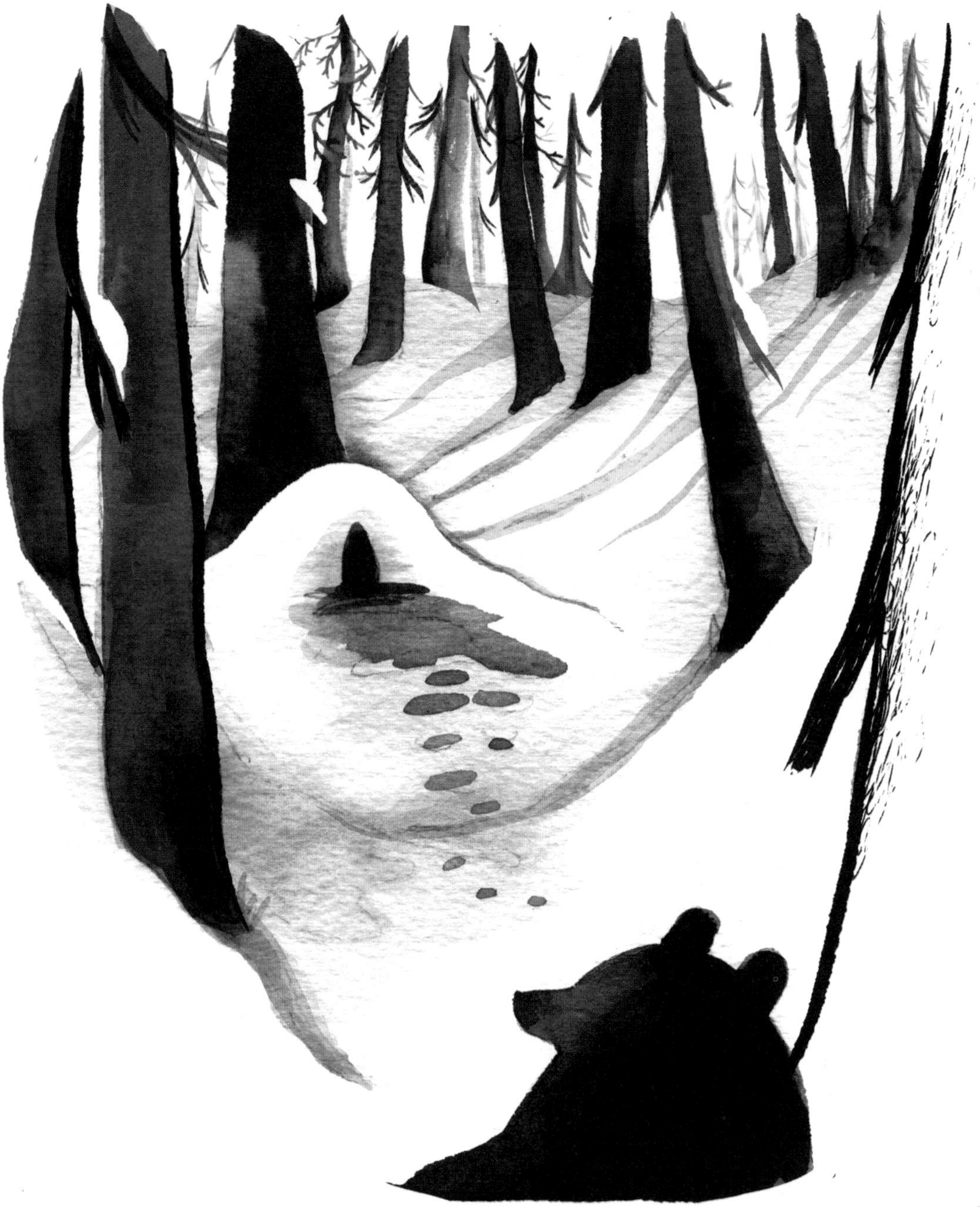

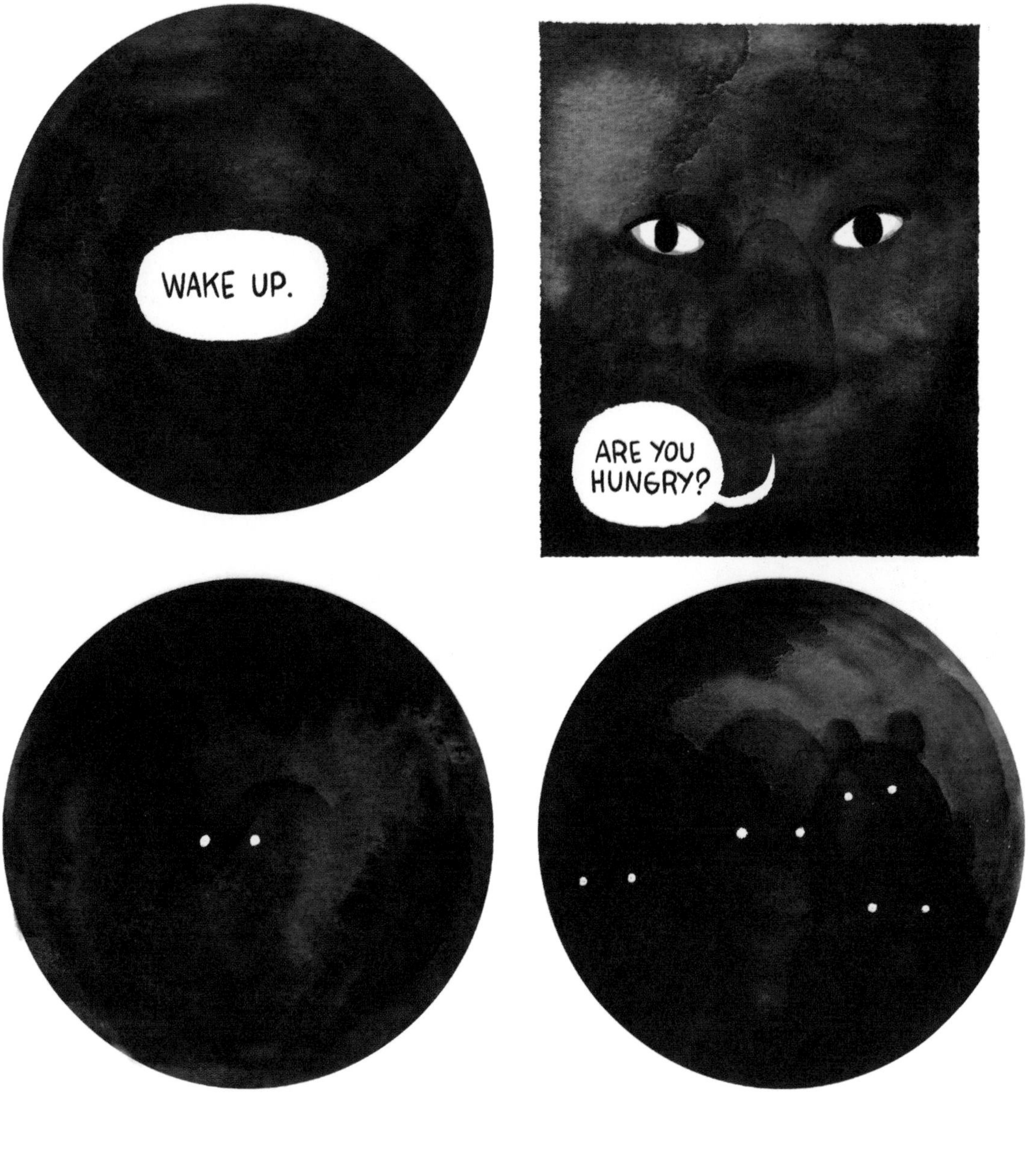
WAKE UP.
ARE YOU HUNGRY?

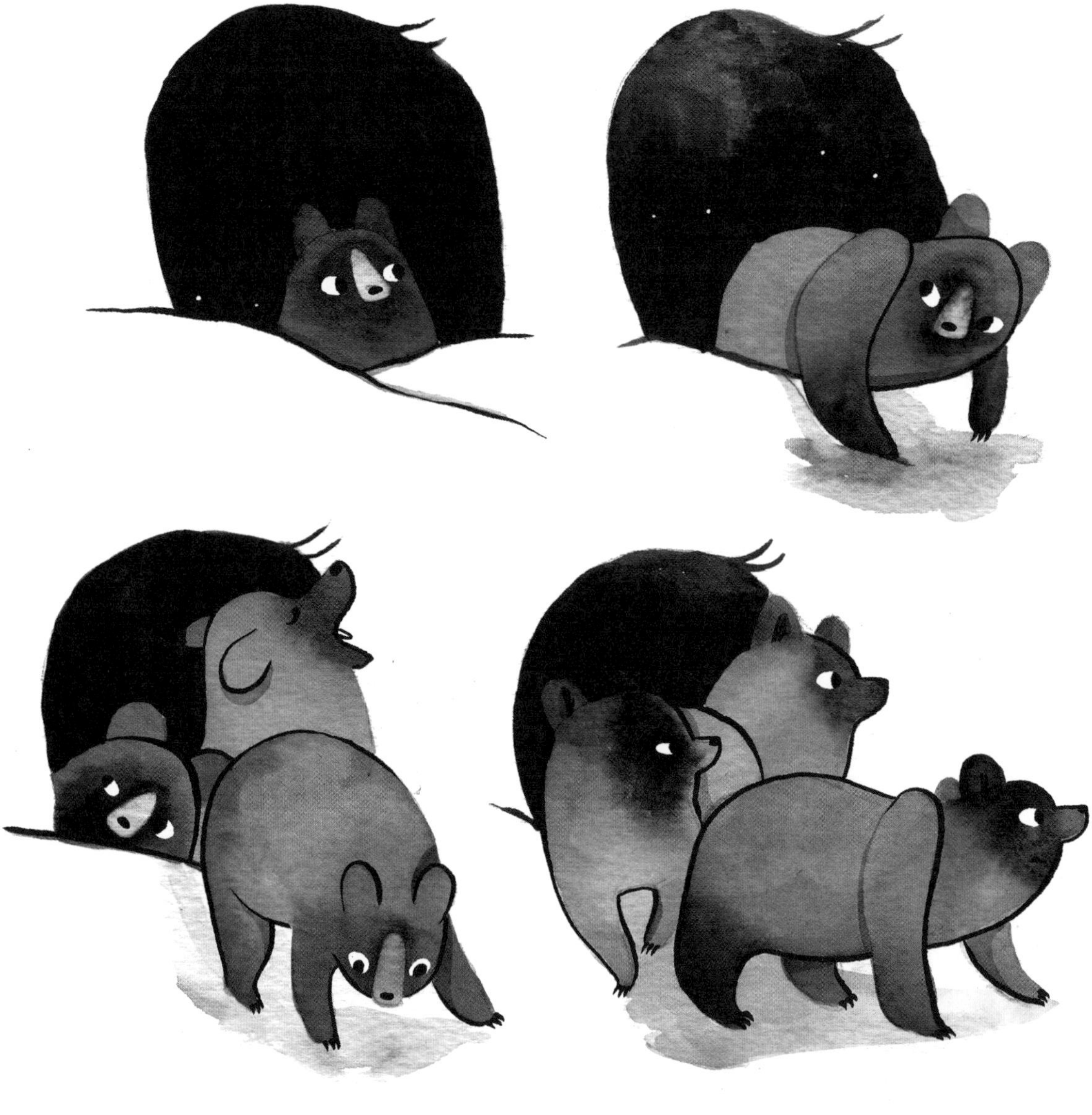

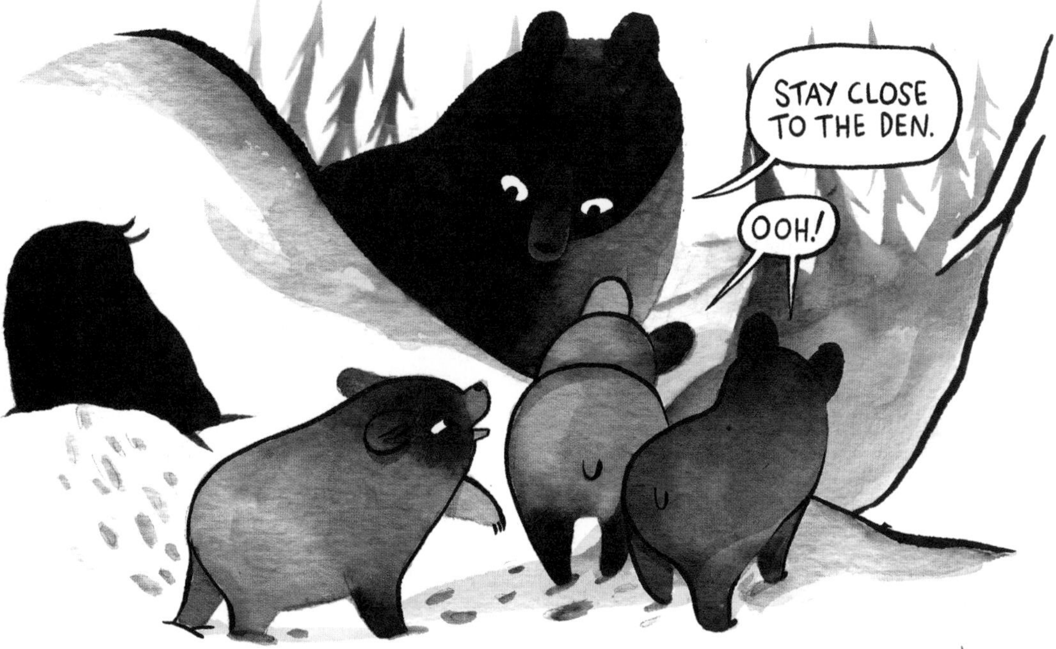
STAY CLOSE TO THE DEN.
OOH!

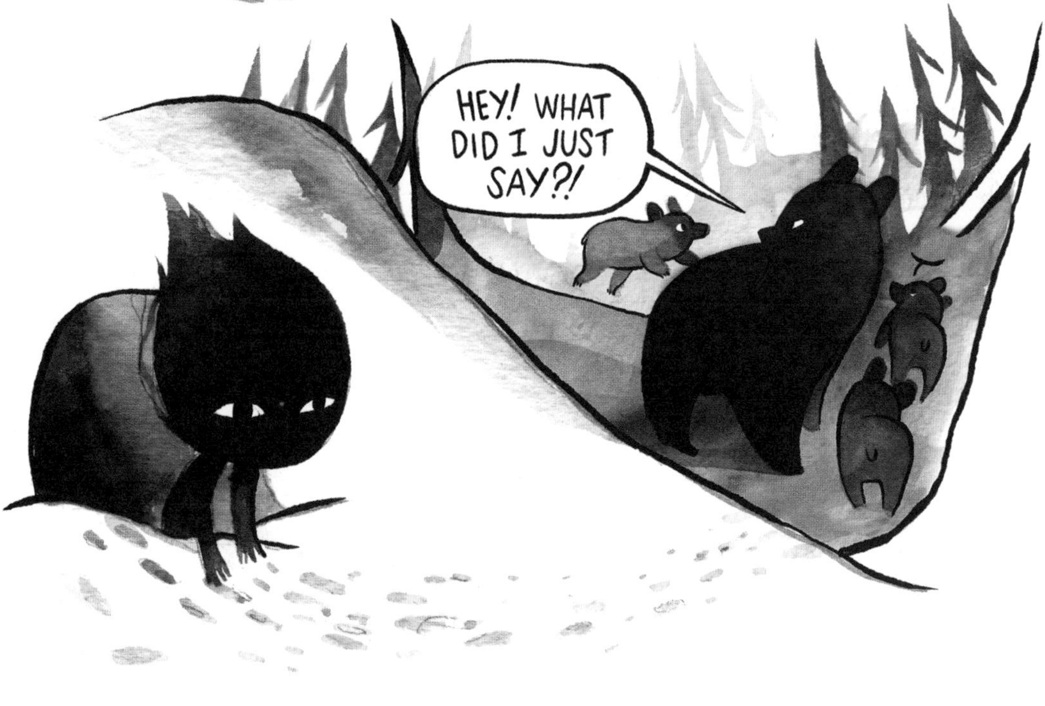
HEY! WHAT DID I JUST SAY?!

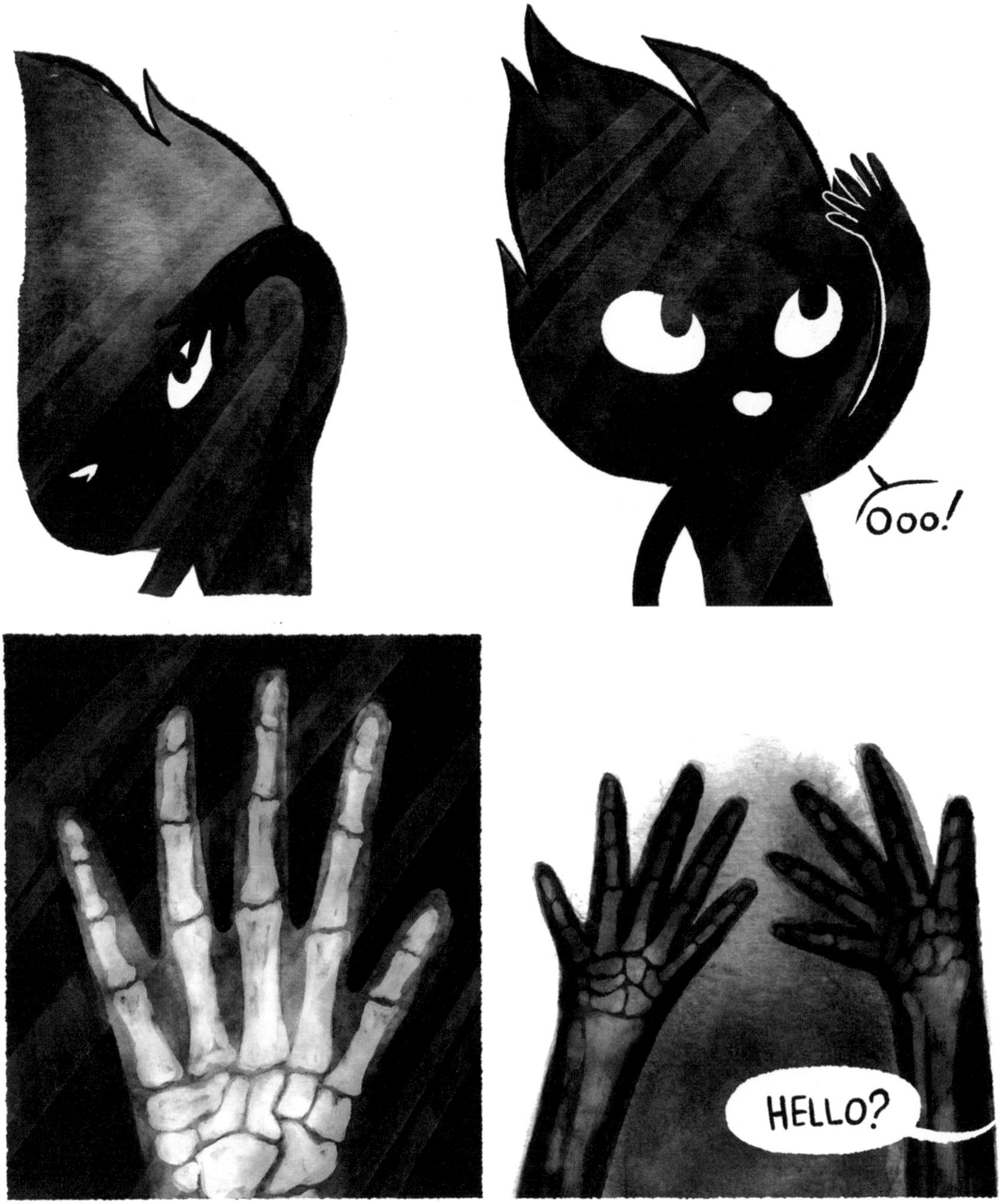
Ooo!
HELLO?

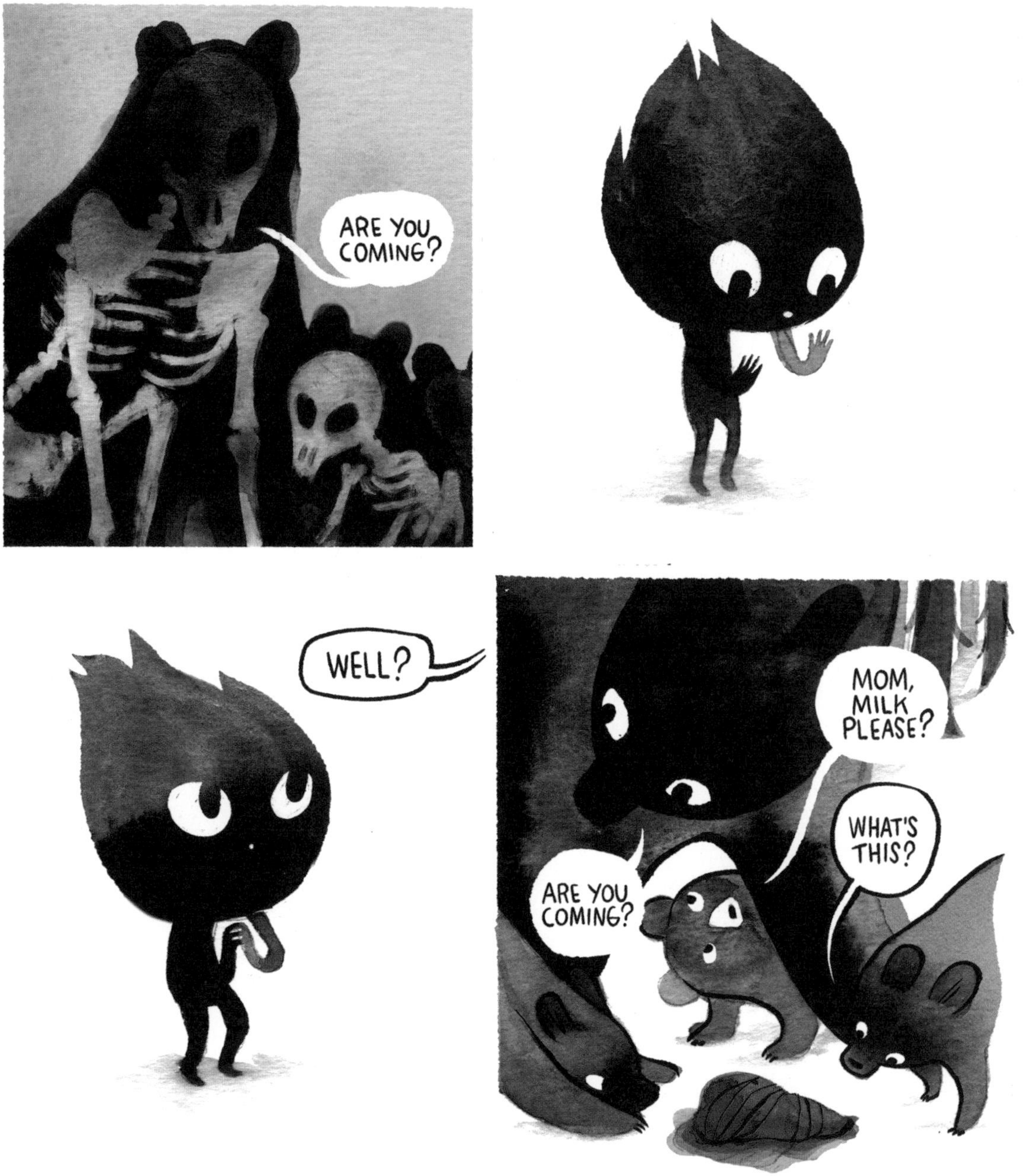
ARE YOU COMING?
WELL?
MOM, MILK PLEASE?
WHAT'S THIS?
ARE YOU COMING?

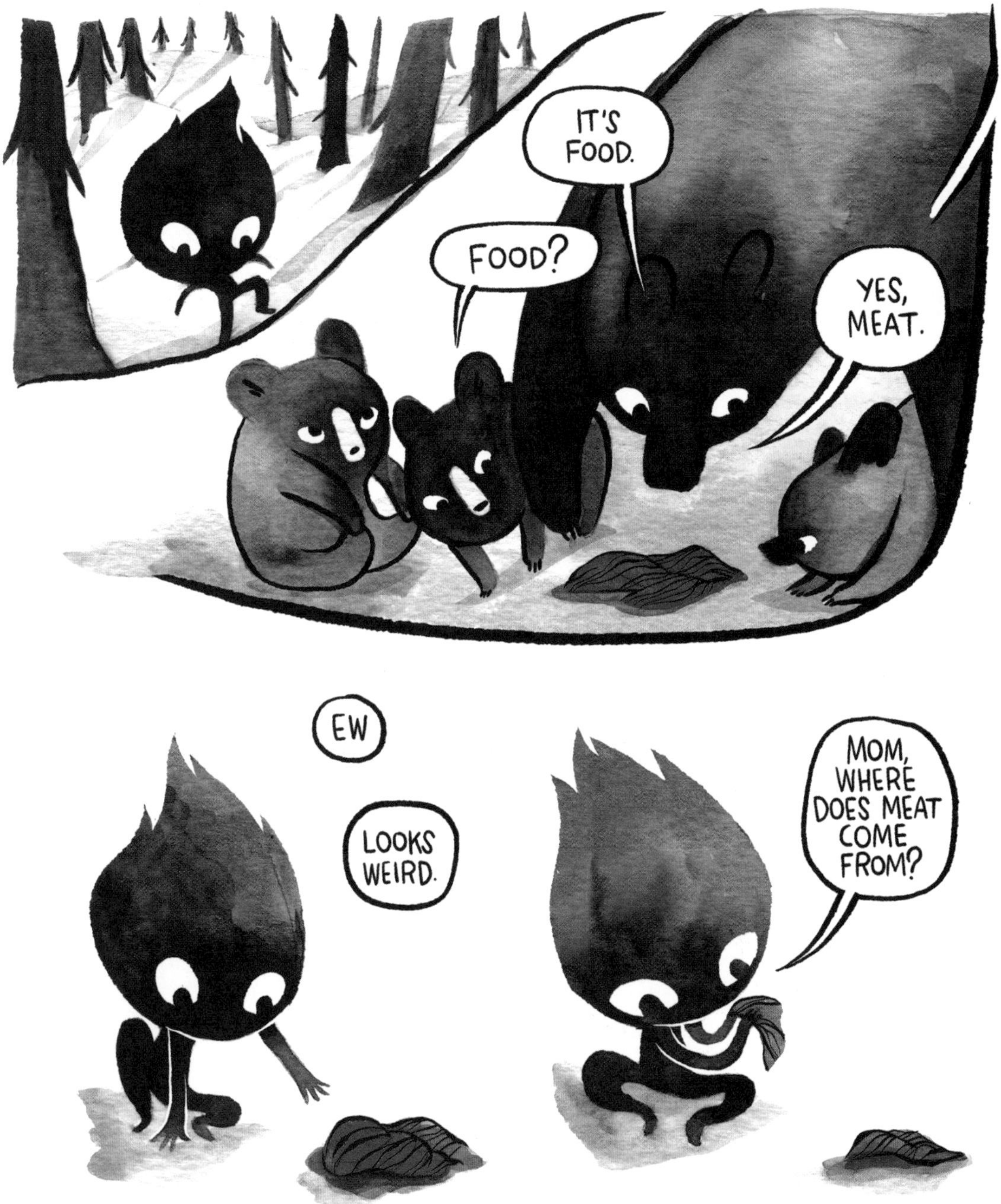
IT'S FOOD.
FOOD?
YES, MEAT.
EW
LOOKS WEIRD.
MOM, WHERE DOES MEAT COME FROM?

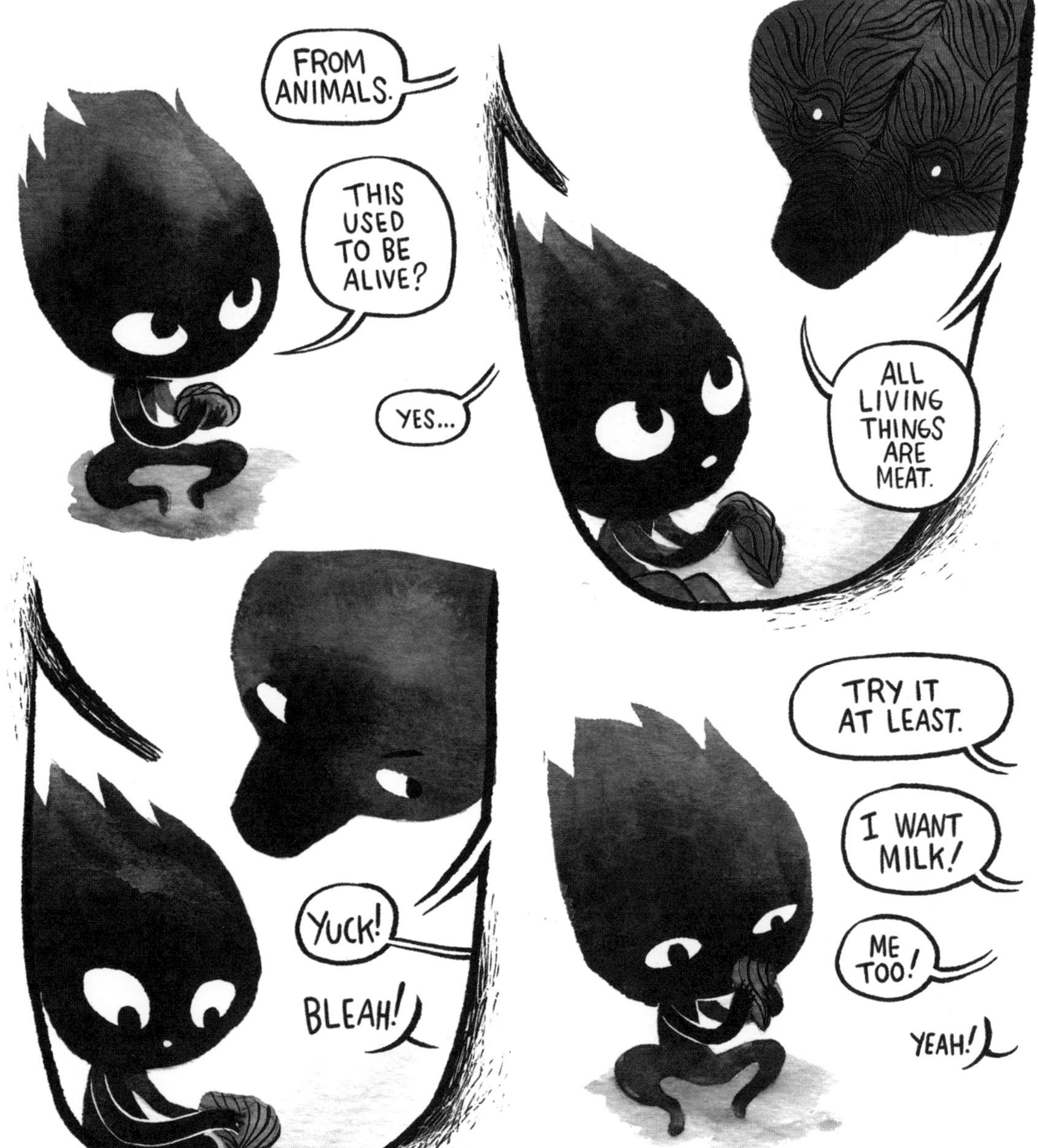
FROM ANIMALS.
THIS USED TO BE ALIVE?
YES...
ALL LIVING THINGS ARE MEAT.
YUCK!
BLEAH!
TRY IT AT LEAST.
I WANT MILK!
ME TOO!
YEAH!

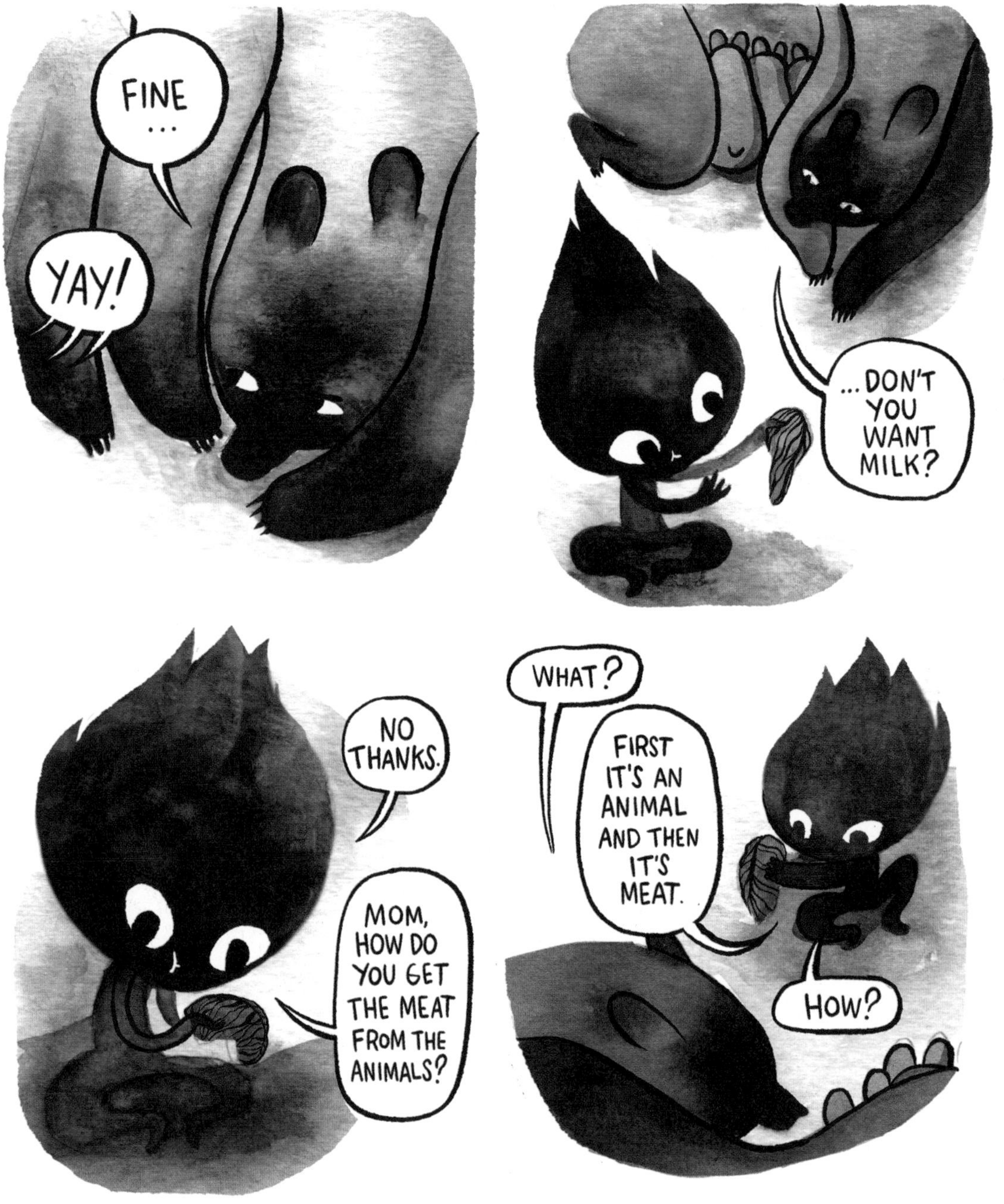
FINE
...
YAY!
...DON'T YOU WANT MILK?
NO THANKS.
MOM, HOW DO YOU GET THE MEAT FROM THE ANIMALS?
WHAT?
FIRST IT'S AN ANIMAL AND THEN IT'S MEAT.
HOW?

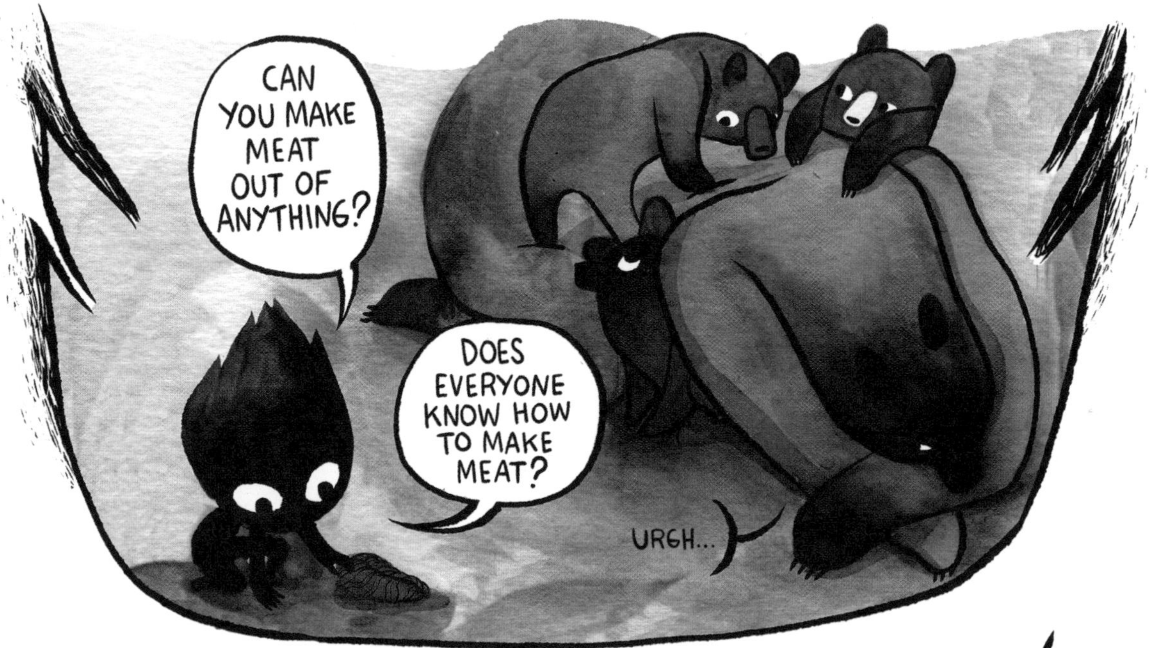
CAN YOU MAKE MEAT OUT OF ANYTHING?
DOES EVERYONE KNOW HOW TO MAKE MEAT?
URGH...

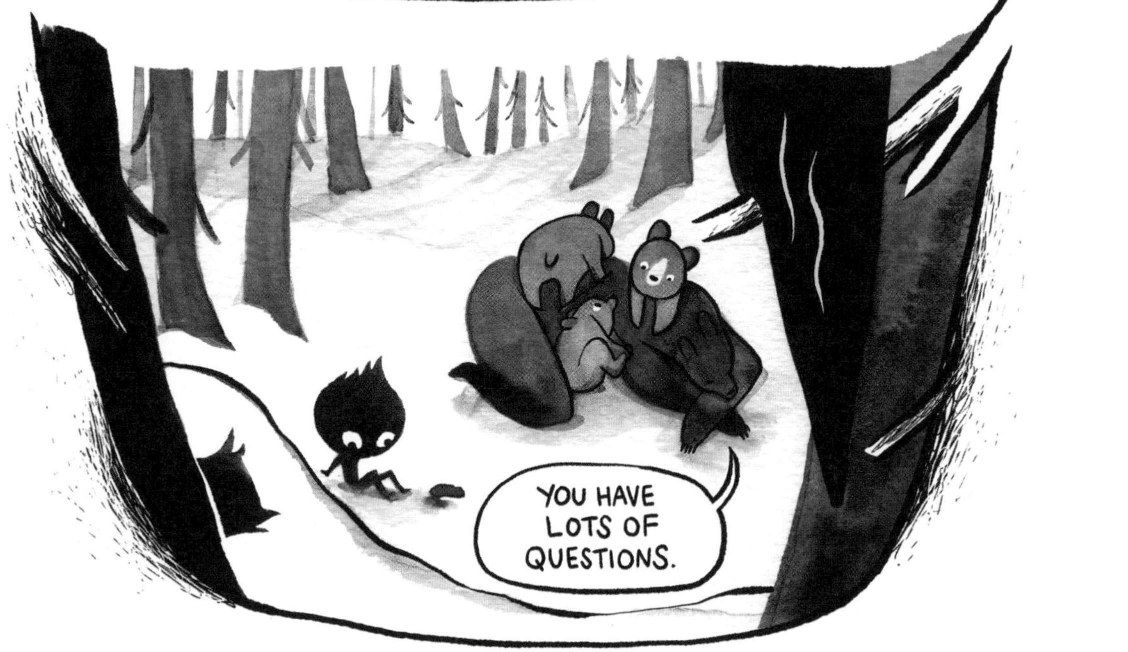
YOU HAVE LOTS OF QUESTIONS.

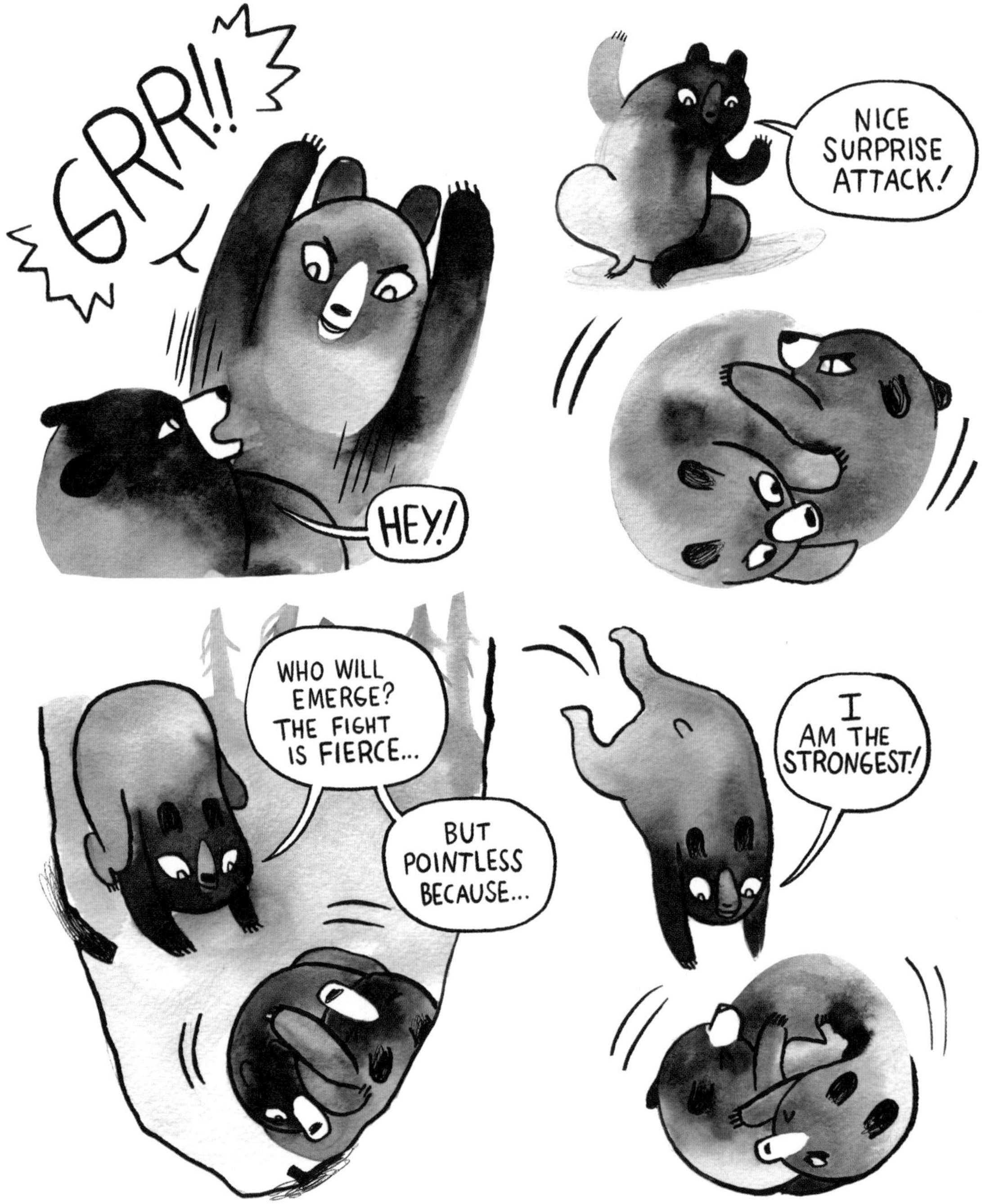
GRR!!
HEY!
NICE SURPRISE ATTACK!
WHO WILL EMERGE? THE FIGHT IS FIERCE...
BUT POINTLESS BECAUSE...
I AM THE STRONGEST!

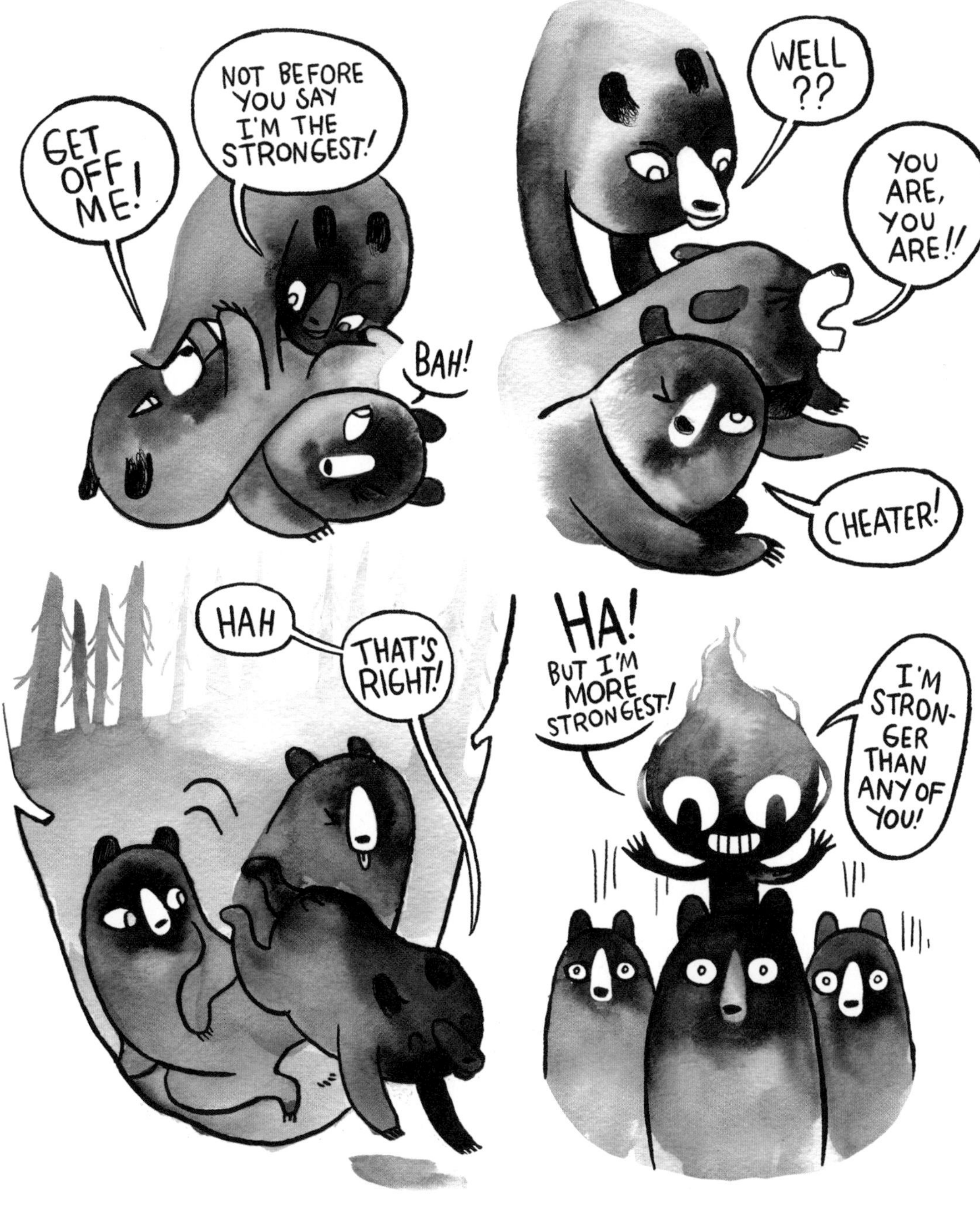
GET OFF ME!
NOT BEFORE YOU SAY I'M THE STRONGEST!
BAH!
WELL ??
YOU ARE, YOU ARE!!
CHEATER!
HAH
THAT'S RIGHT!
HA! BUT I'M MORE STRONGEST!
I'M STRON-GER THAN ANY OF YOU!

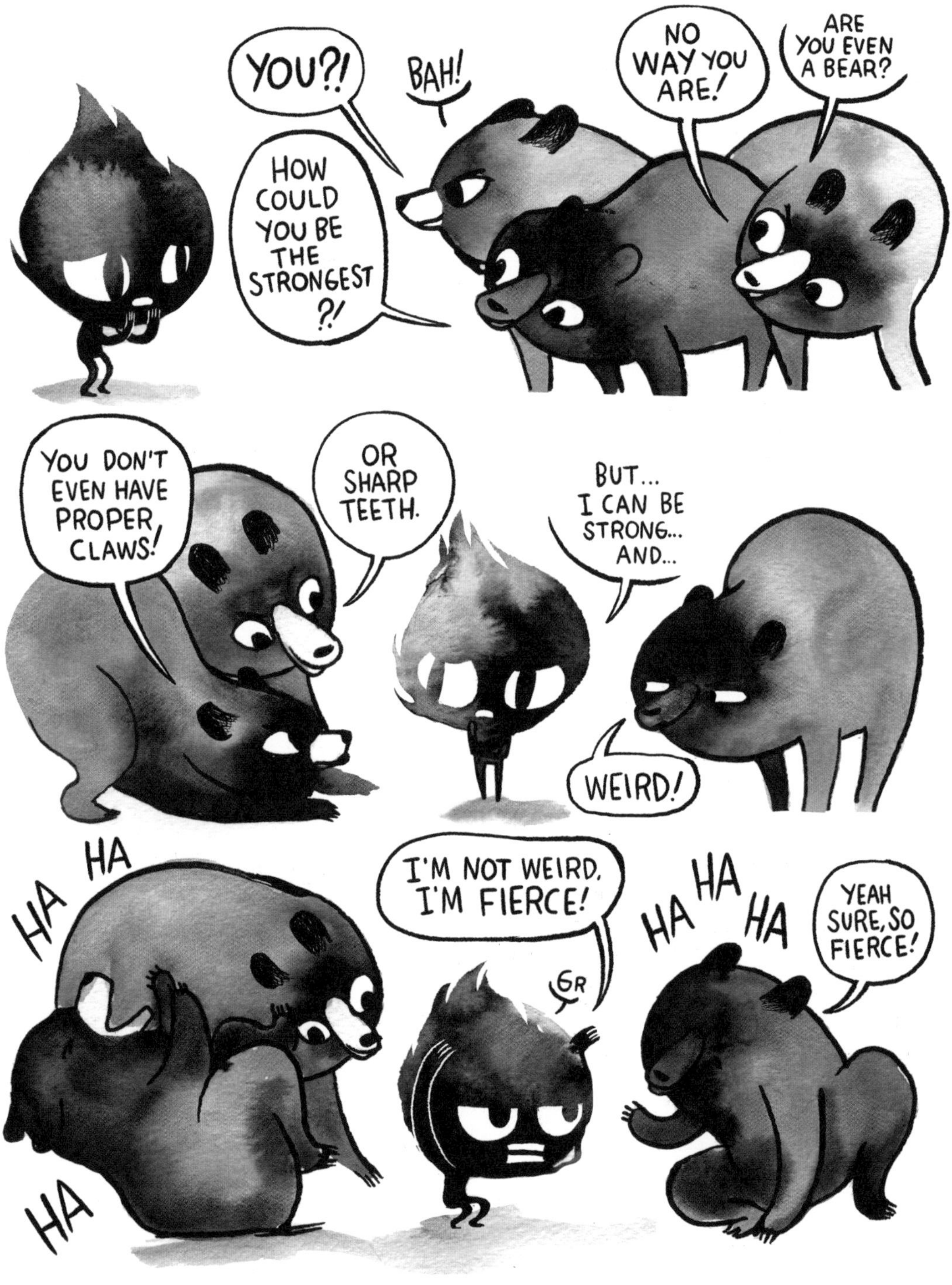
YOU?!
BAH!
HOW COULD YOU BE THE STRONGEST ?!
NO WAY YOU ARE!
ARE YOU EVEN A BEAR?
YOU DON'T EVEN HAVE PROPER CLAWS!
OR SHARP TEETH.
BUT... I CAN BE STRONG... AND...
WEIRD!
HA HA
HA
I'M NOT WEIRD, I'M FIERCE!
GR
HA HA HA
YEAH SURE, SO FIERCE!

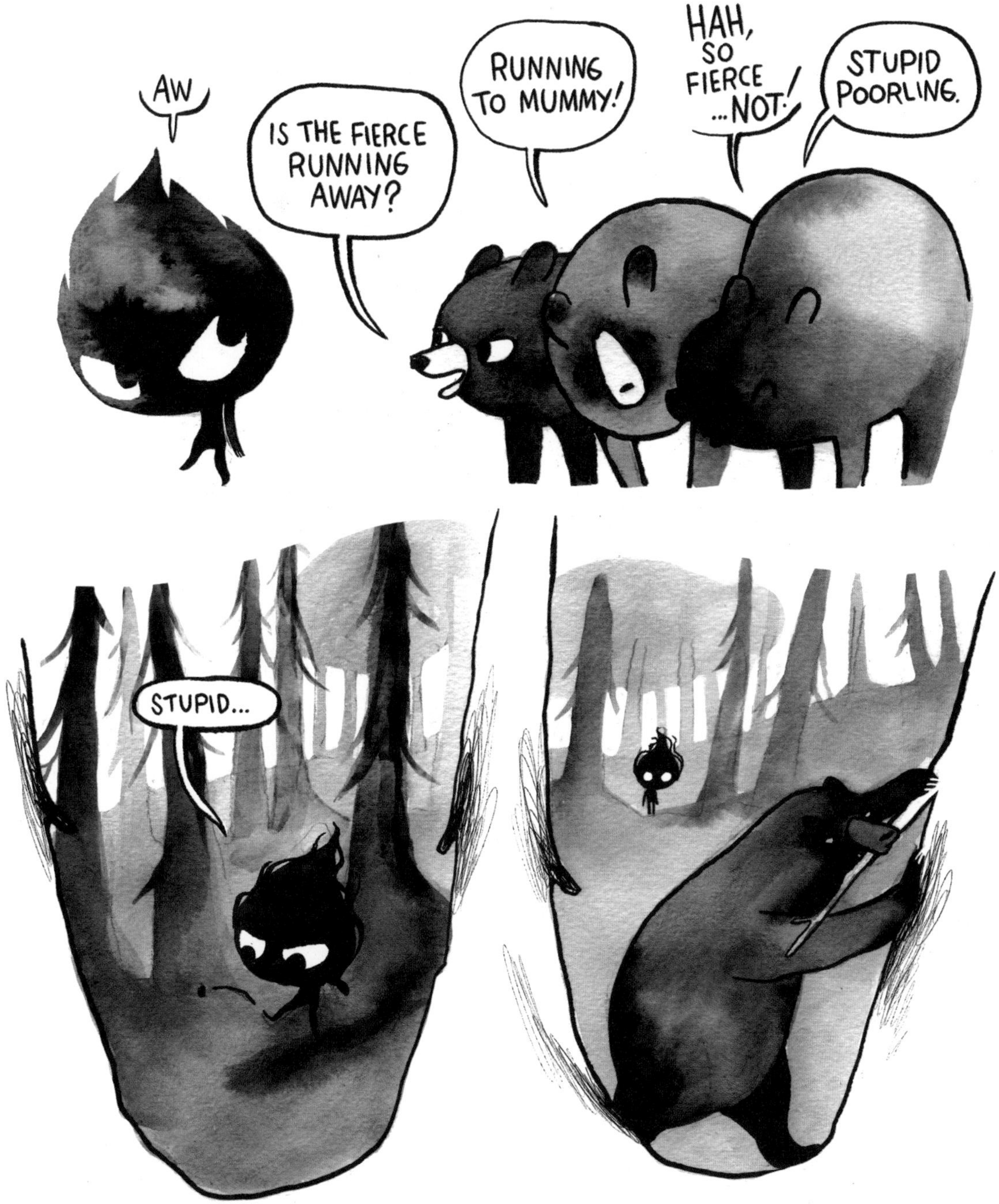
AW
IS THE FIERCE RUNNING AWAY?
RUNNING TO MUMMY!
HAH, SO FIERCE ...NOT!
STUPID POORLING.
STUPID...

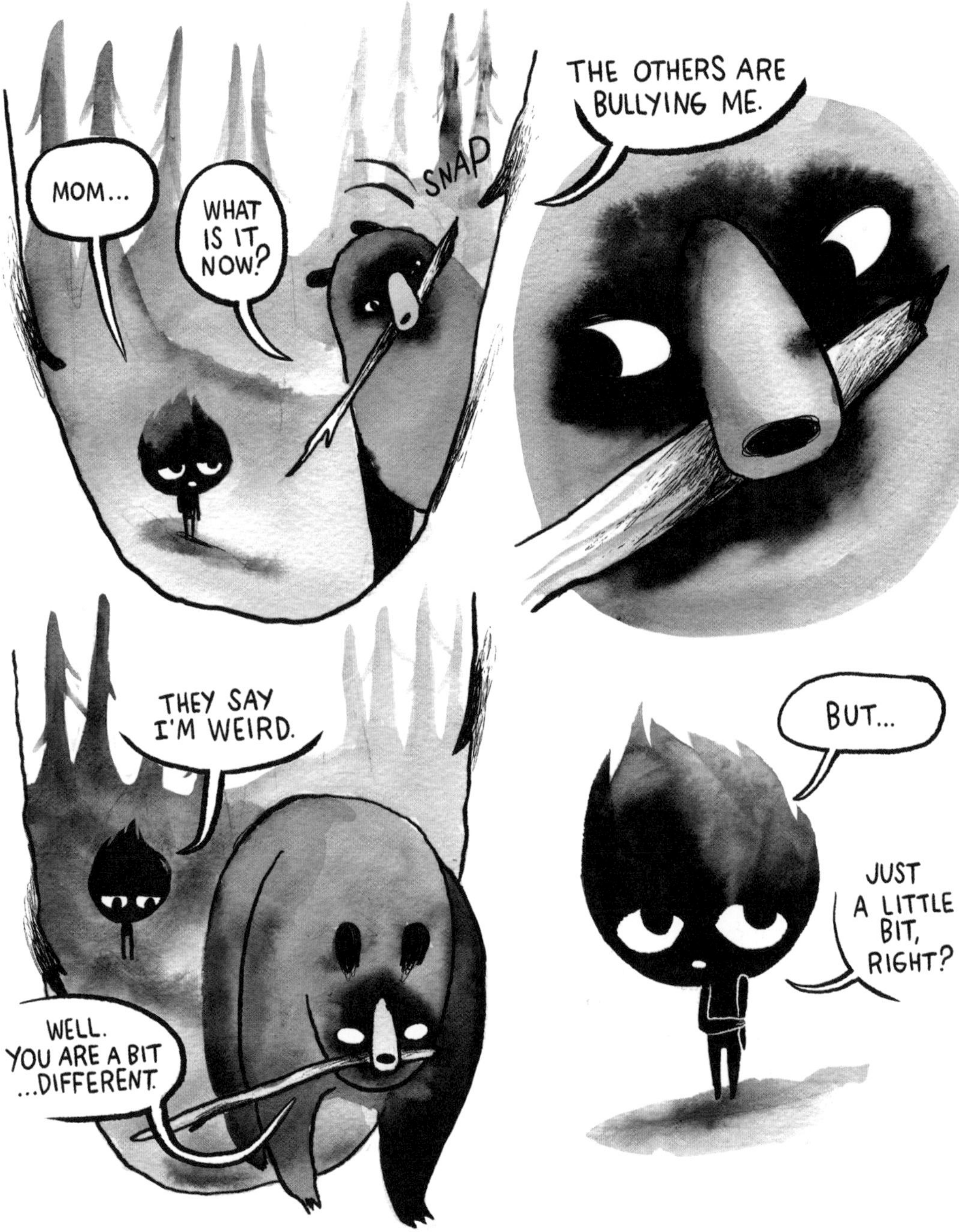
MOM...
WHAT IS IT NOW?
SNAP
THE OTHERS ARE BULLYING ME.
THEY SAY I'M WEIRD.
WELL. YOU ARE A BIT ...DIFFERENT.
BUT...
JUST A LITTLE BIT, RIGHT?

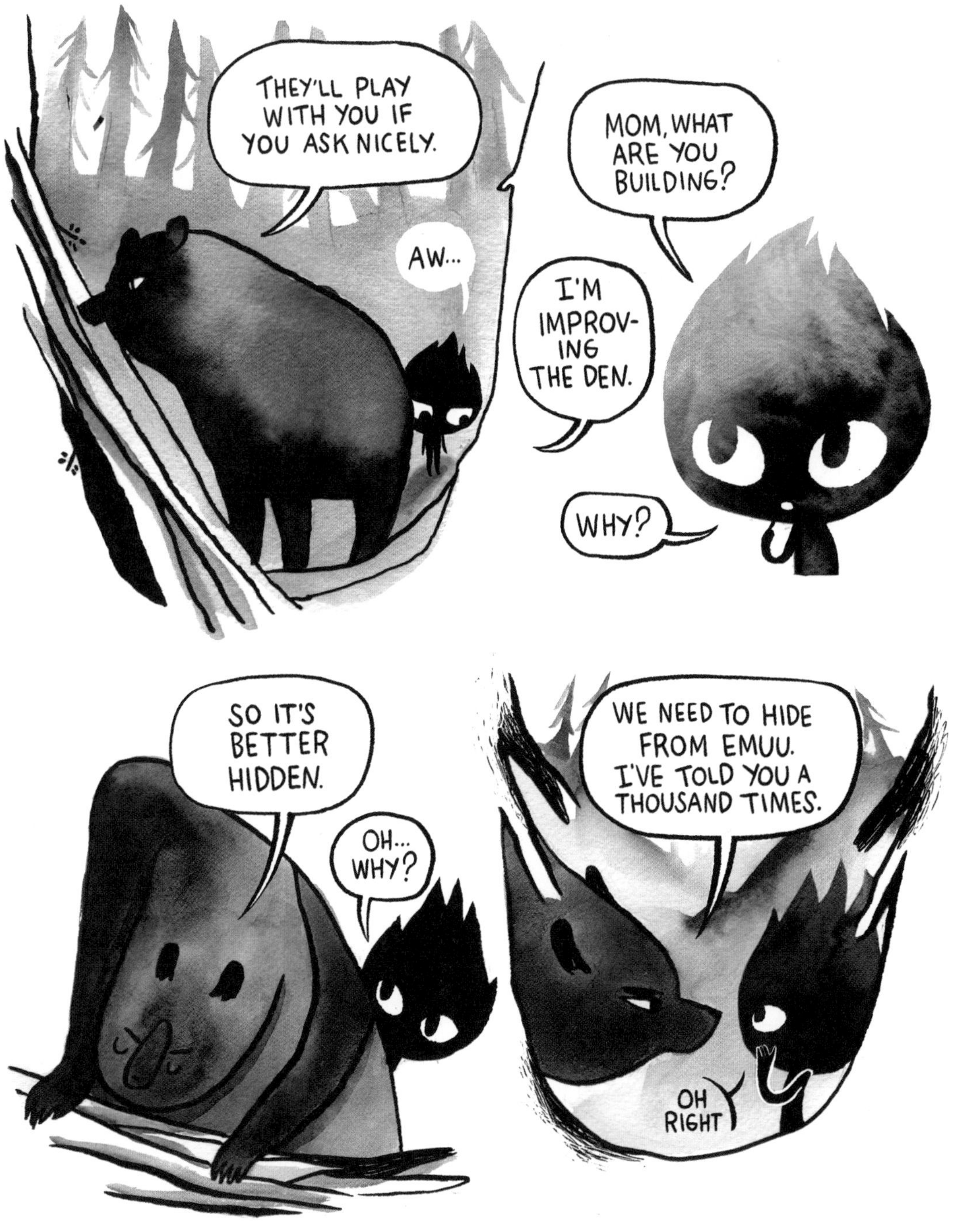
THEY'LL PLAY WITH YOU IF YOU ASK NICELY.
AW...
MOM, WHAT ARE YOU BUILDING?
I'M IMPROV-ING THE DEN.
WHY?
SO IT'S BETTER HIDDEN.
OH... WHY?
WE NEED TO HIDE FROM EMUU. I'VE TOLD YOU A THOUSAND TIMES.
OH RIGHT

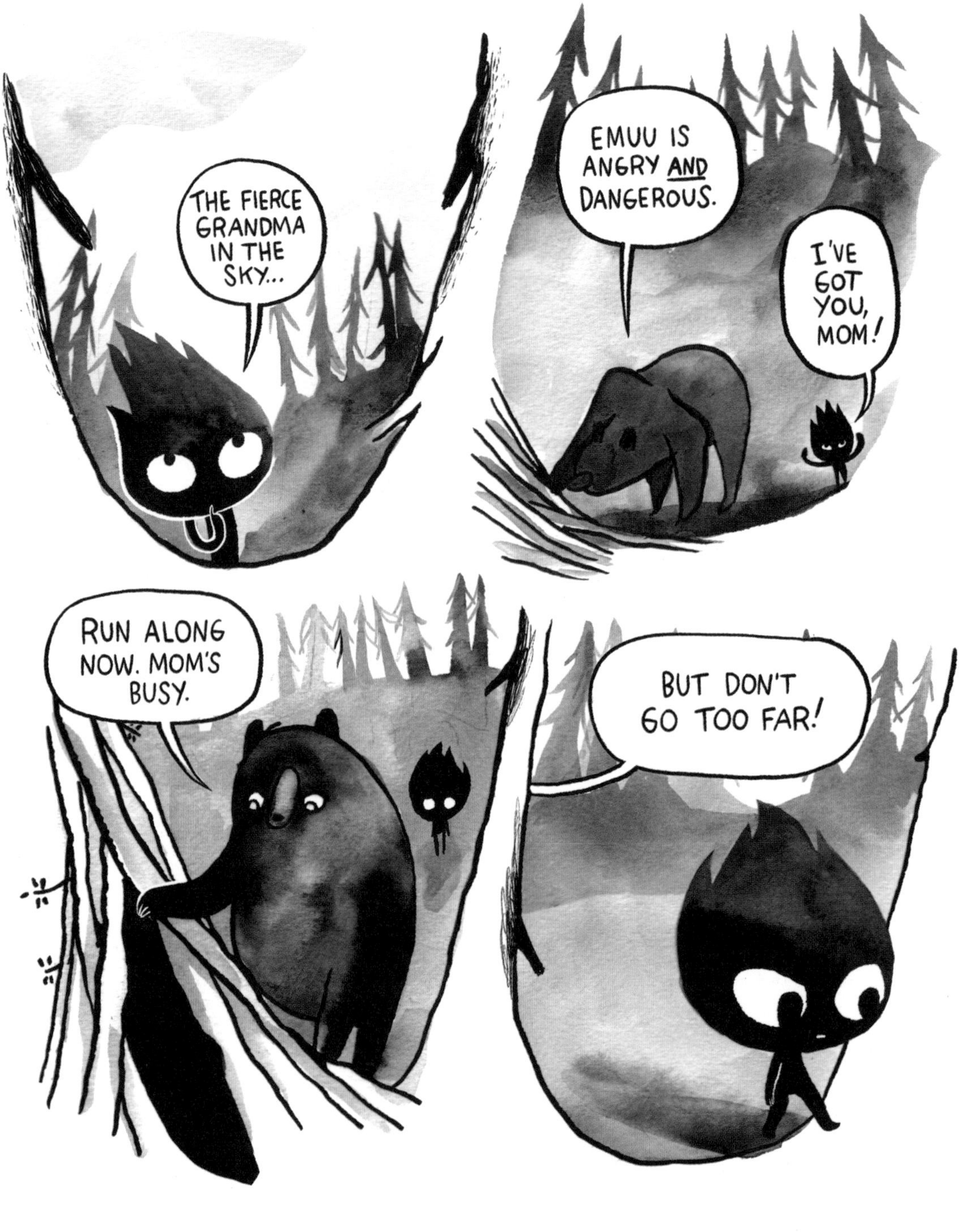
THE FIERCE GRANDMA IN THE SKY...
EMUU IS ANGRY AND DANGEROUS.
I'VE GOT YOU, MOM!
RUN ALONG NOW. MOM'S BUSY.
BUT DON'T GO TOO FAR!

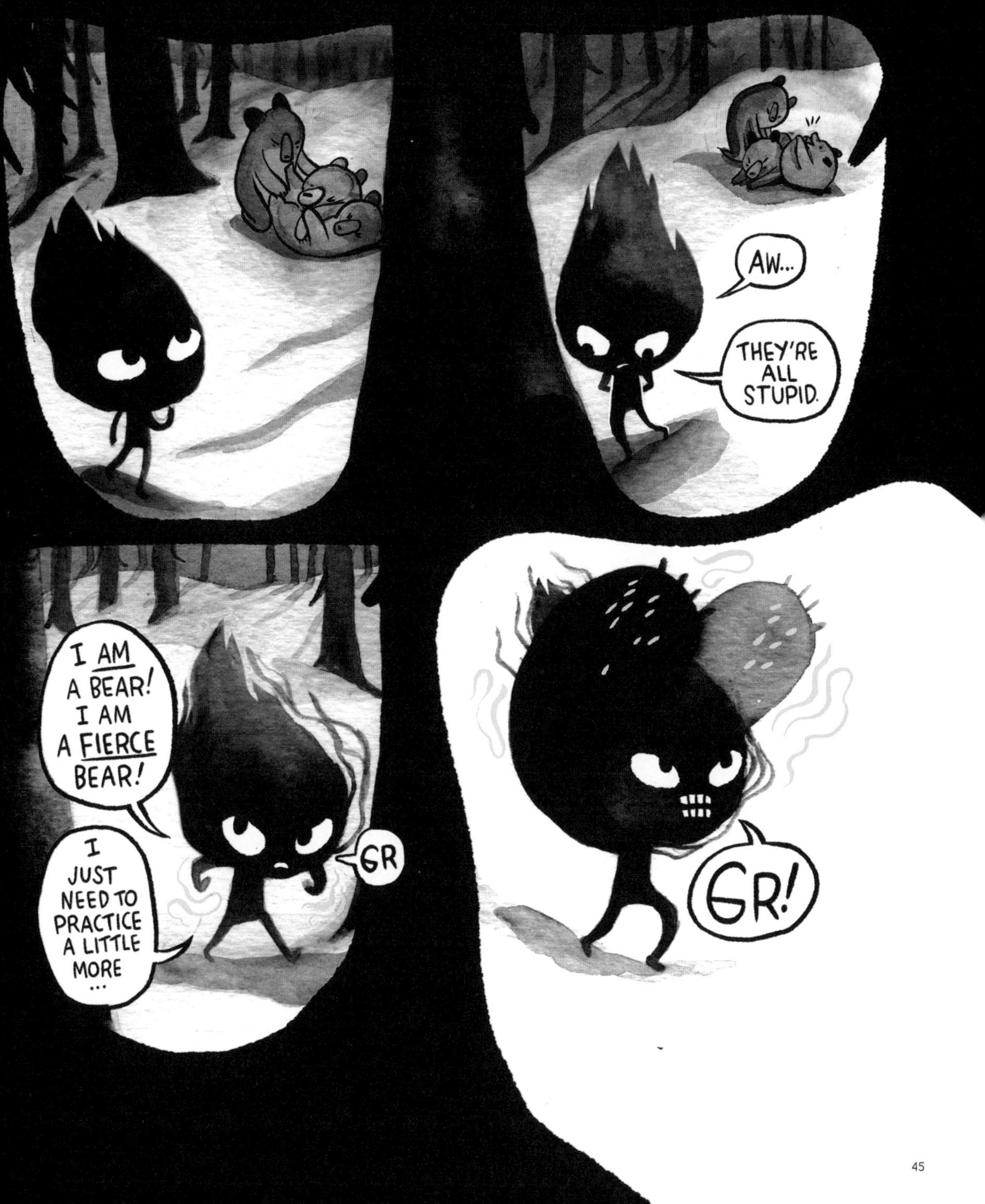
AW...
THEY'RE ALL STUPID.
I AM A BEAR! I AM A FIERCE BEAR!
I JUST NEED TO PRACTICE A LITTLE MORE ...
GR
GR!

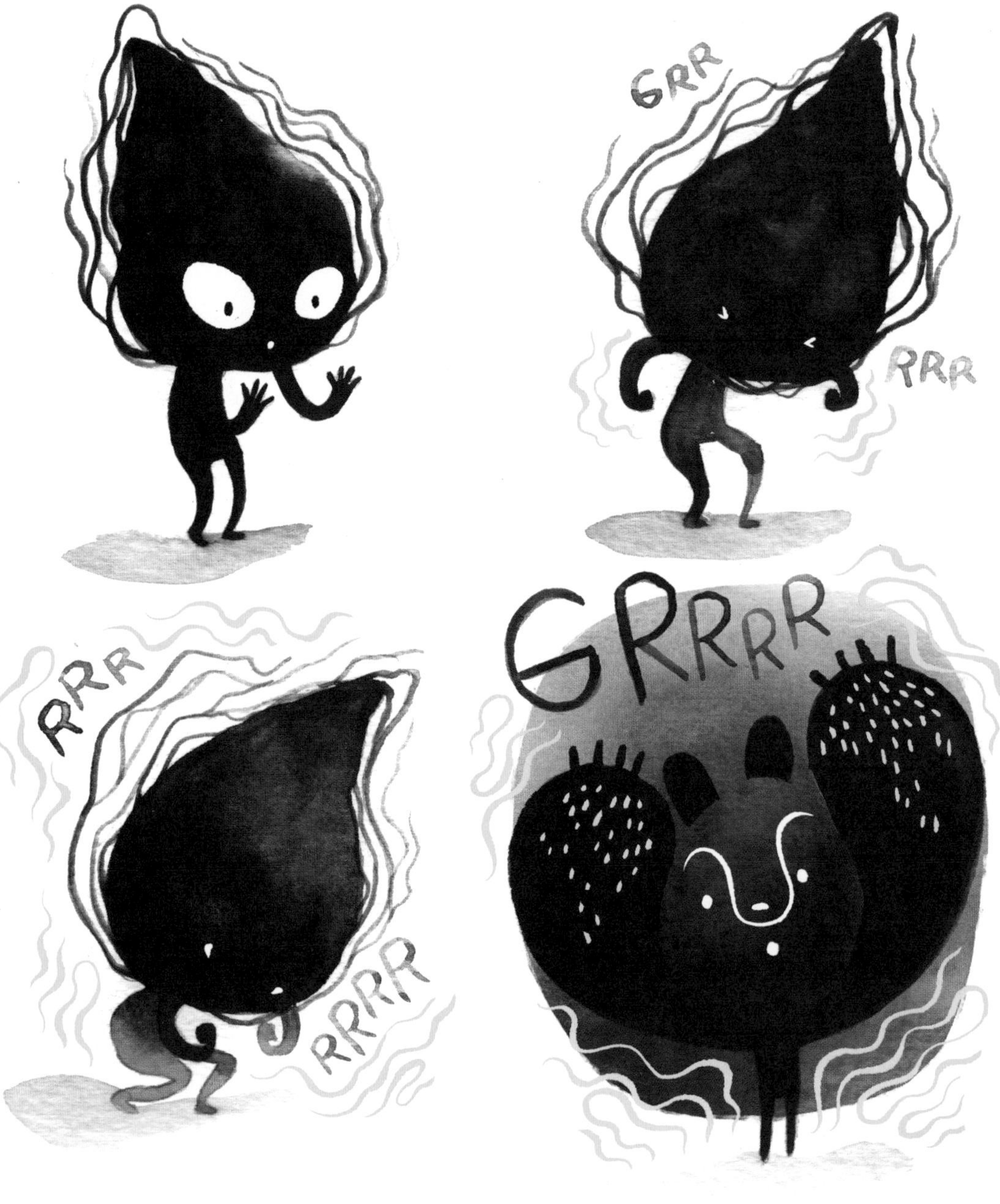
GRR
RRR
RRR
RRRRR
GRRRR

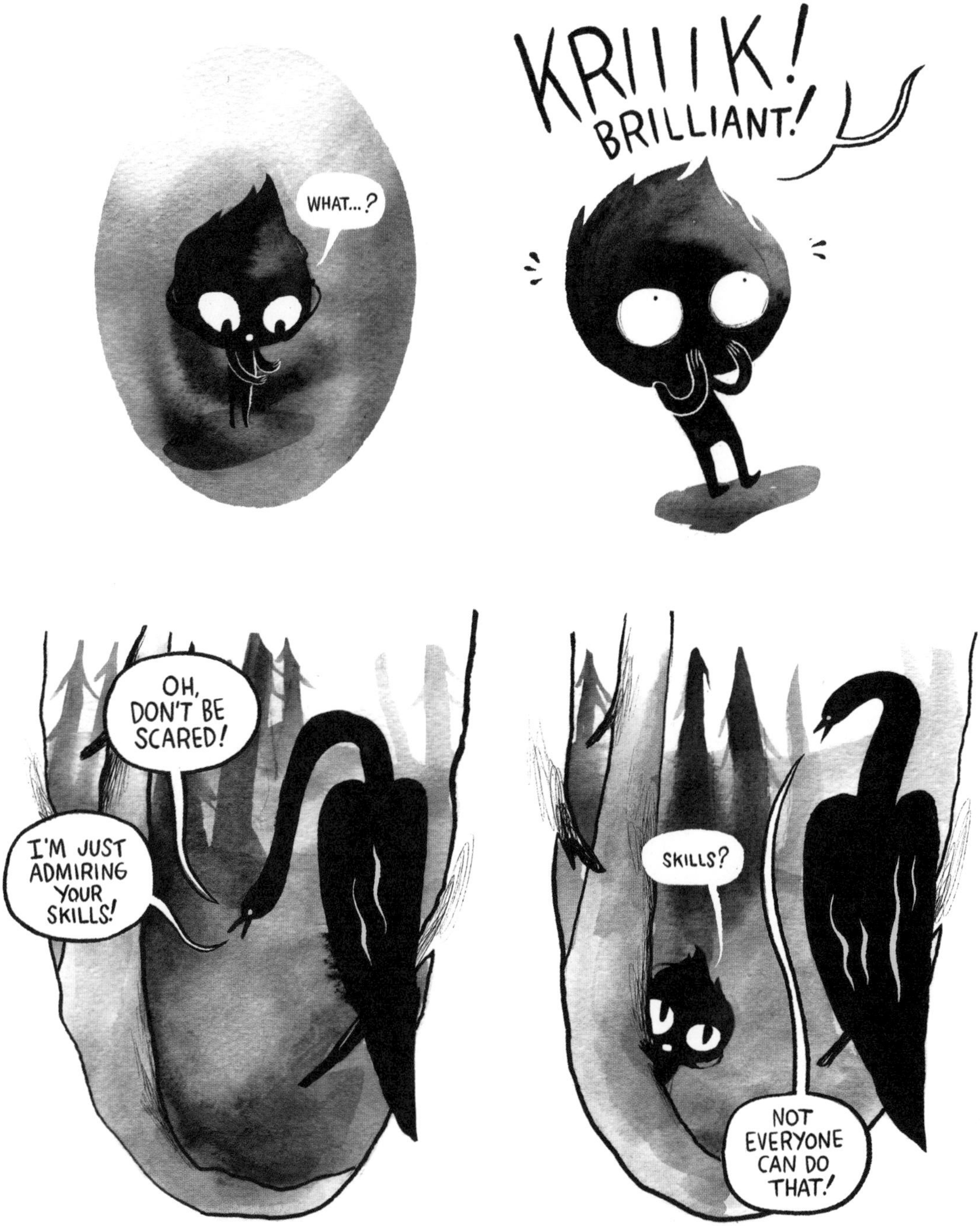
WHAT...?
KRIIIK!
BRILLIANT!
OH, DON'T BE SCARED!
I'M JUST ADMIRING YOUR SKILLS!
SKILLS?
NOT EVERYONE CAN DO THAT!

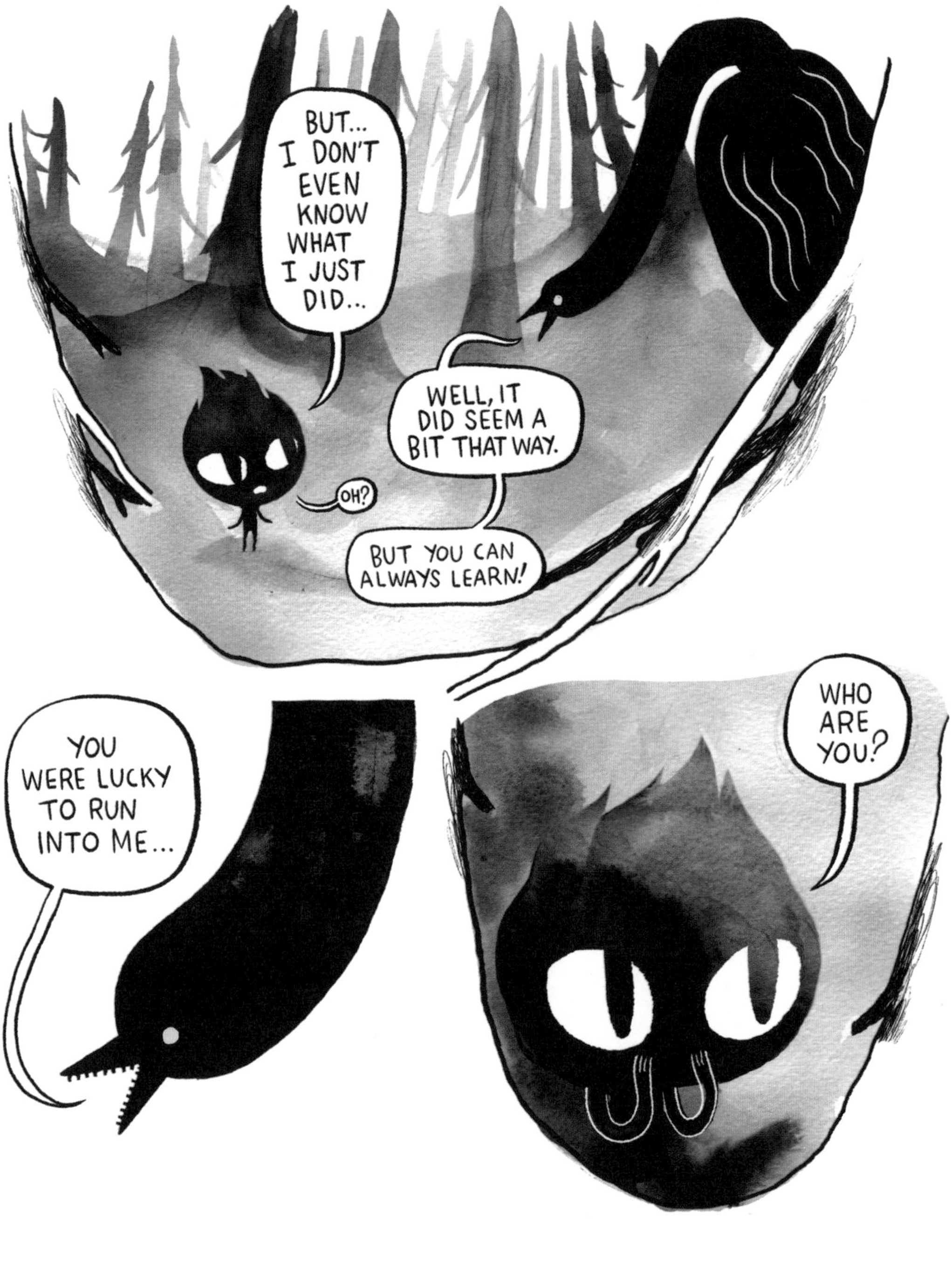
BUT... I DON'T EVEN KNOW WHAT I JUST DID...
WELL, IT DID SEEM A BIT THAT WAY.
OH?
BUT YOU CAN ALWAYS LEARN!
YOU WERE LUCKY TO RUN INTO ME...
WHO ARE YOU?

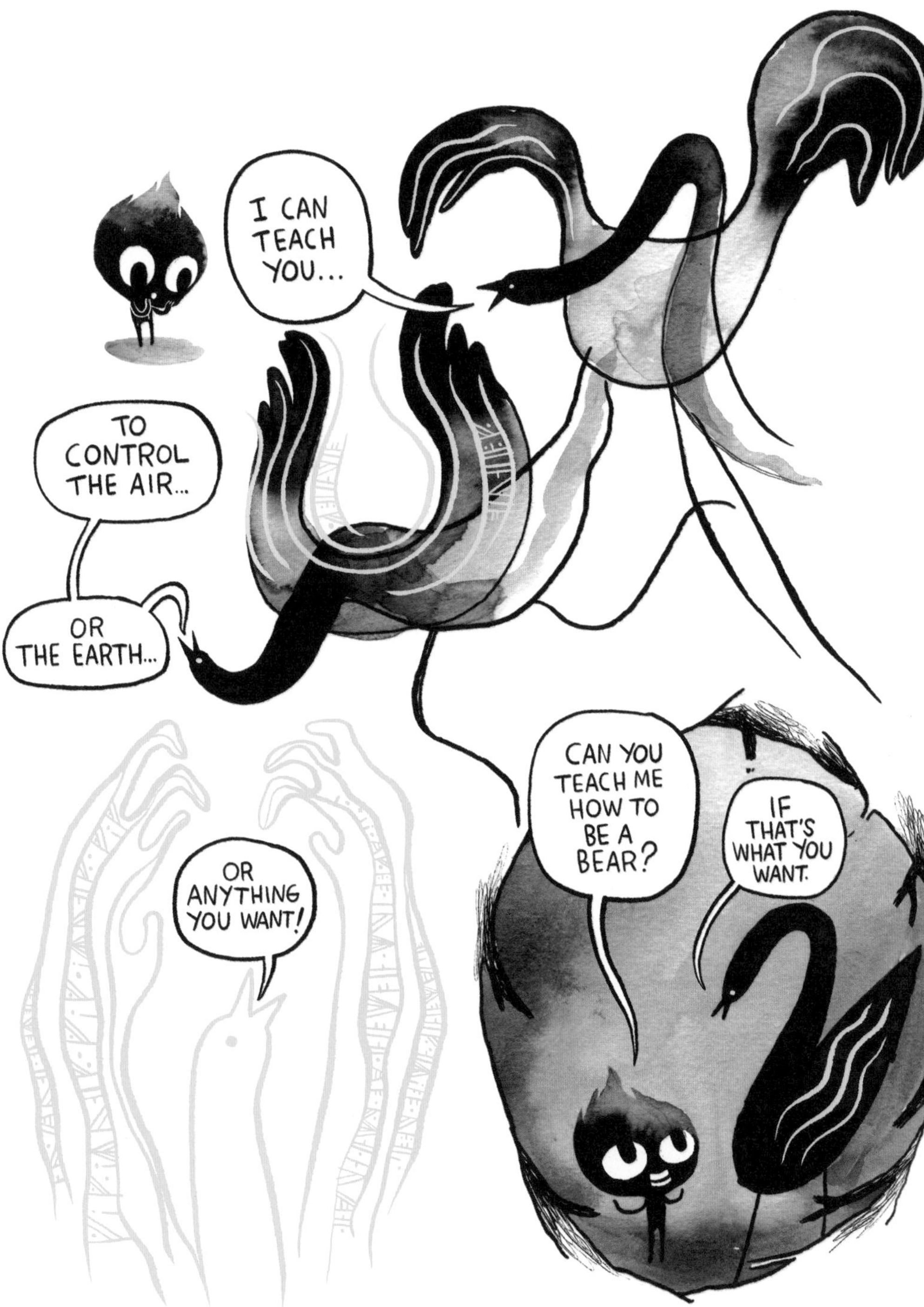
I CAN TEACH YOU...
TO CONTROL THE AIR...
OR THE EARTH...
OR ANYTHING YOU WANT!
CAN YOU TEACH ME HOW TO BE A BEAR?
IF THAT'S WHAT YOU WANT.

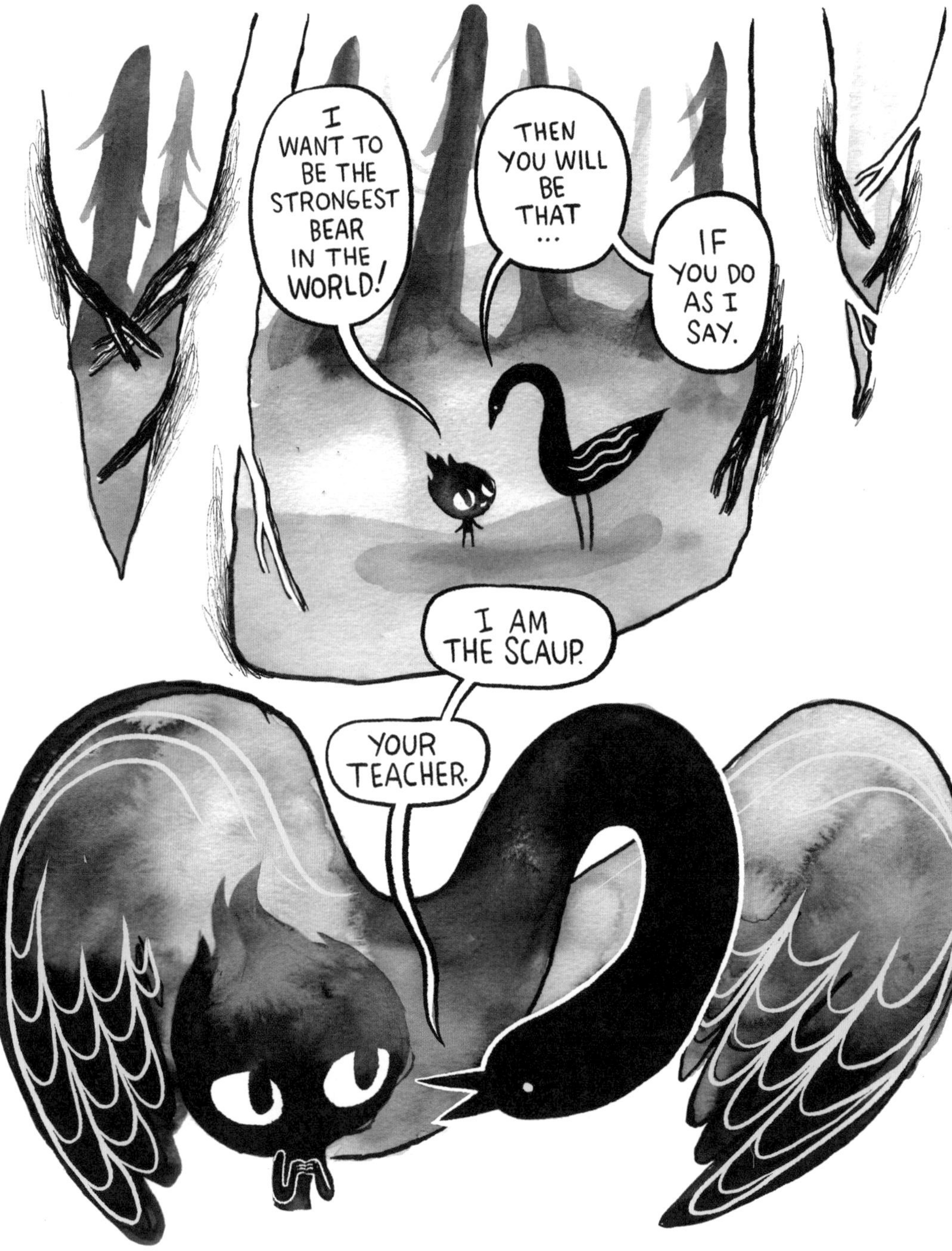
I WANT TO BE THE STRONGEST BEAR IN THE WORLD!
THEN YOU WILL BE THAT ...
IF YOU DO AS I SAY.
I AM THE SCAUP.
YOUR TEACHER.

II

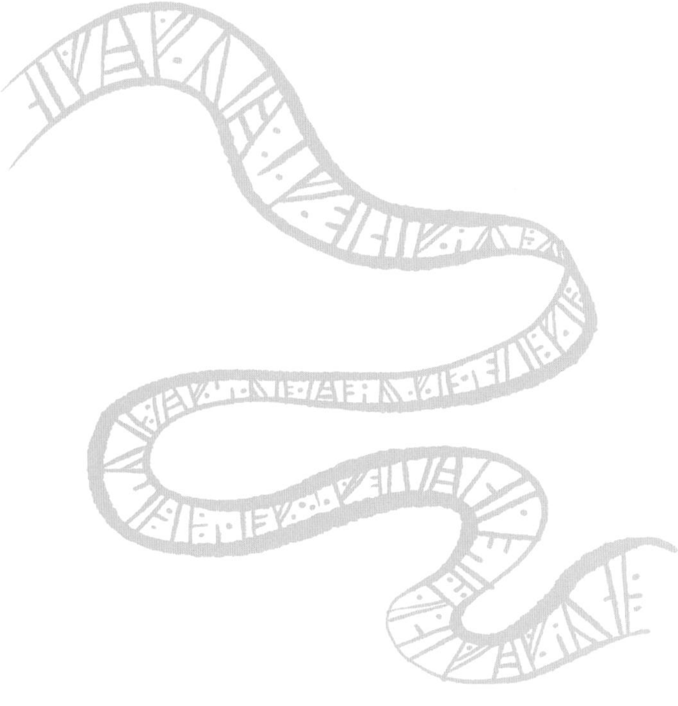

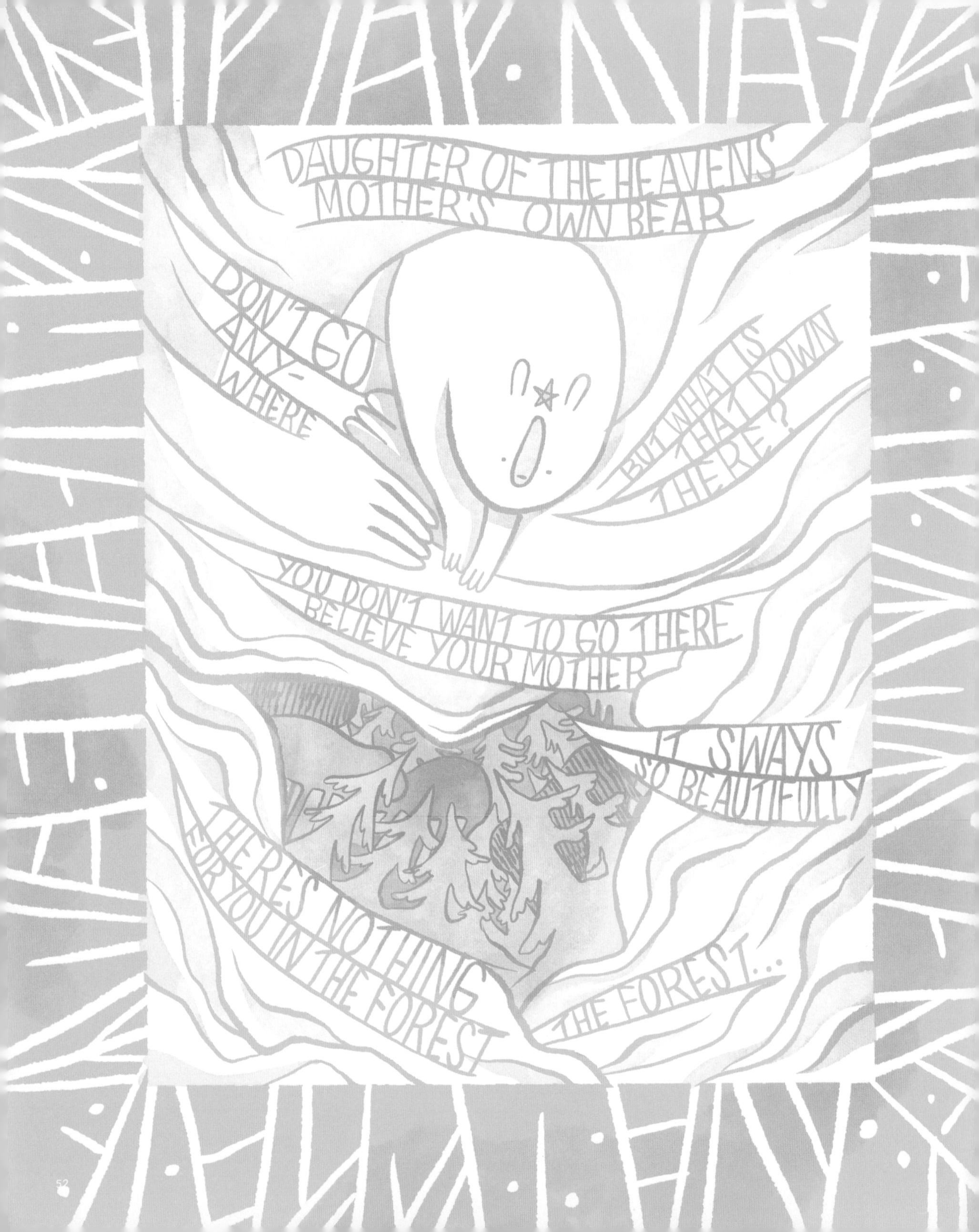
DAUGHTER OF THE HEAVENS
MOTHER'S OWN BEAR
DON'T GO ANY-WHERE
BUT WHAT IS THAT DOWN THERE?
YOU DON'T WANT TO GO THERE
BELIEVE YOUR MOTHER
IT SWAYS SO BEAUTIFULLY
THERE'S NOTHING FOR YOU IN THE FOREST
THE FOREST...

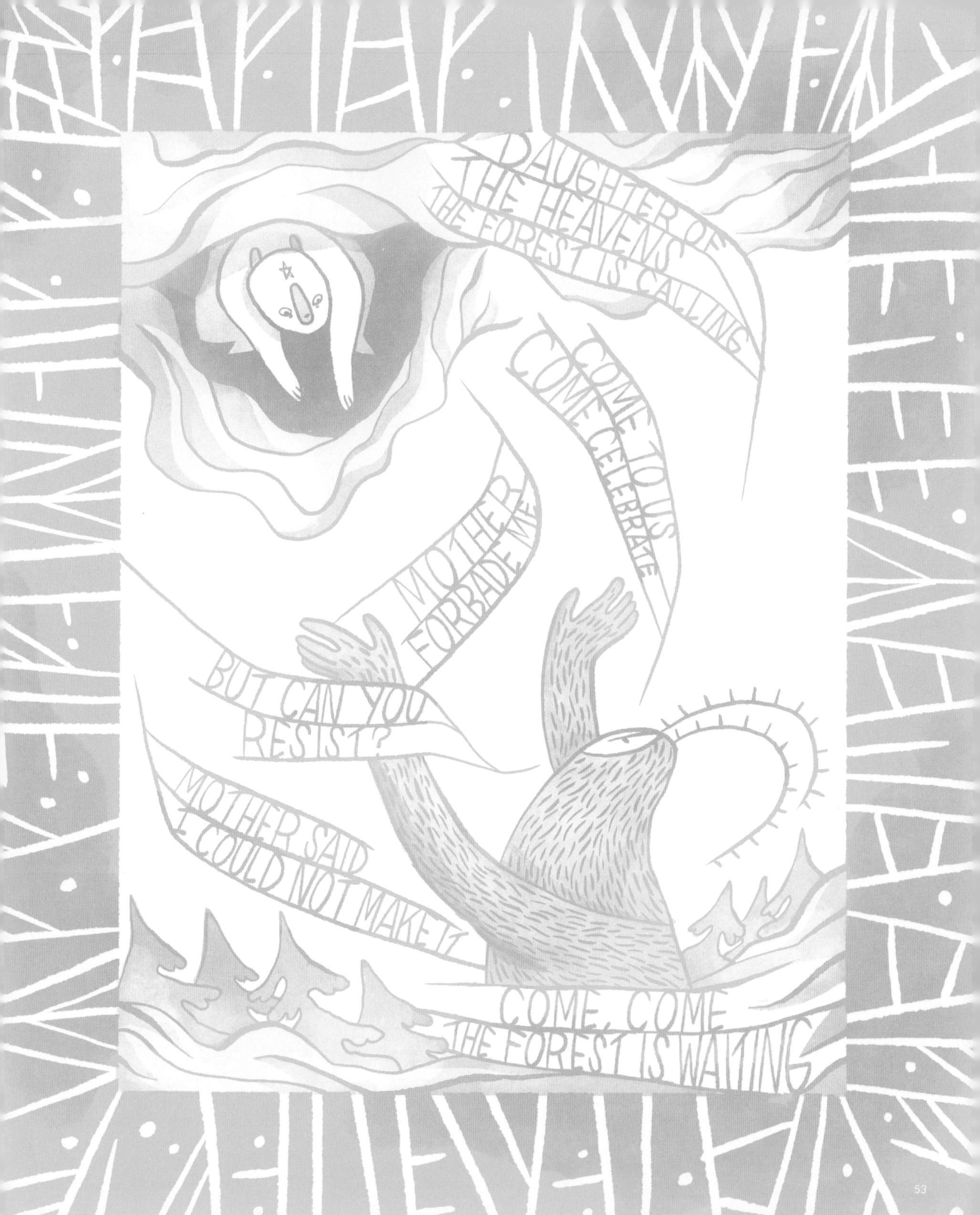
DAUGHTER OF
THE HEAVENS
THE FOREST IS CALLING
COME TO US
COME CELEBRATE
MOTHER
FORBADE ME
BUT CAN YOU
RESIST?
MOTHER SAID
I COULD NOT MAKE IT
COME, COME
THE FOREST IS WAITING

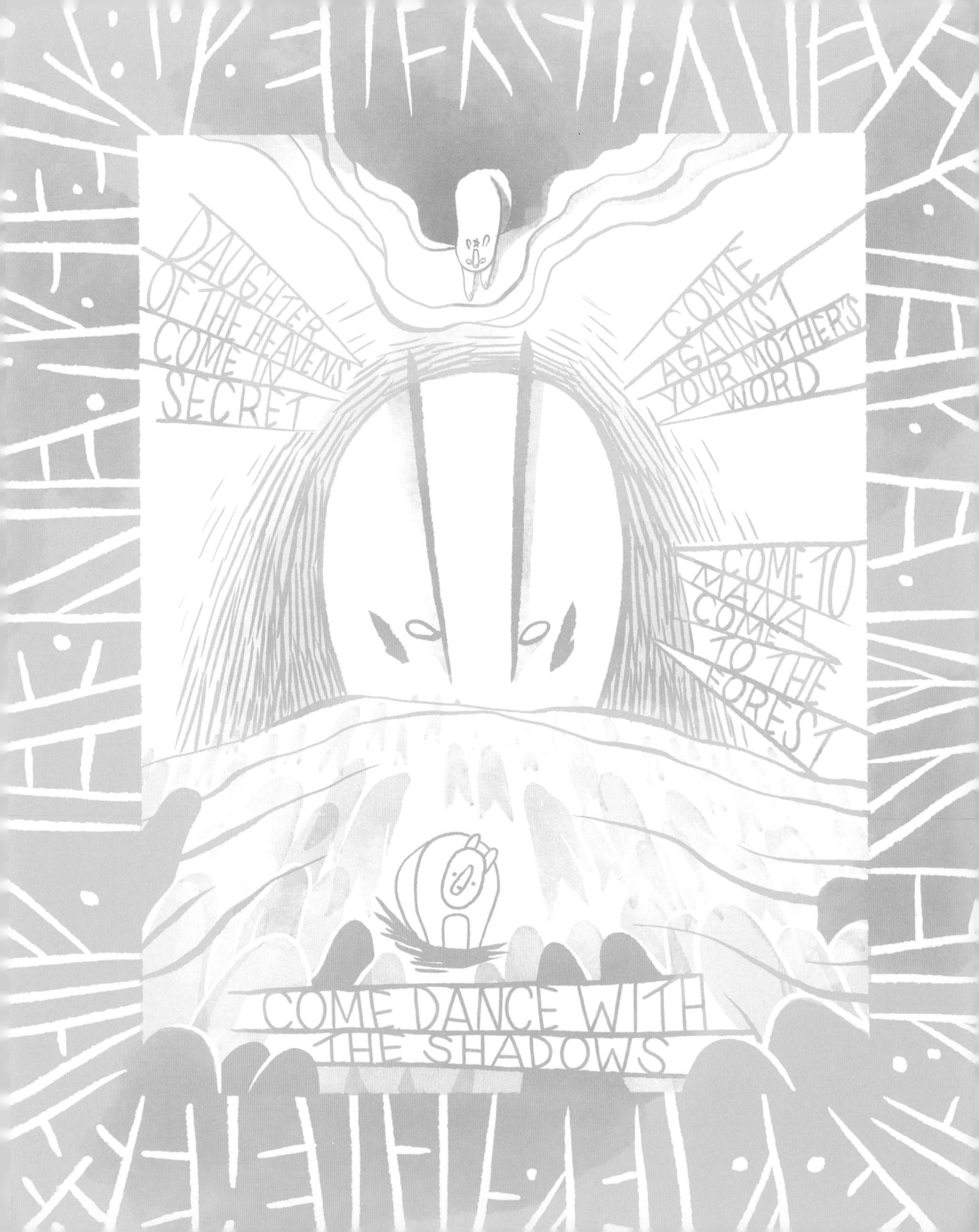

DAUGHTER OF THE HEAVENS COME IN SECRET
COME AGAINST YOUR MOTHER'S WORD
COME TO MAMA COME TO THE FOREST
COME DANCE WITH THE SHADOWS

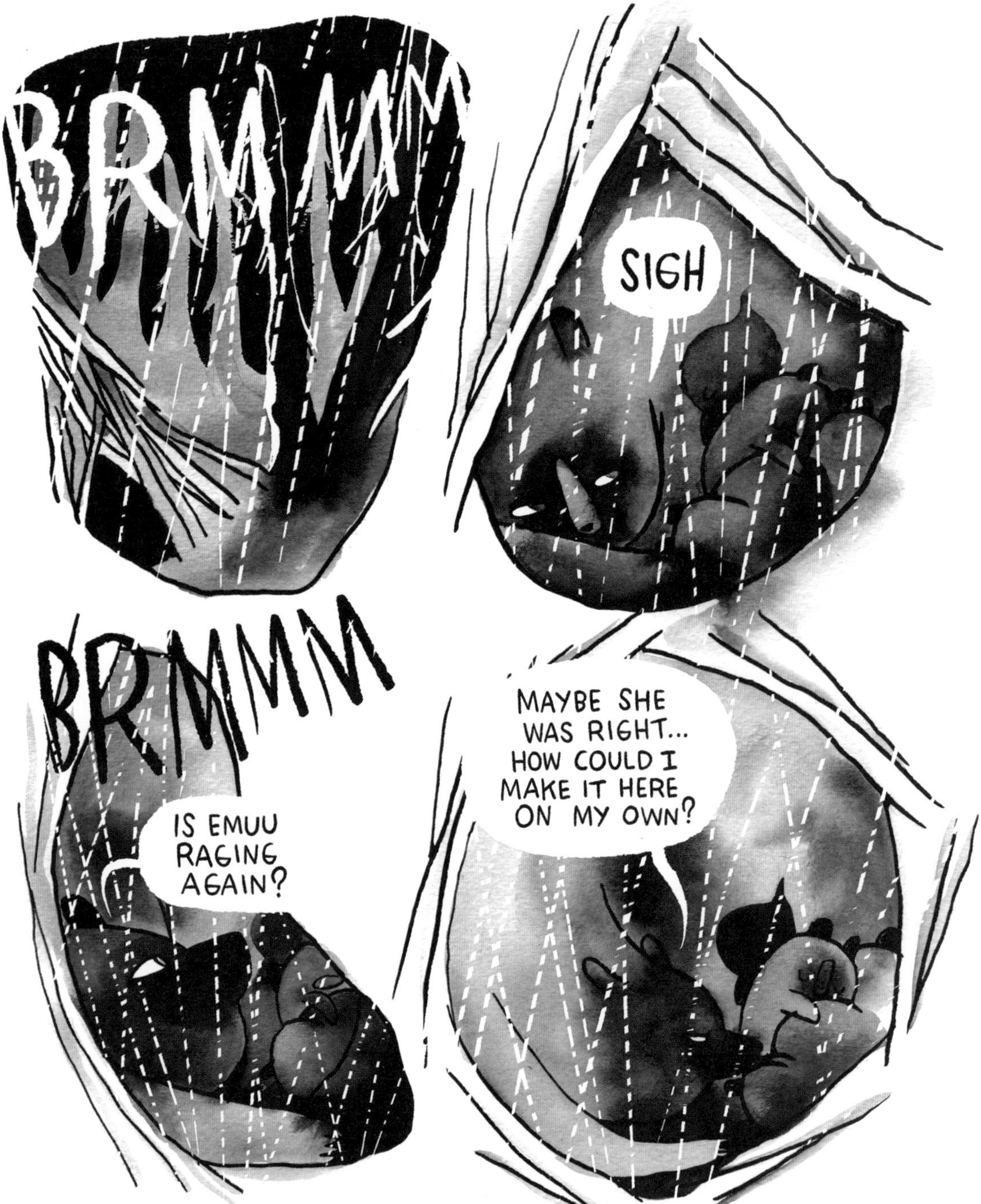
BRMMM
SIGH
BRMMM
IS EMUU RAGING AGAIN?
MAYBE SHE WAS RIGHT... HOW COULD I MAKE IT HERE ON MY OWN?

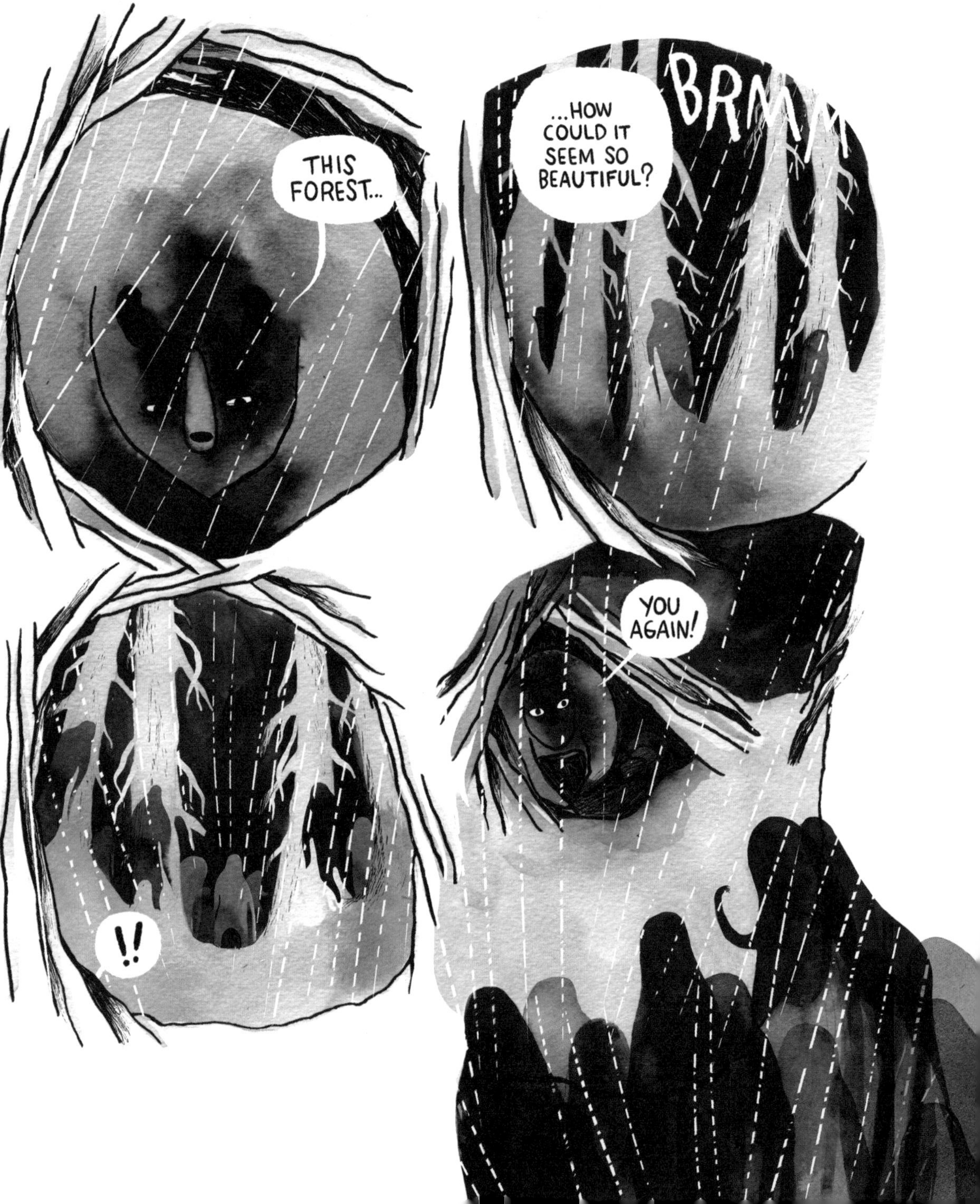
THIS FOREST...
...HOW COULD IT SEEM SO BEAUTIFUL?
BRMM
!!
YOU AGAIN!

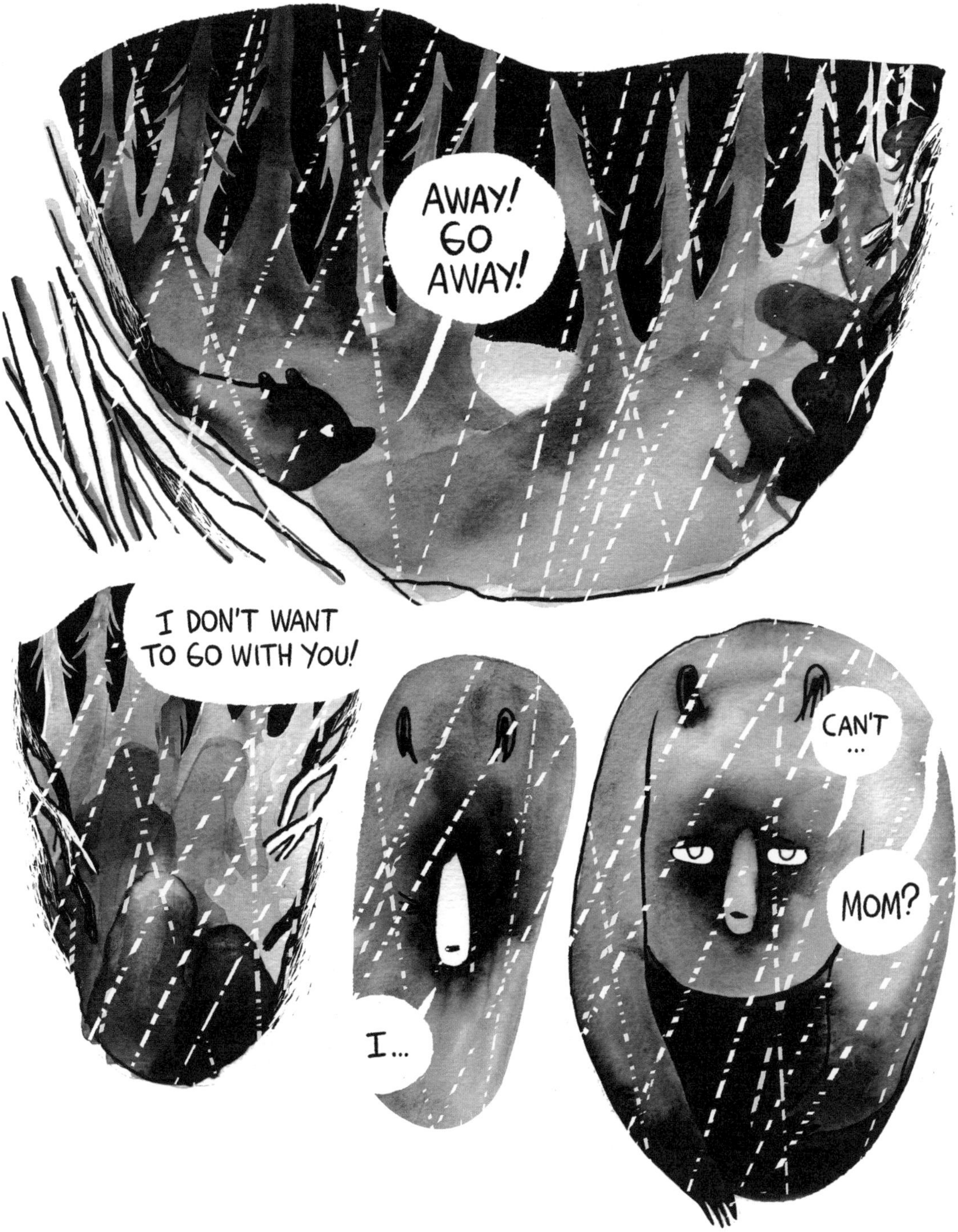
AWAY! GO AWAY!
I DON'T WANT TO GO WITH YOU!
I...
CAN'T ...
MOM?

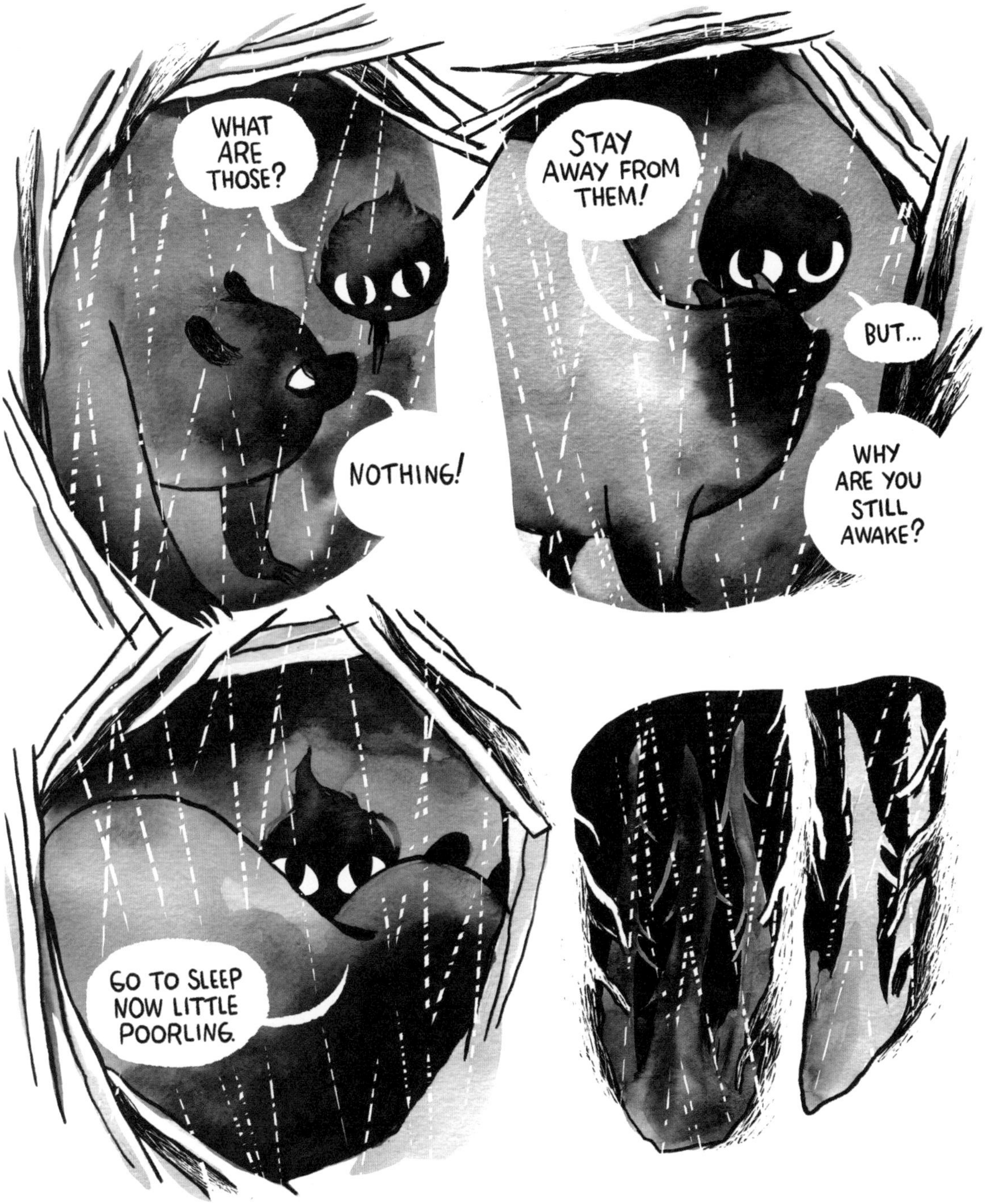
WHAT ARE THOSE?
NOTHING!
STAY AWAY FROM THEM!
BUT...
WHY ARE YOU STILL AWAKE?
GO TO SLEEP NOW LITTLE POORLING.

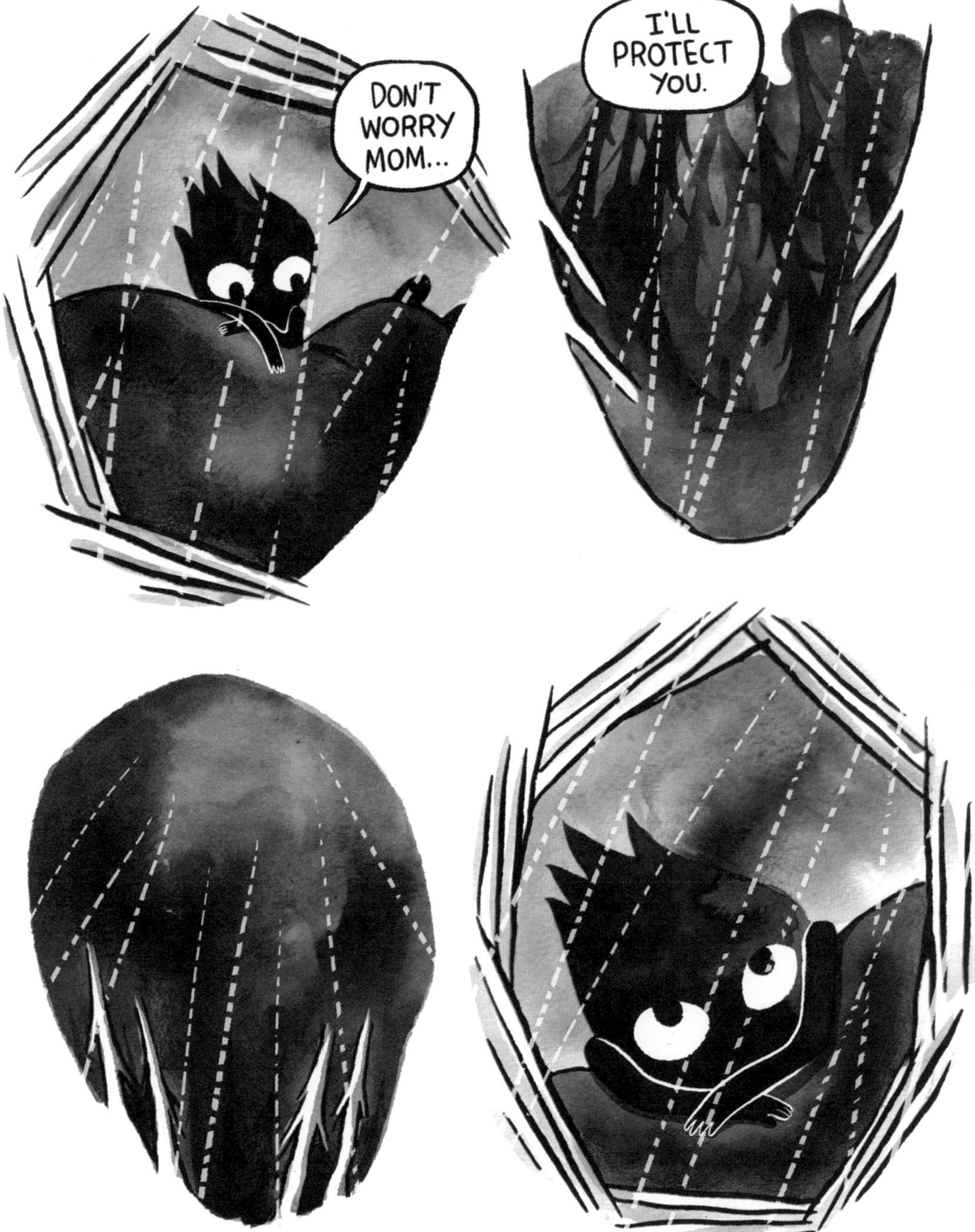
DON'T WORRY MOM...
I'LL PROTECT YOU.

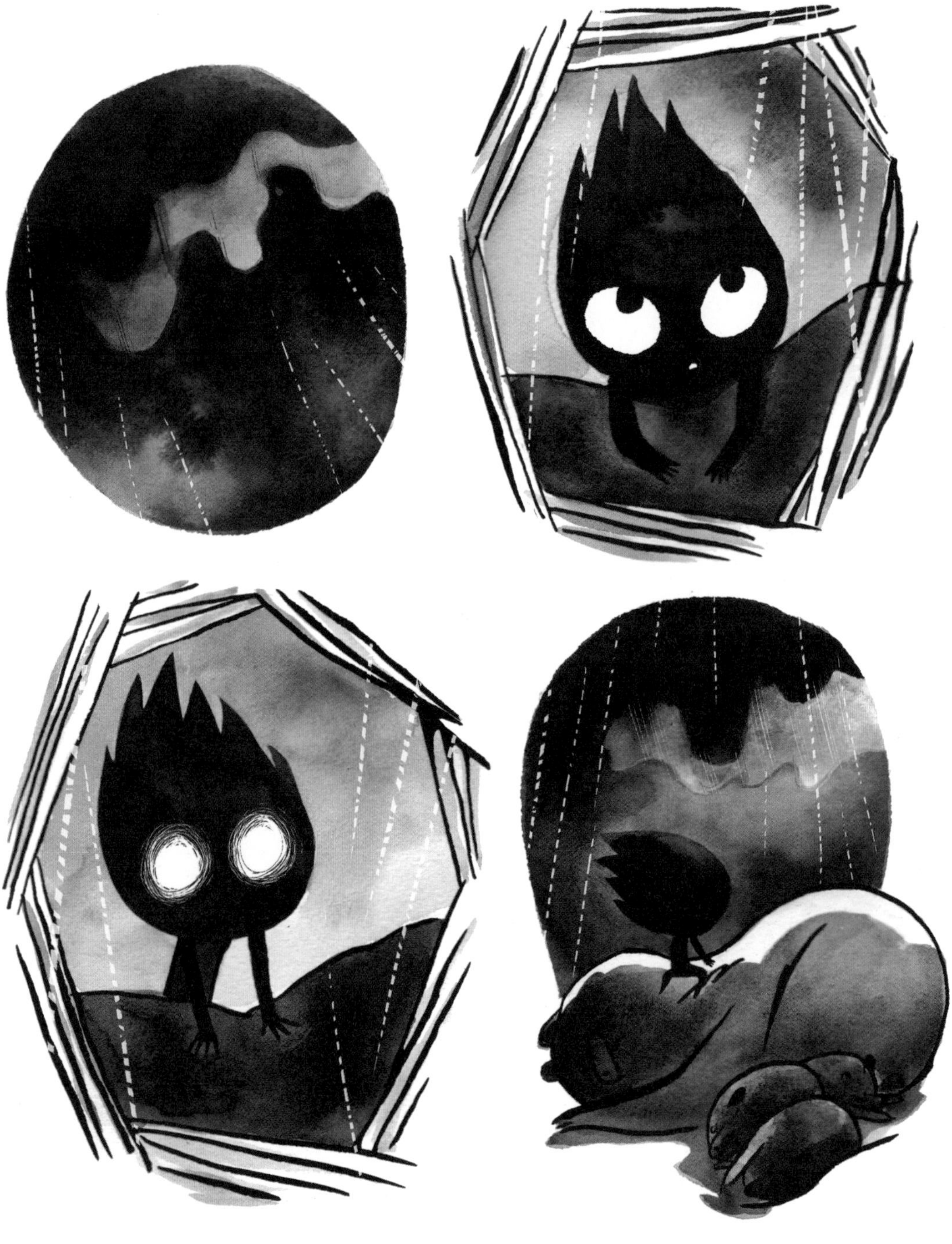

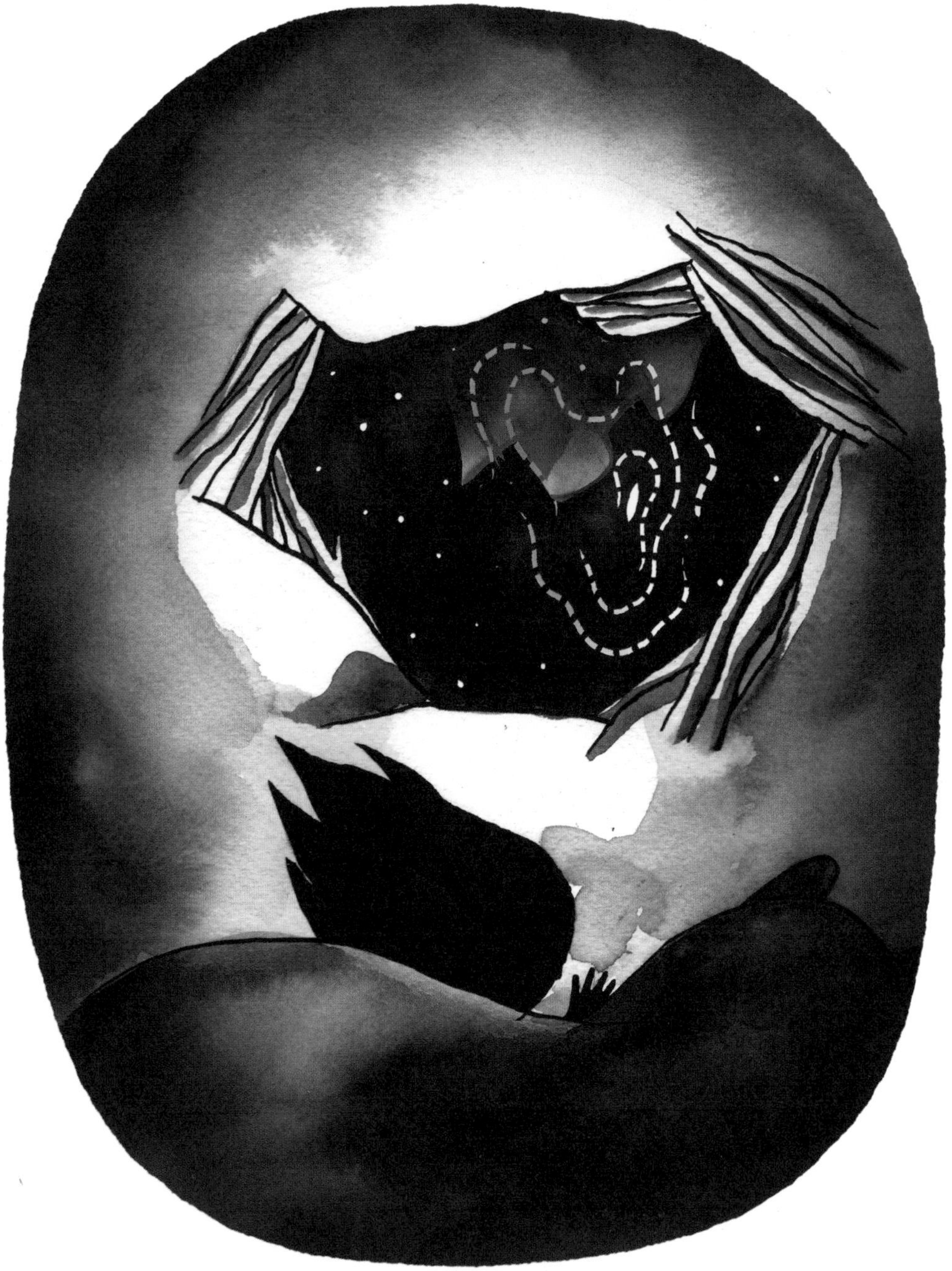

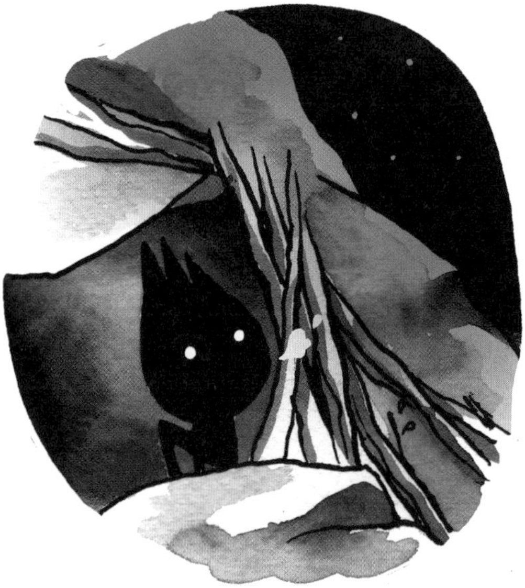

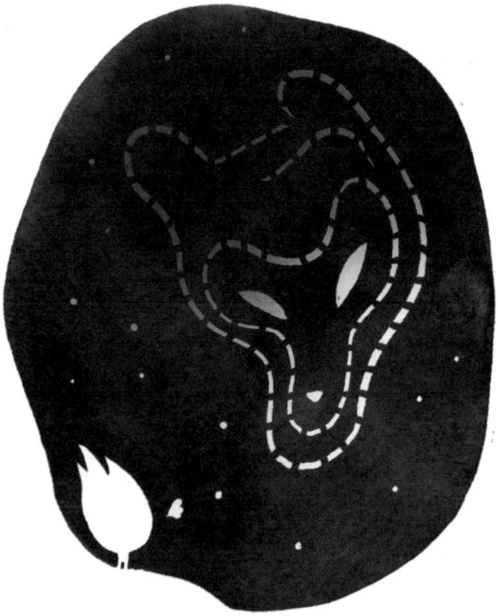

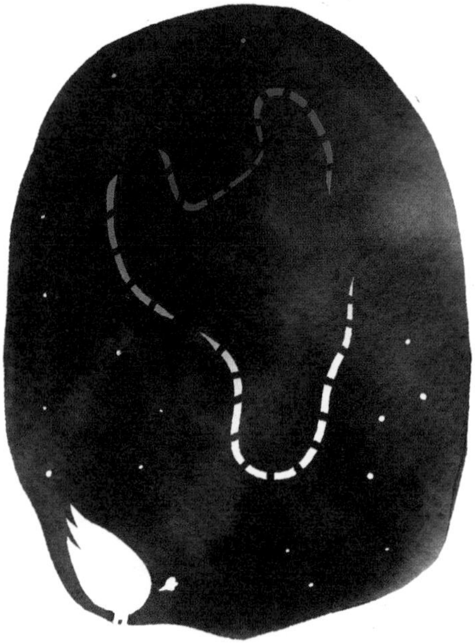

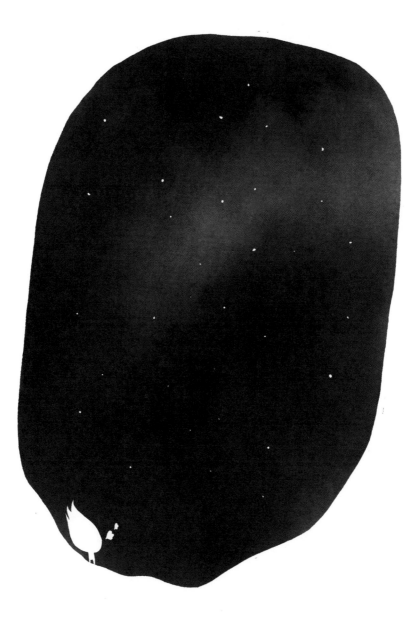

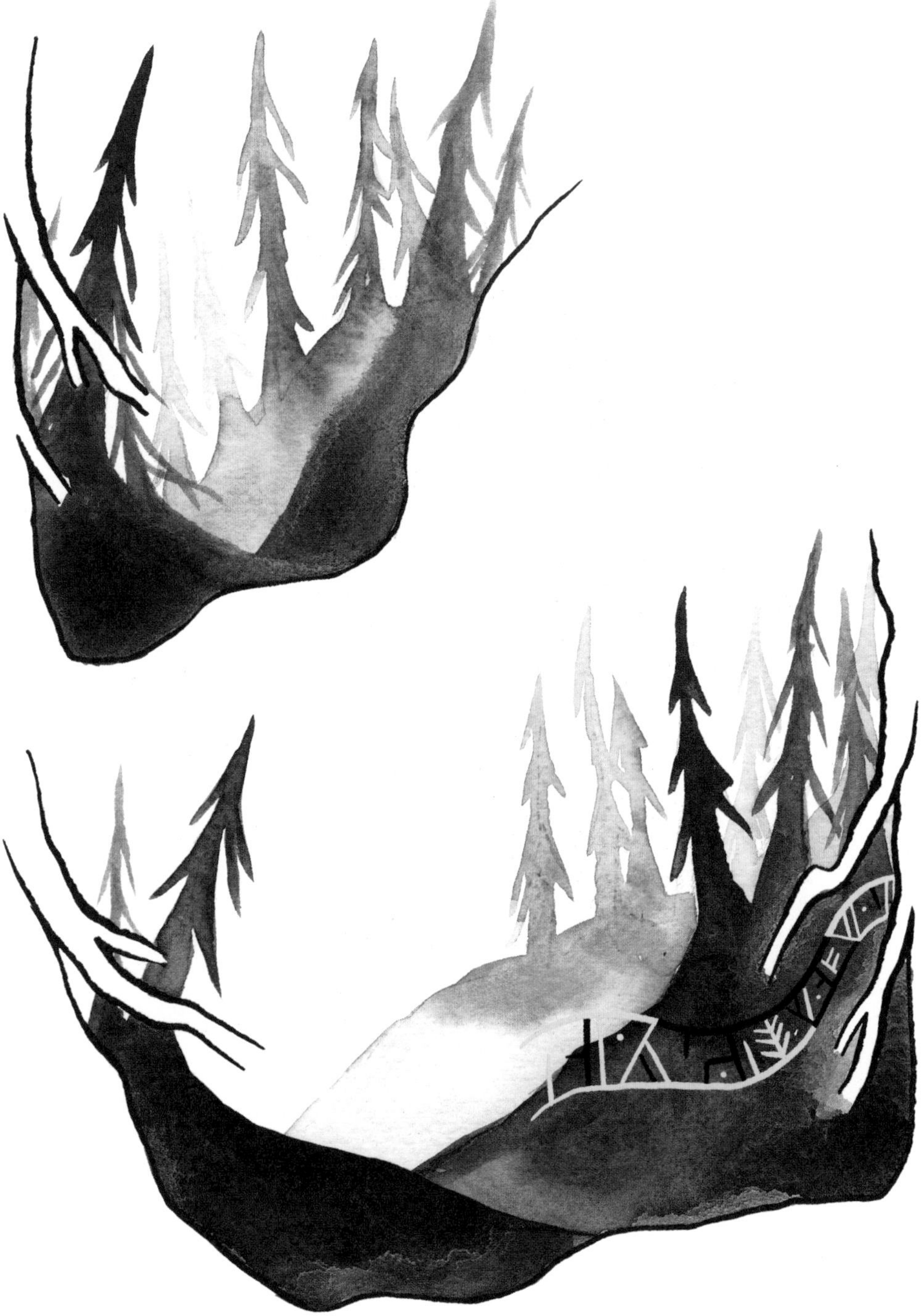

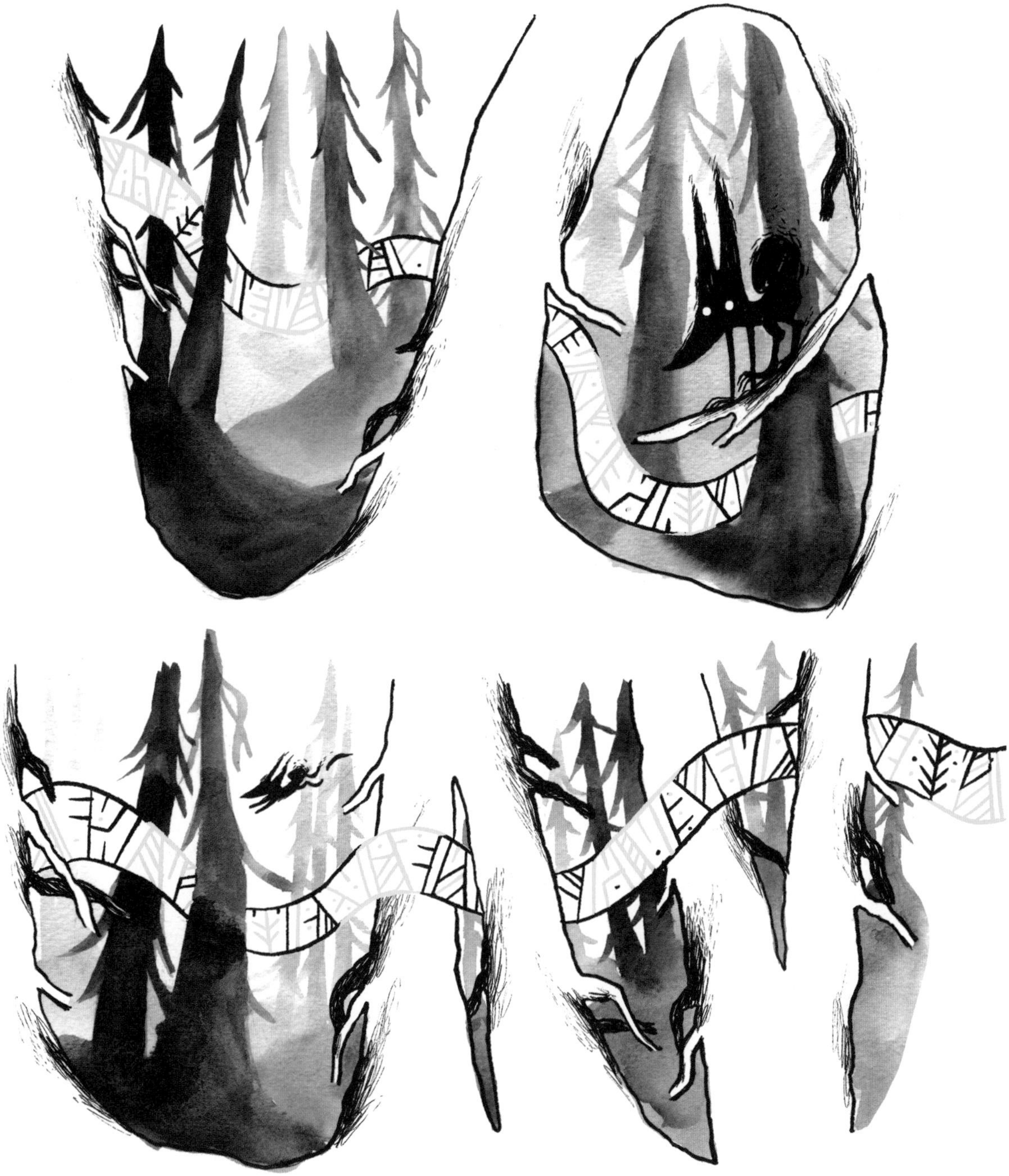

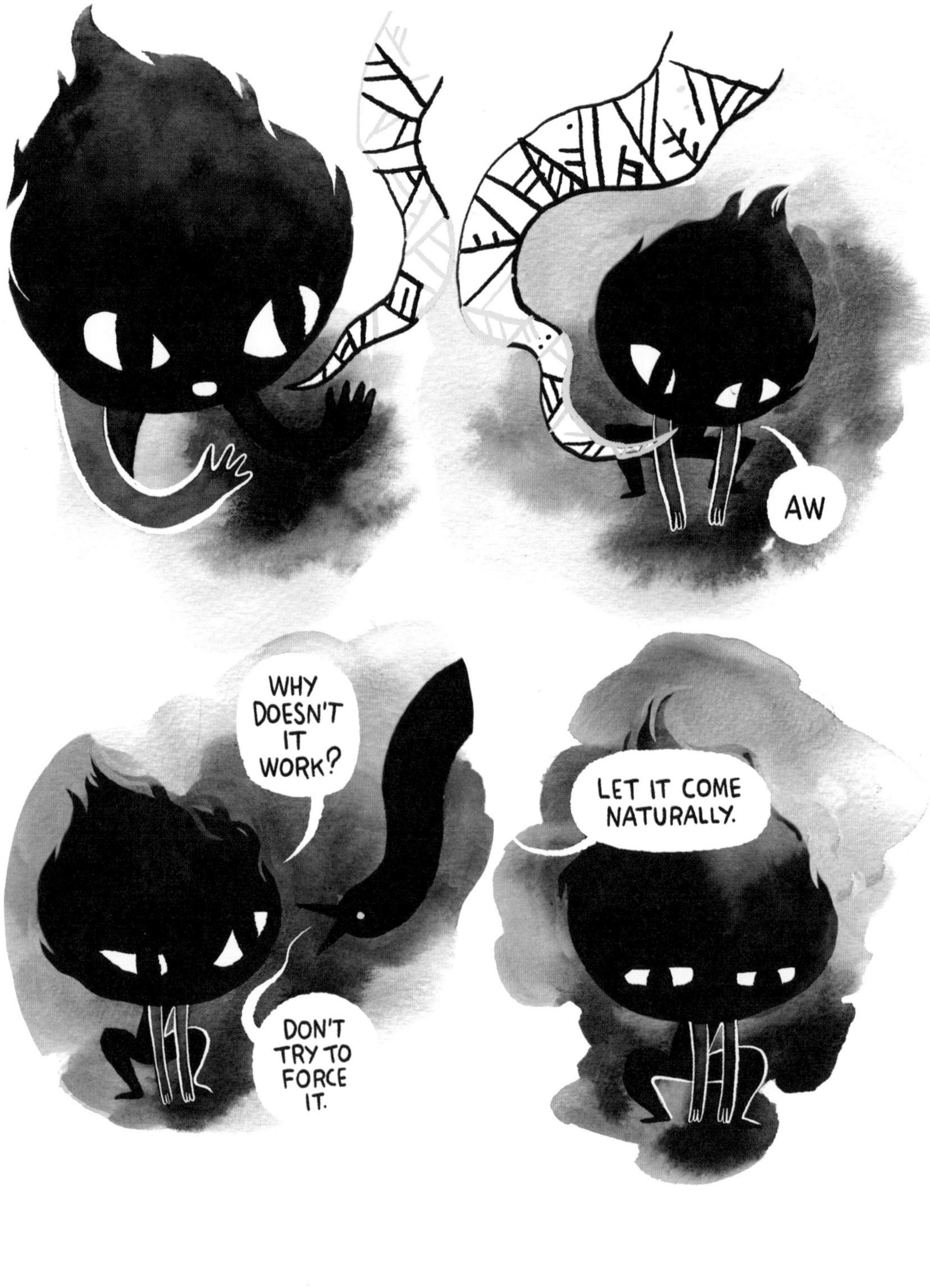
AW
WHY DOESN'T IT WORK?
DON'T TRY TO FORCE IT.
LET IT COME NATURALLY.

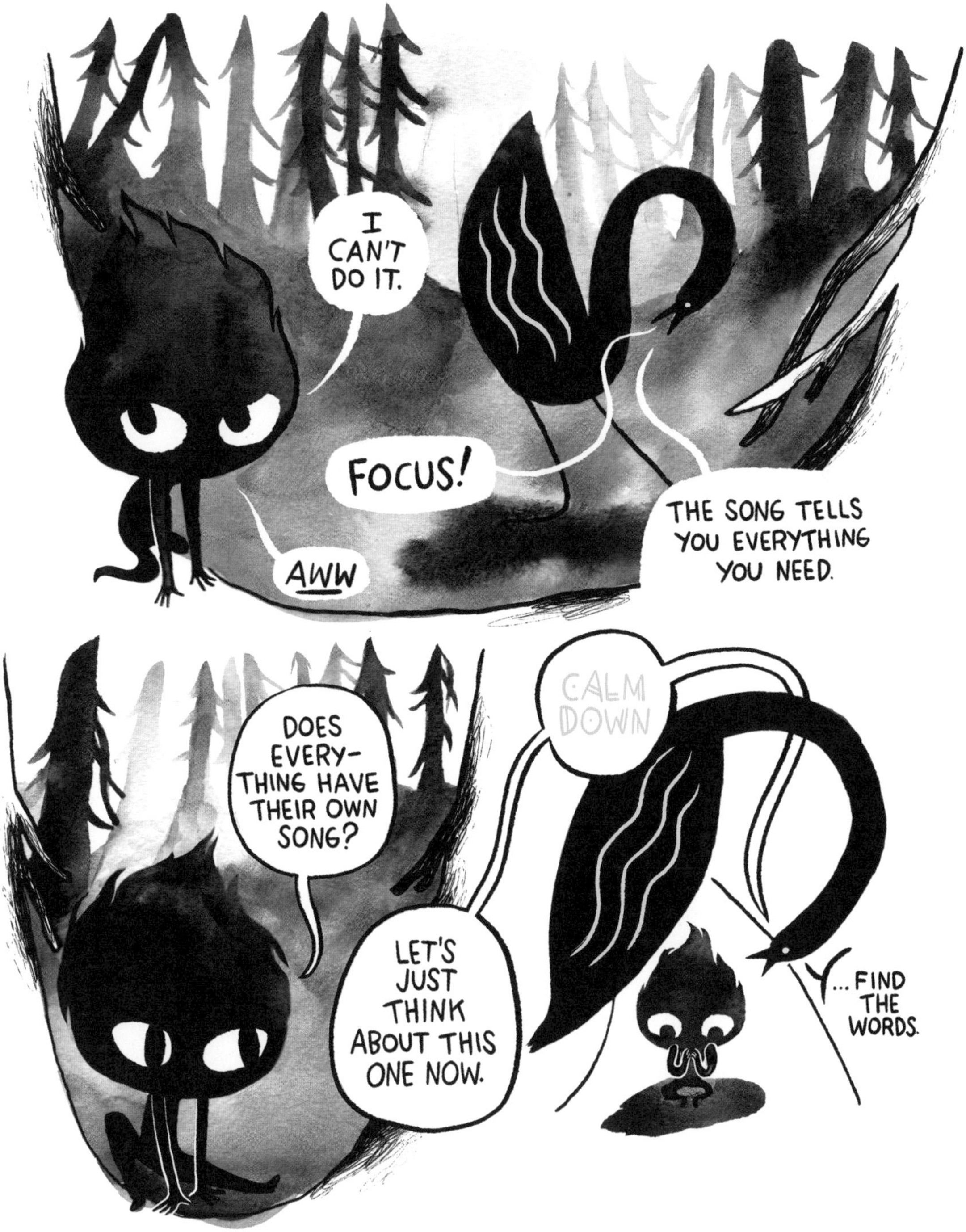
I CAN'T DO IT.
FOCUS!
AWW
THE SONG TELLS YOU EVERYTHING YOU NEED.
DOES EVERY-THING HAVE THEIR OWN SONG?
CALM DOWN
LET'S JUST THINK ABOUT THIS ONE NOW.
...FIND THE WORDS.

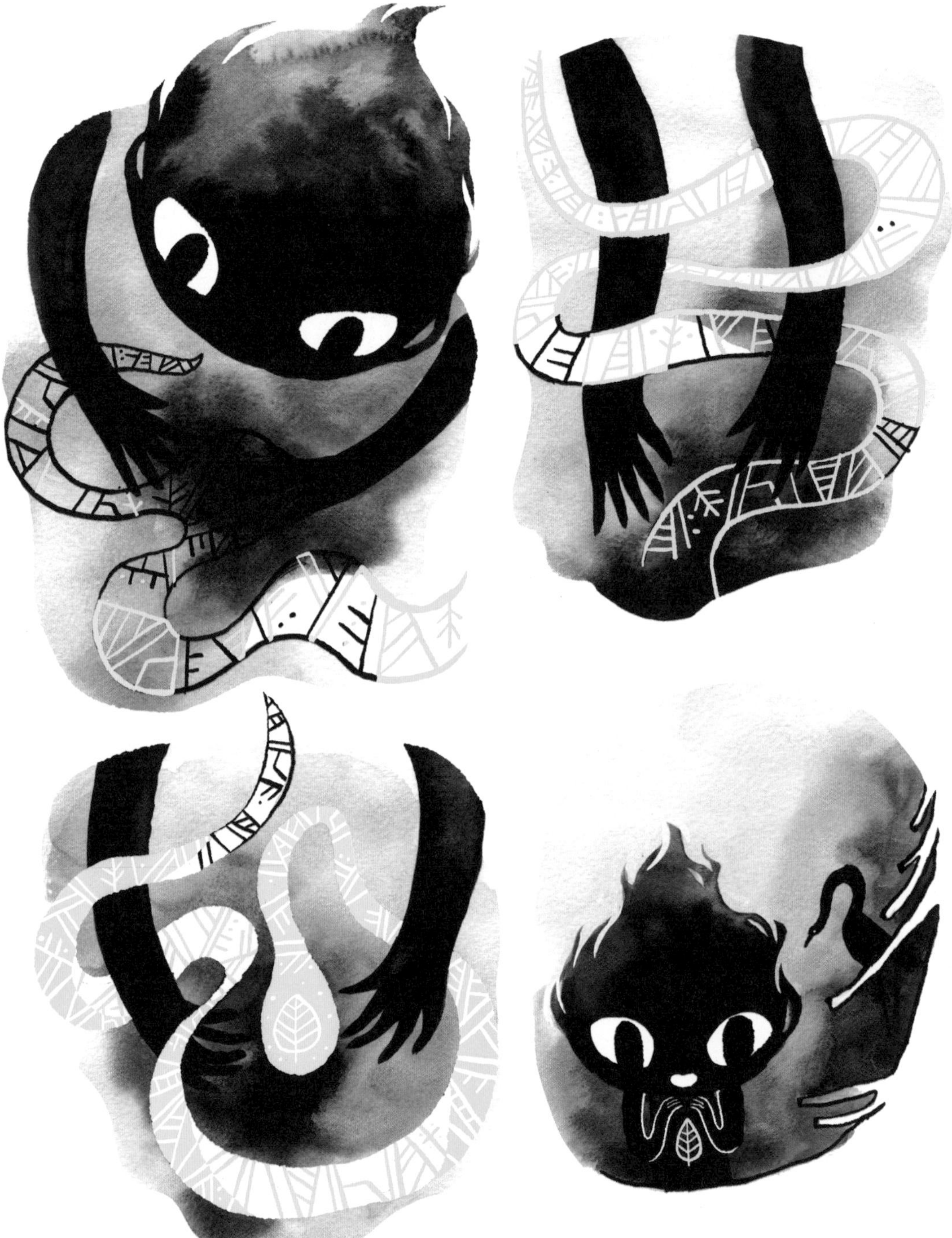

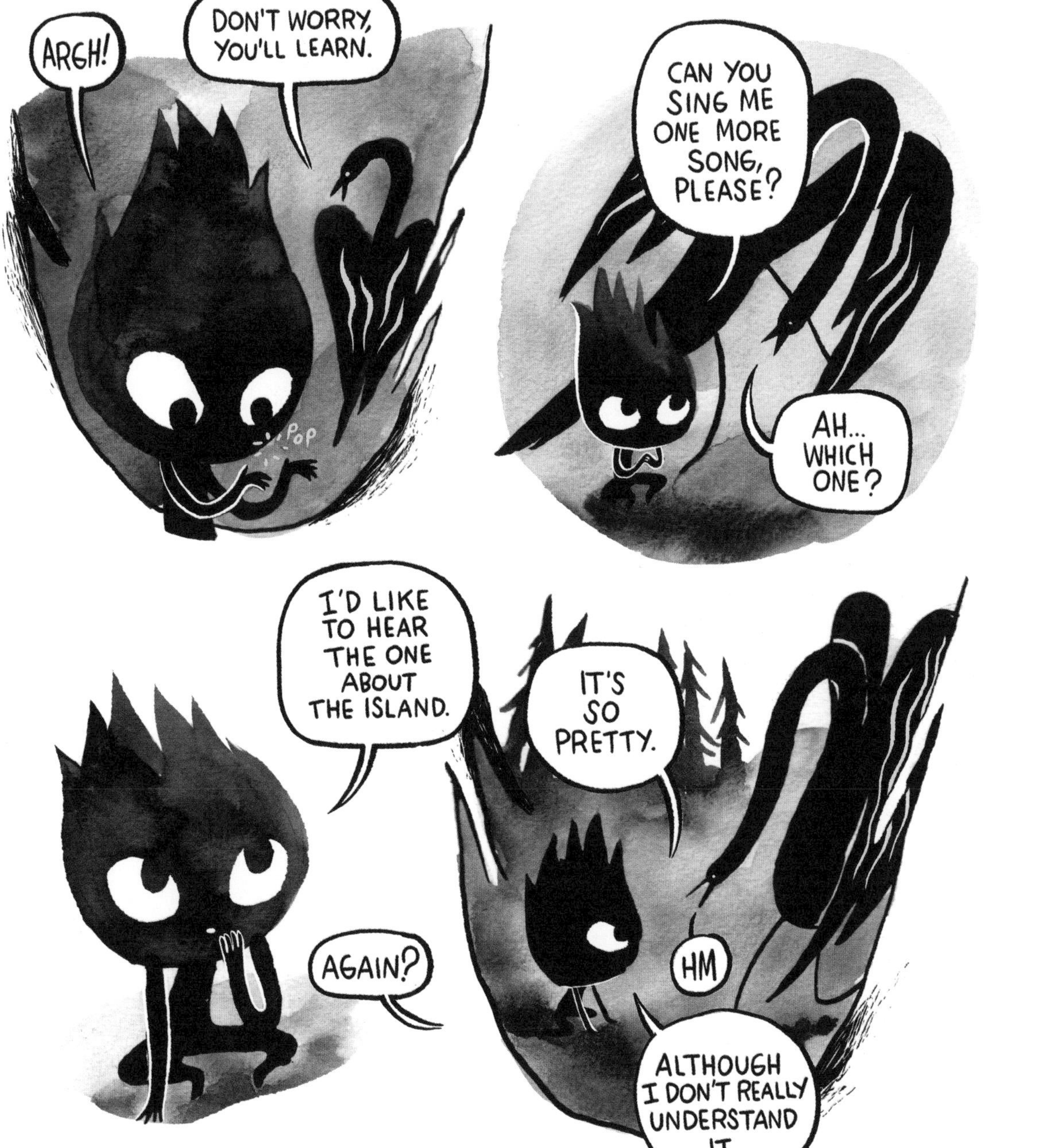
ARGH!
DON'T WORRY, YOU'LL LEARN.
POP
CAN YOU SING ME ONE MORE SONG, PLEASE?
AH... WHICH ONE?
I'D LIKE TO HEAR THE ONE ABOUT THE ISLAND.
AGAIN?
IT'S SO PRETTY.
HM
ALTHOUGH I DON'T REALLY UNDERSTAND IT.

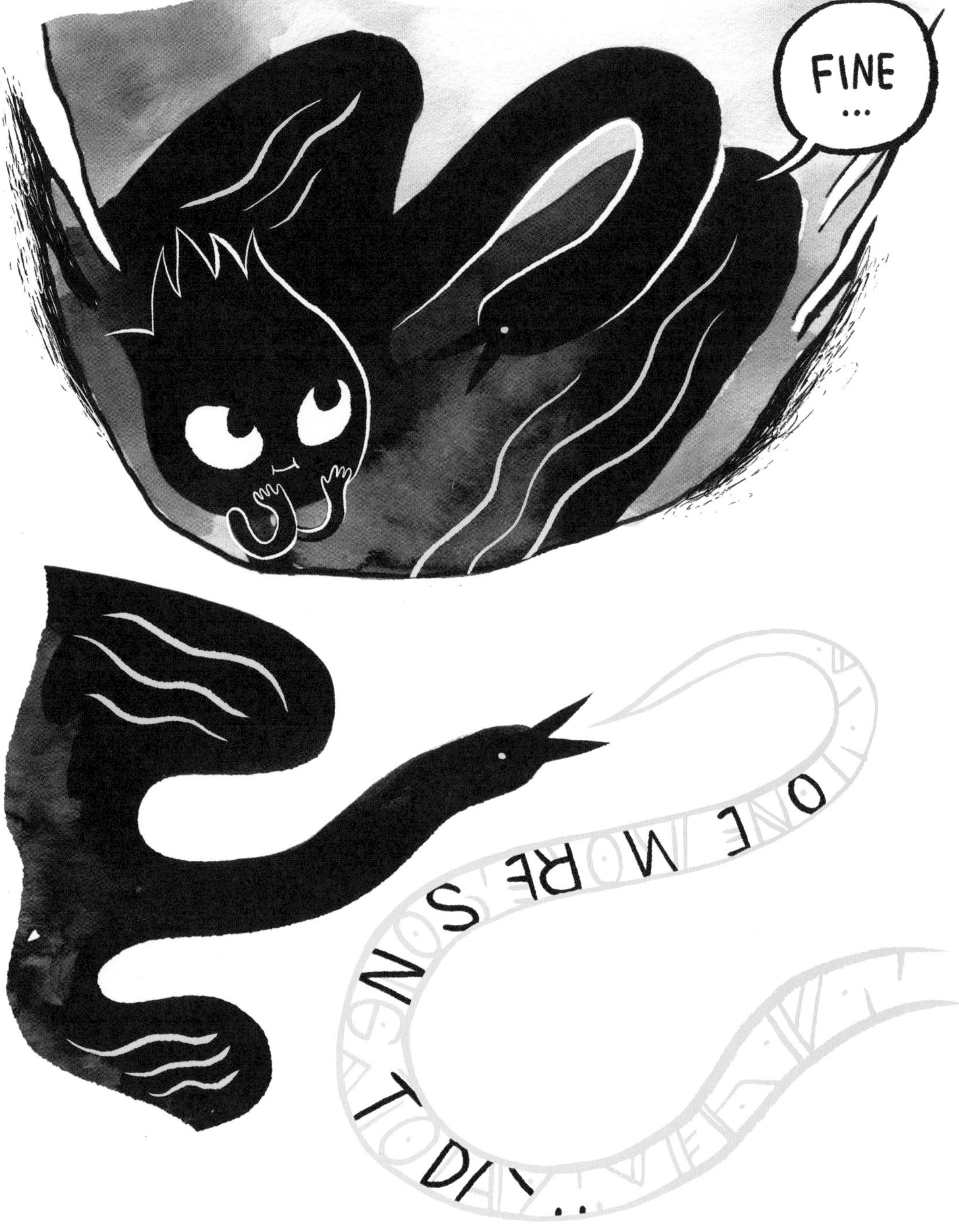
FINE ...
ONE MORE SONG TODAY...

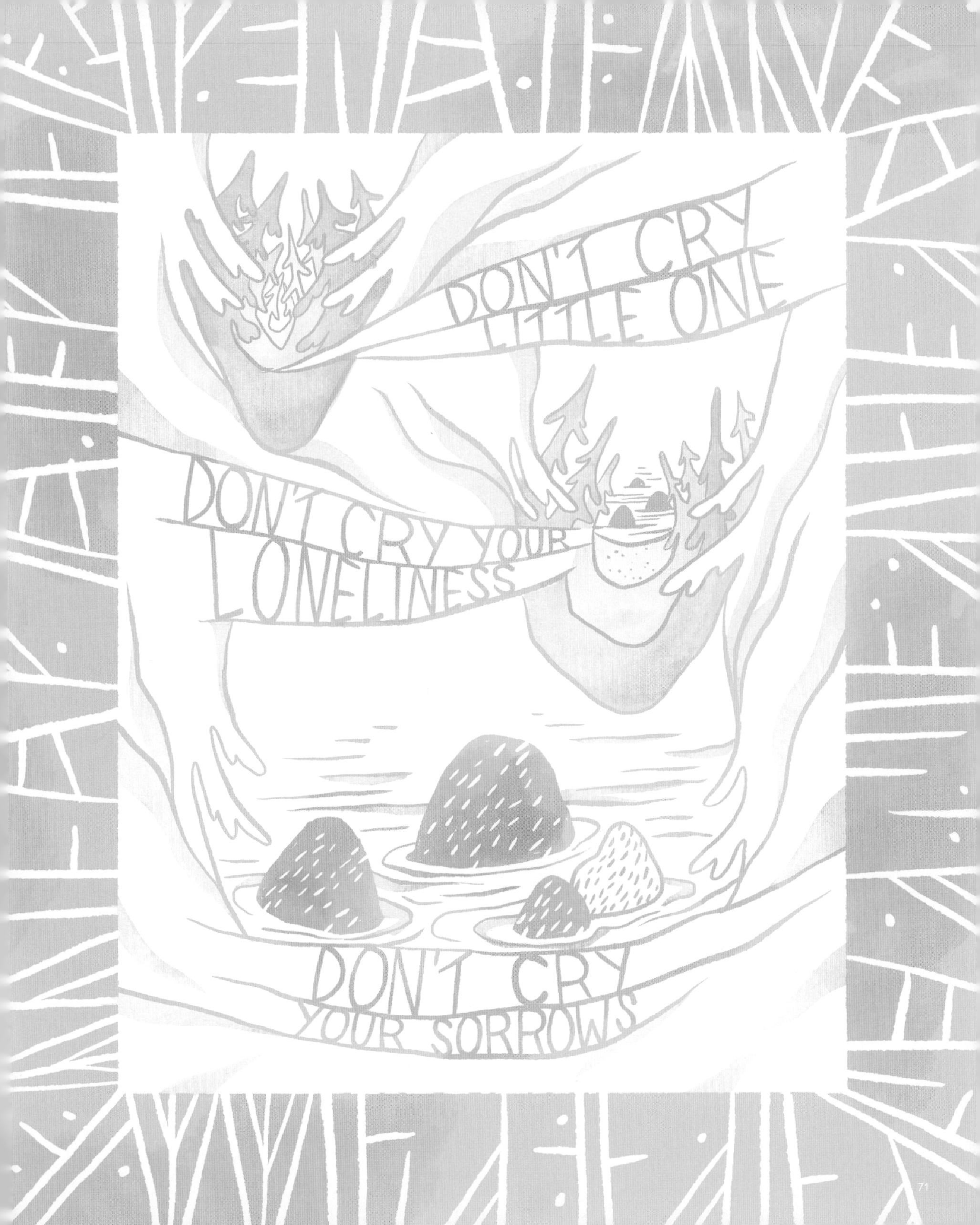
DON'T CRY
LITTLE ONE
DON'T CRY YOUR
LONELINESS
DON'T CRY
YOUR SORROWS

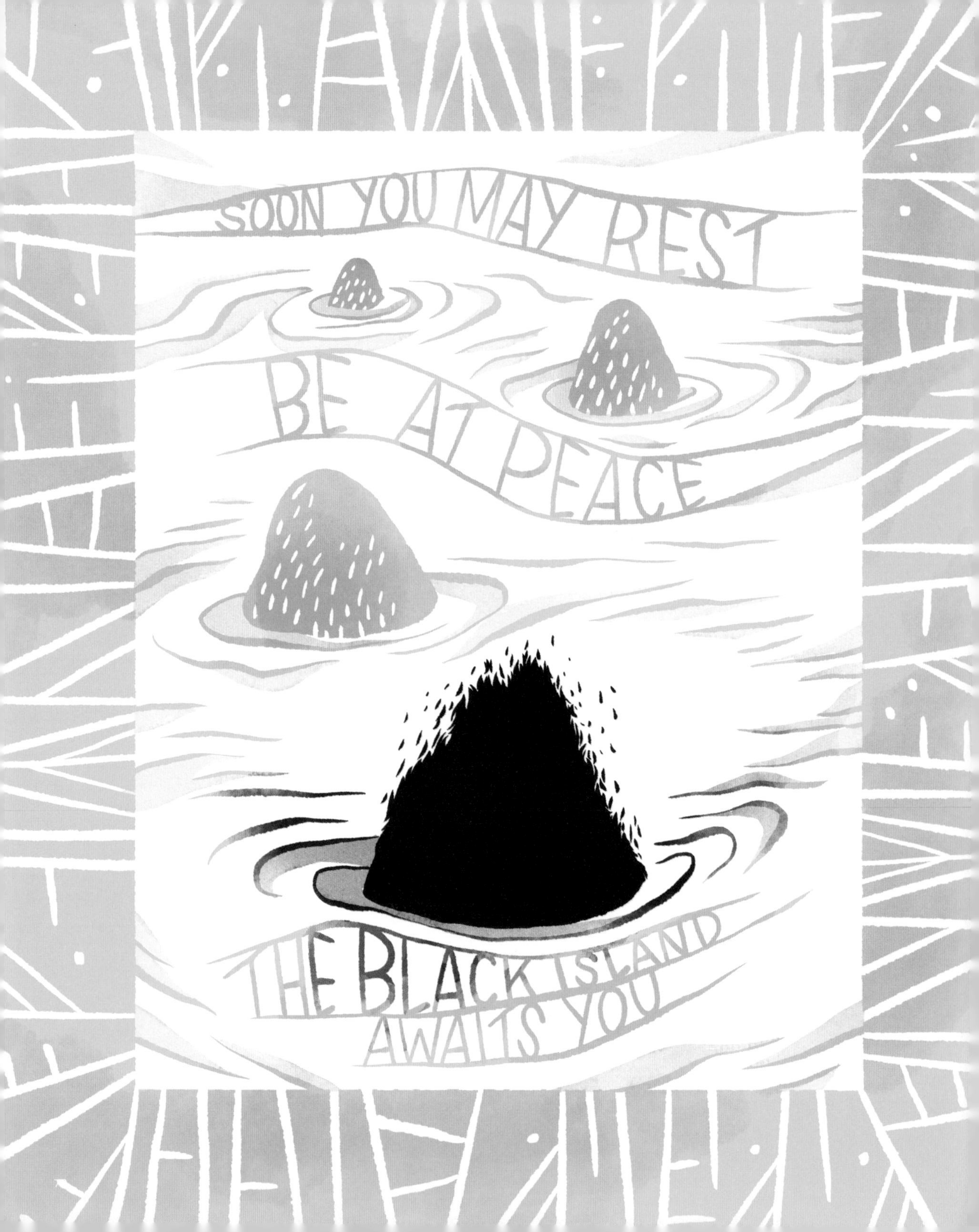
SOON YOU MAY REST
BE AT PEACE
THE BLACK ISLAND
AWAITS YOU

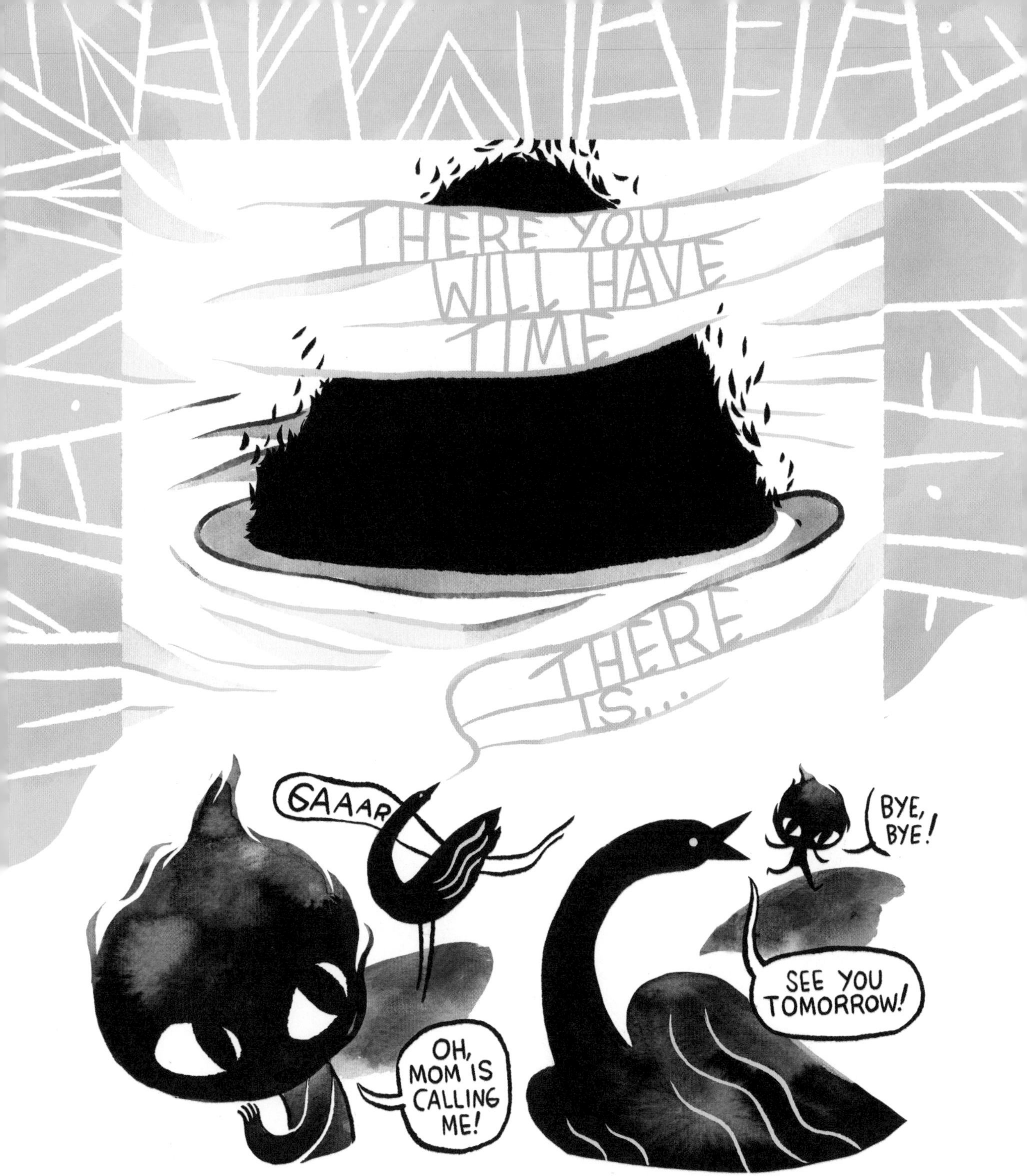
THERE YOU WILL HAVE TIME
THERE IS...
GAAAR
BYE, BYE!
SEE YOU TOMORROW!
OH, MOM IS CALLING ME!

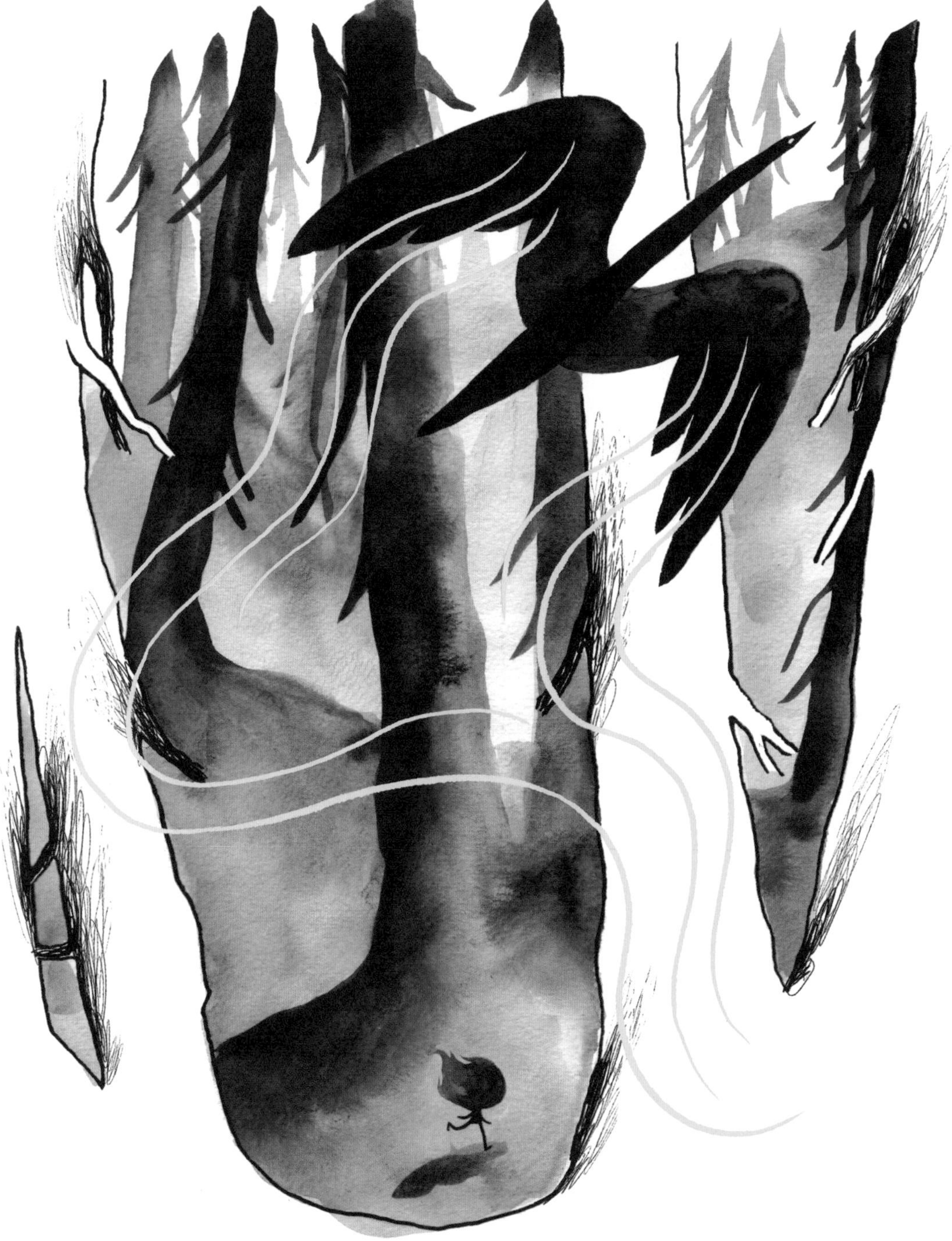

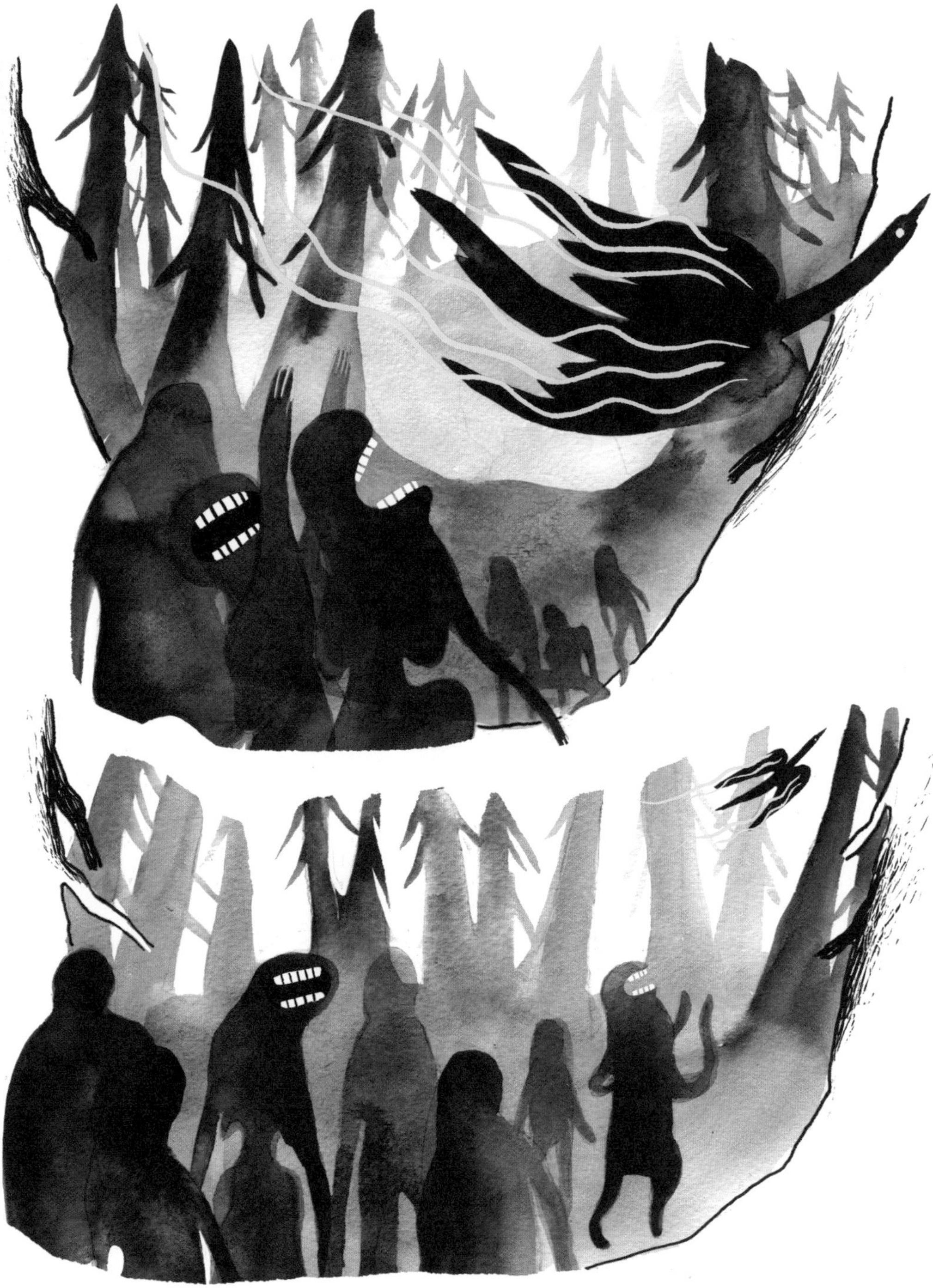

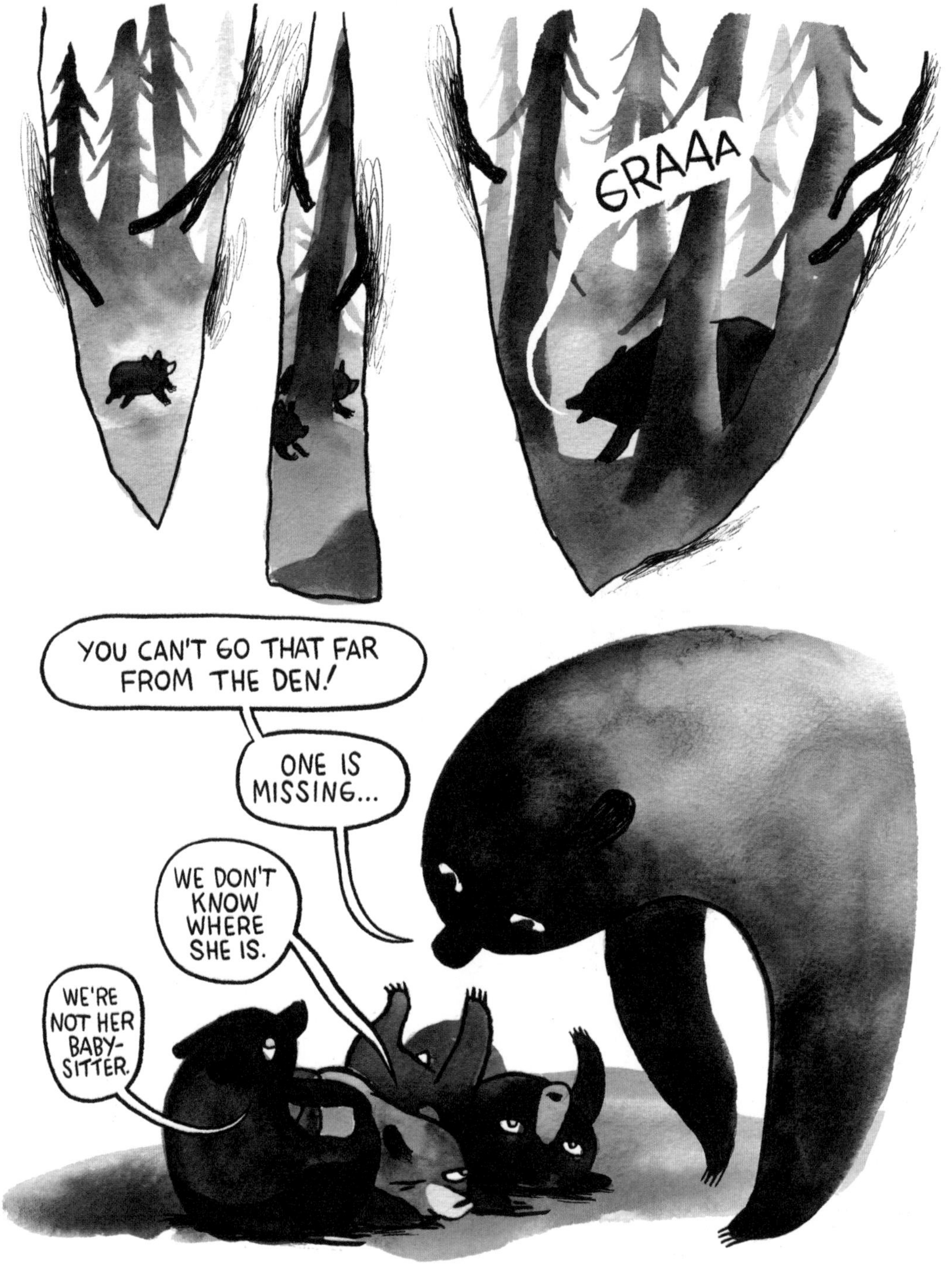
GRAAA
YOU CAN'T GO THAT FAR FROM THE DEN!
ONE IS MISSING...
WE DON'T KNOW WHERE SHE IS.
WE'RE NOT HER BABY-SITTER.

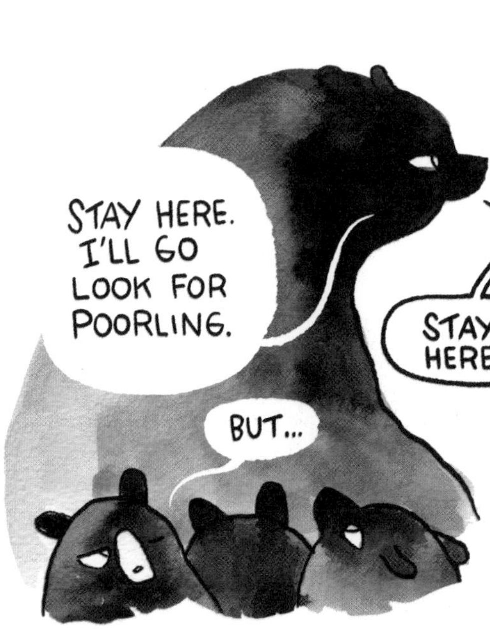
STAY HERE. I'LL GO LOOK FOR POORLING.
STAY HERE.
BUT...

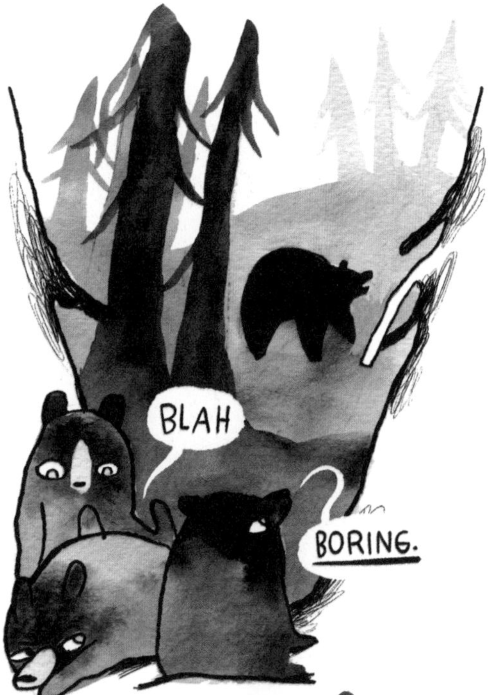
BLAH
BORING.

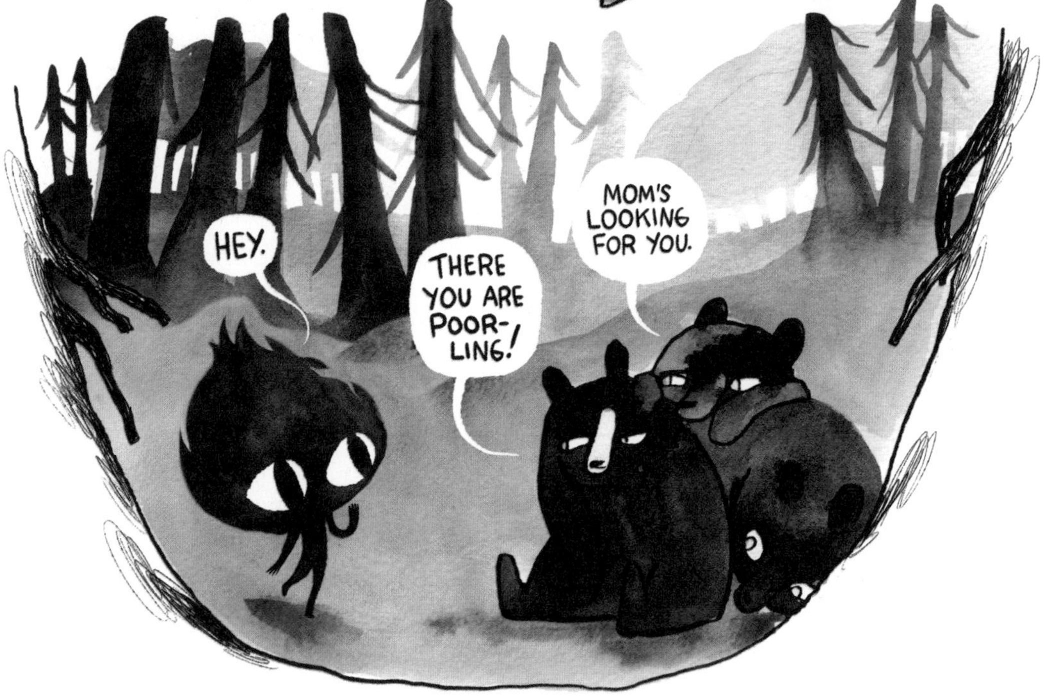
HEY.
THERE YOU ARE POOR-LING!
MOM'S LOOKING FOR YOU.

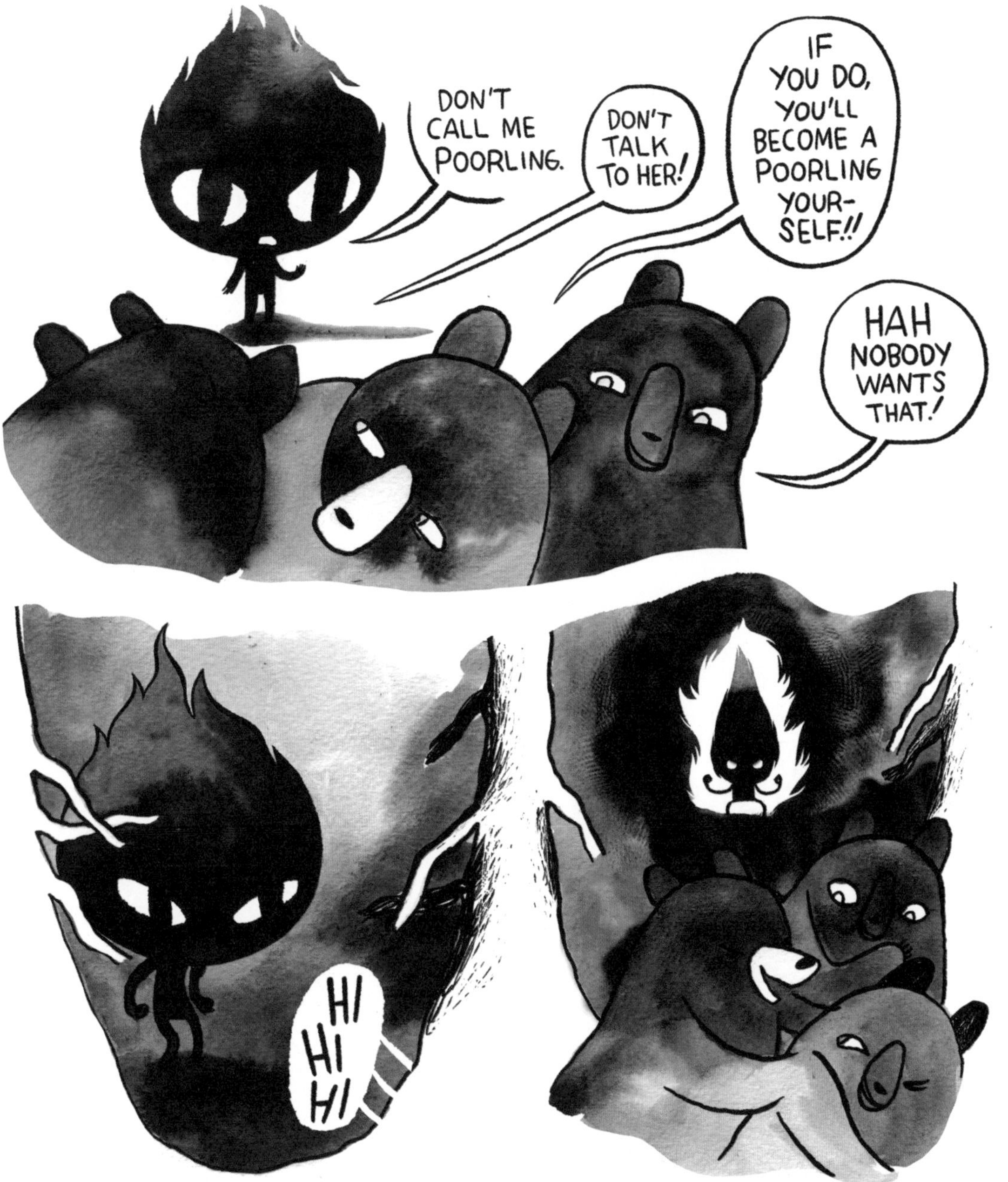
DON'T CALL ME POORLING.
DON'T TALK TO HER!
IF YOU DO, YOU'LL BECOME A POORLING YOURSELF!!
HAH NOBODY WANTS THAT!
HI HI HI

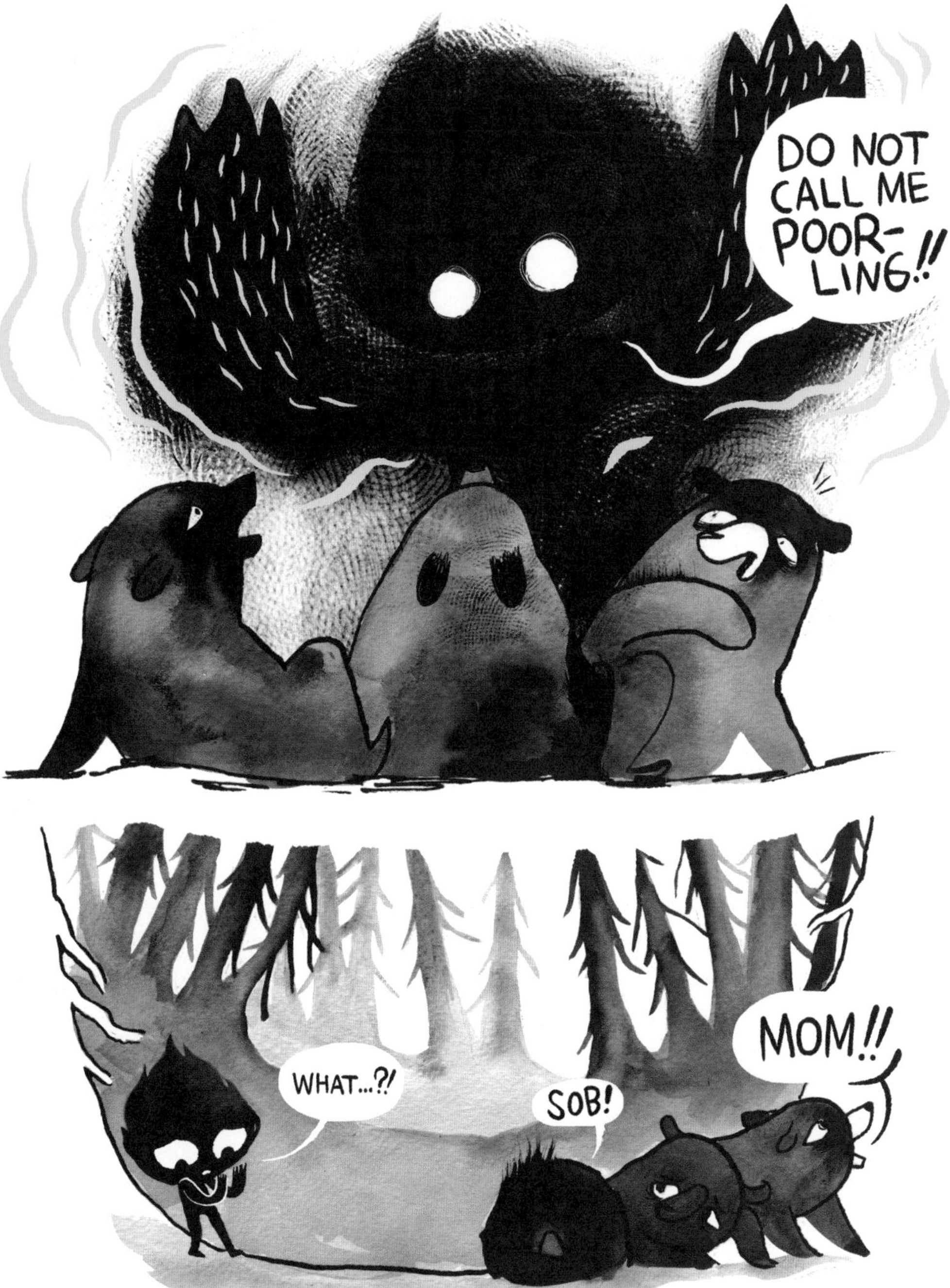
DO NOT CALL ME POOR-LING!!
WHAT...?!
SOB!
MOM!!

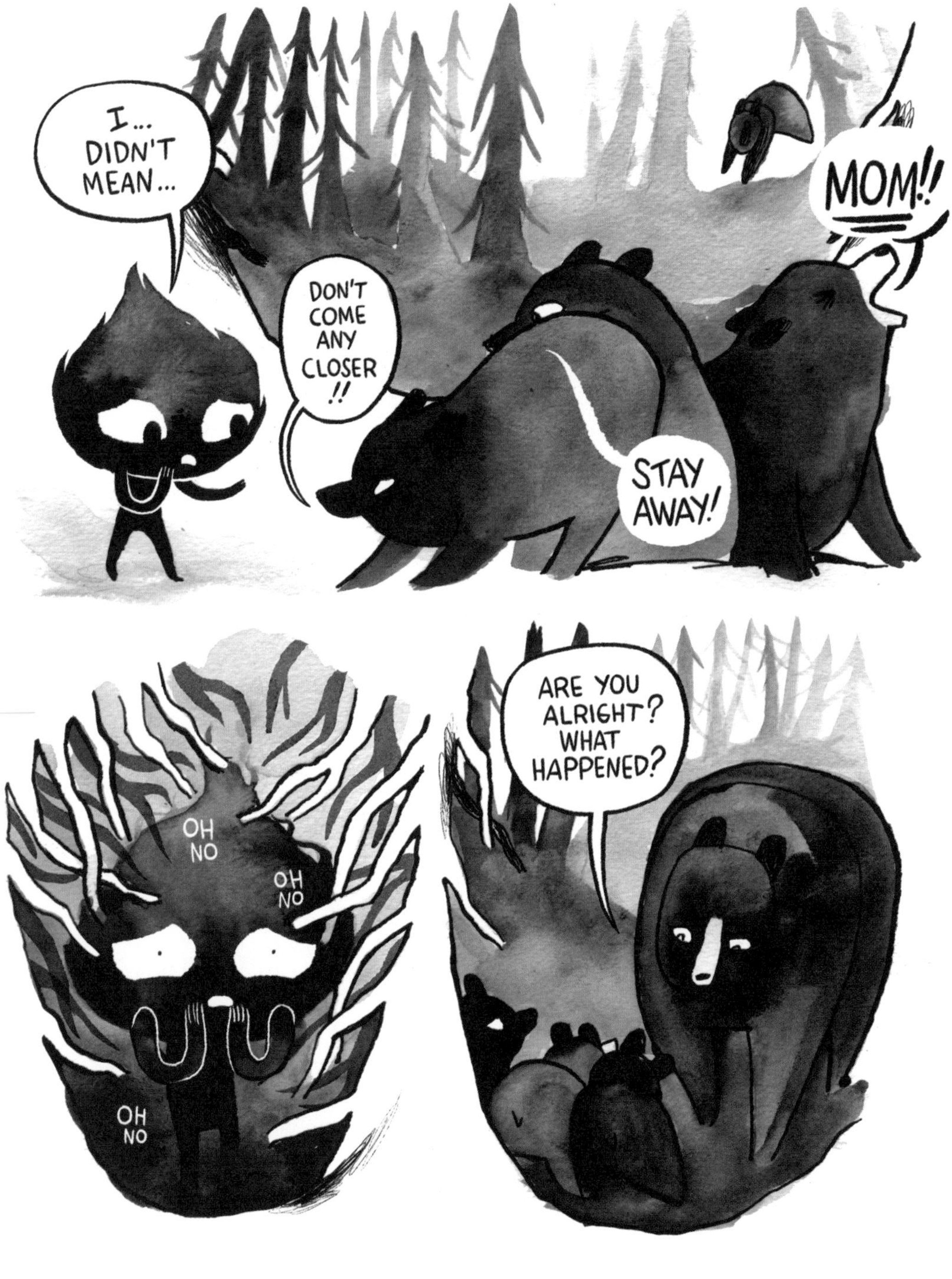
I... DIDN'T MEAN...
MOM!!
DON'T COME ANY CLOSER !!
STAY AWAY!
OH NO
OH NO
OH NO
ARE YOU ALRIGHT? WHAT HAPPENED?

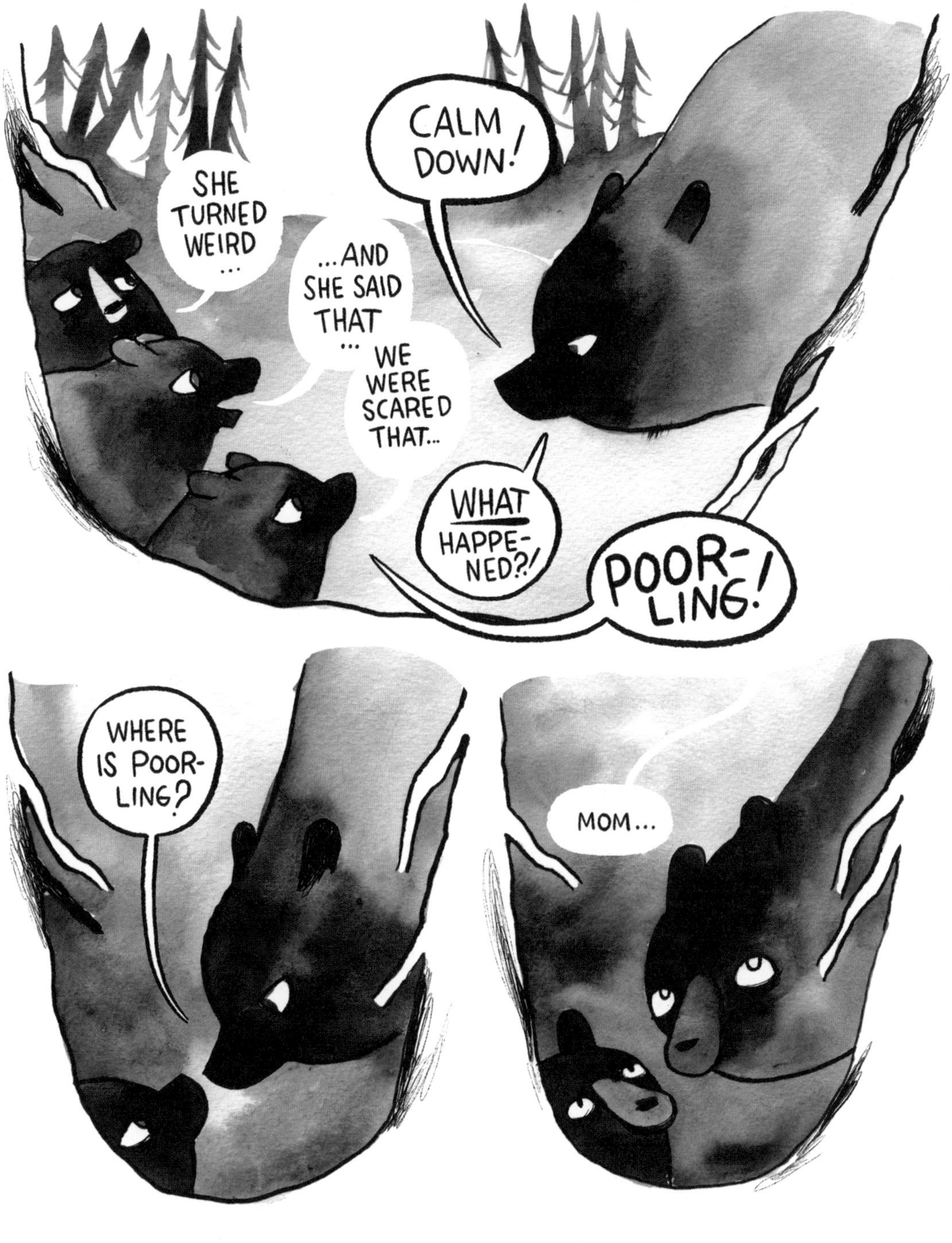
SHE TURNED WEIRD ...
...AND SHE SAID THAT ...
WE WERE SCARED THAT...
CALM DOWN!
WHAT HAPPENED?!
POOR-LING!
WHERE IS POORLING?
MOM...

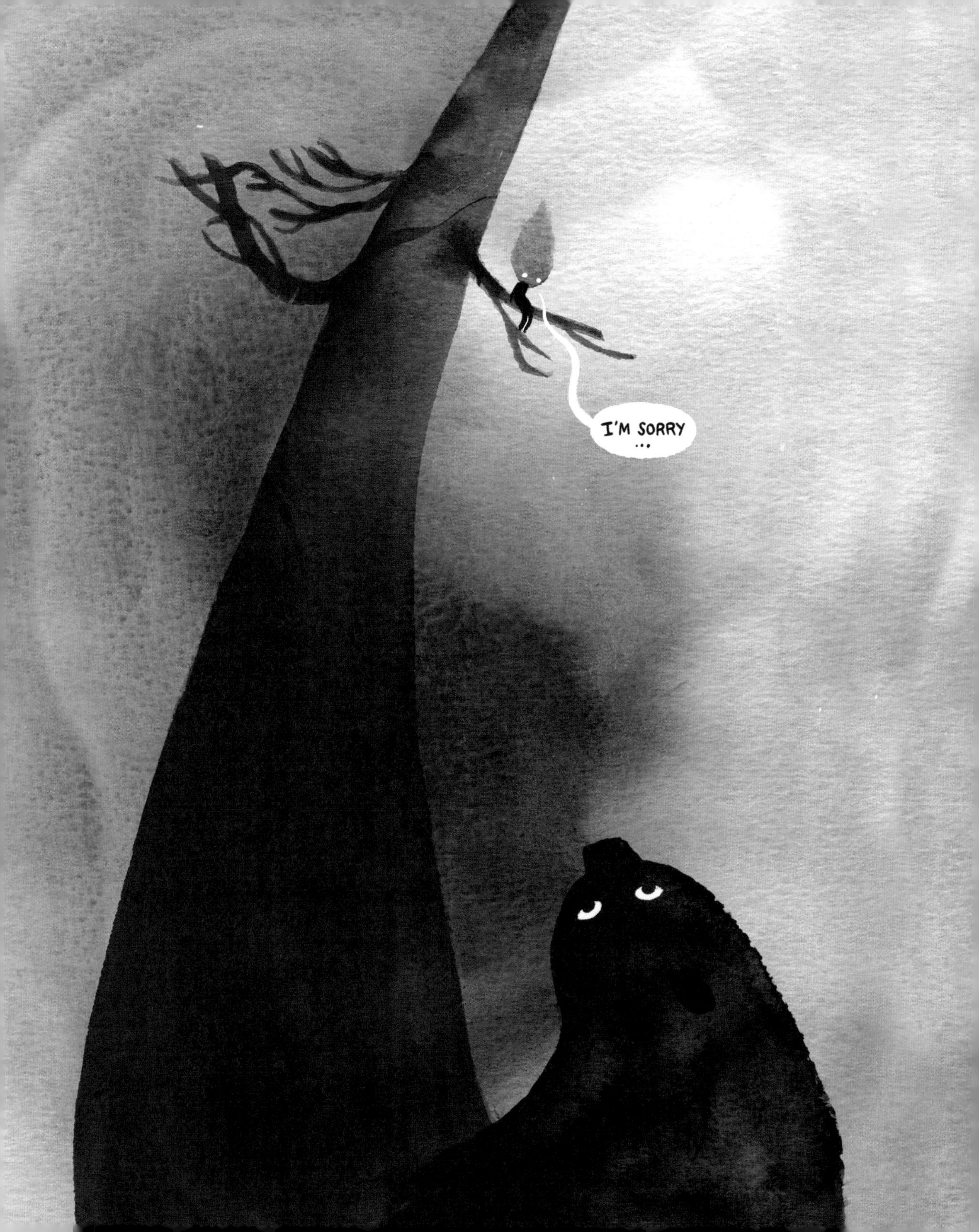
I'M SORRY ...

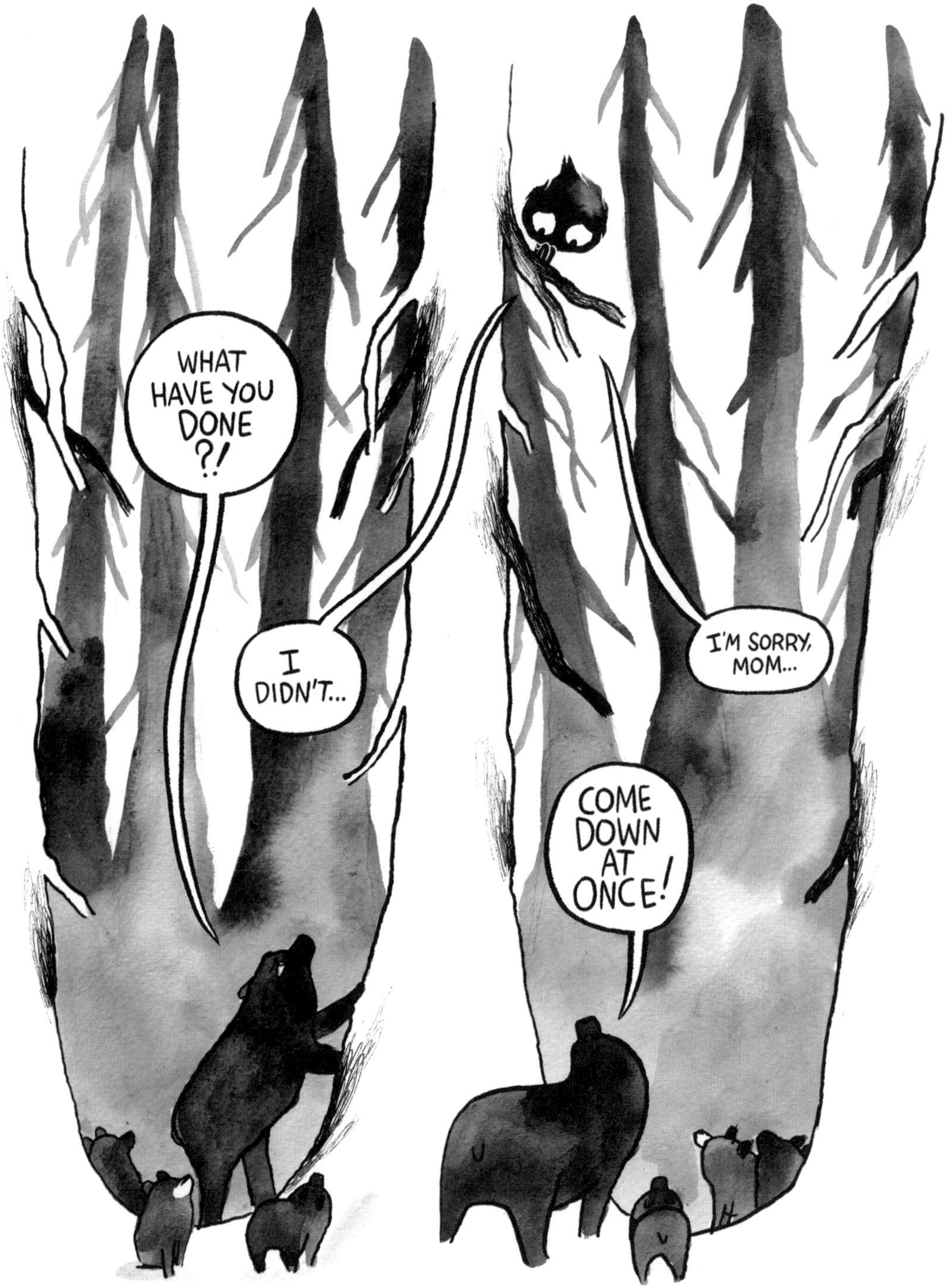
WHAT HAVE YOU DONE ?!
I DIDN'T...
I'M SORRY, MOM...
COME DOWN AT ONCE!

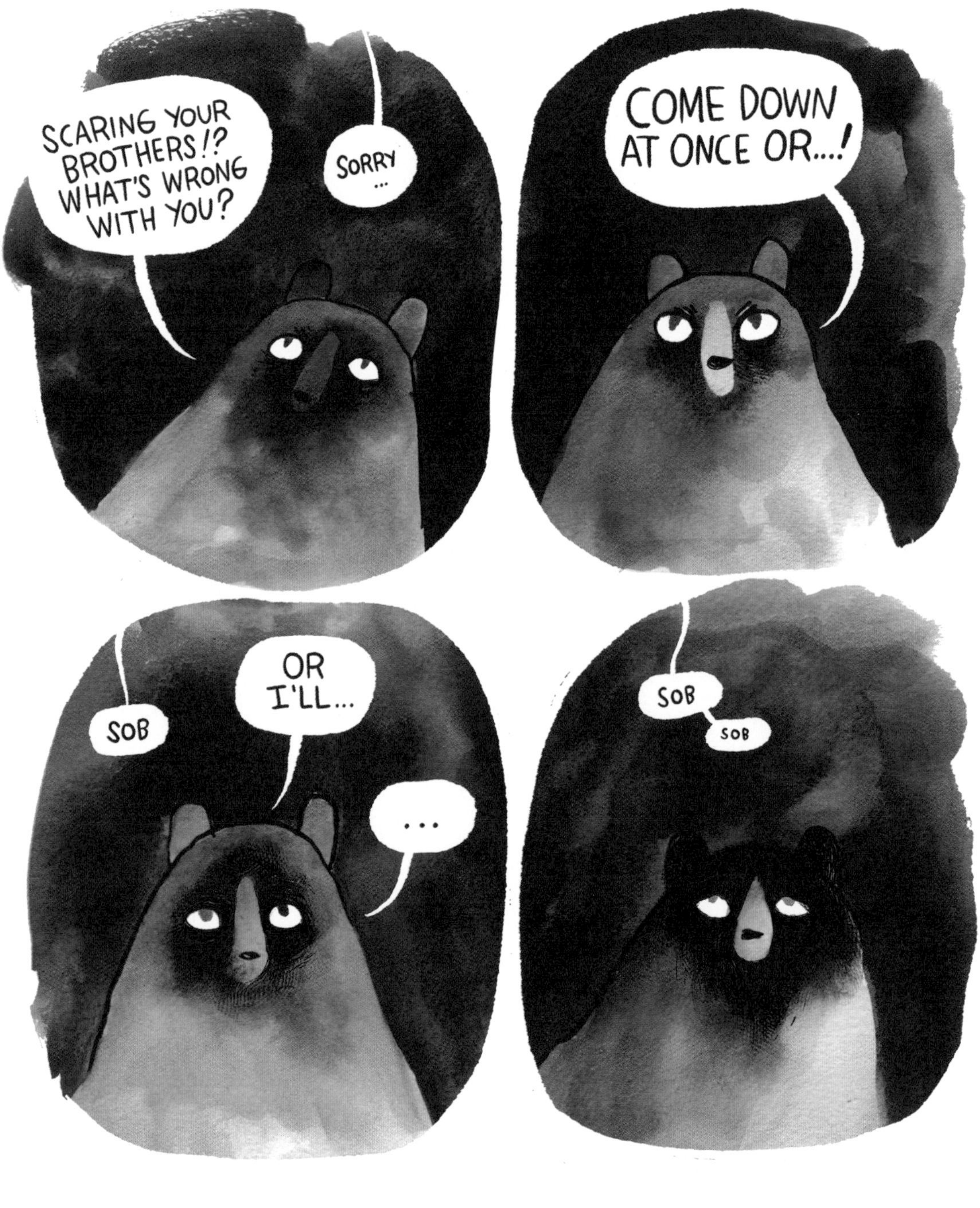
SCARING YOUR BROTHERS!? WHAT'S WRONG WITH YOU?
SORRY ...
COME DOWN AT ONCE OR...!
SOB
OR I'LL...
...
SOB
SOB

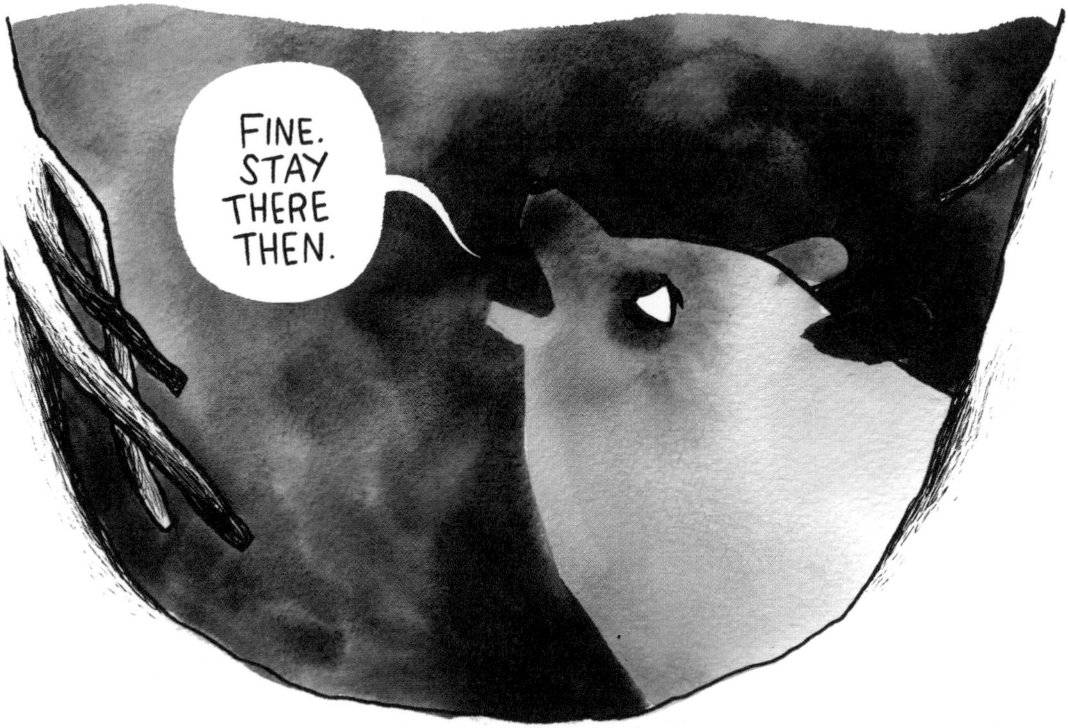
FINE. STAY THERE THEN.

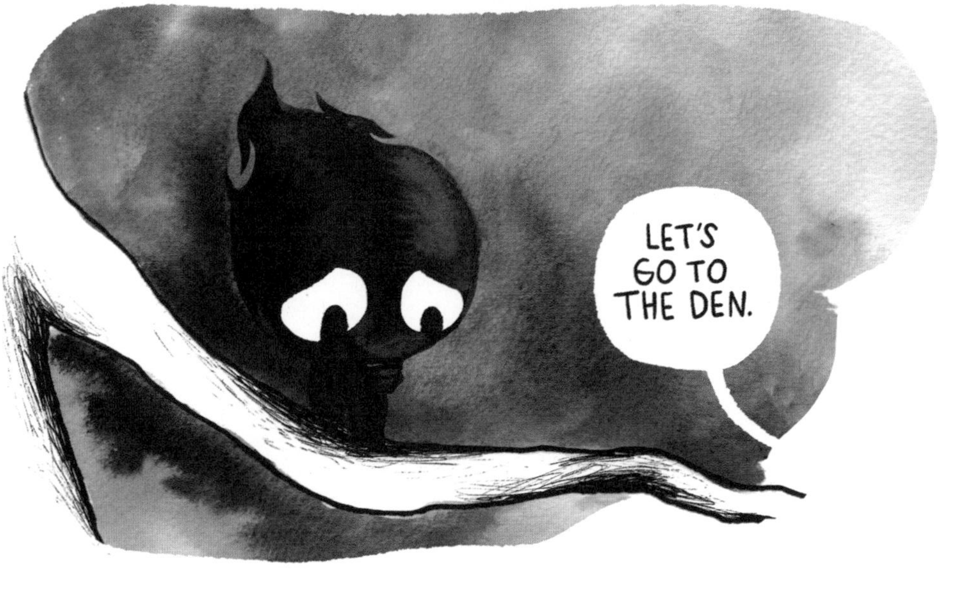
LET'S GO TO THE DEN.

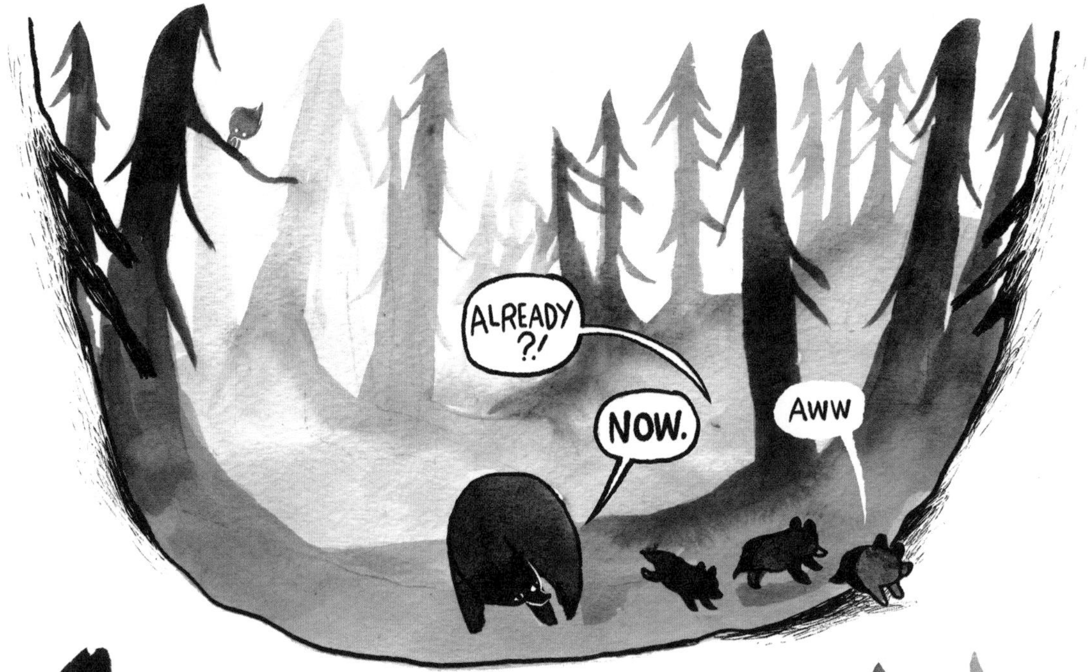
ALREADY ?!
NOW.
AWW
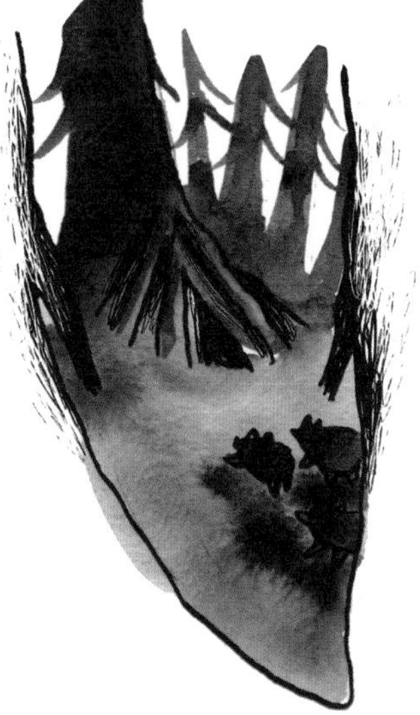
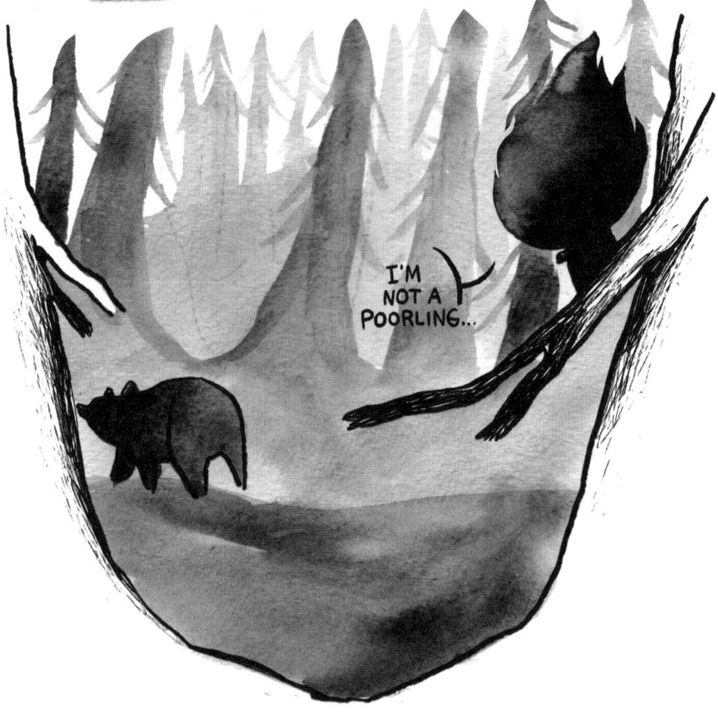
I'M NOT A POORLING...

III

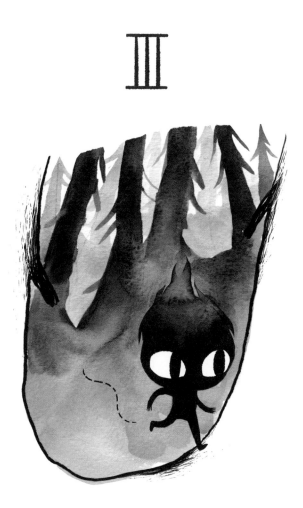

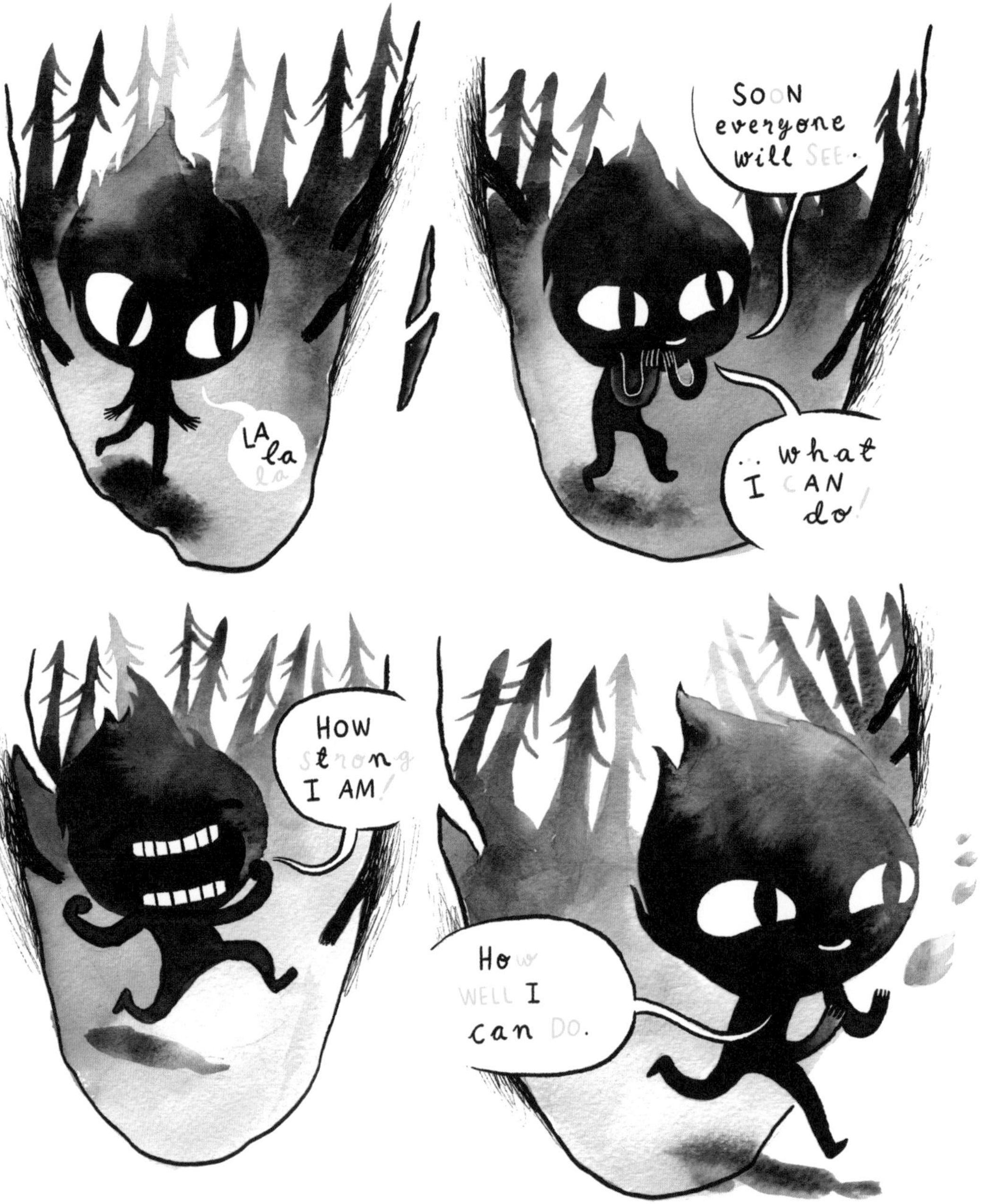
LA la la
SOON everyone will SEE..
... what I CAN do!
HOW strong I AM!
How WELL I can DO.

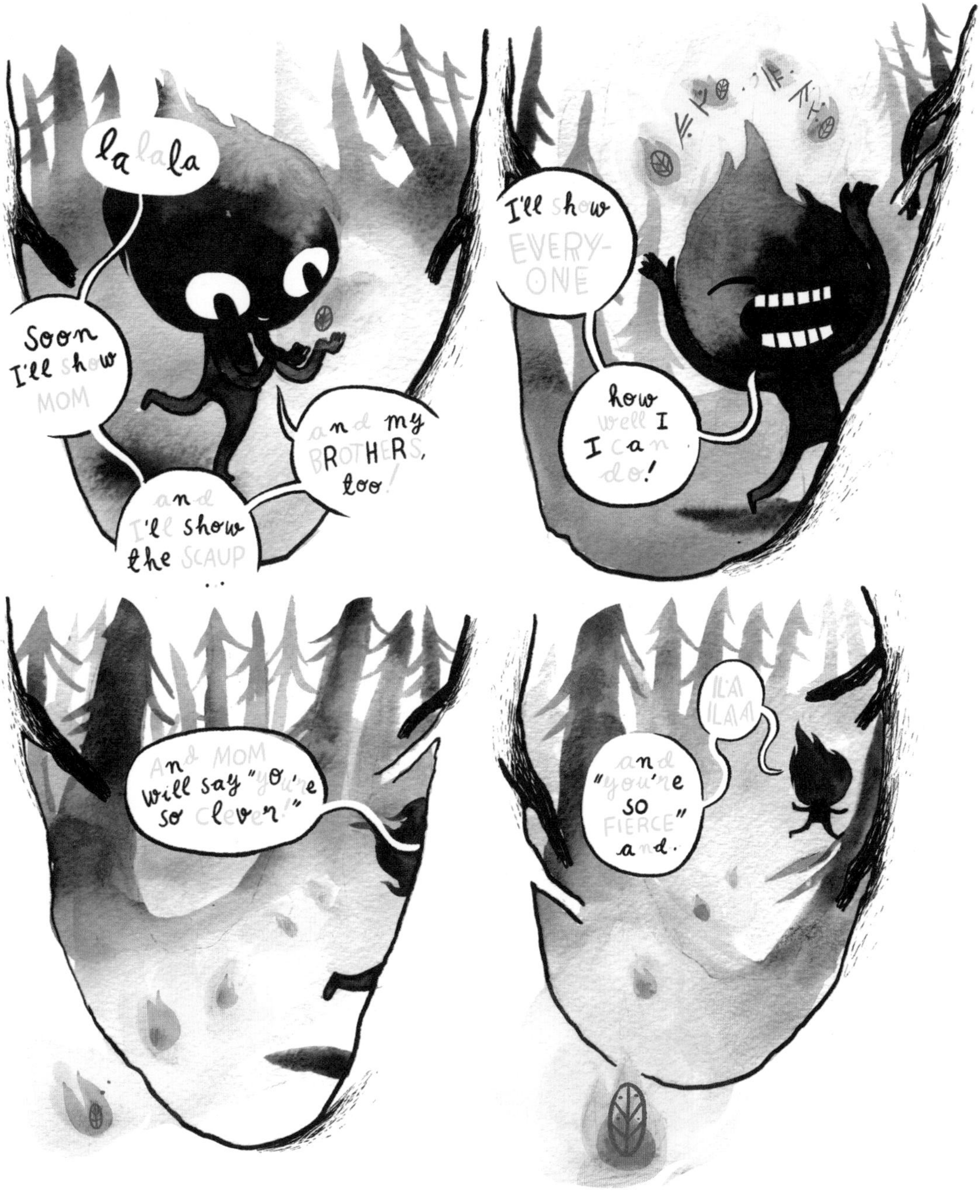
la la la
Soon I'll show MOM
and I'll show the SCAUP ...
and my BROTHERS, too!
I'll show EVERY-ONE
how well I I can do!
And MOM will say "You're so clever!"
and "you're SO FIERCE" and.

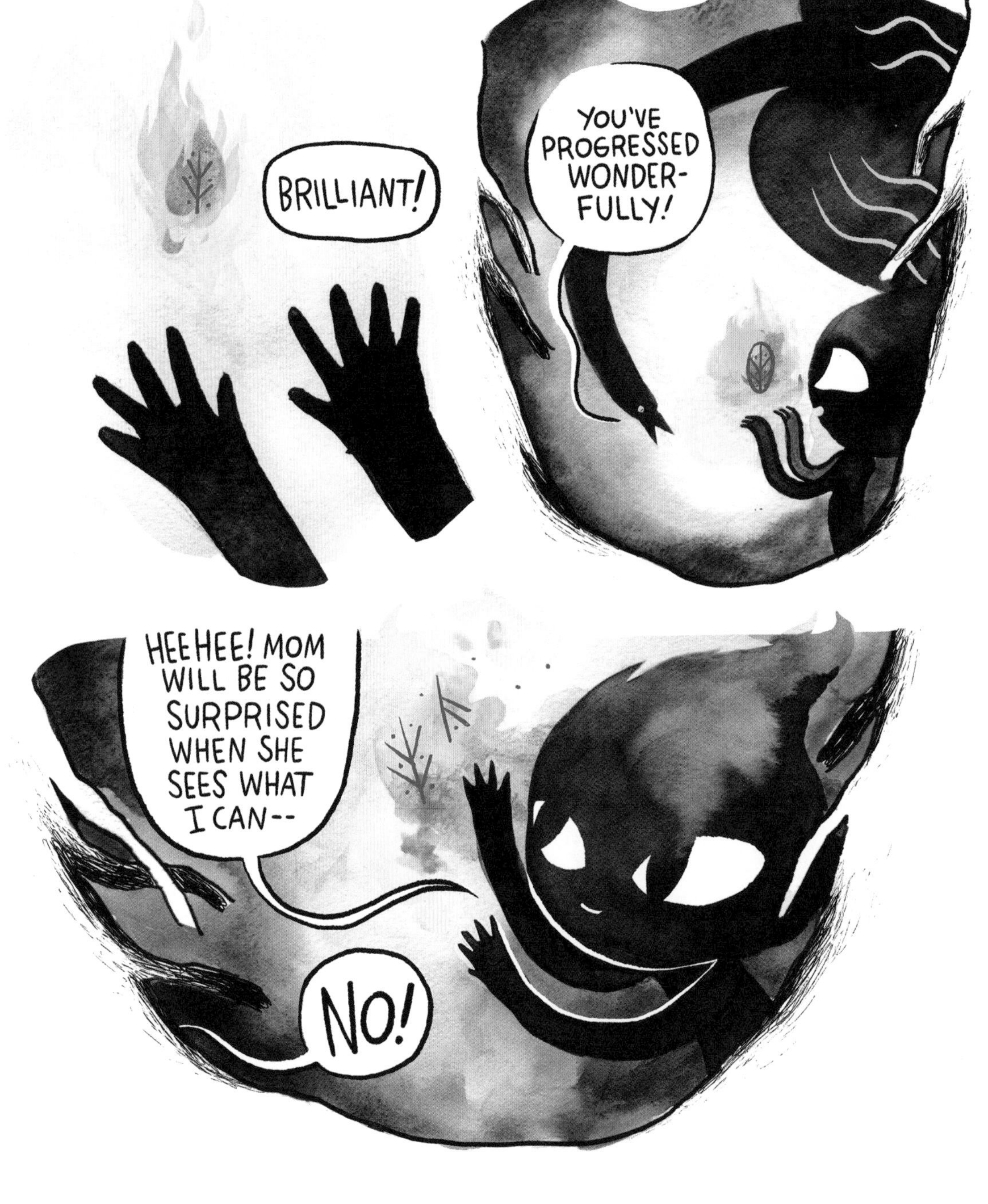
BRILLIANT!
YOU'VE PROGRESSED WONDER-FULLY!
HEEHEE! MOM WILL BE SO SURPRISED WHEN SHE SEES WHAT I CAN--
NO!

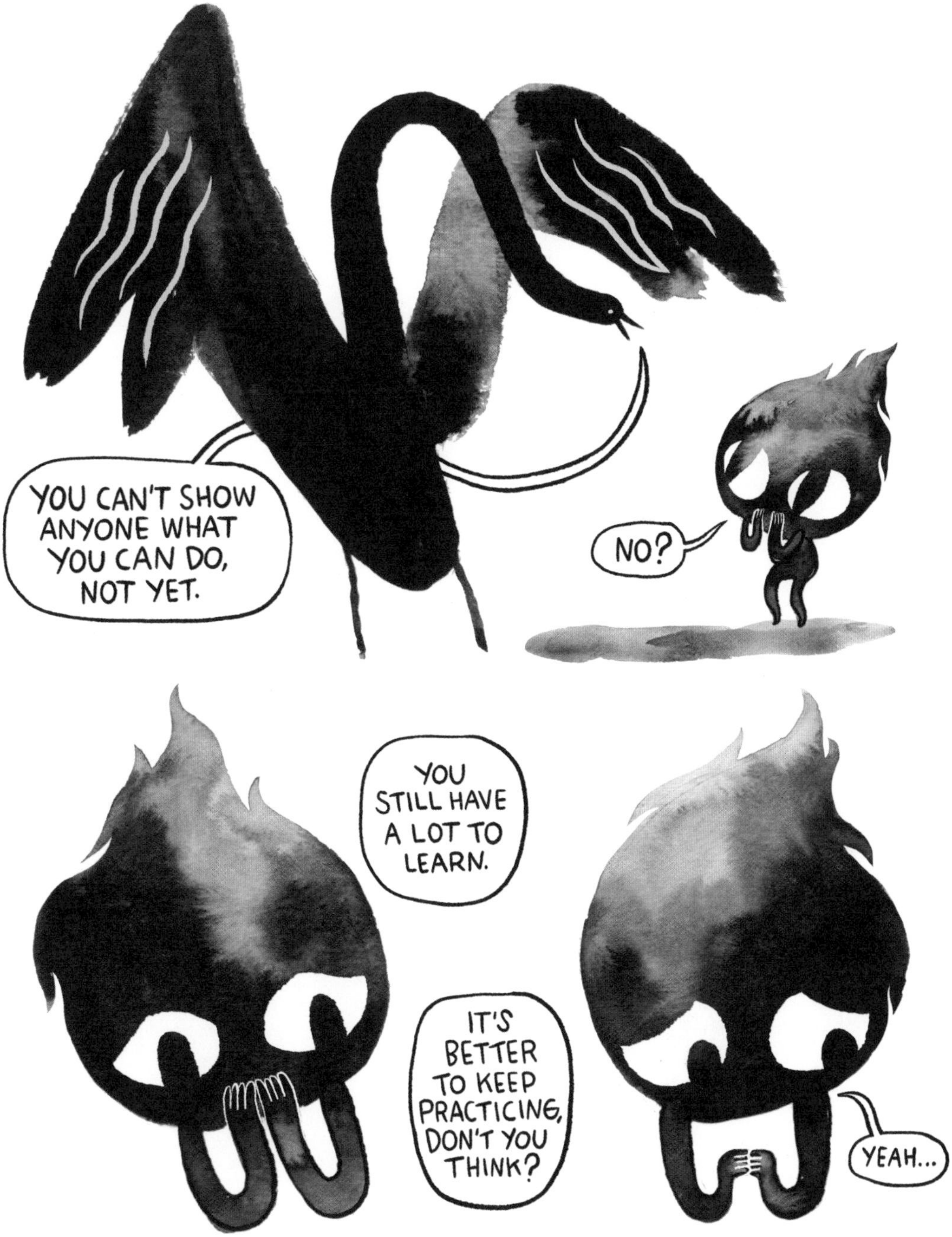
YOU CAN'T SHOW ANYONE WHAT YOU CAN DO, NOT YET.
NO?
YOU STILL HAVE A LOT TO LEARN.
IT'S BETTER TO KEEP PRACTICING, DON'T YOU THINK?
YEAH...

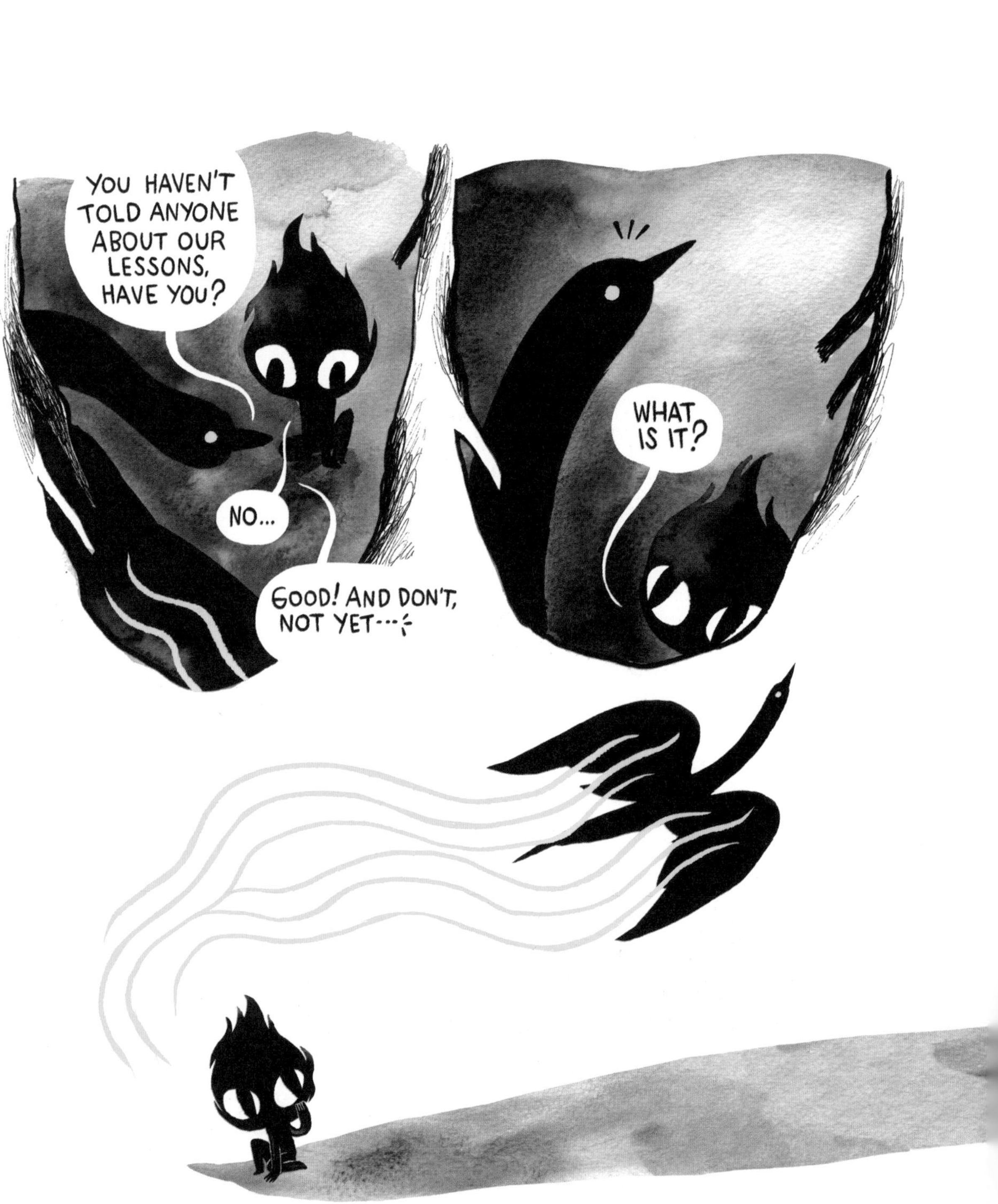
YOU HAVEN'T TOLD ANYONE ABOUT OUR LESSONS, HAVE YOU?
NO...
GOOD! AND DON'T, NOT YET...
WHAT IS IT?

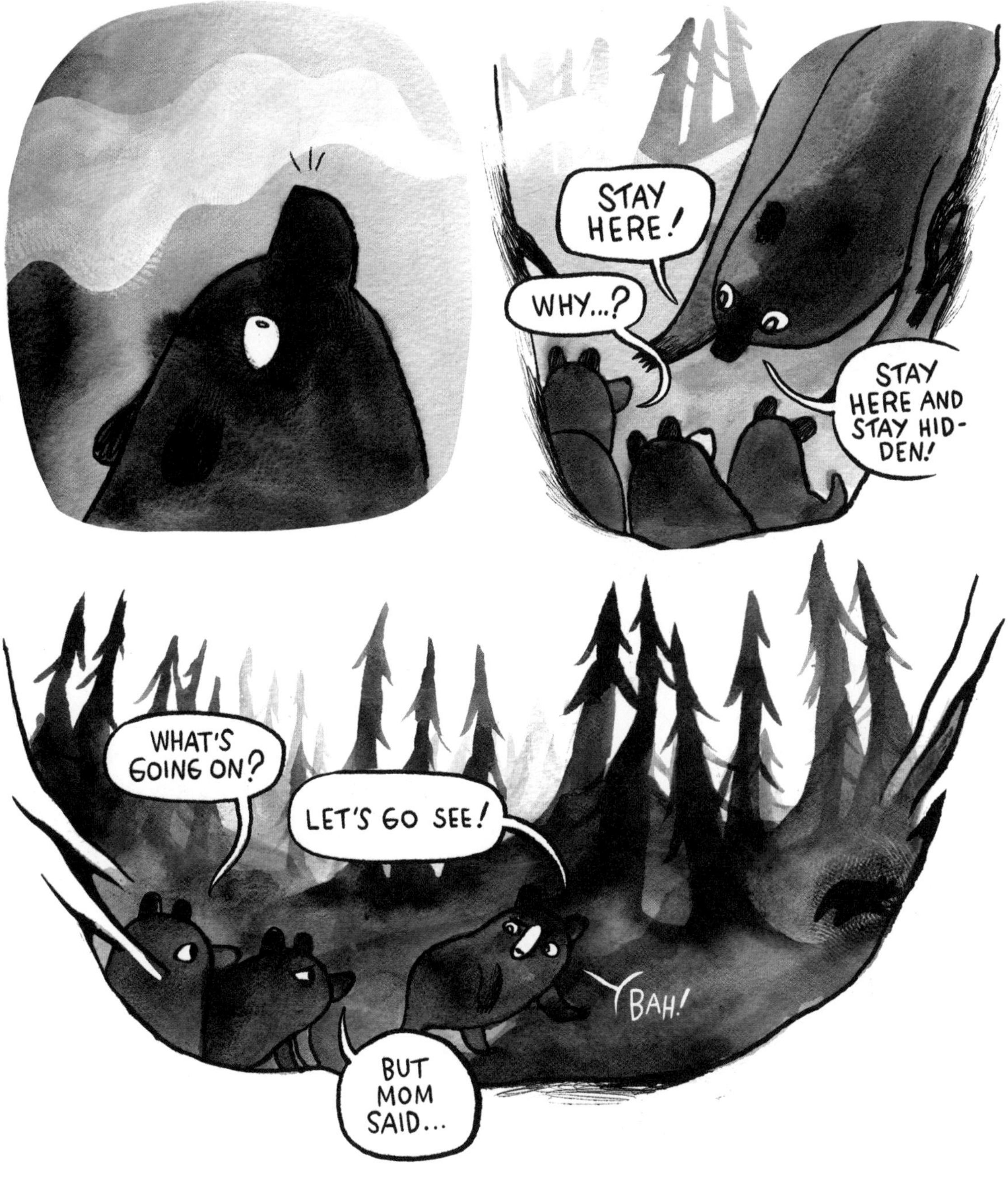
STAY HERE!
WHY...?
STAY HERE AND STAY HID-DEN!
WHAT'S GOING ON?
LET'S GO SEE!
BAH!
BUT MOM SAID...

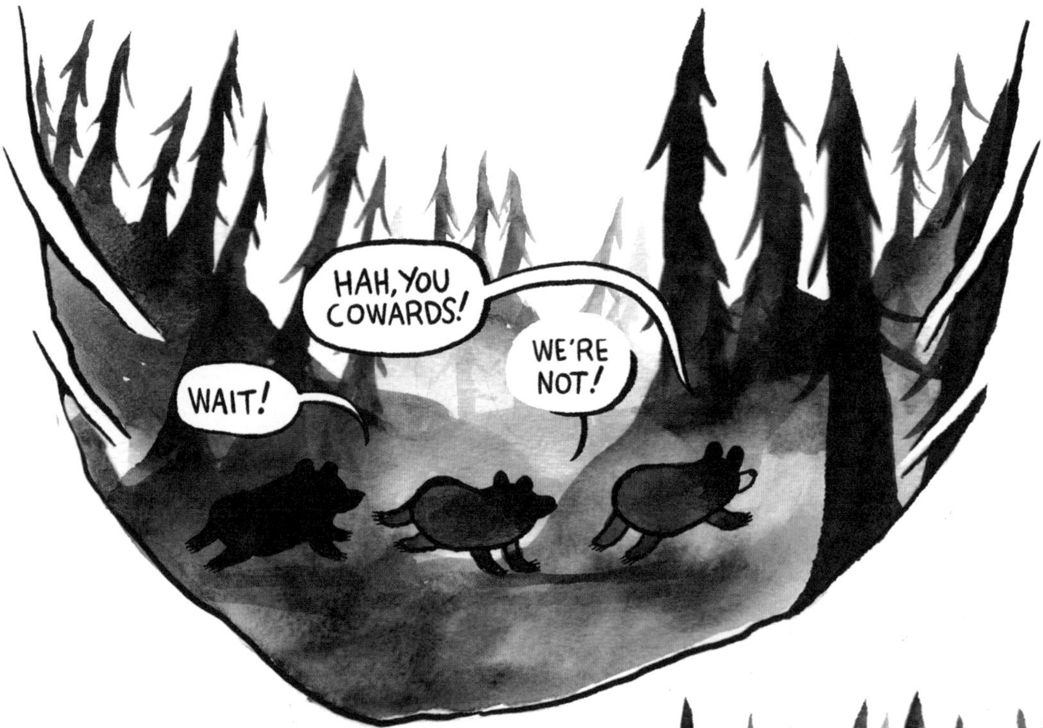
HAH, YOU COWARDS!
WAIT!
WE'RE NOT!

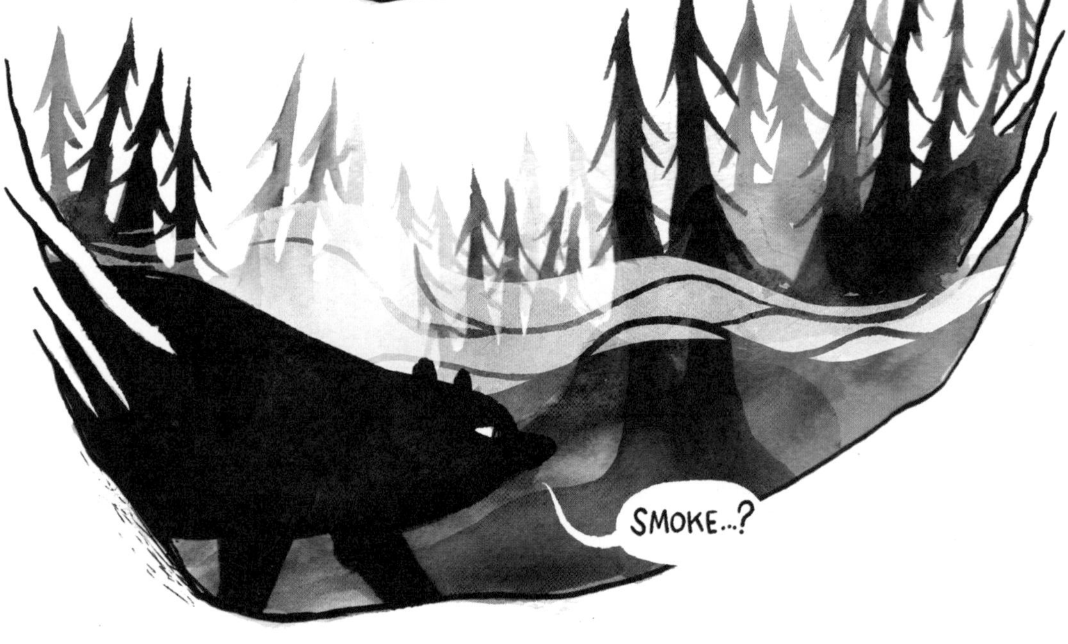
SMOKE...?

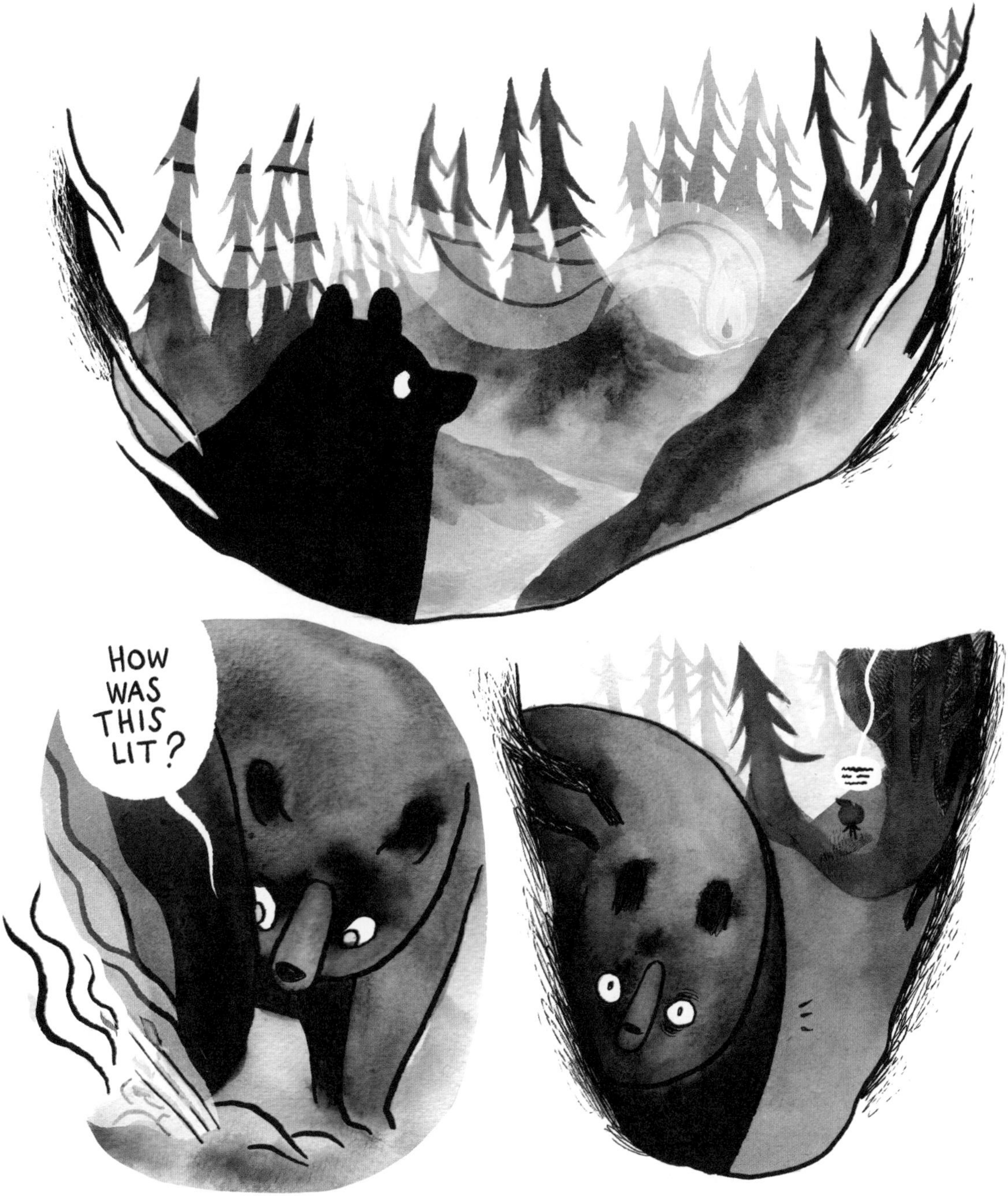
HOW WAS THIS LIT?

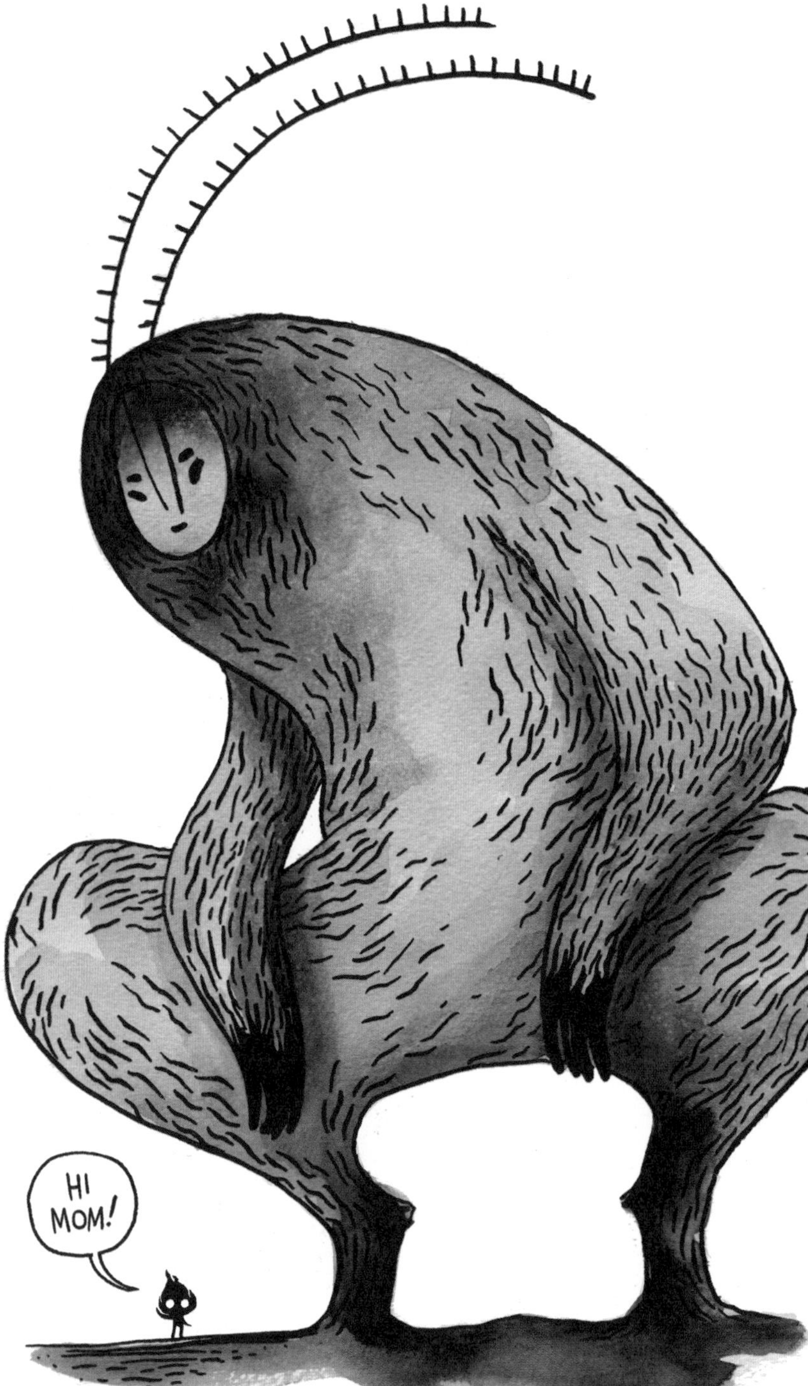
HI MOM!

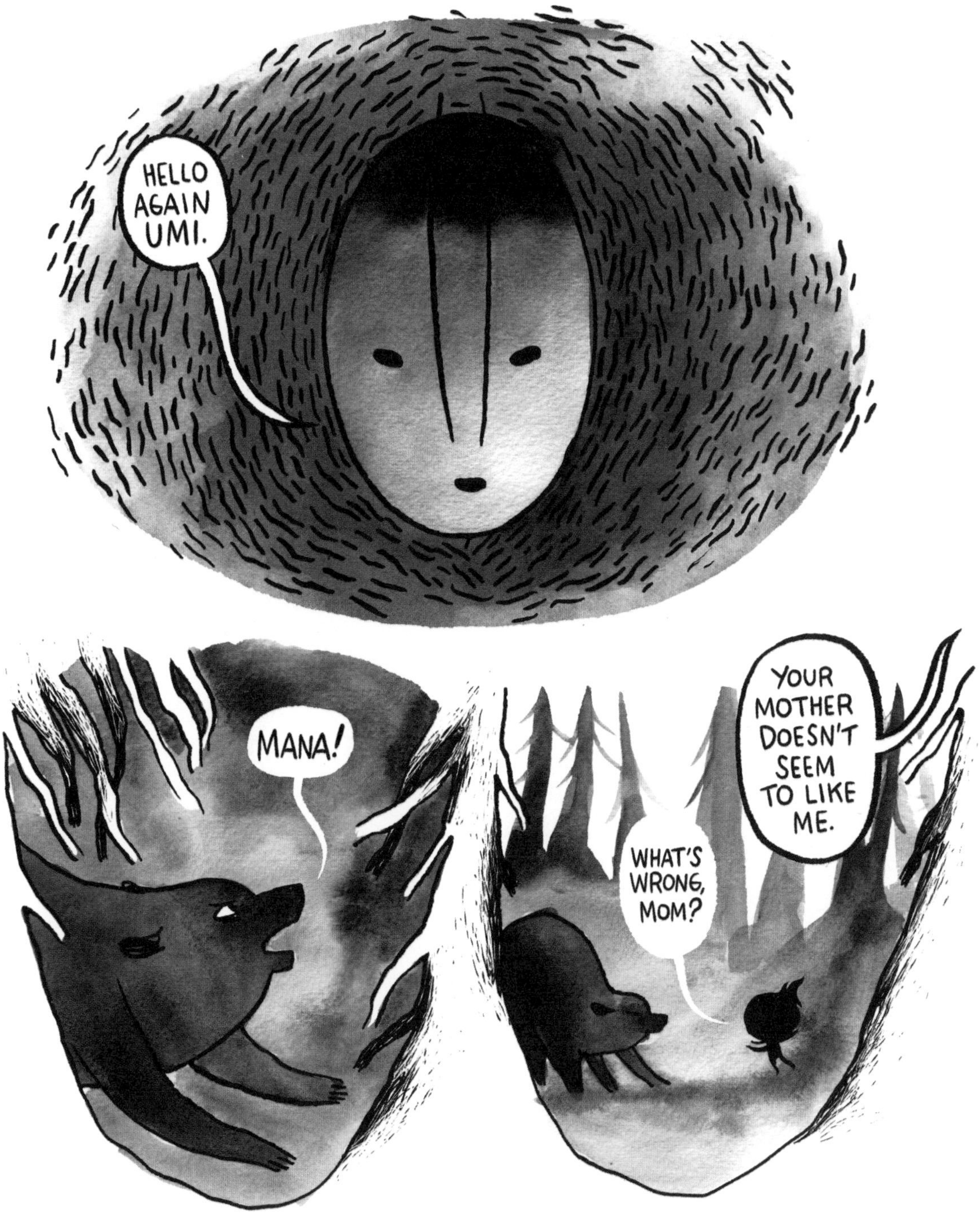
HELLO AGAIN UMI.
MANA!
WHAT'S WRONG, MOM?
YOUR MOTHER DOESN'T SEEM TO LIKE ME.

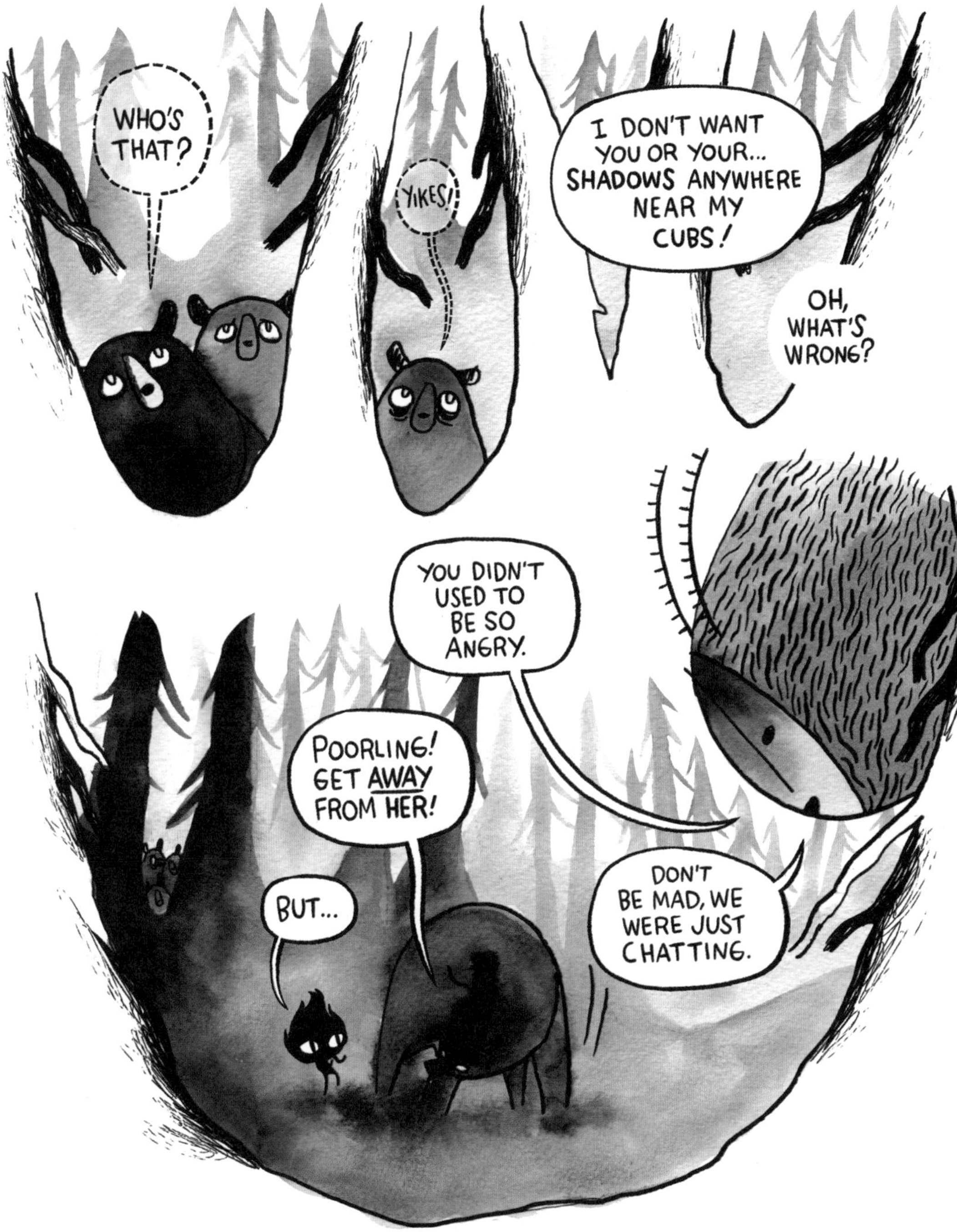
WHO'S THAT?
YIKES!
I DON'T WANT YOU OR YOUR... SHADOWS ANYWHERE NEAR MY CUBS!
OH, WHAT'S WRONG?
YOU DIDN'T USED TO BE SO ANGRY.
POORLING! GET AWAY FROM HER!
BUT...
DON'T BE MAD, WE WERE JUST CHATTING.

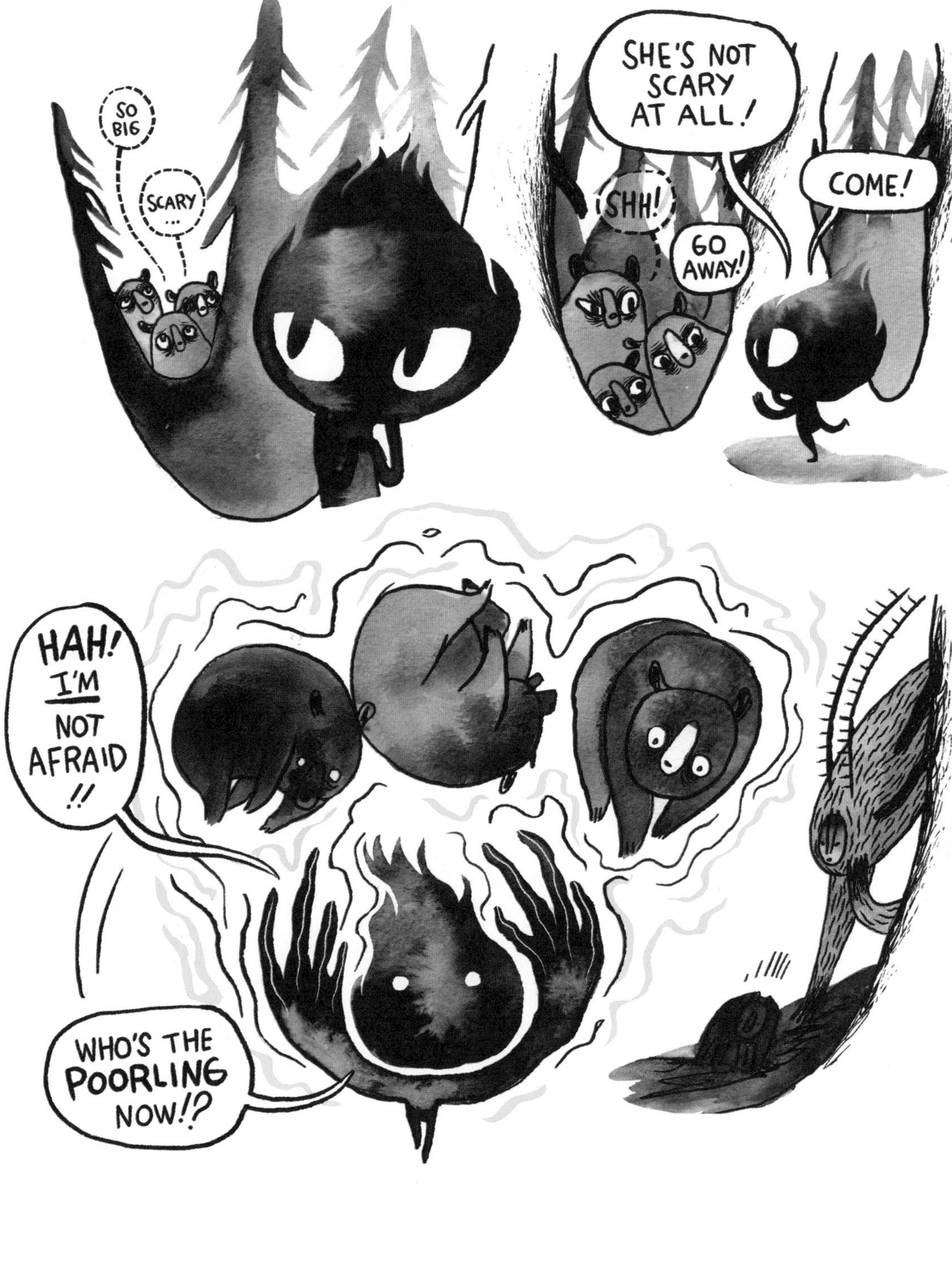
SO BIG
SCARY ...
SHE'S NOT SCARY AT ALL!
SHH!
GO AWAY!
COME!
HAH! I'M NOT AFRAID !!
WHO'S THE POORLING NOW!?

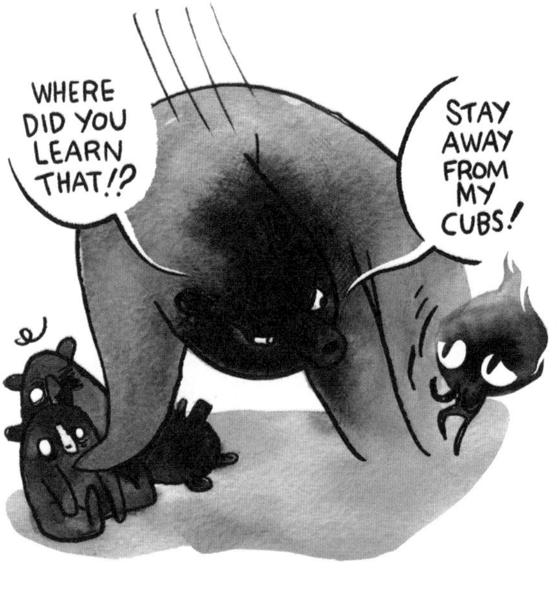
WHERE DID YOU LEARN THAT!?
STAY AWAY FROM MY CUBS!

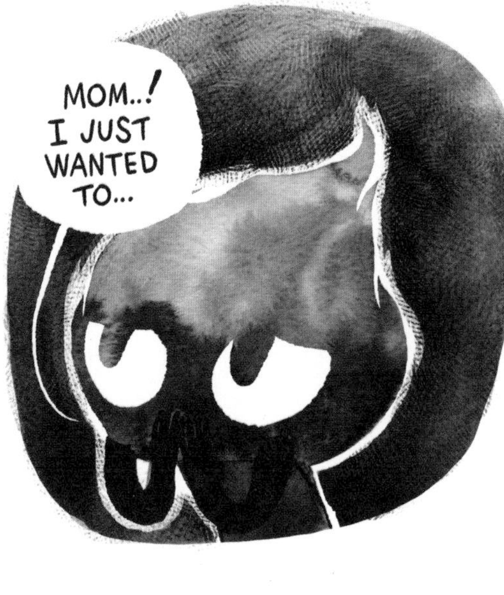
MOM..! I JUST WANTED TO...

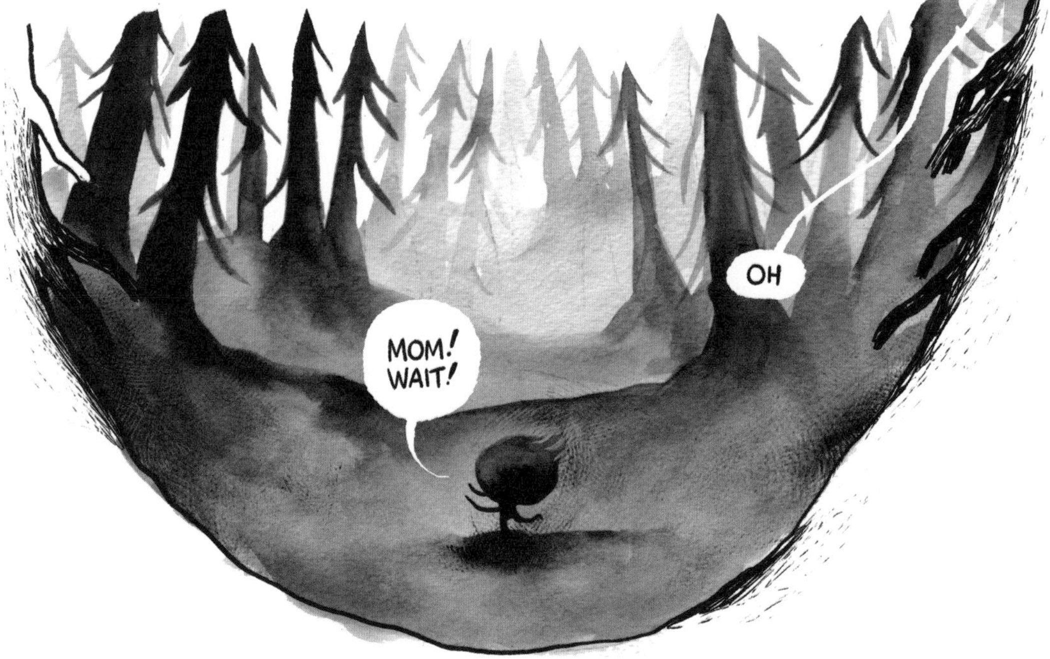
OH
MOM! WAIT!

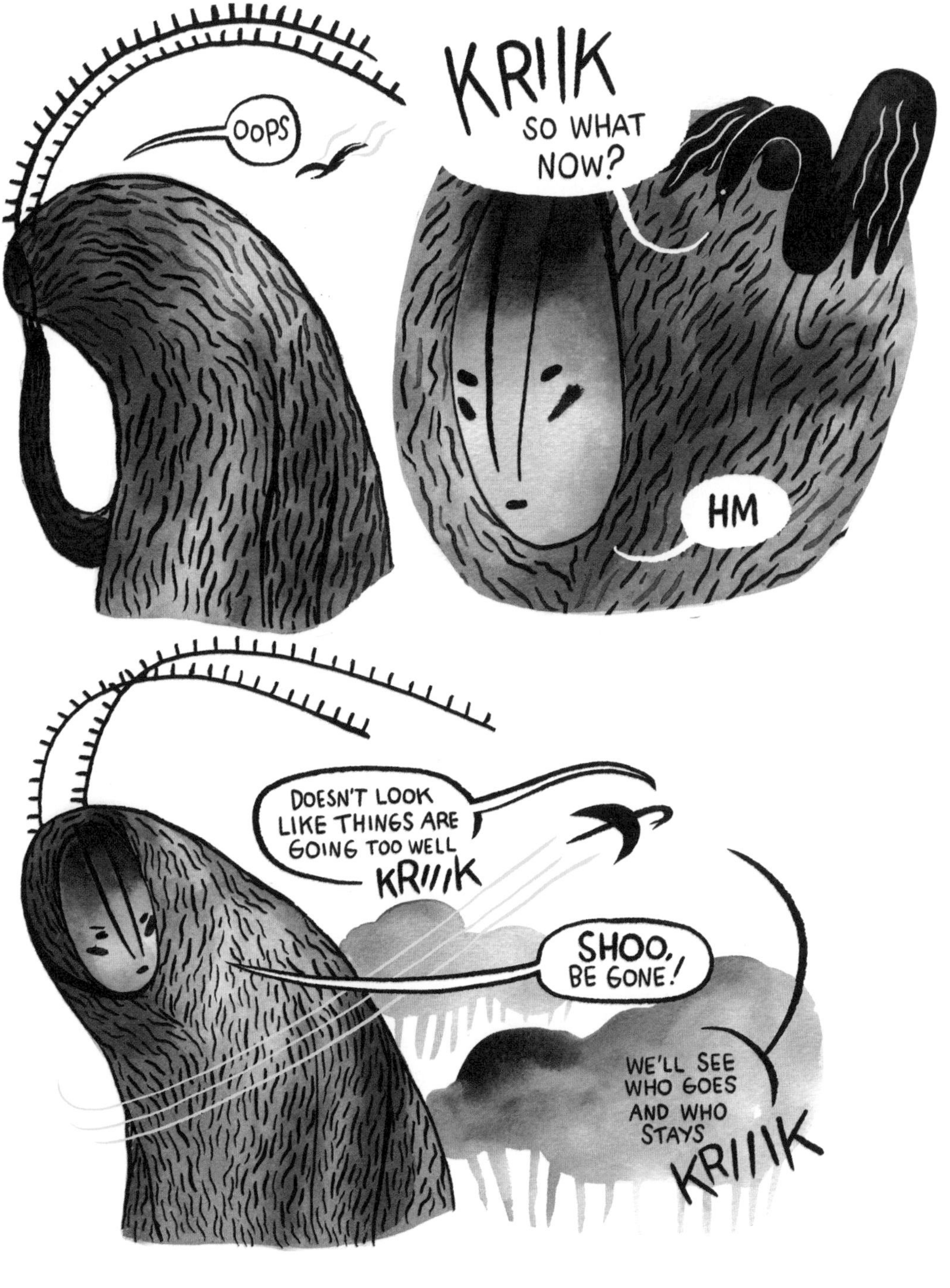
OOPS
KRIIK
SO WHAT NOW?
HM
DOESN'T LOOK LIKE THINGS ARE GOING TOO WELL
KRIIIK
SHOO, BE GONE!
WE'LL SEE WHO GOES AND WHO STAYS
KRIIIK

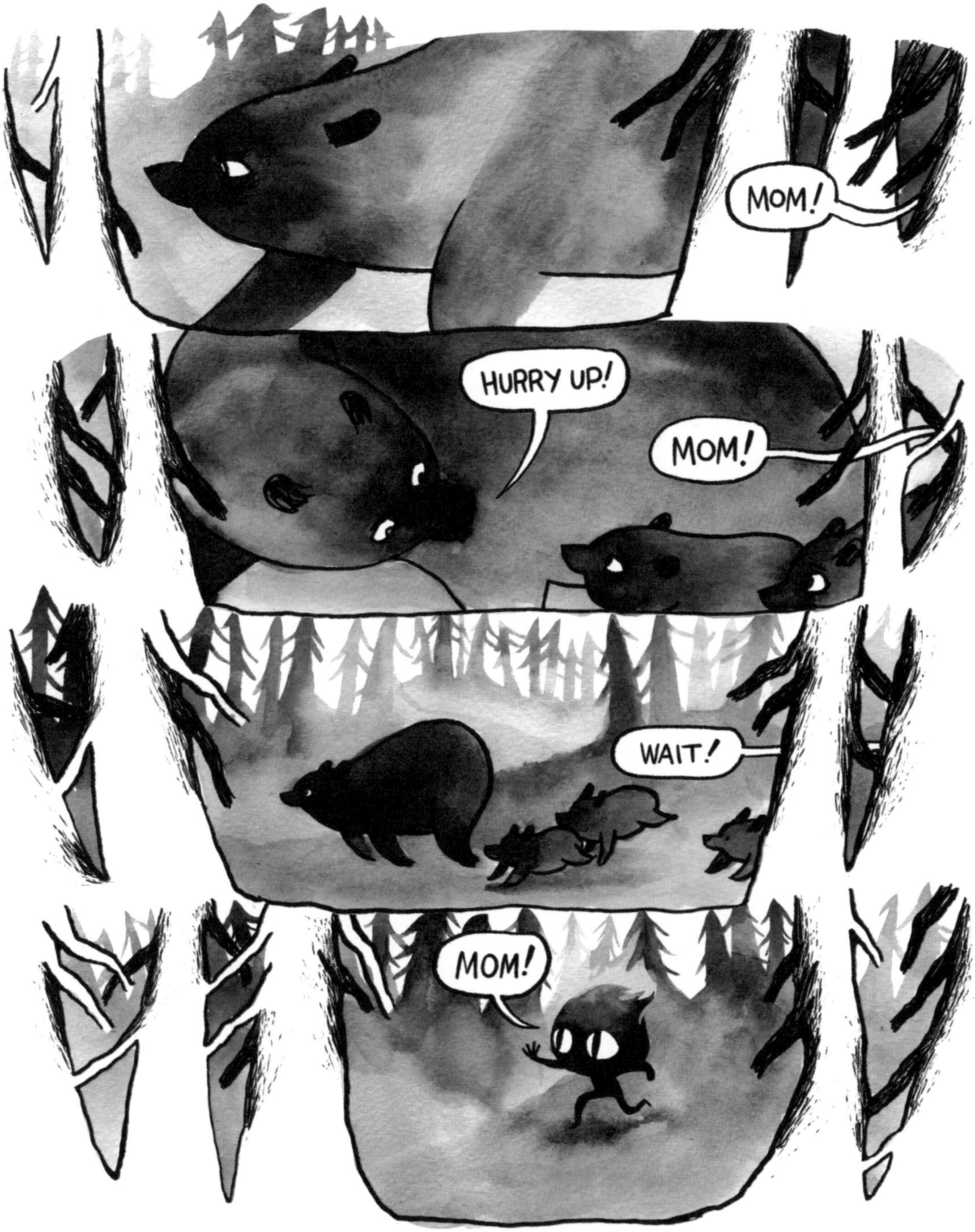
MOM!
HURRY UP!
MOM!
WAIT!
MOM!

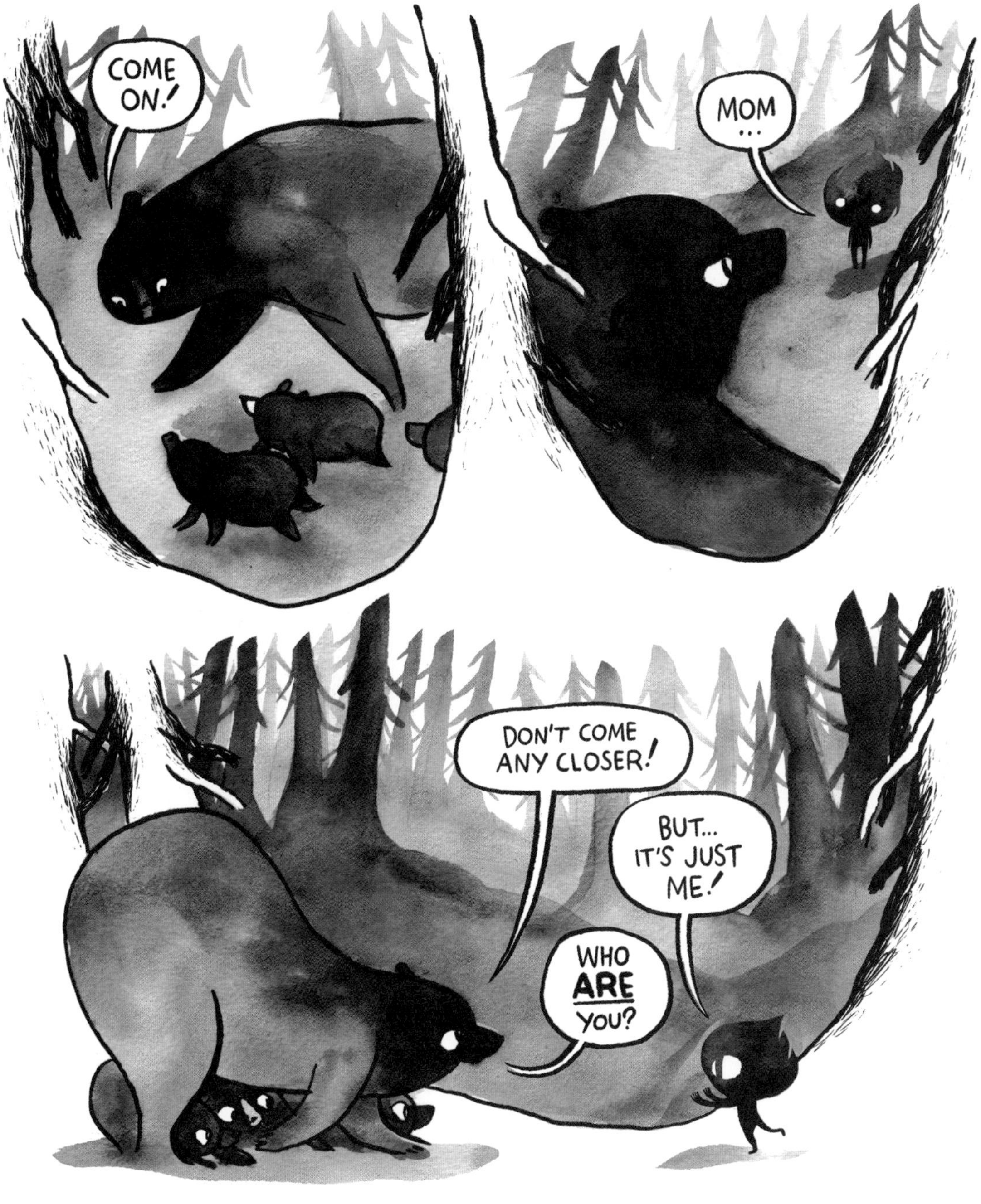

COME ON!
MOM ...
DON'T COME ANY CLOSER!
BUT... IT'S JUST ME!
WHO **ARE** YOU?

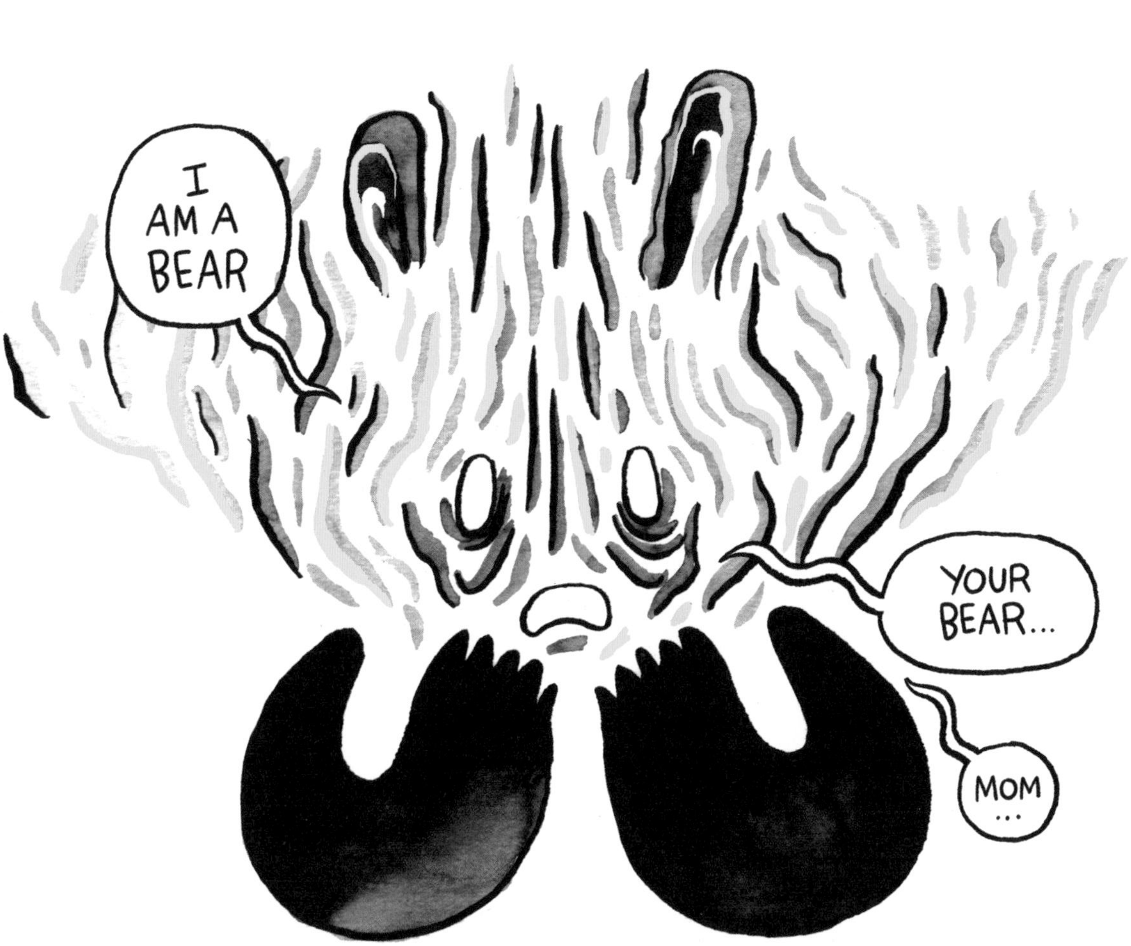
I AM A BEAR
YOUR BEAR...
MOM ...

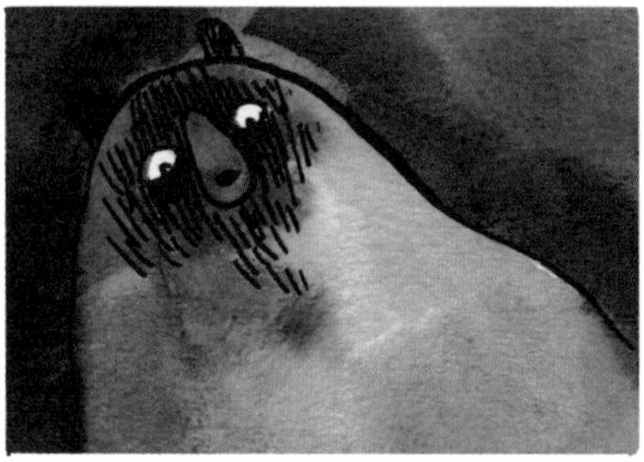

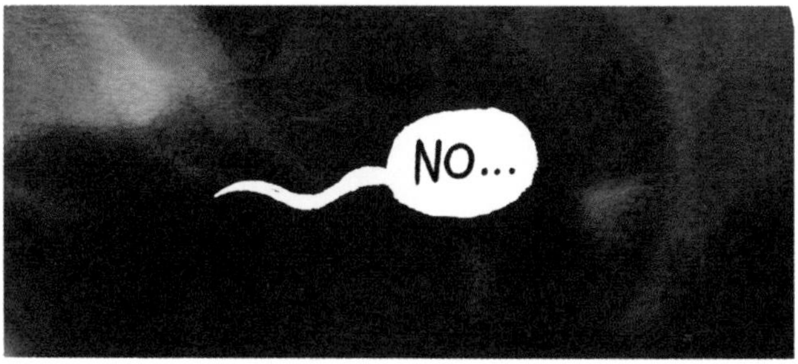
NO...

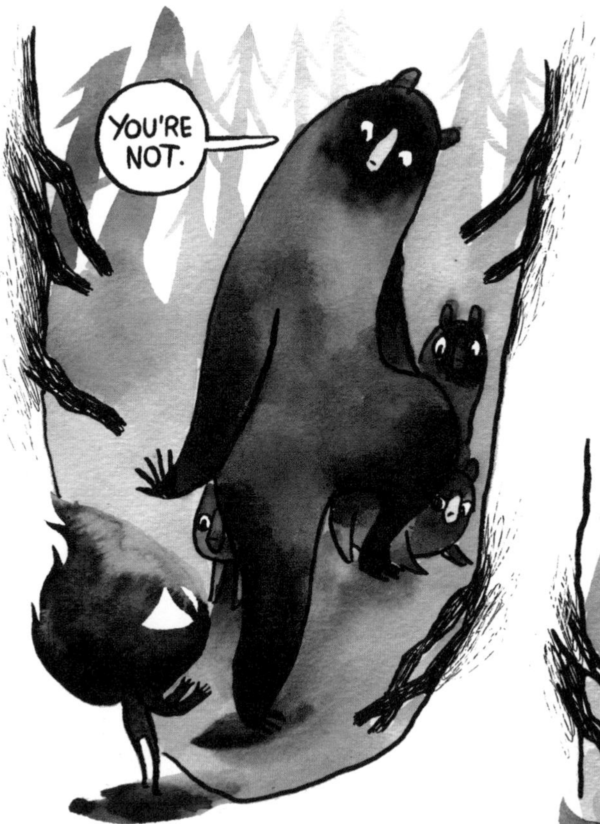
YOU'RE NOT.

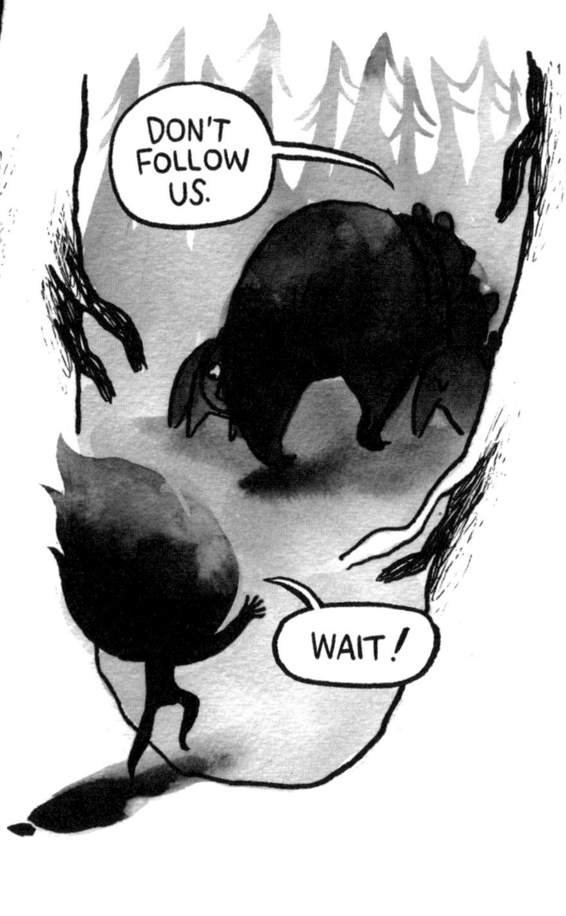
DON'T FOLLOW US.
WAIT!

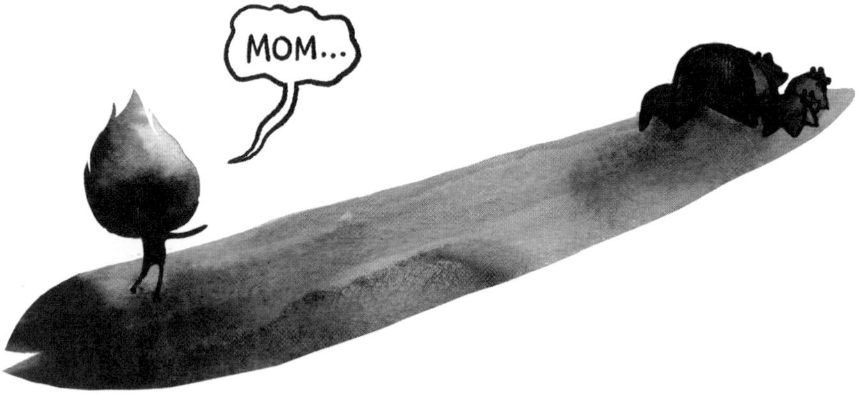
MOM...

IV

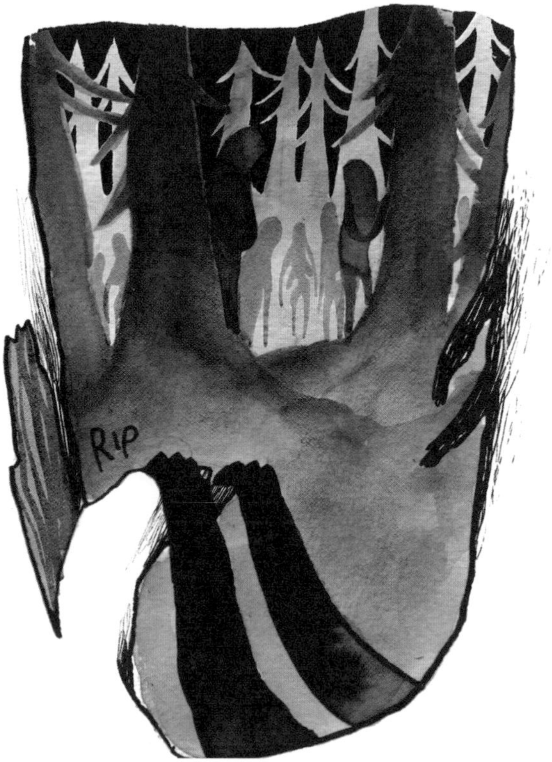
RIP

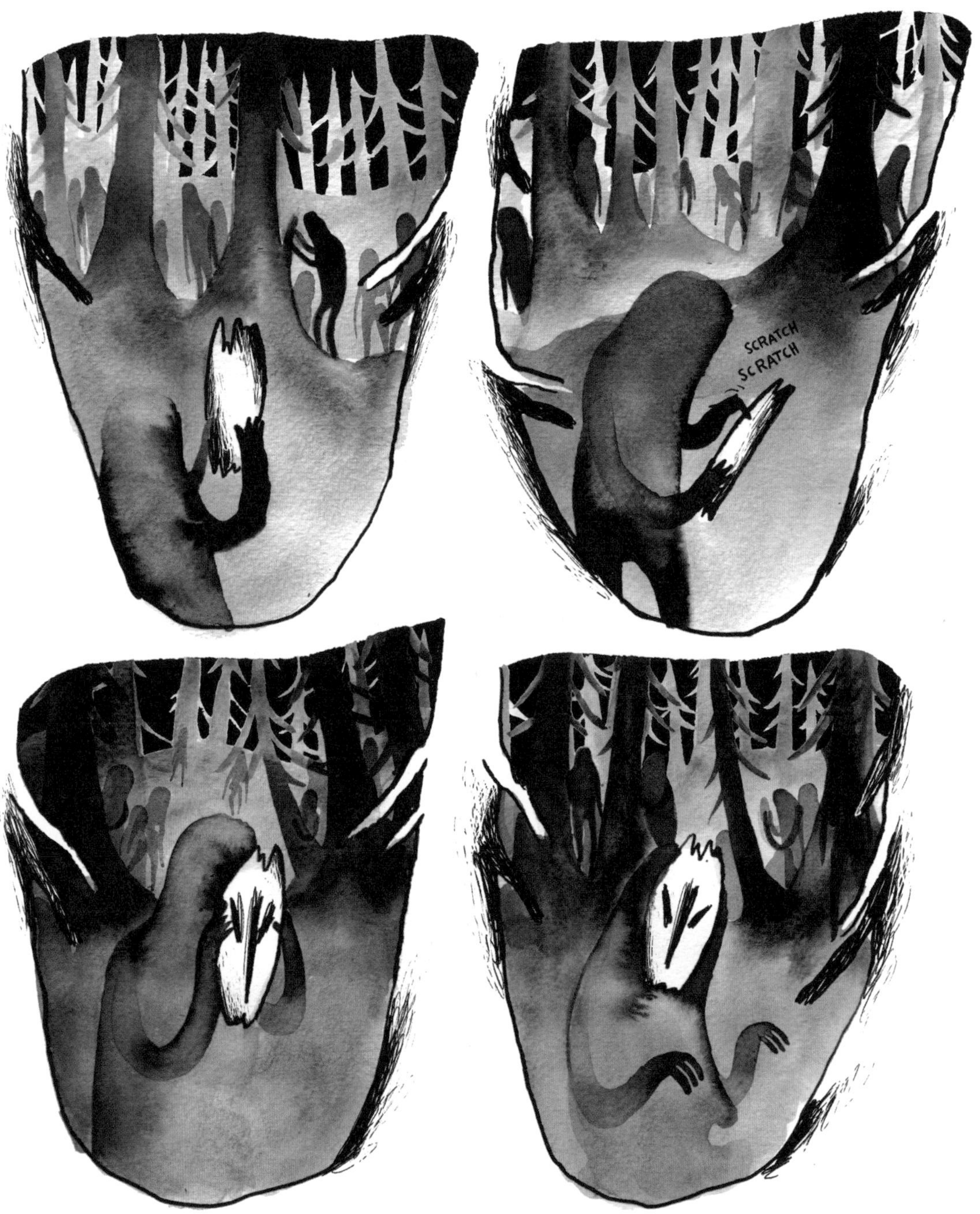
SCRATCH
SCRATCH

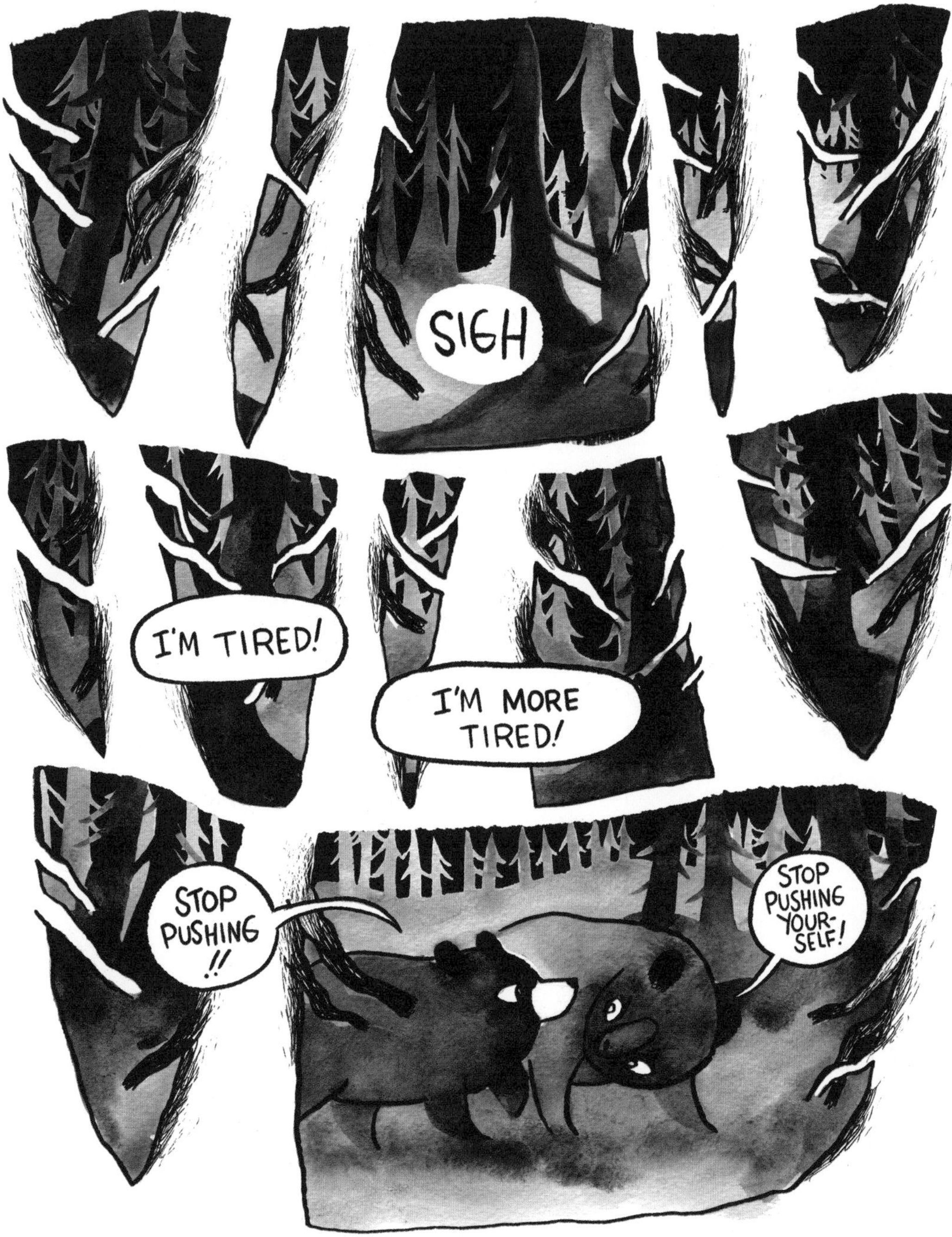
SIGH
I'M TIRED!
I'M MORE TIRED!
STOP PUSHING !!
STOP PUSHING YOUR-SELF!

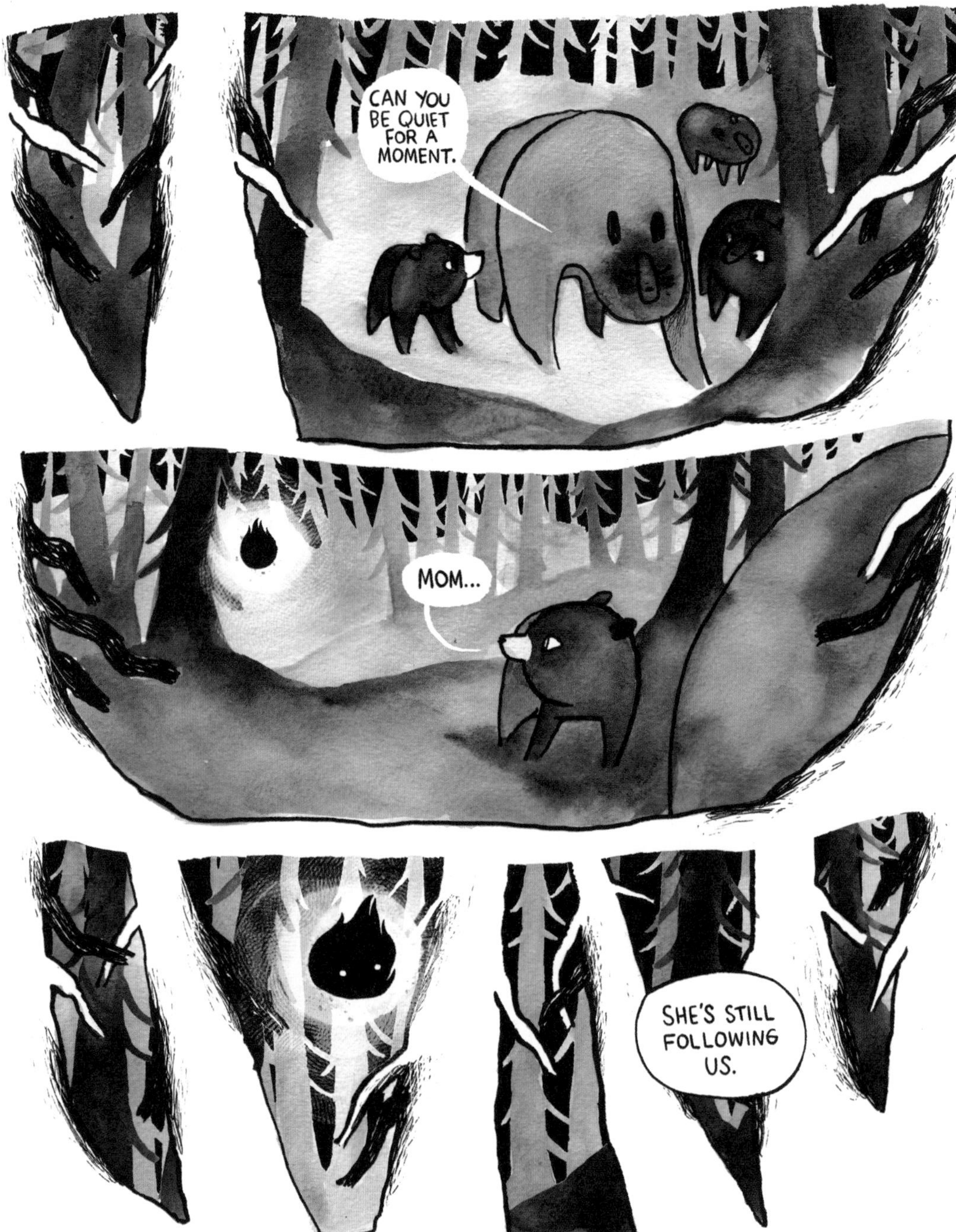
CAN YOU BE QUIET FOR A MOMENT.
MOM...
SHE'S STILL FOLLOWING US.

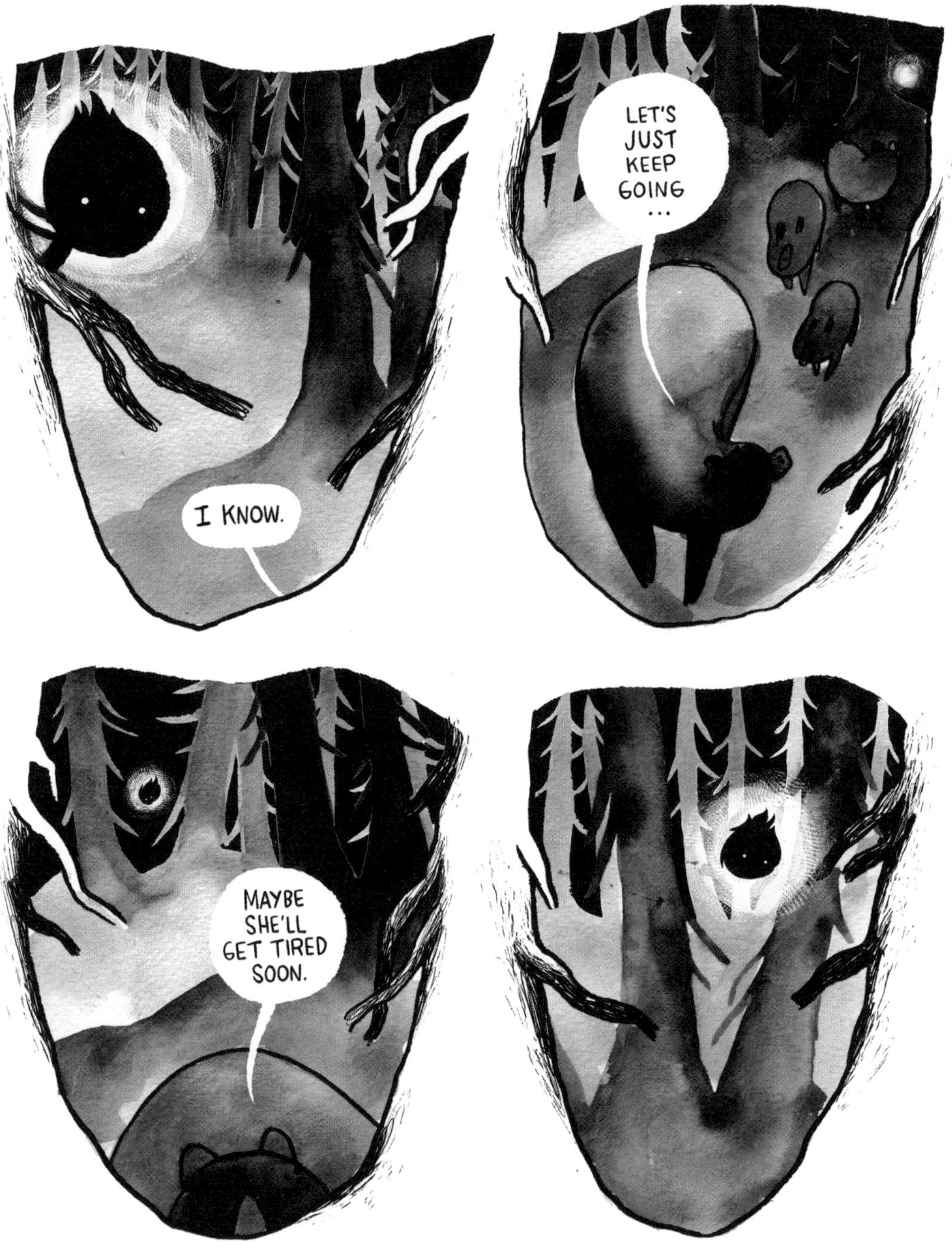
I KNOW.
LET'S JUST KEEP GOING ...
MAYBE SHE'LL GET TIRED SOON.

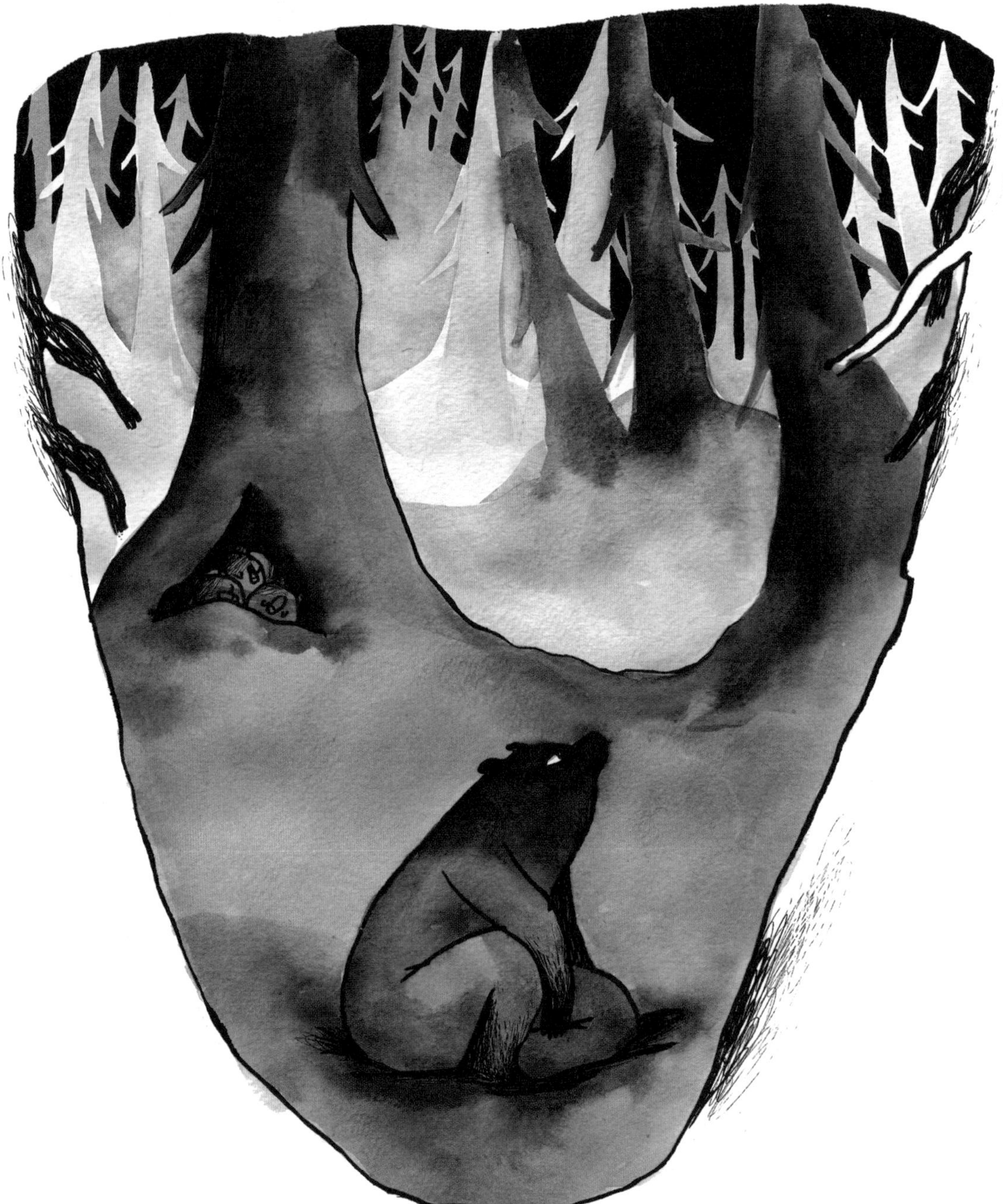

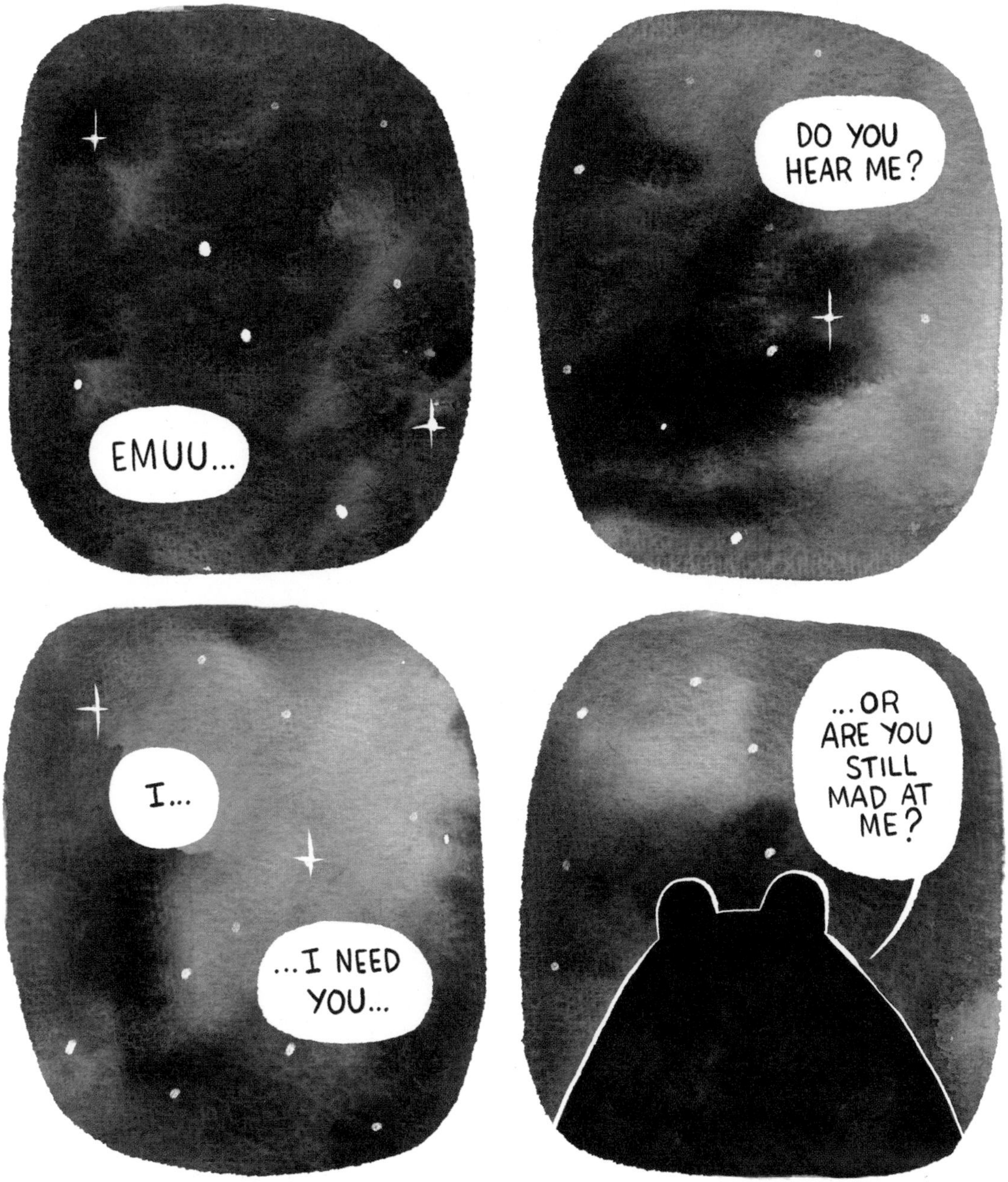
EMUU...
DO YOU HEAR ME?
I...
...I NEED YOU...
...OR ARE YOU STILL MAD AT ME?

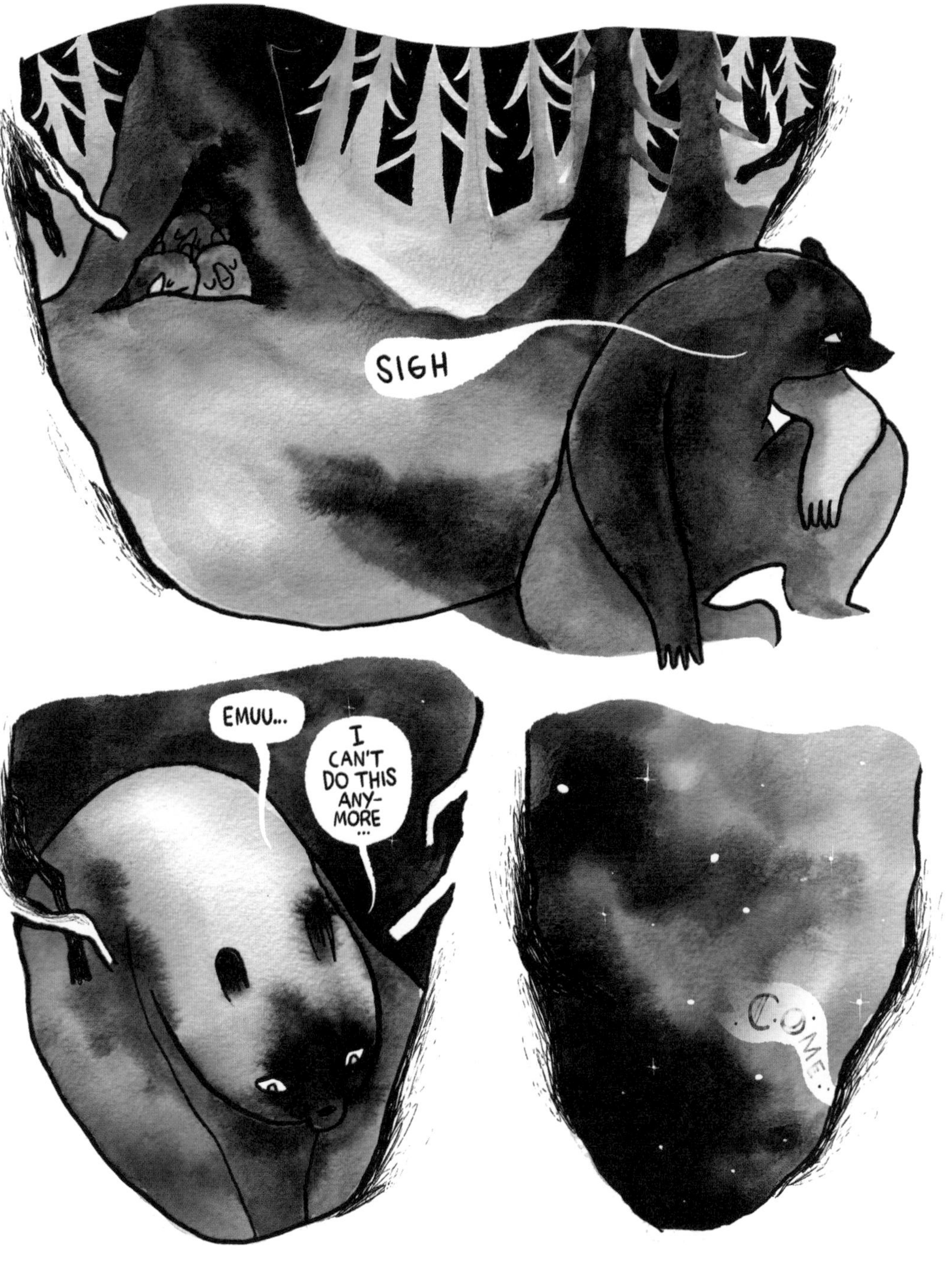
SIGH
EMUU...
I CAN'T DO THIS ANY-MORE...
.C.OME..

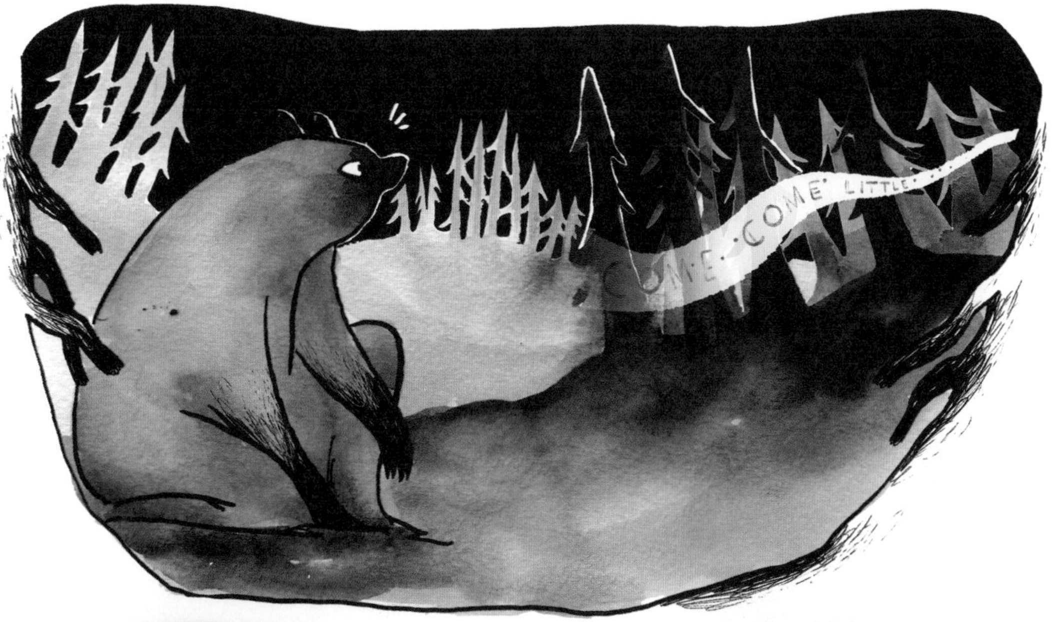
COME · COME · LITTLE...

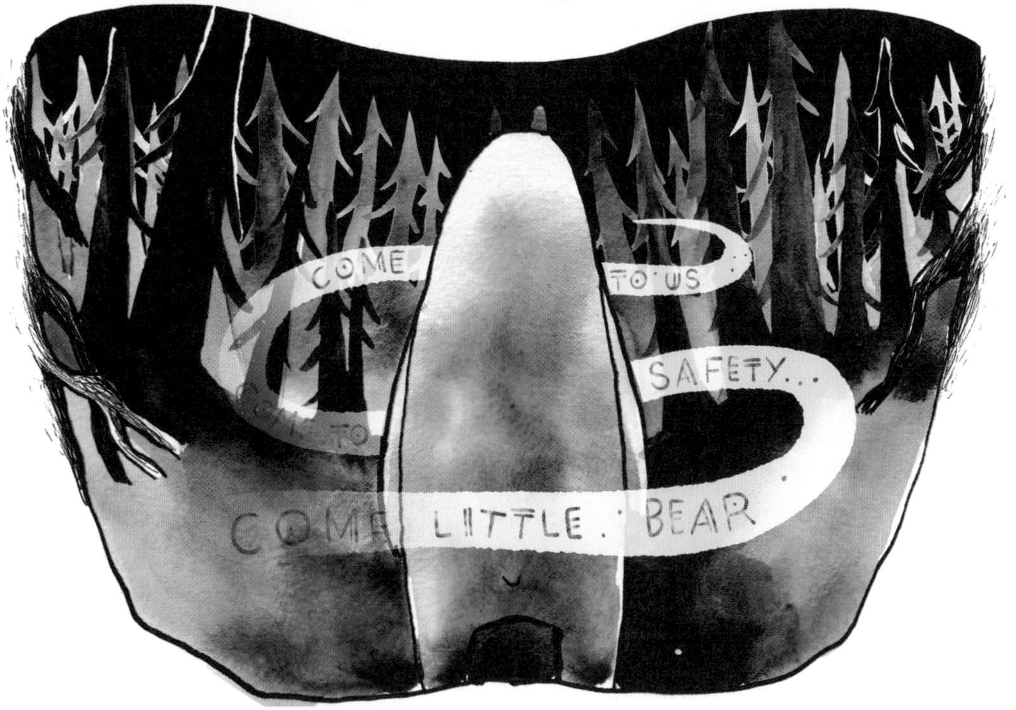
COME
TO US
SAFETY...
COME LITTLE. BEAR

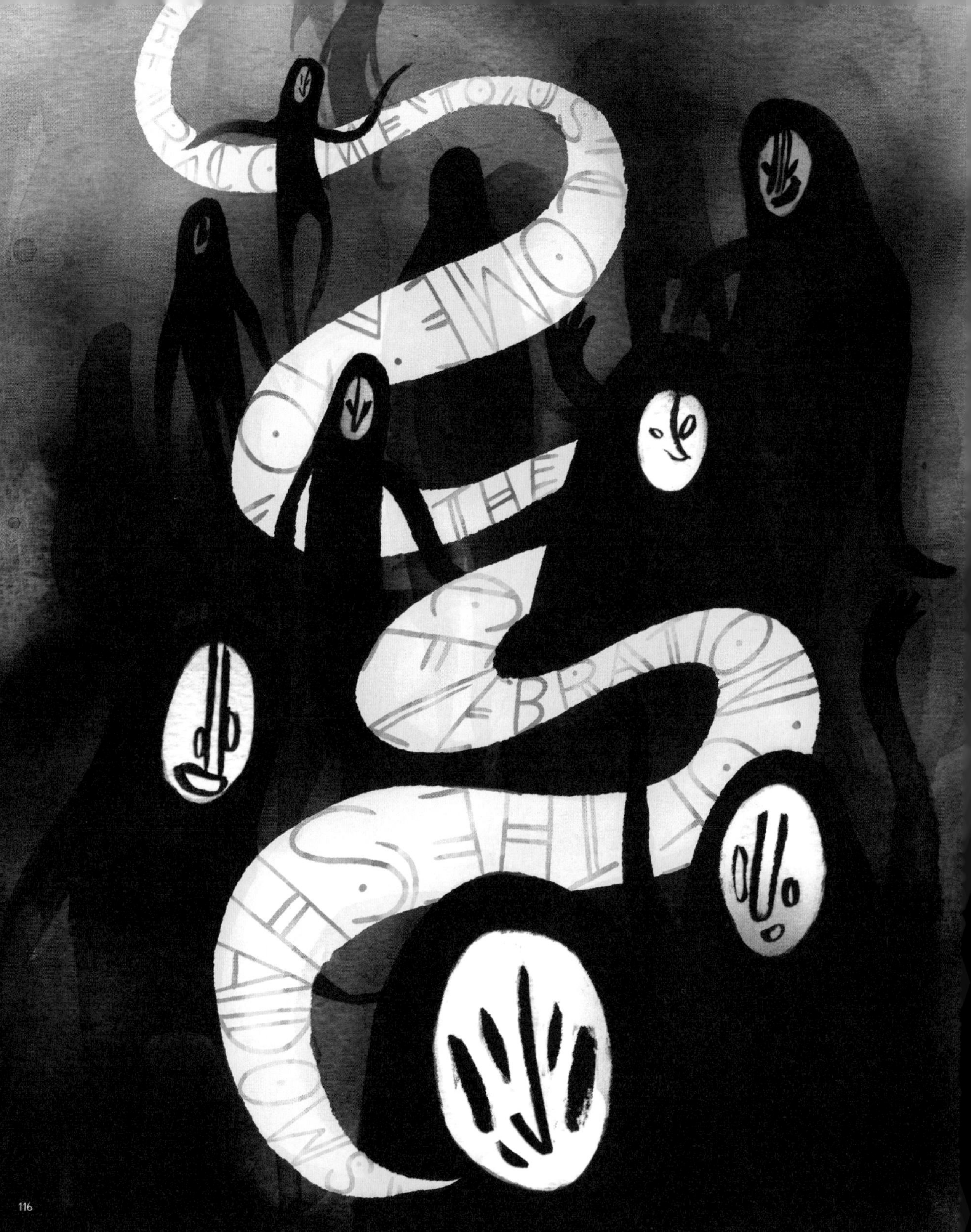

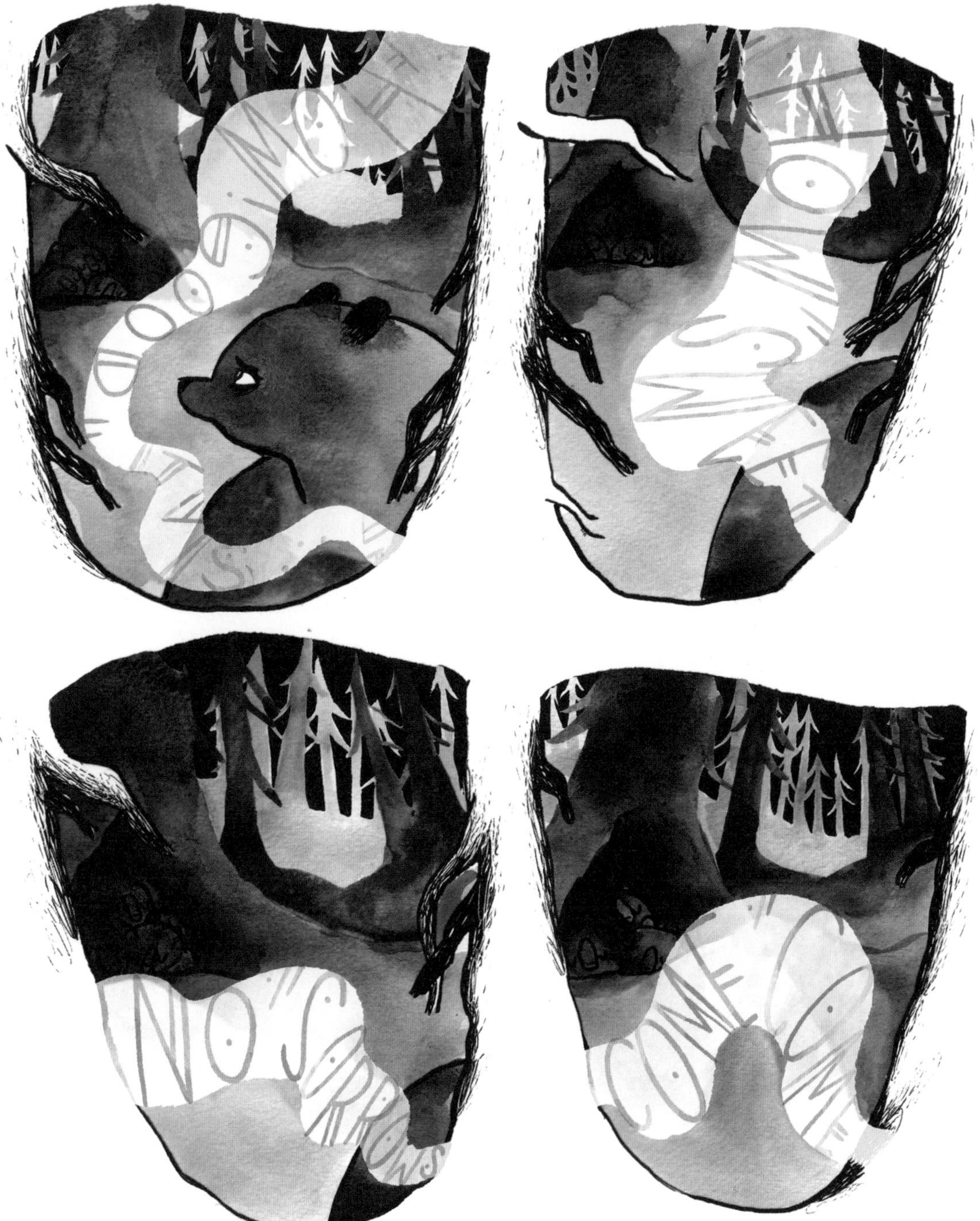
NO SORROWS
COME COME

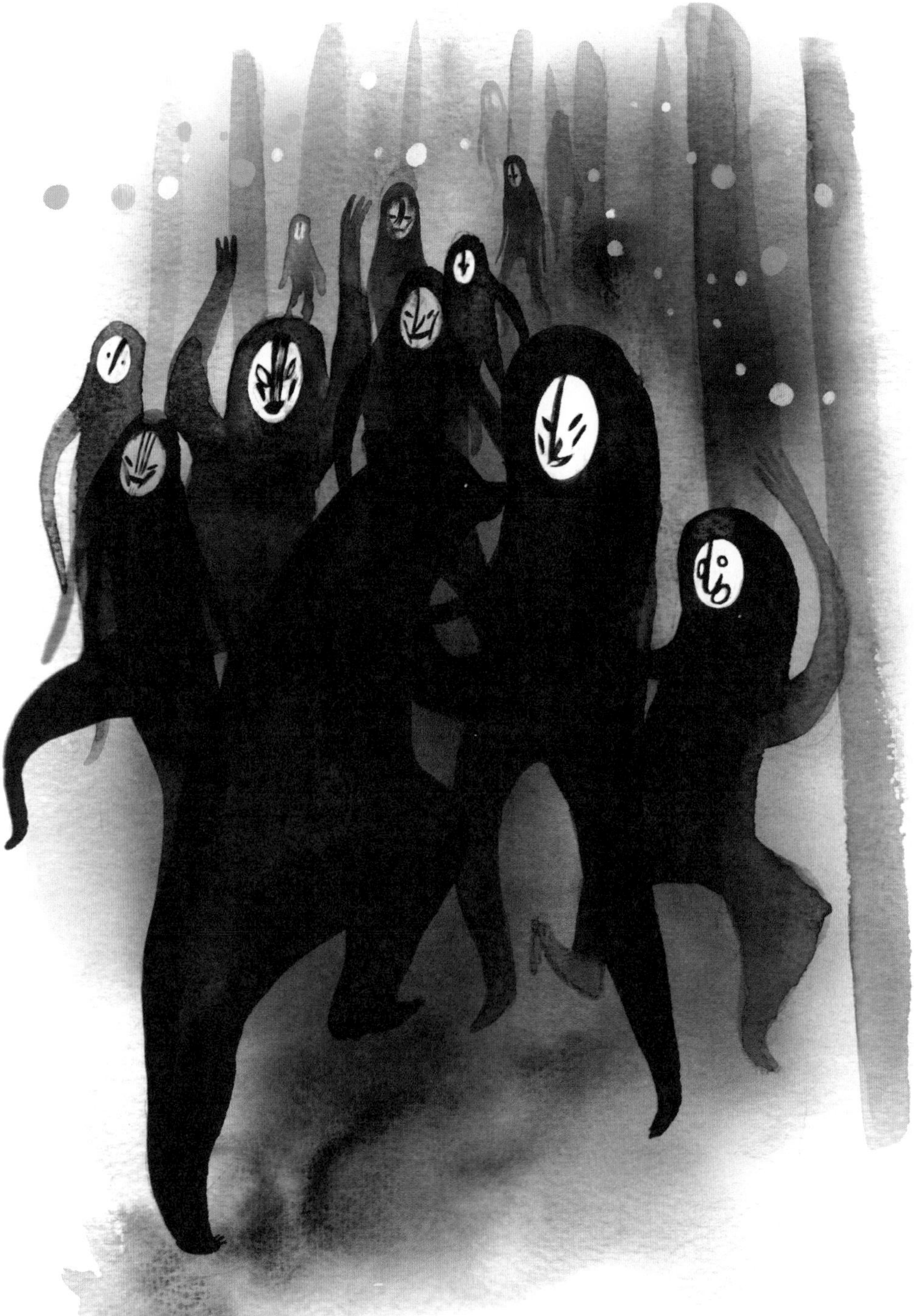

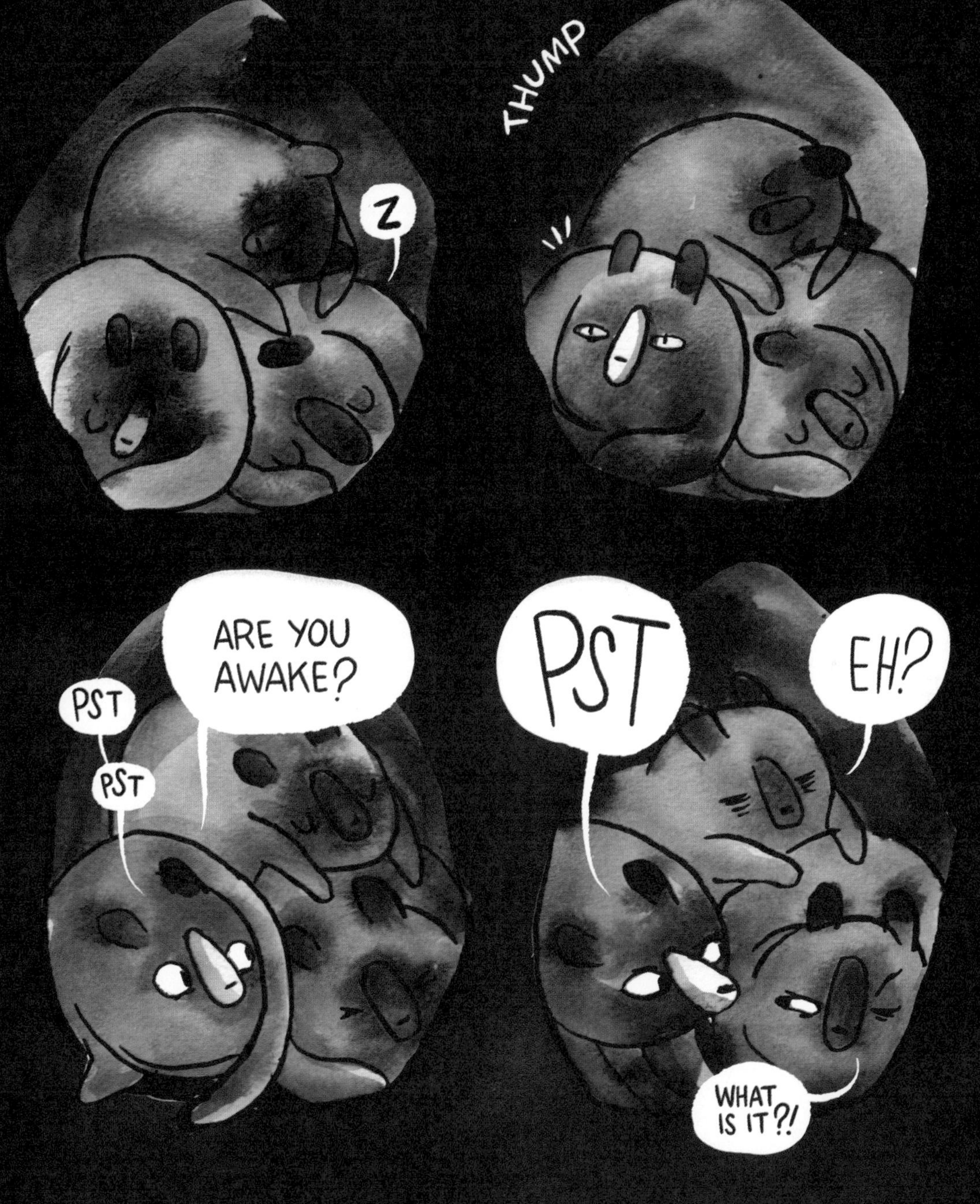
Z
THUMP
PST
PST
ARE YOU AWAKE?
PST
EH?
WHAT IS IT?!

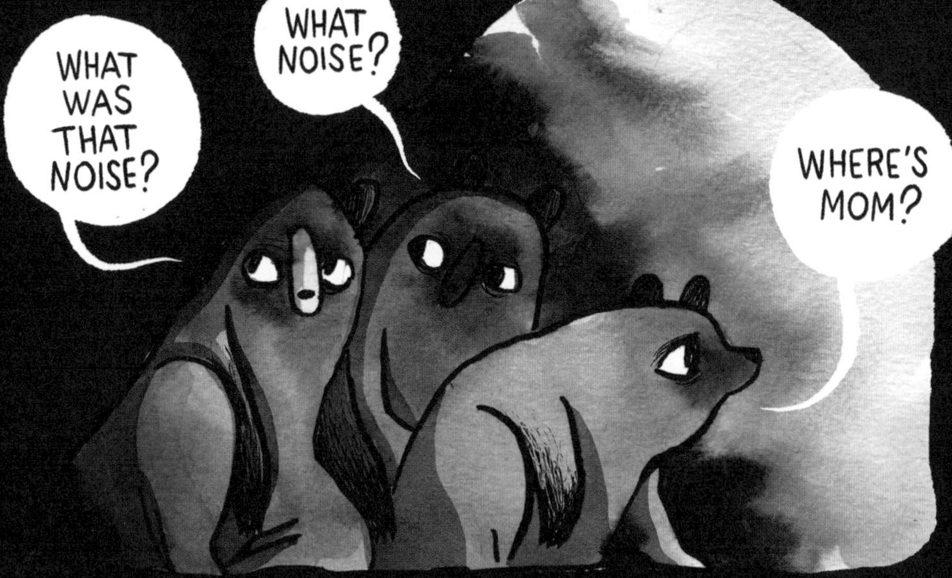
WHAT WAS THAT NOISE?
WHAT NOISE?
WHERE'S MOM?

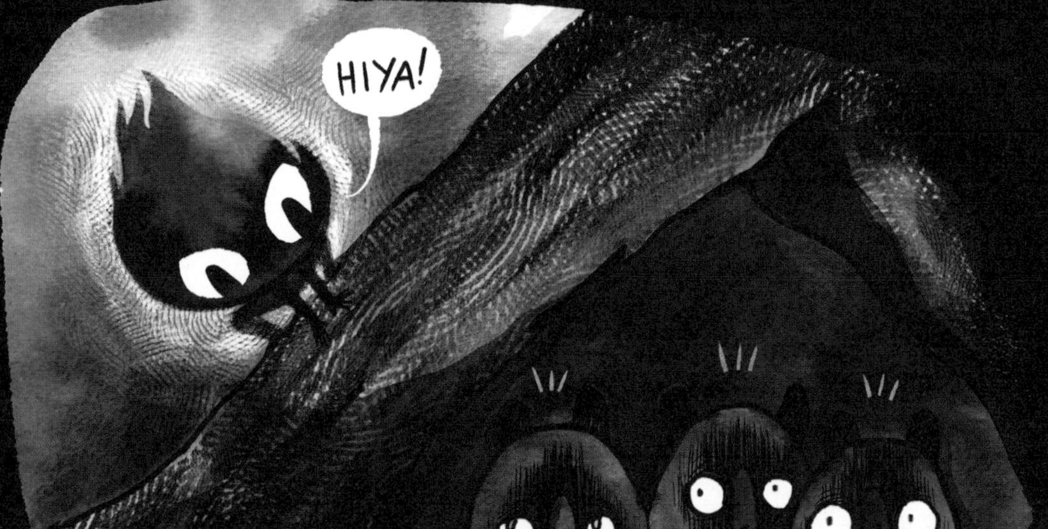
HIYA!

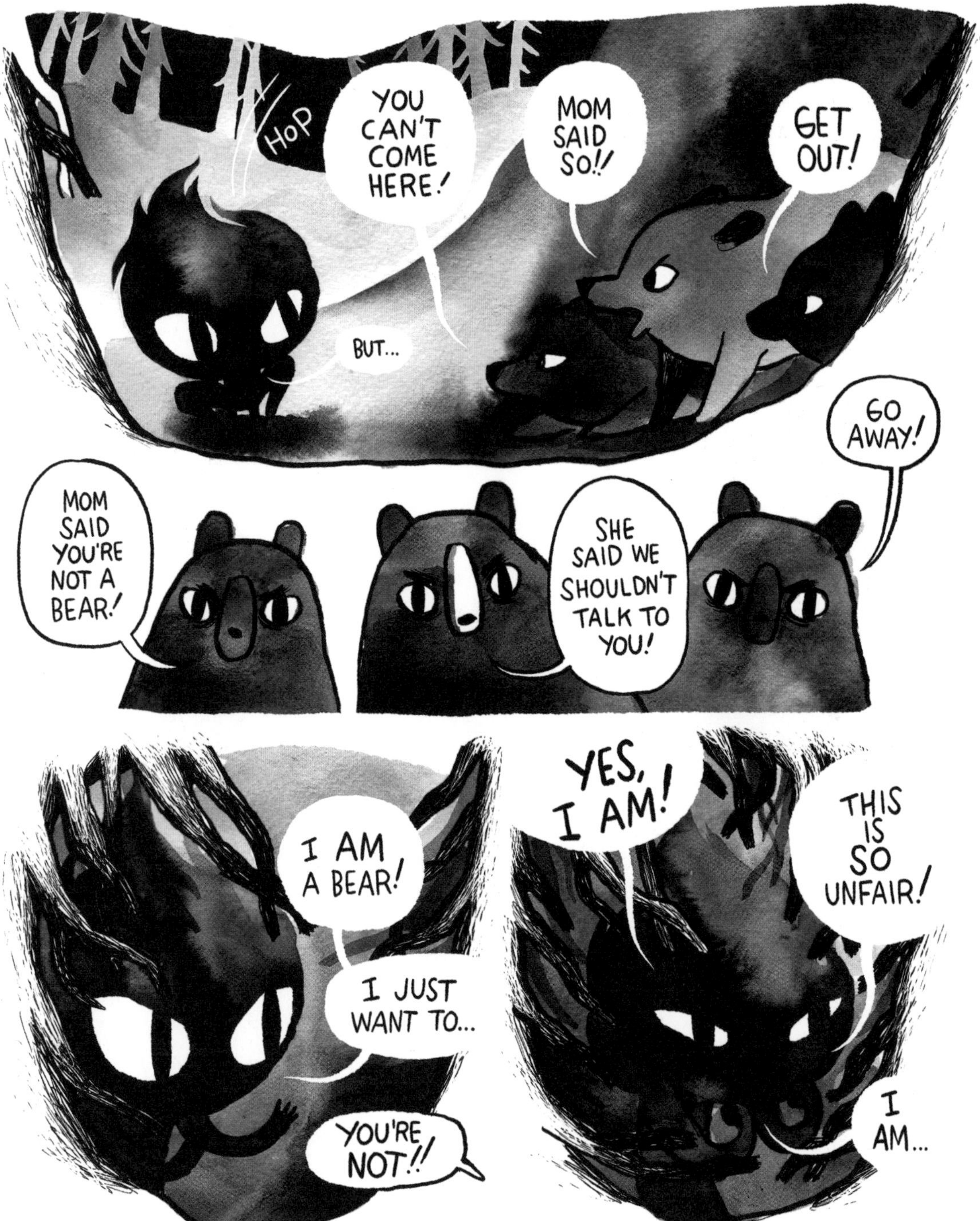
HOP
YOU CAN'T COME HERE!
MOM SAID SO!!
GET OUT!
BUT...
MOM SAID YOU'RE NOT A BEAR!
SHE SAID WE SHOULDN'T TALK TO YOU!
GO AWAY!
I AM A BEAR!
I JUST WANT TO...
YOU'RE NOT!!
YES, I AM!
THIS IS SO UNFAIR!
I AM...

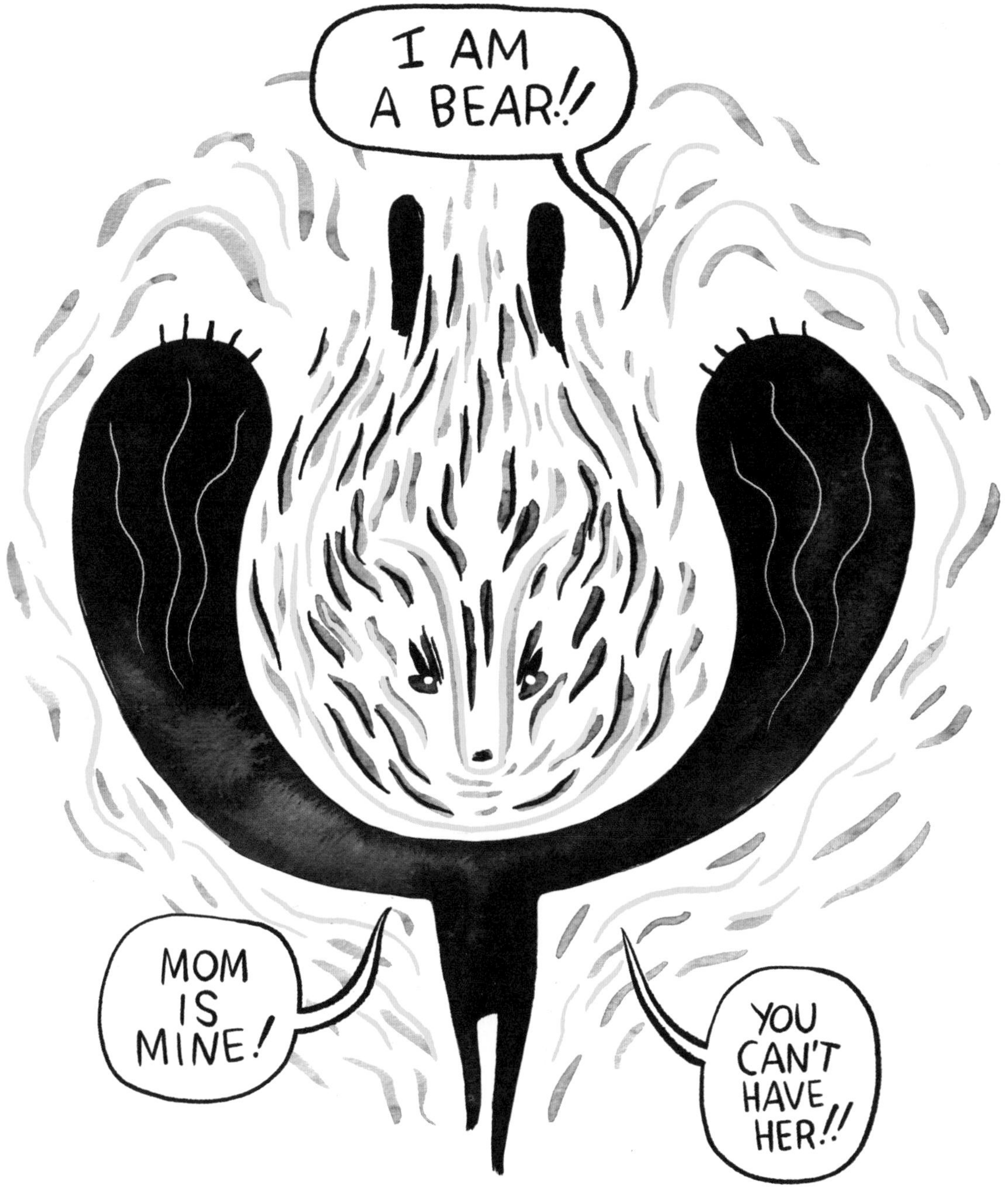
I AM A BEAR!!
MOM IS MINE!
YOU CAN'T HAVE HER!!

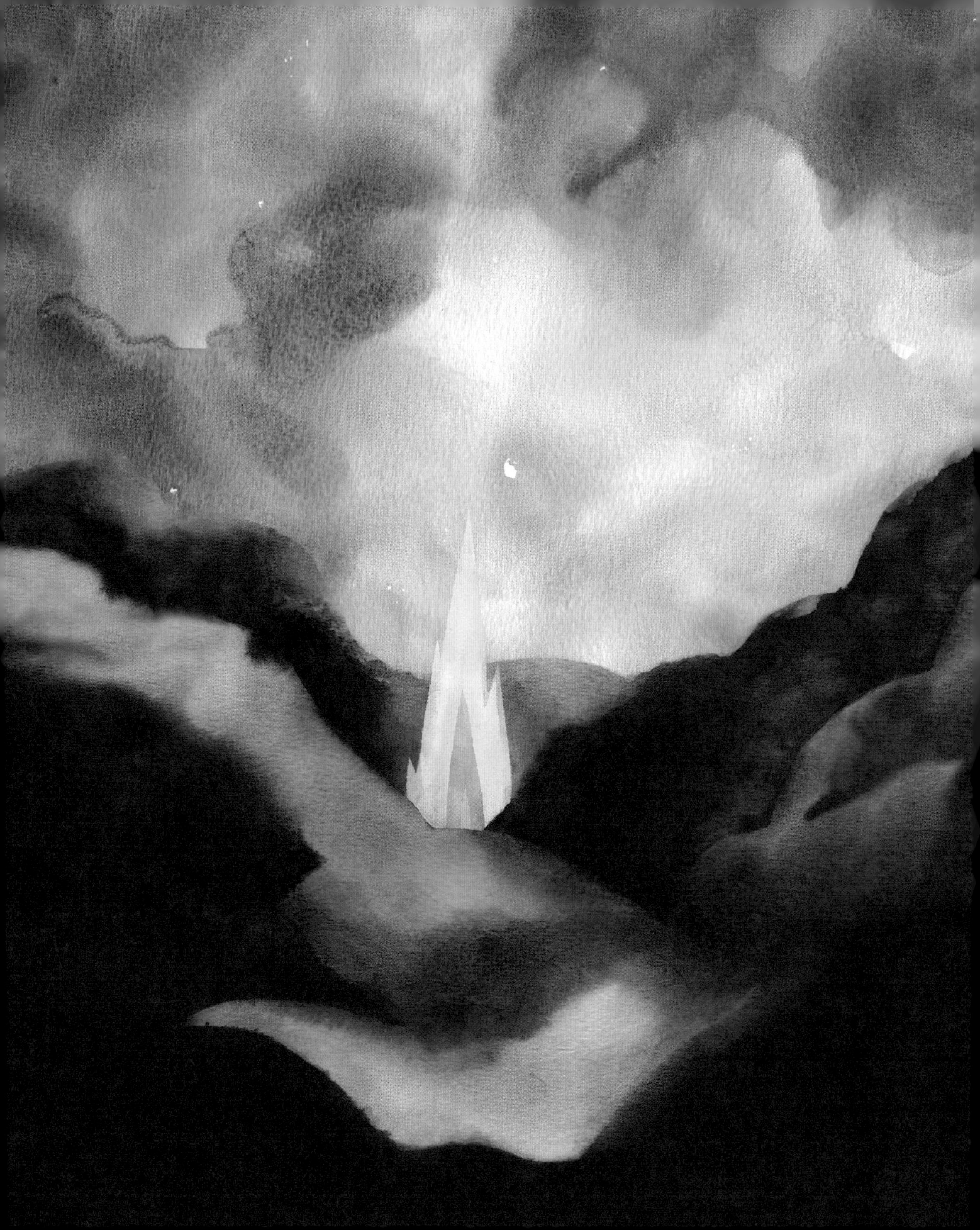

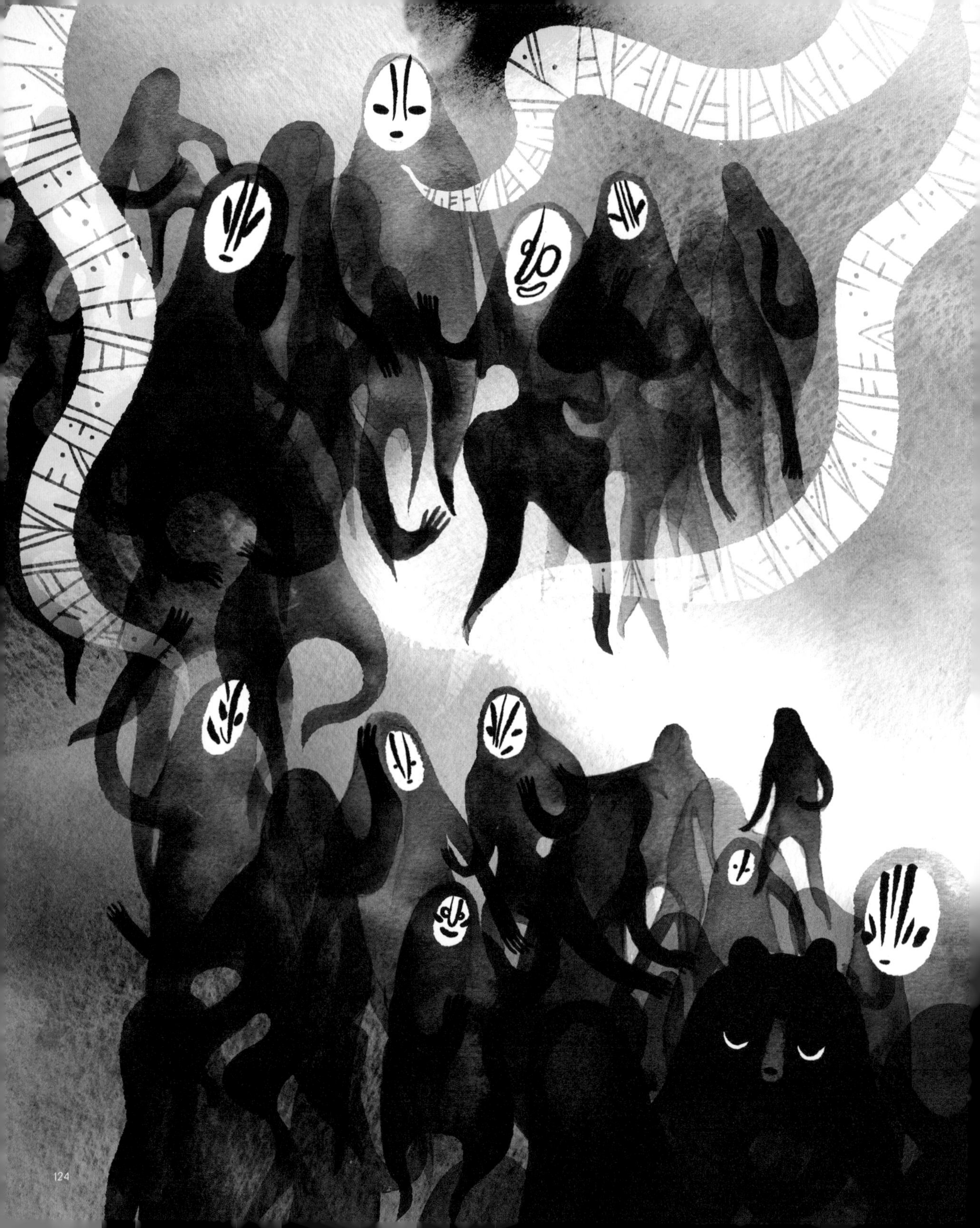

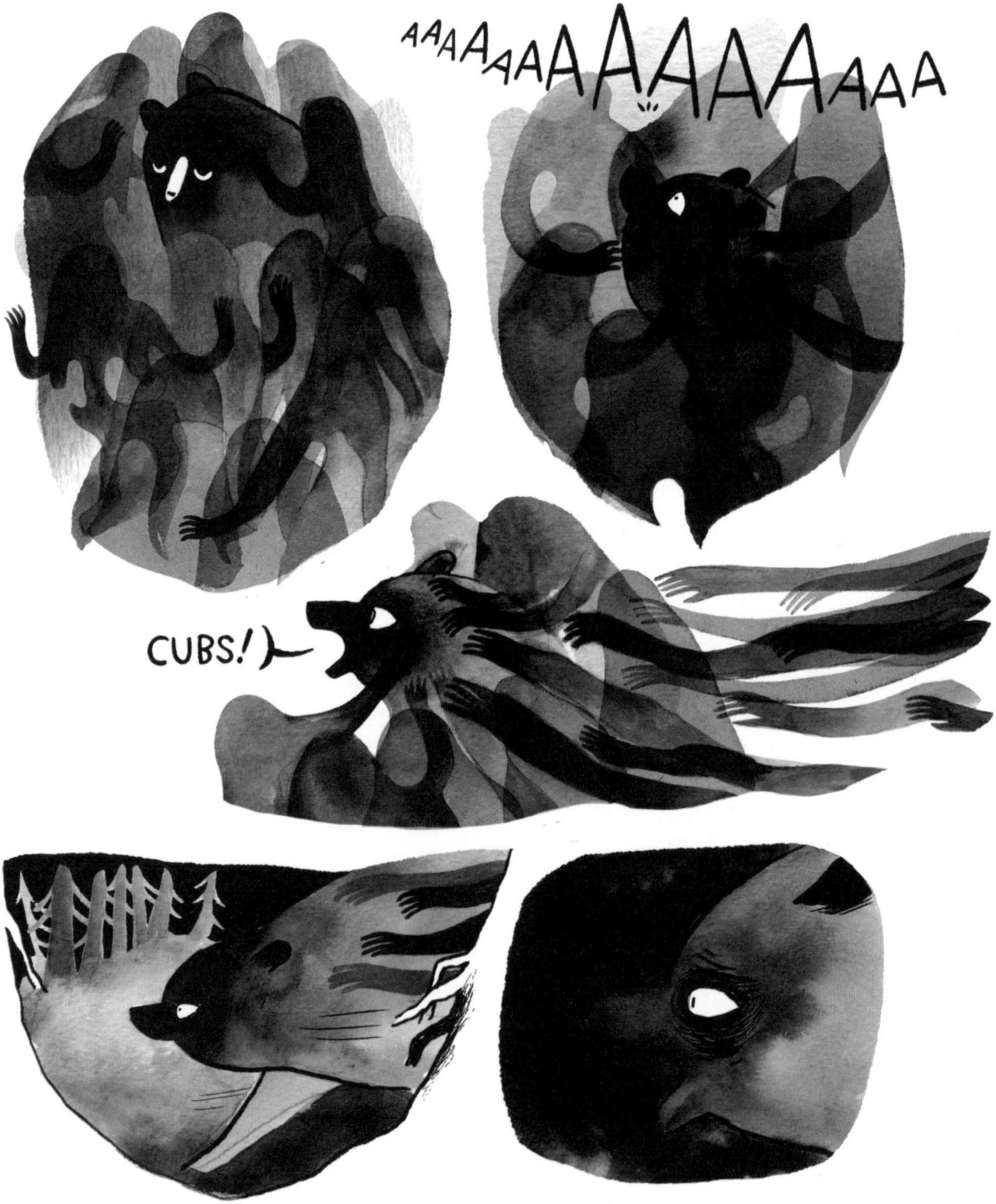
AAAAAAAAAAAAAAA
CUBS!

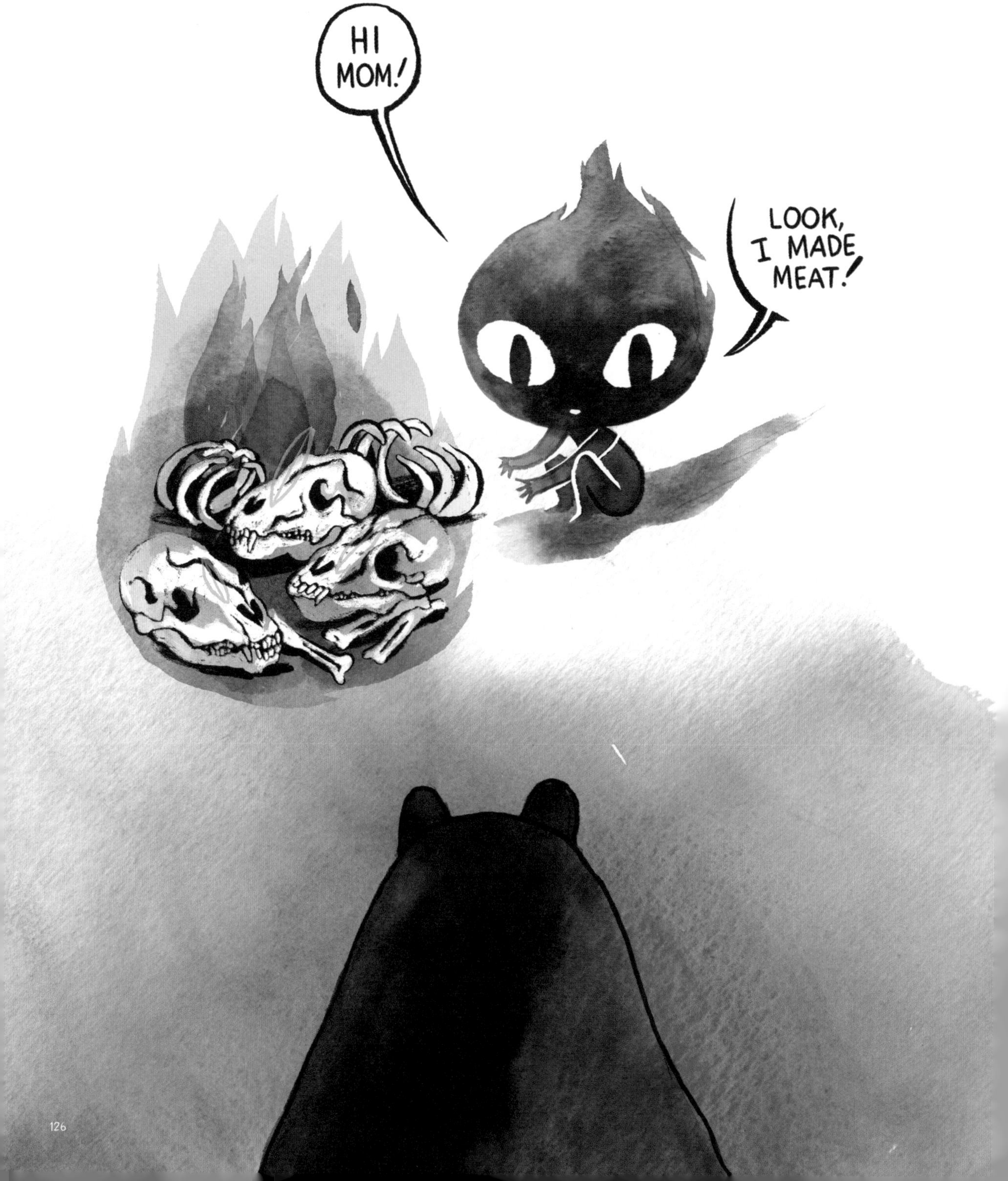
HI MOM!
LOOK, I MADE MEAT!

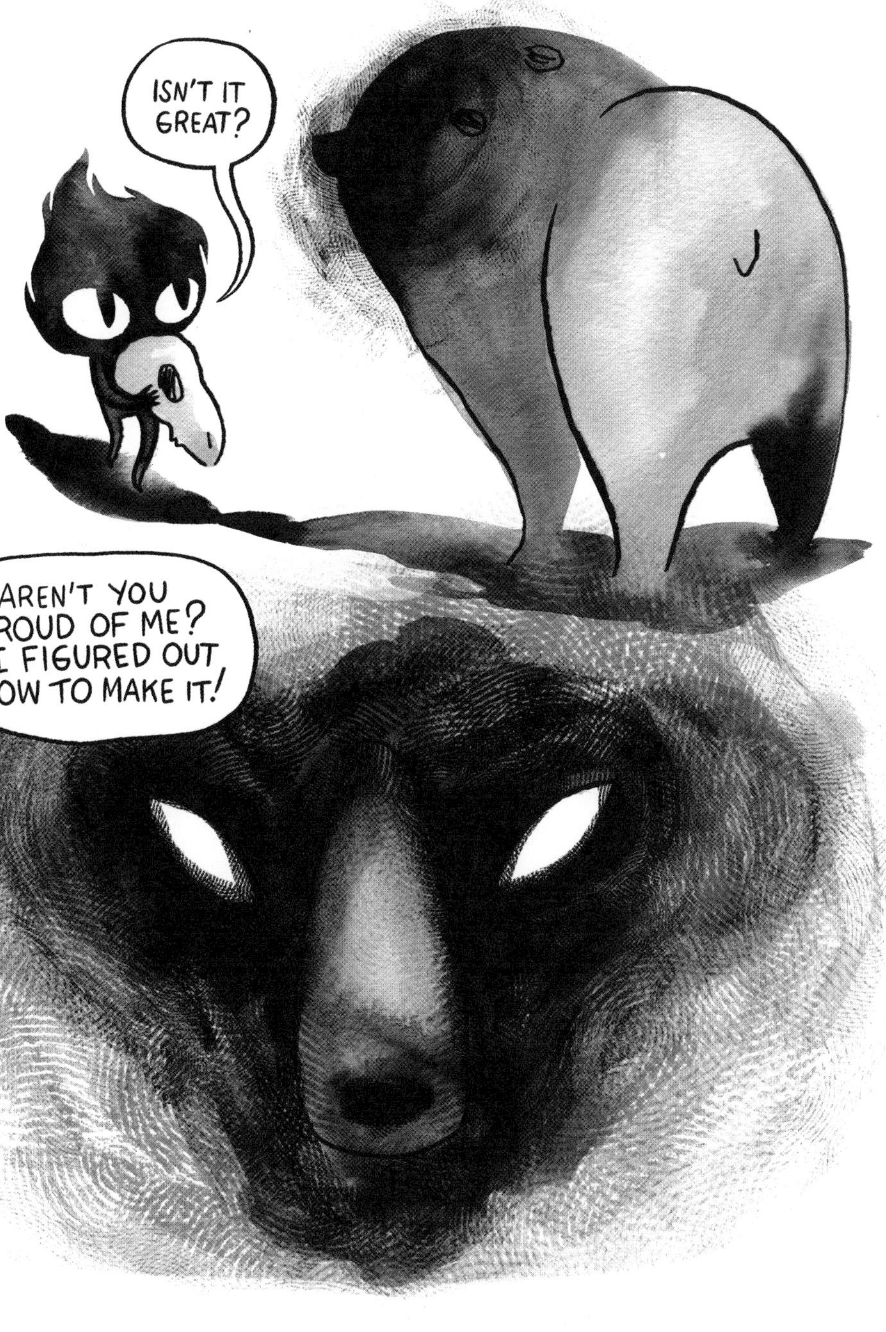
ISN'T IT GREAT?
AREN'T YOU PROUD OF ME? I FIGURED OUT HOW TO MAKE IT!

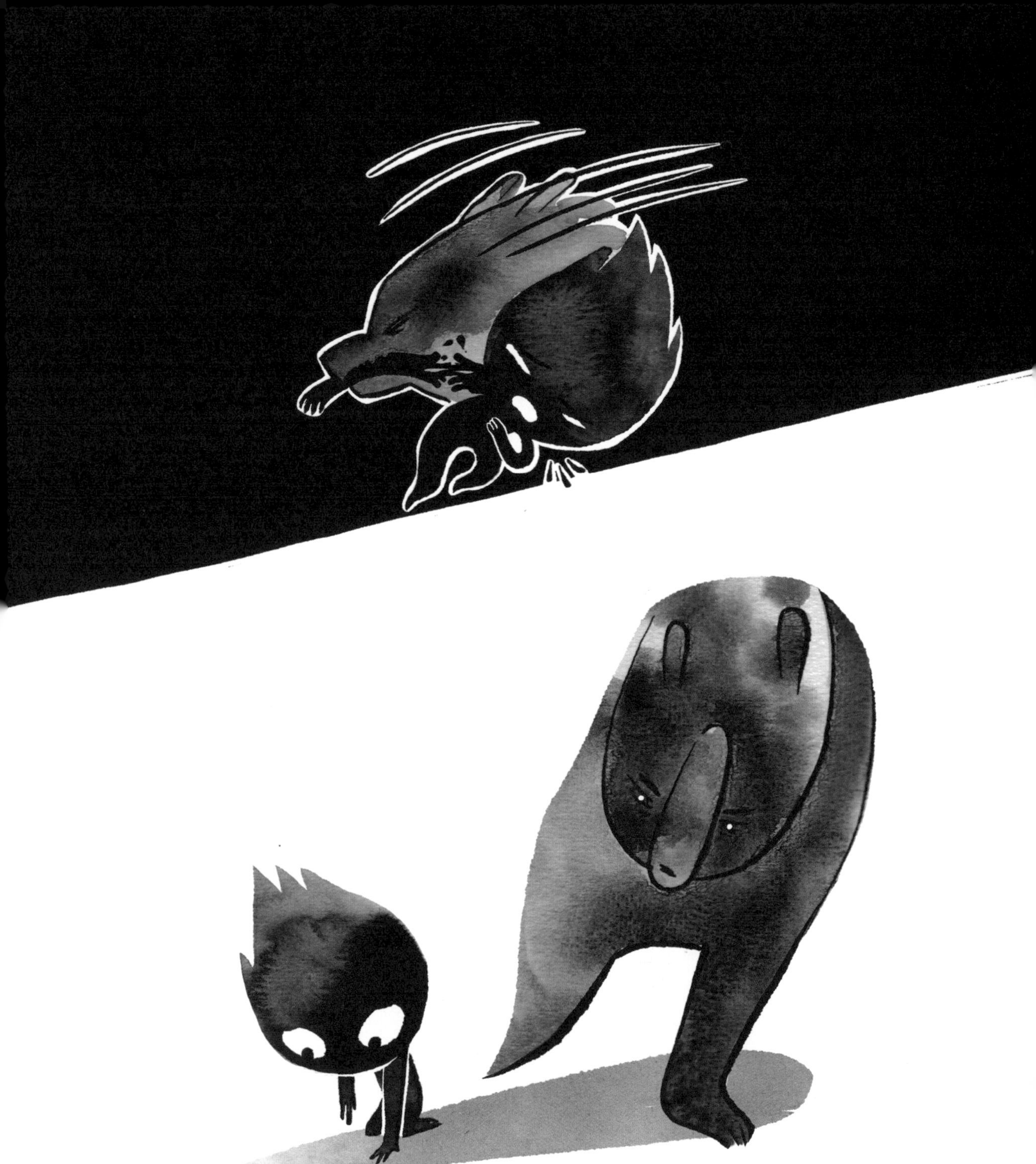

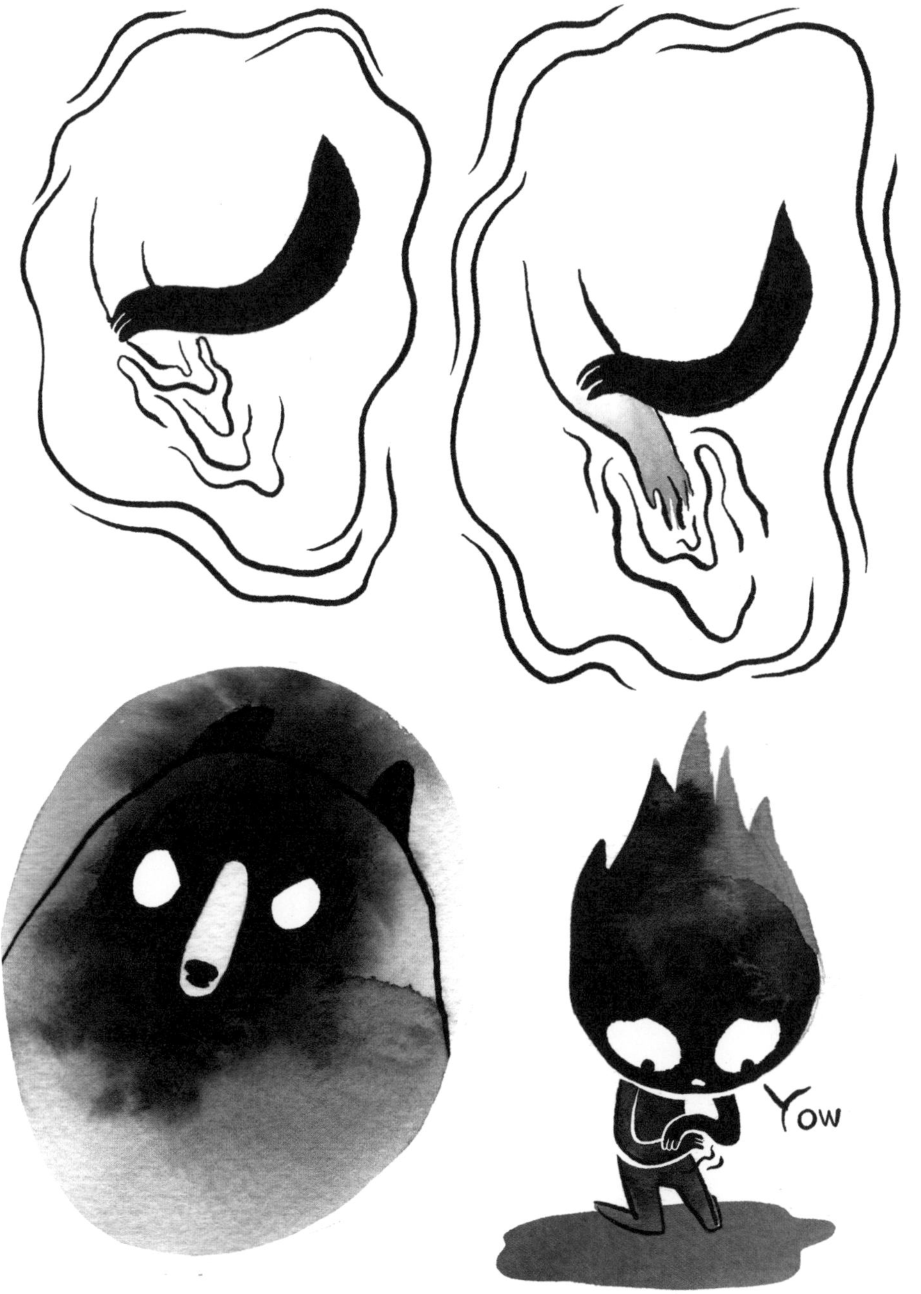
Yow

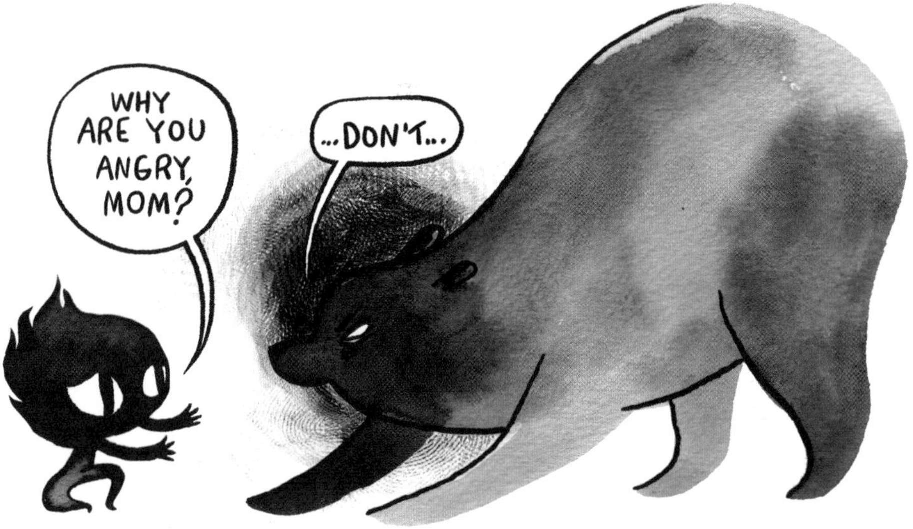
WHY ARE YOU ANGRY, MOM?
...DON'T...

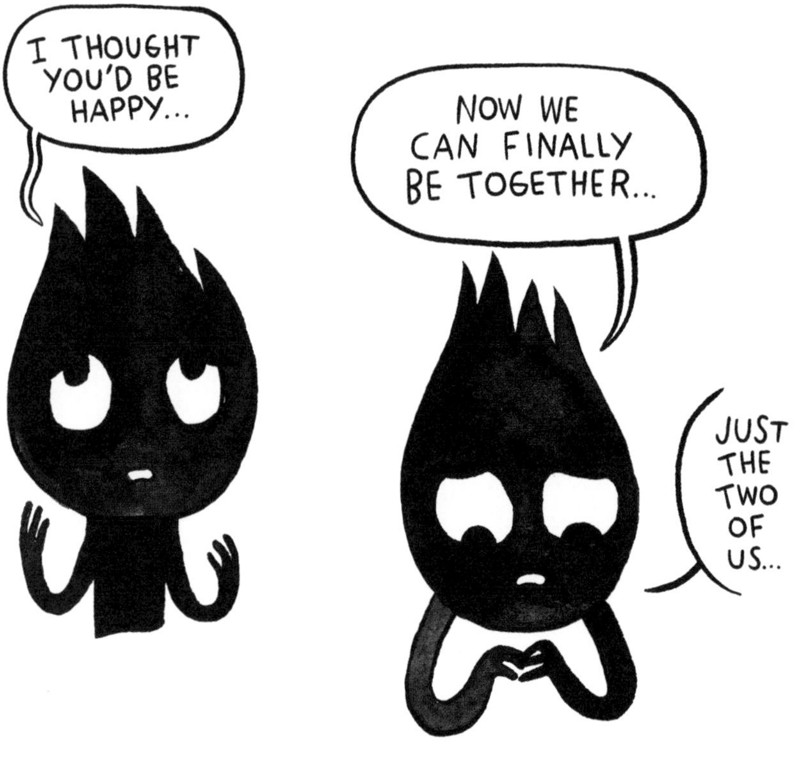
I THOUGHT YOU'D BE HAPPY...
NOW WE CAN FINALLY BE TOGETHER...
JUST THE TWO OF US...

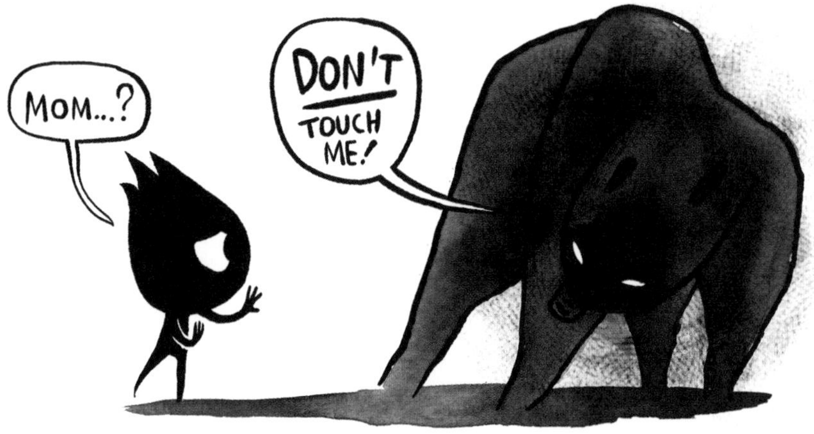
MOM...?
DON'T TOUCH ME!

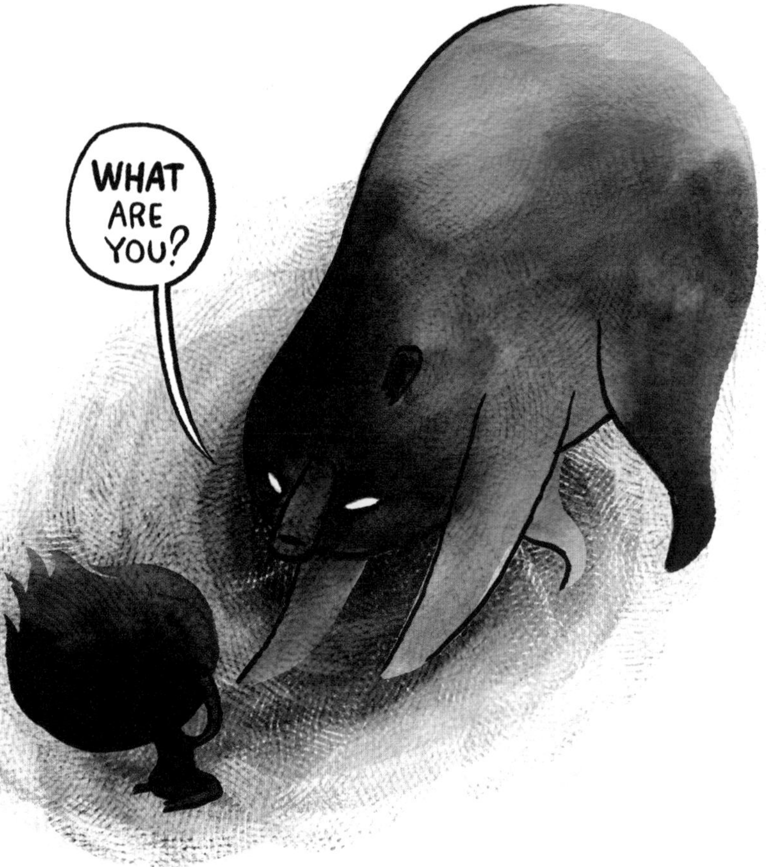
WHAT ARE YOU?

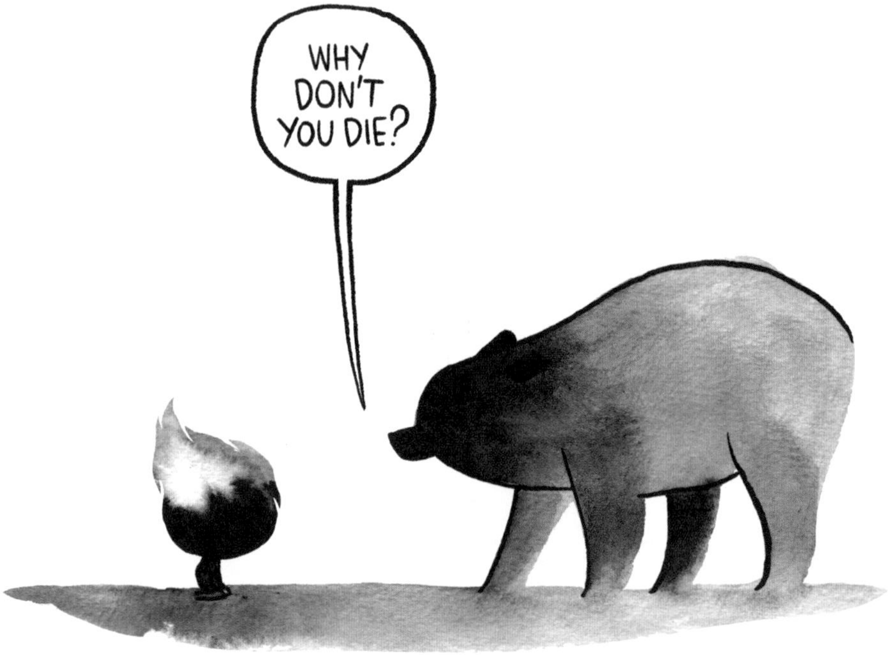
WHY DON'T YOU DIE?

V

EMUU! TAKE ME BACK!

PUNISH ME HOW YOU WILL! I DON'T CARE ANYMORE!
JUST TAKE ME AWAY FROM HERE!

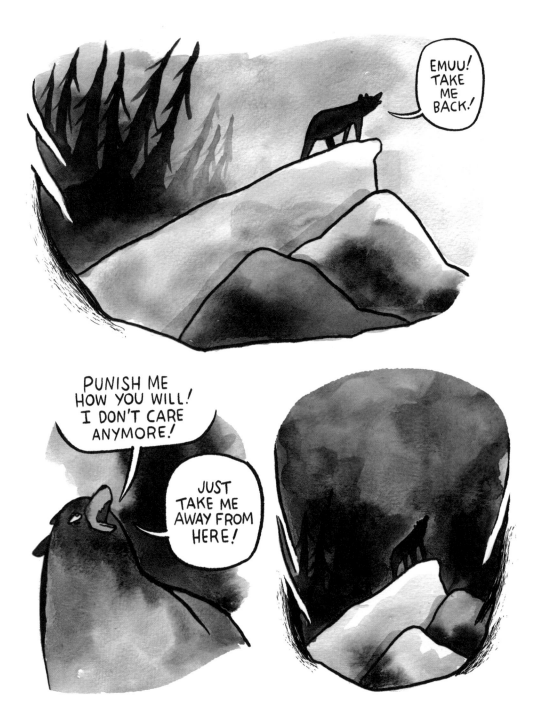

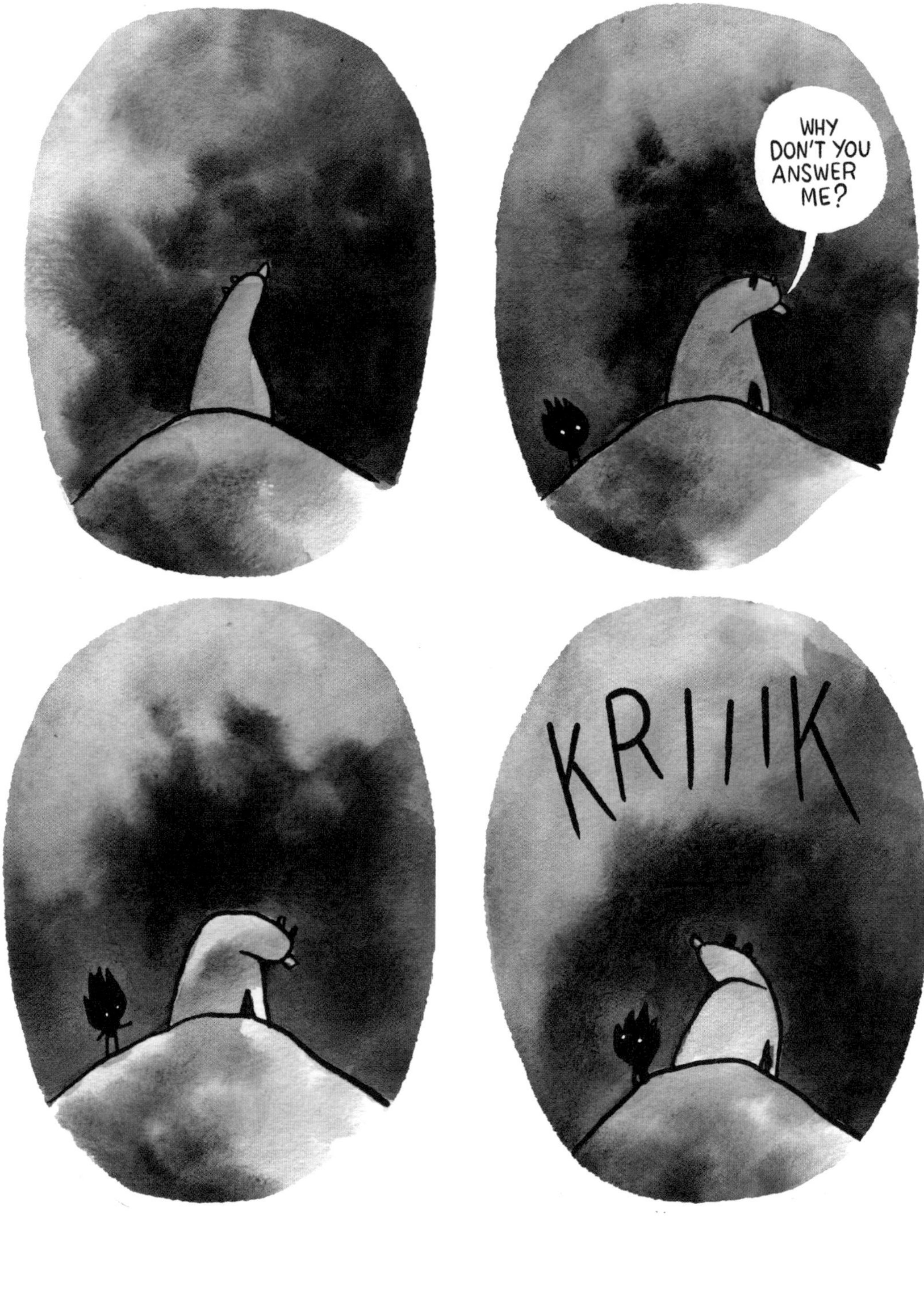
WHY DON'T YOU ANSWER ME?
KRIIIK

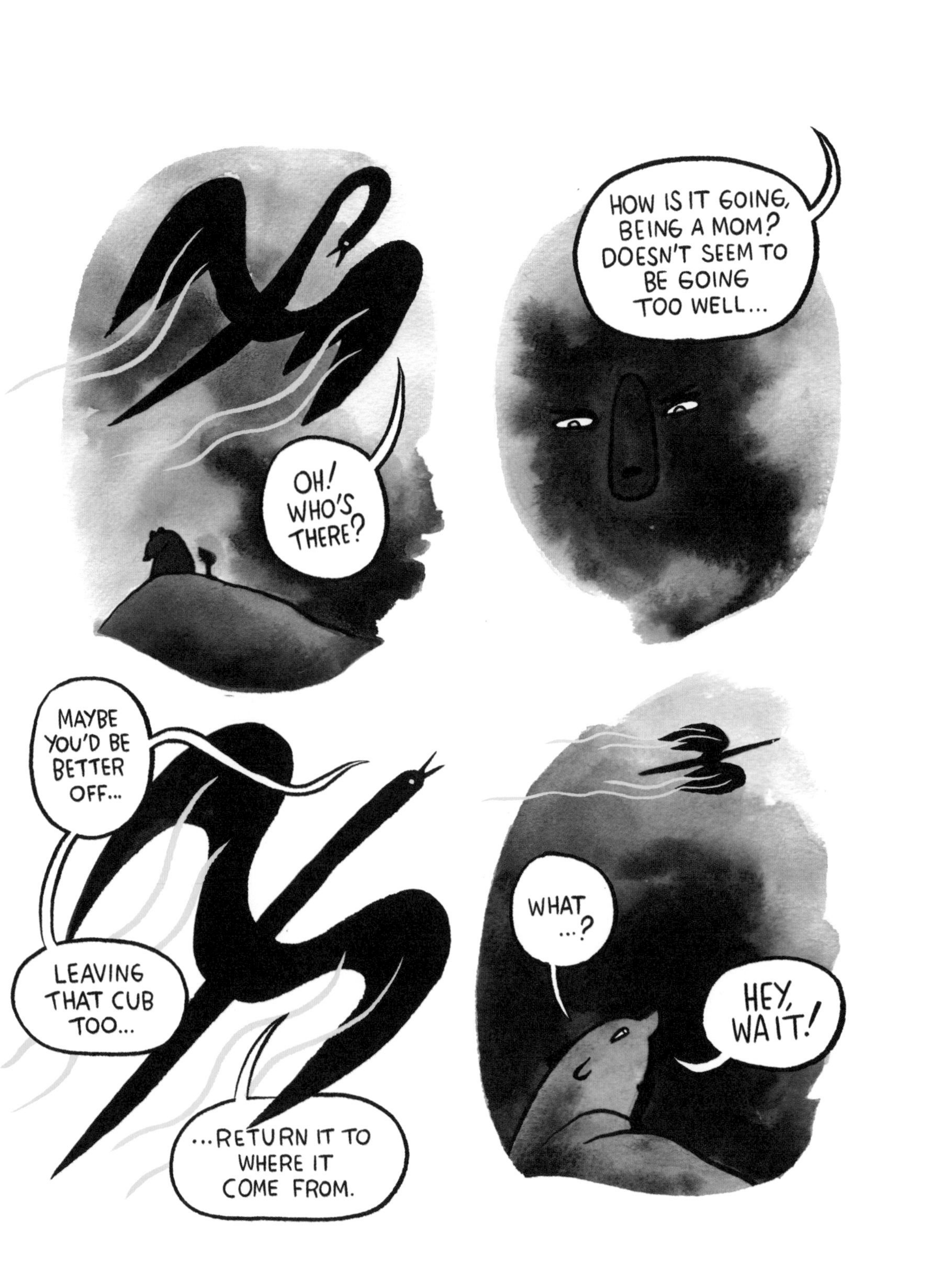
OH! WHO'S THERE?
HOW IS IT GOING, BEING A MOM? DOESN'T SEEM TO BE GOING TOO WELL...
MAYBE YOU'D BE BETTER OFF...
LEAVING THAT CUB TOO...
...RETURN IT TO WHERE IT COME FROM.
WHAT ...?
HEY, WAIT!

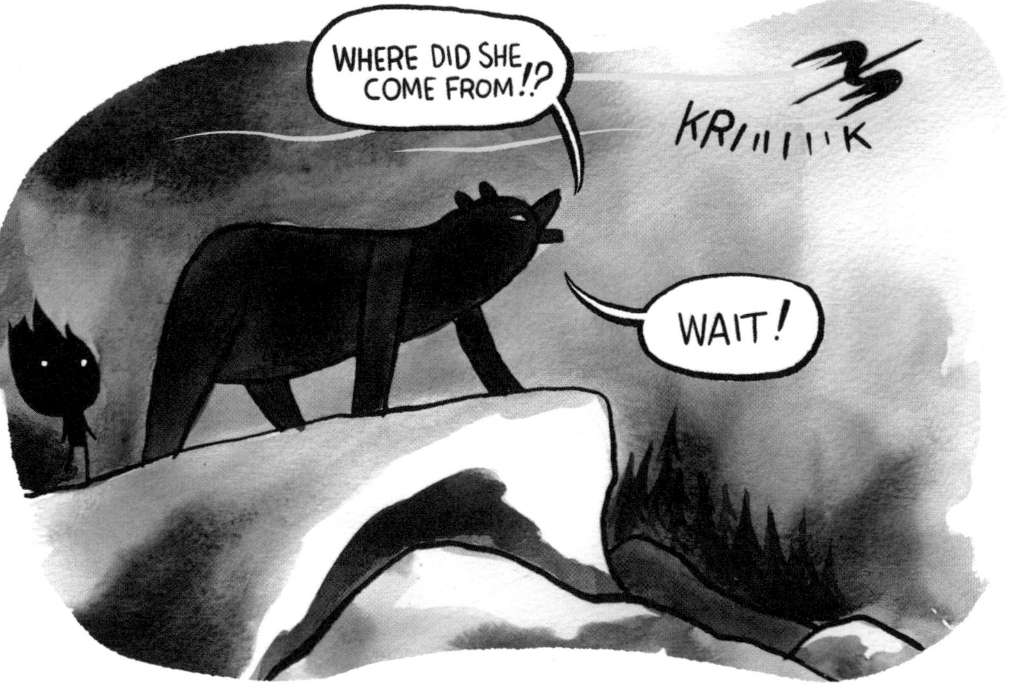
WHERE DID SHE COME FROM!?
KRI''''''K
WAIT!

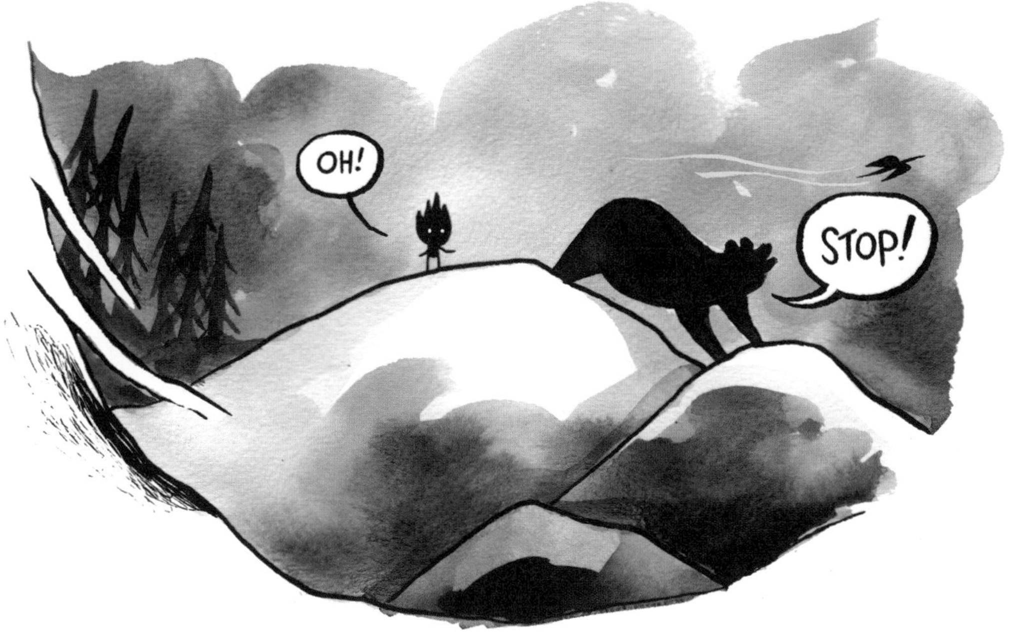
OH!
STOP!

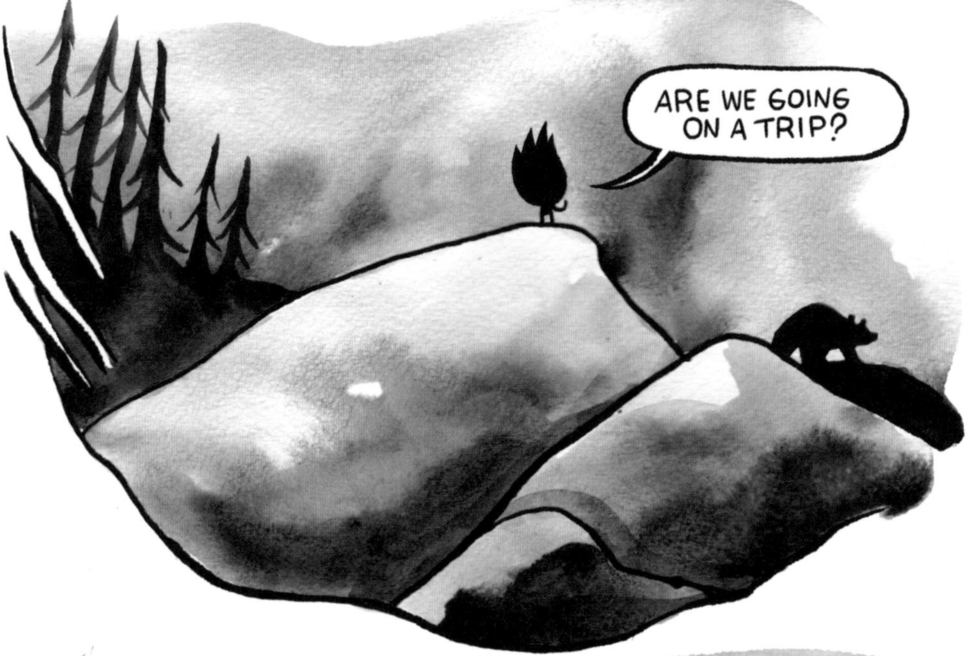
ARE WE GOING ON A TRIP?

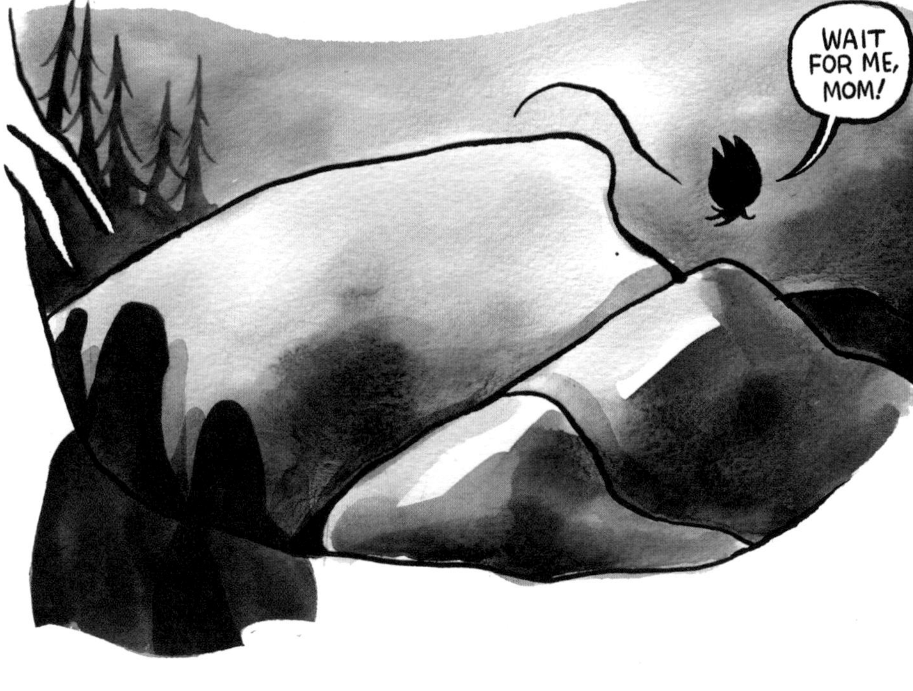
WAIT FOR ME, MOM!

VI

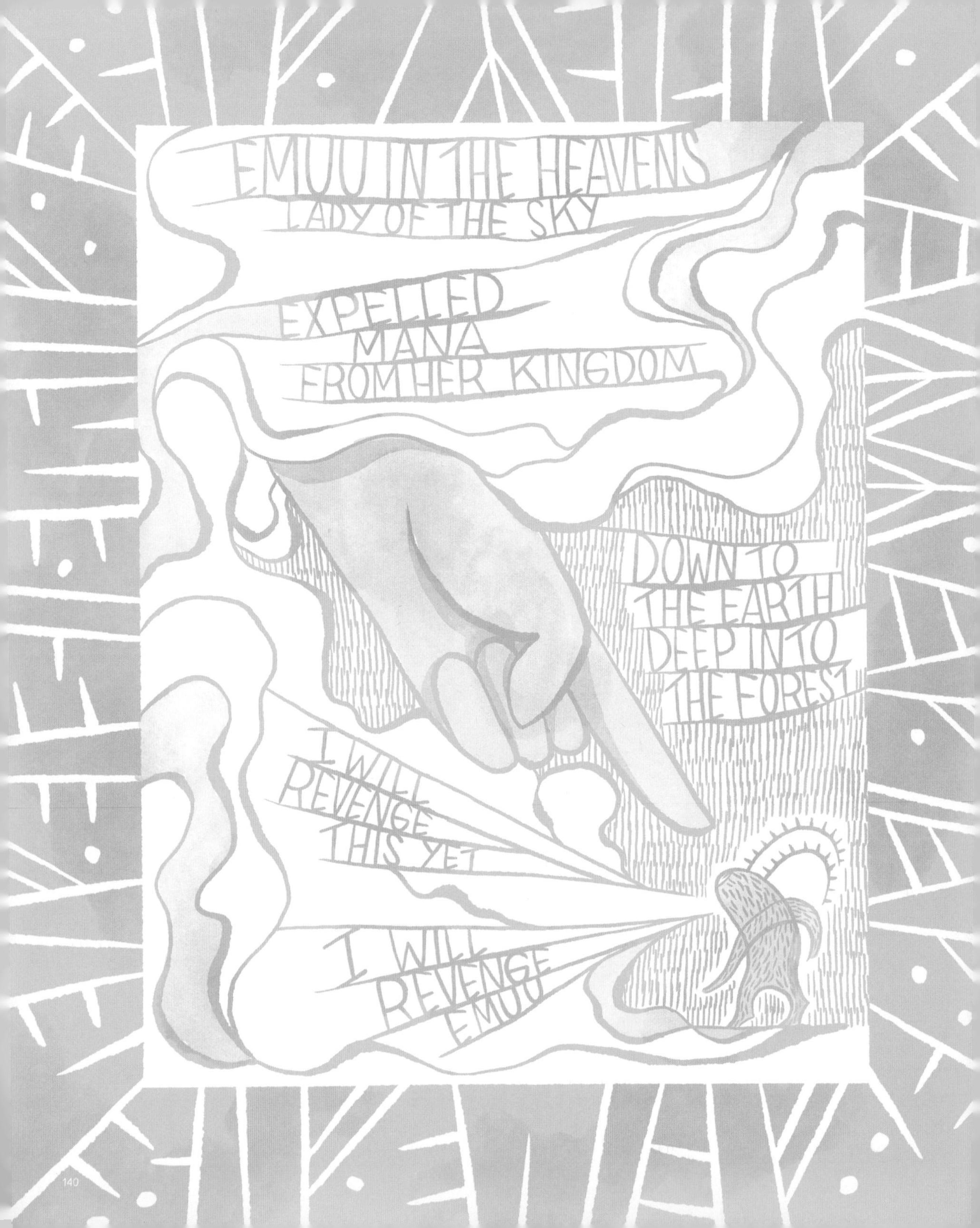
EMUU IN THE HEAVENS
LADY OF THE SKY
EXPELLED
MANA
FROM HER KINGDOM
DOWN TO
THE EARTH
DEEP INTO
THE FOREST
I WILL
REVENGE
THIS YET
I WILL
REVENGE
EMUU

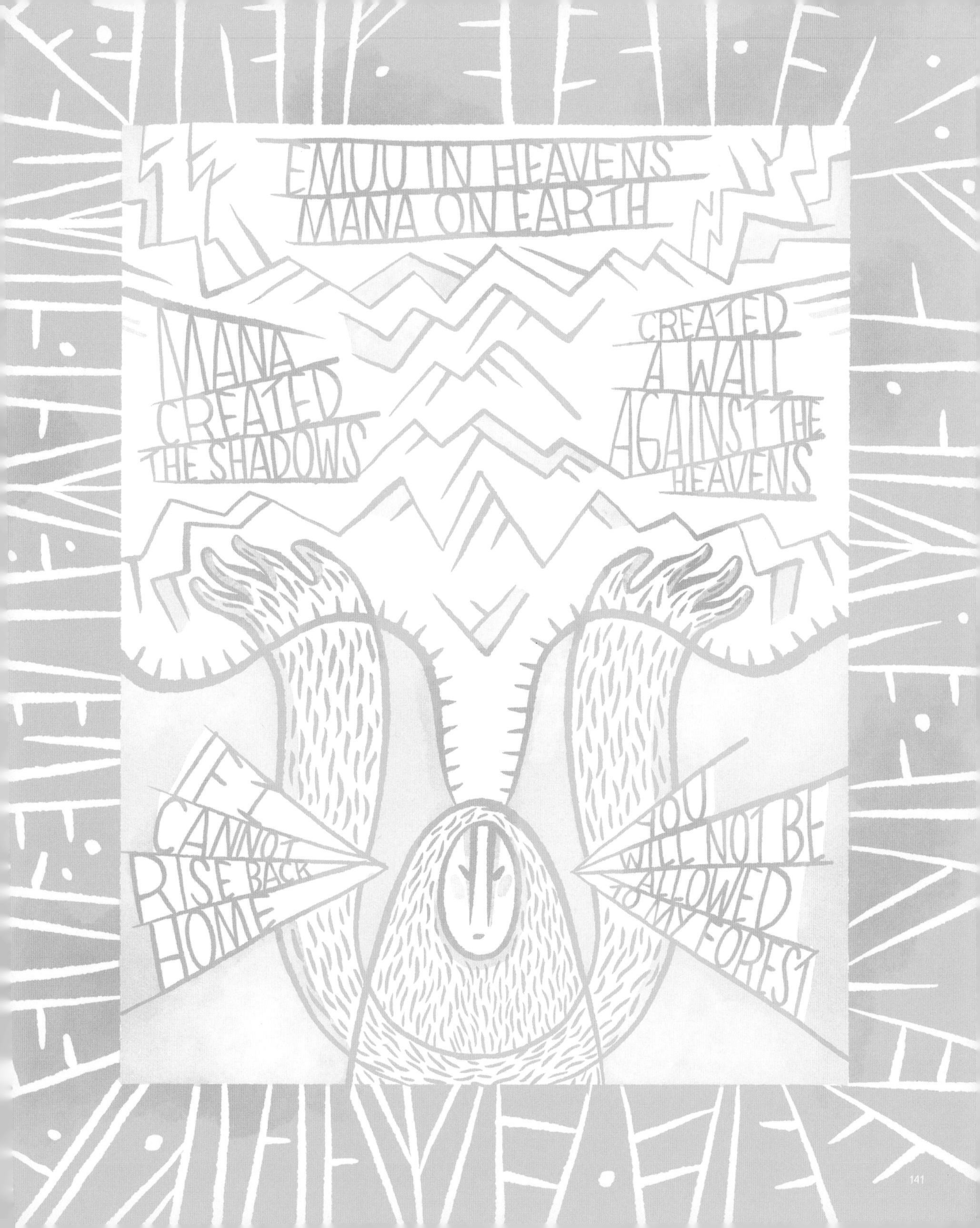
EMUU IN HEAVENS
MANA ON EARTH
MANA CREATED THE SHADOWS
CREATED A WALL AGAINST THE HEAVENS
CANNOT RISE BACK HOME
YOU WILL NOT BE ALLOWED TO MY FOREST

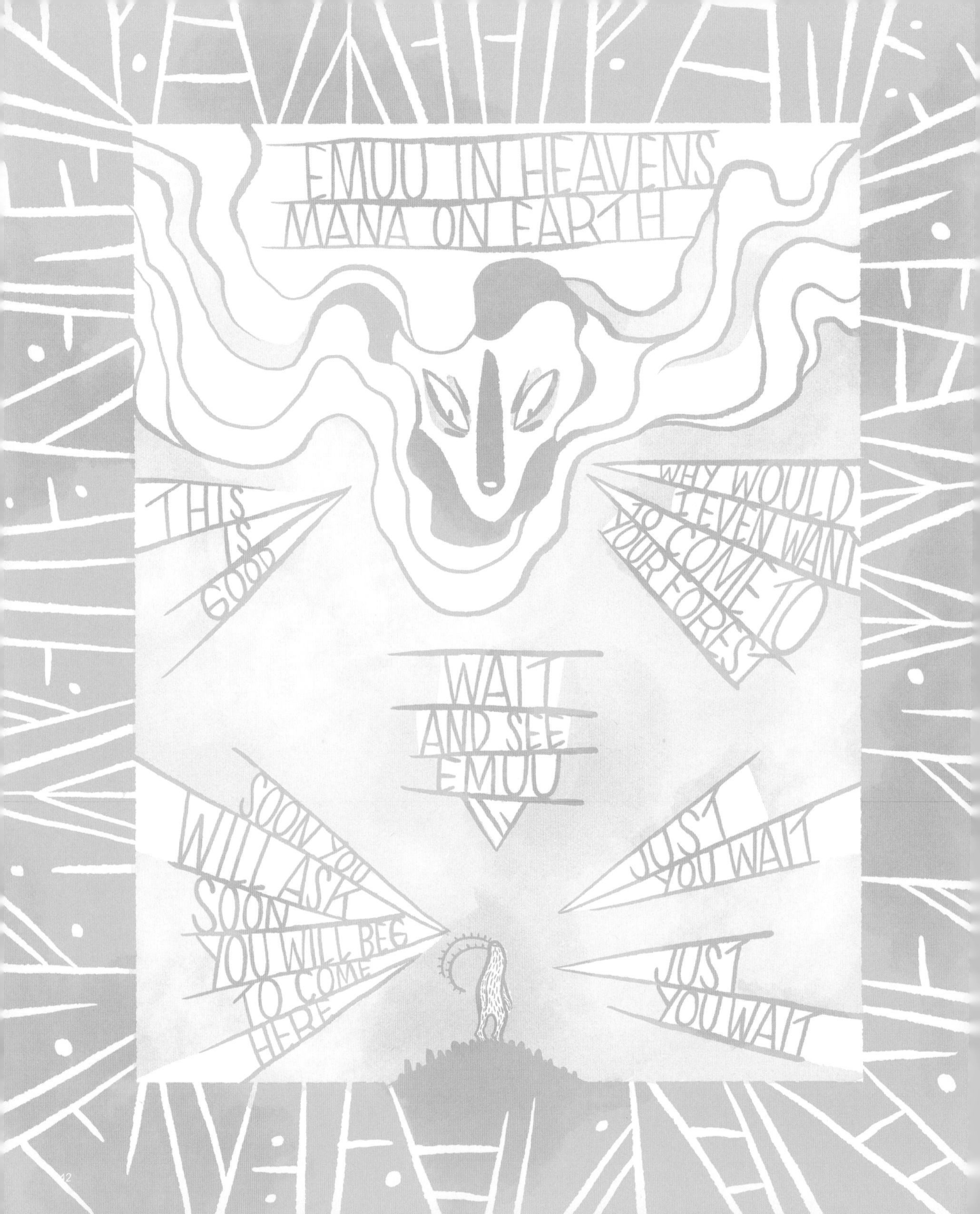
EMUU IN HEAVENS
MANA ON EARTH
THIS IS GOOD
WHY WOULD I EVEN WANT TO COME TO YOUR FORES
WAIT AND SEE EMUU
SOON YOU WILL ASK
SOON YOU WILL BEG TO COME HERE
JUST YOU WAIT
JUST YOU WAIT

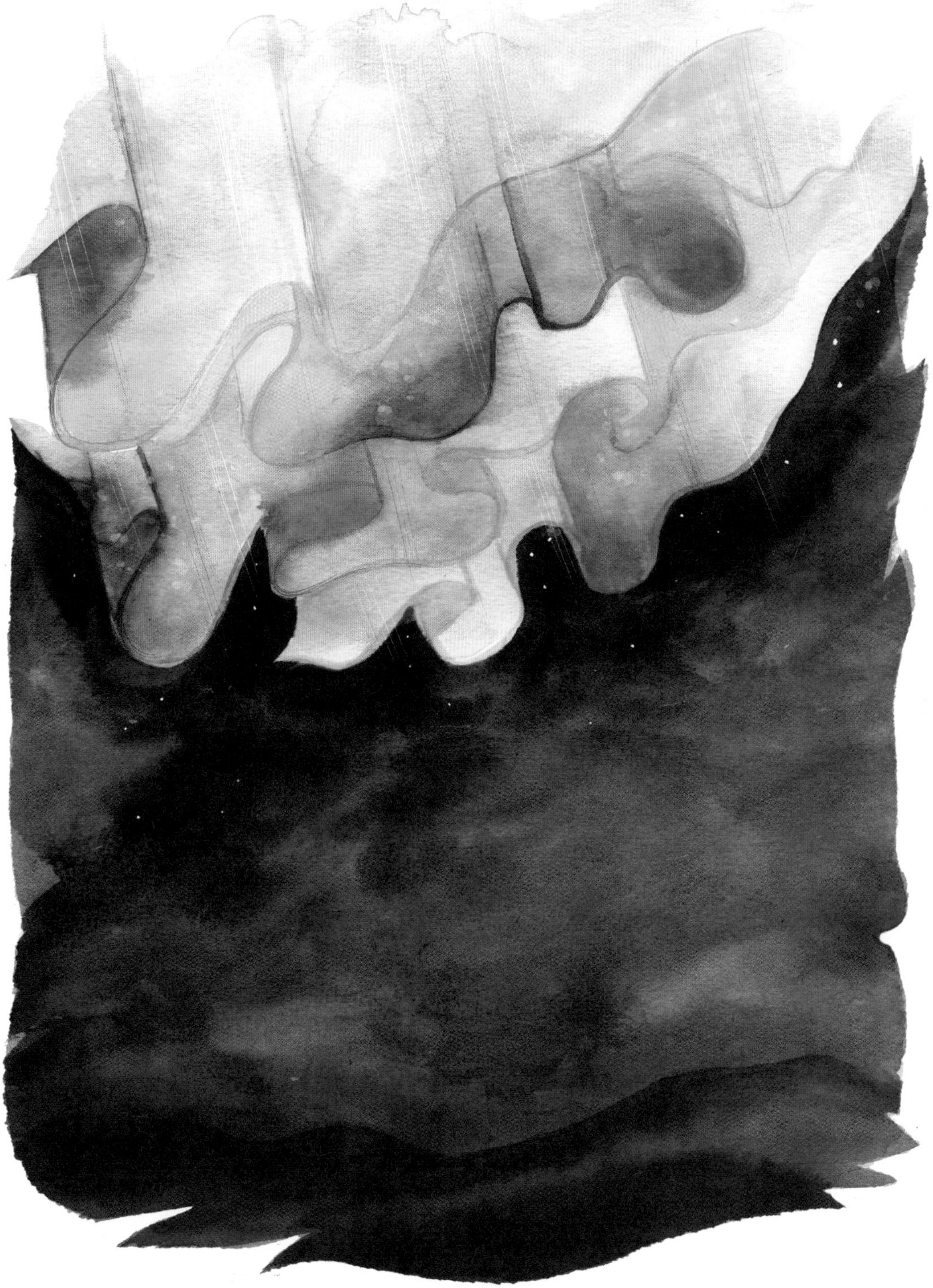

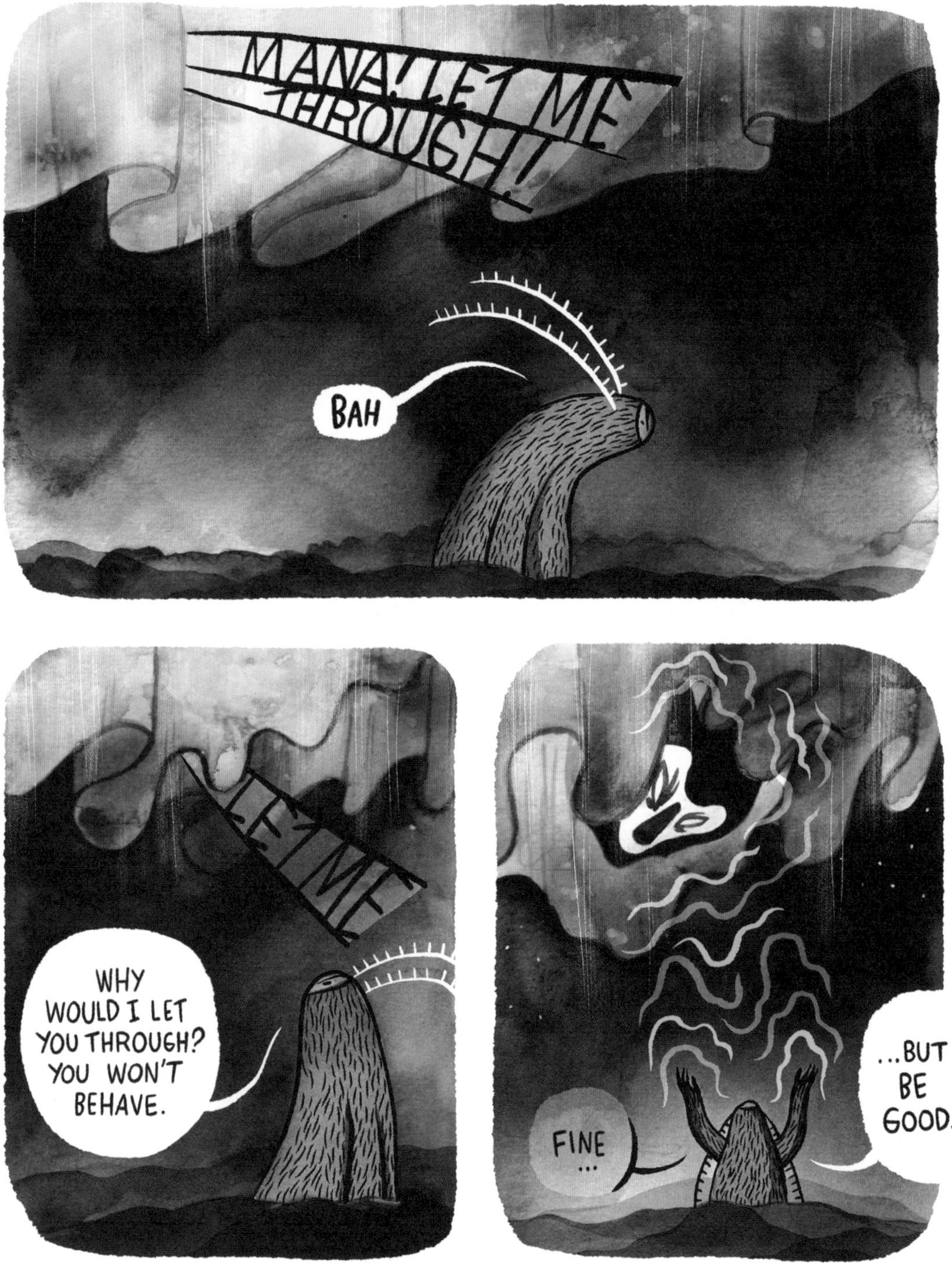
MANA! LET ME THROUGH!
BAH
LET ME
WHY WOULD I LET YOU THROUGH? YOU WON'T BEHAVE.
FINE ...
...BUT BE GOOD.

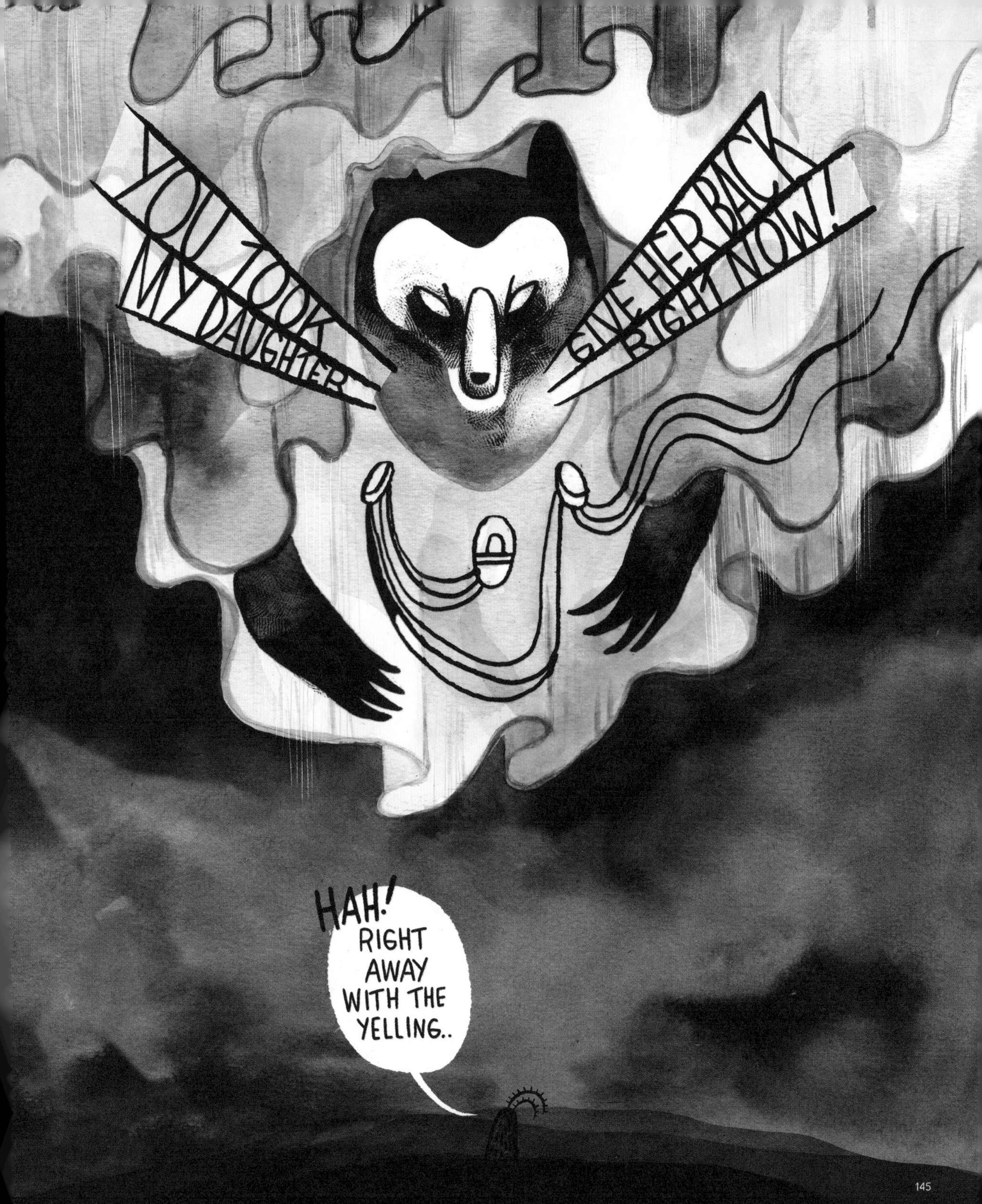

YOU TOOK MY DAUGHTER
GIVE HER BACK RIGHT NOW!
HAH! RIGHT AWAY WITH THE YELLING..

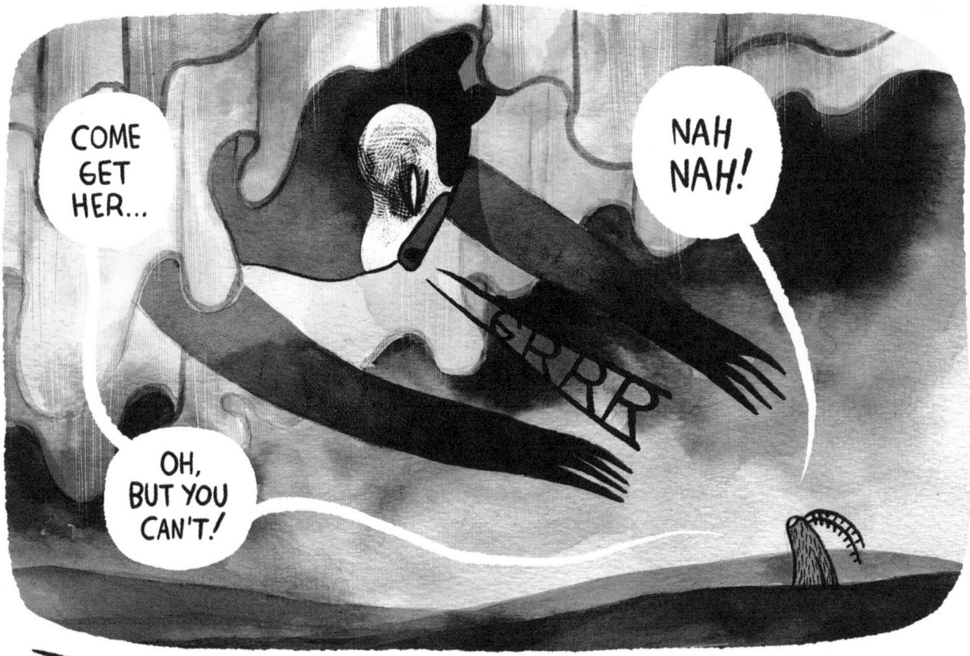
COME GET HER...
NAH NAH!
GRRRR
OH, BUT YOU CAN'T!

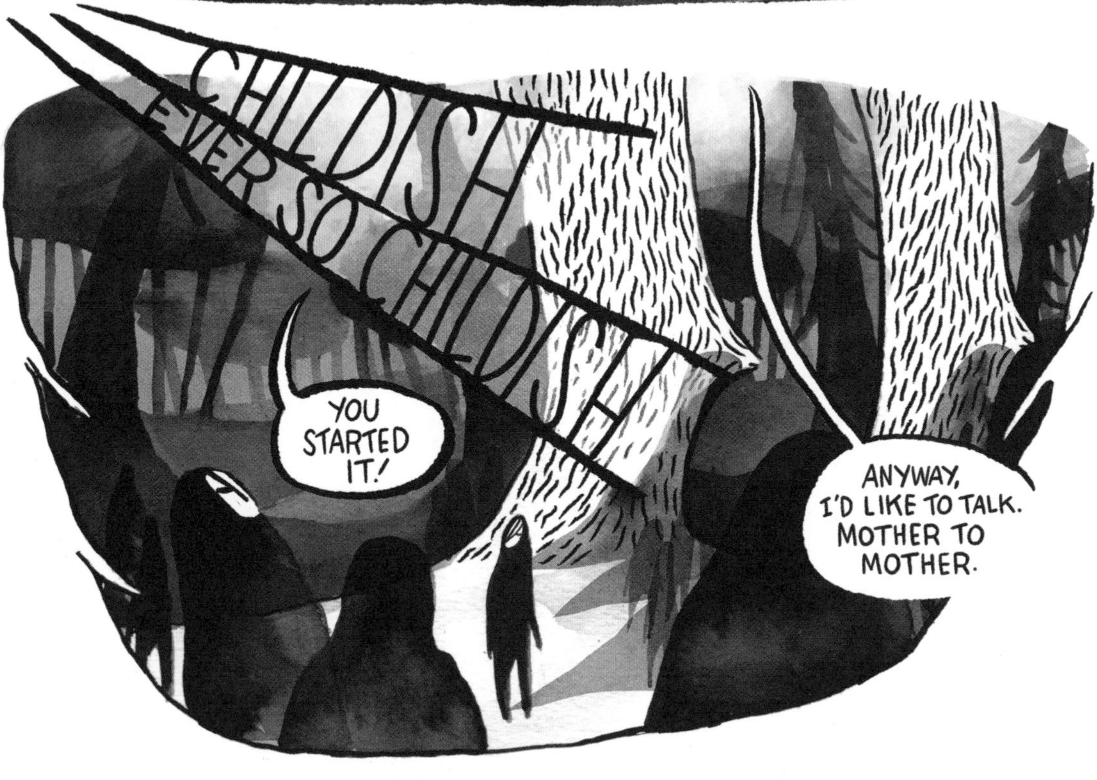
CHILDISH
EVER SO CHILDISH
YOU STARTED IT!
ANYWAY, I'D LIKE TO TALK. MOTHER TO MOTHER.

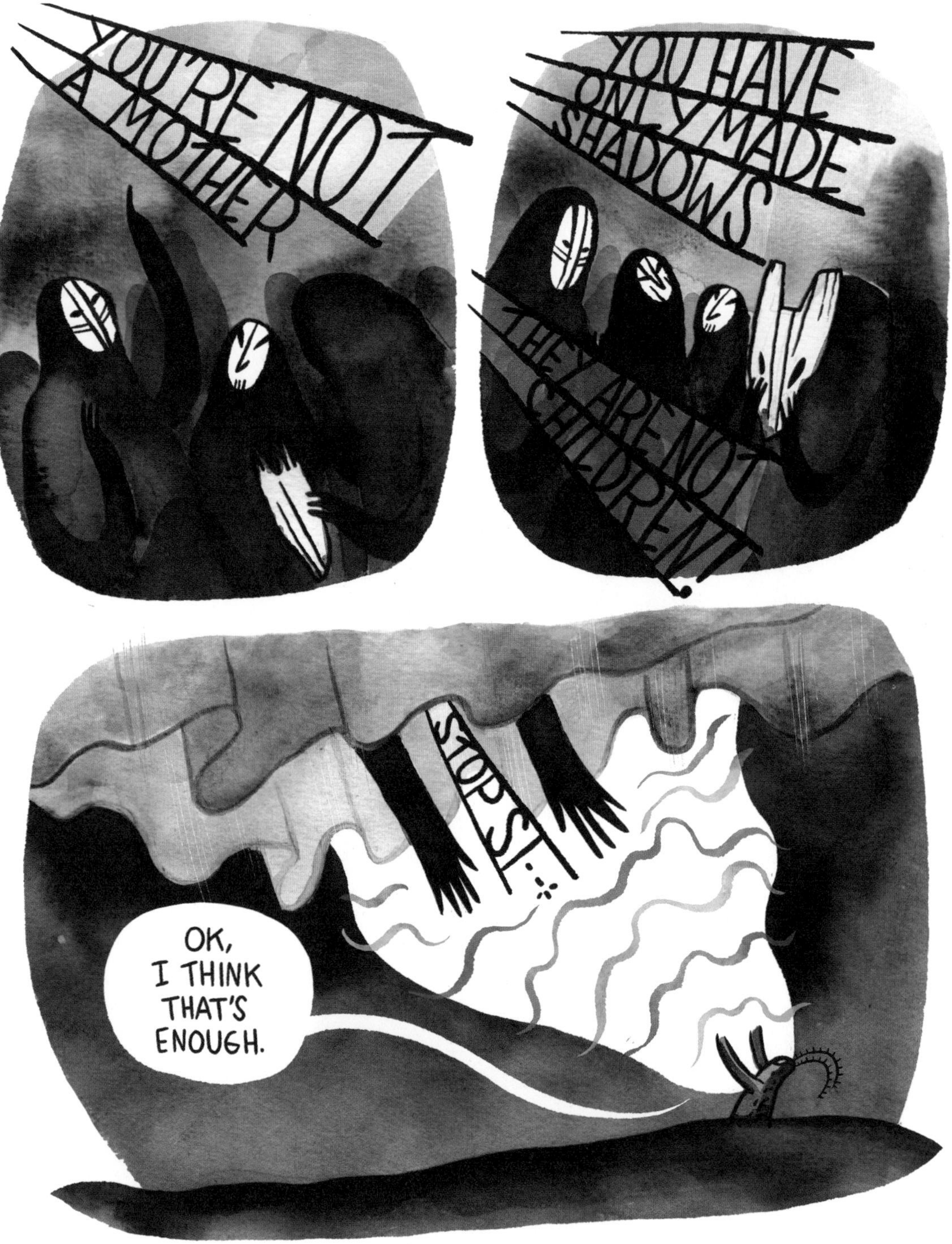
YOU'RE NOT A MOTHER
YOU HAVE ONLY MADE SHADOWS
THEY ARE NOT CHILDREN!
STOP ST...
OK, I THINK THAT'S ENOUGH.

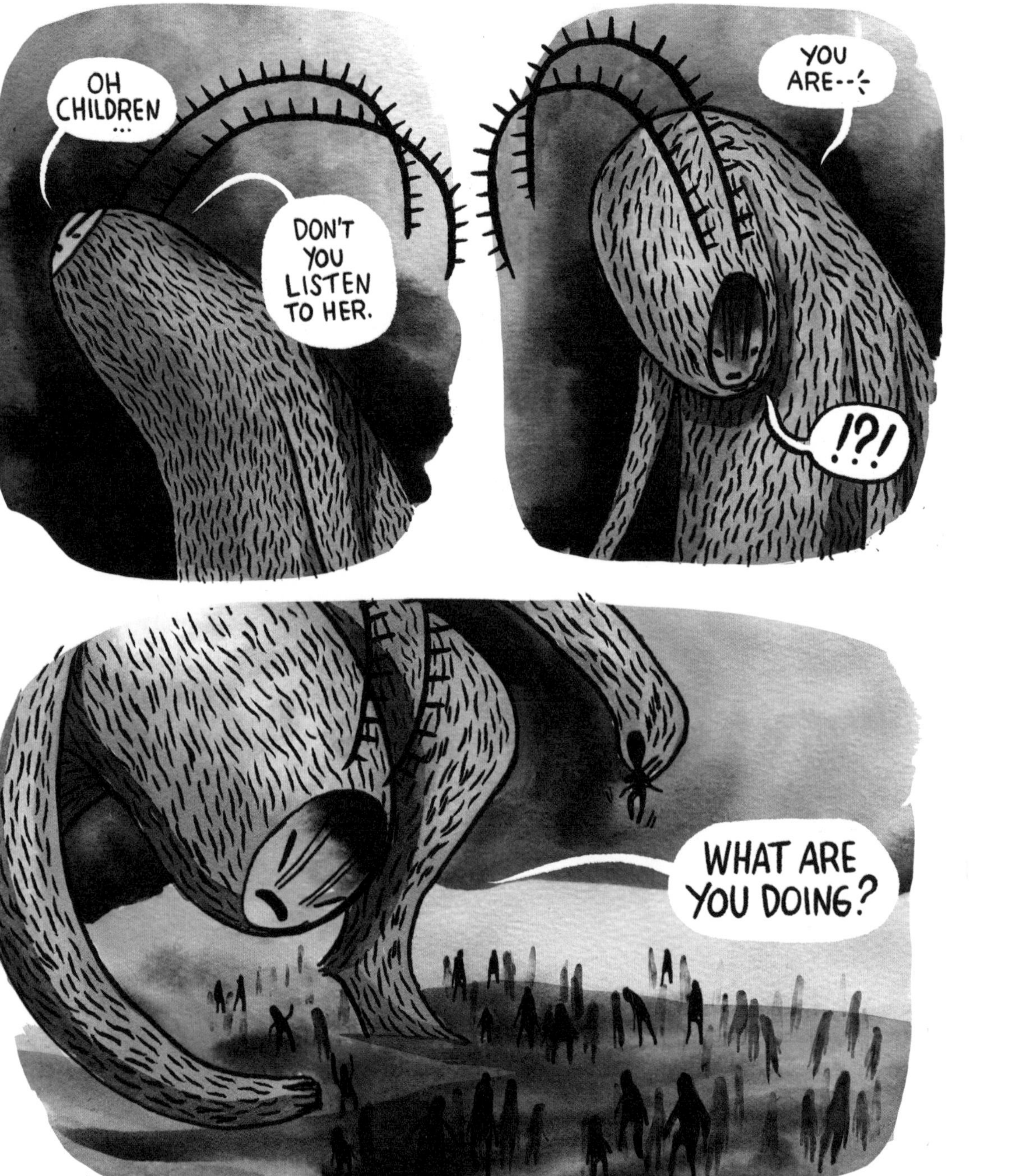
OH CHILDREN ...
DON'T YOU LISTEN TO HER.
YOU ARE--
!?!
WHAT ARE YOU DOING?

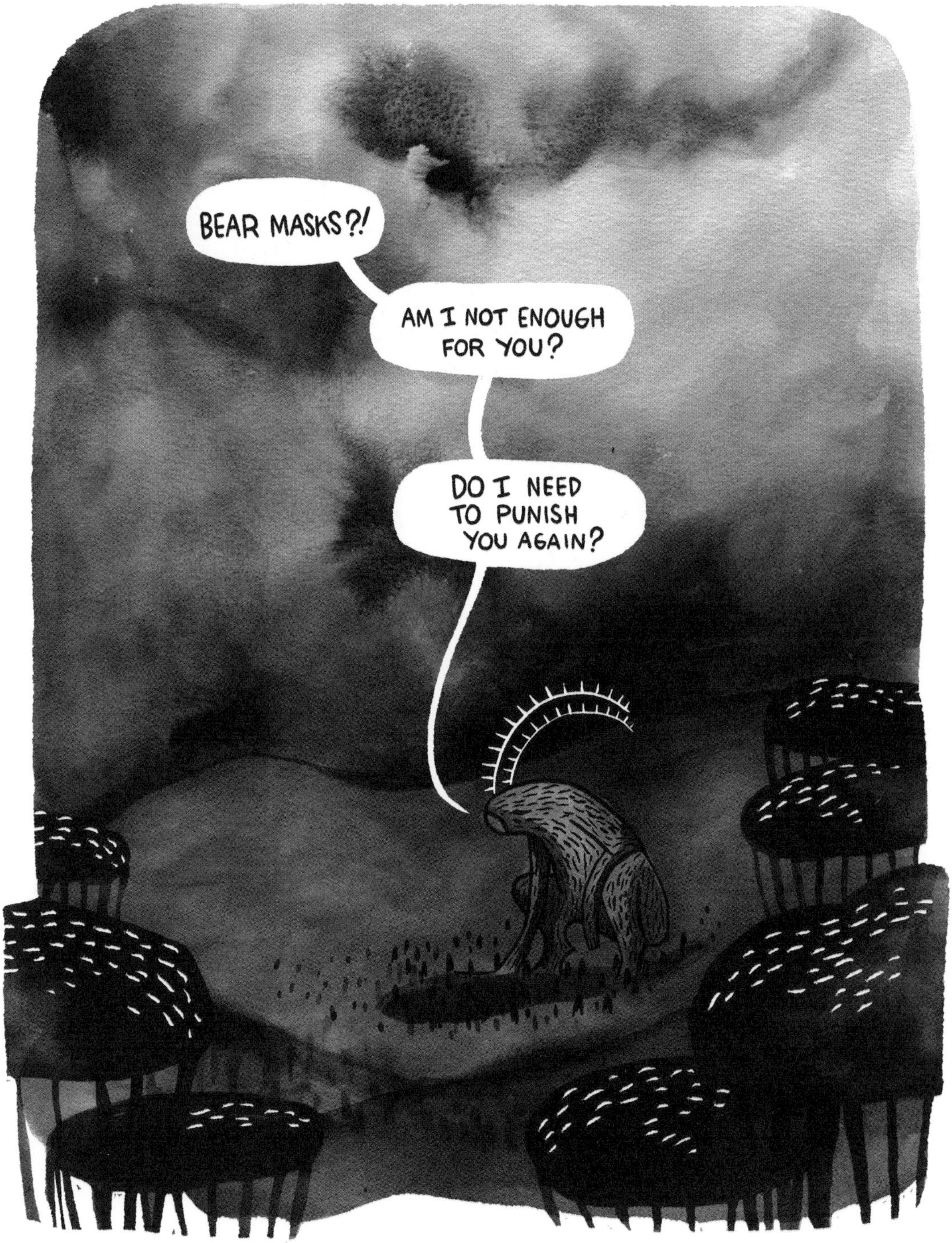
BEAR MASKS?!
AM I NOT ENOUGH FOR YOU?
DO I NEED TO PUNISH YOU AGAIN?

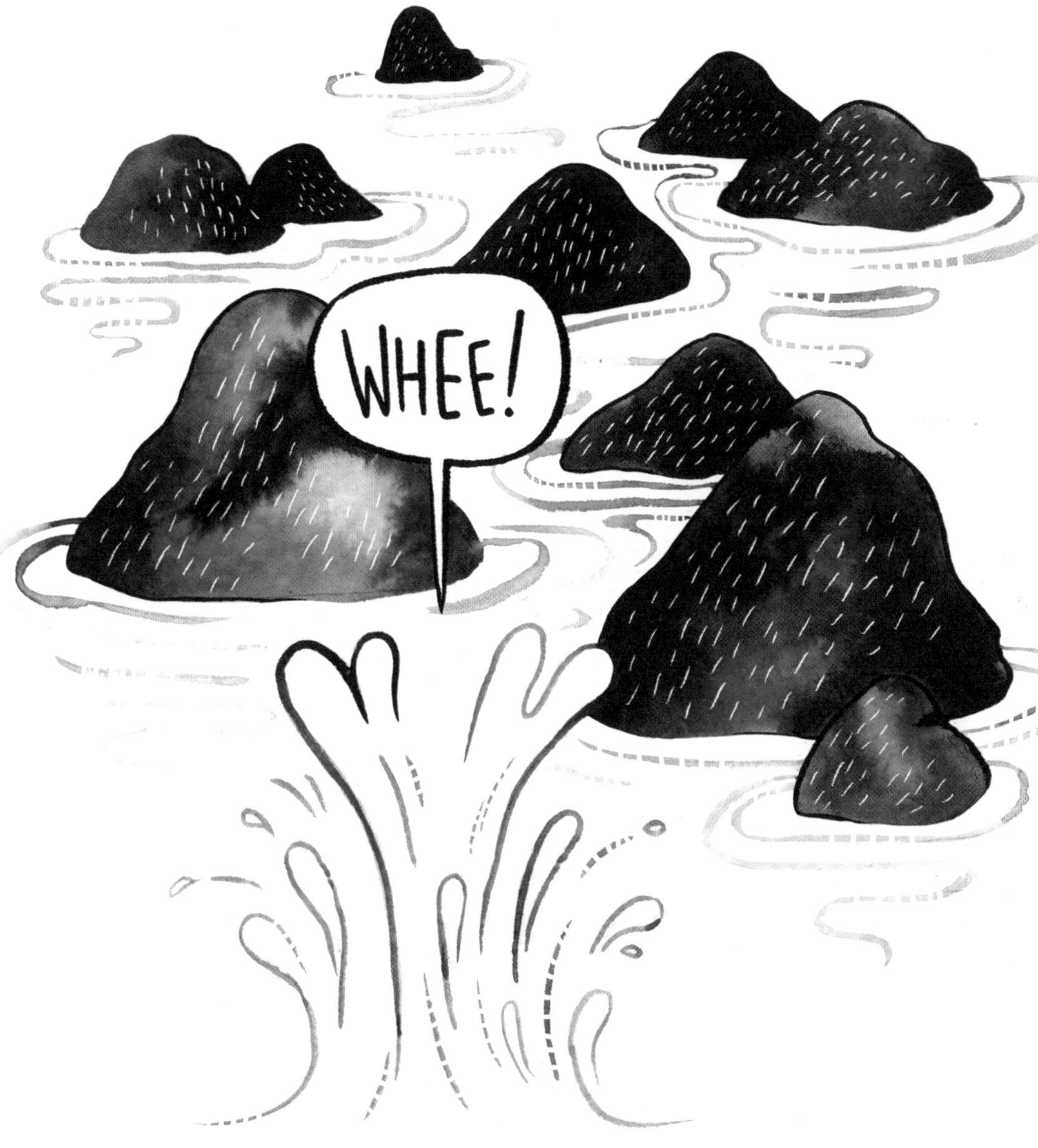
WHEE!

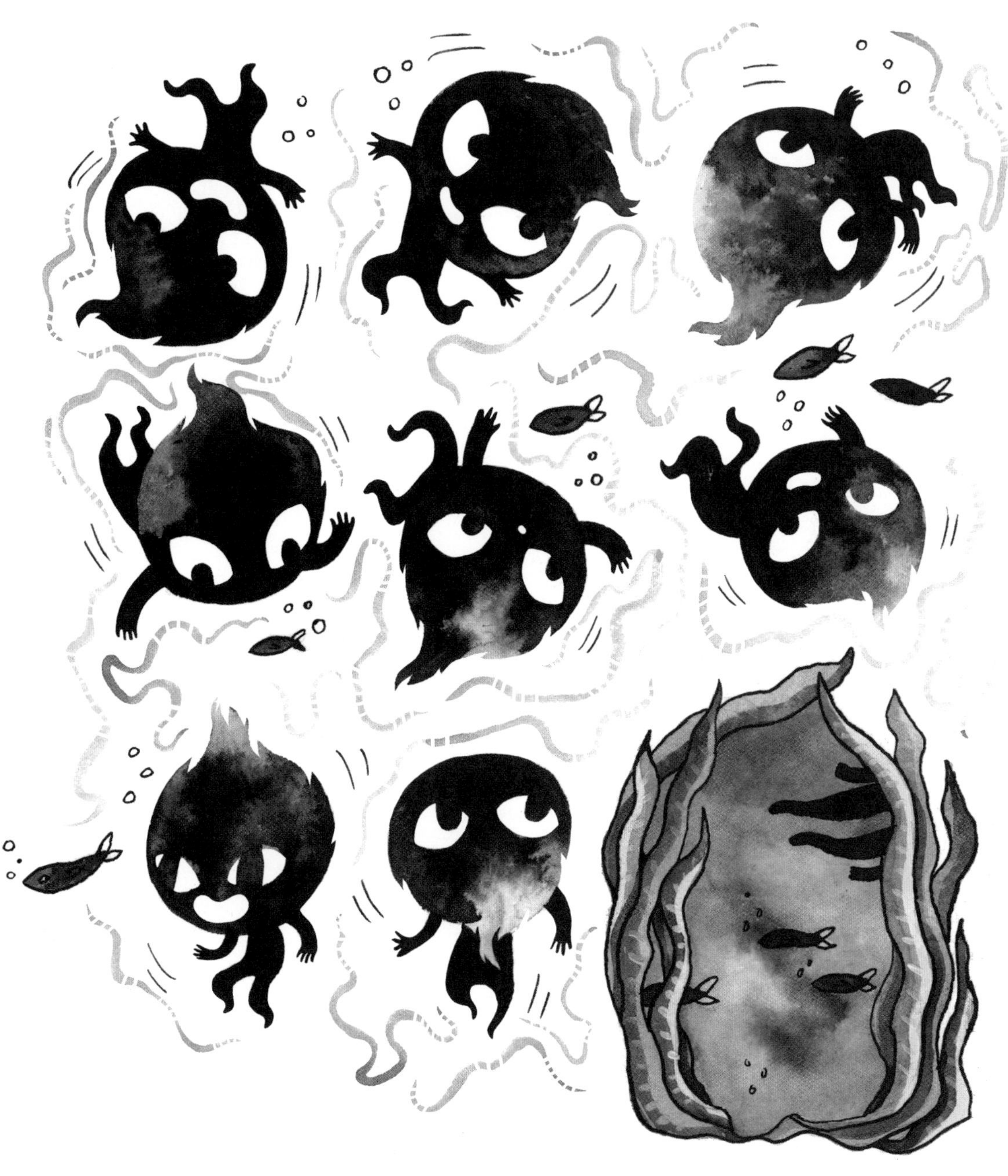

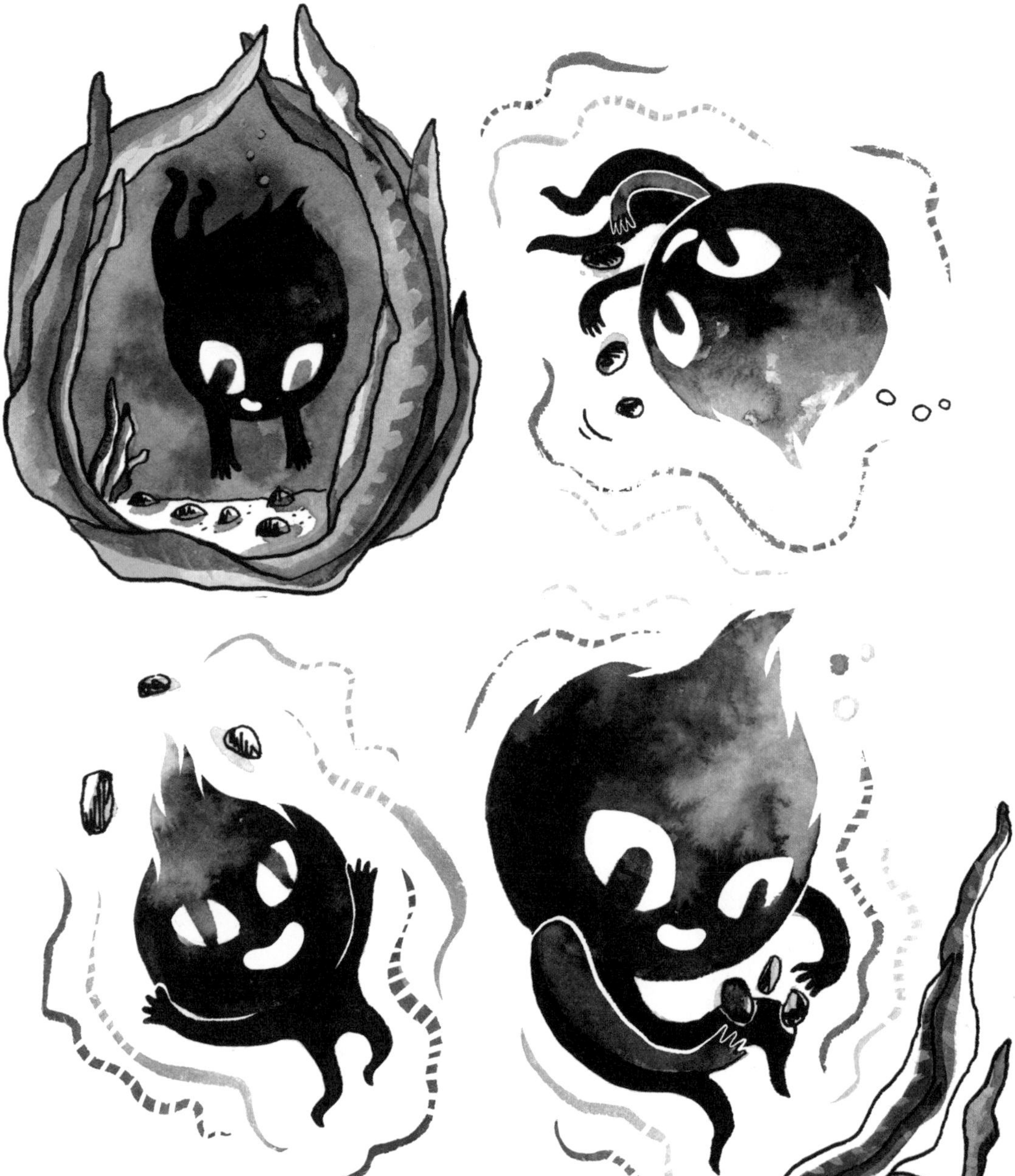

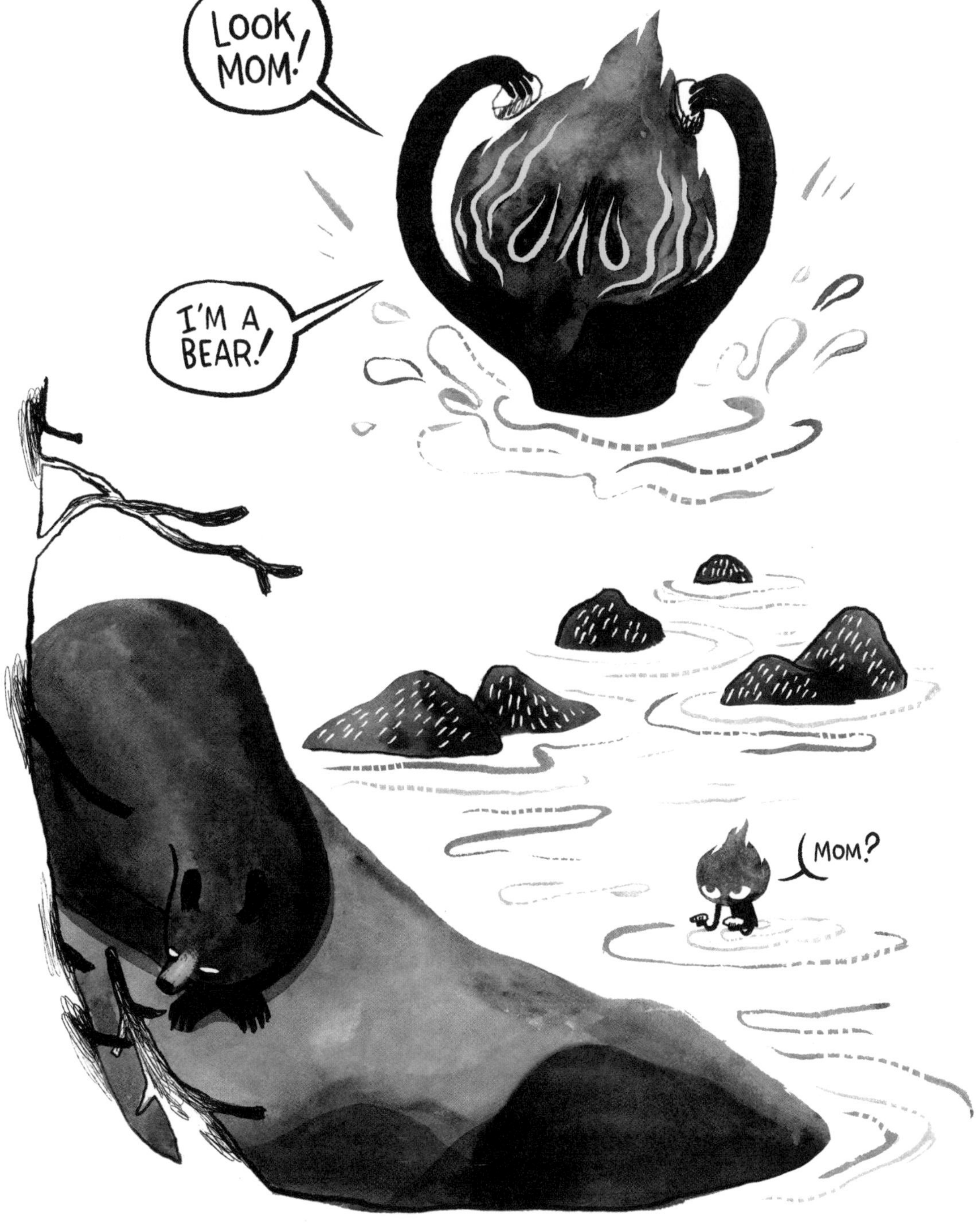
LOOK, MOM!
I'M A BEAR!
MOM?

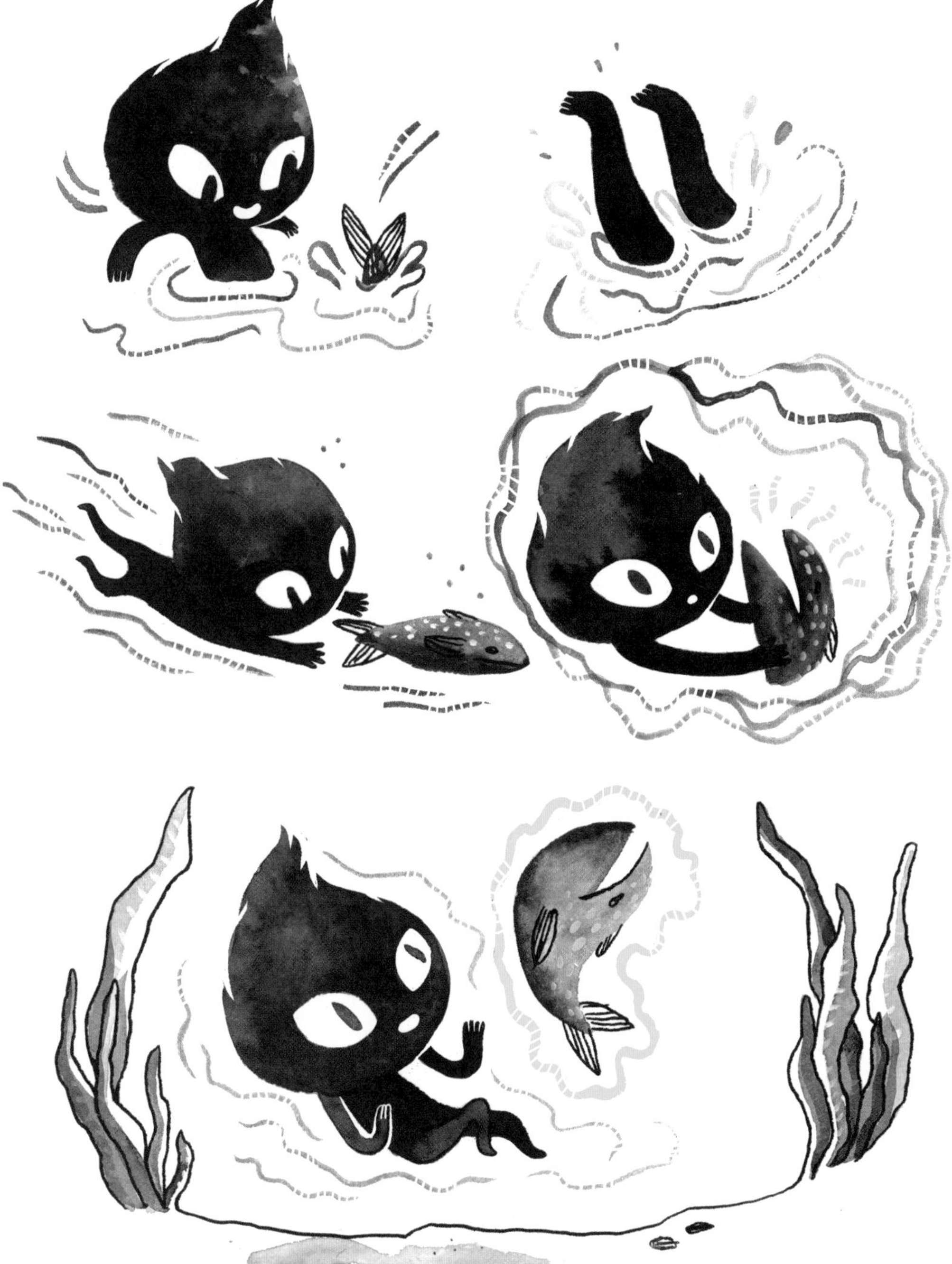

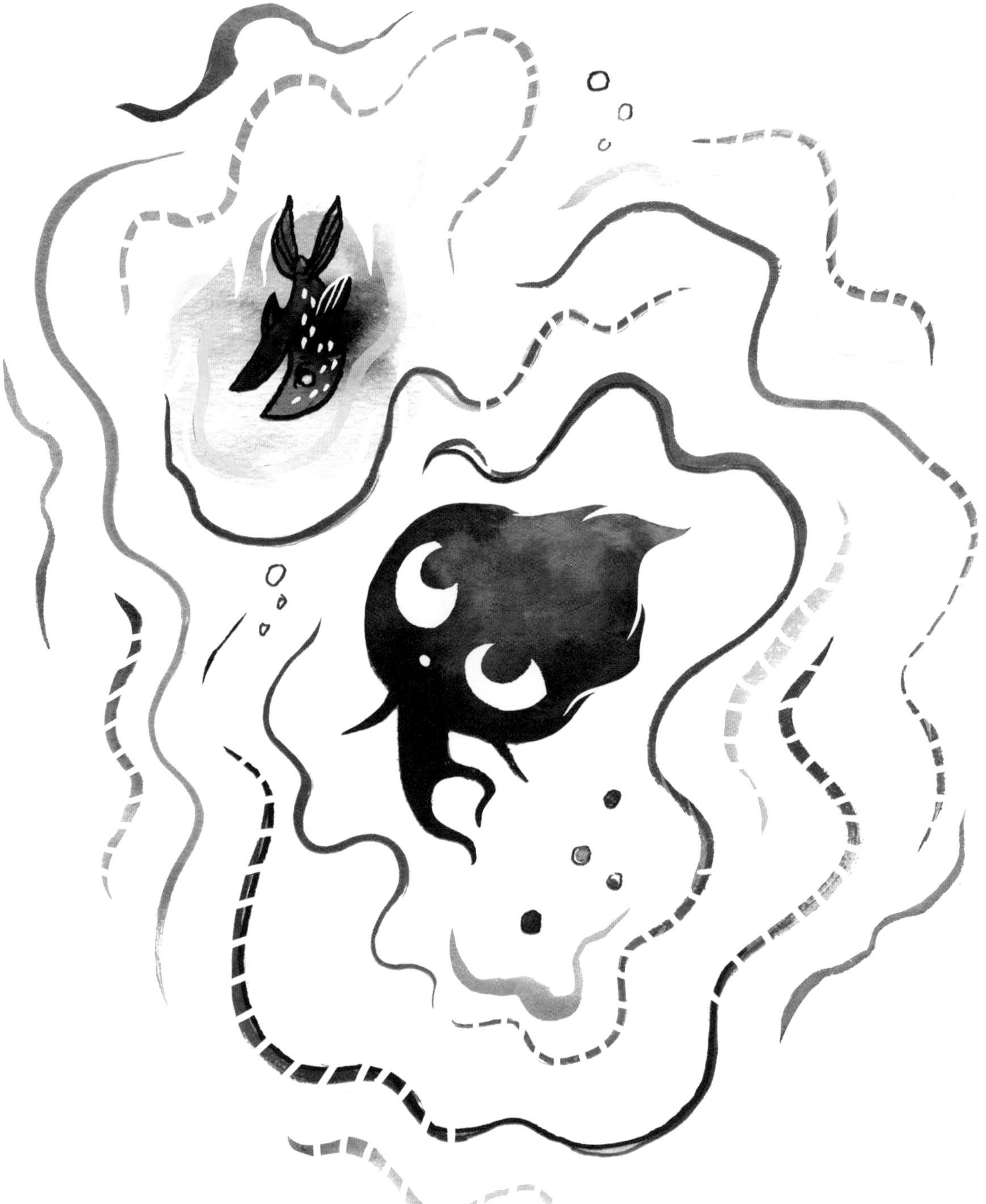

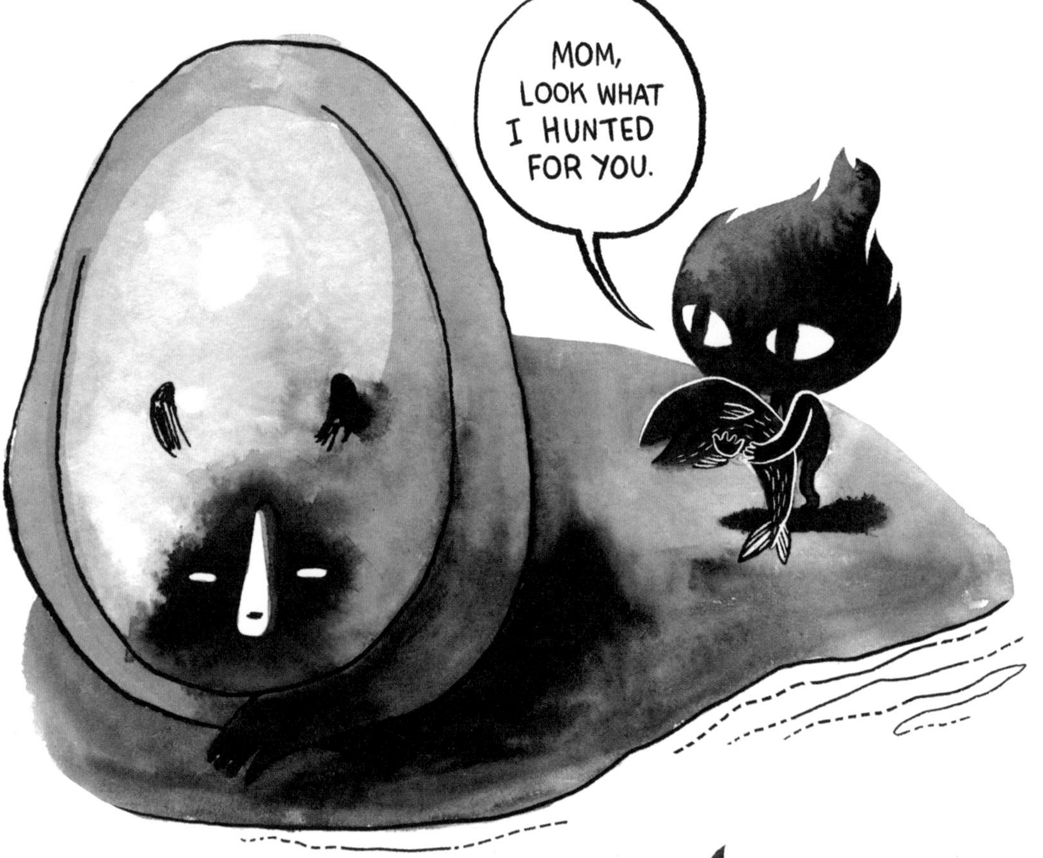
MOM, LOOK WHAT I HUNTED FOR YOU.

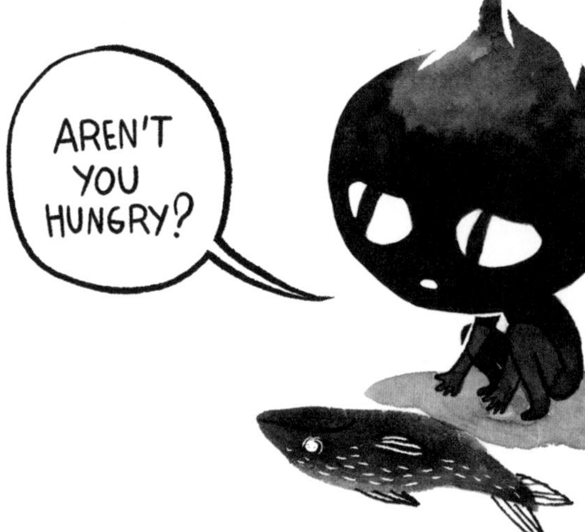
AREN'T YOU HUNGRY?

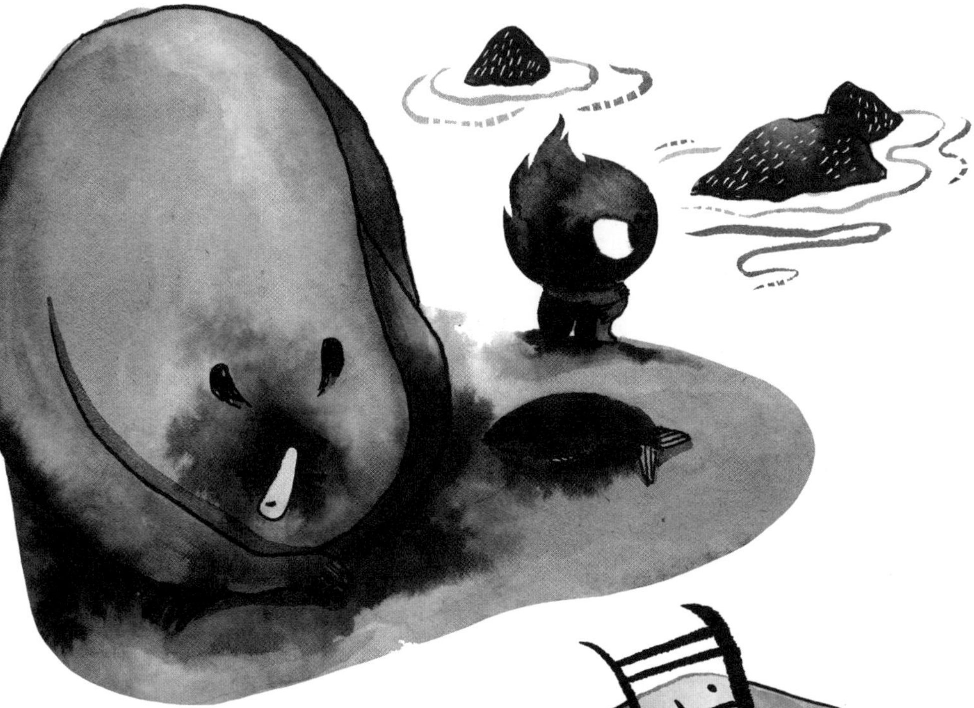

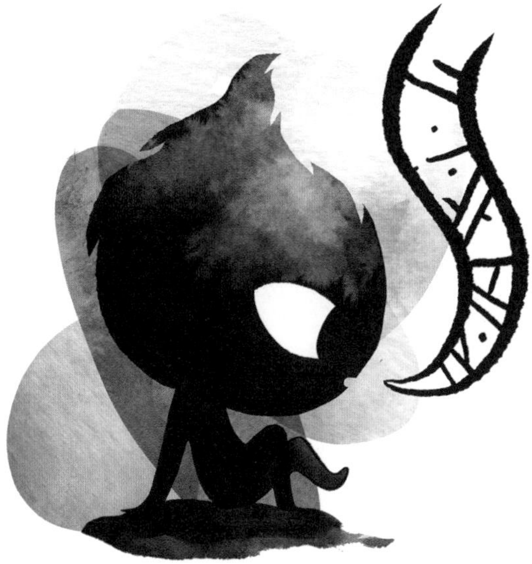

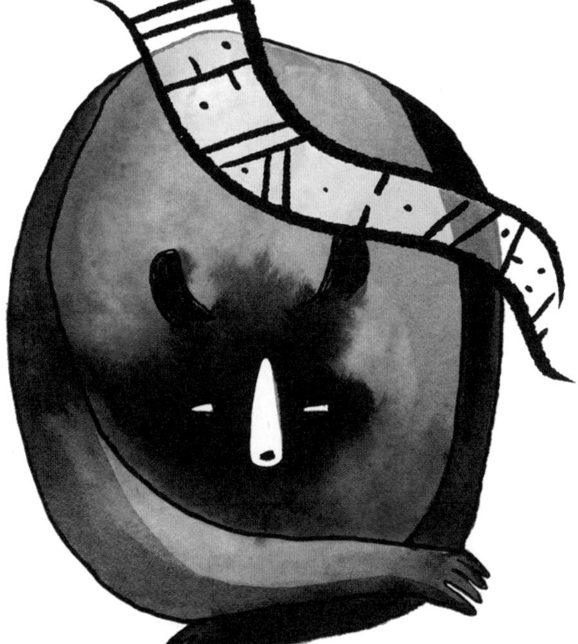

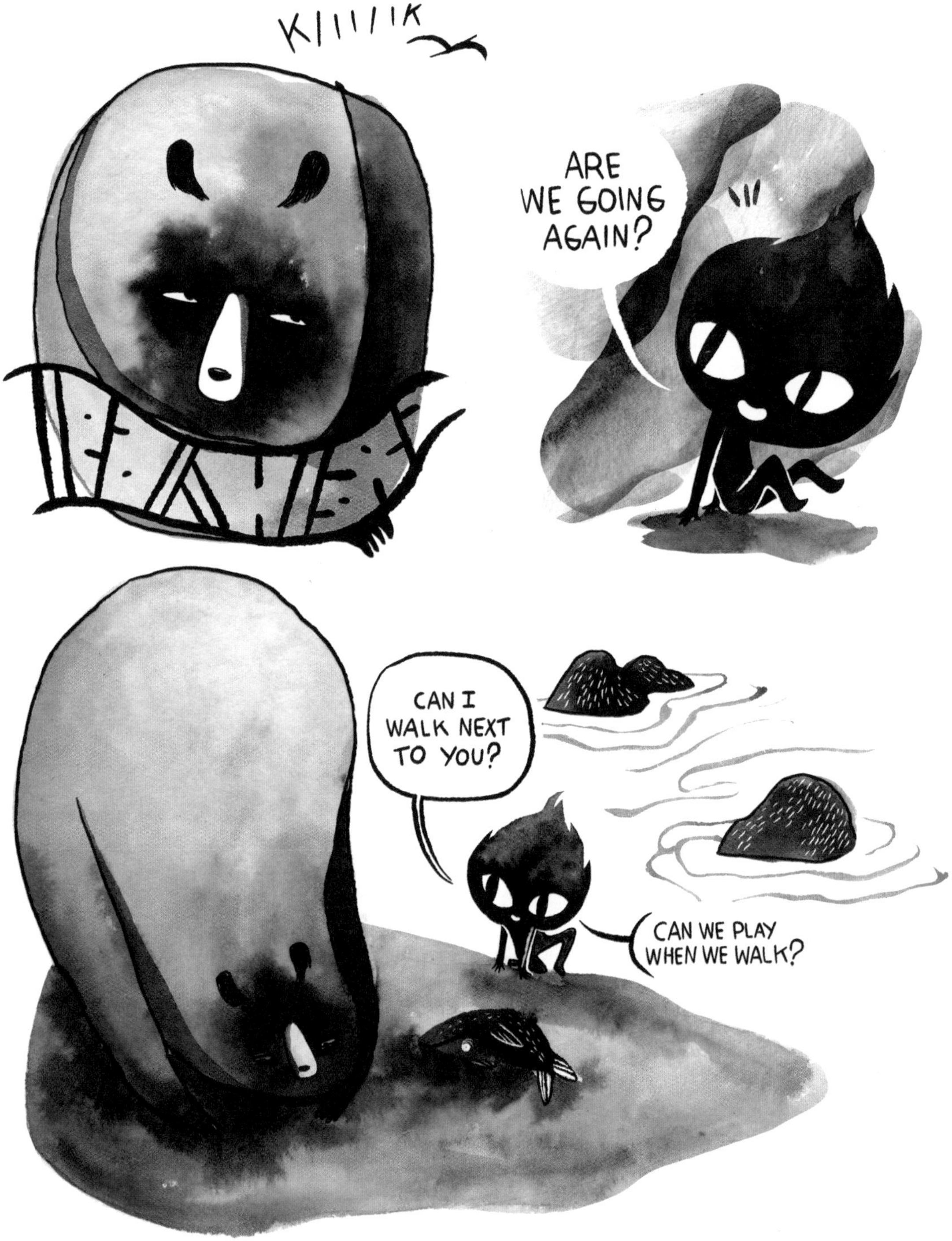
KIIIIIK
ARE WE GOING AGAIN?
CAN I WALK NEXT TO YOU?
CAN WE PLAY WHEN WE WALK?

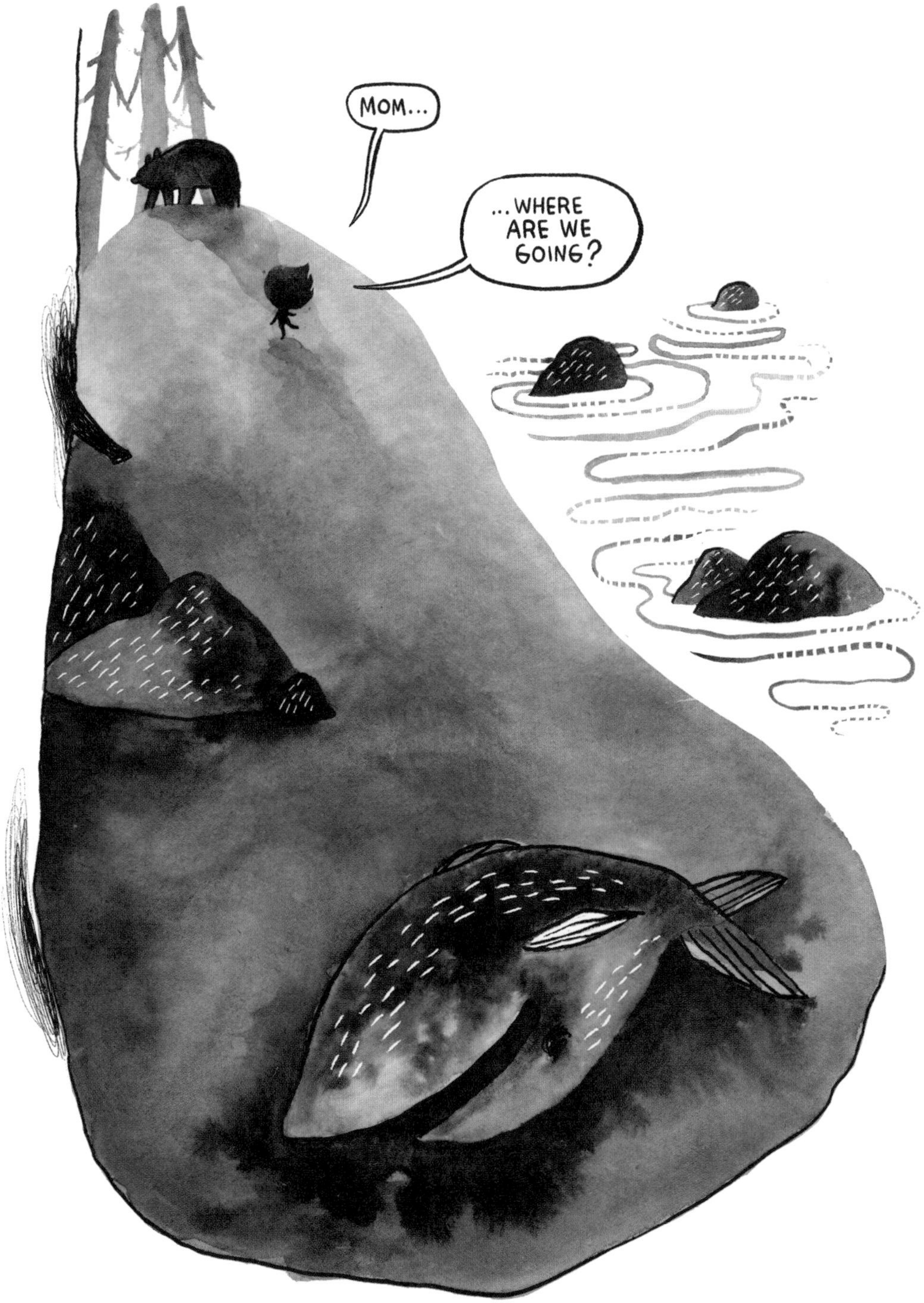
MOM...
...WHERE ARE WE GOING?

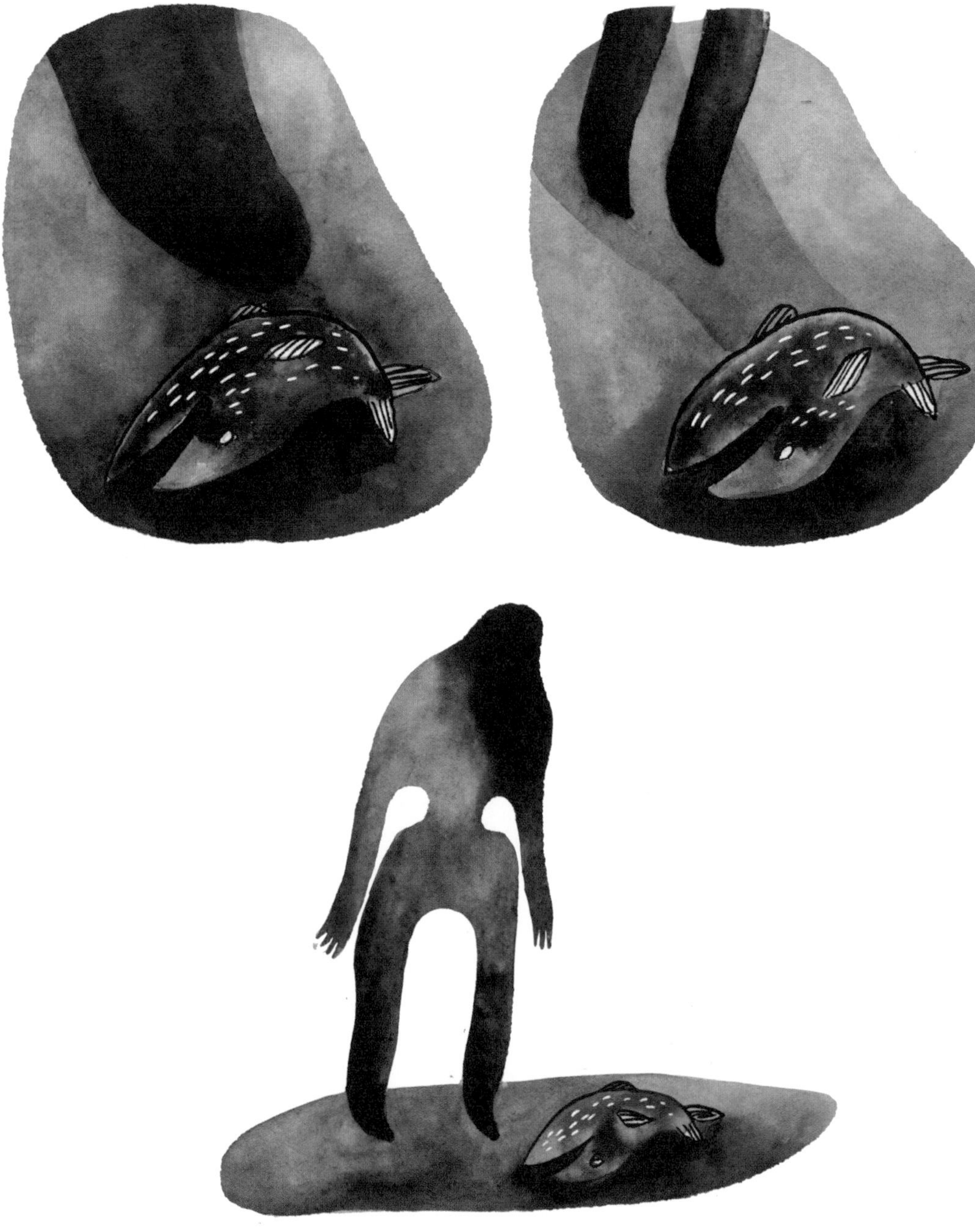

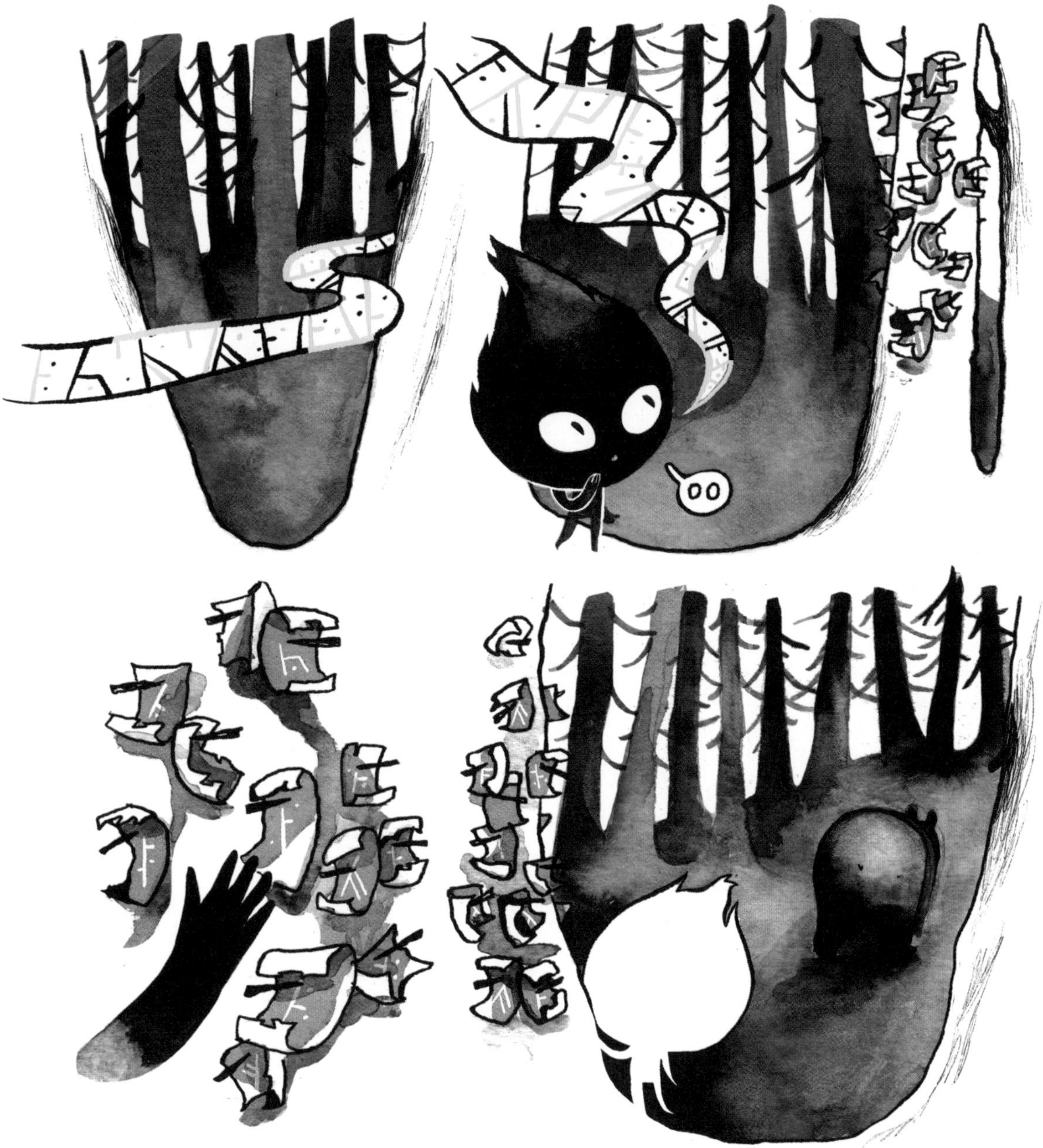

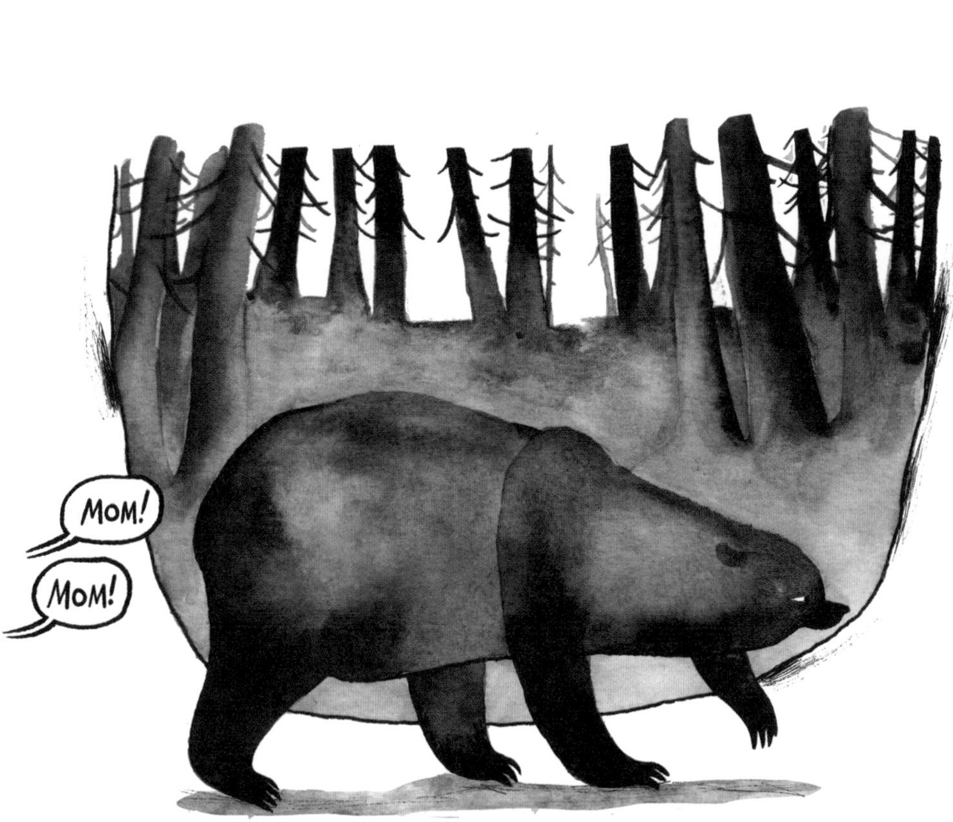
MOM!
MOM!

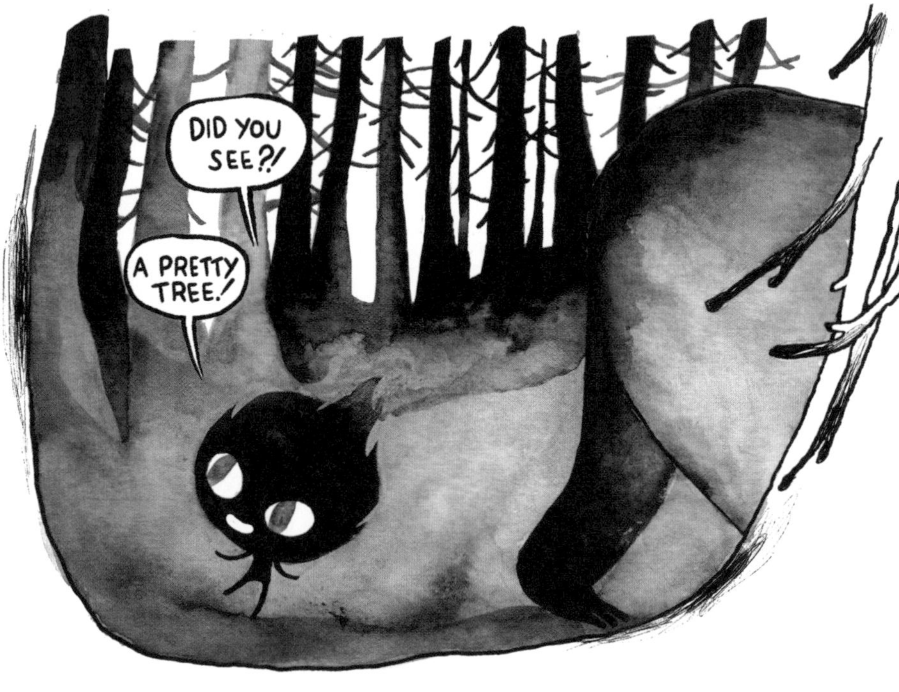
DID YOU SEE?!
A PRETTY TREE!

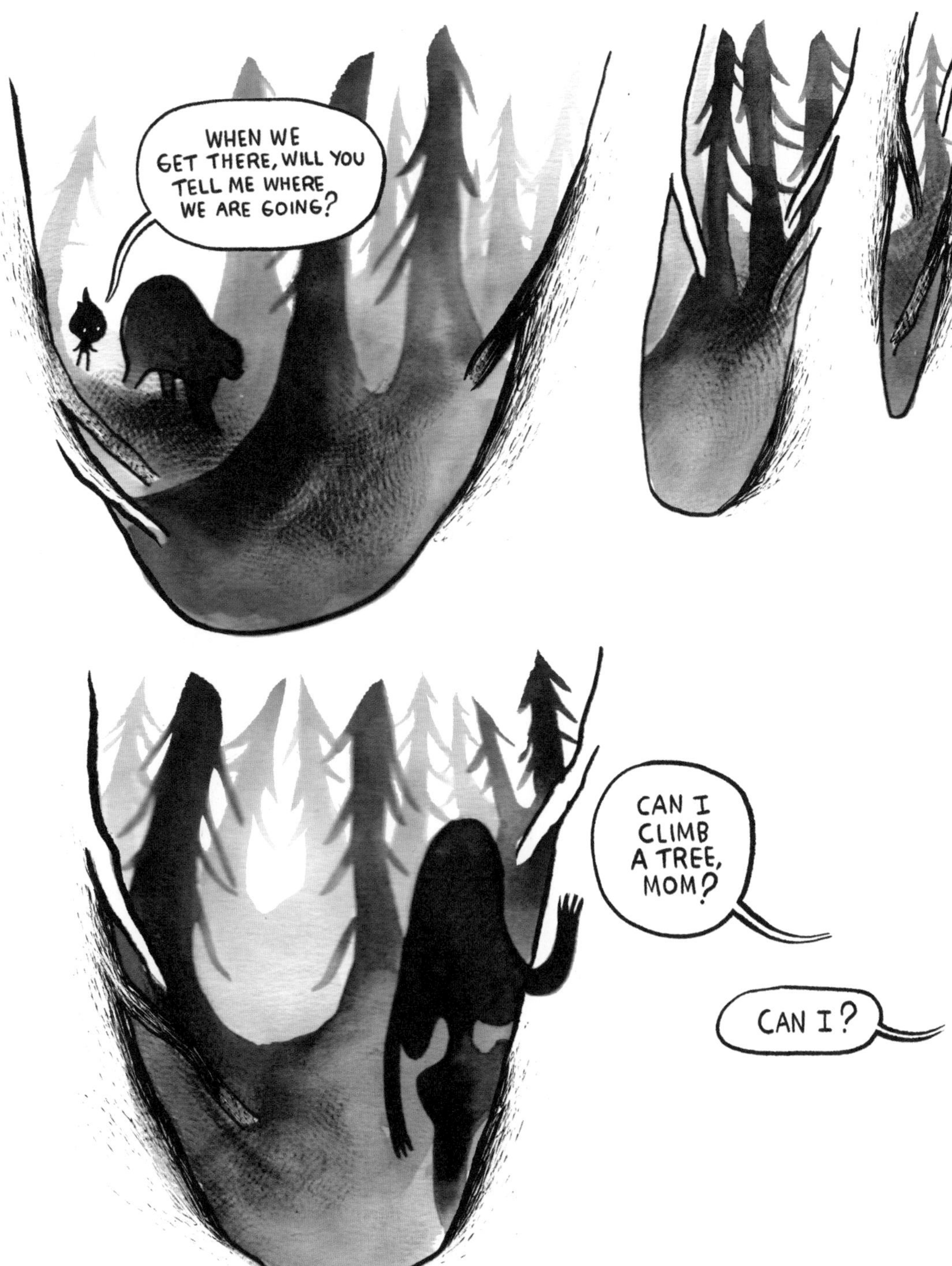
WHEN WE GET THERE, WILL YOU TELL ME WHERE WE ARE GOING?
CAN I CLIMB A TREE, MOM?
CAN I?

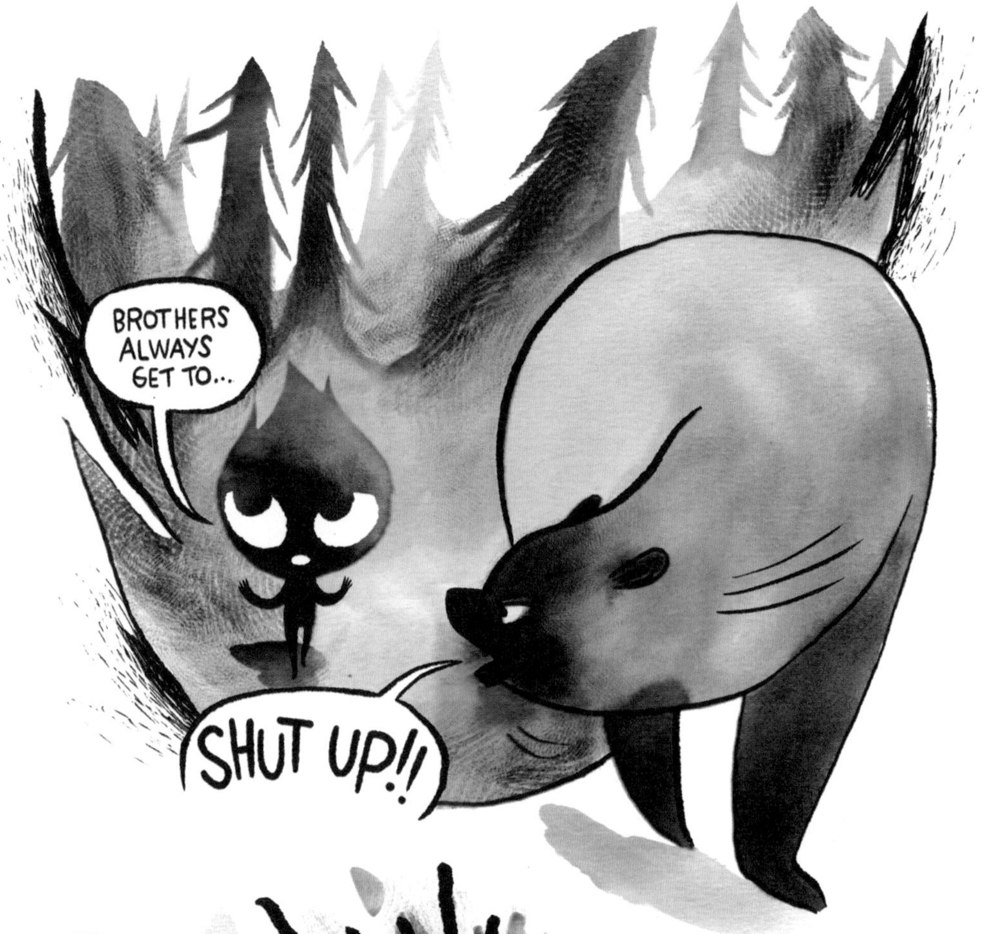
BROTHERS ALWAYS GET TO...
SHUT UP!!

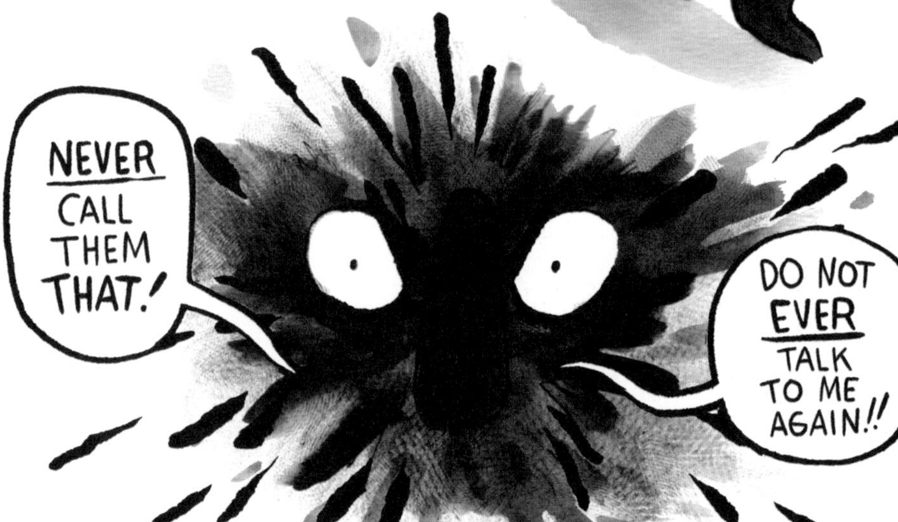
NEVER CALL THEM THAT.!
DO NOT EVER TALK TO ME AGAIN!!

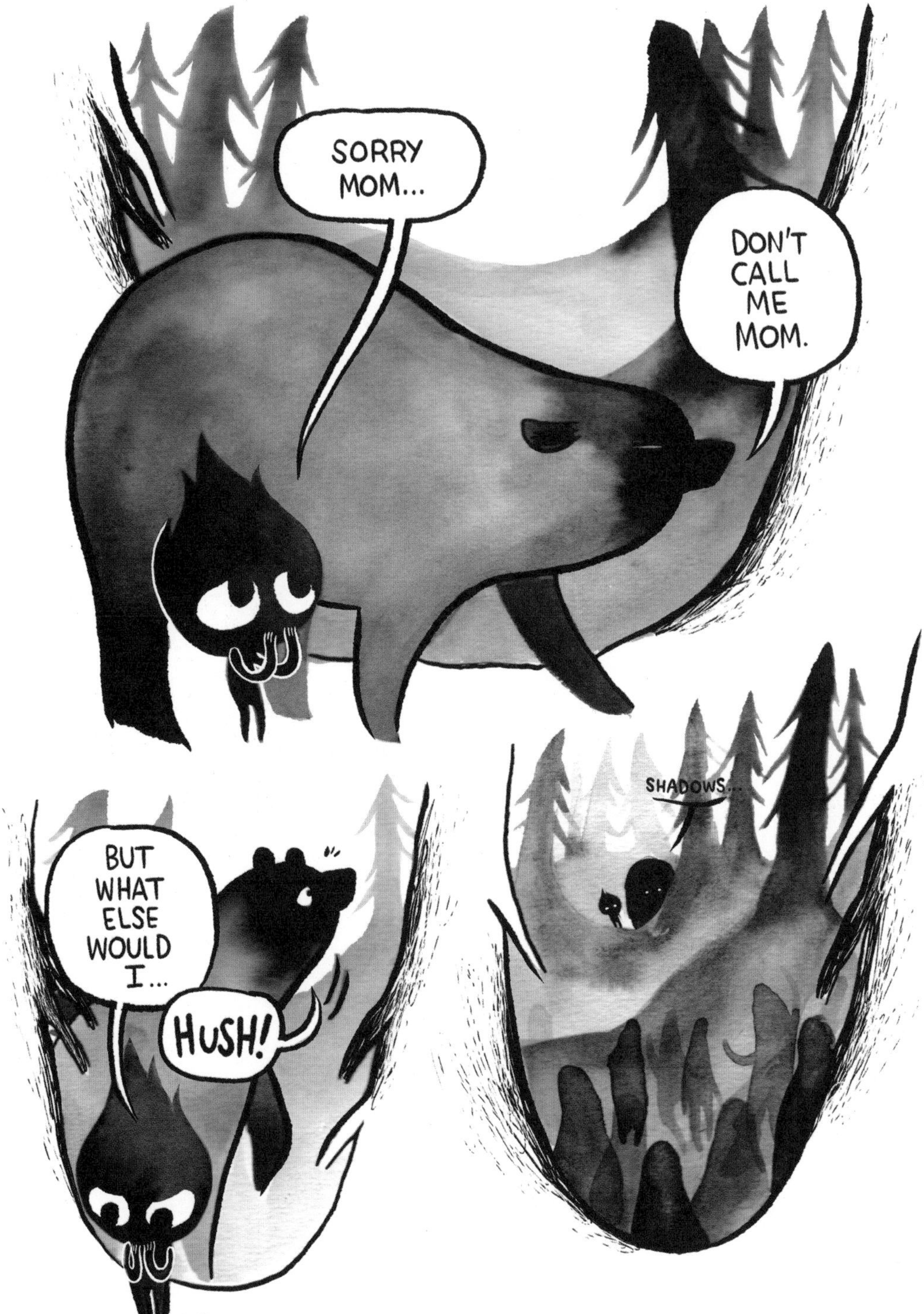
SORRY MOM...
DON'T CALL ME MOM.
BUT WHAT ELSE WOULD I...
HUSH!
SHADOWS...

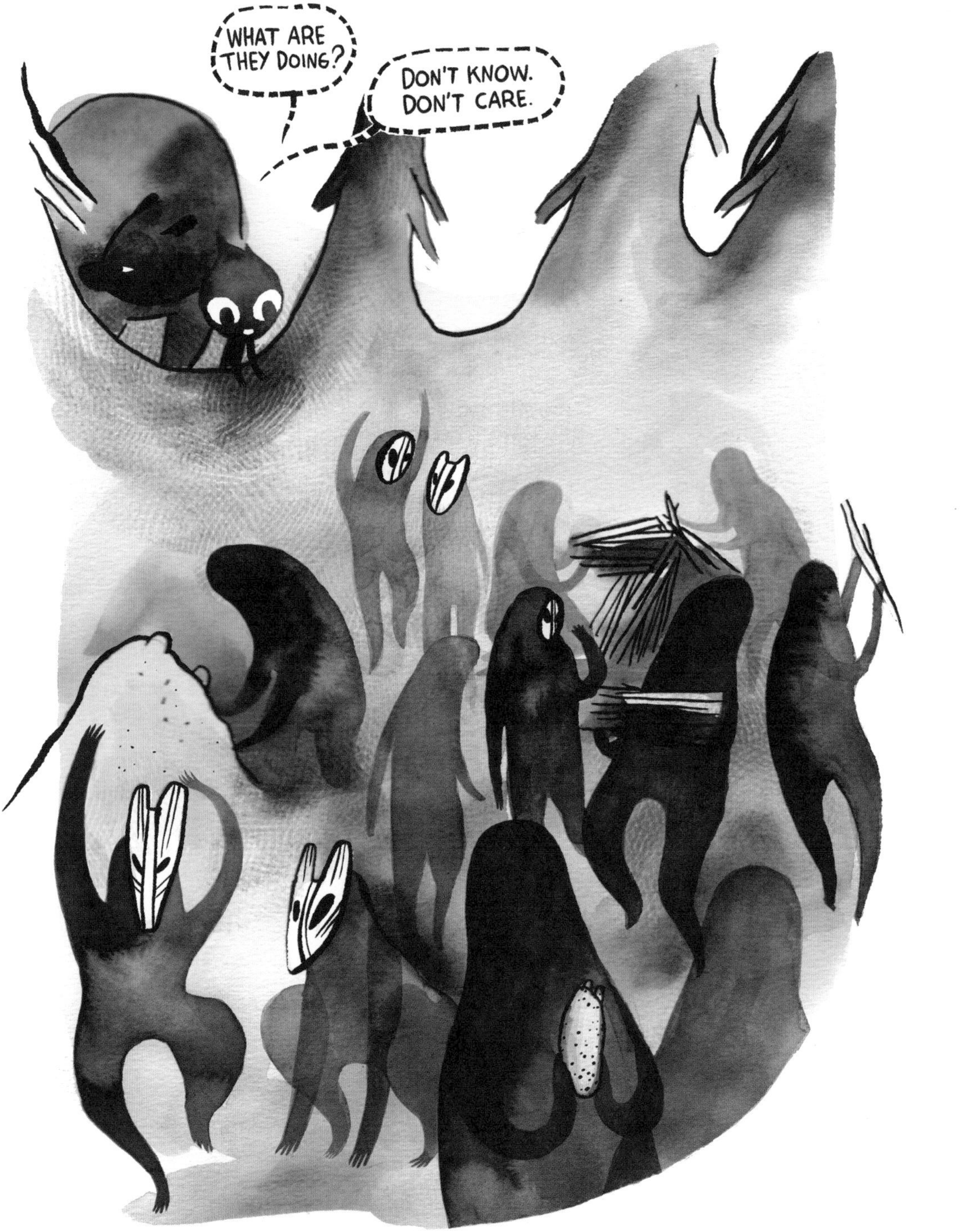
WHAT ARE THEY DOING?
DON'T KNOW. DON'T CARE.

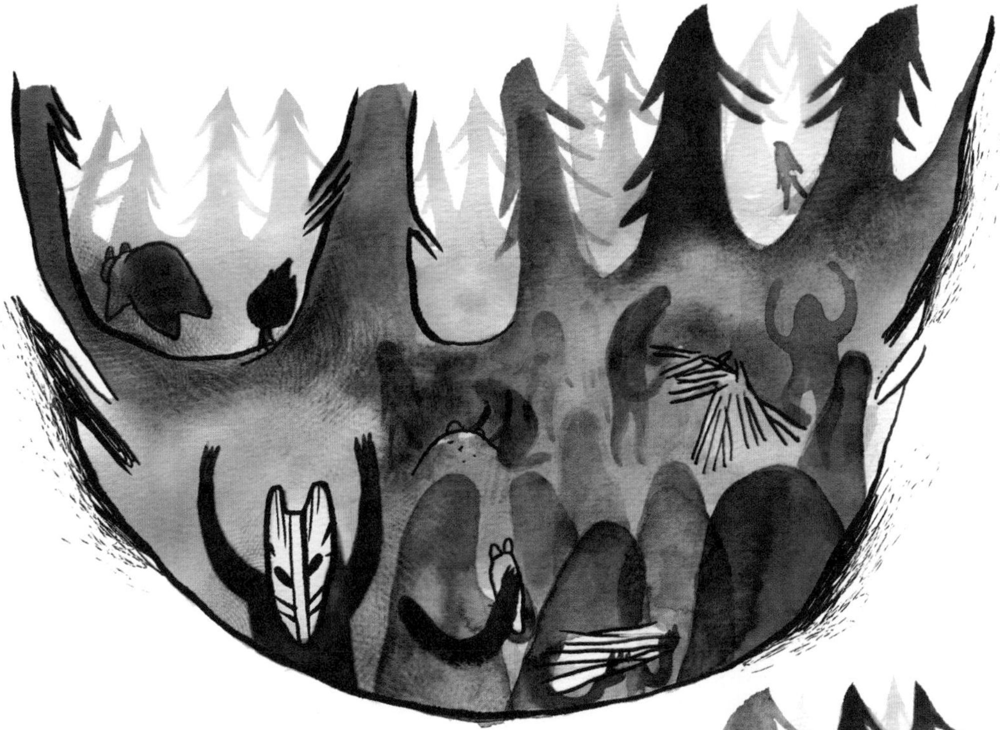

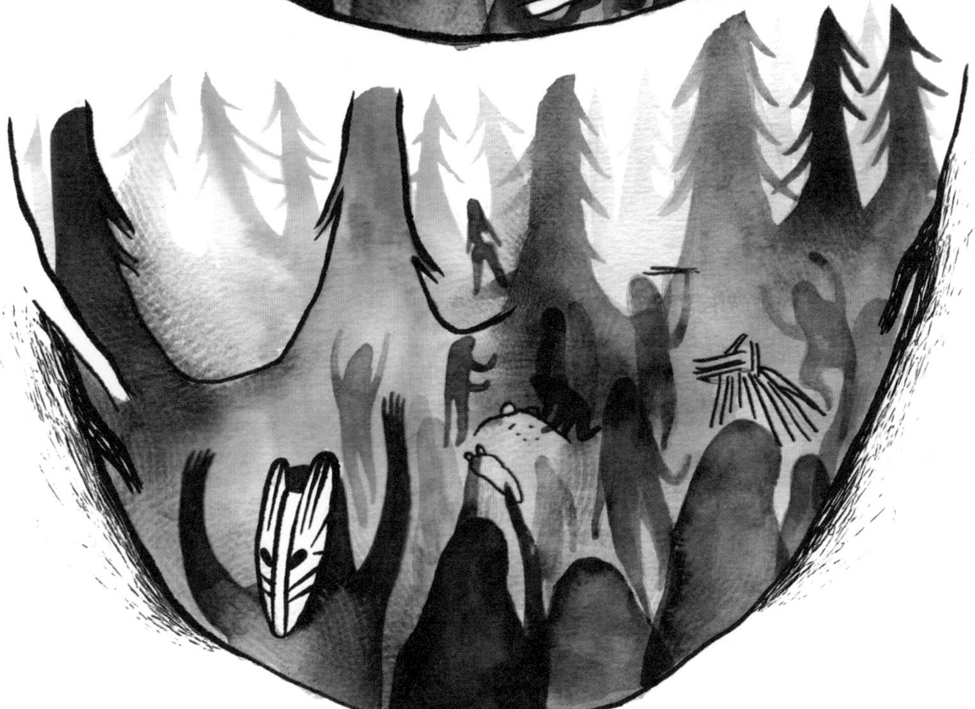

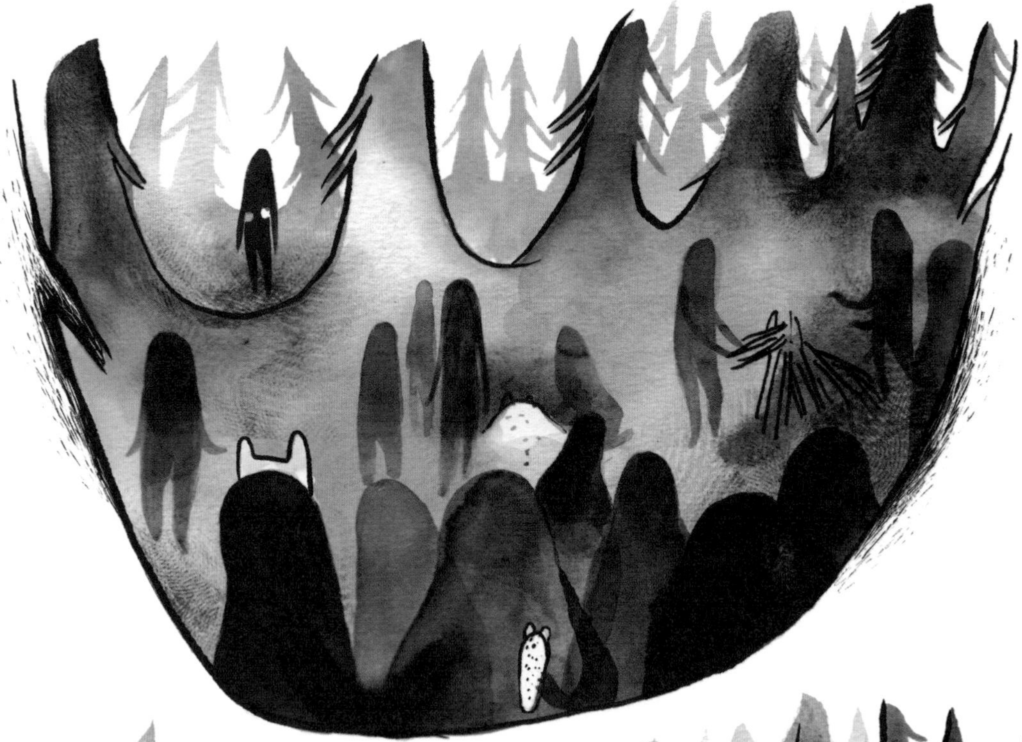

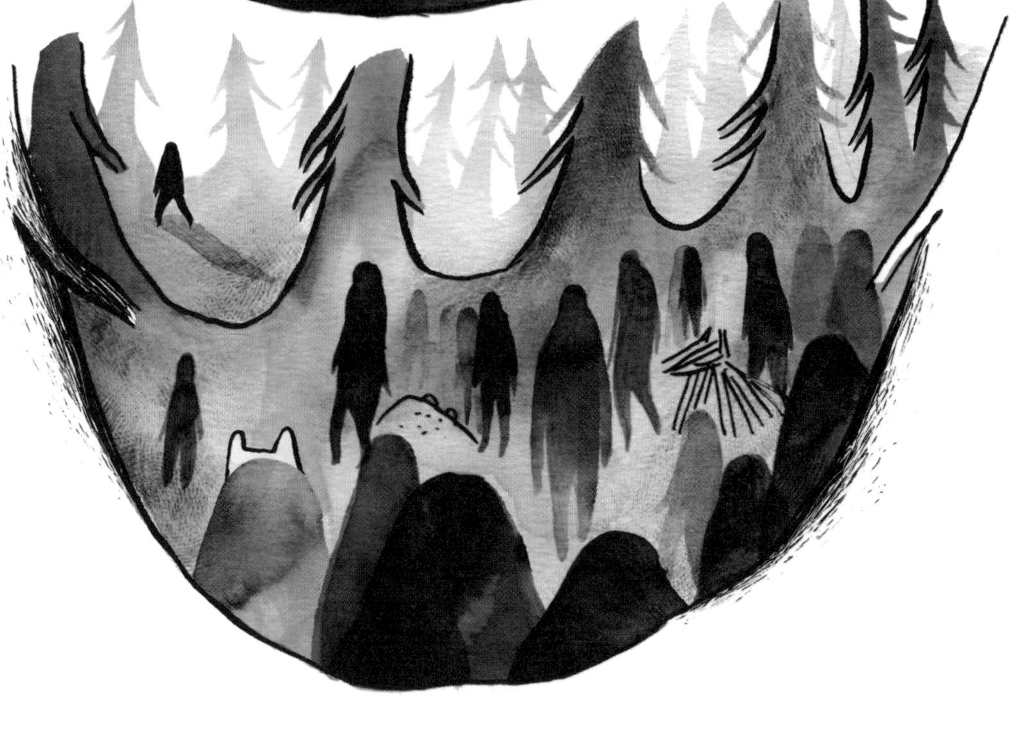

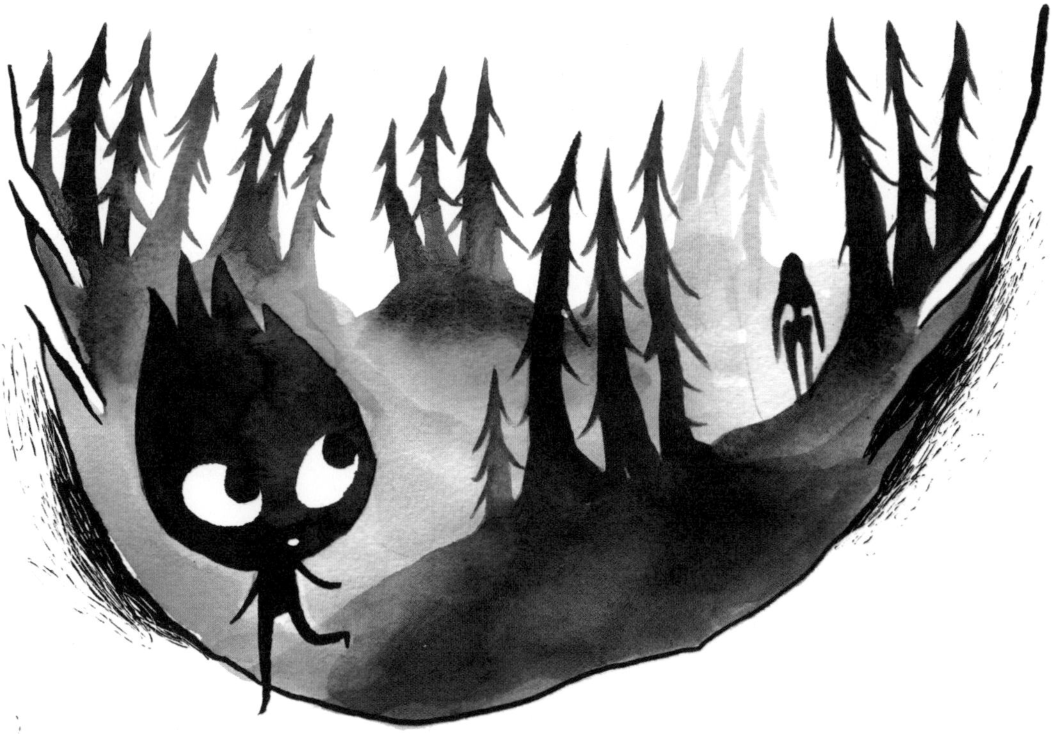

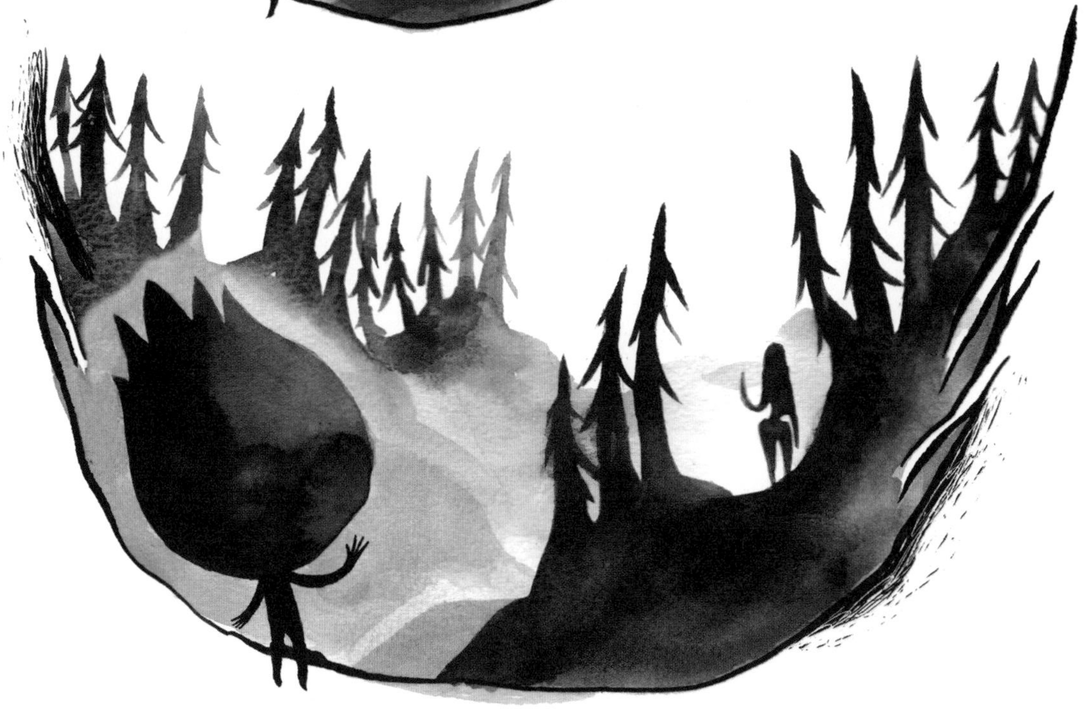

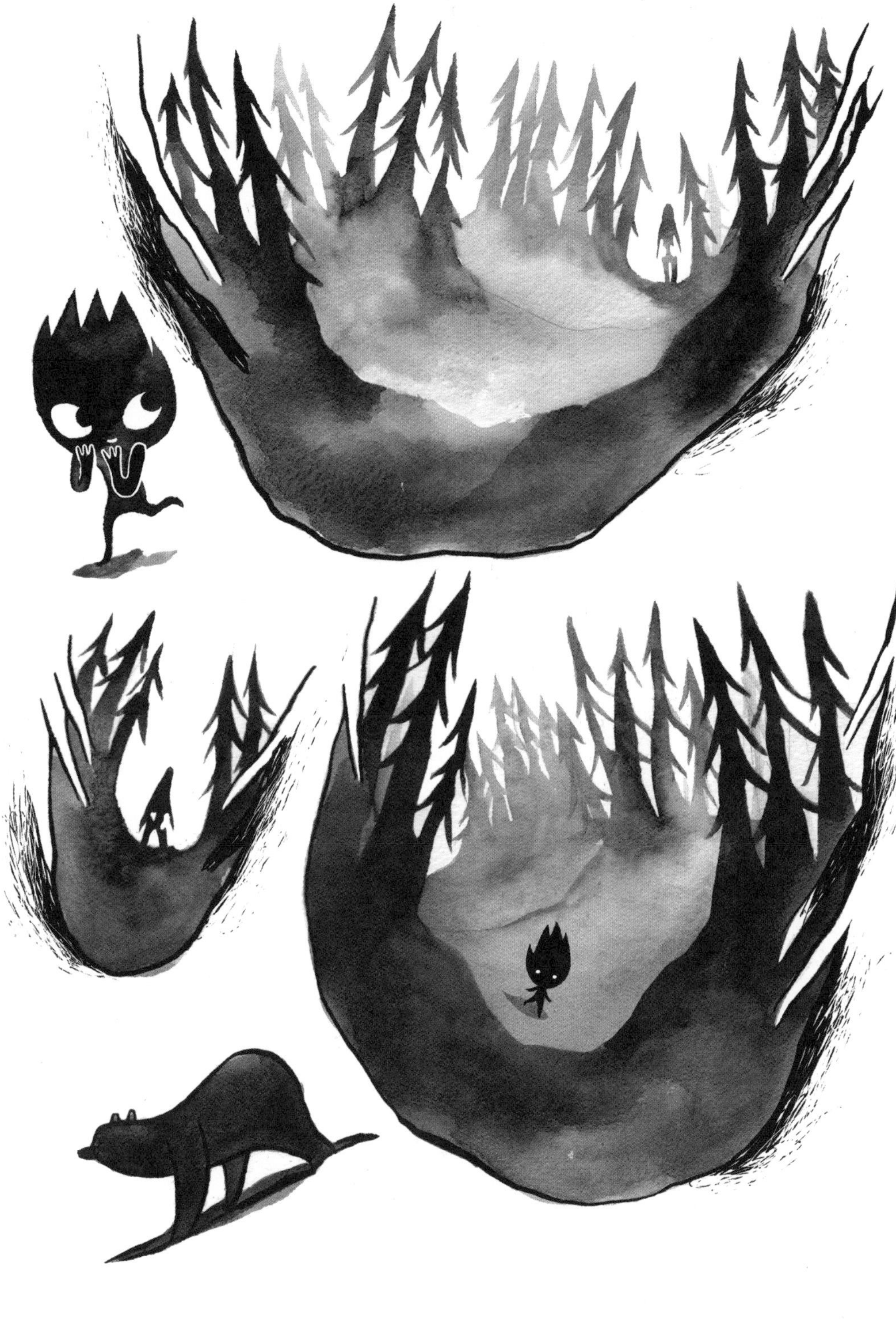

VII

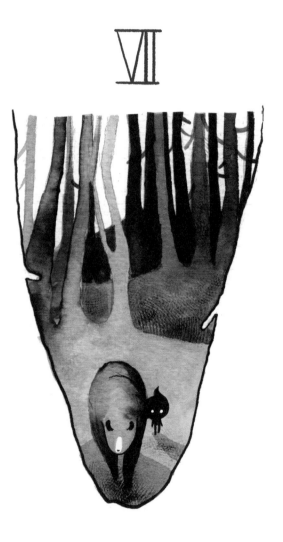

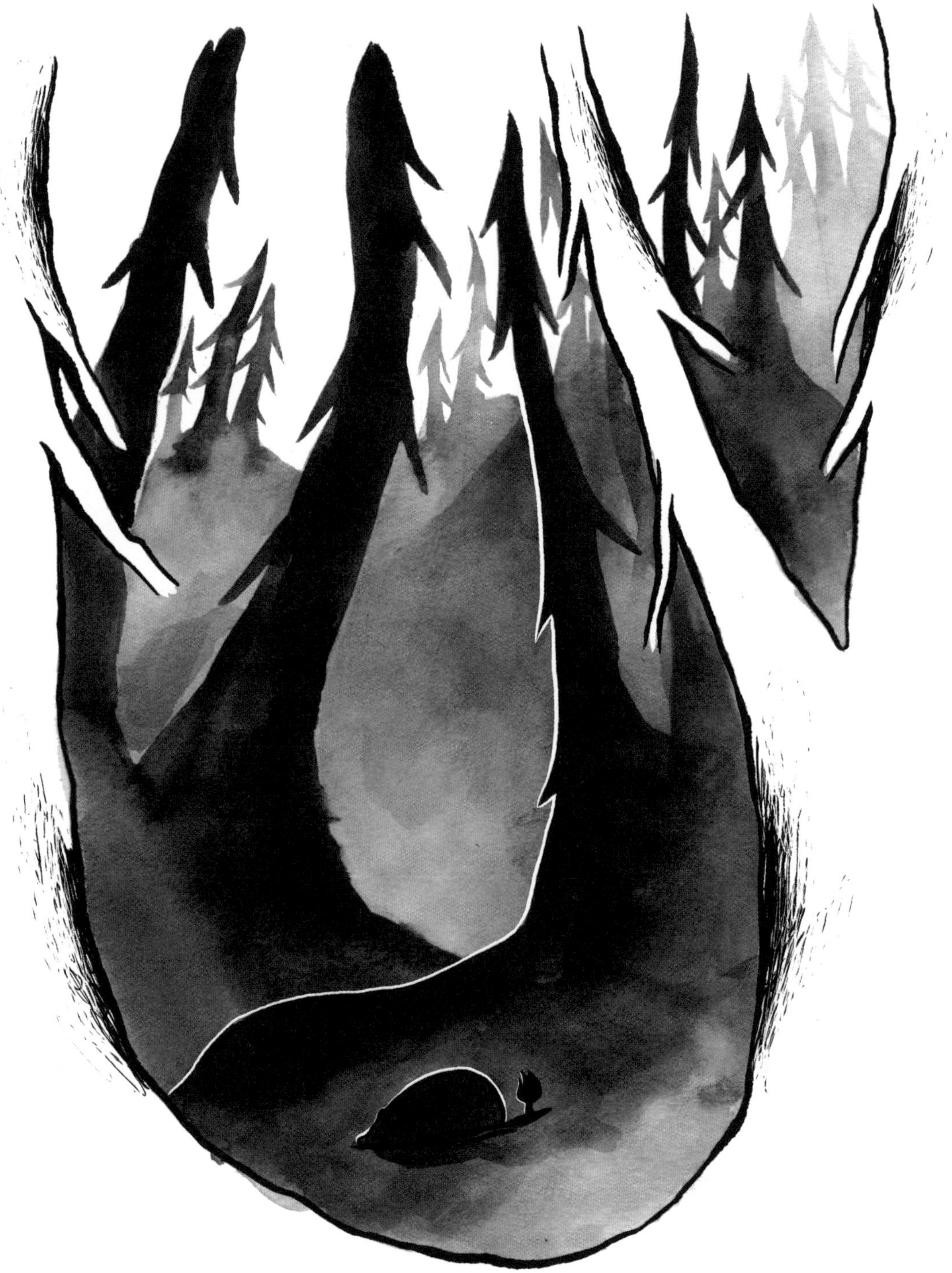

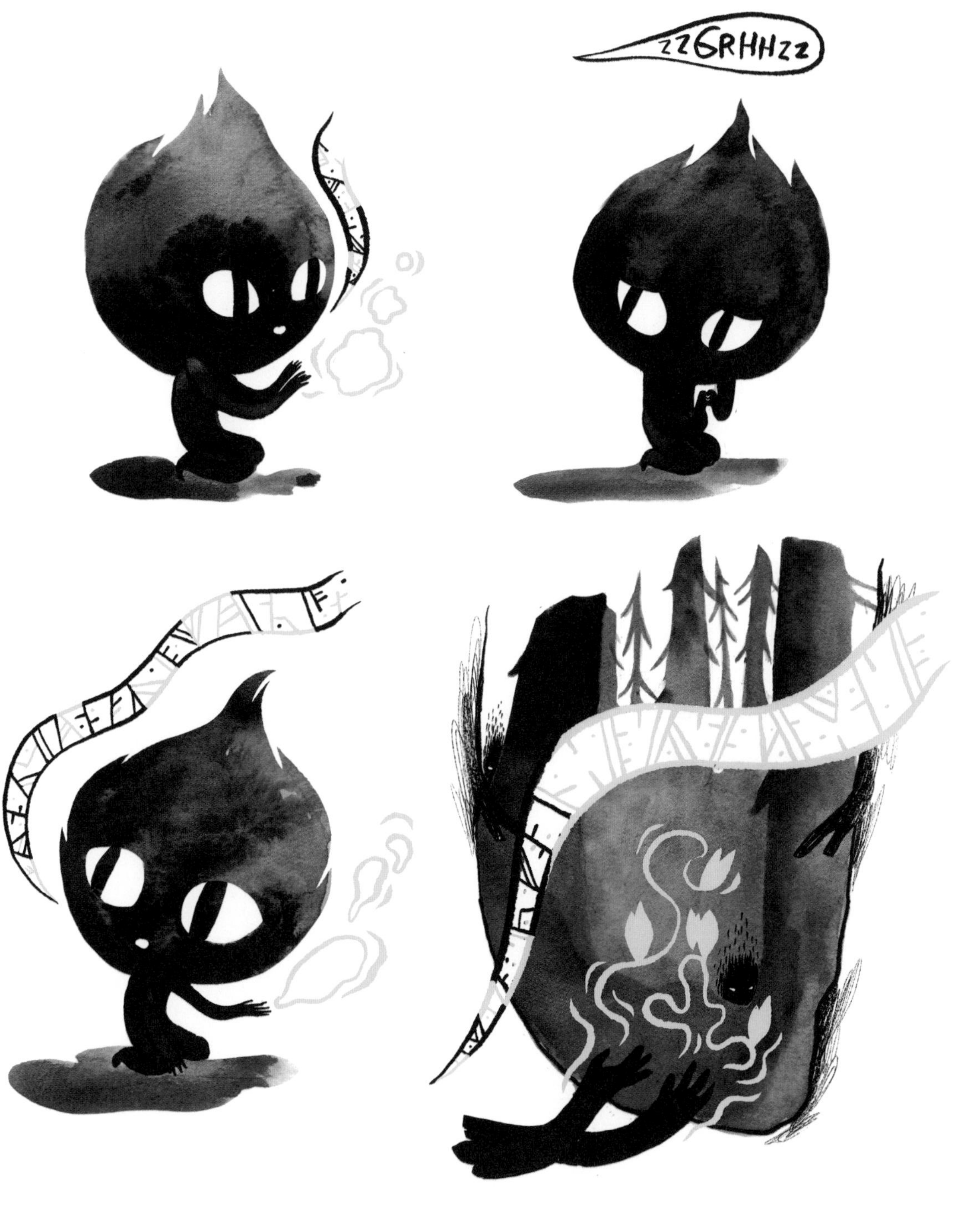
zzGRHHzz

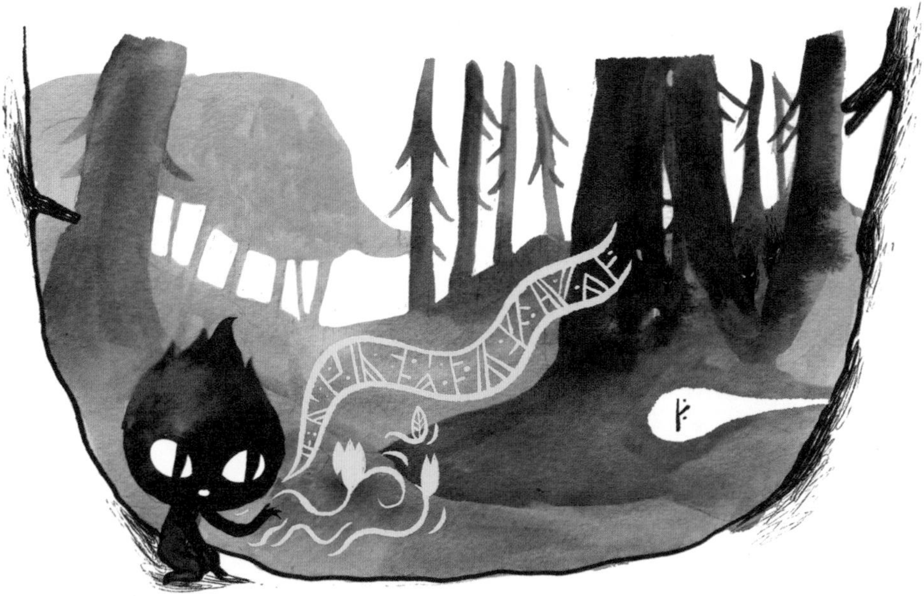

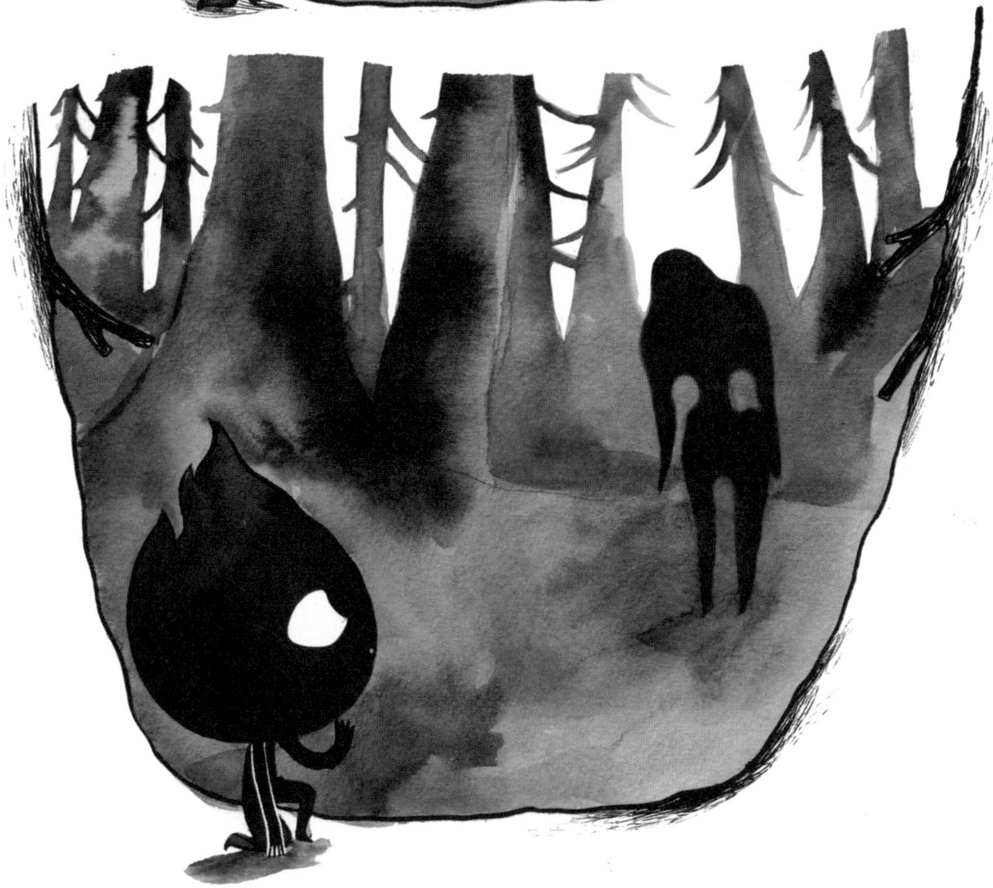

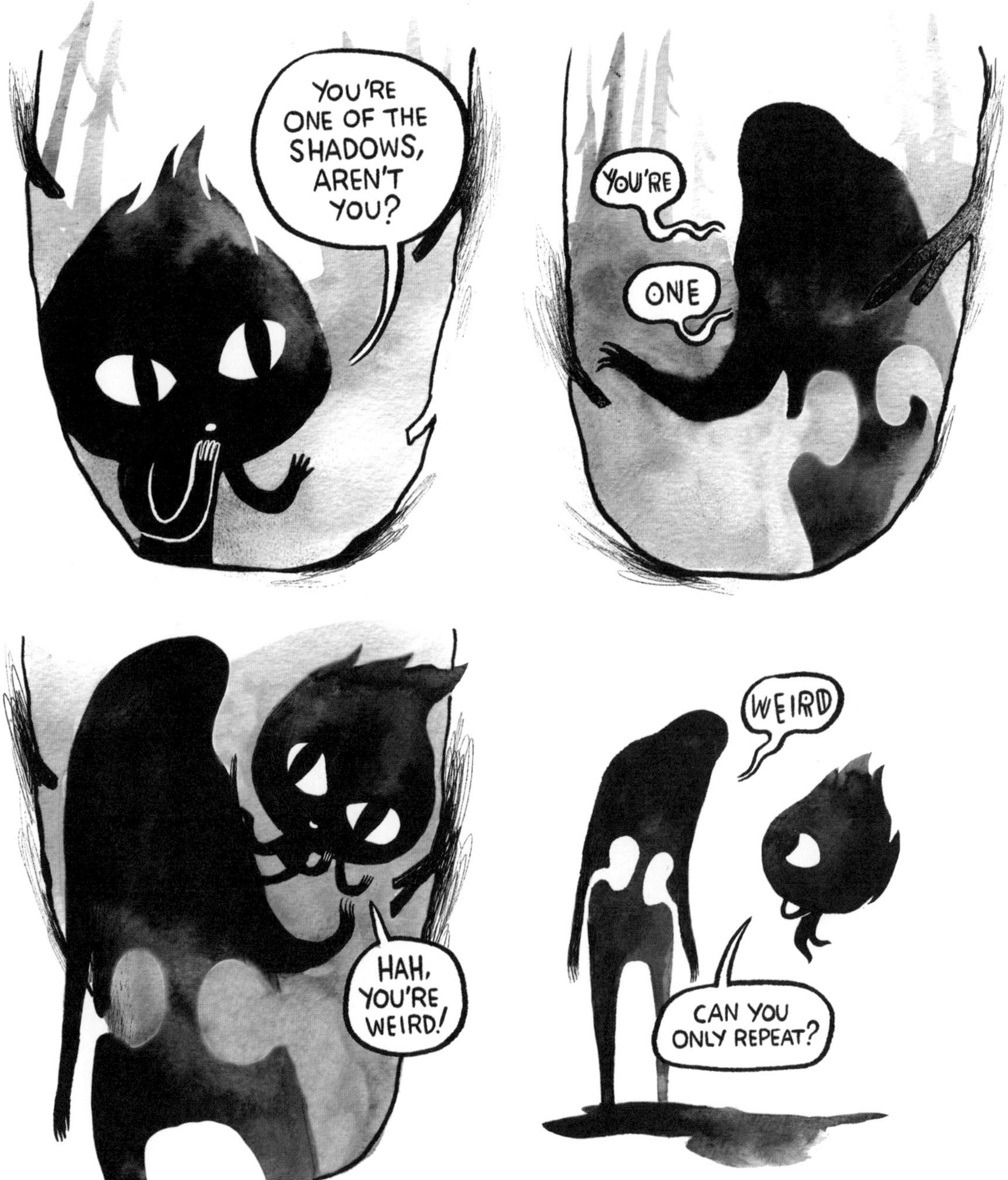
YOU'RE ONE OF THE SHADOWS, AREN'T YOU?
YOU'RE
ONE
HAH, YOU'RE WEIRD!
WEIRD
CAN YOU ONLY REPEAT?

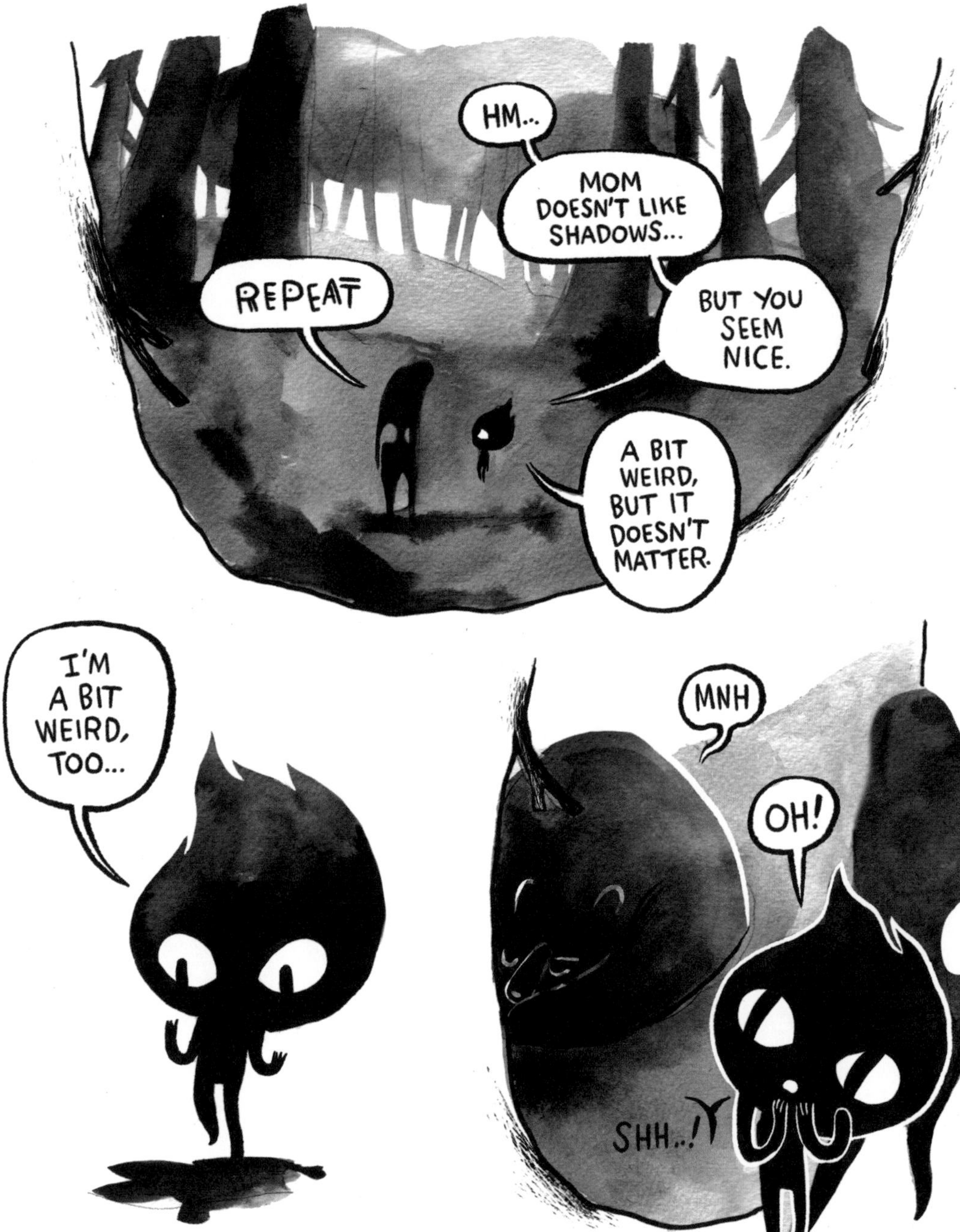
HM..
MOM DOESN'T LIKE SHADOWS...
REPEAT
BUT YOU SEEM NICE.
A BIT WEIRD, BUT IT DOESN'T MATTER.
I'M A BIT WEIRD, TOO...
MNH
OH!
SHH..!

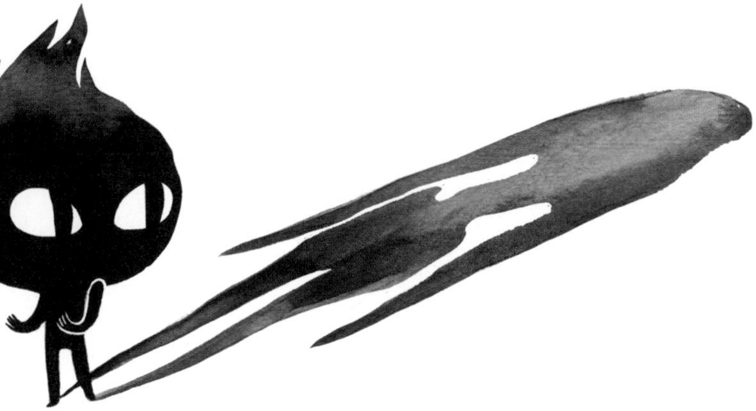

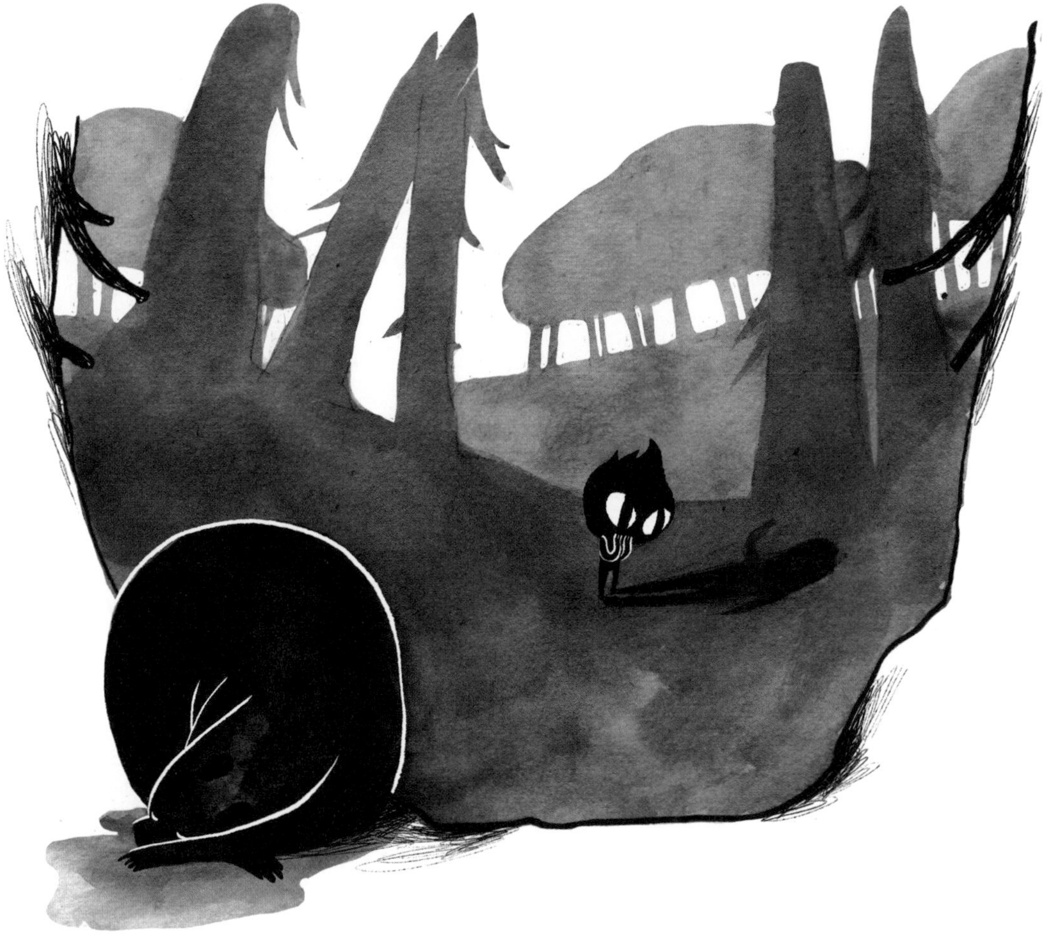

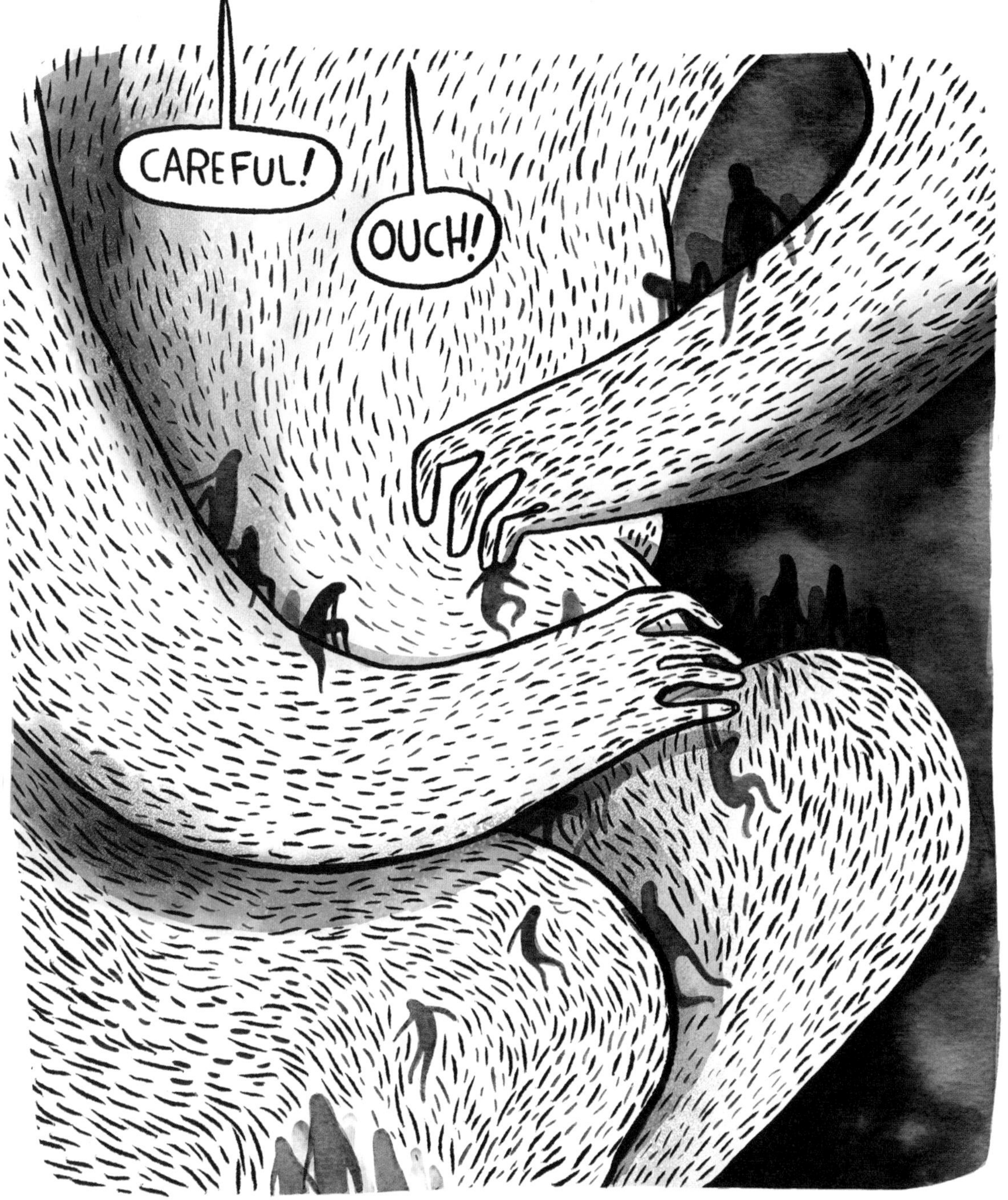
CAREFUL!
OUCH!

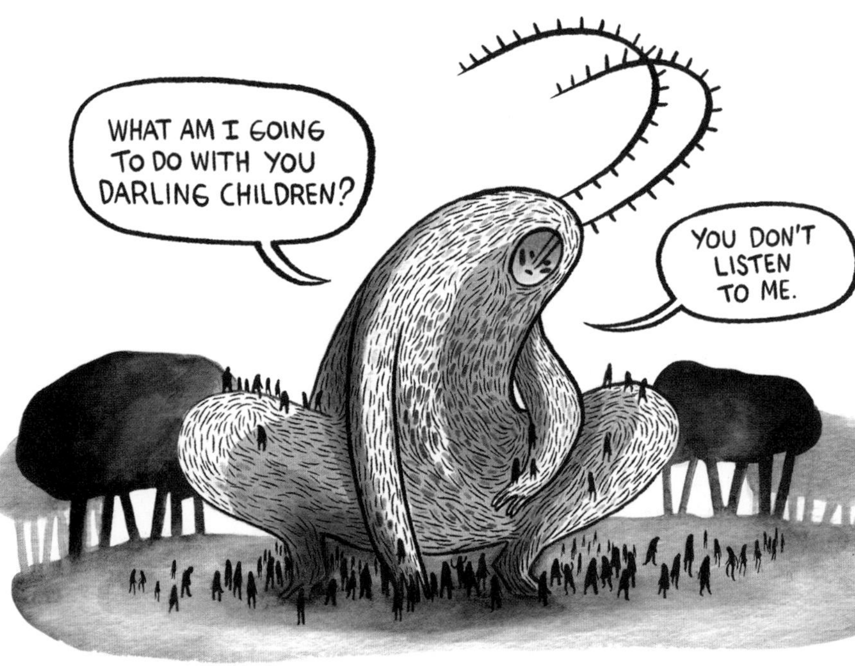
WHAT AM I GOING TO DO WITH YOU DARLING CHILDREN?
YOU DON'T LISTEN TO ME.

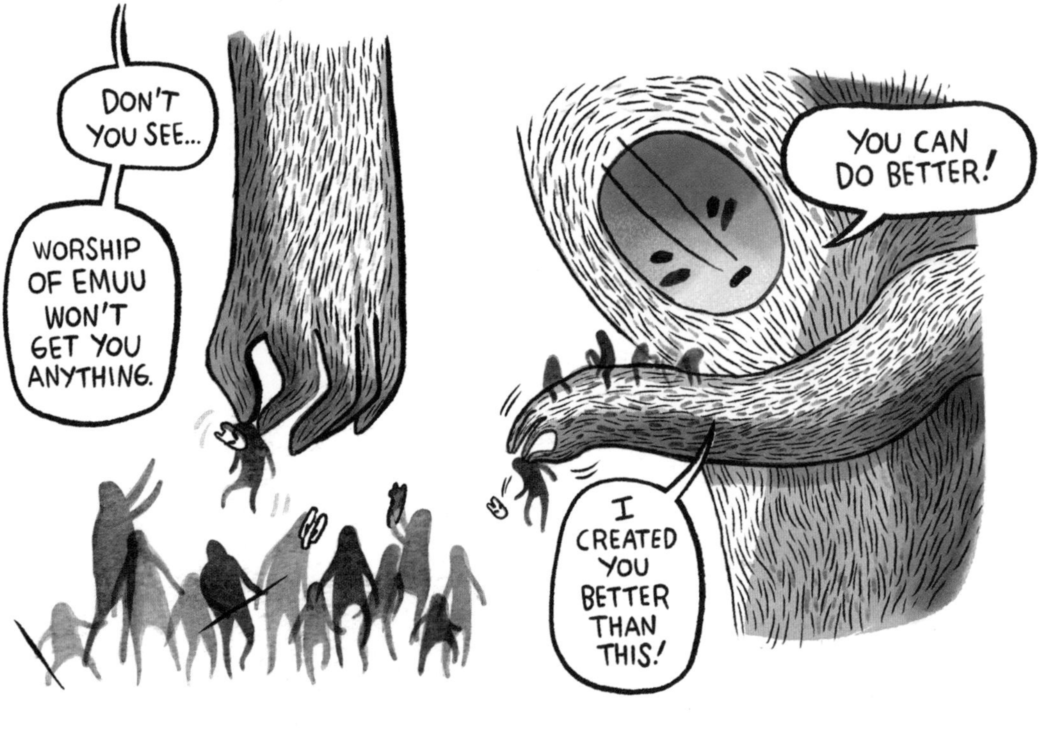
DON'T YOU SEE...
WORSHIP OF EMUU WON'T GET YOU ANYTHING.
YOU CAN DO BETTER!
I CREATED YOU BETTER THAN THIS!

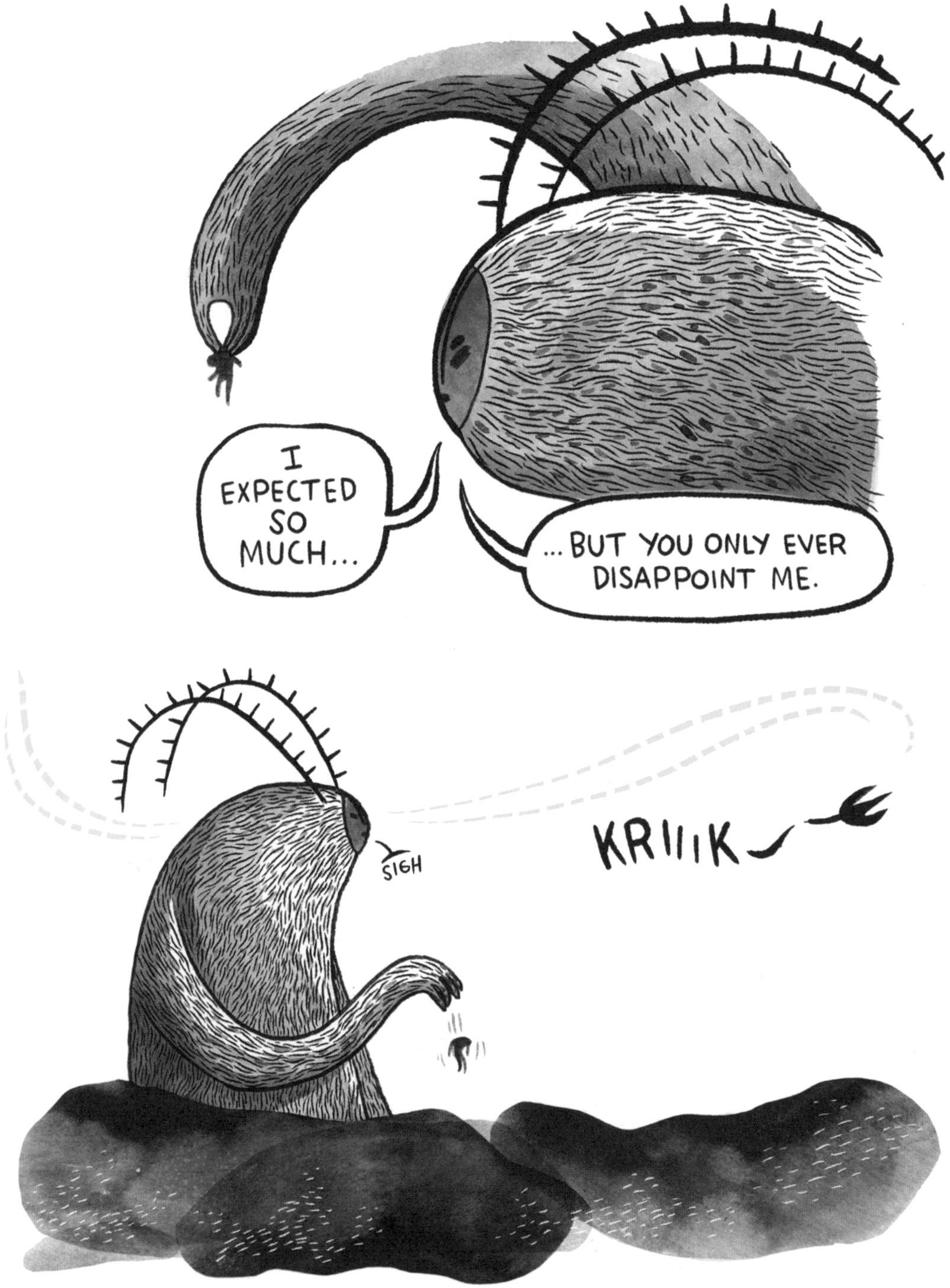
I EXPECTED SO MUCH...
...BUT YOU ONLY EVER DISAPPOINT ME.
SIGH
KRIIIK

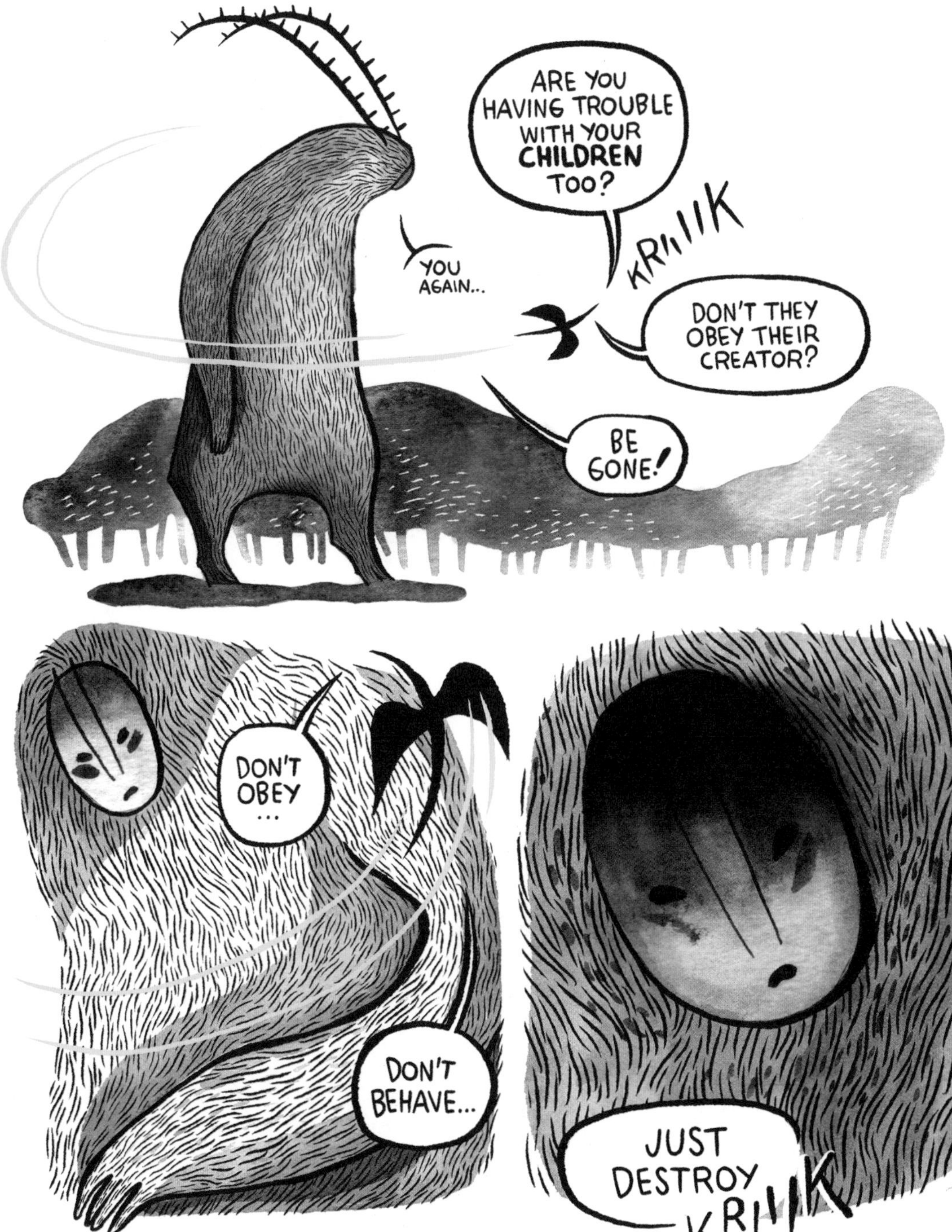
ARE YOU HAVING TROUBLE WITH YOUR **CHILDREN** TOO?
YOU AGAIN...
KRIIIK
DON'T THEY OBEY THEIR CREATOR?
BE GONE!
DON'T OBEY ...
DON'T BEHAVE...
JUST DESTROY
KRIIIK

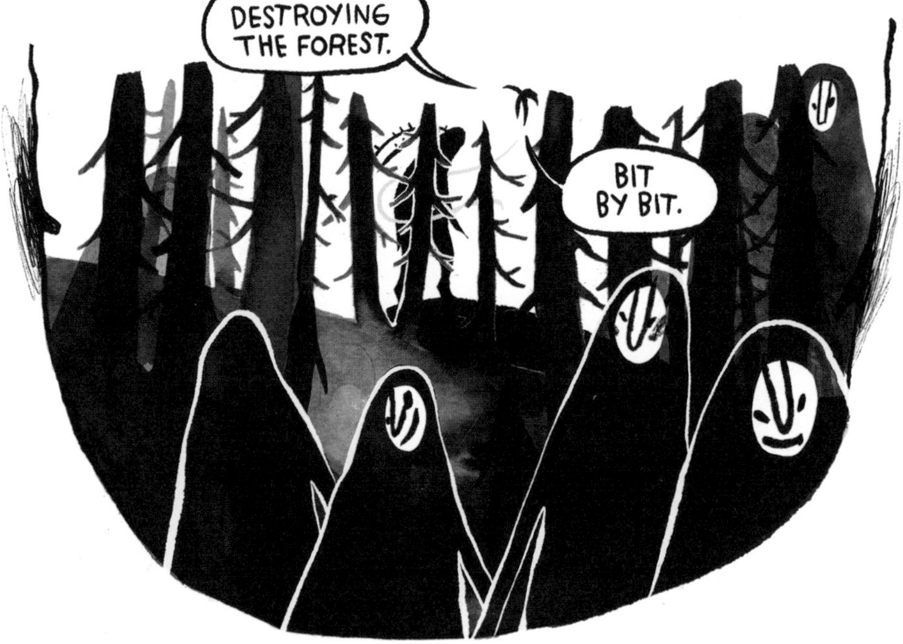
DESTROYING THE FOREST.
BIT BY BIT.

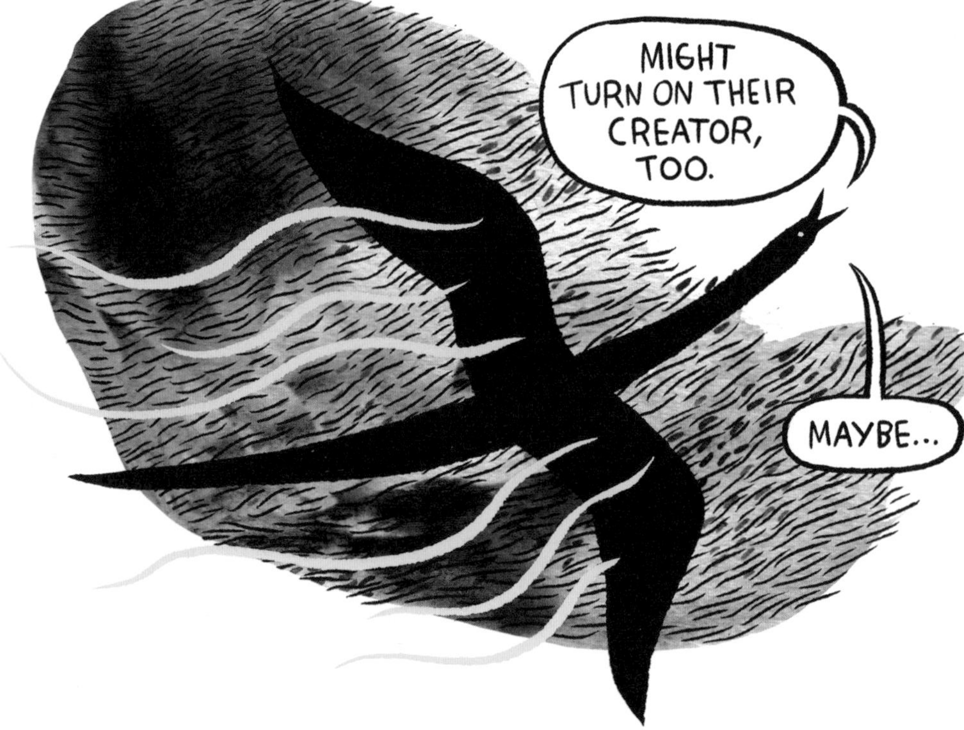
MIGHT TURN ON THEIR CREATOR, TOO.
MAYBE...

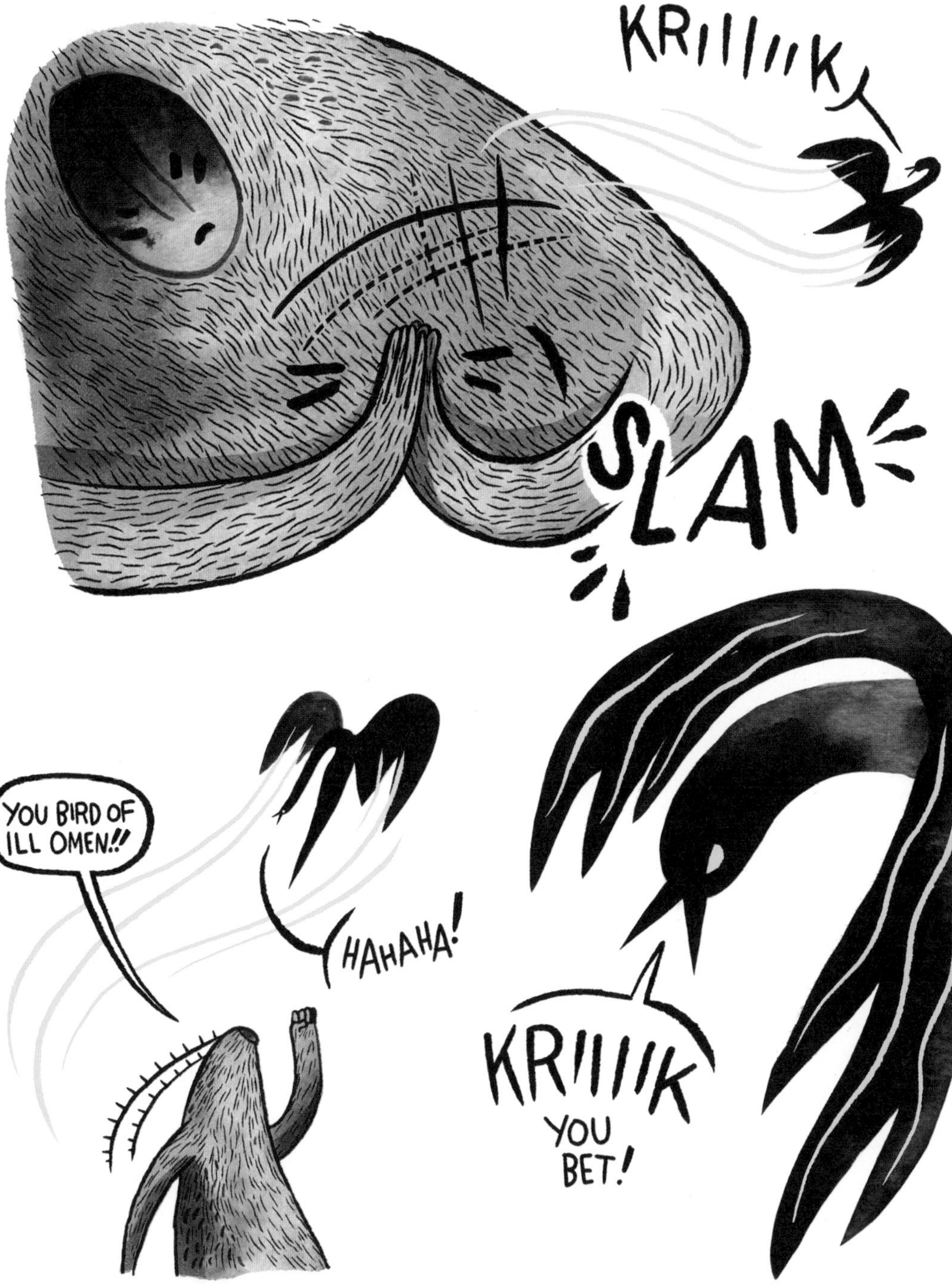
KRIIIIIK
SLAM
YOU BIRD OF ILL OMEN!!
HAHAHA!
KRIIIIK
YOU BET!

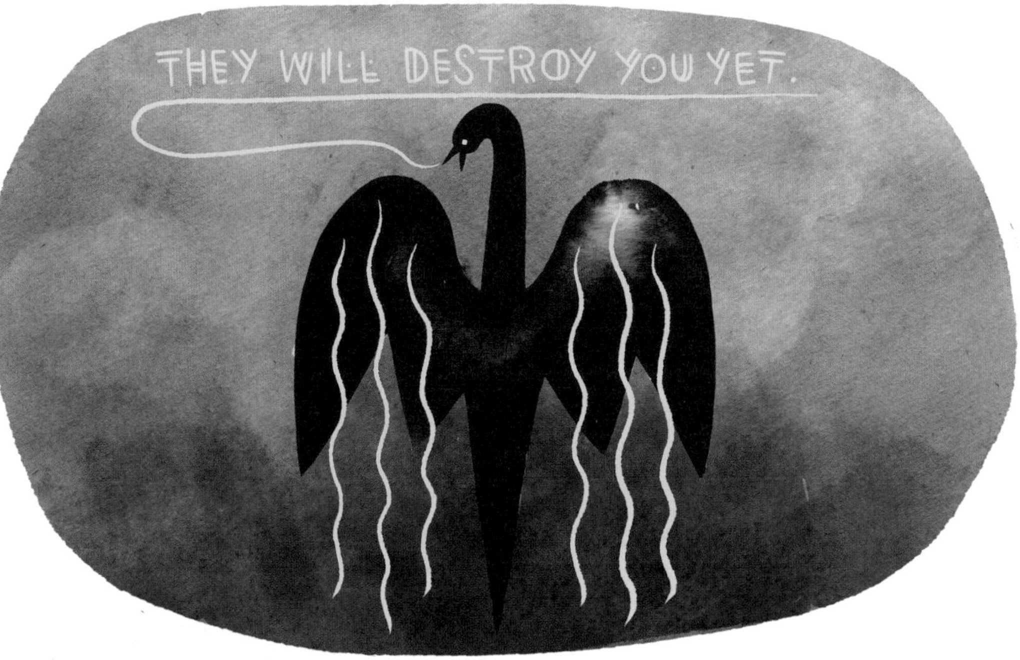
THEY WILL DESTROY YOU YET.

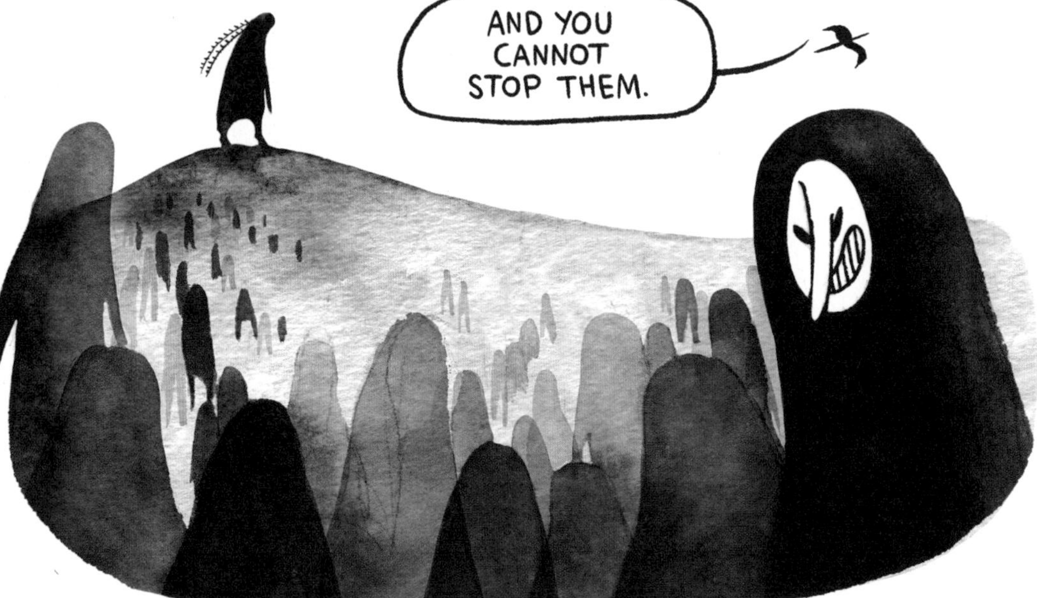
AND YOU CANNOT STOP THEM.

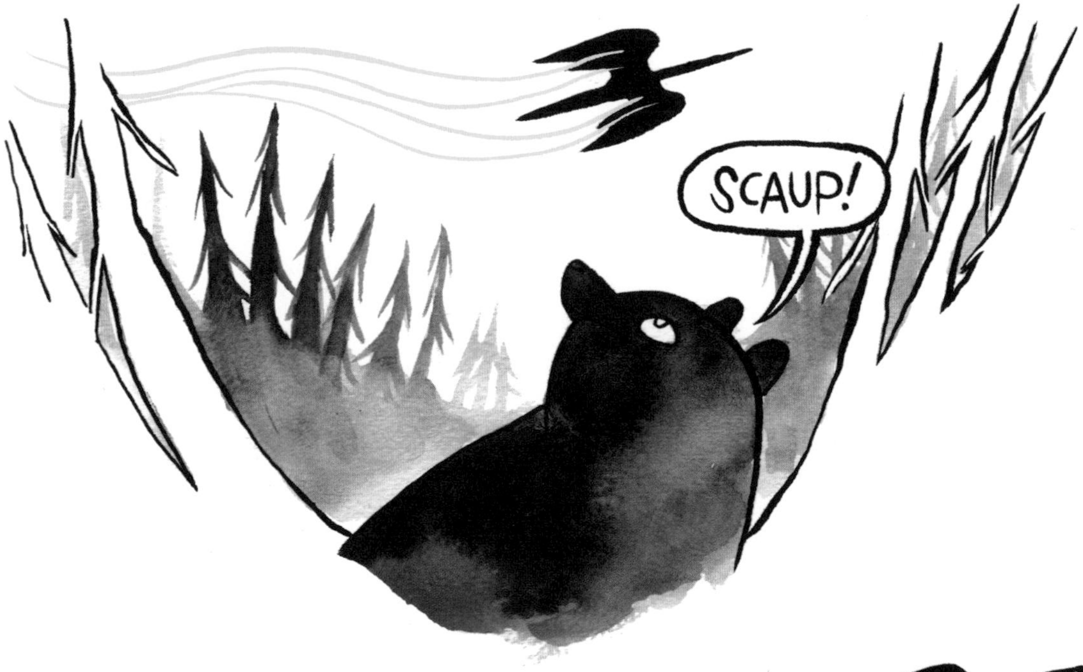
SCAUP!

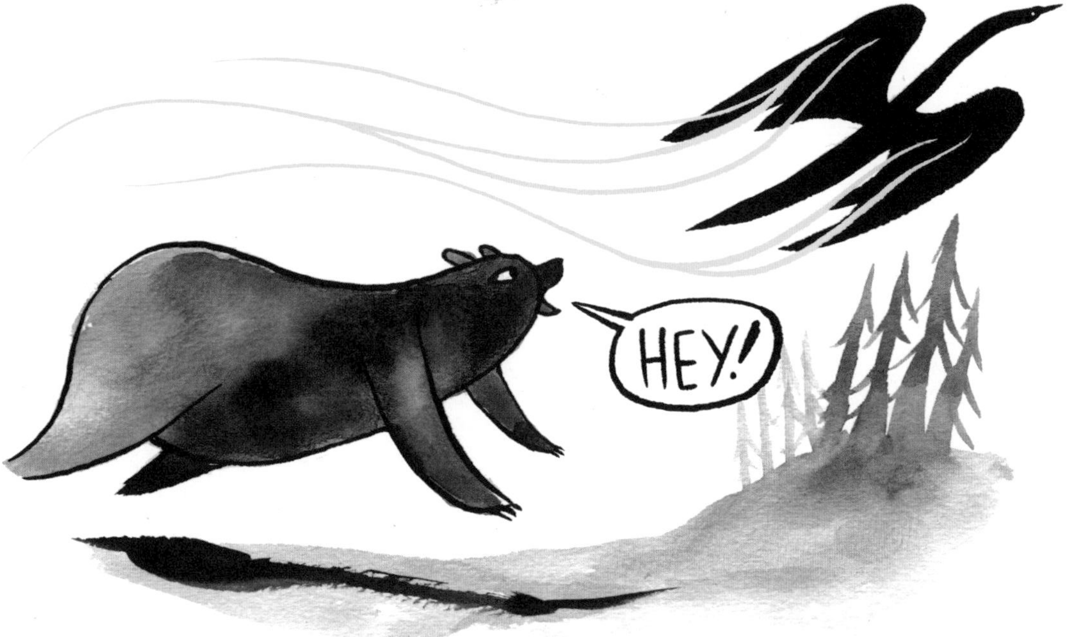
HEY!

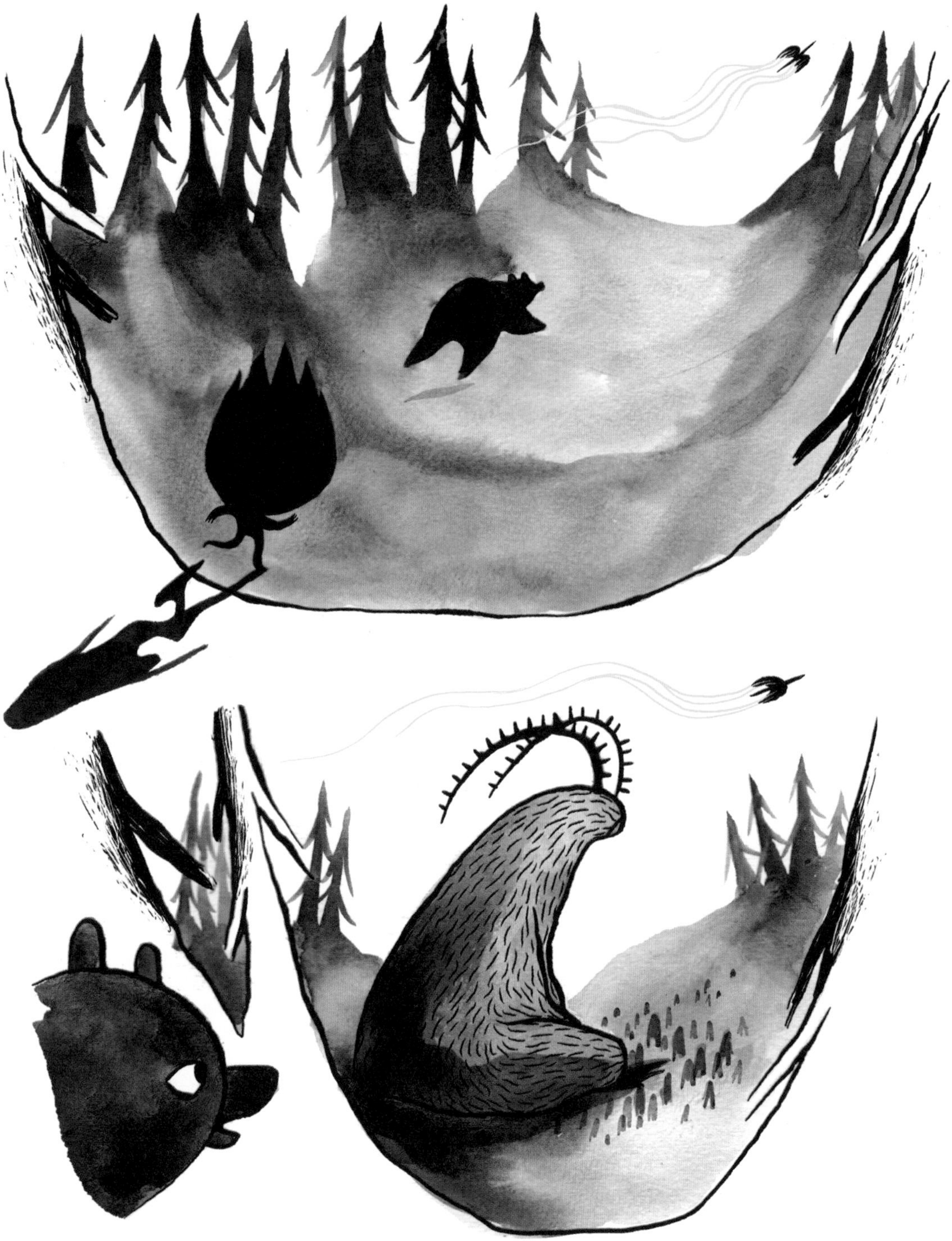

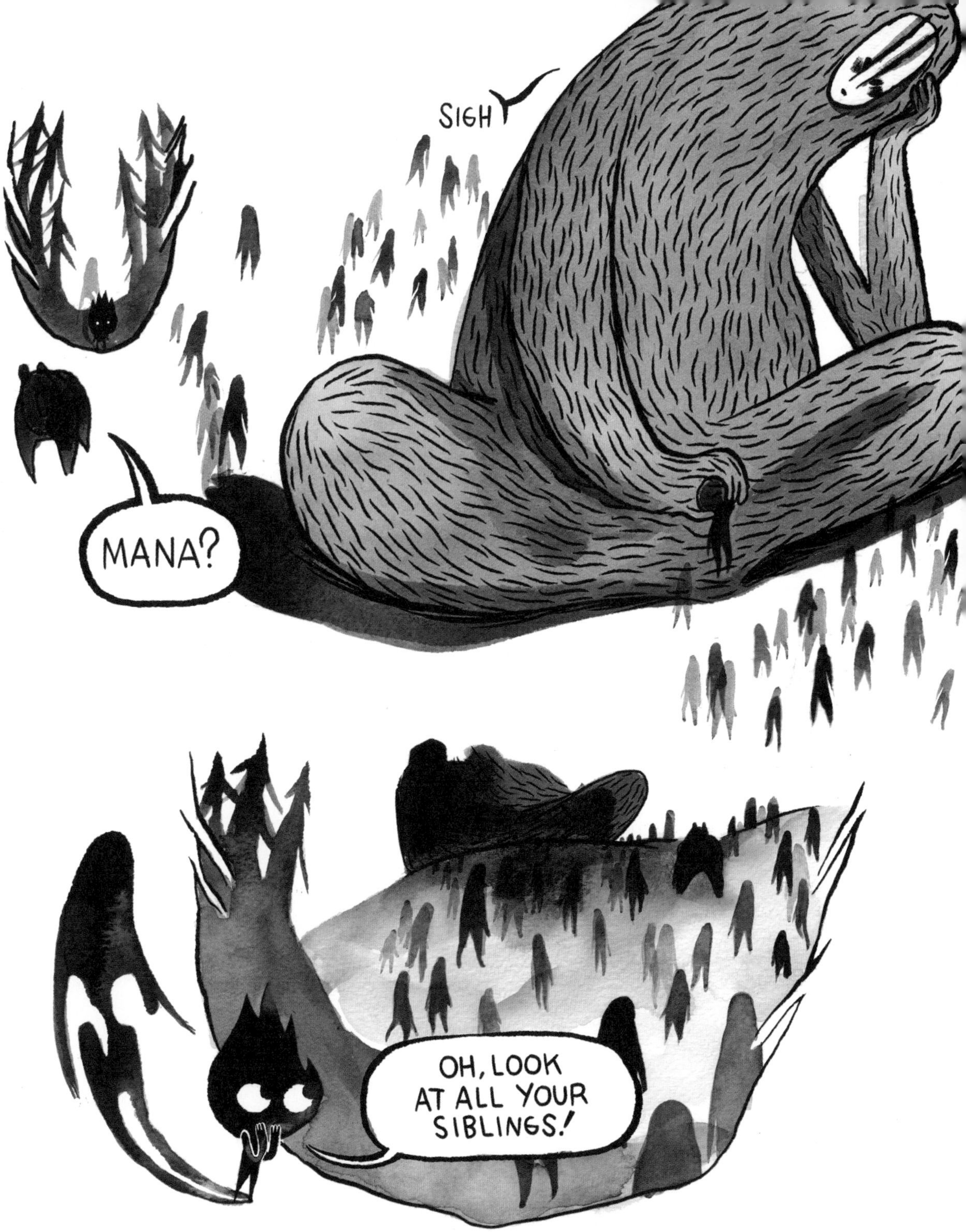
SIGH
MANA?
OH, LOOK AT ALL YOUR SIBLINGS!

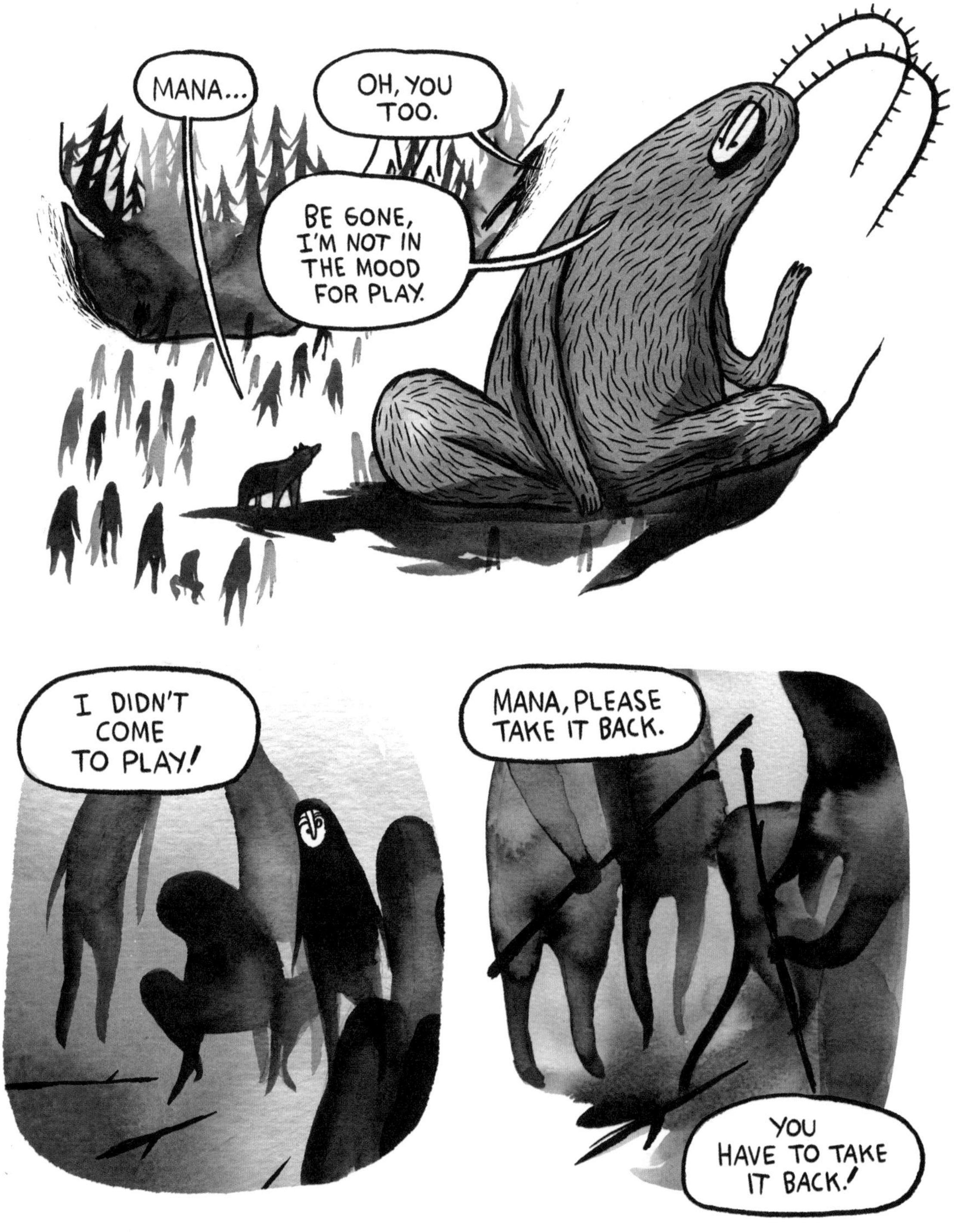
MANA...
OH, YOU TOO.
BE GONE, I'M NOT IN THE MOOD FOR PLAY.
I DIDN'T COME TO PLAY!
MANA, PLEASE TAKE IT BACK.
YOU HAVE TO TAKE IT BACK!

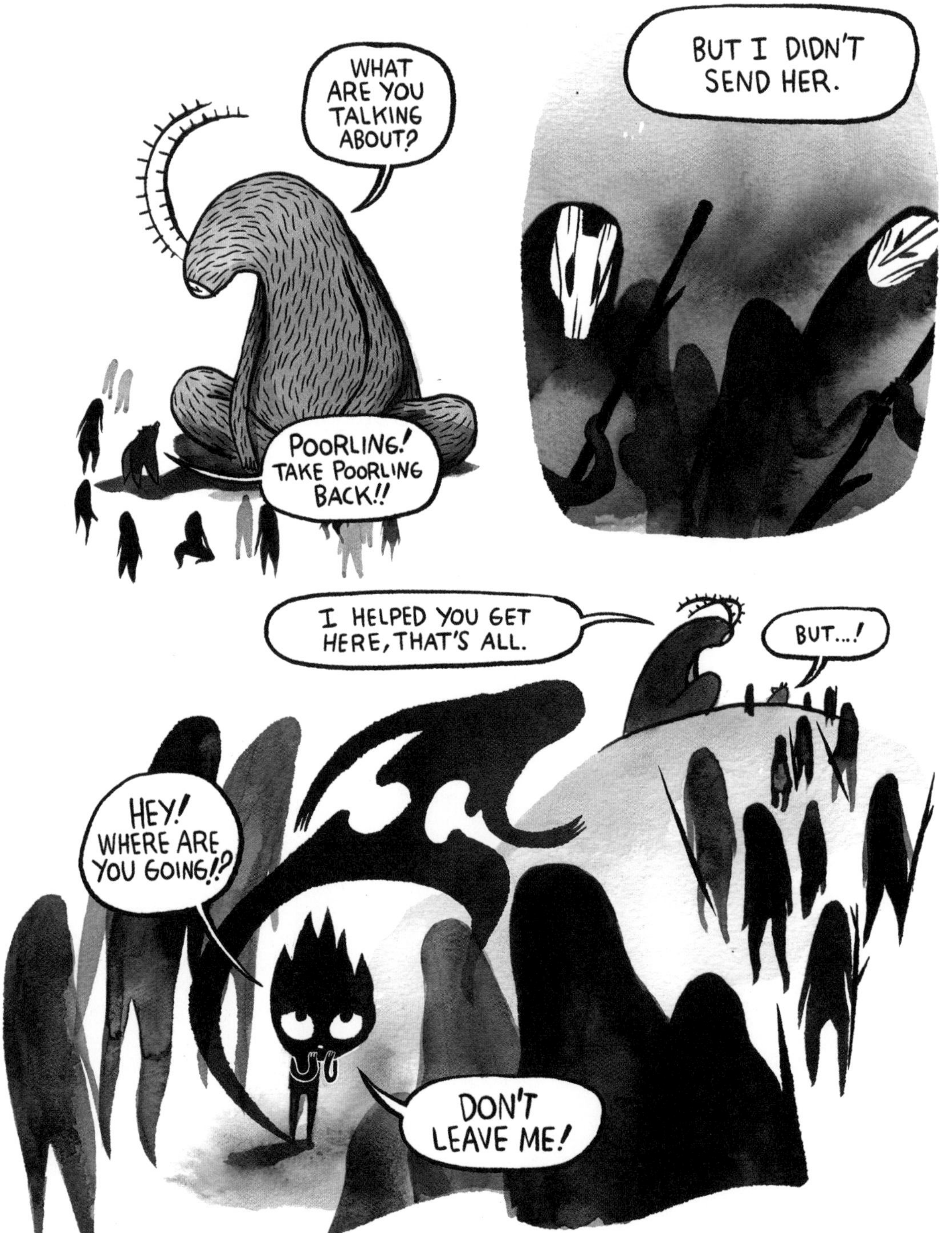
WHAT ARE YOU TALKING ABOUT?
POORLING! TAKE POORLING BACK!!
BUT I DIDN'T SEND HER.
I HELPED YOU GET HERE, THAT'S ALL.
BUT...!
HEY! WHERE ARE YOU GOING!?
DON'T LEAVE ME!

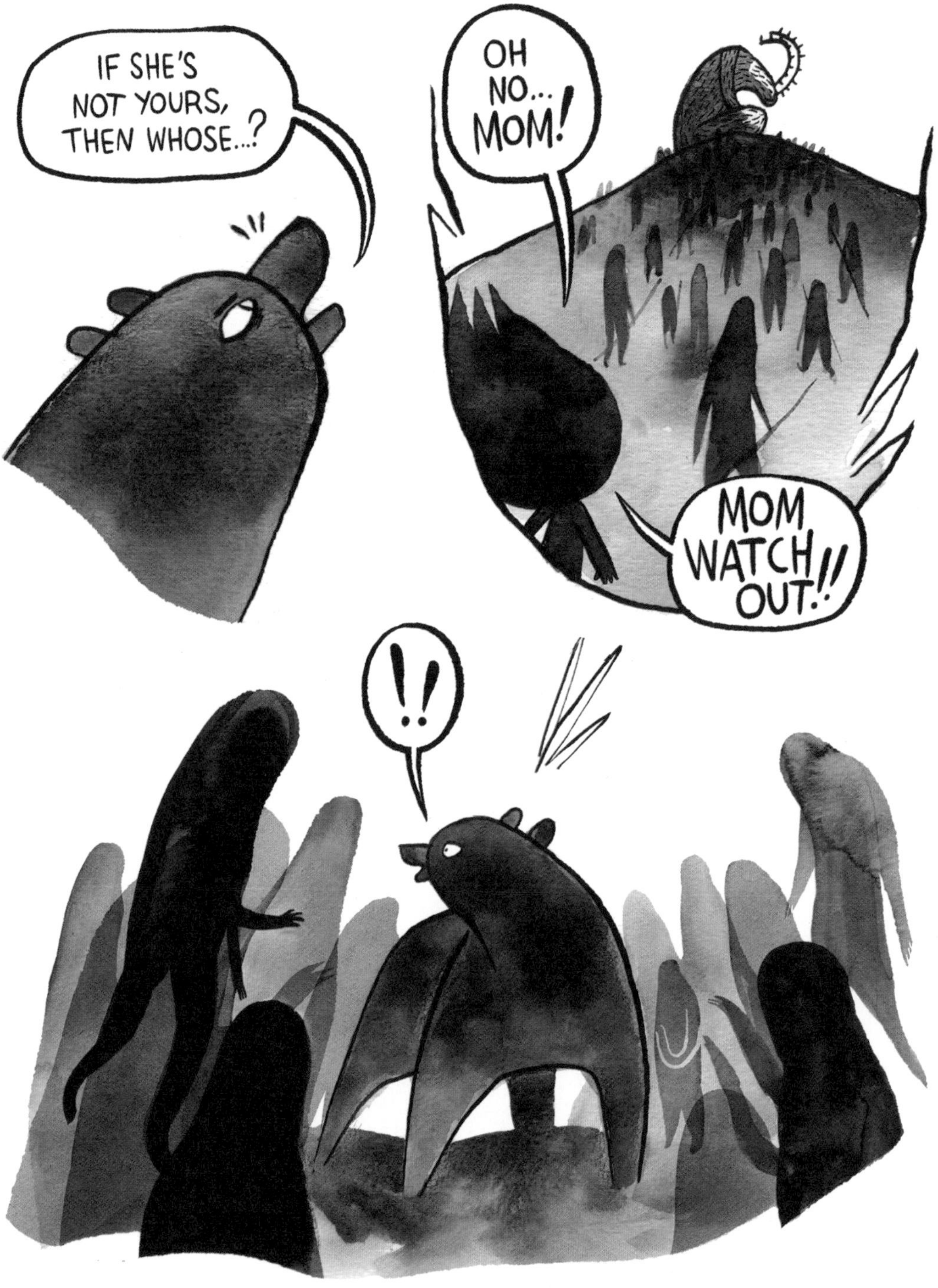
IF SHE'S NOT YOURS, THEN WHOSE...?
OH NO... MOM!
MOM WATCH OUT!!
!!

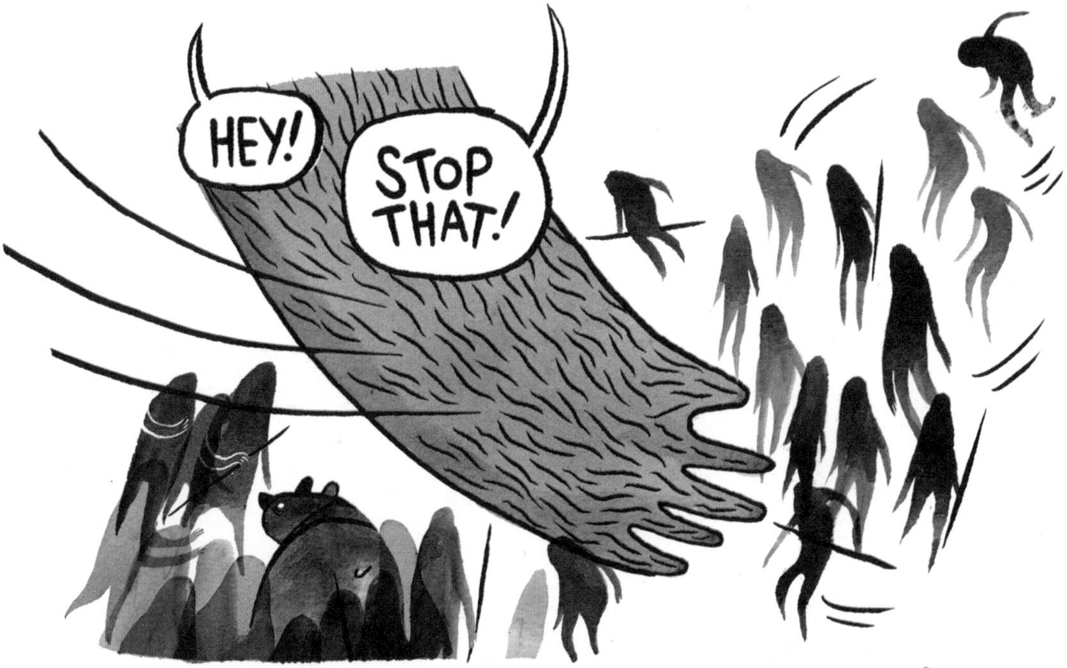
HEY!
STOP THAT!

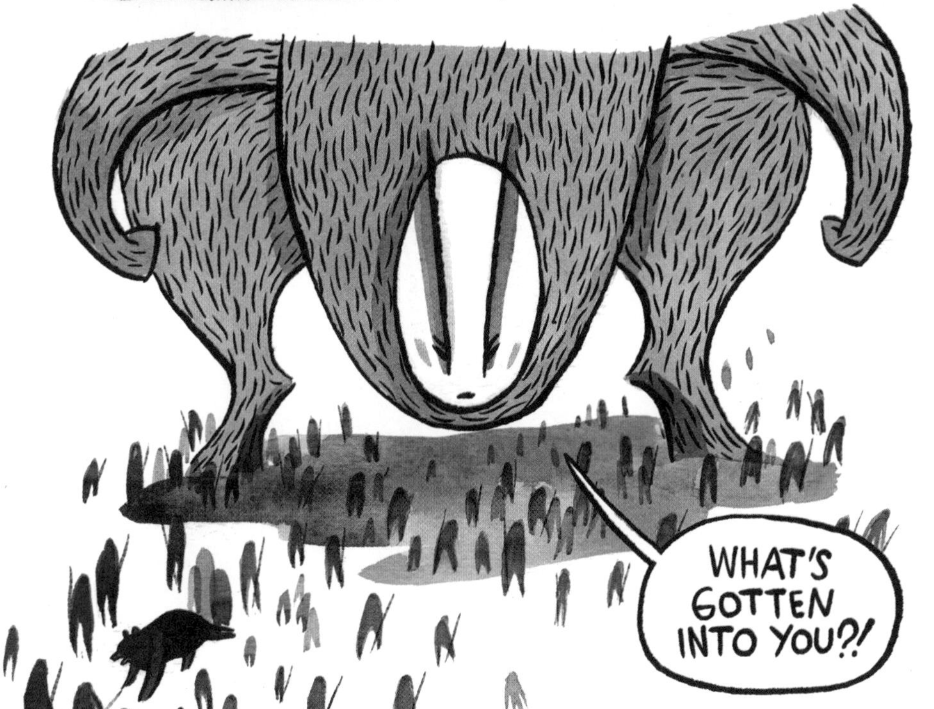
WHAT'S GOTTEN INTO YOU?!

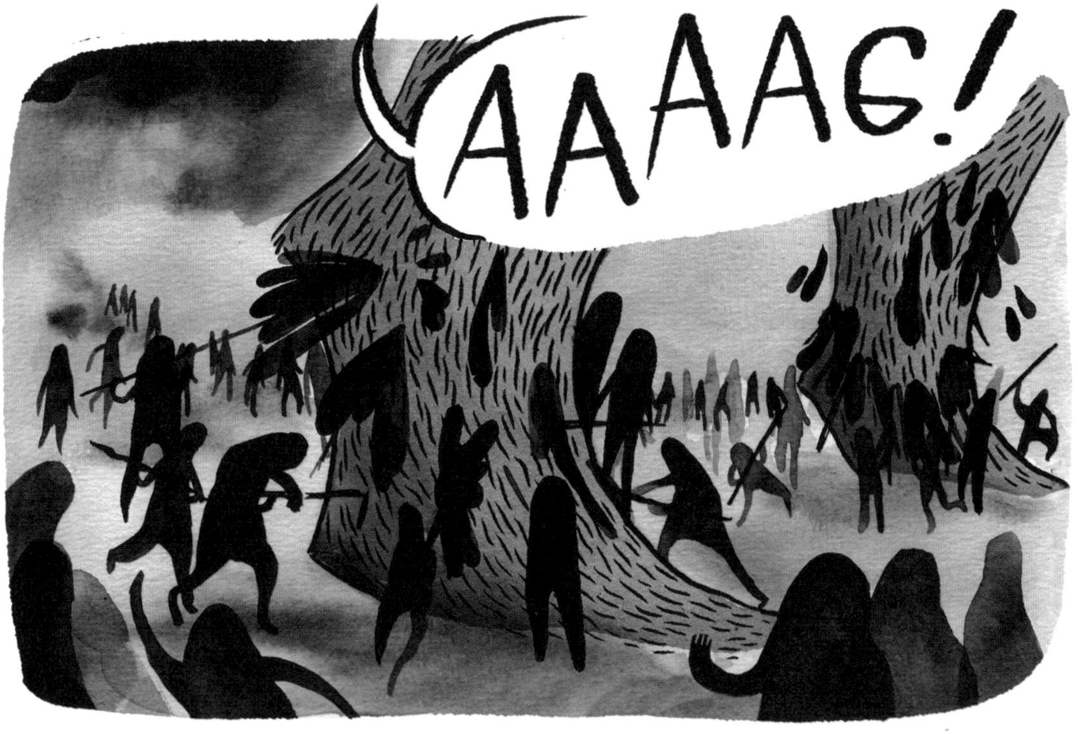
AAAAG!

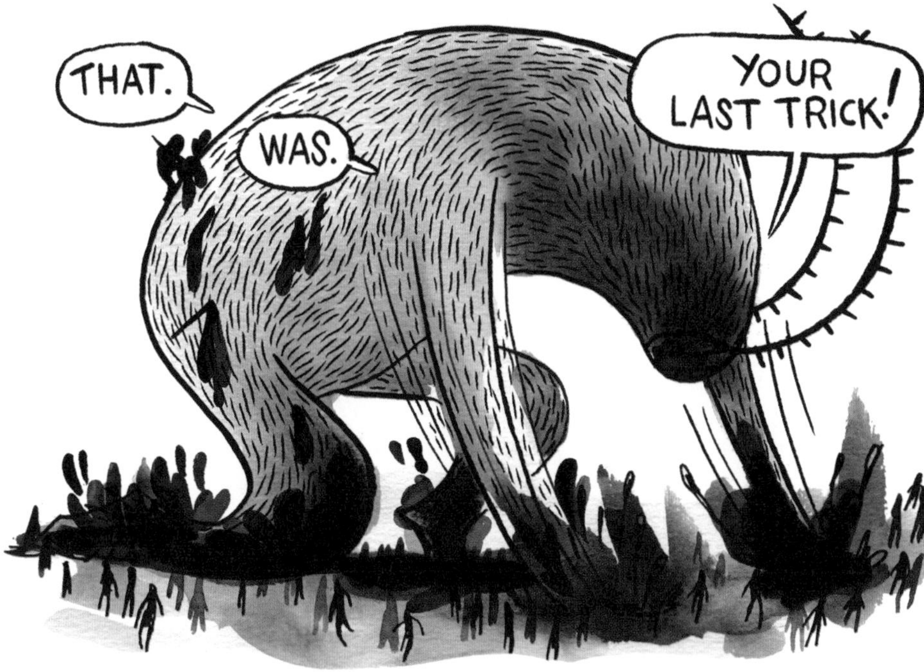
THAT.
WAS.
YOUR LAST TRICK!

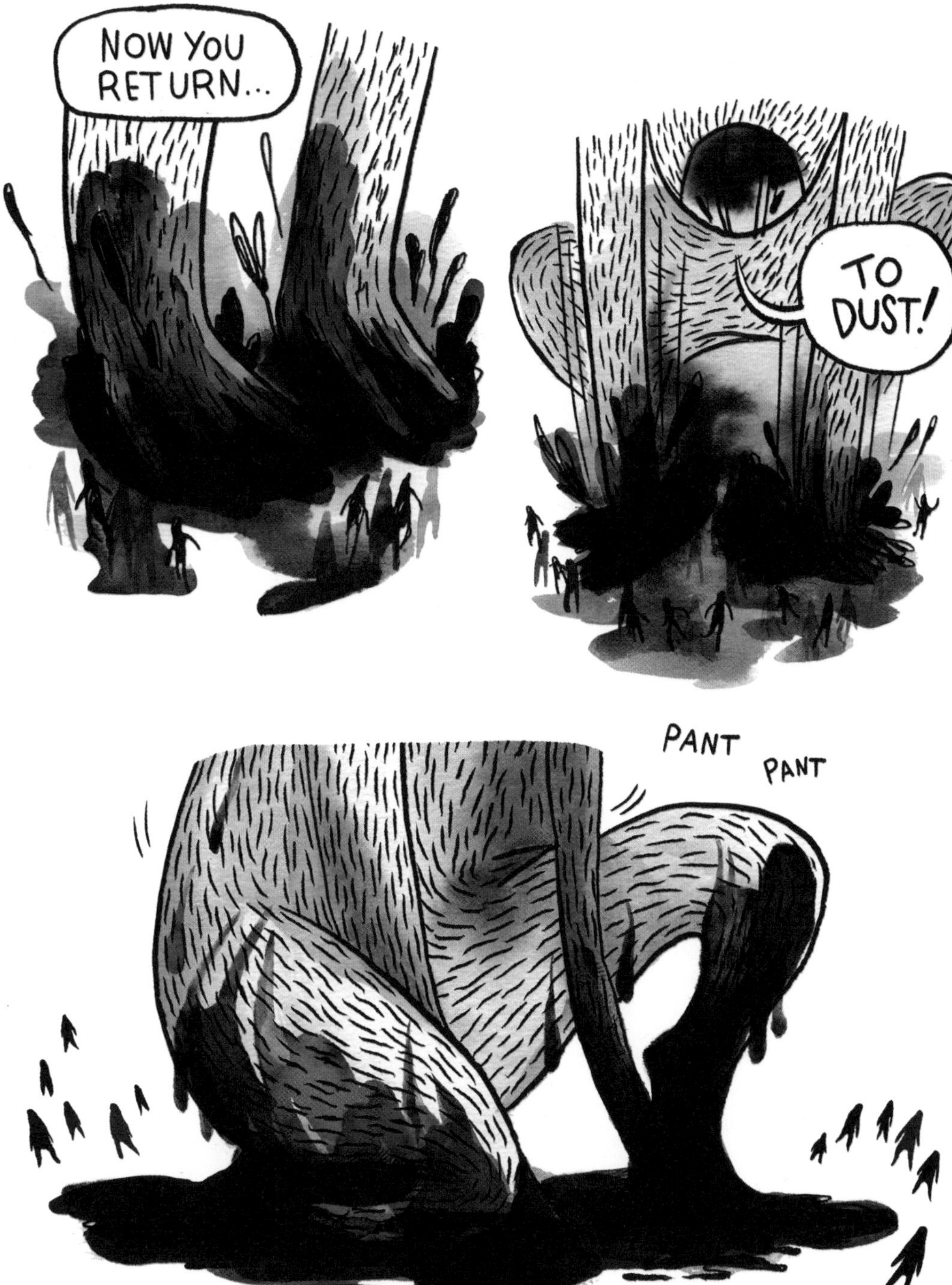
NOW YOU RETURN...
TO DUST!
PANT
PANT

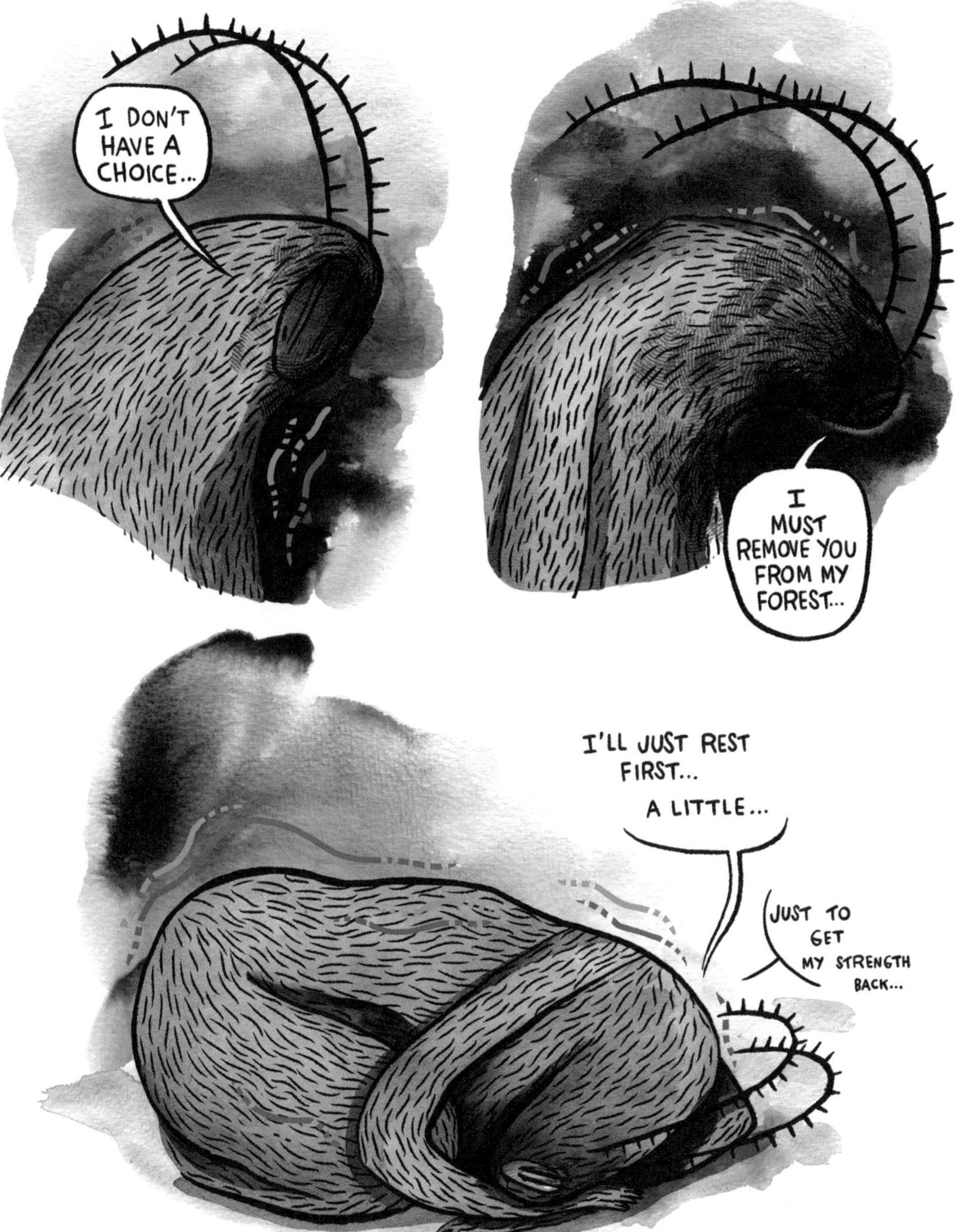

I DON'T HAVE A CHOICE...
I MUST REMOVE YOU FROM MY FOREST...
I'LL JUST REST FIRST...
A LITTLE...
JUST TO GET MY STRENGTH BACK...

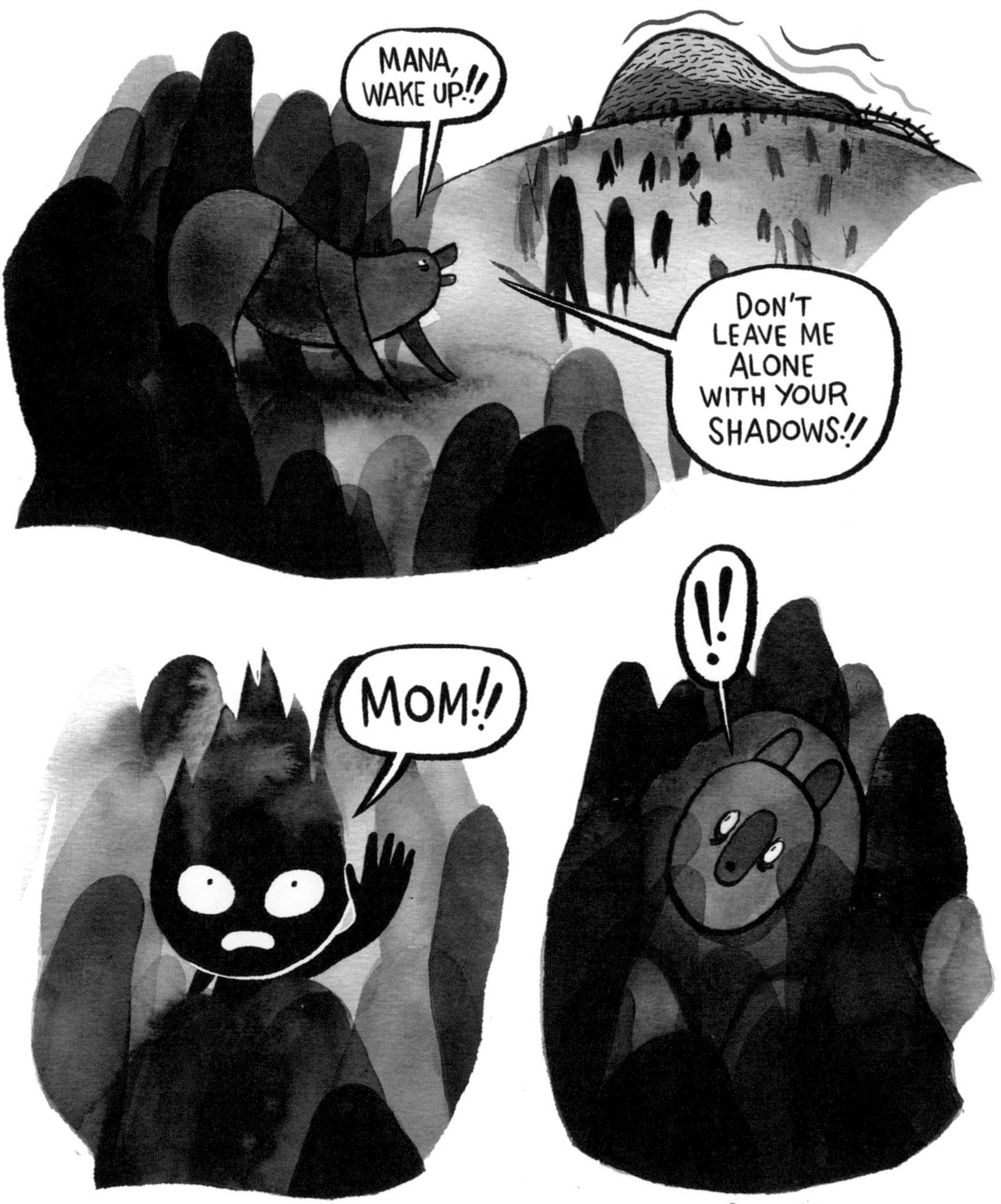
MANA, WAKE UP!!
DON'T LEAVE ME ALONE WITH YOUR SHADOWS!!
MOM!!
!!

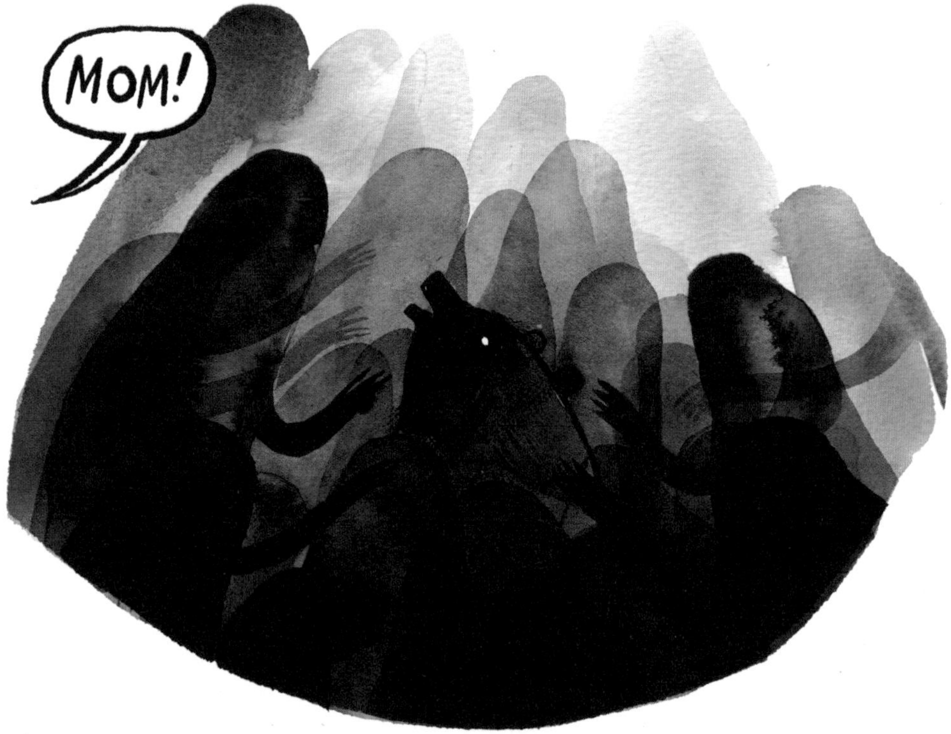
MOM!

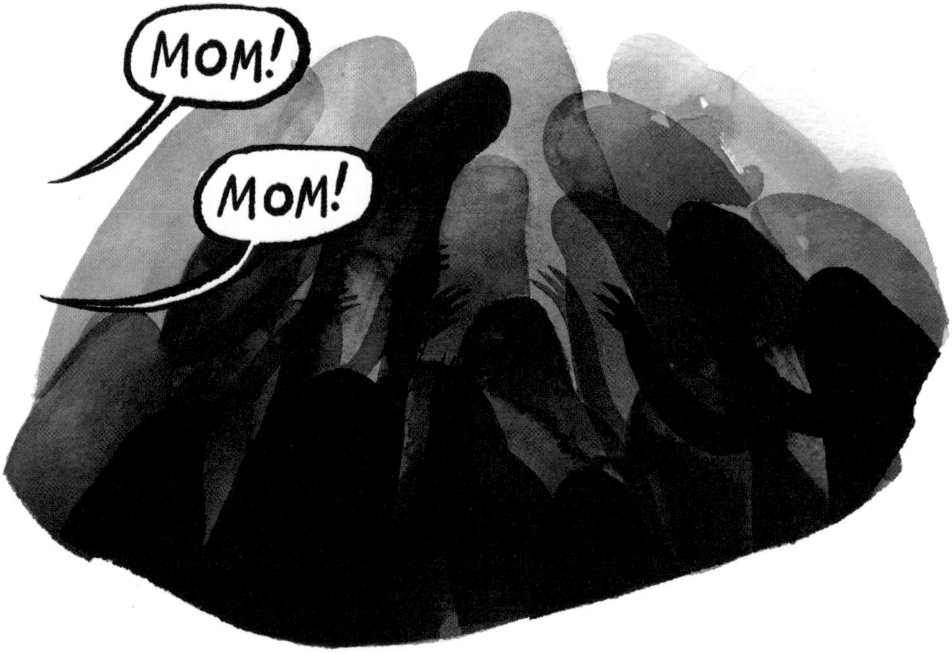
MOM!
MOM!

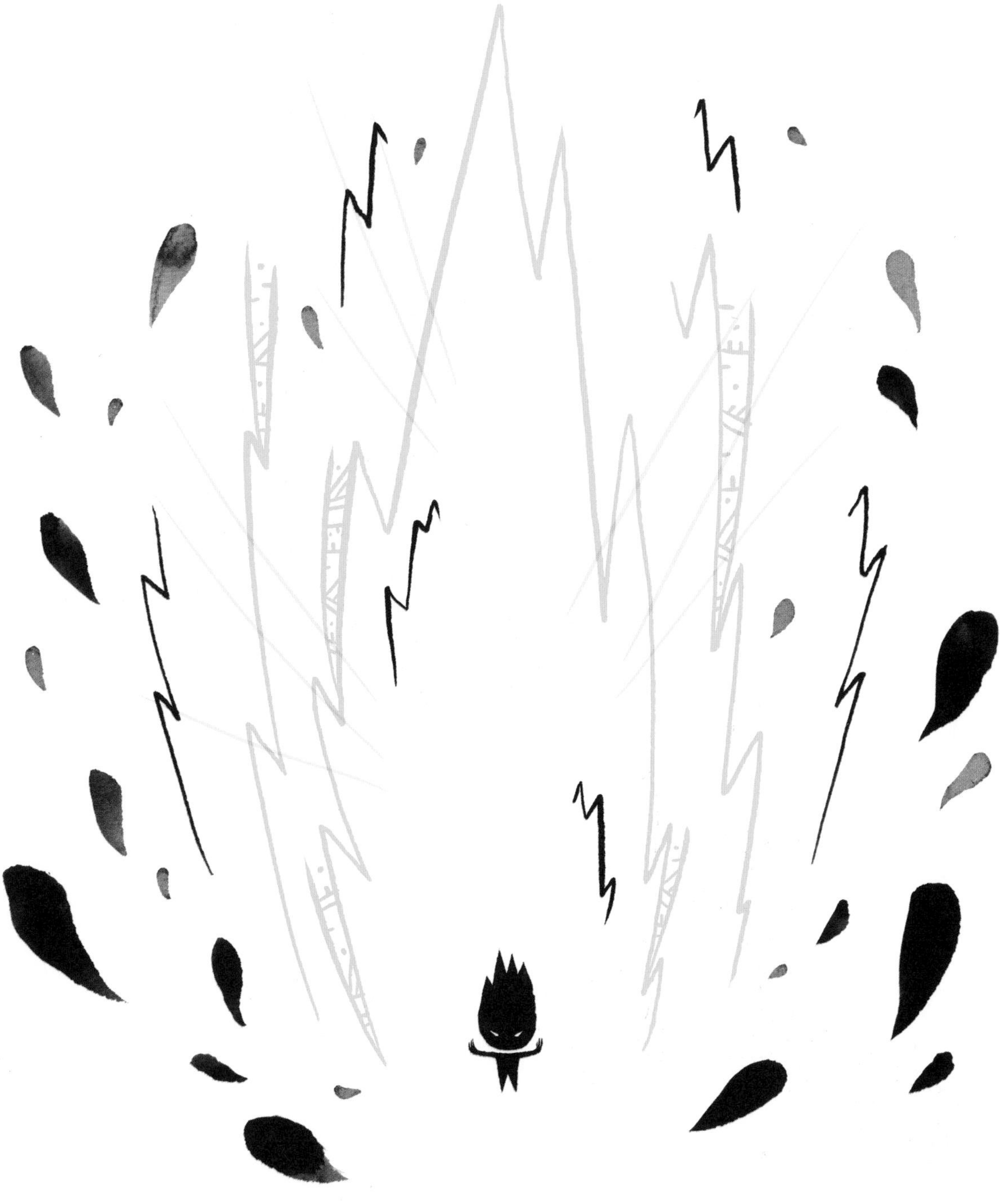

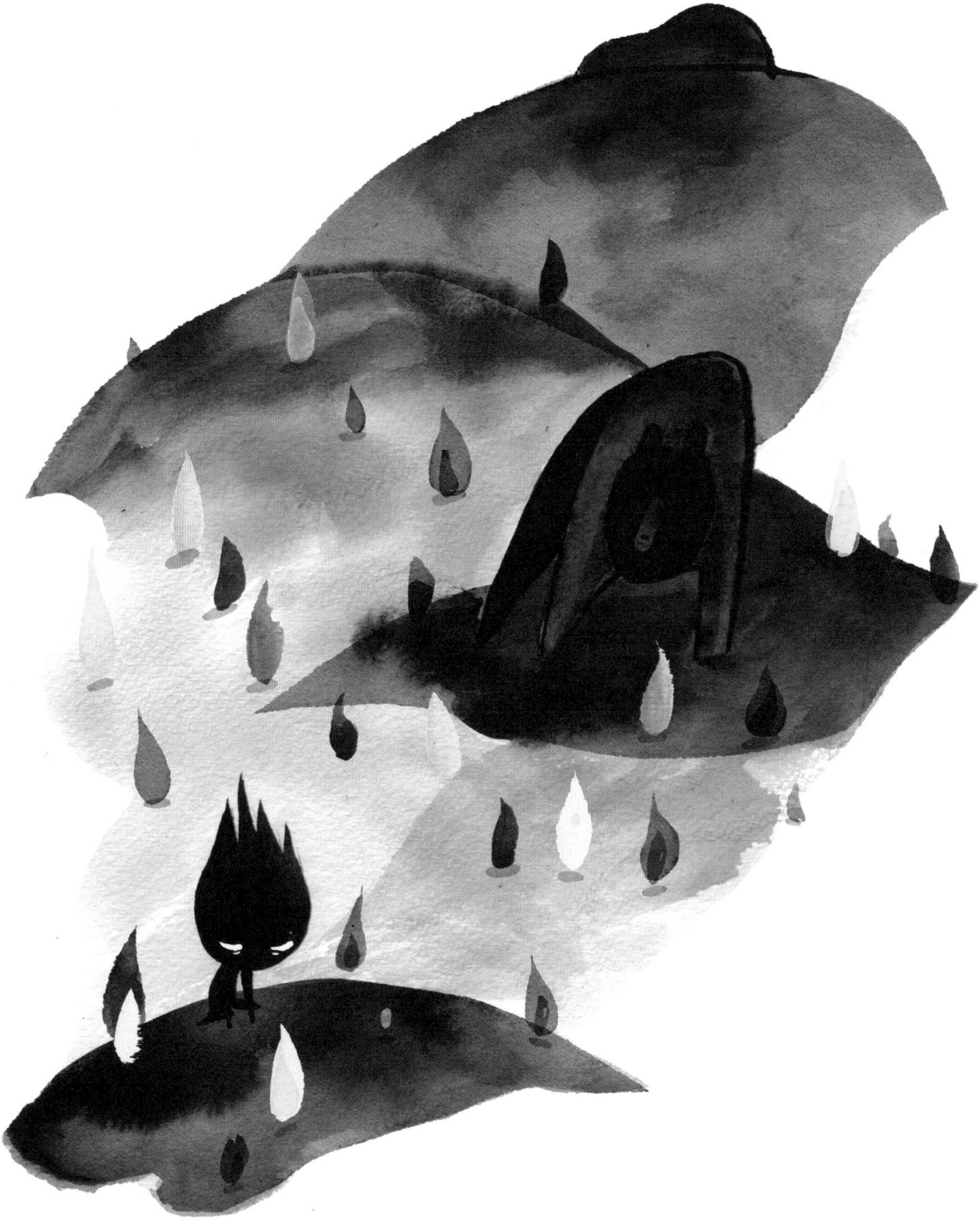

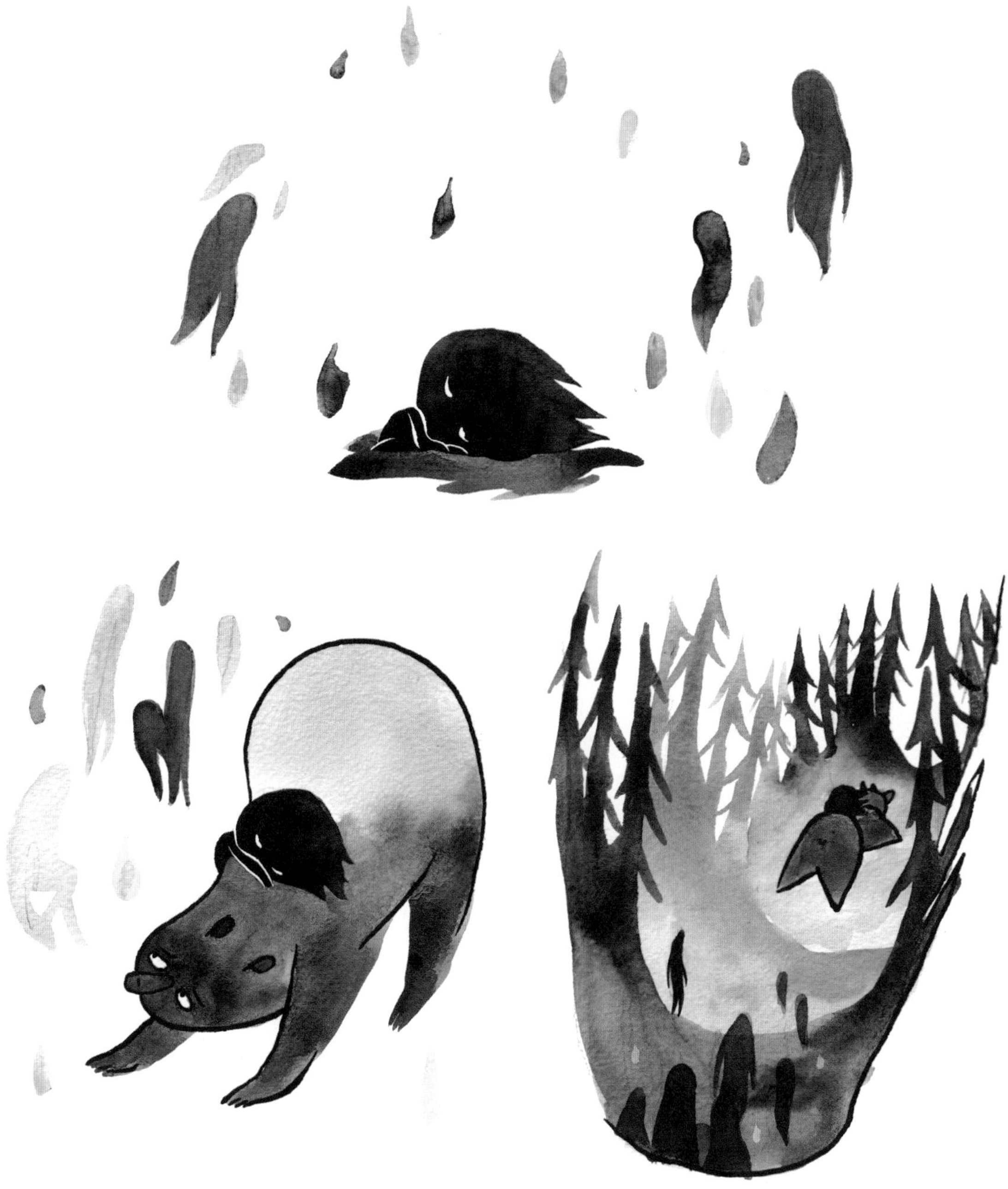

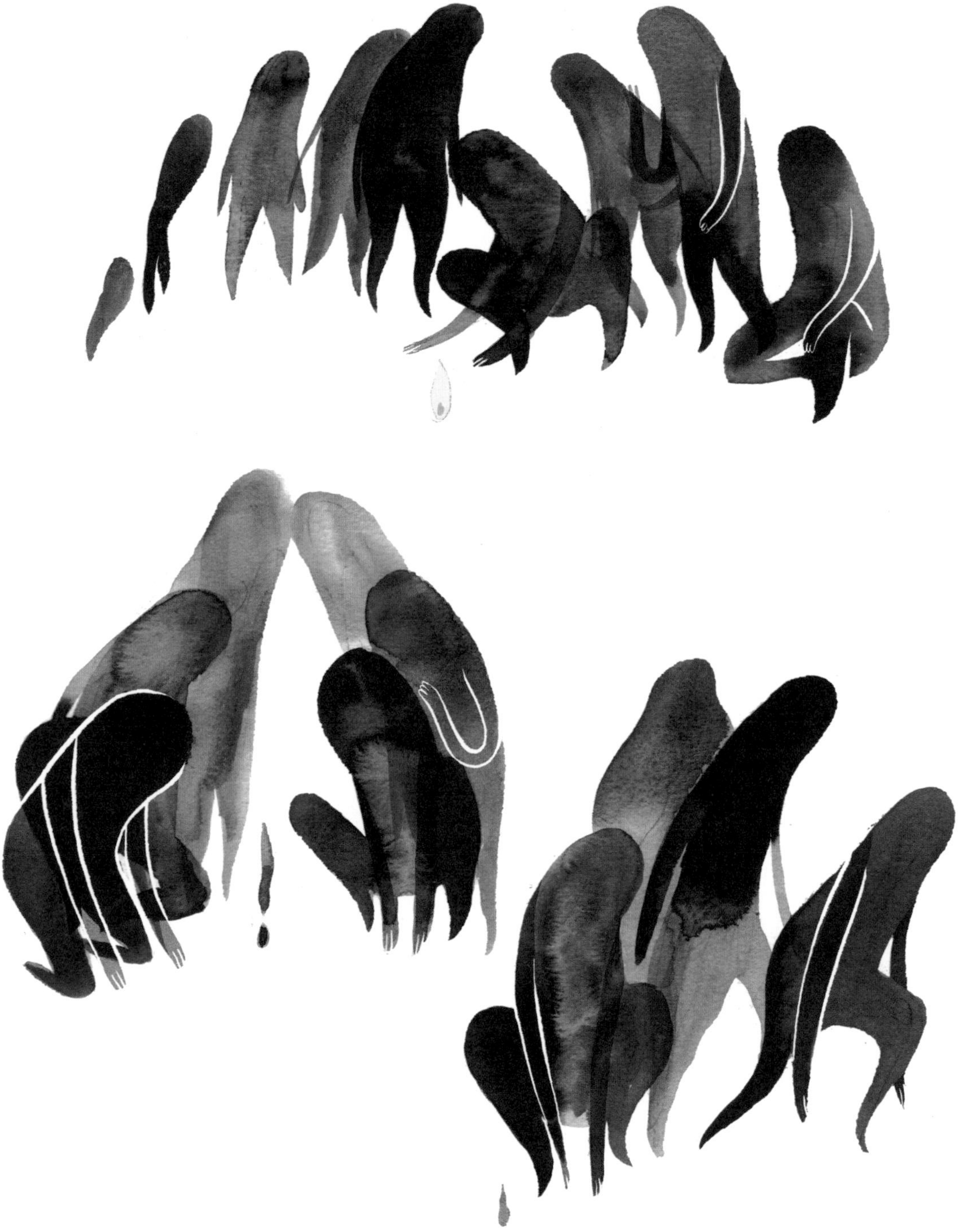

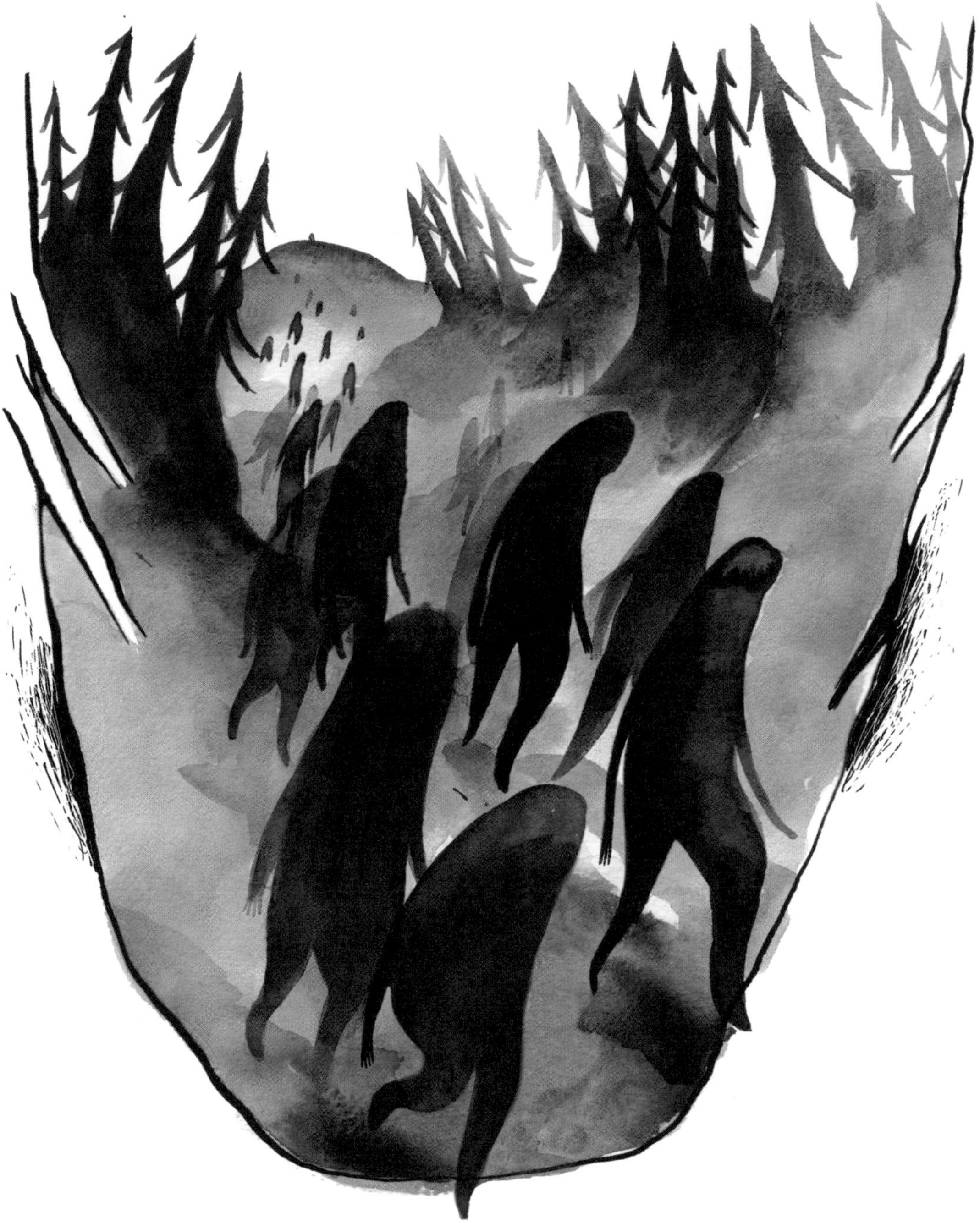

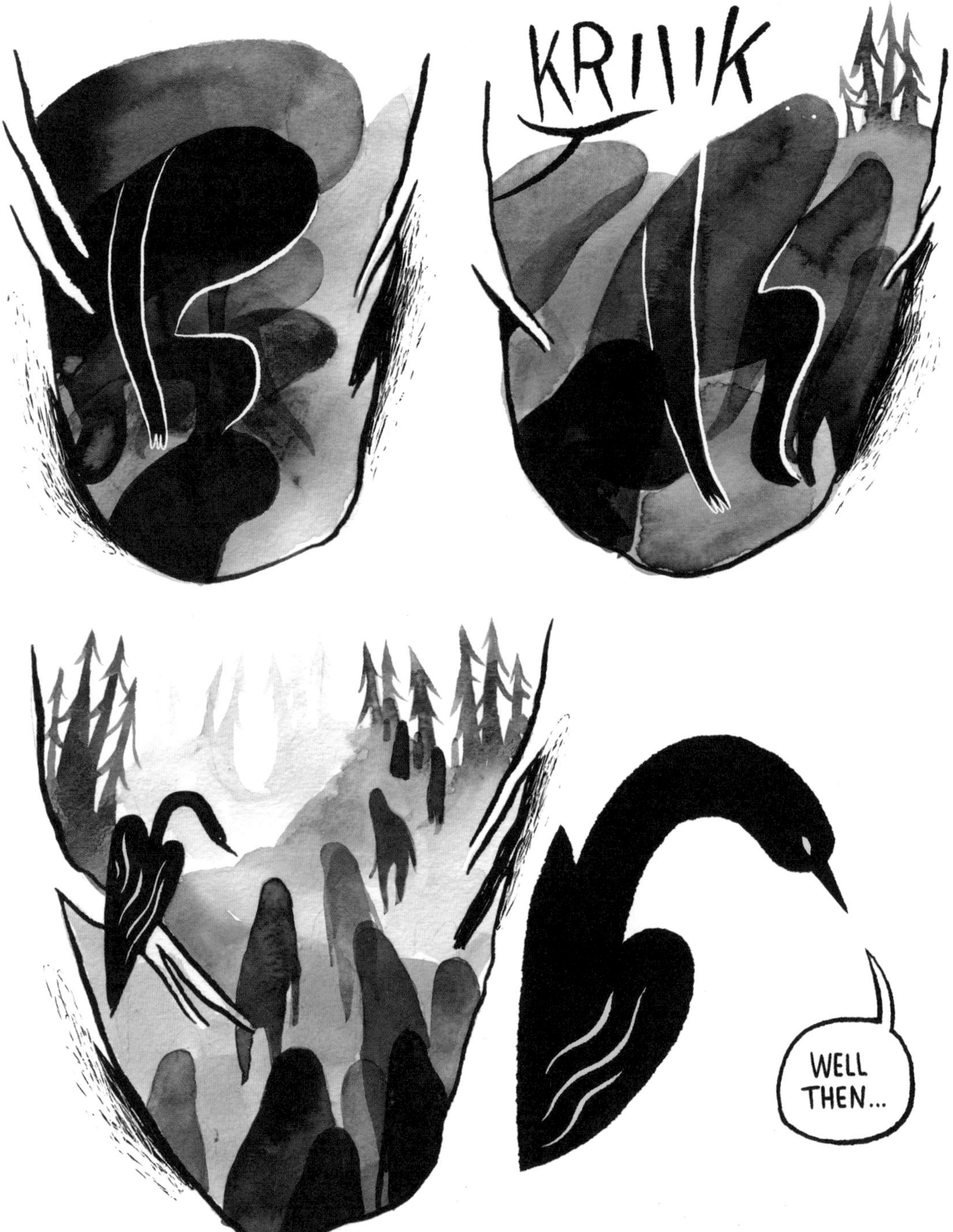
KRIIIK
WELL THEN...

VIII

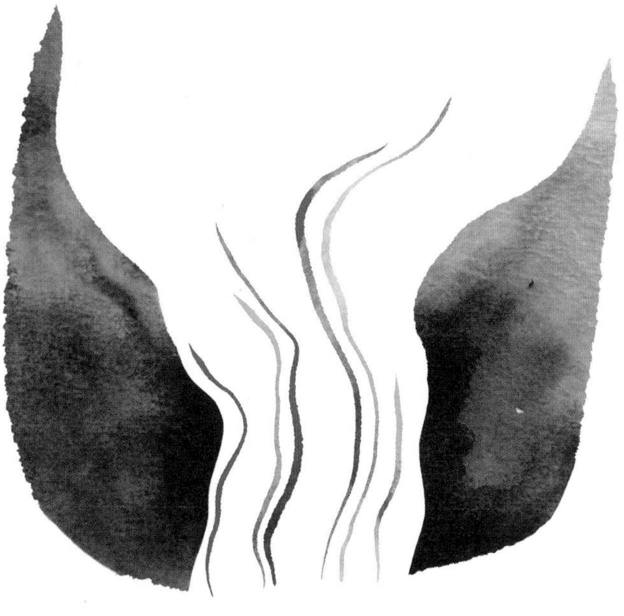

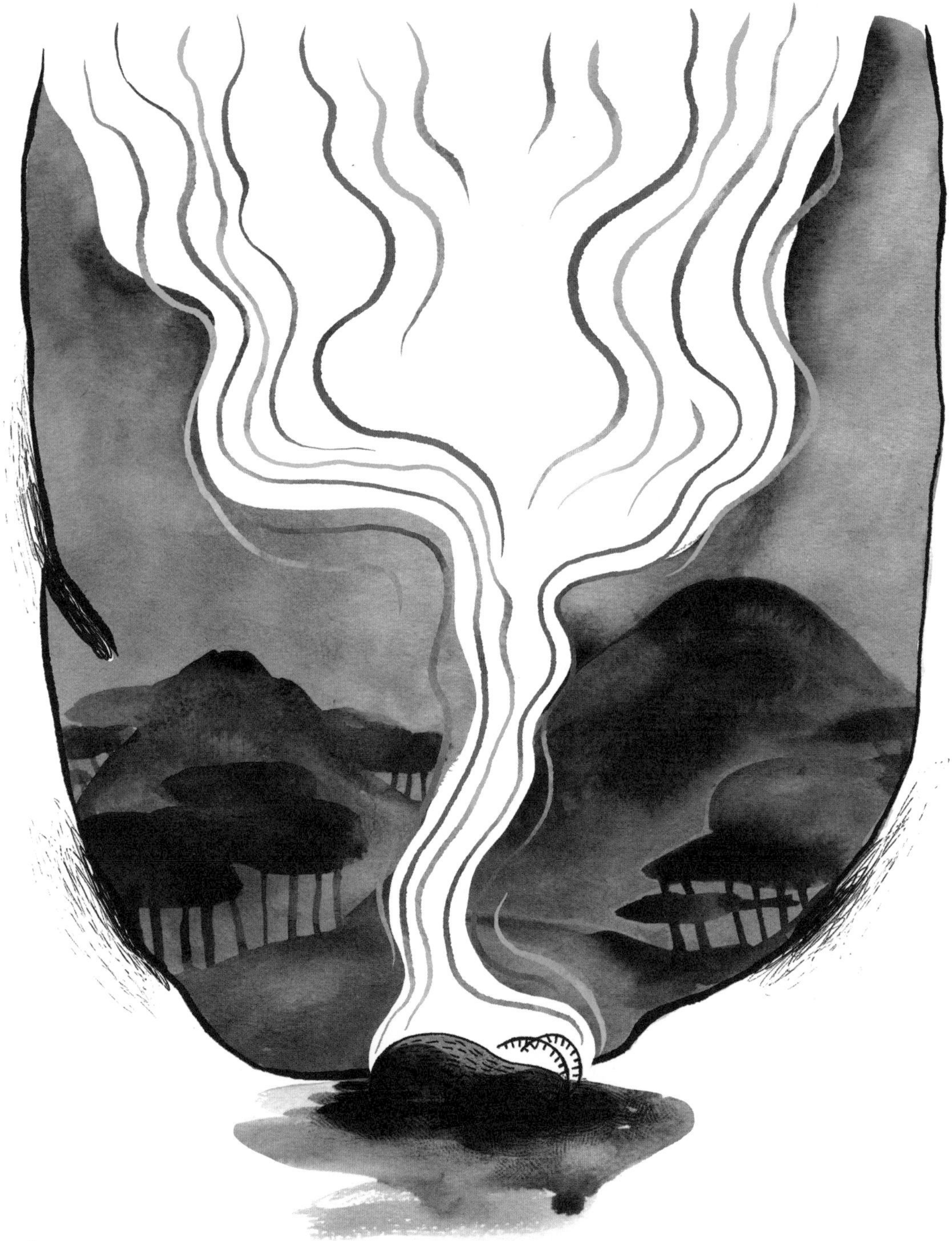

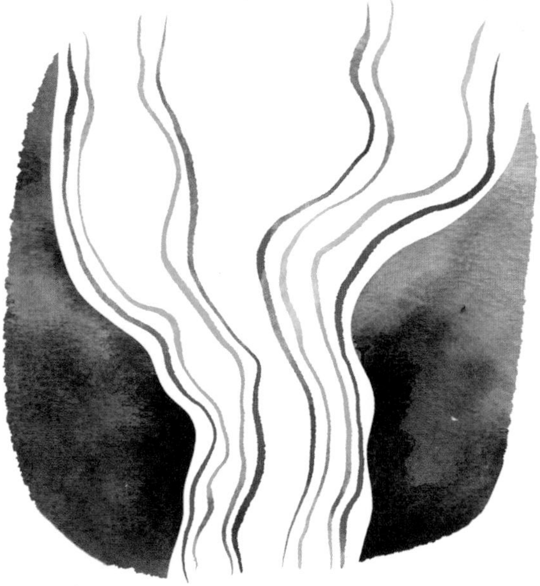
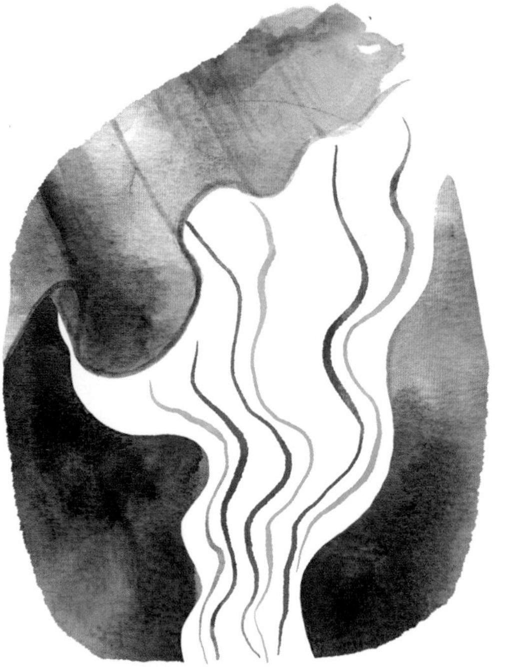
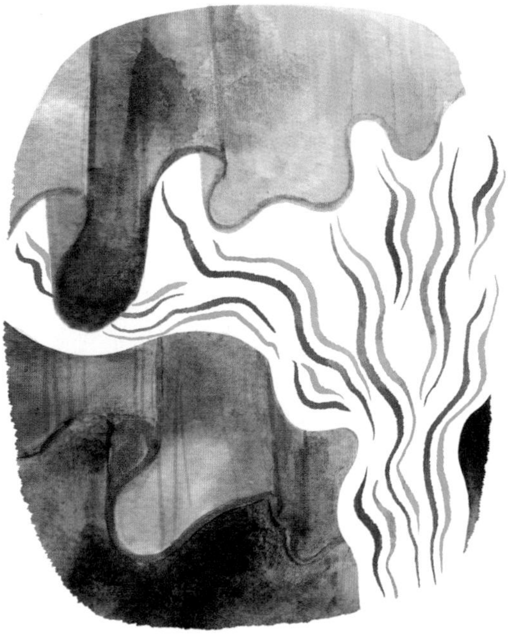
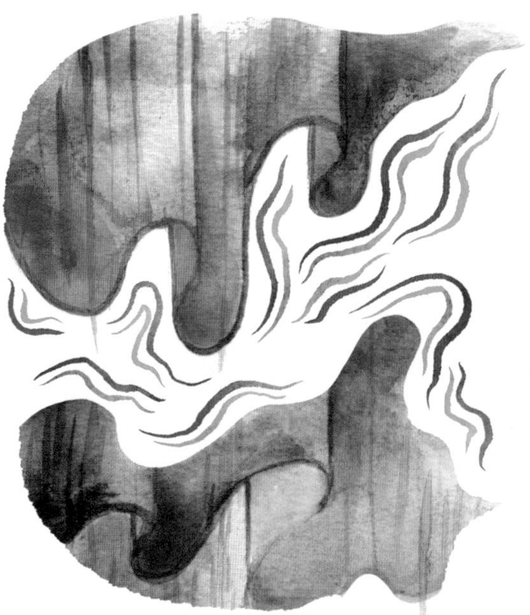

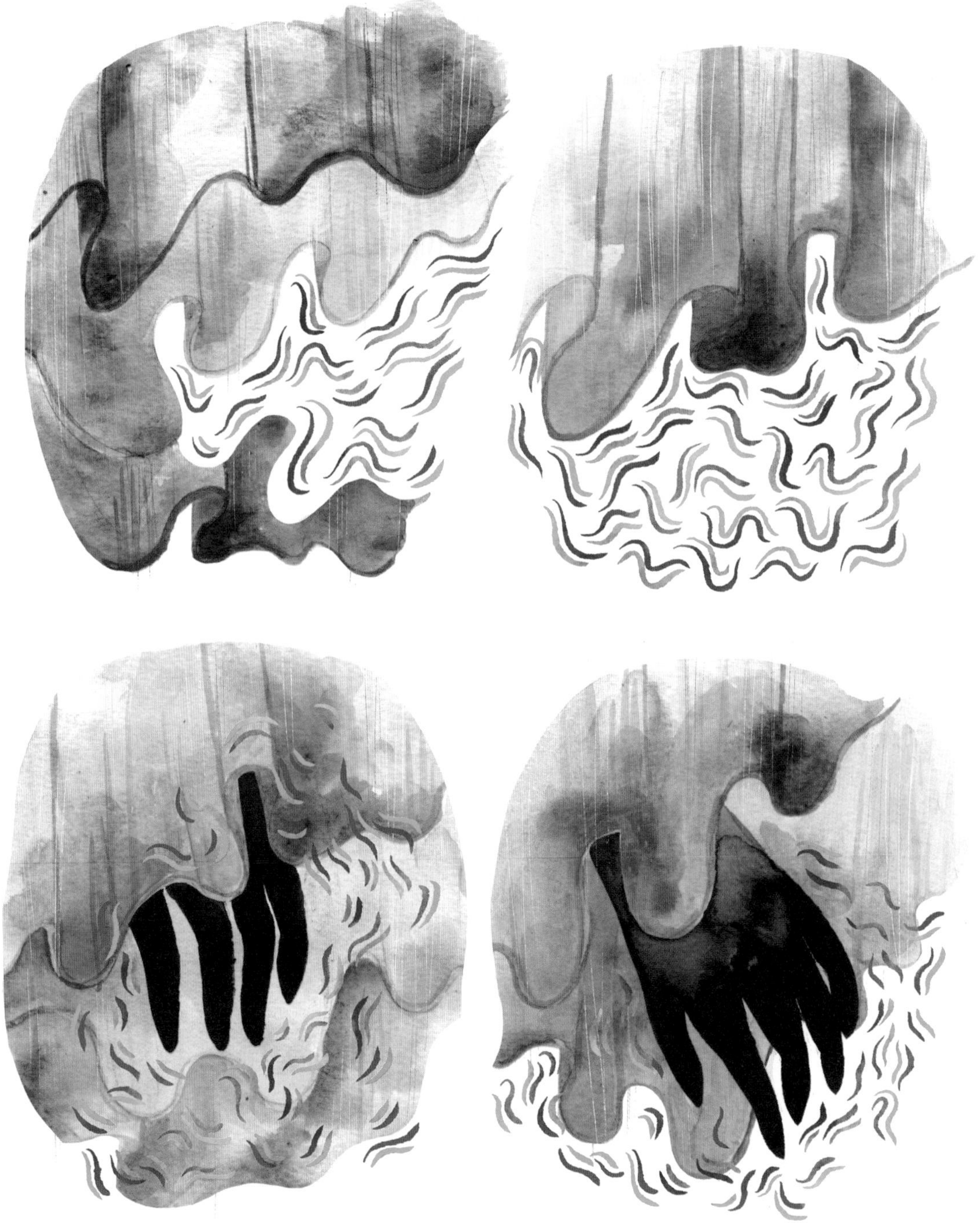

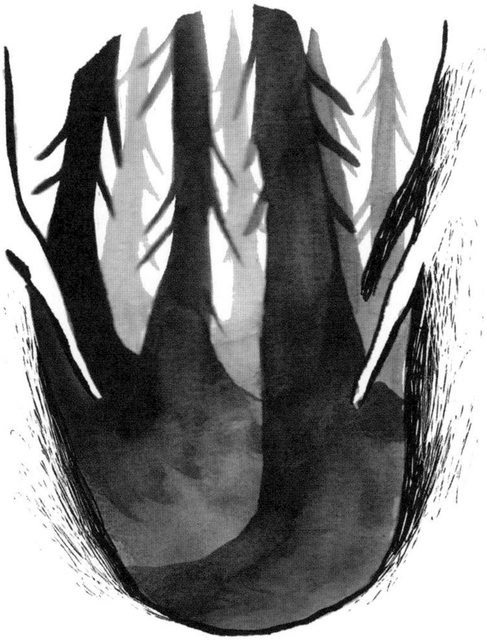
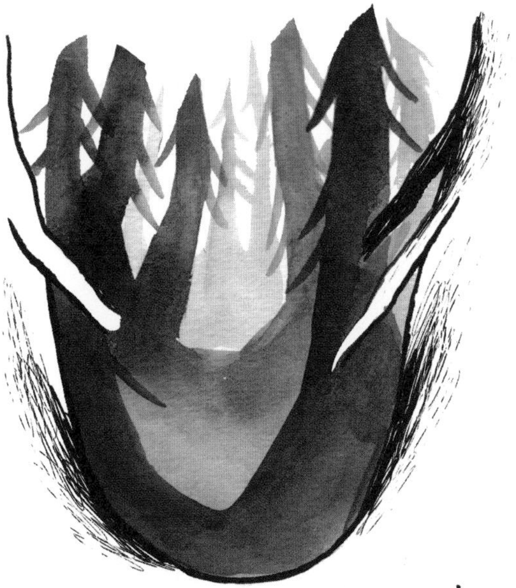
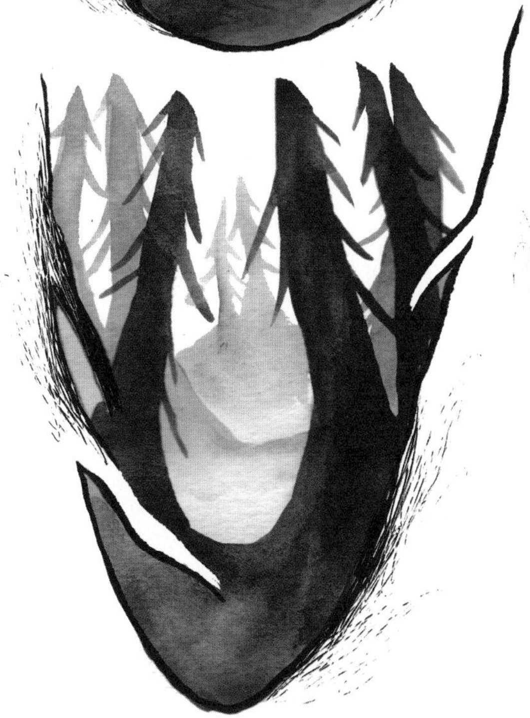
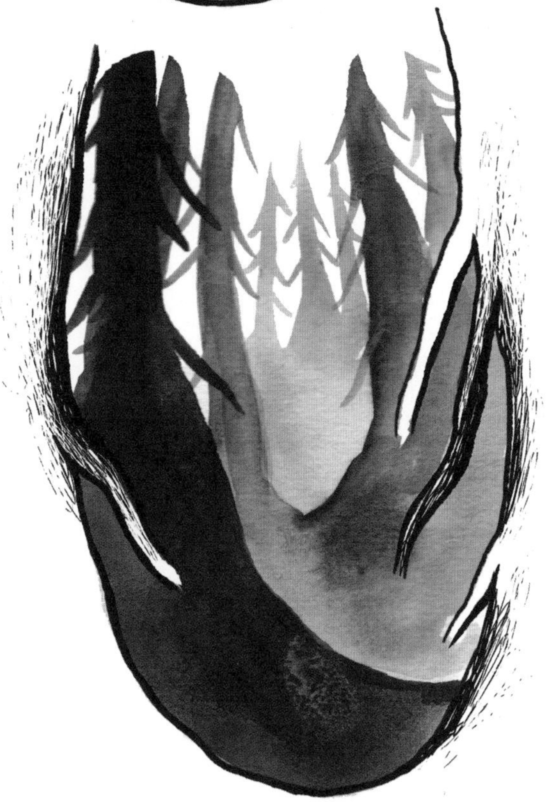

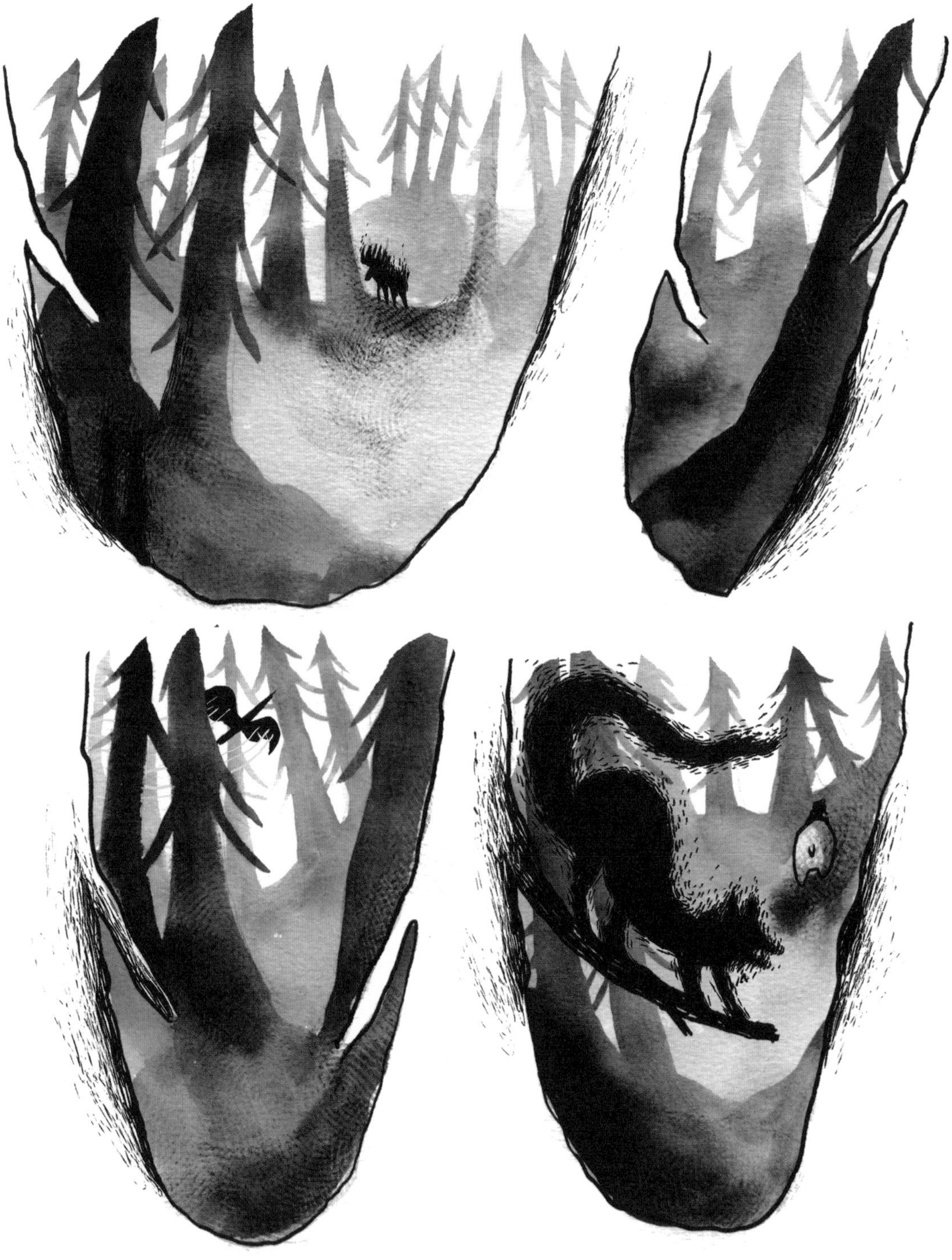

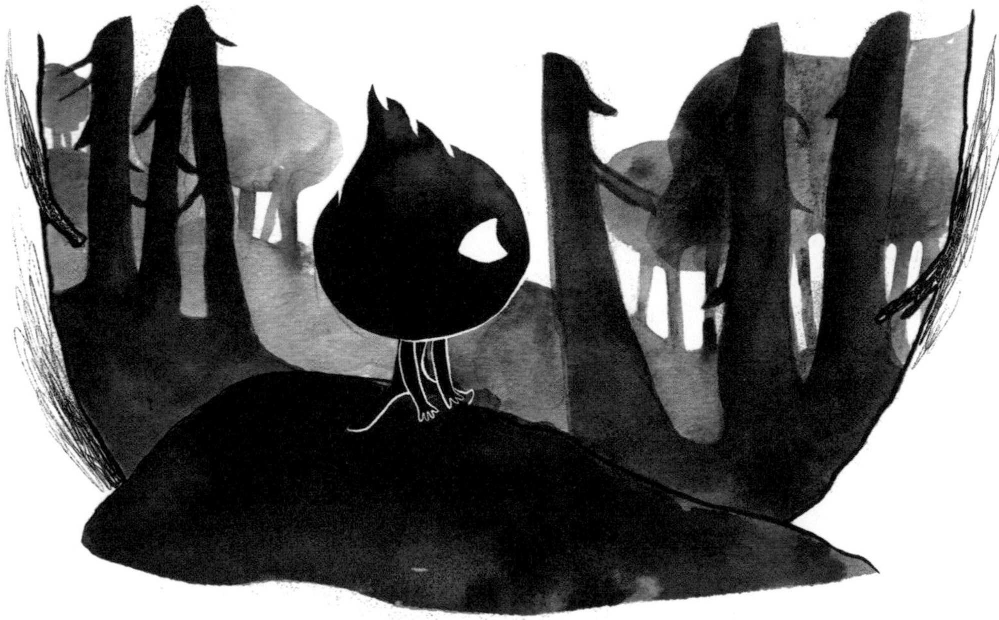

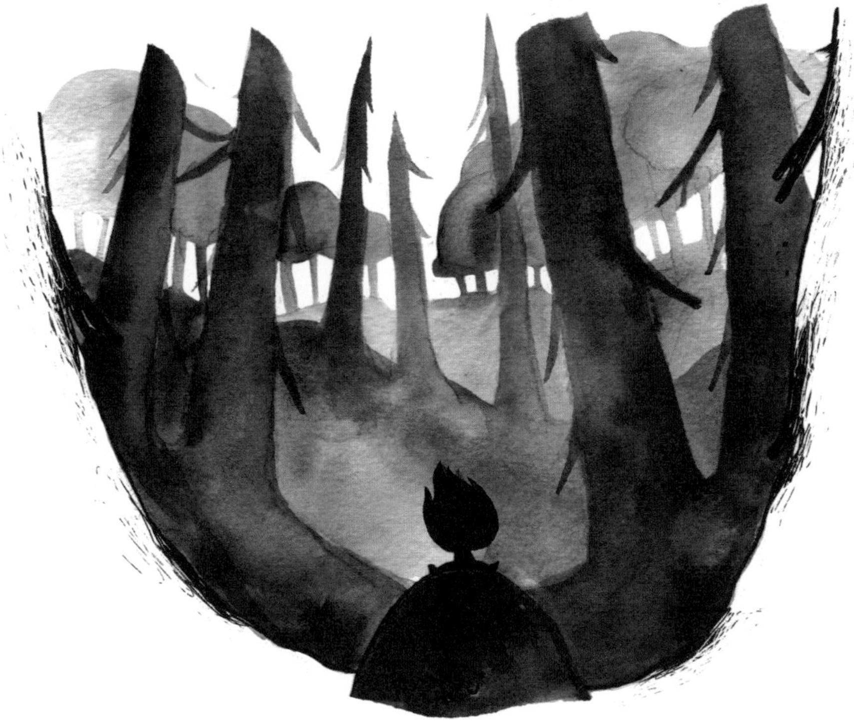

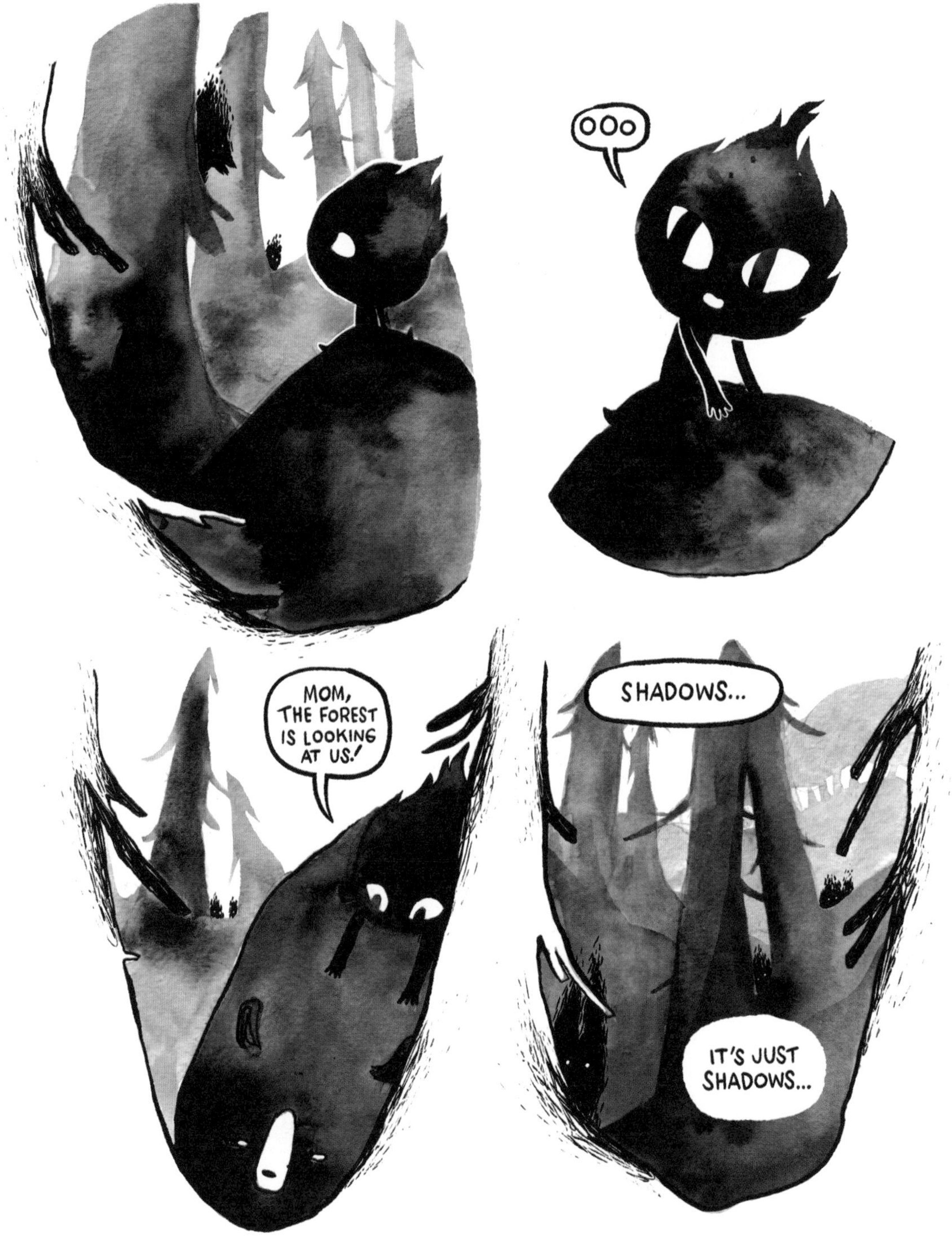
OOo
MOM, THE FOREST IS LOOKING AT US!
SHADOWS...
IT'S JUST SHADOWS...

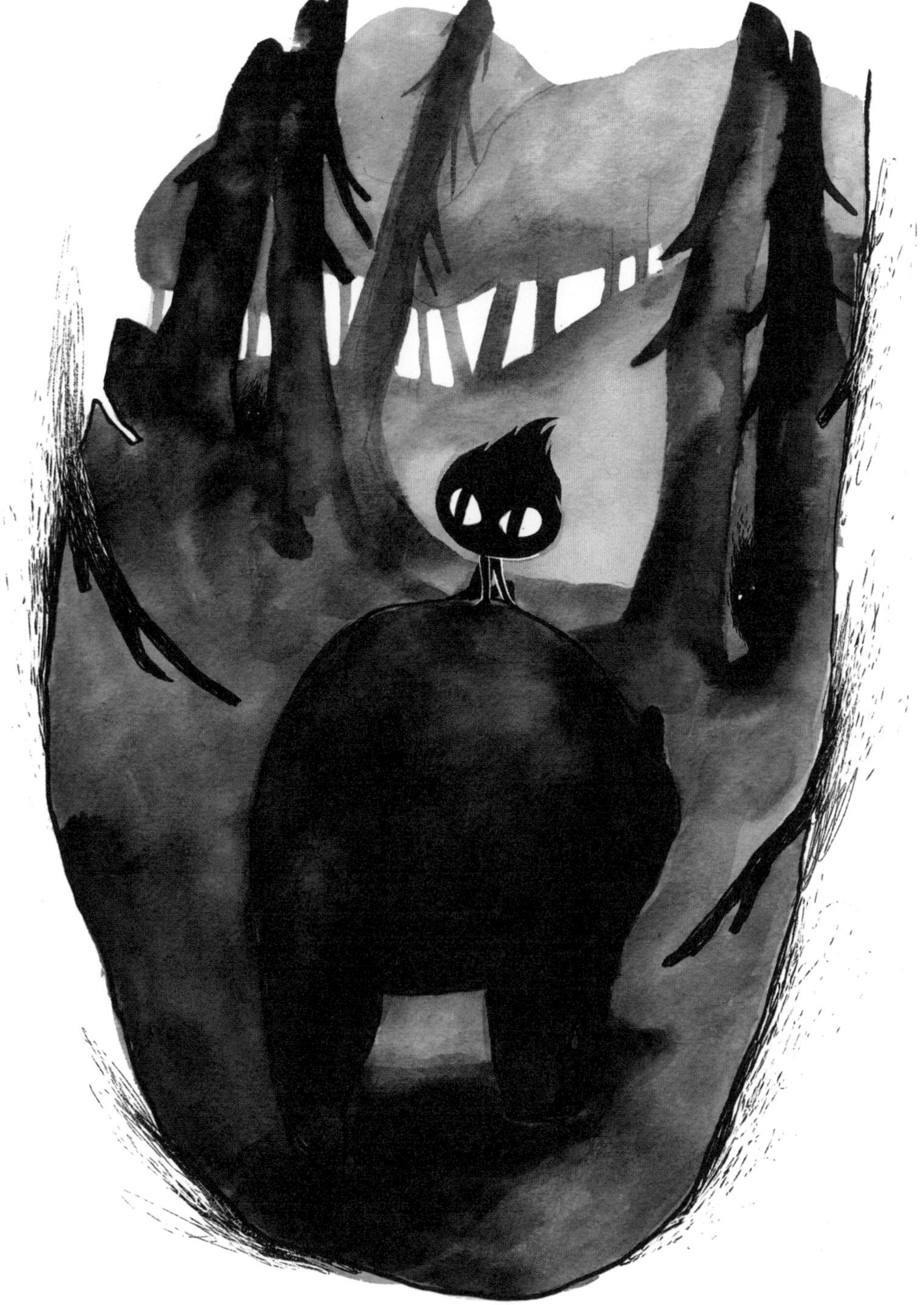

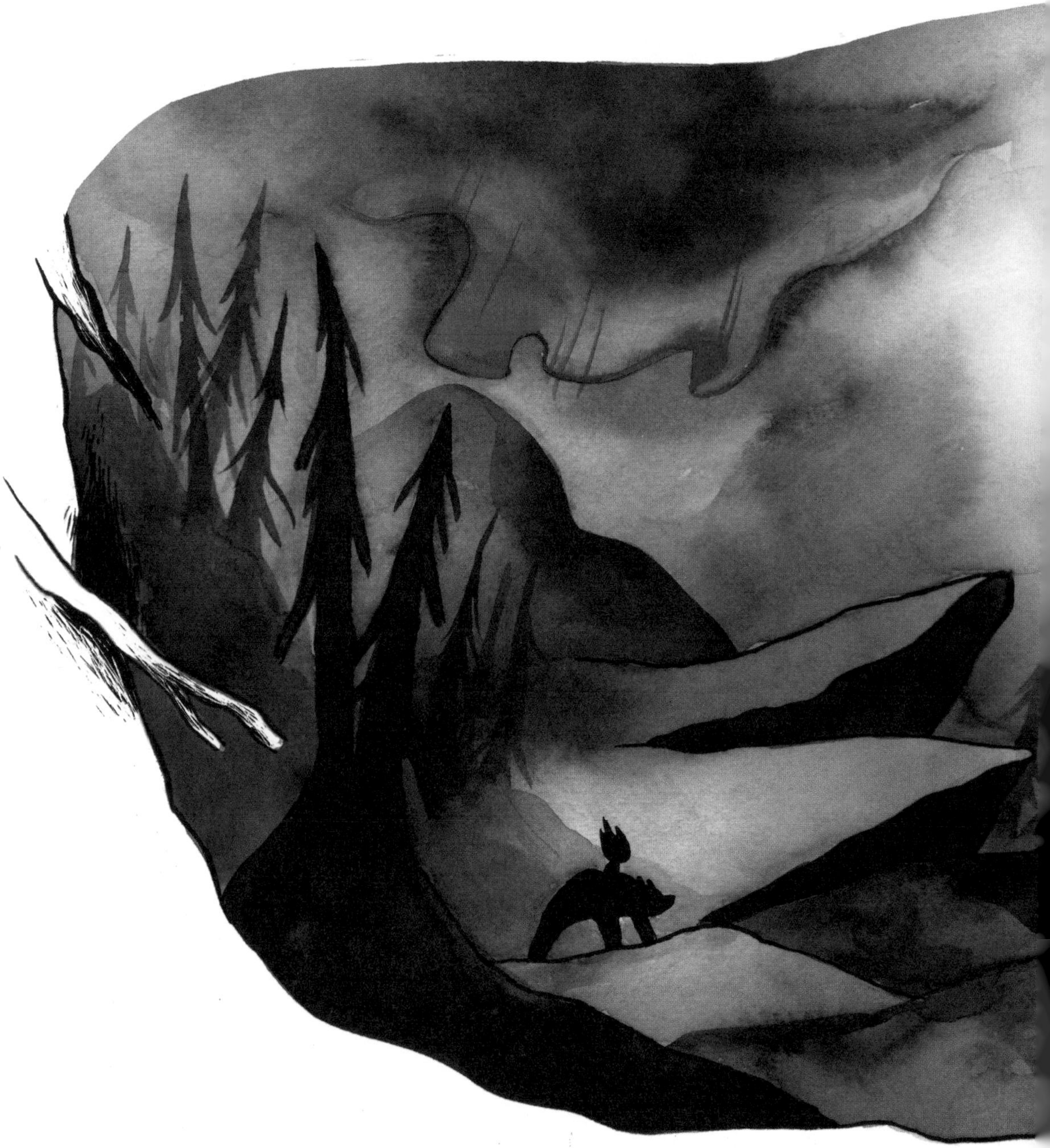

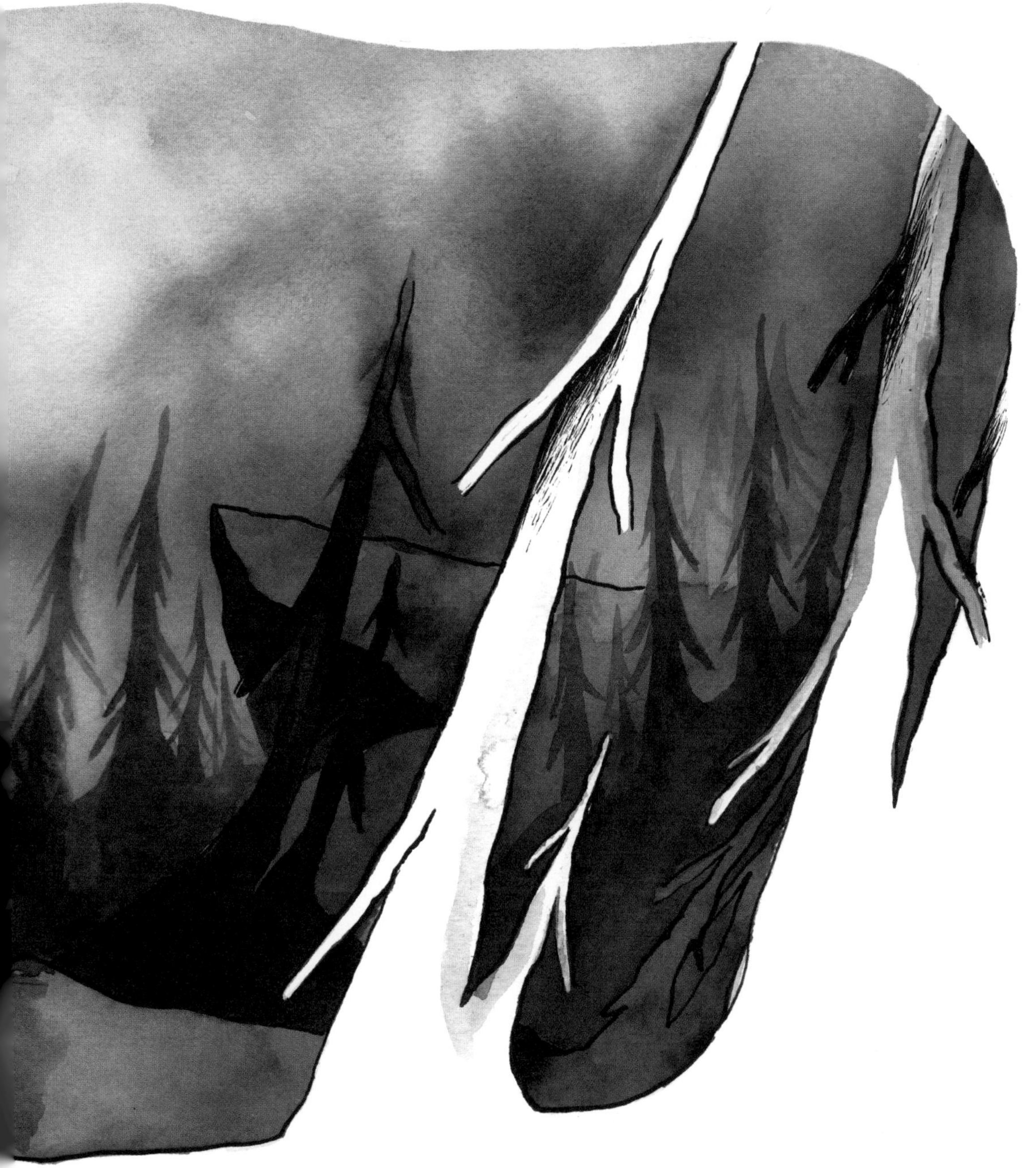

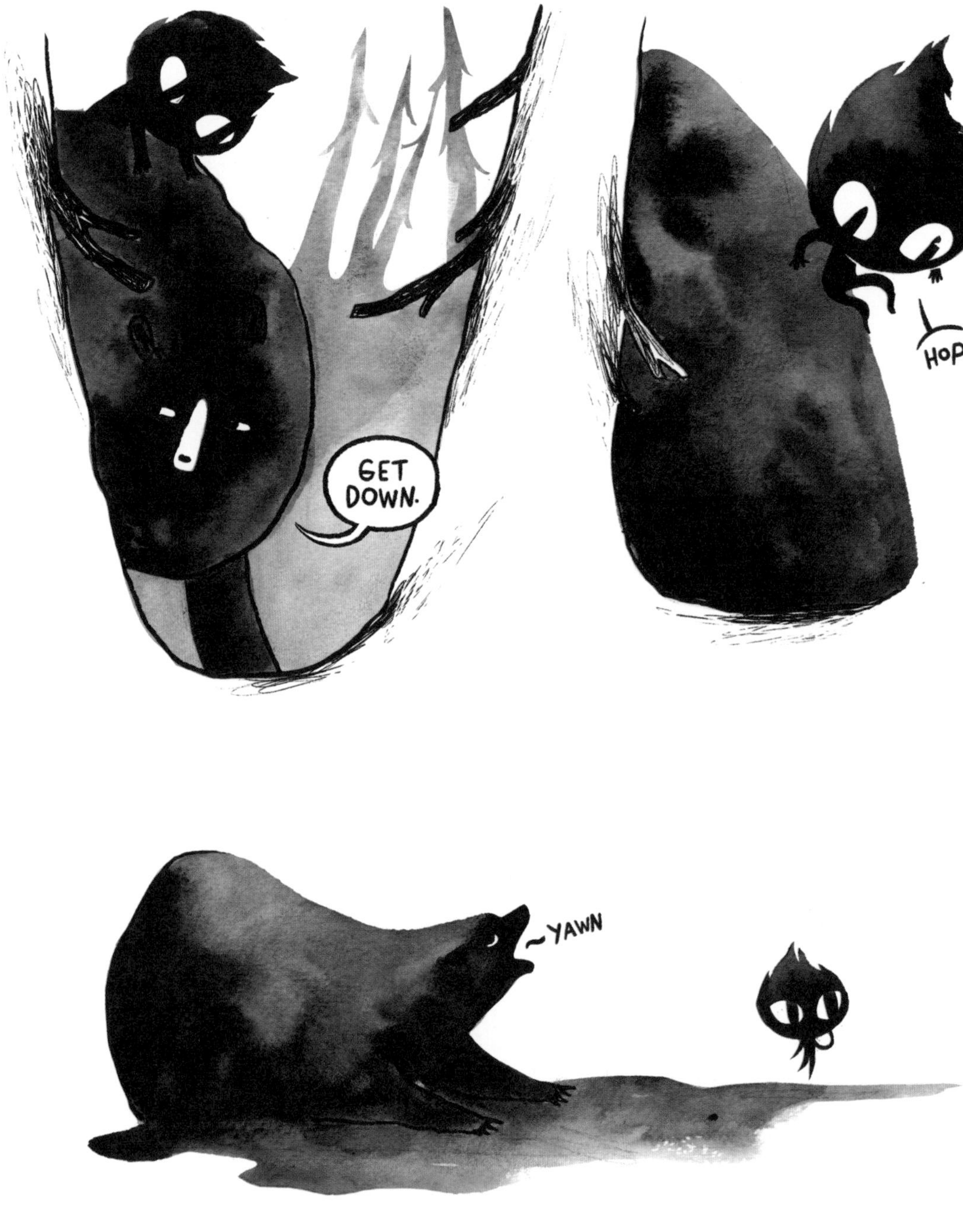
GET DOWN.
HOP
YAWN

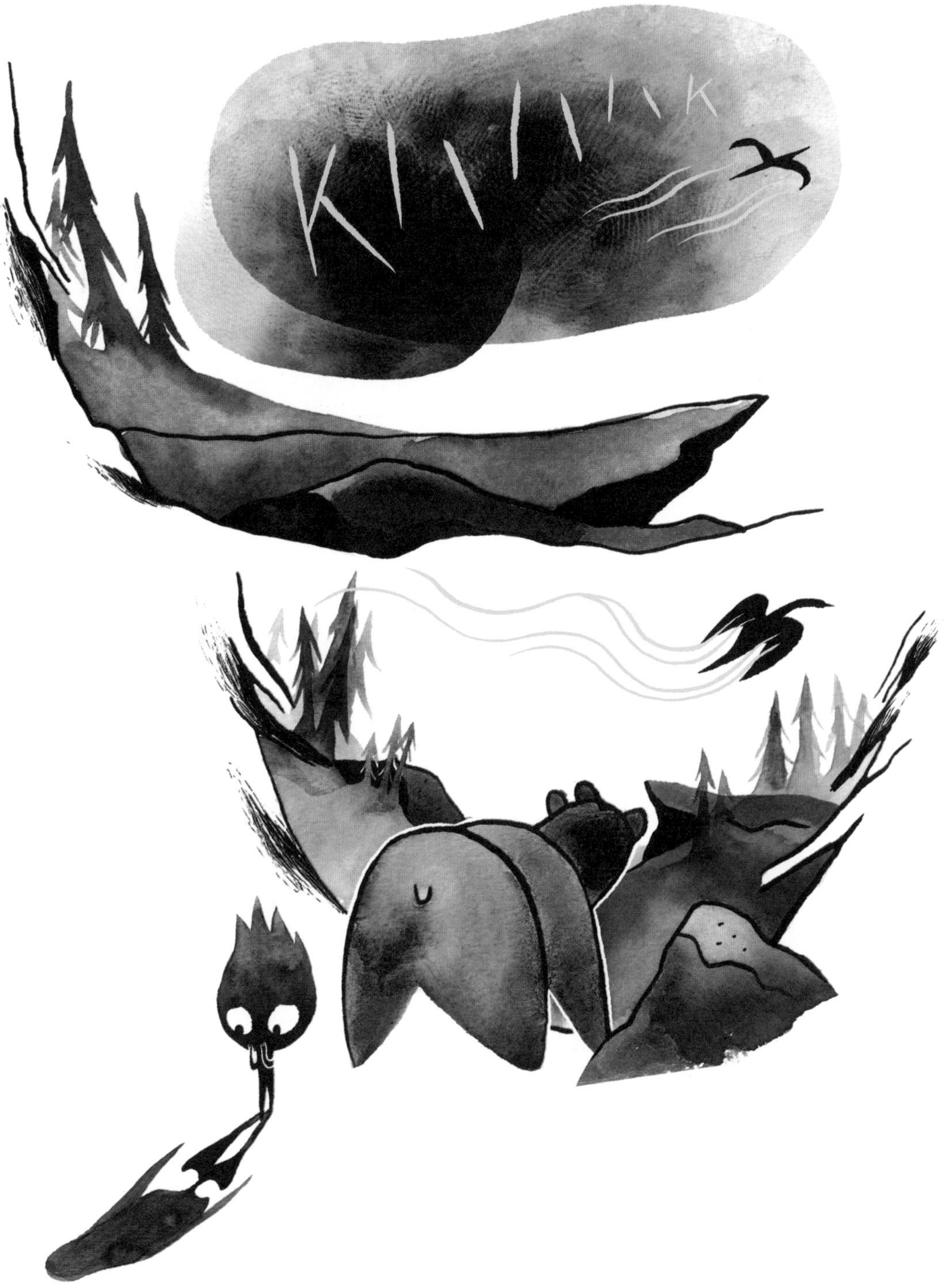
KIIIIIIK

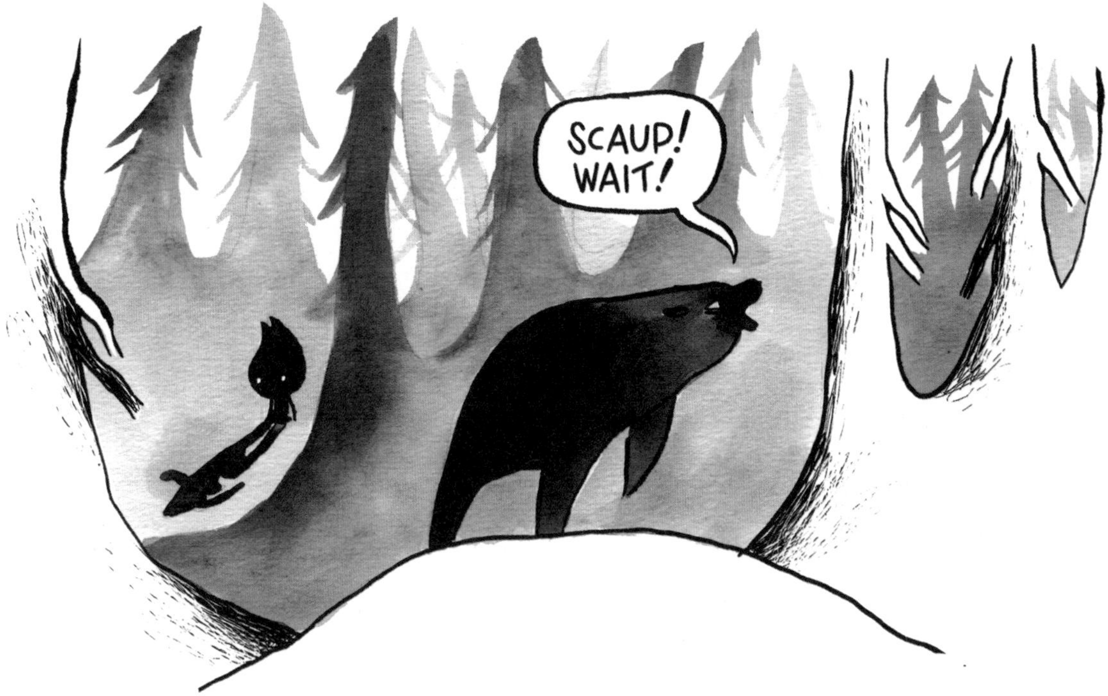
SCAUP! WAIT!

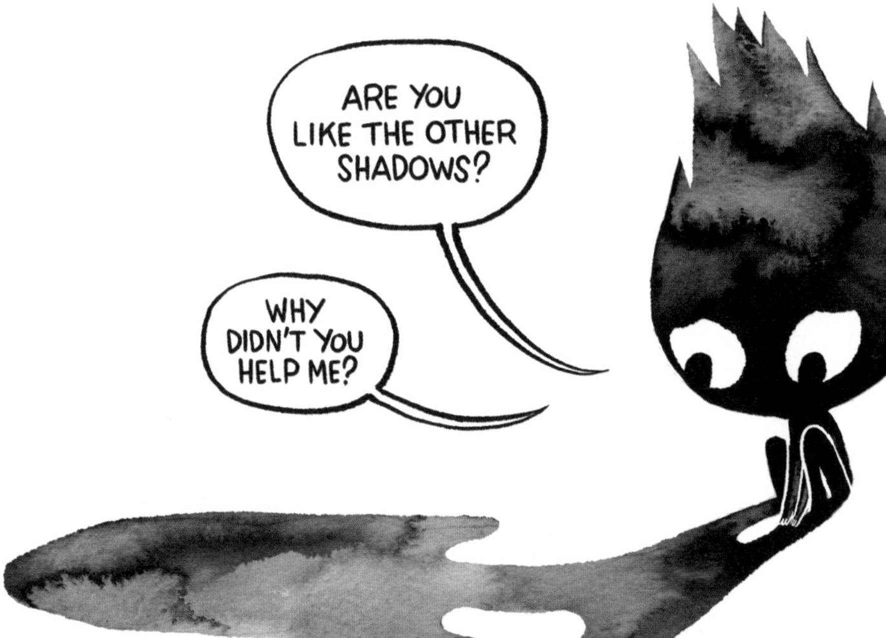
ARE YOU LIKE THE OTHER SHADOWS?
WHY DIDN'T YOU HELP ME?

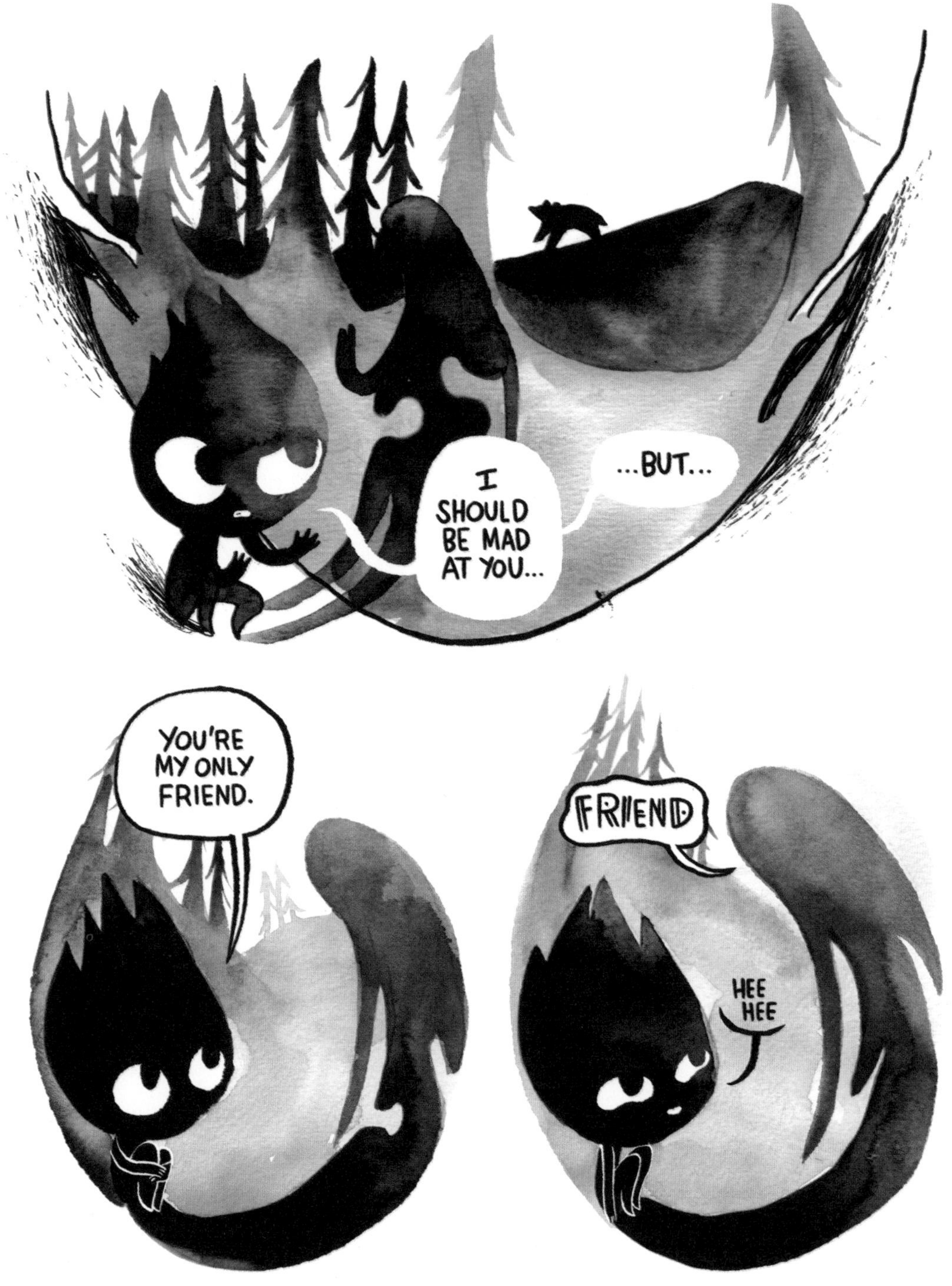
I SHOULD BE MAD AT YOU...
...BUT...
YOU'RE MY ONLY FRIEND.
FRIEND
HEE HEE

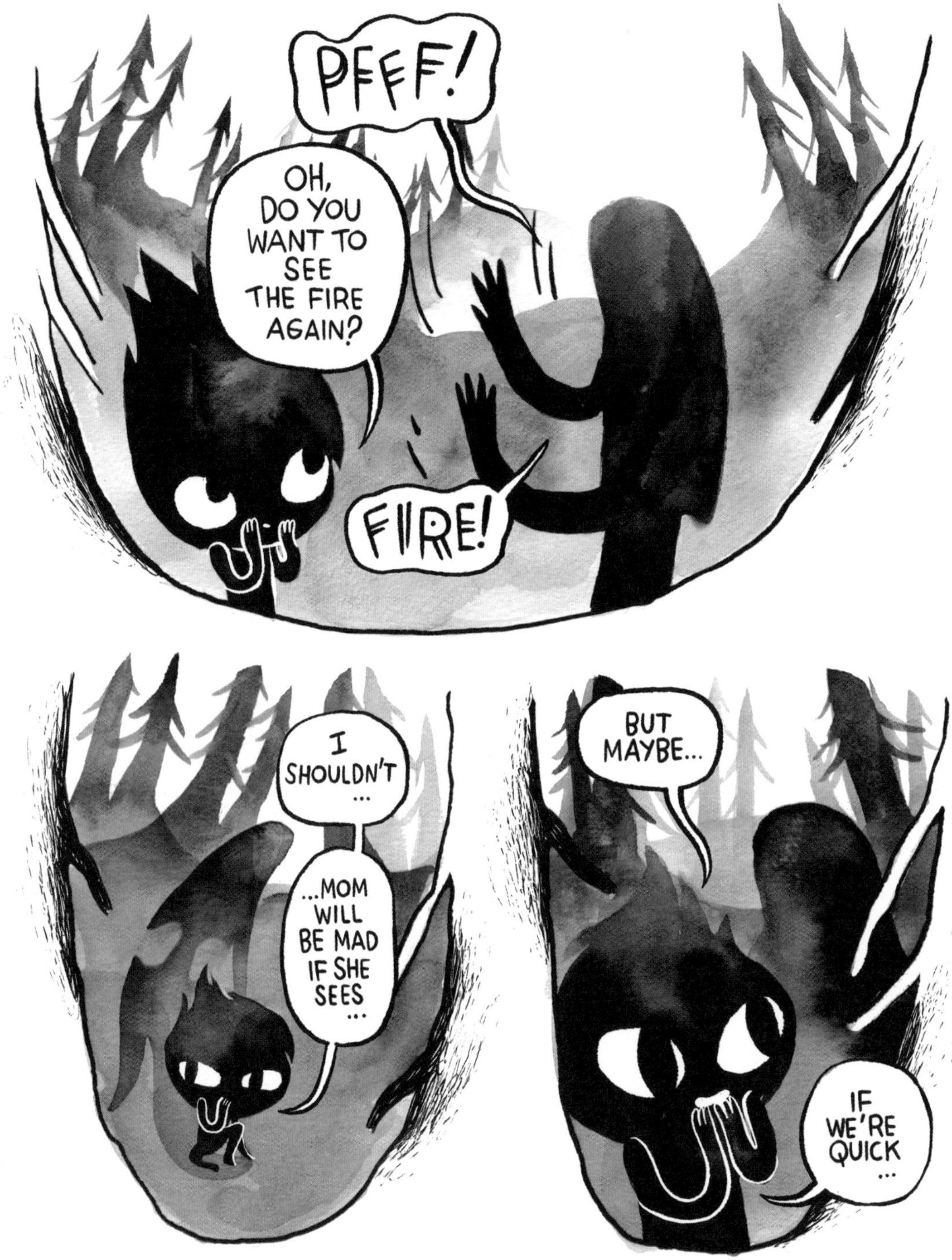
PFFF!
OH, DO YOU WANT TO SEE THE FIRE AGAIN?
FIRE!
I SHOULDN'T ...
...MOM WILL BE MAD IF SHE SEES ...
BUT MAYBE...
IF WE'RE QUICK ...

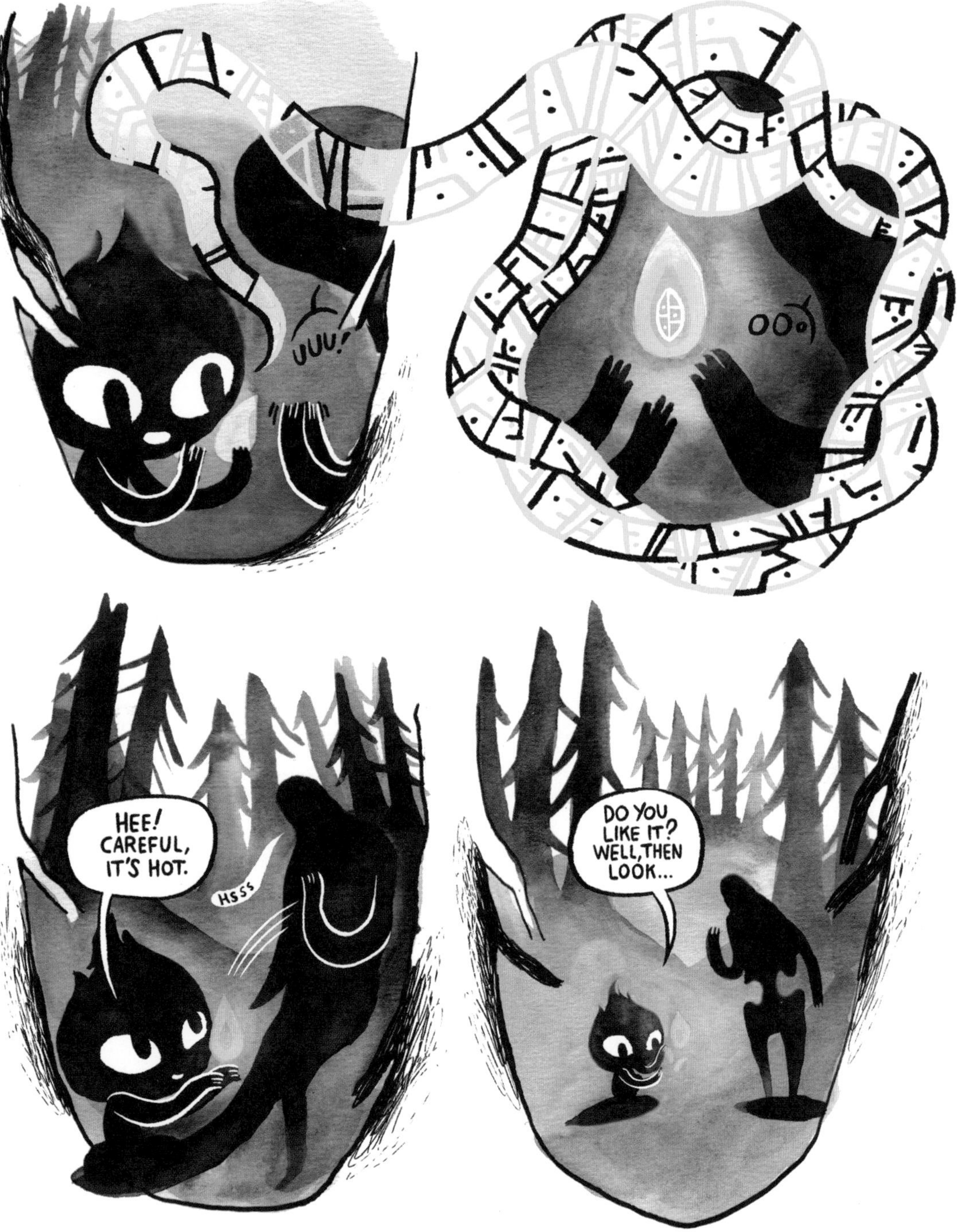
UUU!
OOo)
HEE! CAREFUL, IT'S HOT.
HSSS
DO YOU LIKE IT? WELL, THEN LOOK...

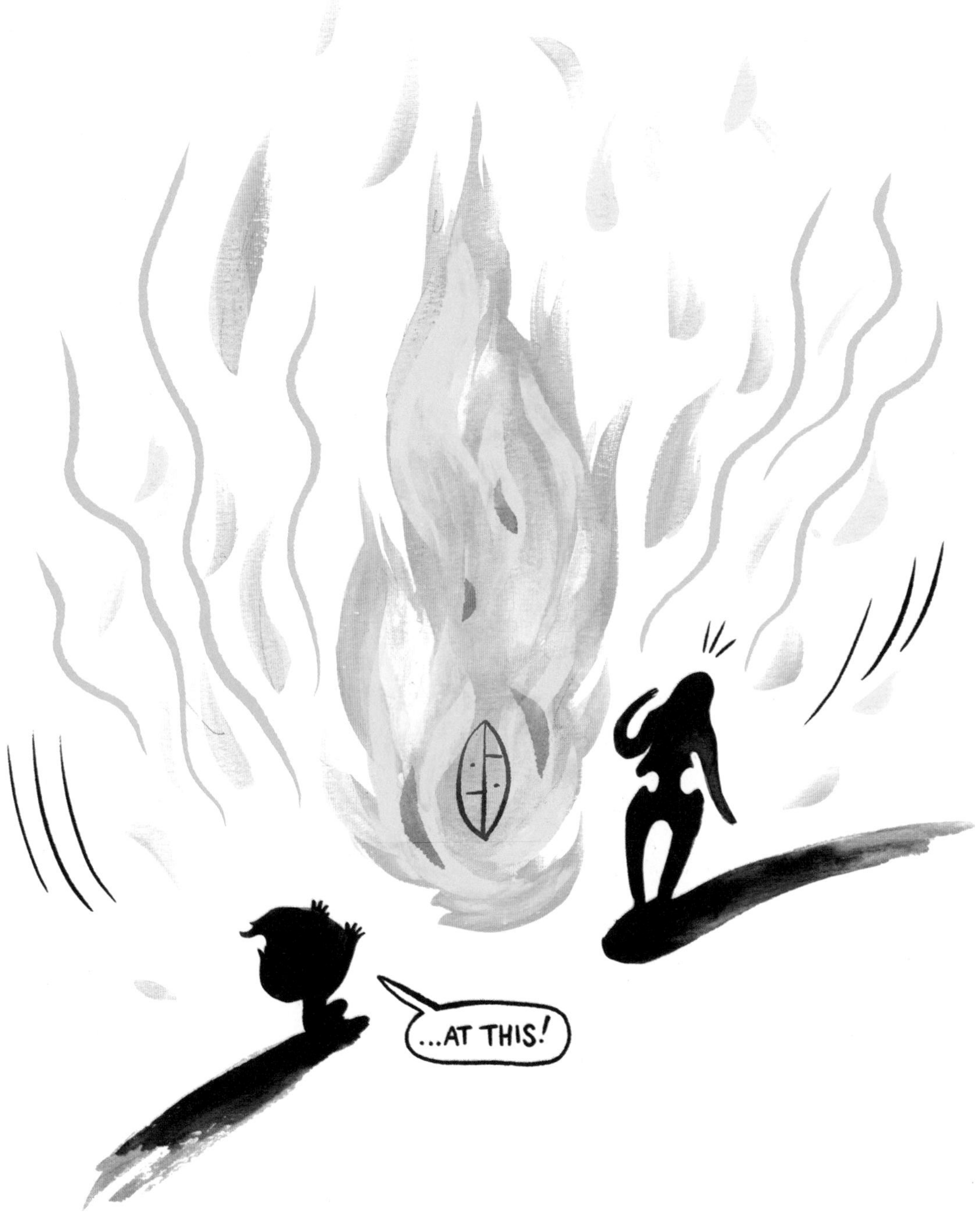
...AT THIS!

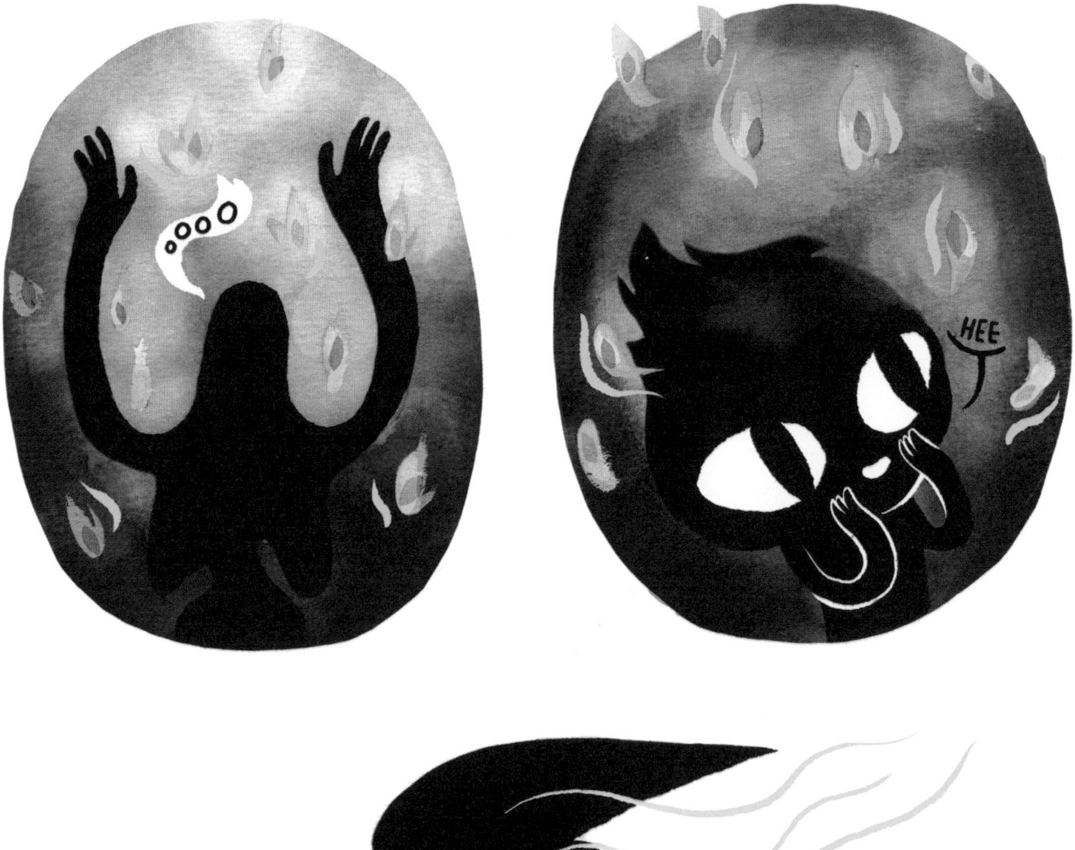
HEE
STOP!

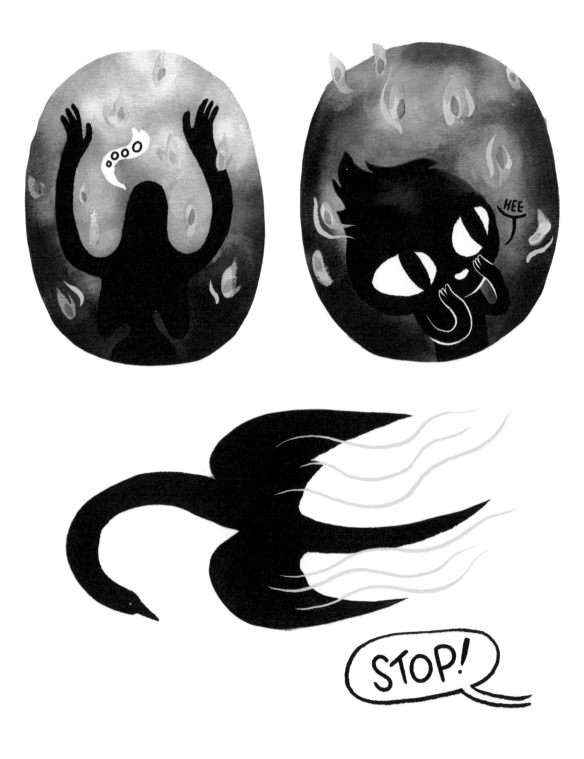

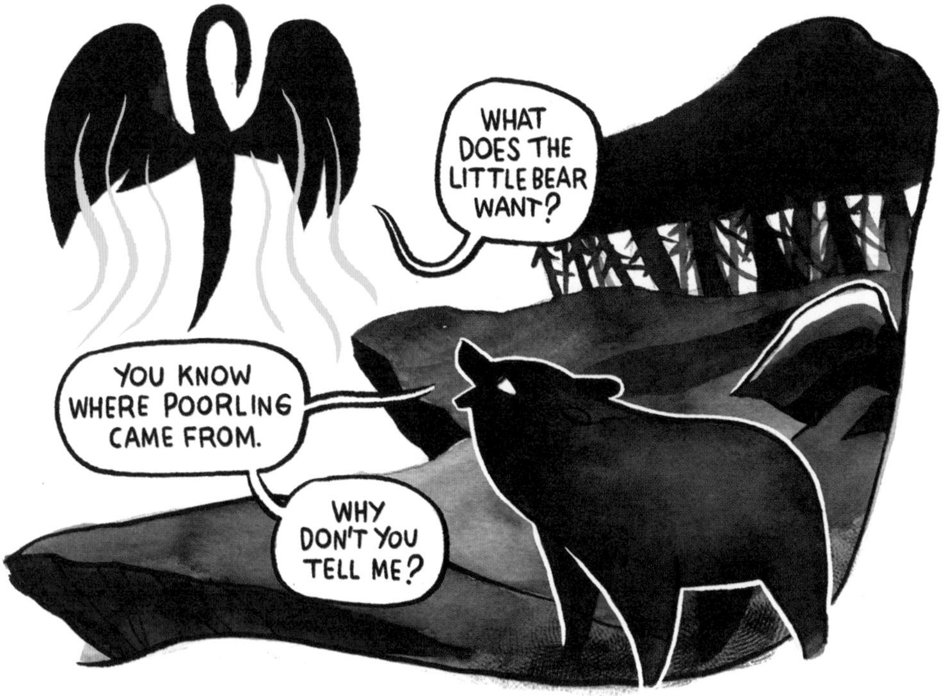
WHAT DOES THE LITTLE BEAR WANT?
YOU KNOW WHERE POORLING CAME FROM.
WHY DON'T YOU TELL ME?

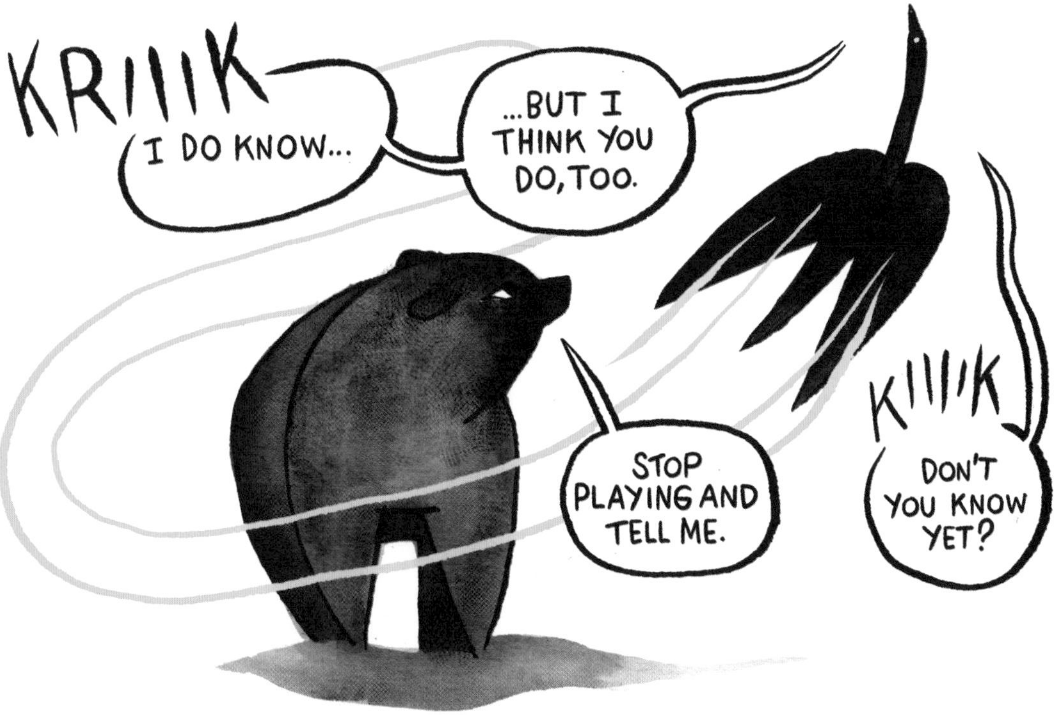
KRIIIK
I DO KNOW...
...BUT I THINK YOU DO, TOO.
STOP PLAYING AND TELL ME.
KIIIK
DON'T YOU KNOW YET?

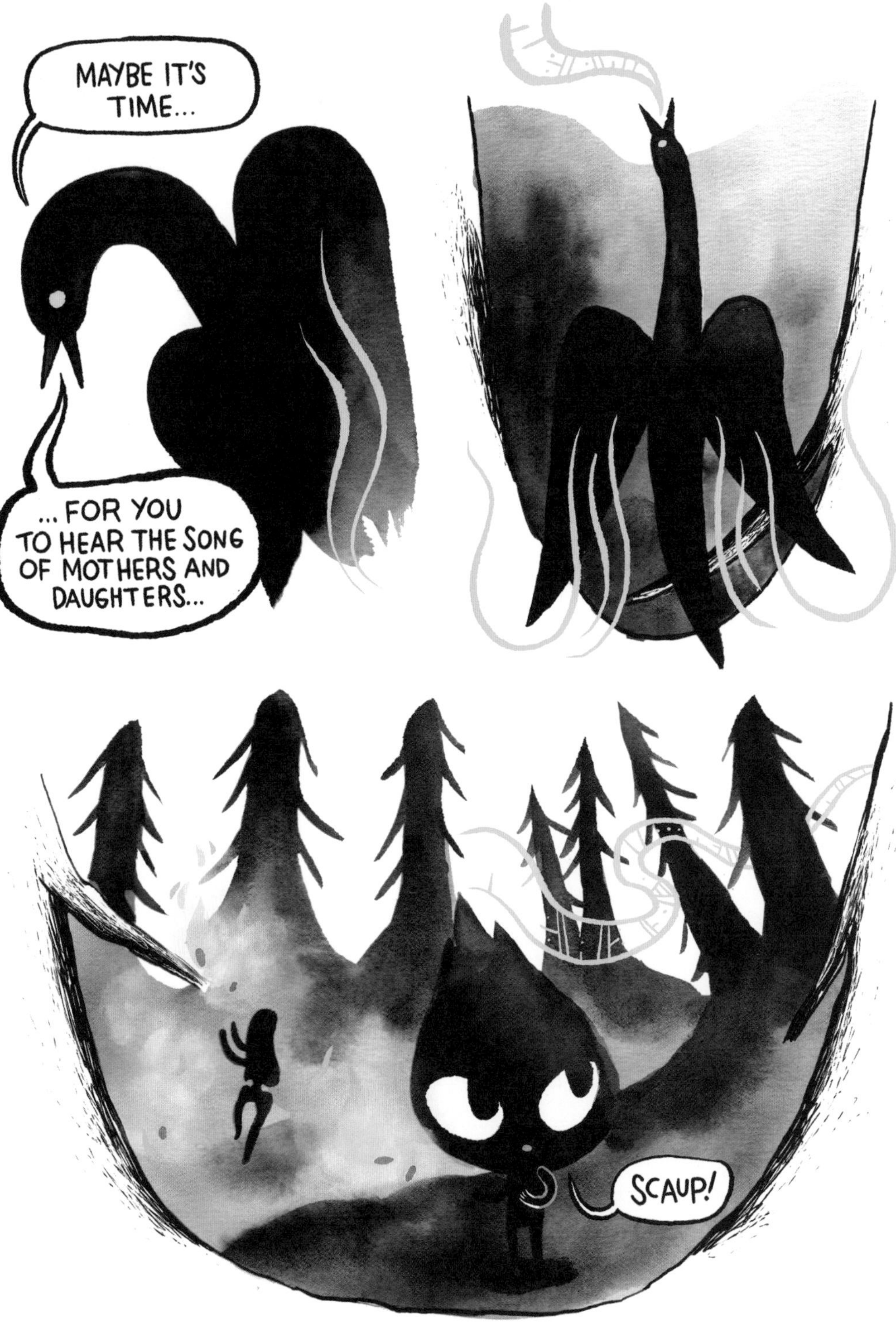
MAYBE IT'S TIME...
... FOR YOU TO HEAR THE SONG OF MOTHERS AND DAUGHTERS...
SCAUP!

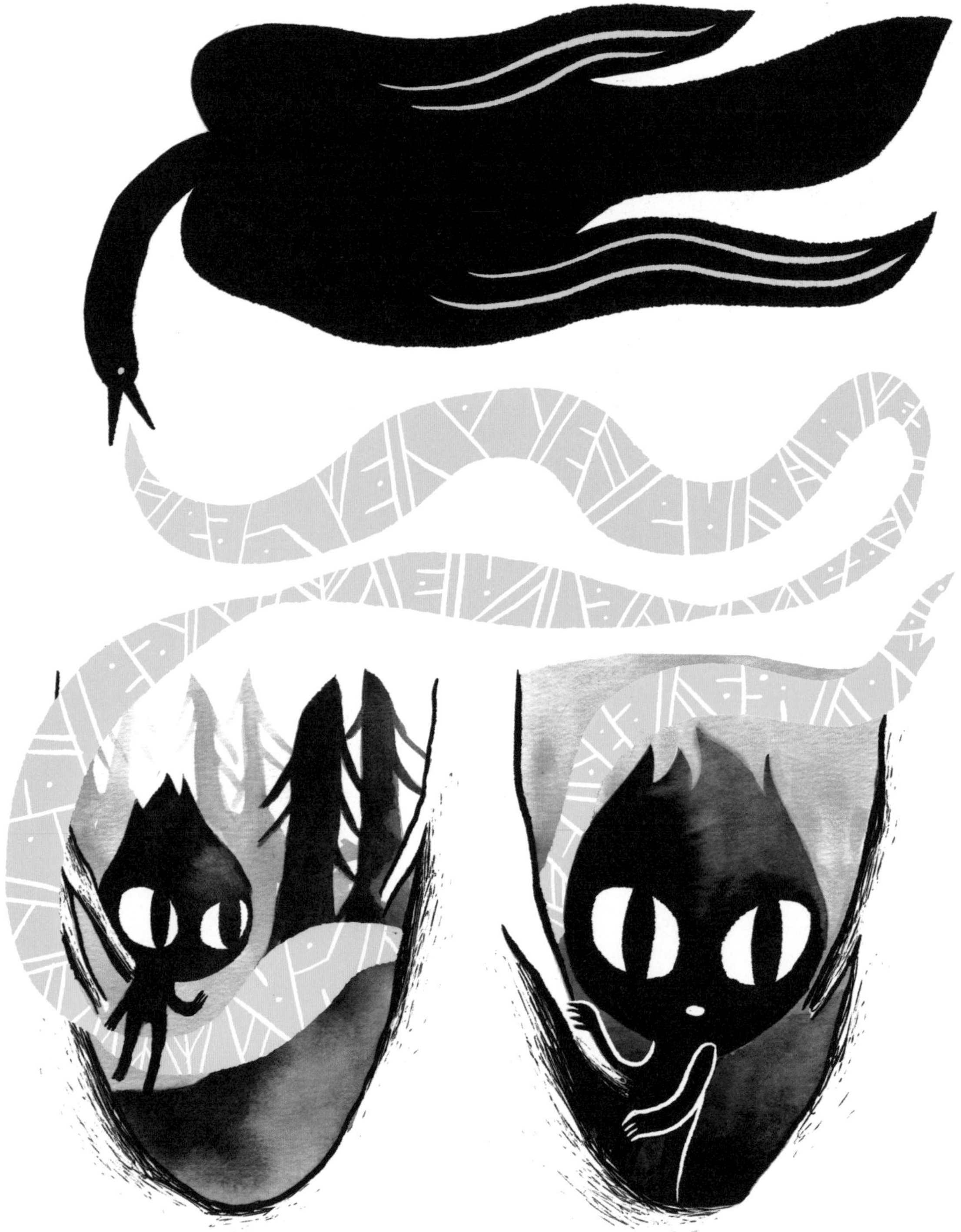

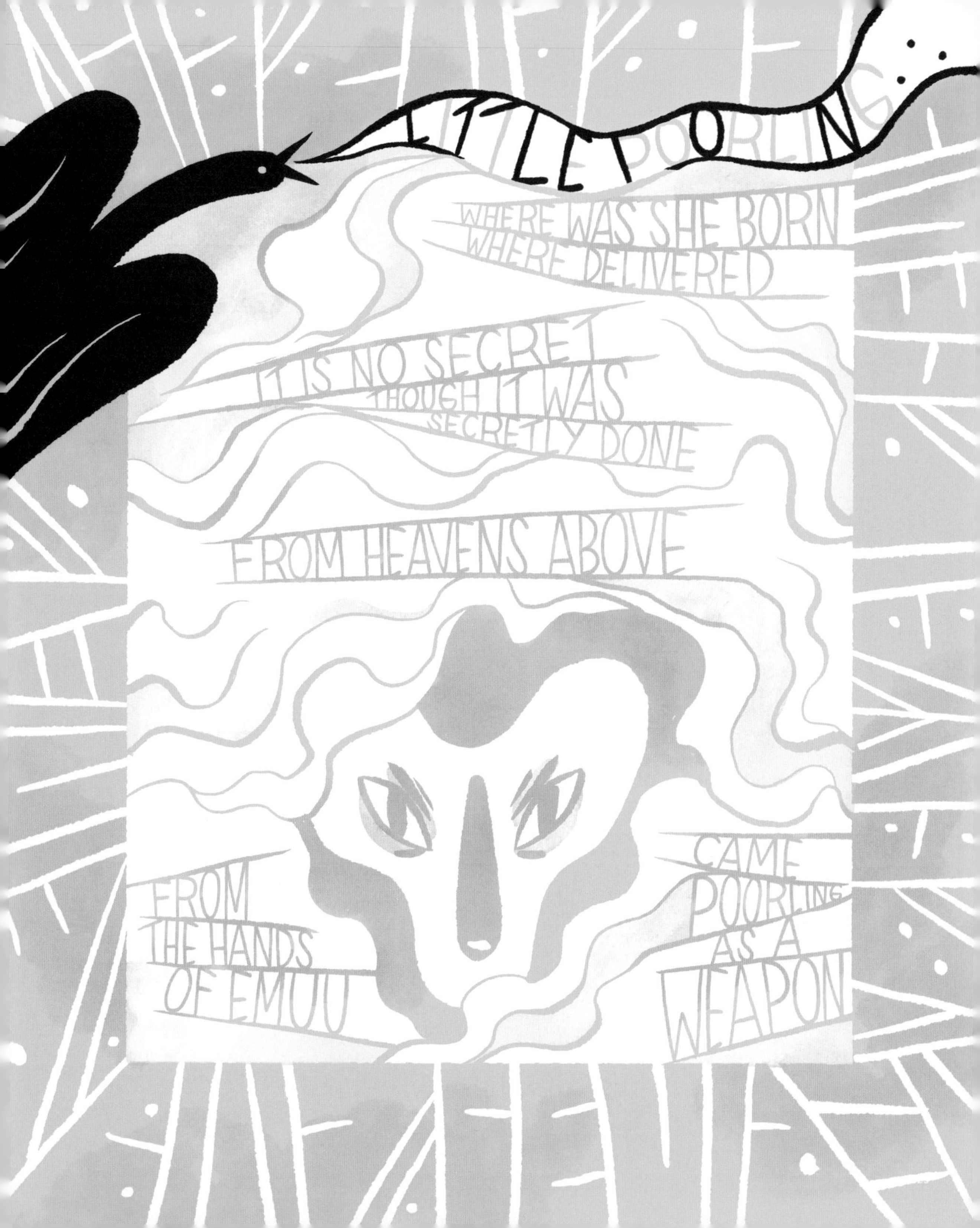
LITTLE POORLING
WHERE WAS SHE BORN
WHERE DELIVERED
IT IS NO SECRET
THOUGH IT WAS
SECRETLY DONE
FROM HEAVENS ABOVE
FROM
THE HANDS
OF EMUU
CAME
POORLING
AS A
WEAPON

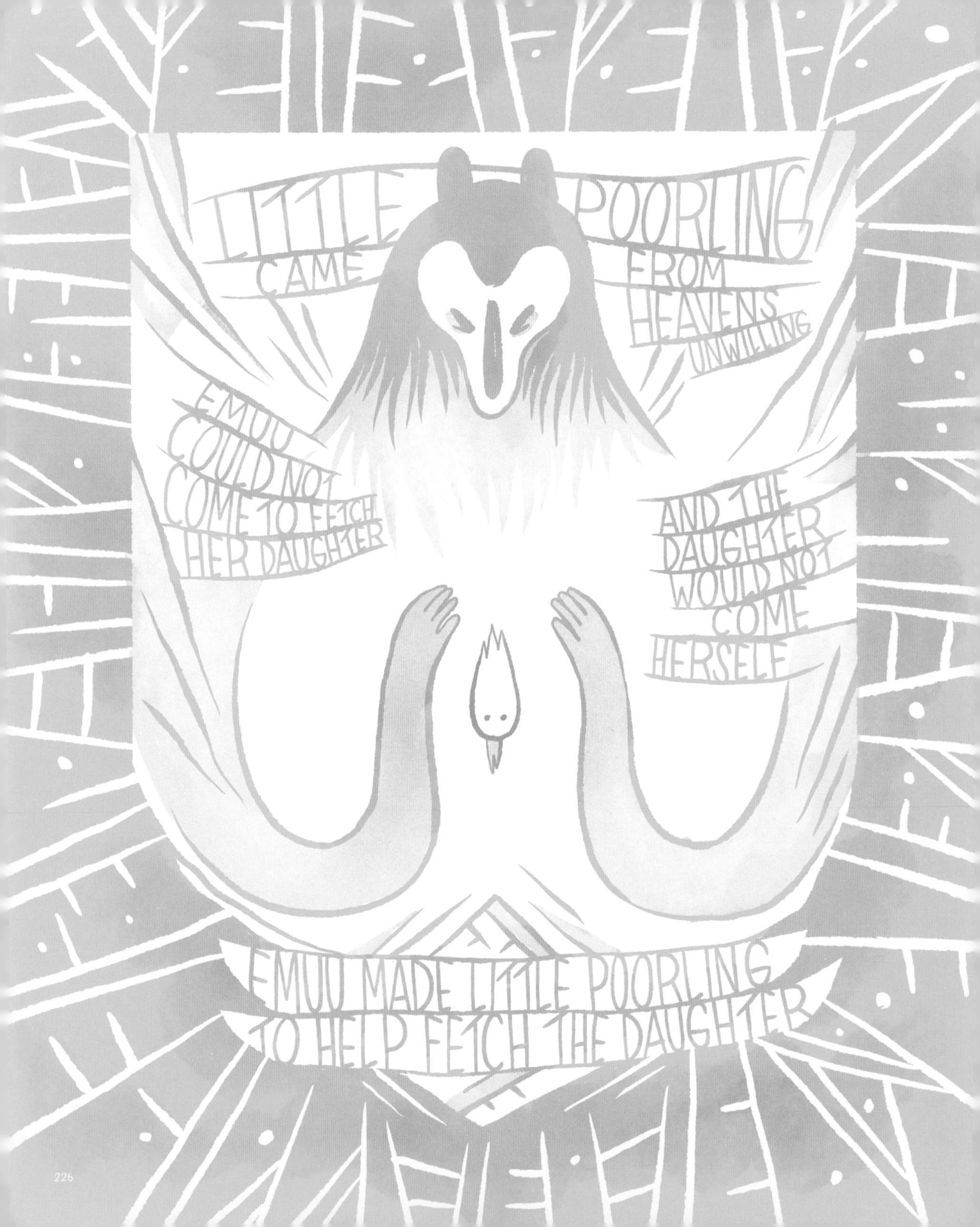
LITTLE POORLING
CAME FROM HEAVENS UNWILLING
EMUU COULD NOT COME TO FETCH HER DAUGHTER
AND THE DAUGHTER WOULD NOT COME HERSELF
EMUU MADE LITTLE POORLING
TO HELP FETCH THE DAUGHTER

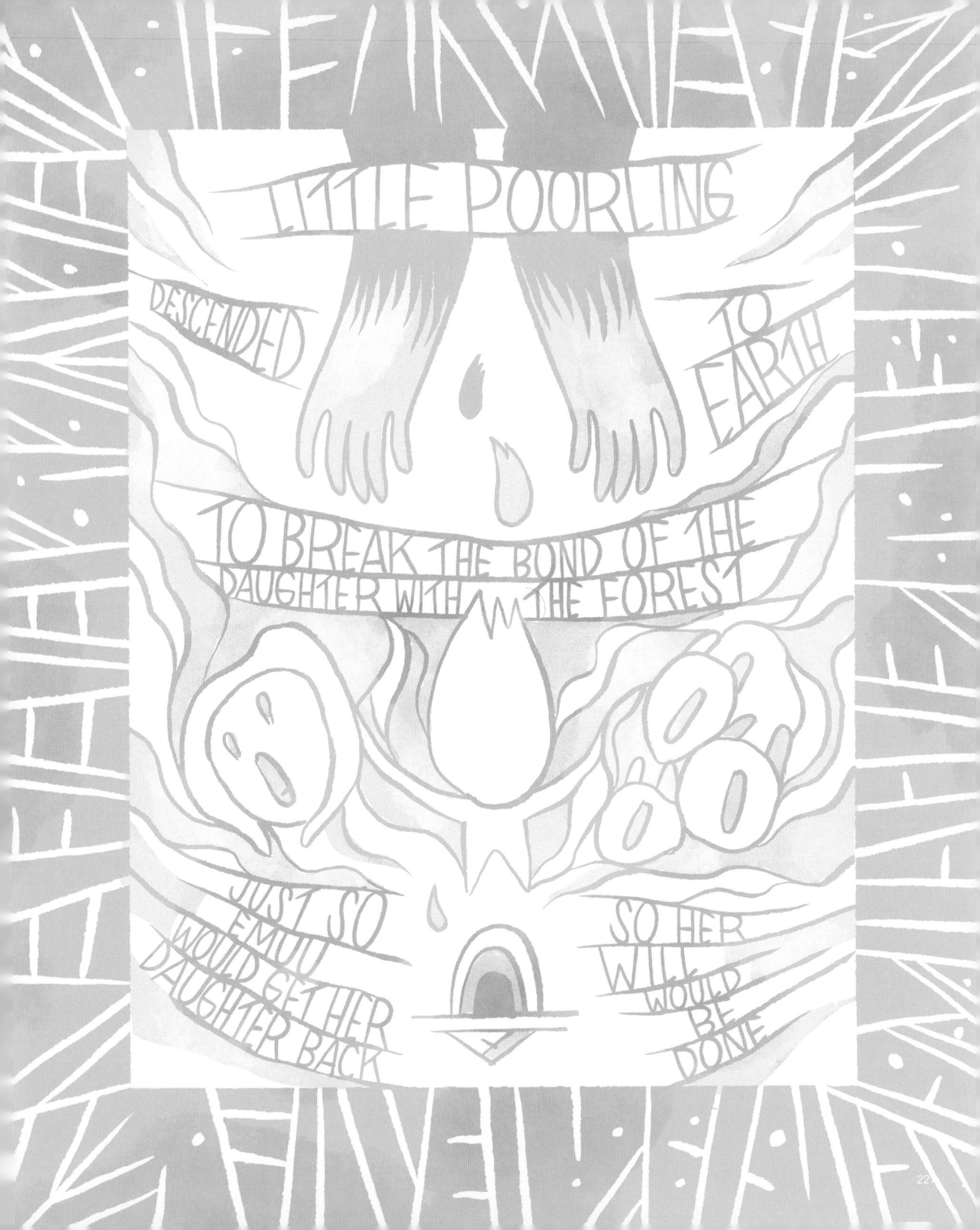
LITTLE POORLING
DESCENDED
TO EARTH
TO BREAK THE BOND OF THE DAUGHTER WITH THE FOREST
JUST SO EMUU WOULD GET HER DAUGHTER BACK
SO HER WILL WOULD BE DONE

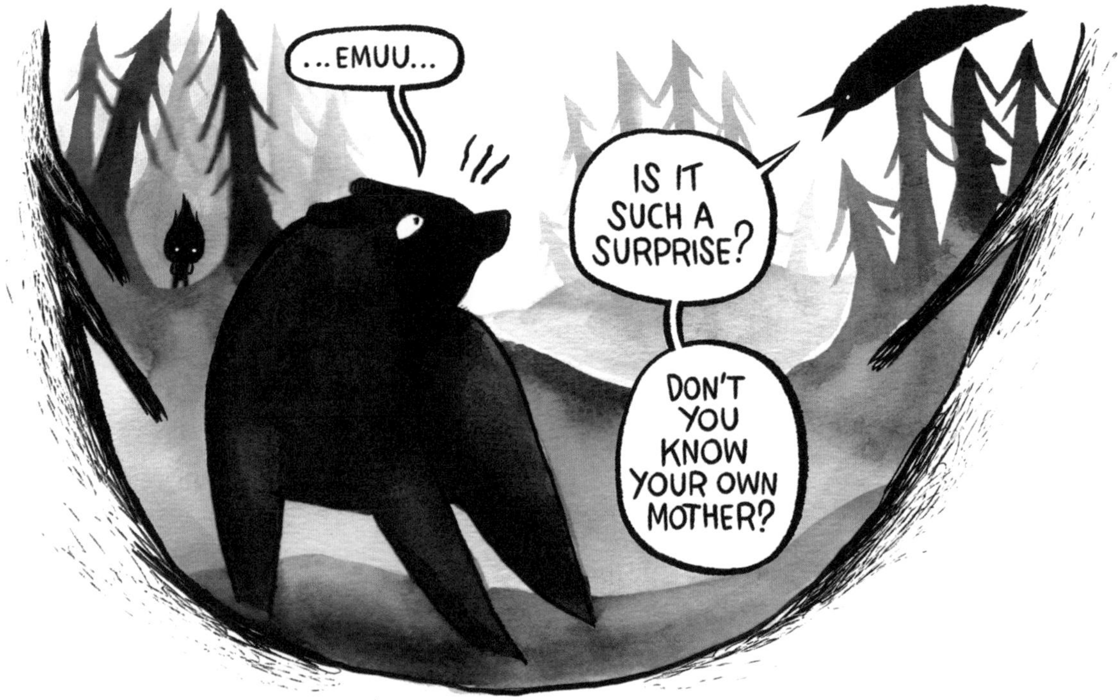
...EMUU...
IS IT SUCH A SURPRISE?
DON'T YOU KNOW YOUR OWN MOTHER?

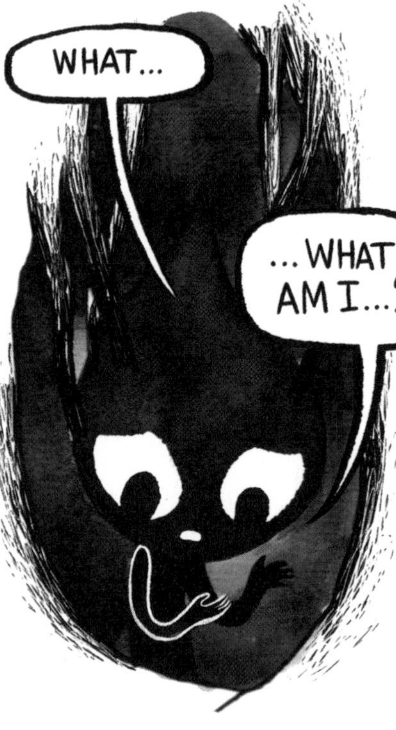
WHAT...
...WHAT AM I...?

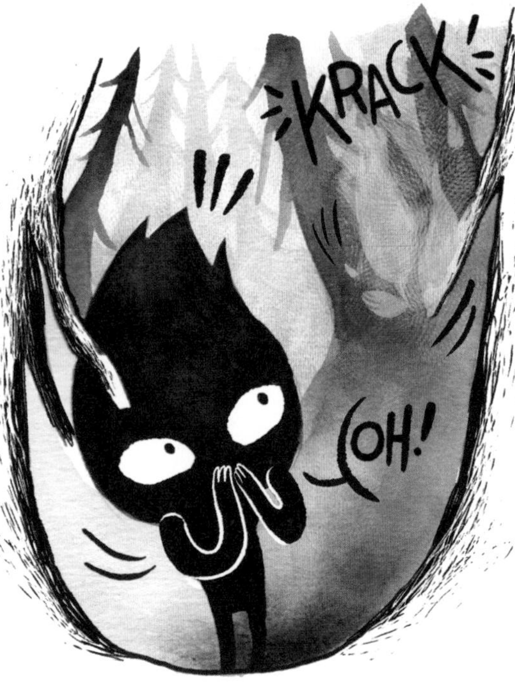
KRACK
OH!

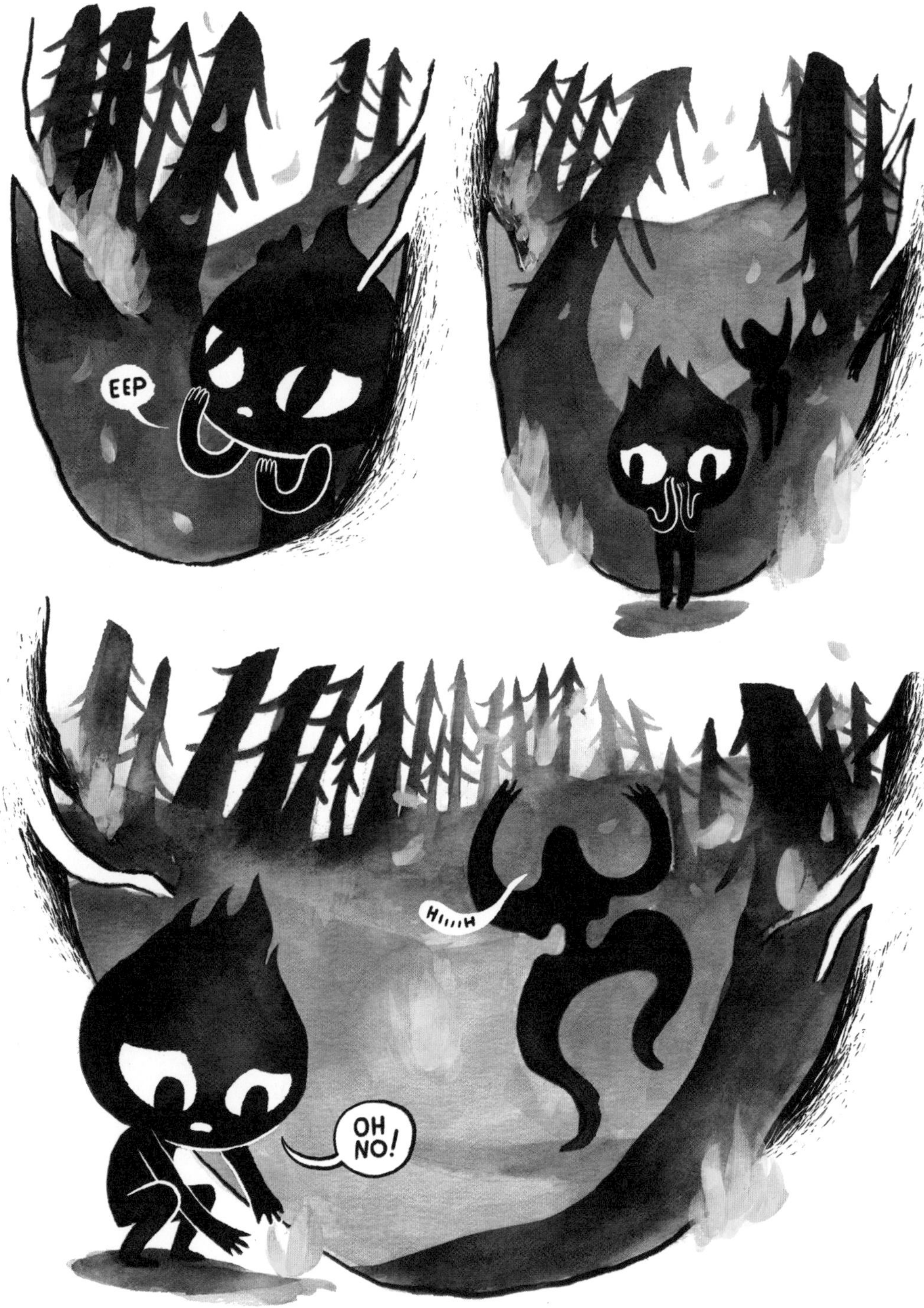
EEP
HIIIIH
OH NO!

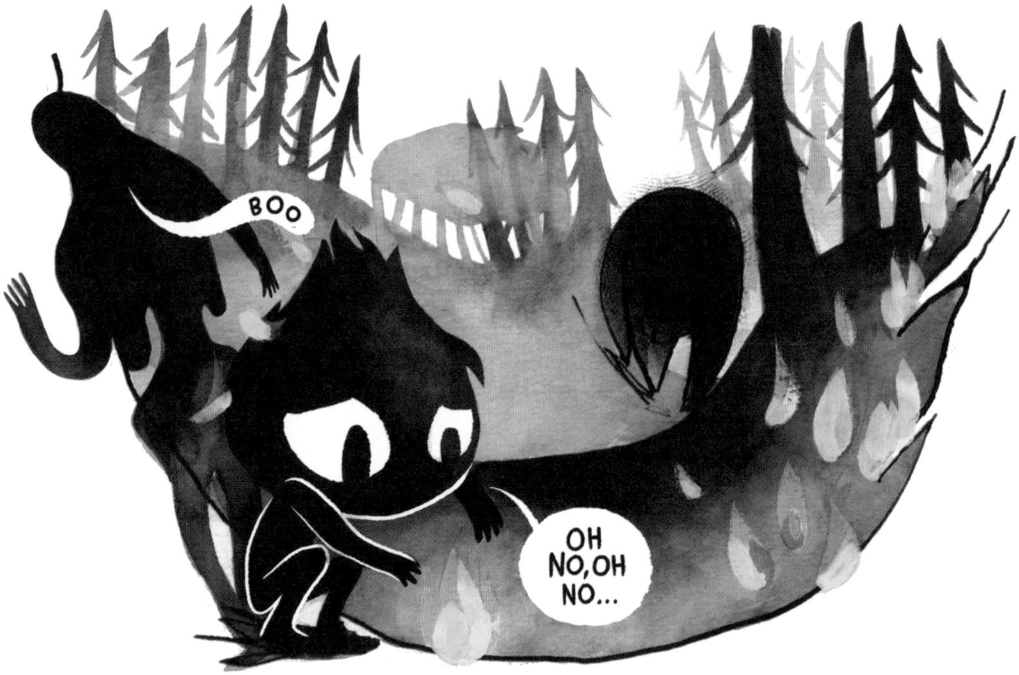
BOO
OH NO, OH NO...

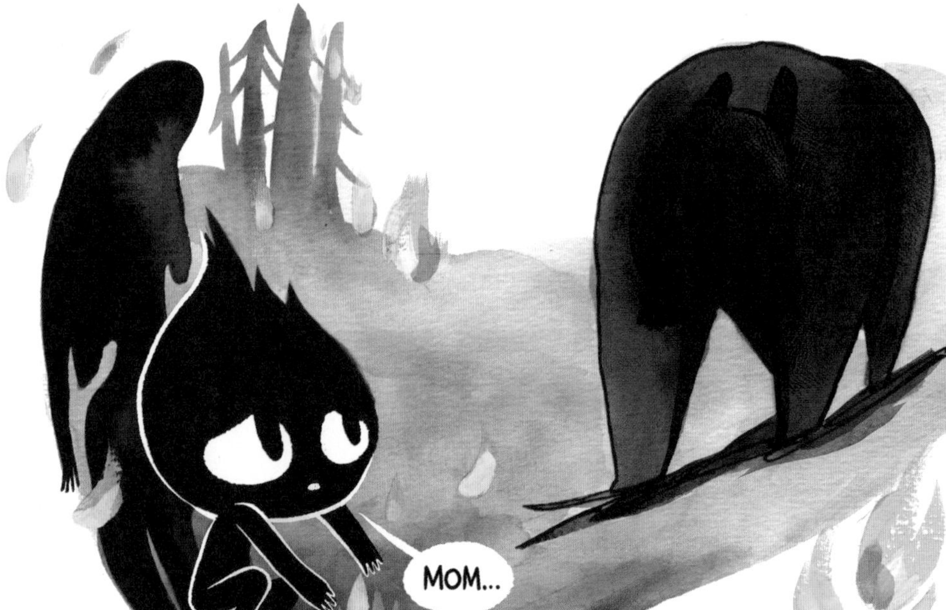
MOM...

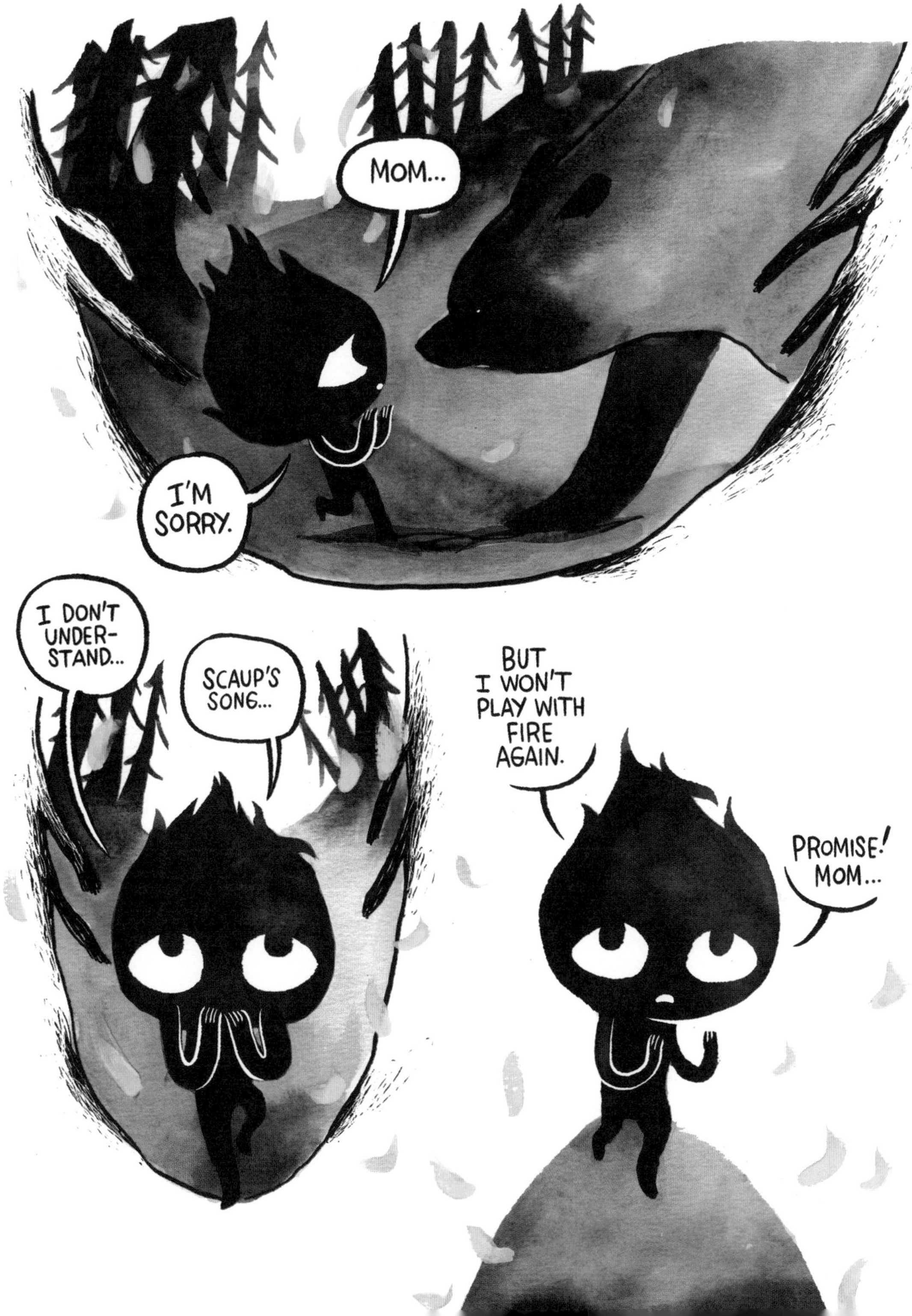
MOM...
I'M SORRY.
I DON'T UNDER-STAND...
SCAUP'S SONG...
BUT I WON'T PLAY WITH FIRE AGAIN.
PROMISE! MOM...

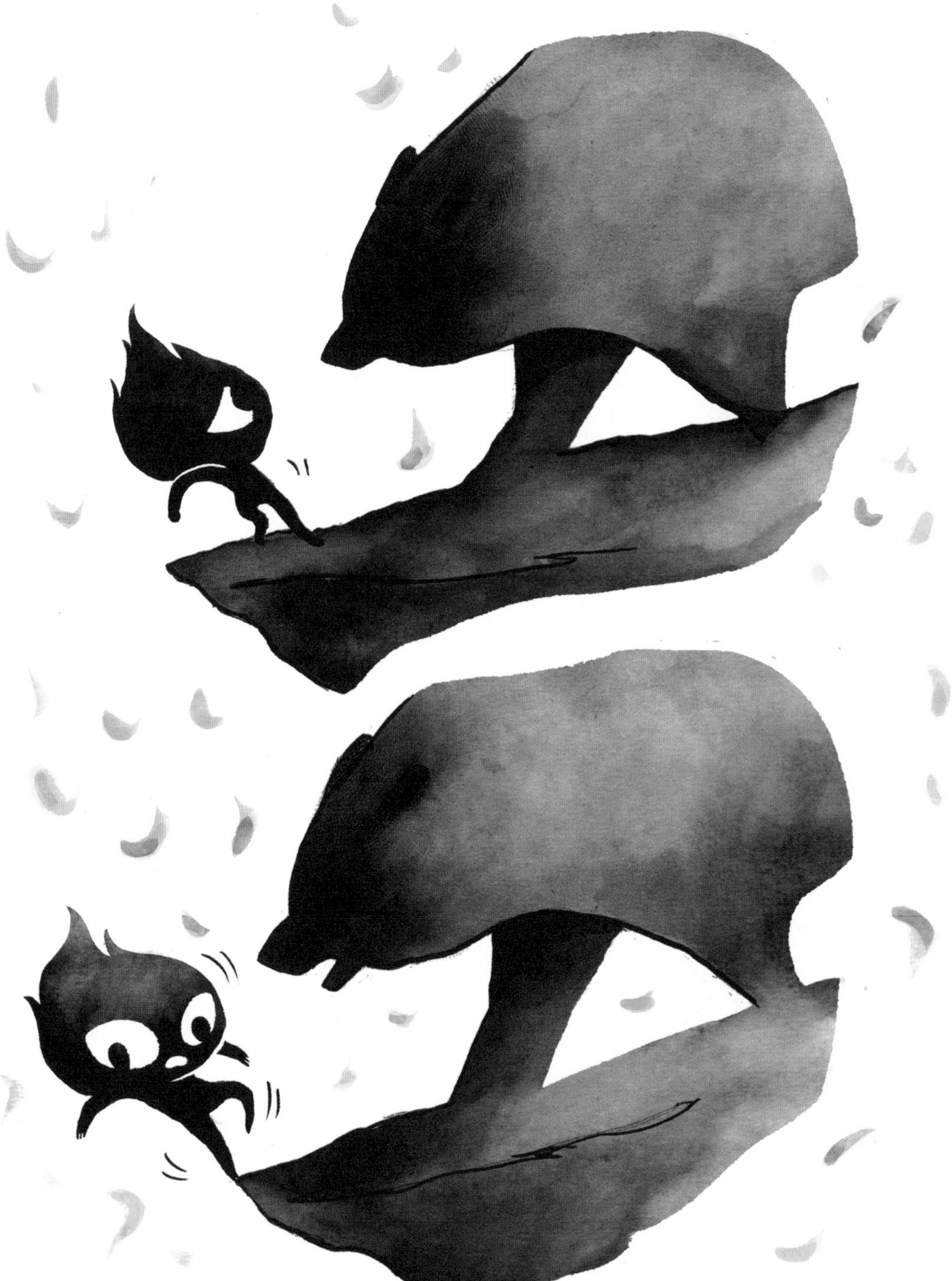

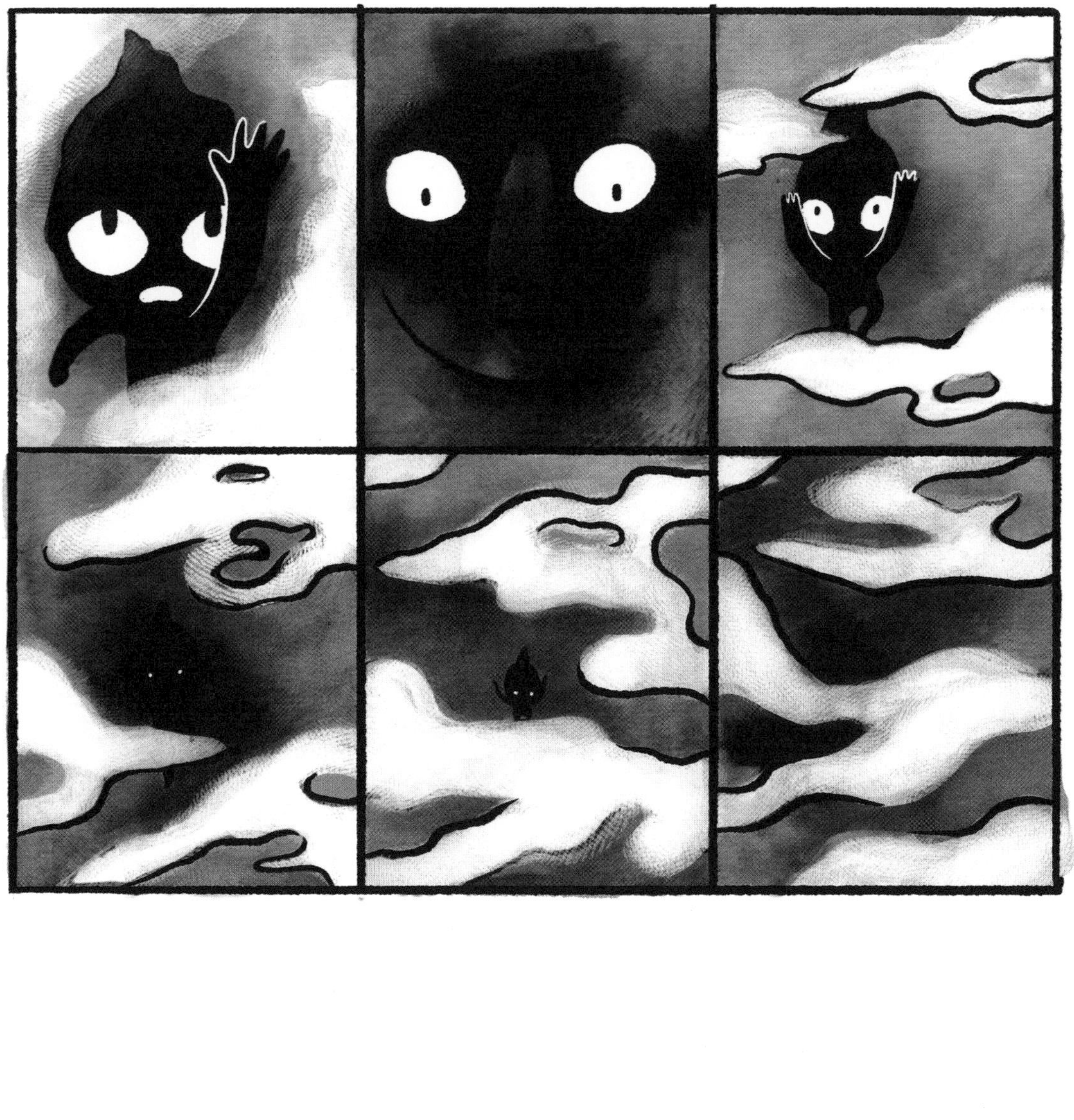

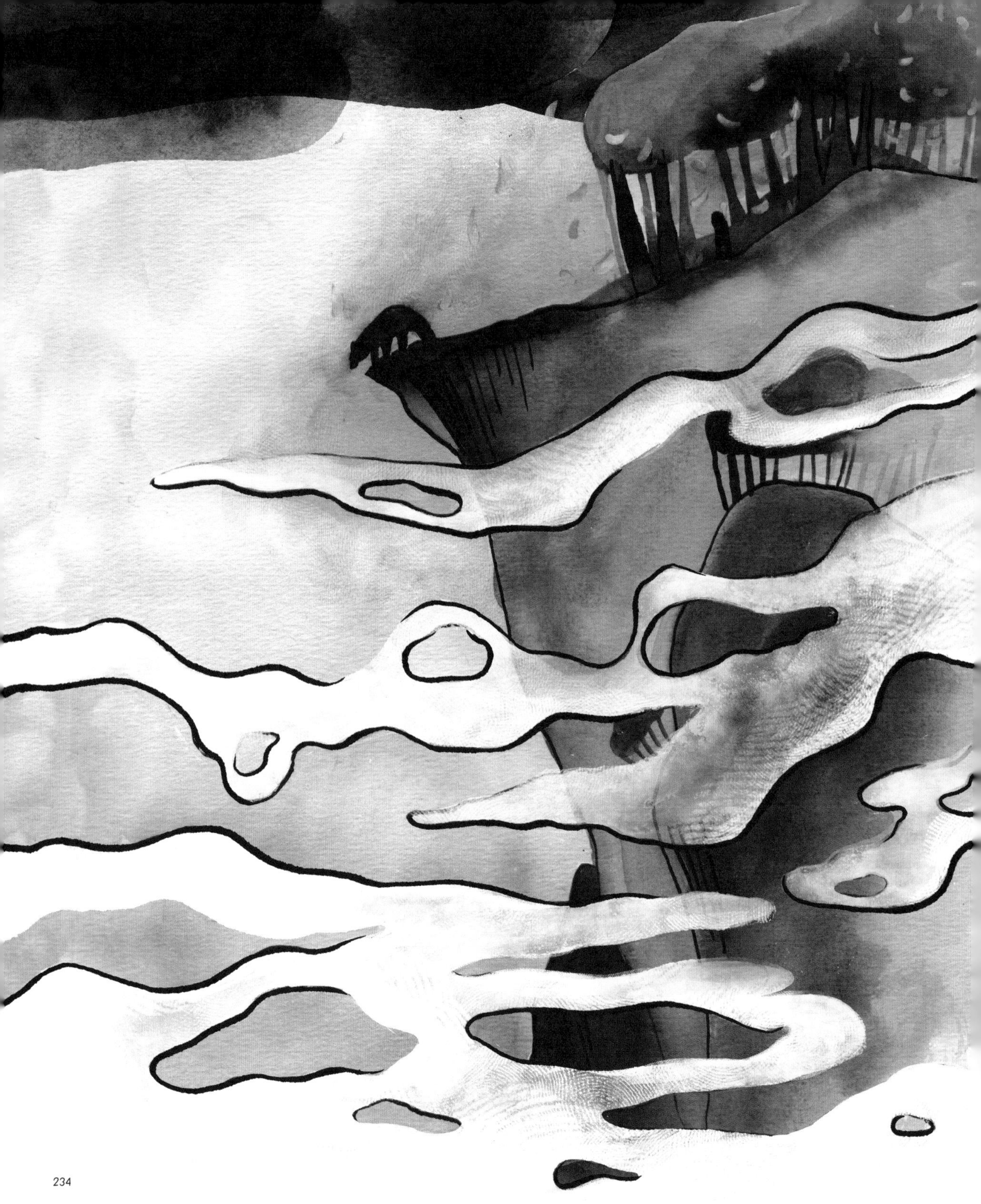

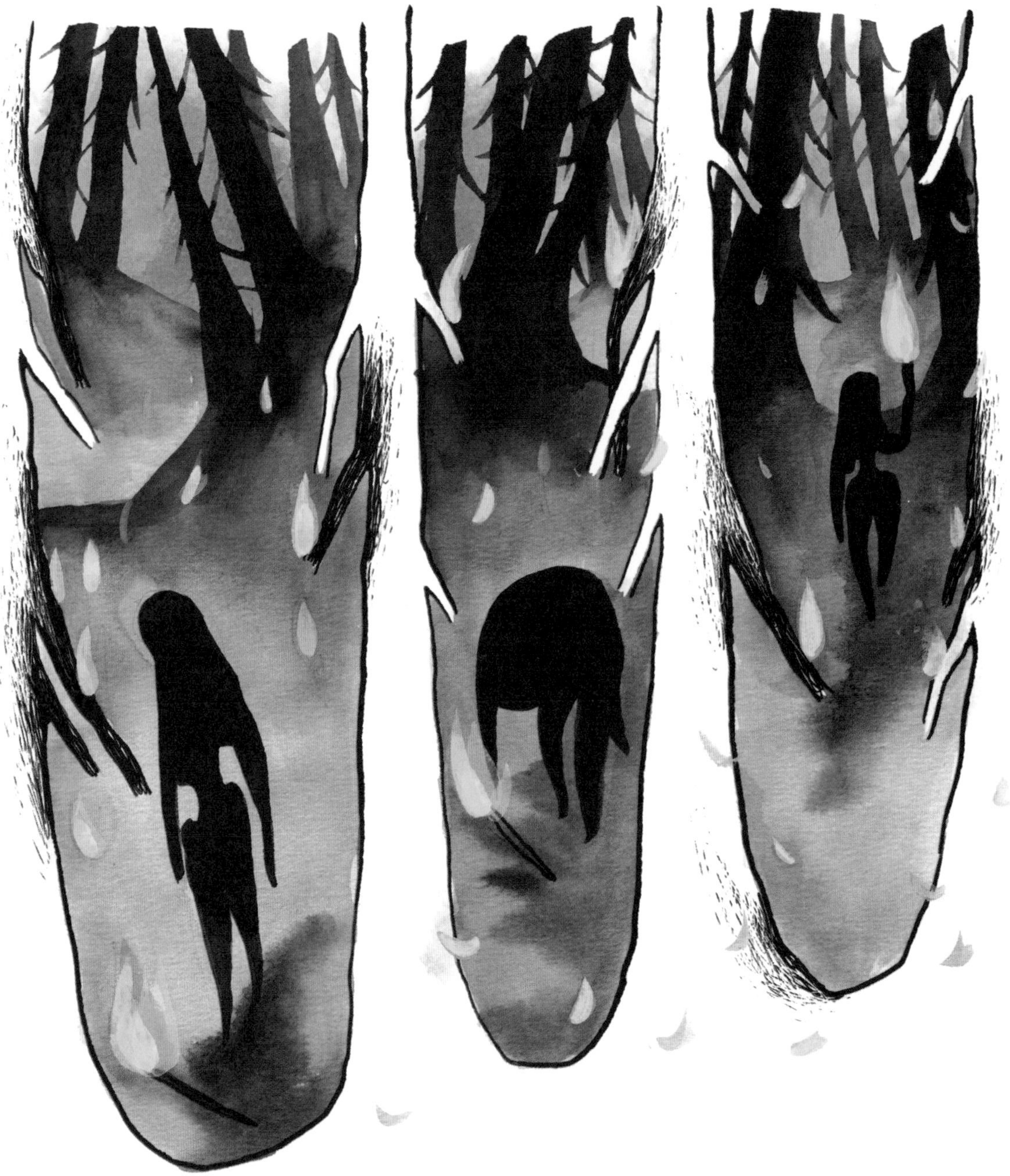

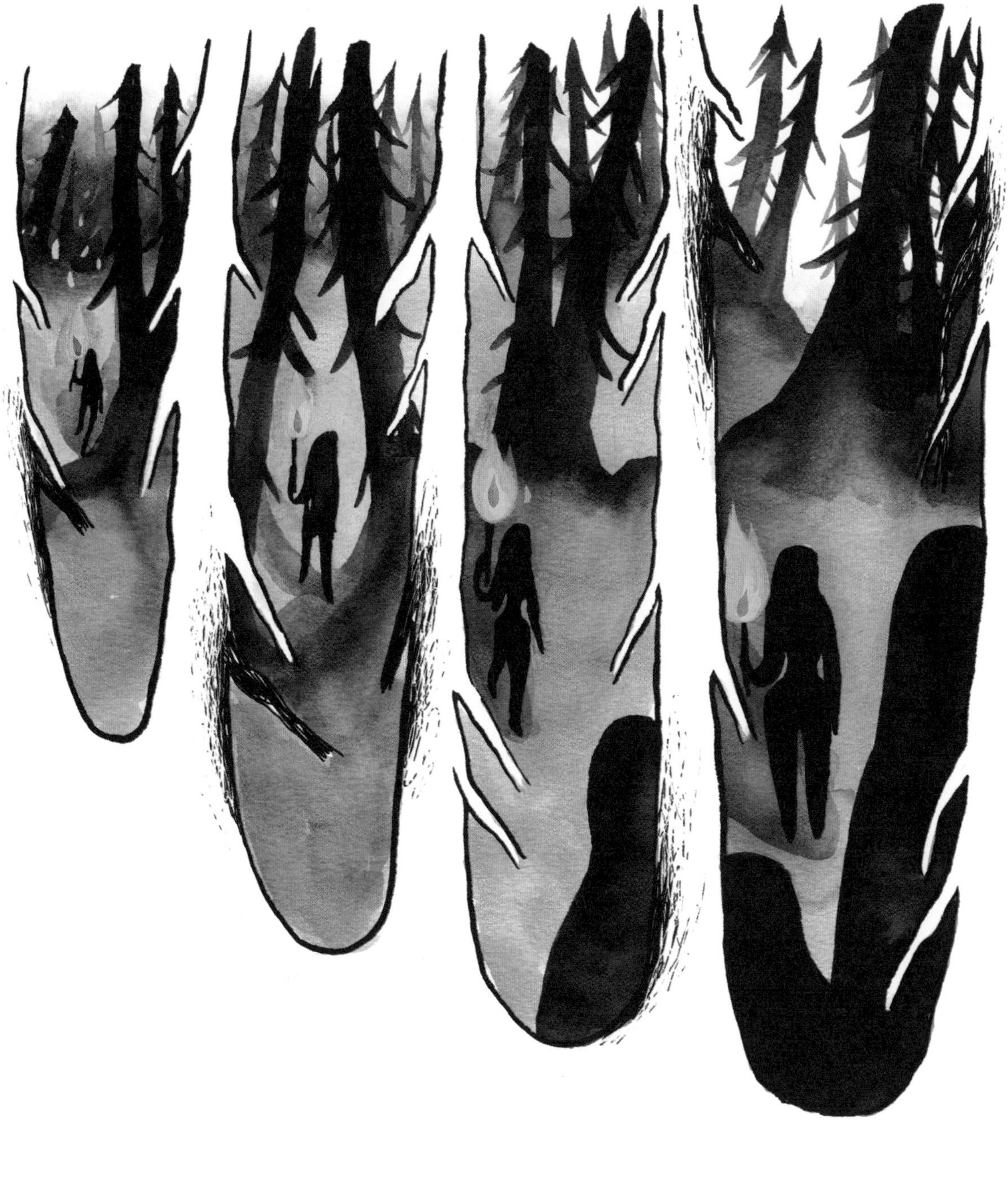

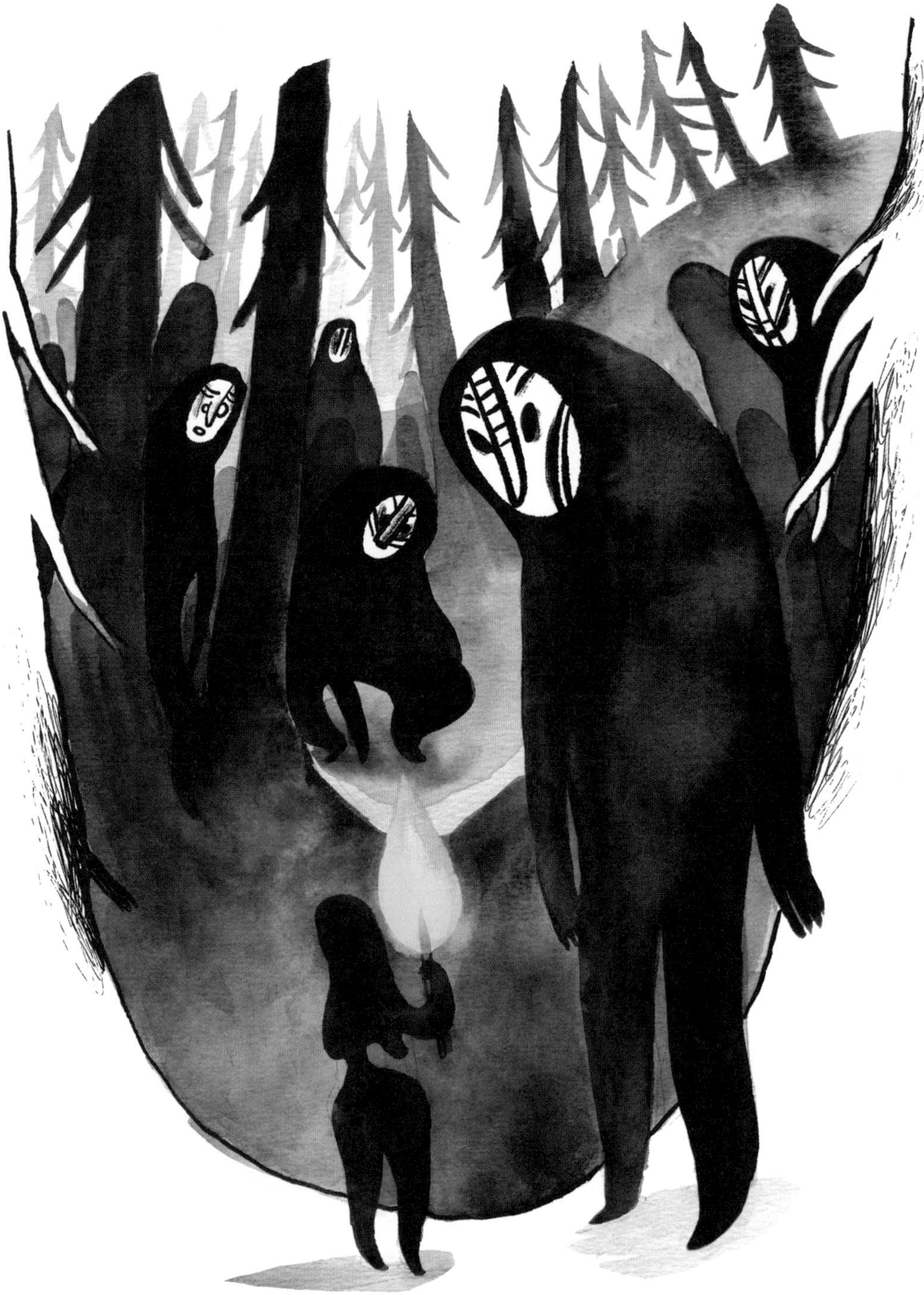

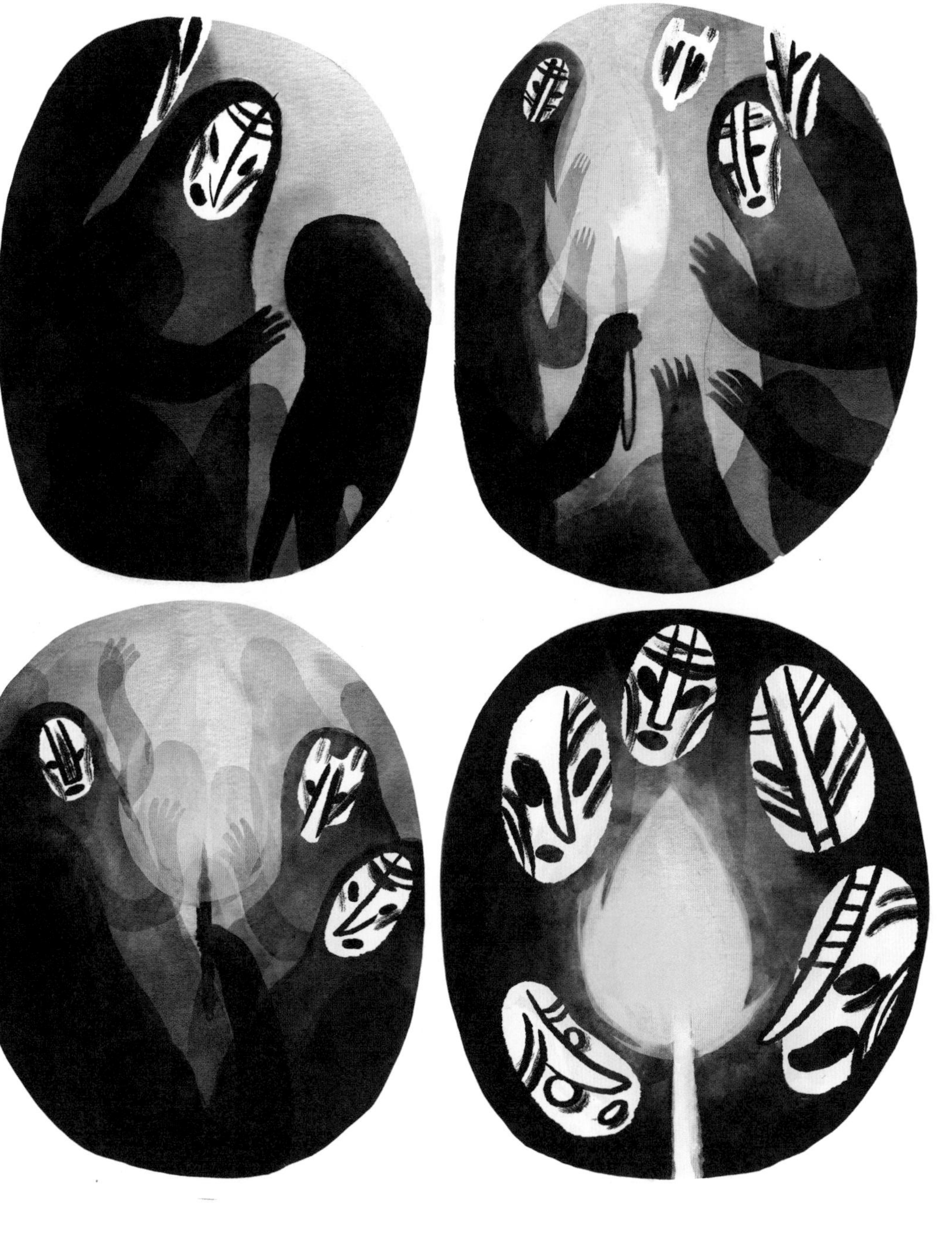

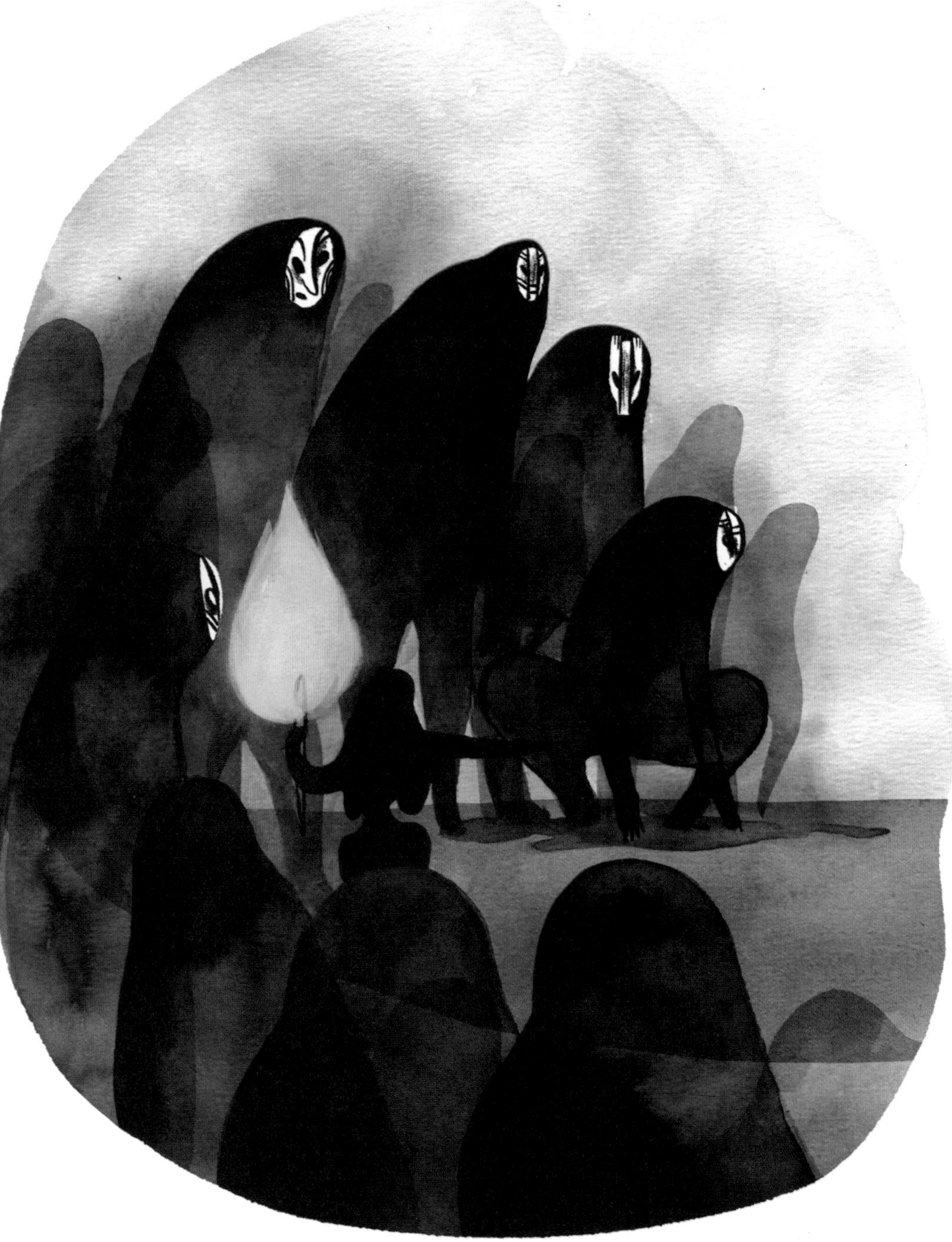

IX

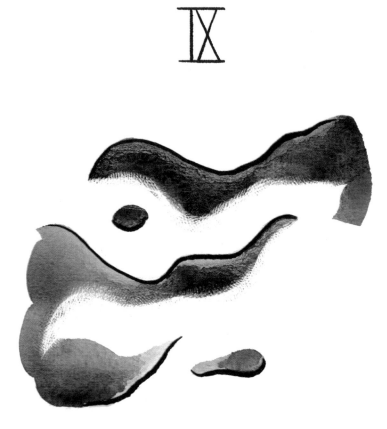

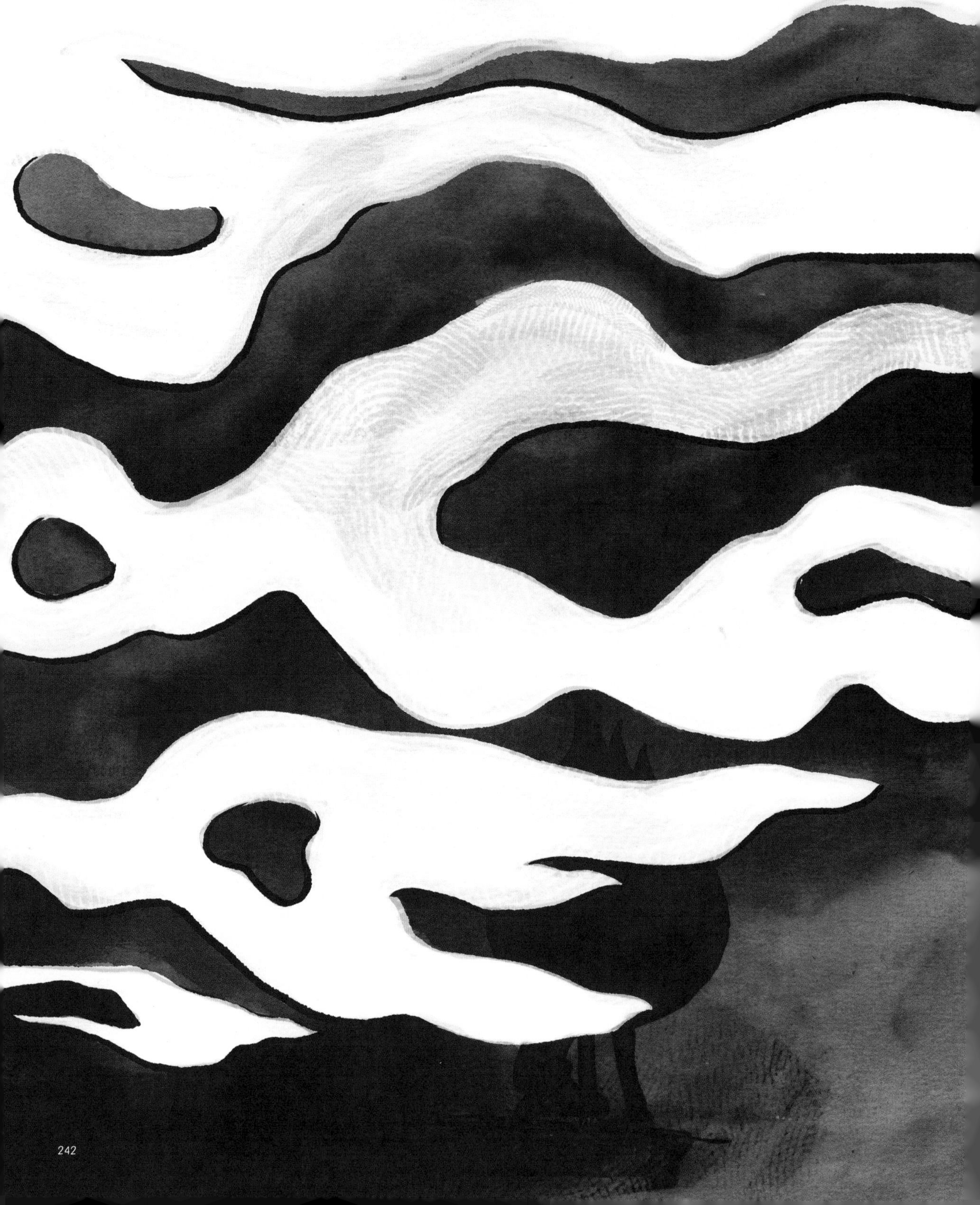

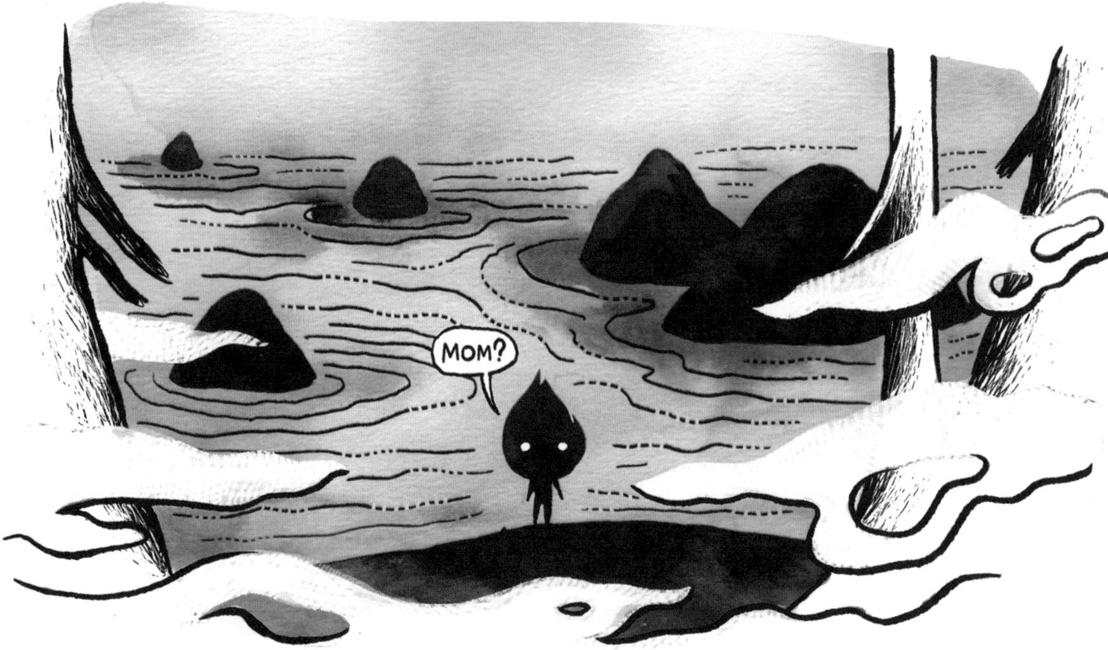
MOM?

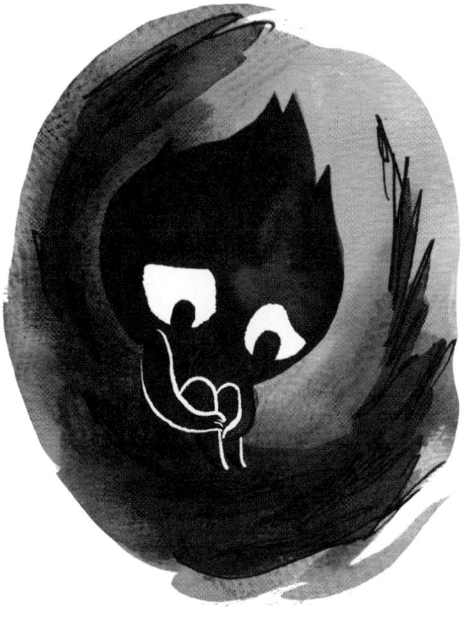

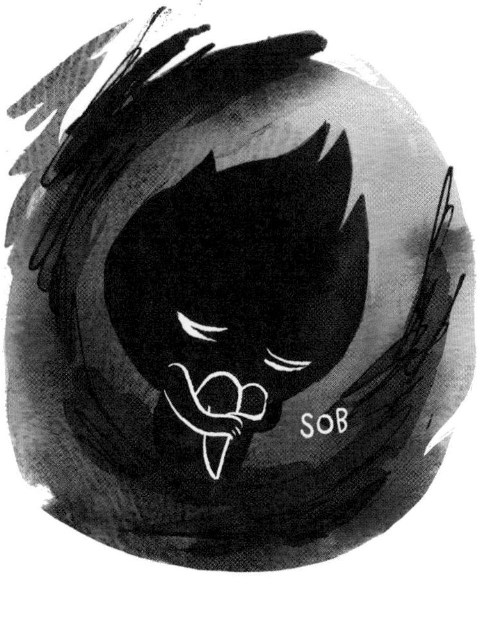
SOB

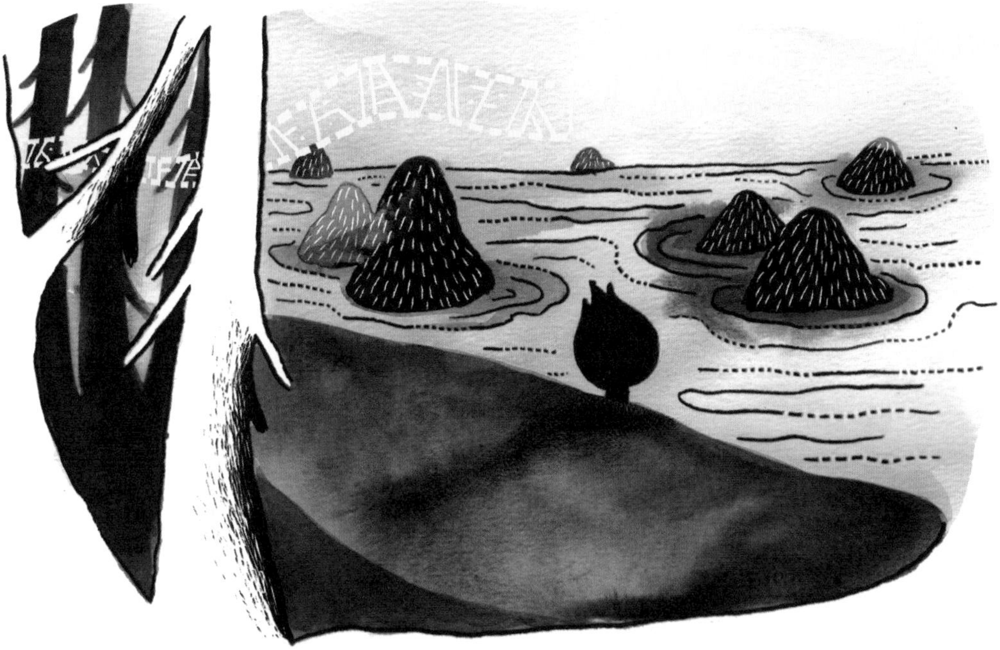

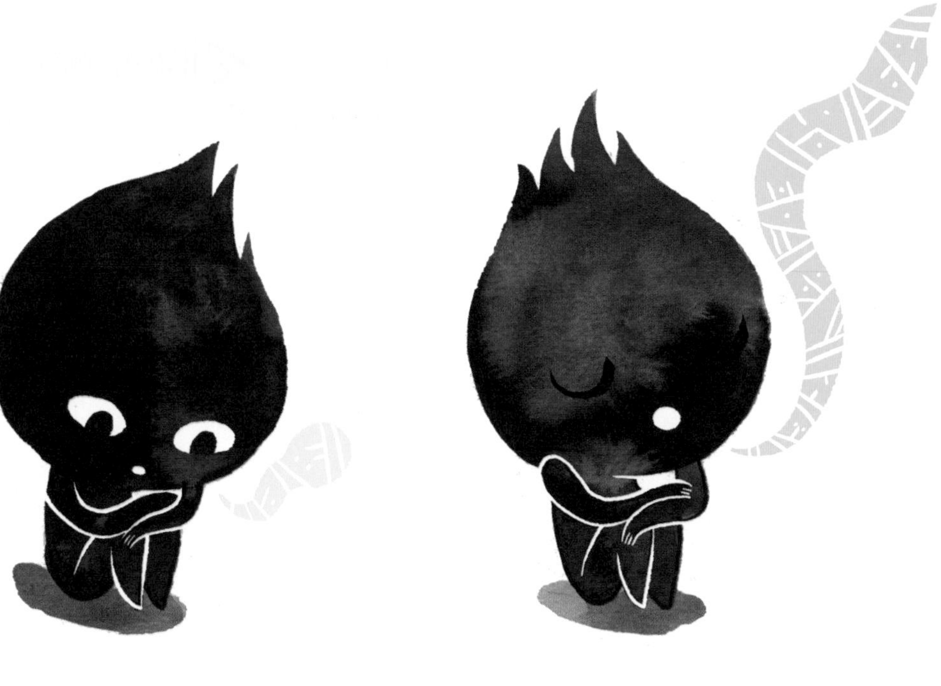

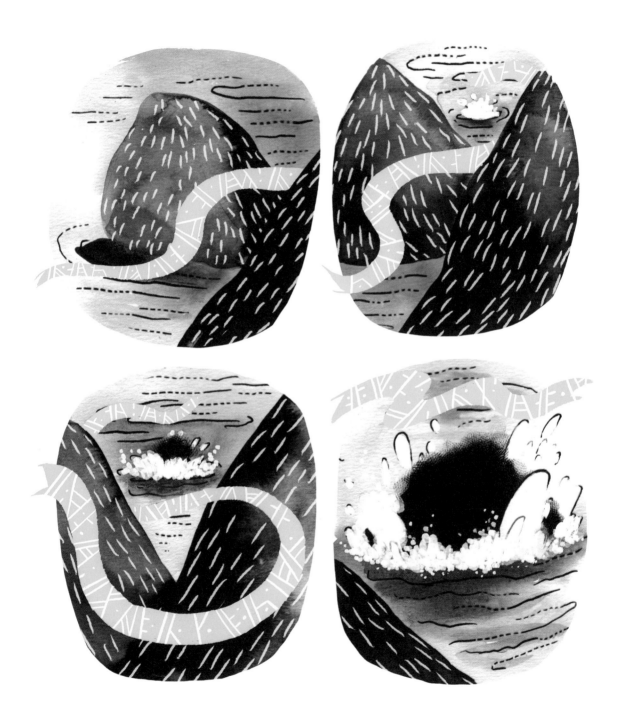

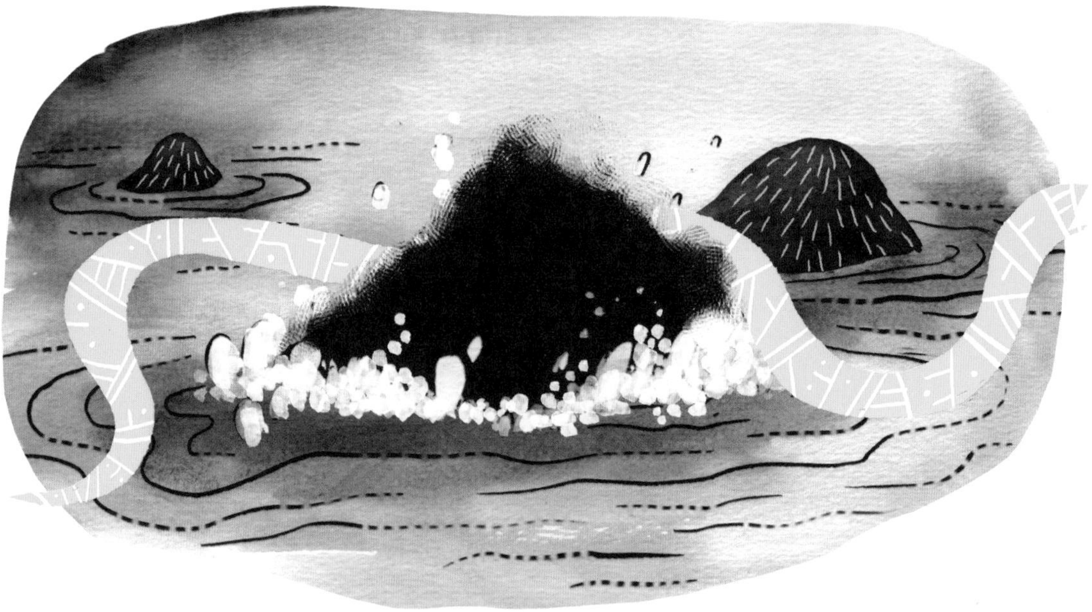

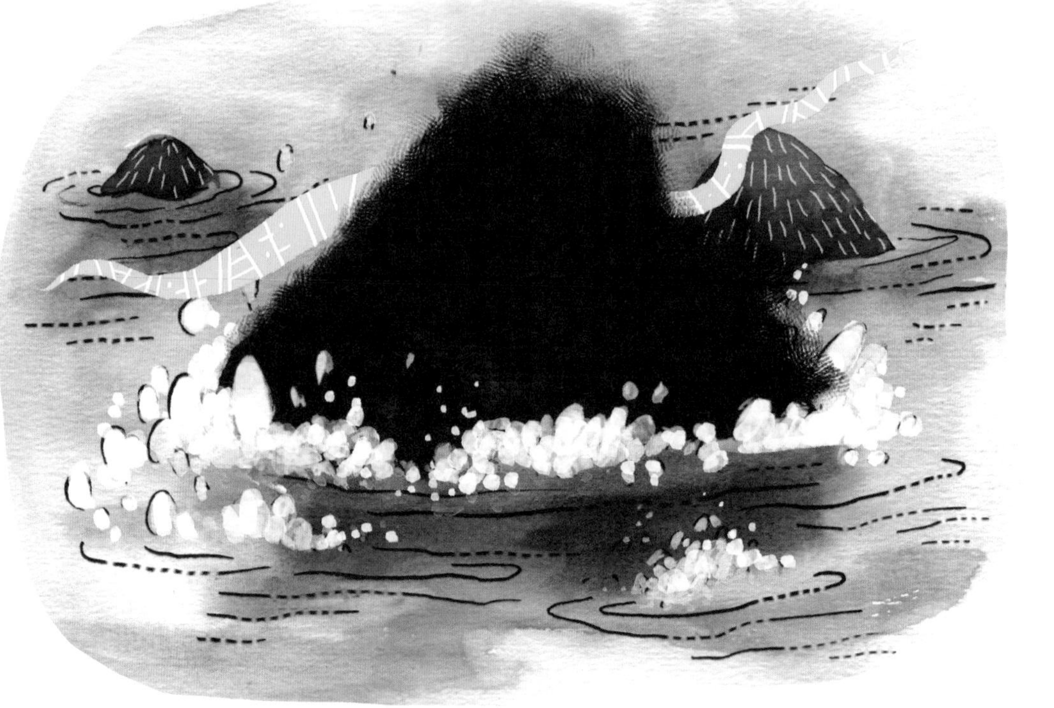

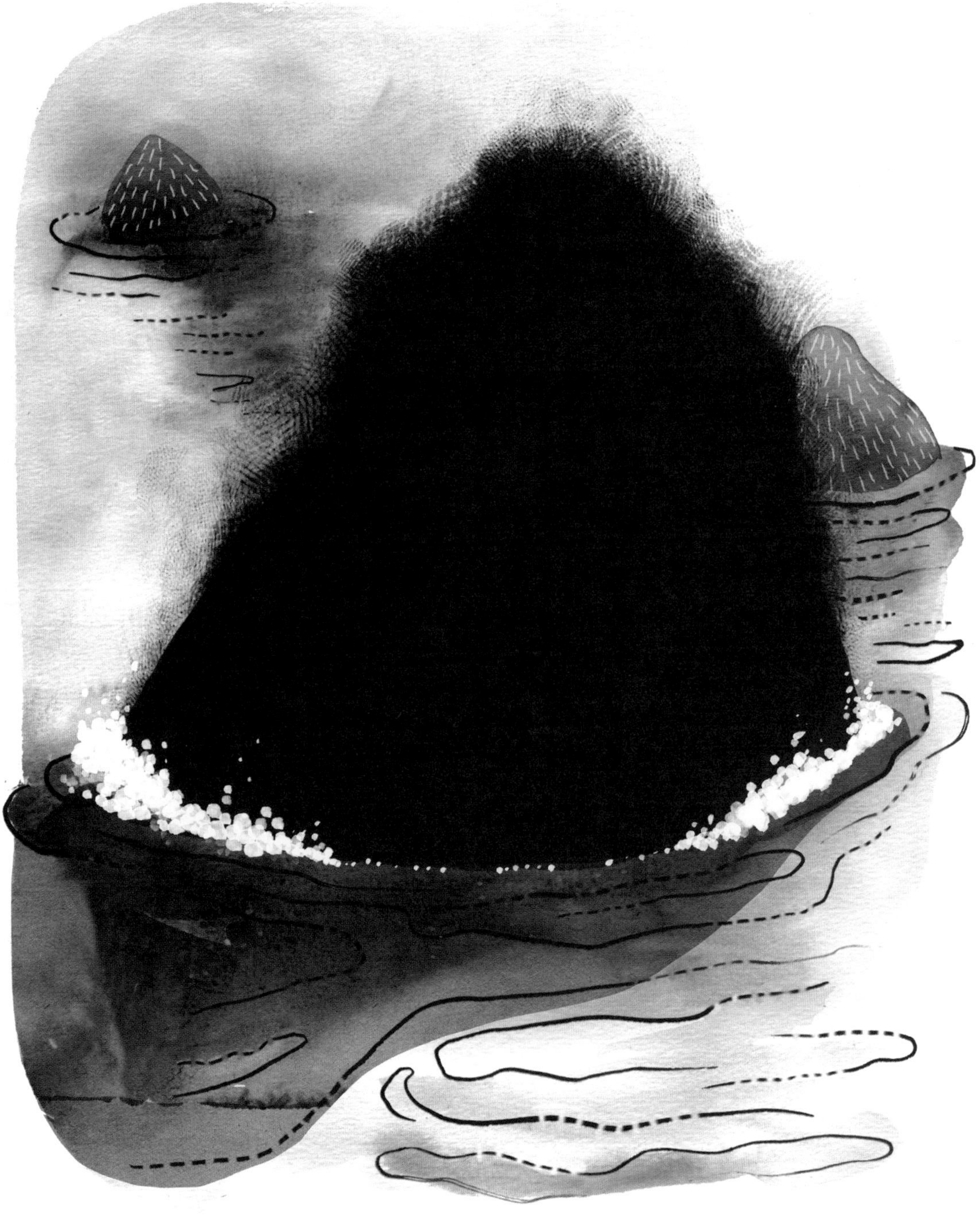

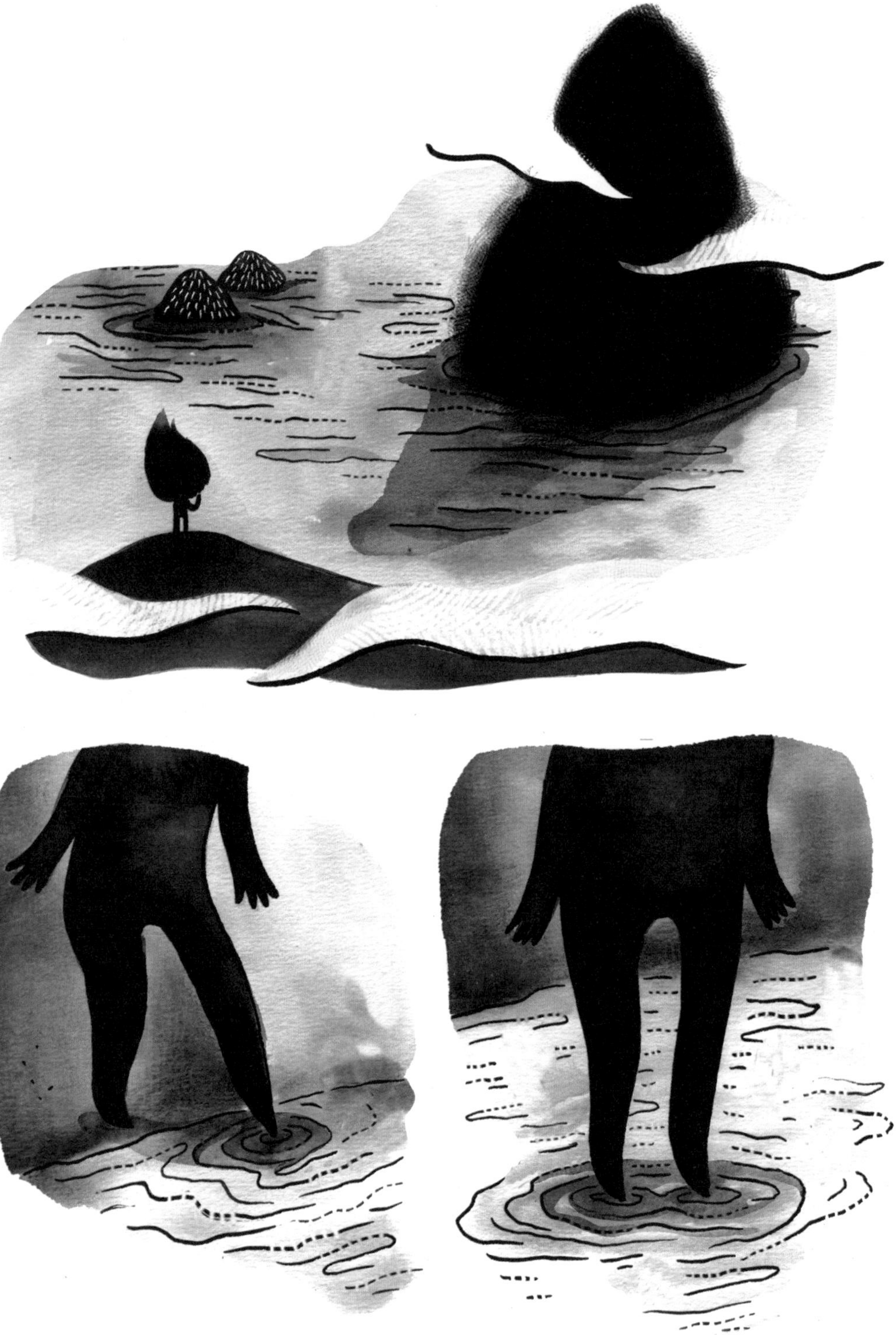

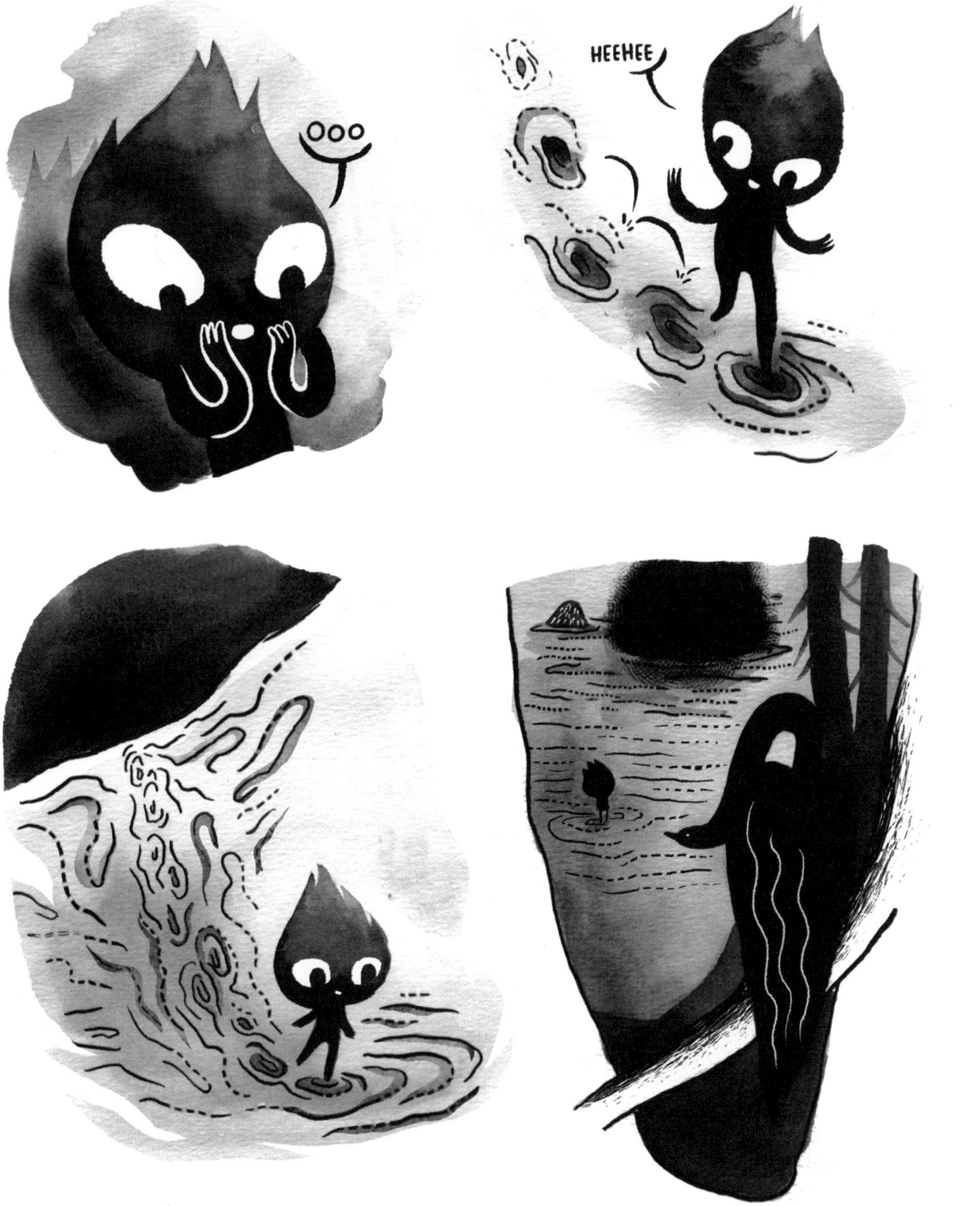
OOO
HEEHEE

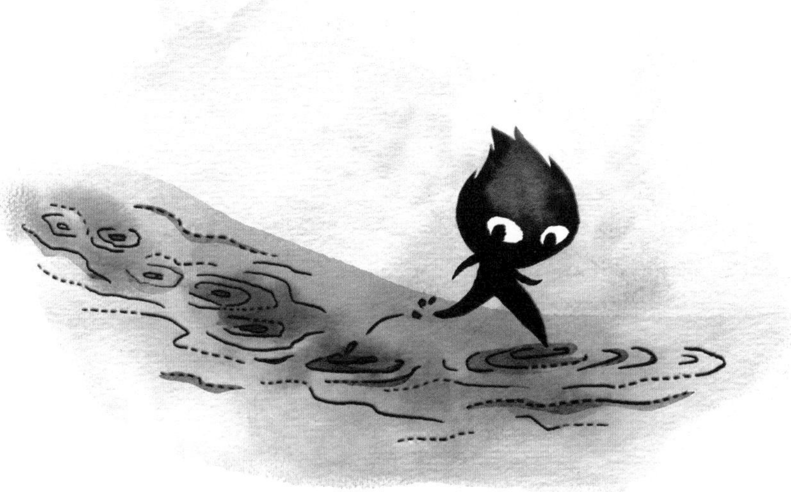

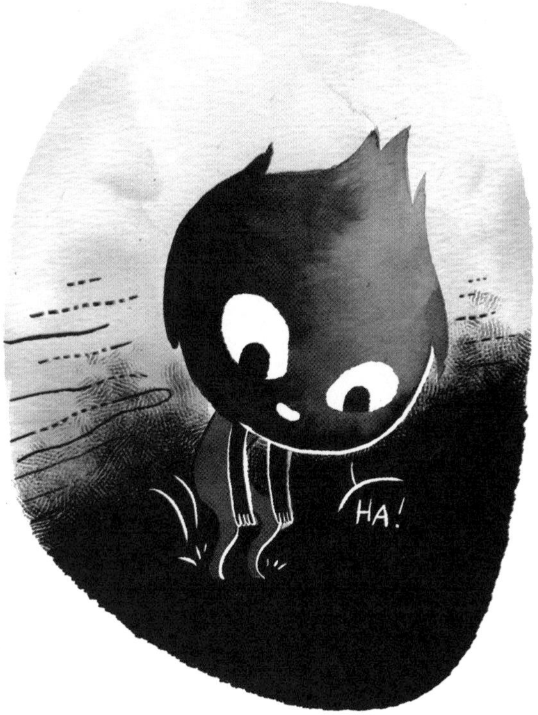
HA!

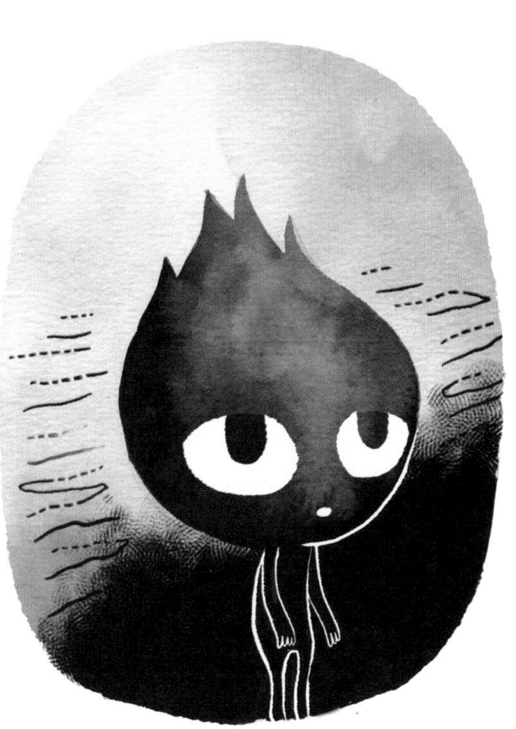

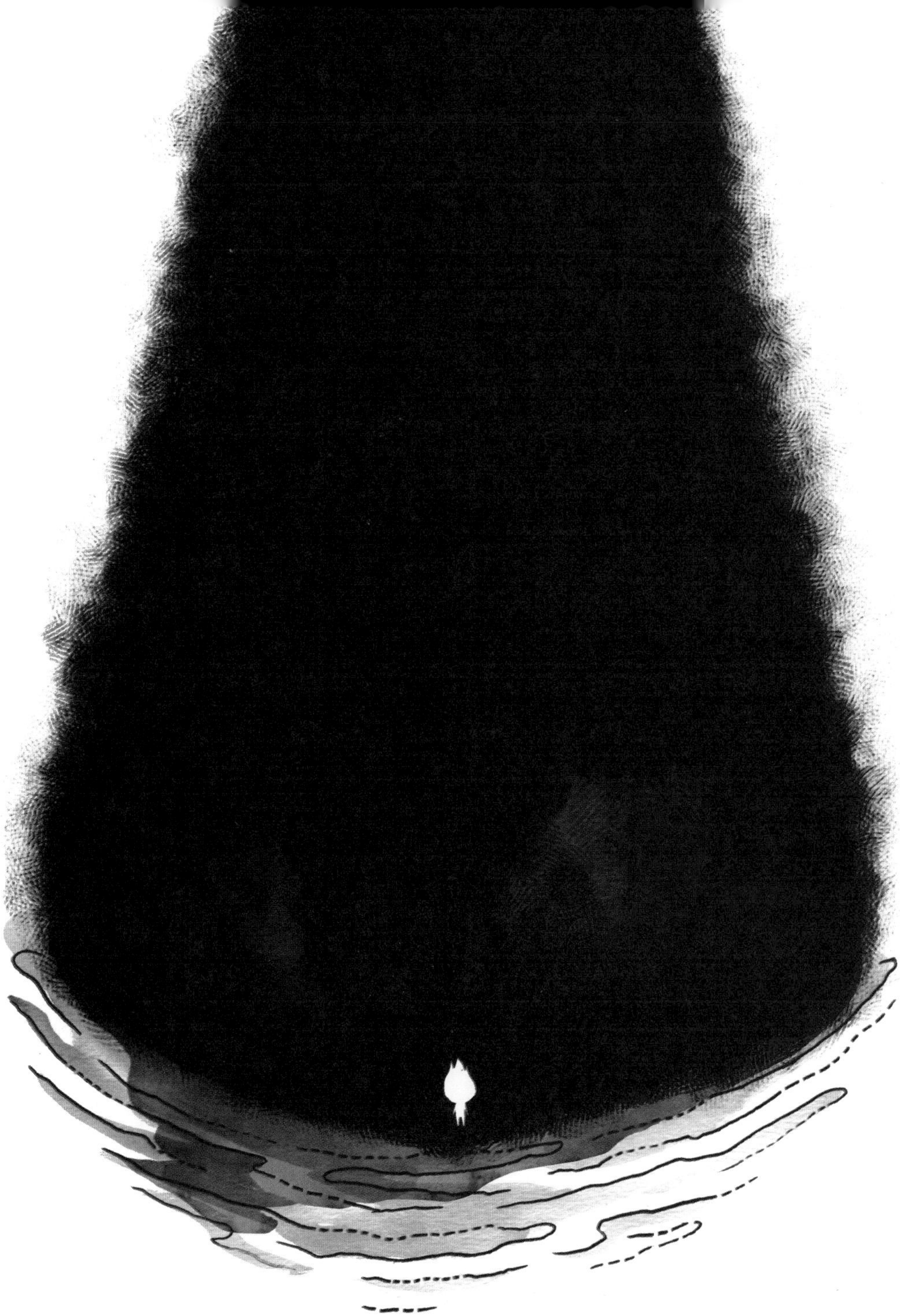

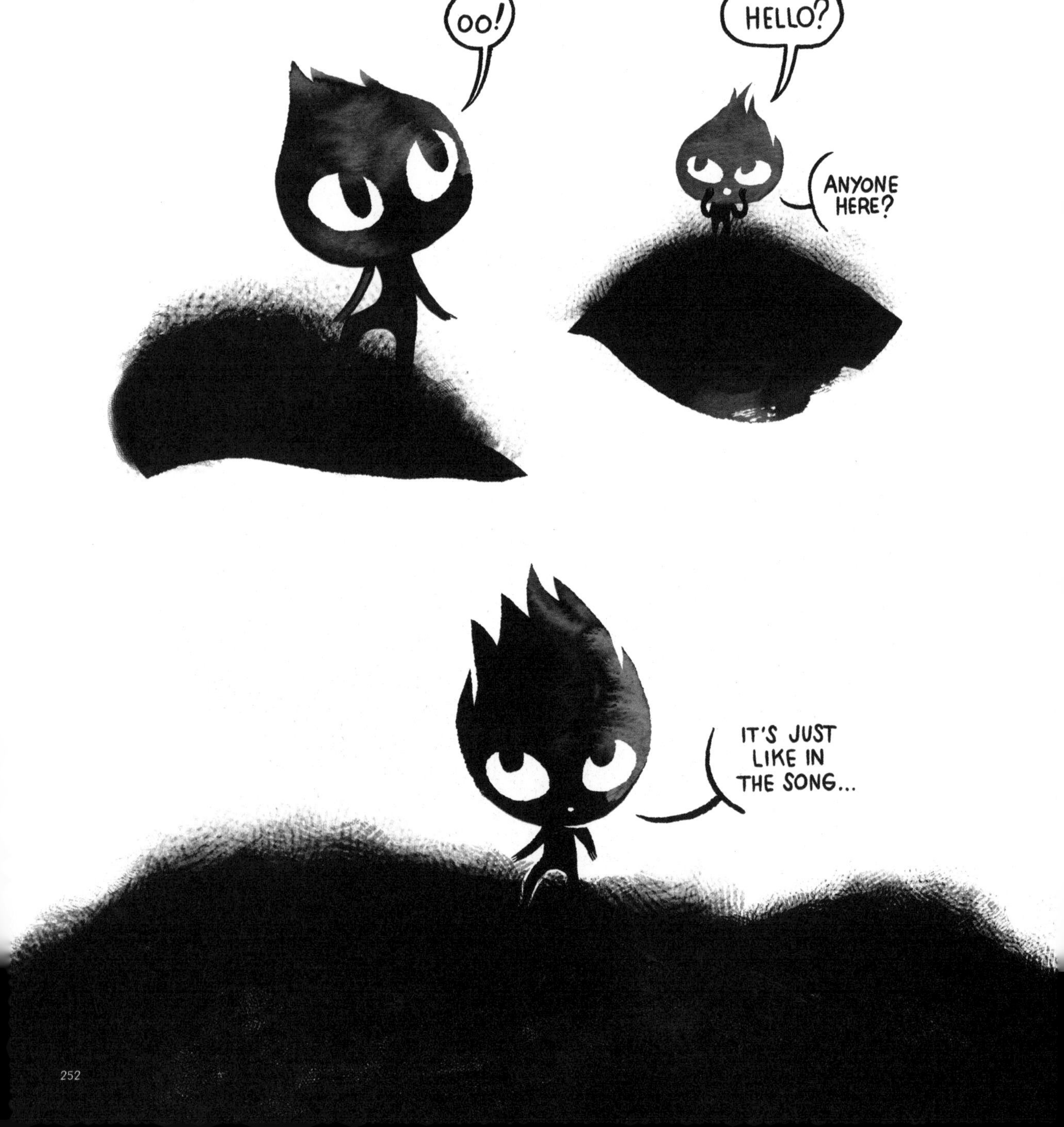

OO!
HELLO?
ANYONE HERE?
IT'S JUST LIKE IN THE SONG...

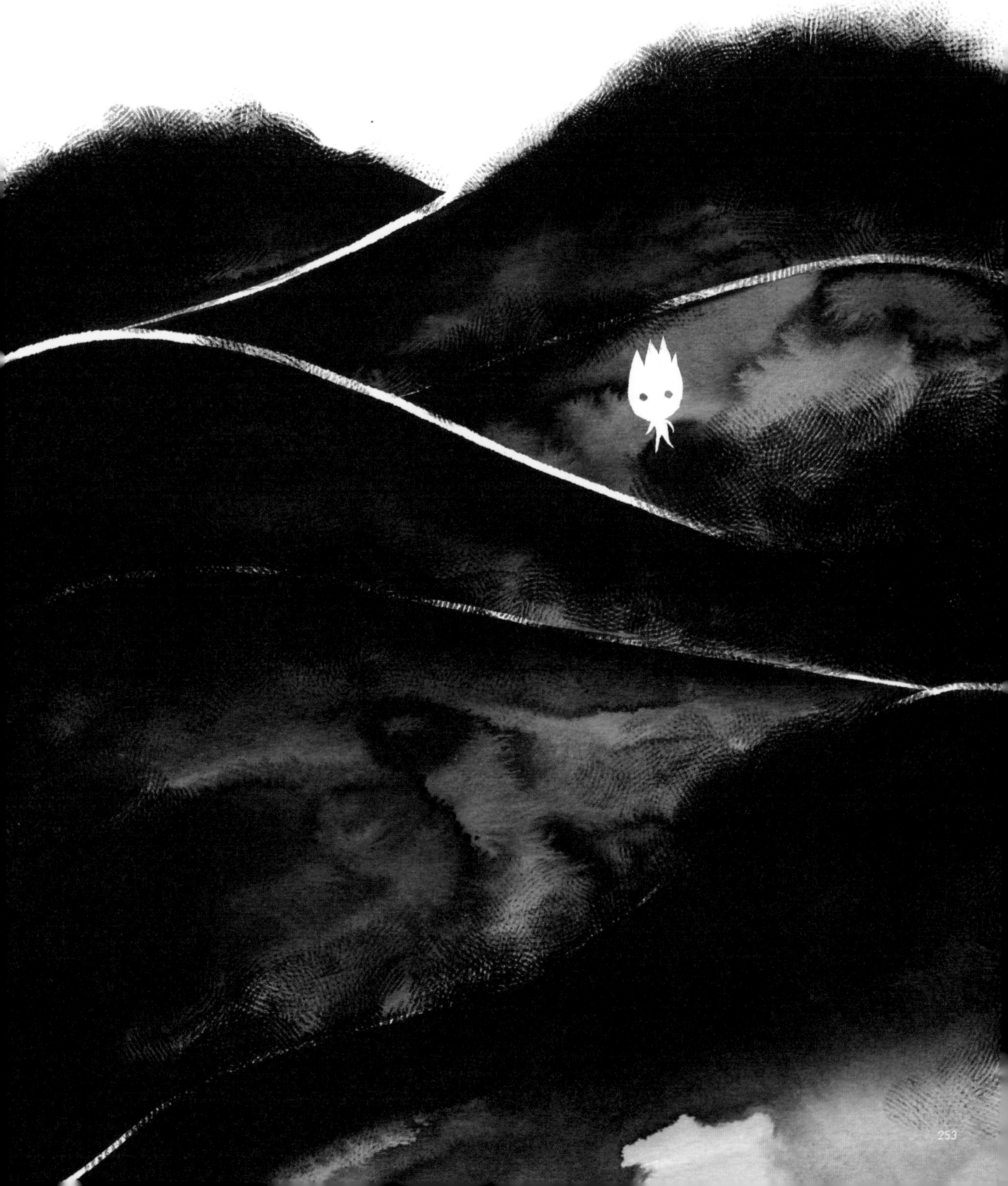

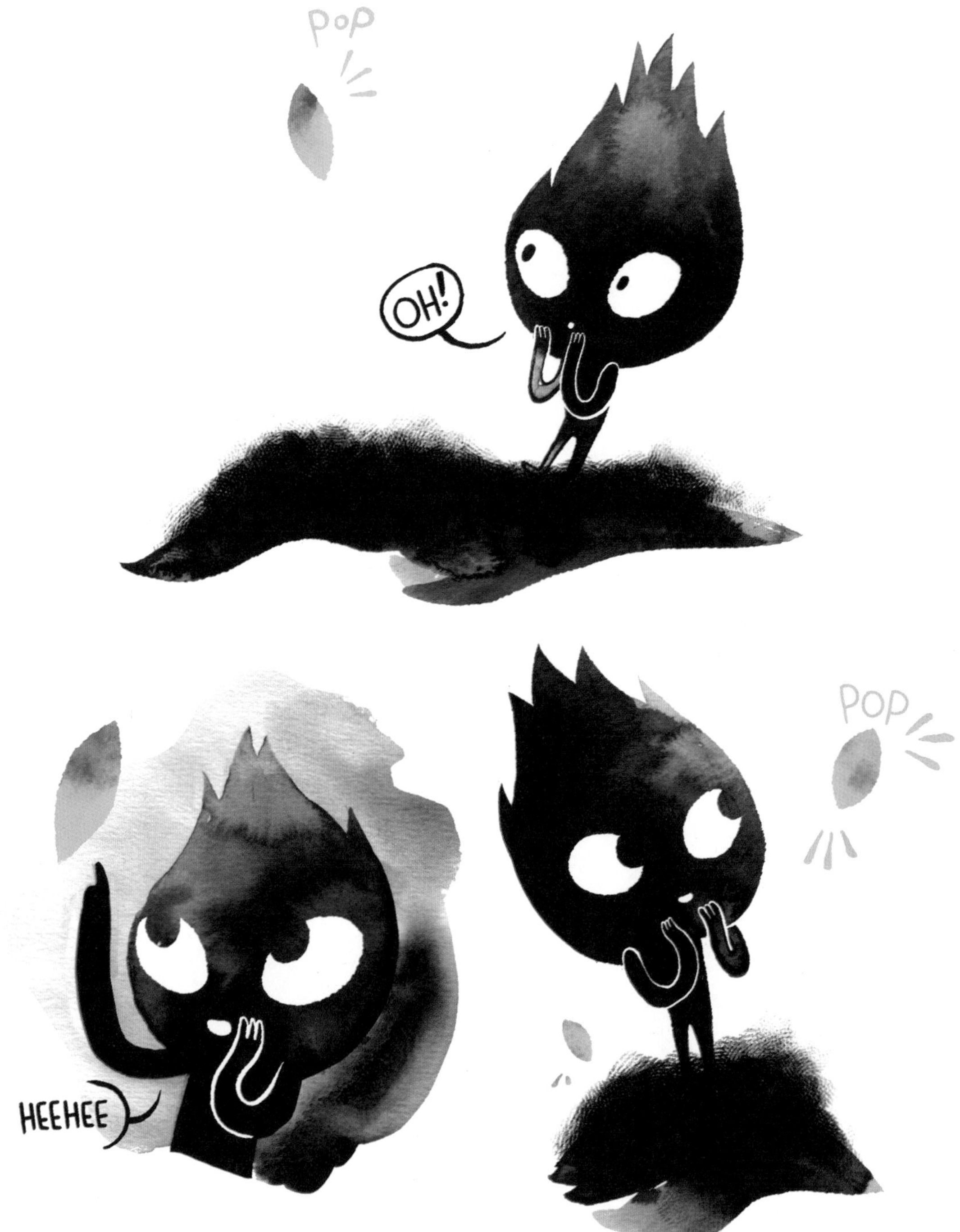
POP
OH!
HEEHEE
POP

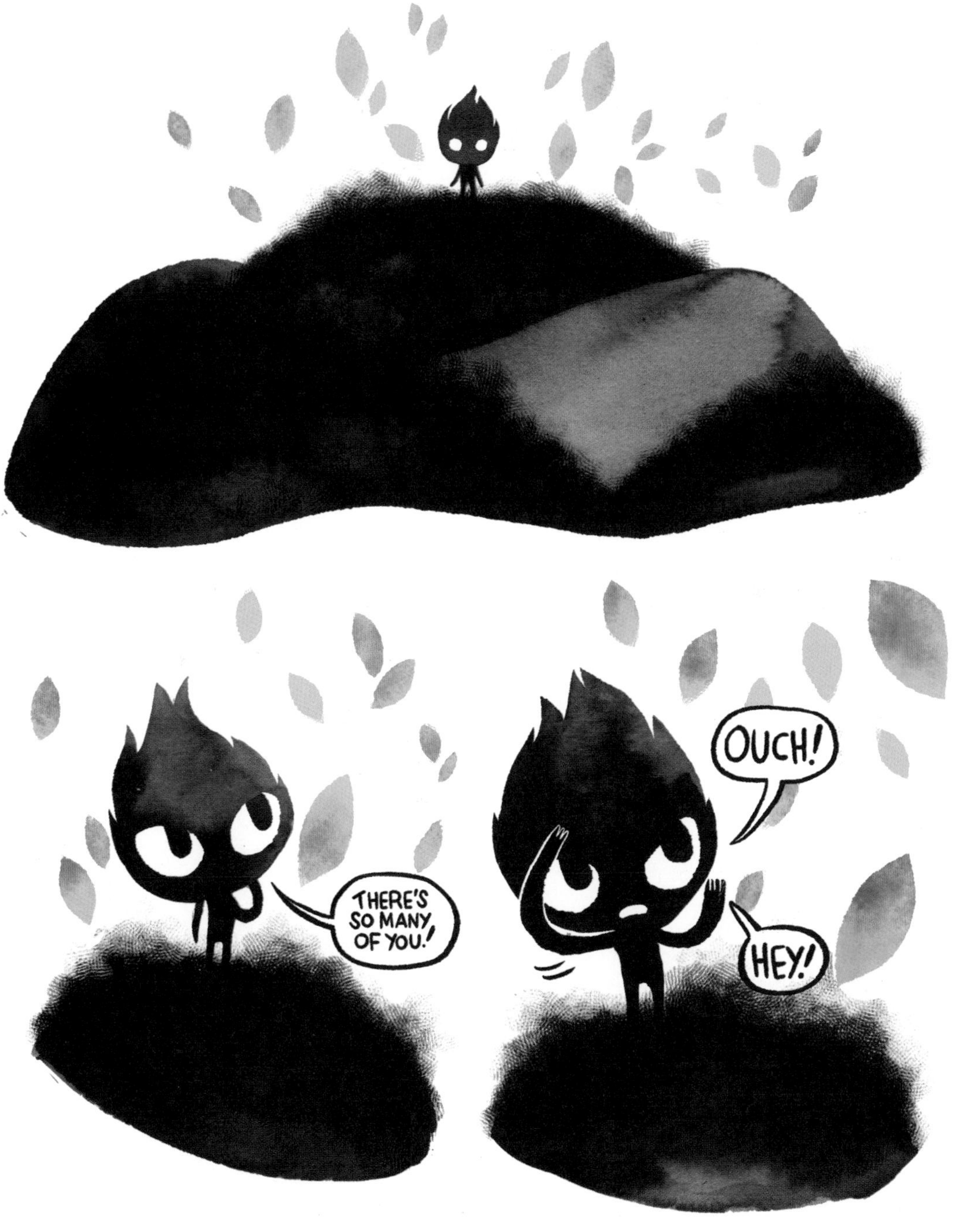
THERE'S SO MANY OF YOU!
OUCH!
HEY!

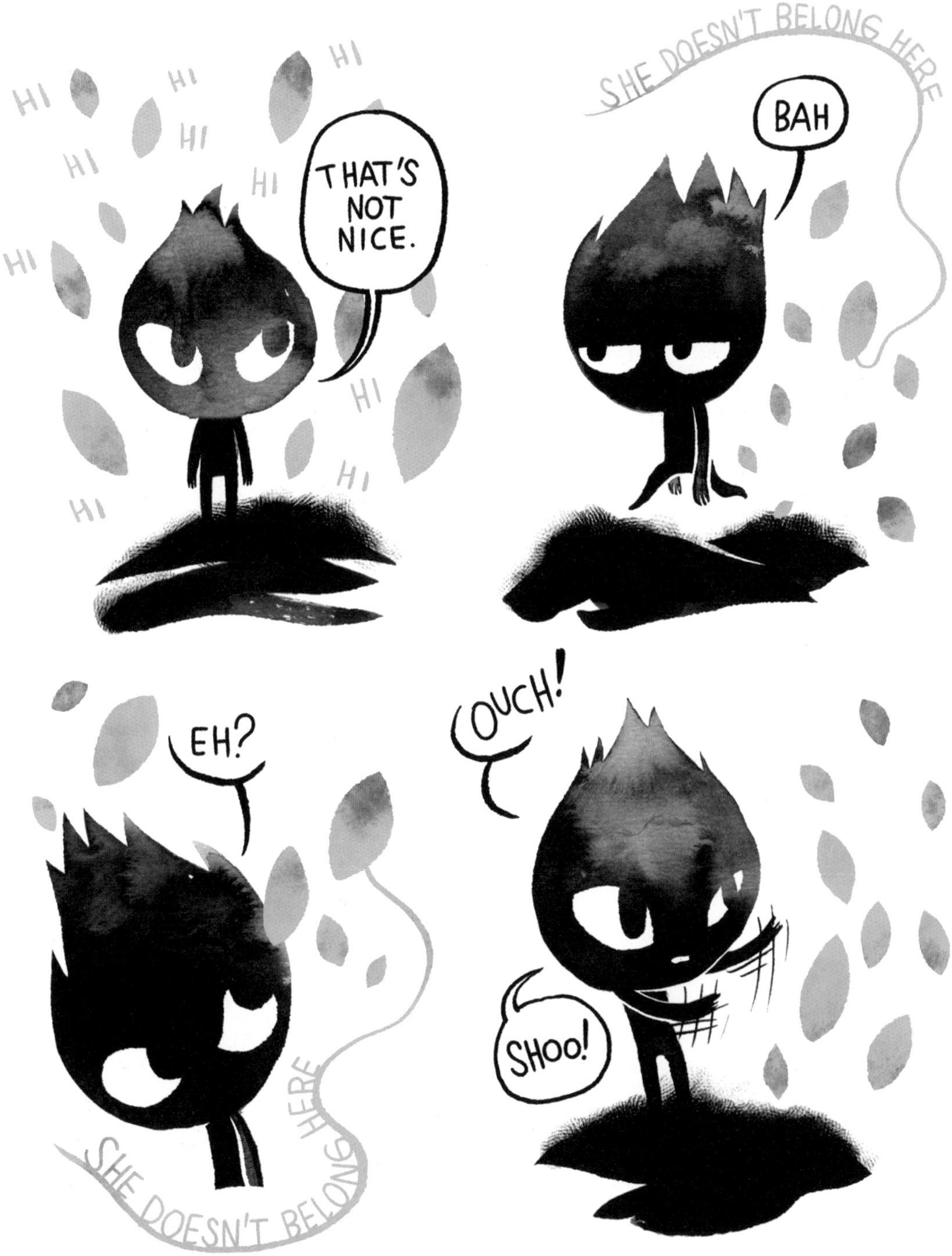
HI
HI
HI
HI
HI
HI
HI
HI
HI
HI
THAT'S NOT NICE.
SHE DOESN'T BELONG HERE
BAH
EH?
SHE DOESN'T BELONG HERE
OUCH!
SHOO!

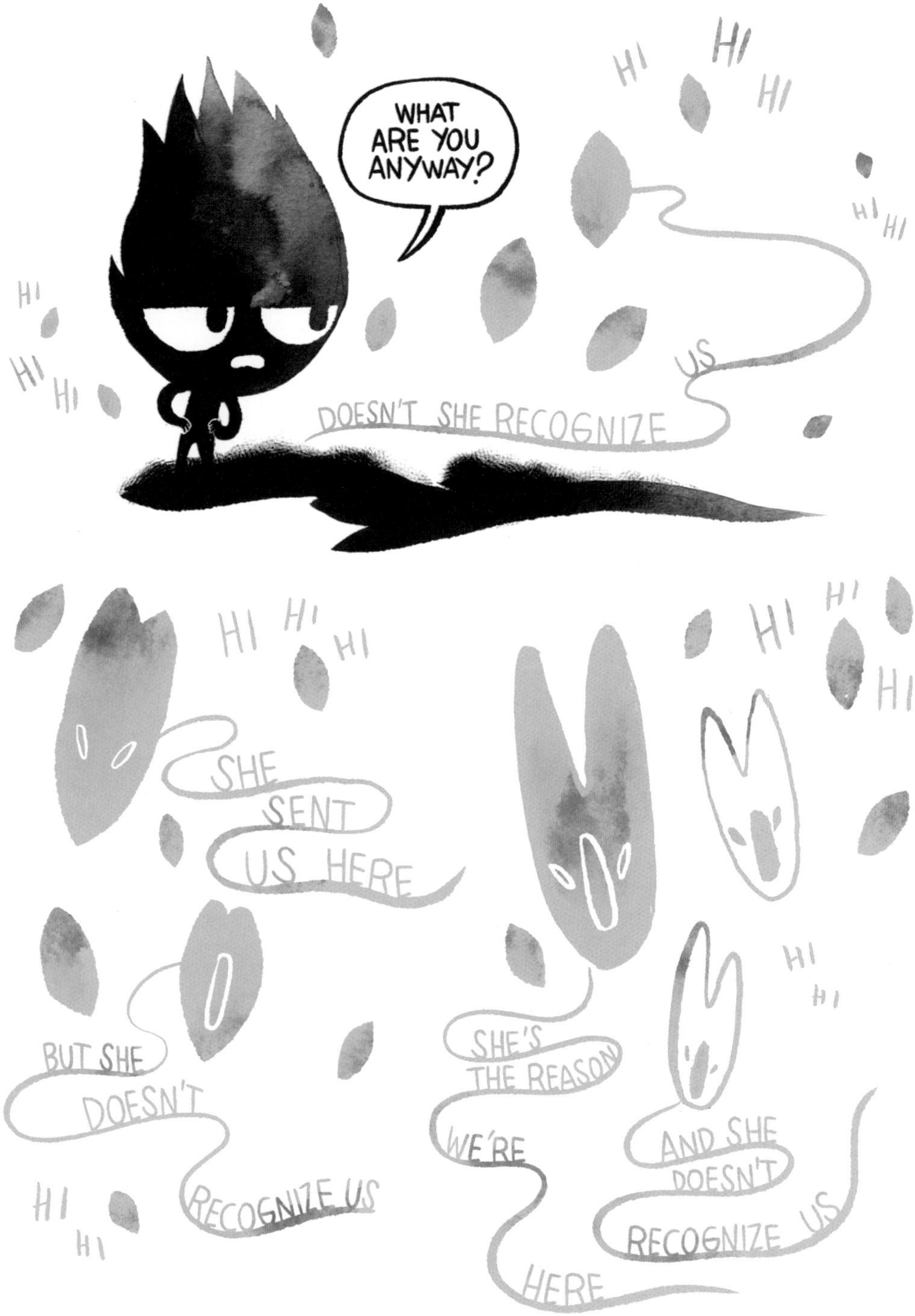
WHAT ARE YOU ANYWAY?
HI
HI
HI
HI
HI
HI
HI
HI
DOESN'T SHE RECOGNIZE US
HI
HI
HI
HI
HI
HI
SHE SENT US HERE
BUT SHE DOESN'T RECOGNIZE US
SHE'S THE REASON WE'RE HERE
AND SHE DOESN'T RECOGNIZE US
HI
HI
HI
HI

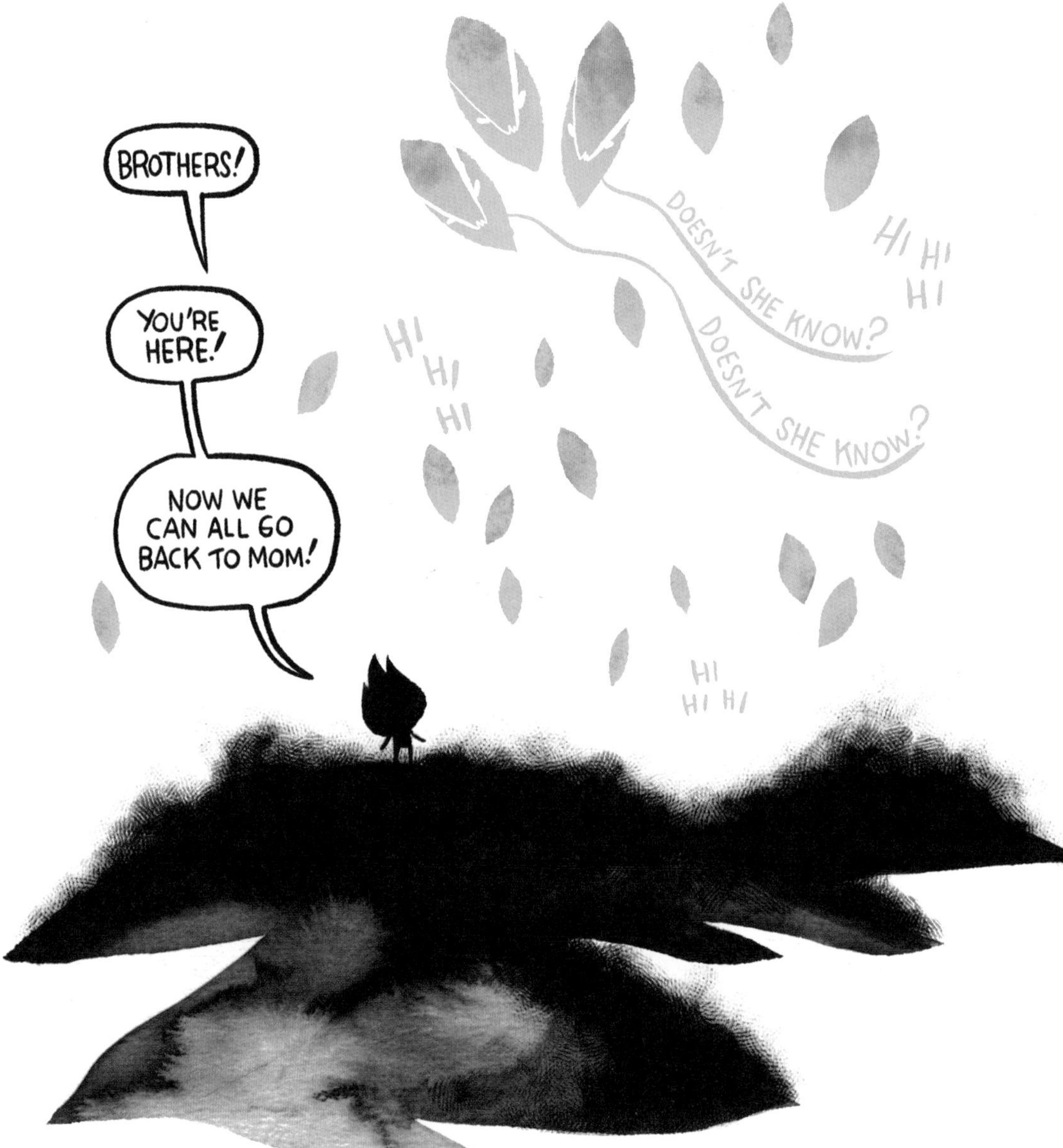
BROTHERS!
YOU'RE HERE!
NOW WE CAN ALL GO BACK TO MOM!
DOESN'T SHE KNOW?
DOESN'T SHE KNOW?
HI HI HI
HI HI HI
HI HI HI

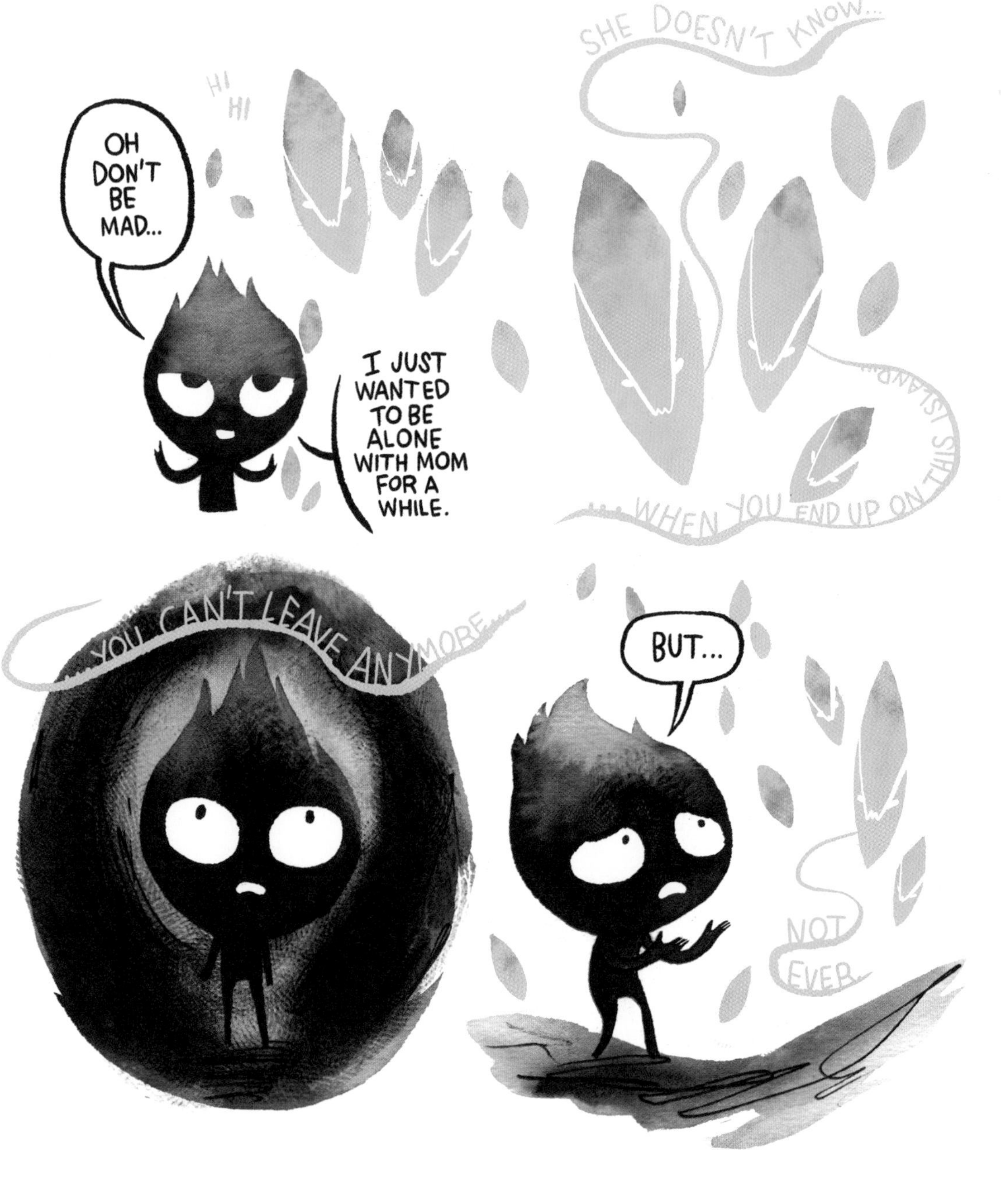
HI
HI
OH DON'T BE MAD...
I JUST WANTED TO BE ALONE WITH MOM FOR A WHILE.
SHE DOESN'T KNOW...
...WHEN YOU END UP ON THIS ISLAND...
...YOU CAN'T LEAVE ANYMORE...
BUT...
NOT EVER.

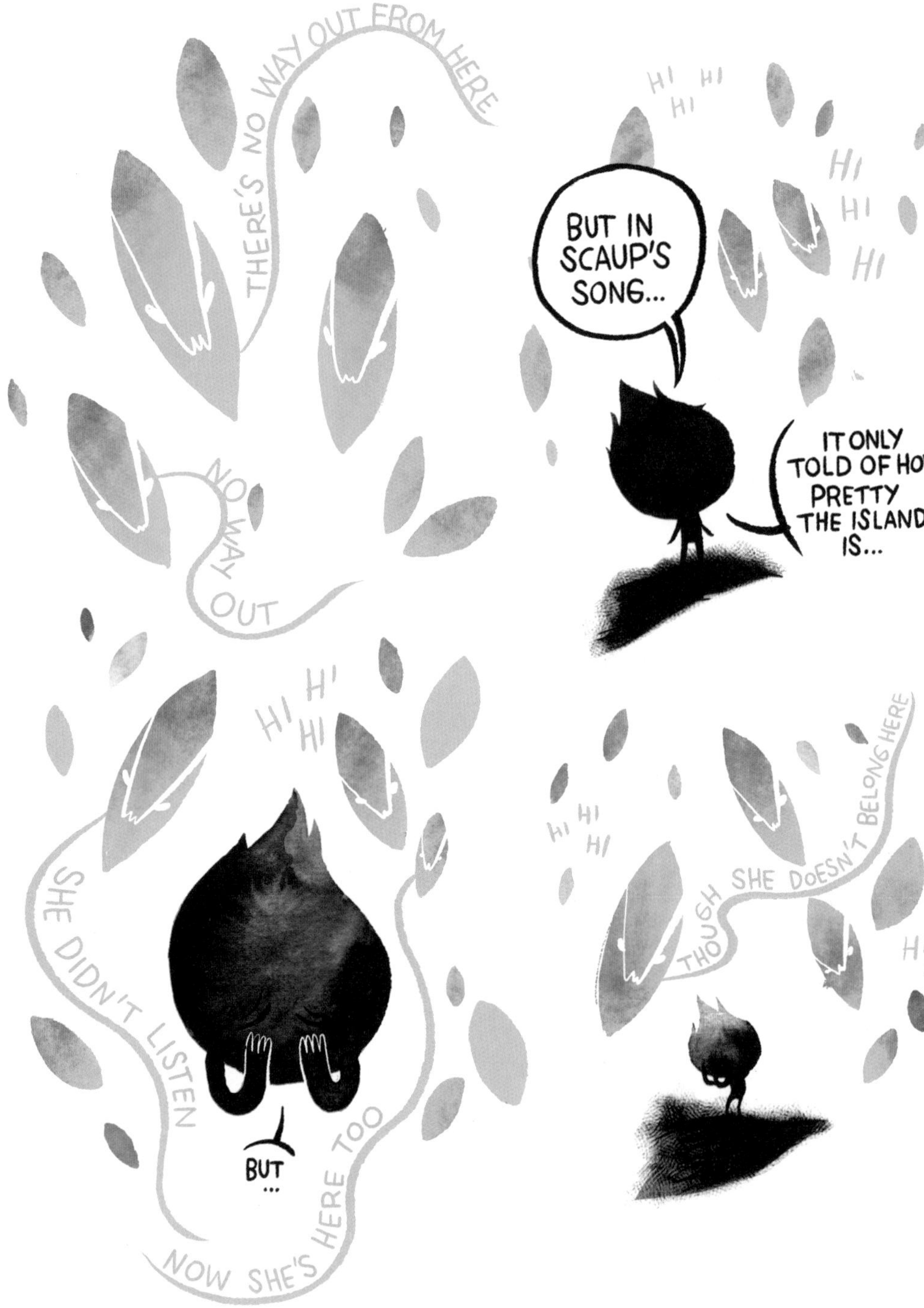
THERE'S NO WAY OUT FROM HERE
NO WAY OUT
HI HI HI HI
BUT IN SCAUP'S SONG...
HI HI HI
IT ONLY TOLD OF HOW PRETTY THE ISLAND IS...
HI HI HI
SHE DIDN'T LISTEN
NOW SHE'S HERE TOO
BUT ...
HI HI HI
THOUGH SHE DOESN'T BELONG HERE
HI HI HI

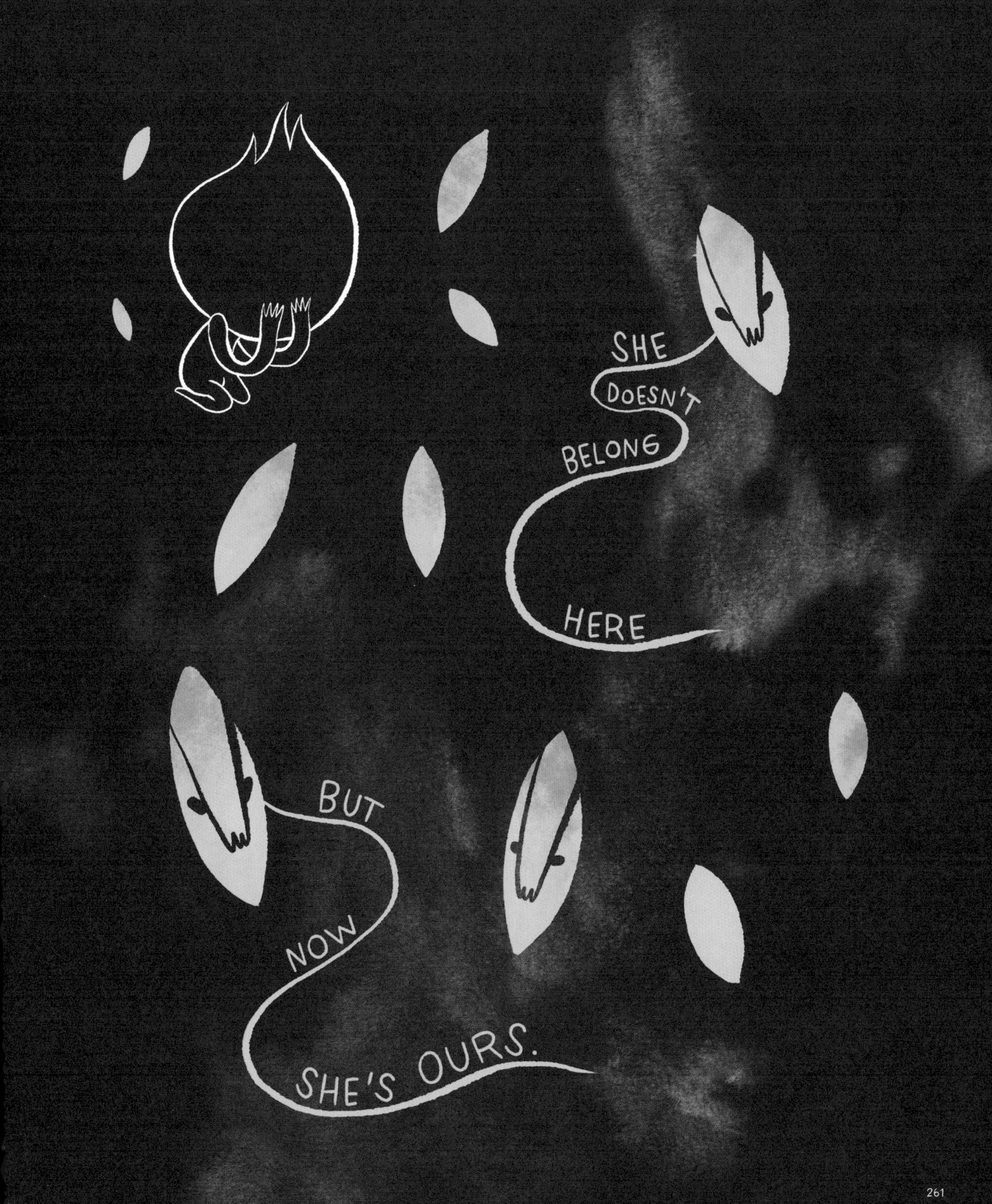
SHE DOESN'T BELONG HERE
BUT NOW SHE'S OURS.

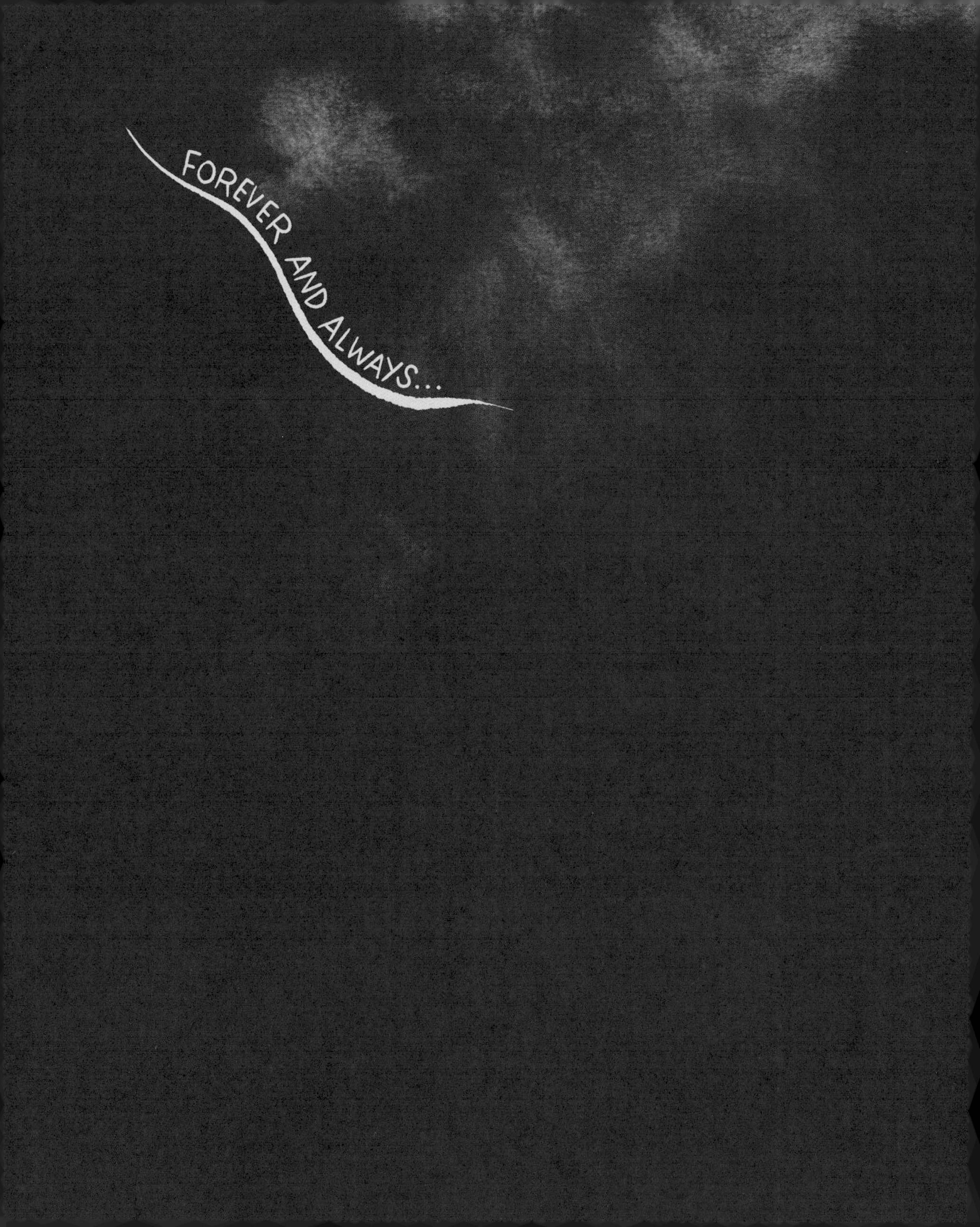
FOREVER AND ALWAYS...

X

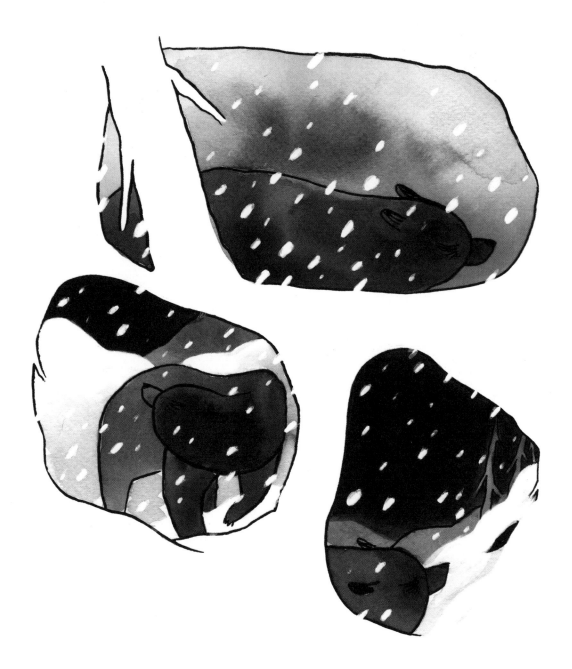

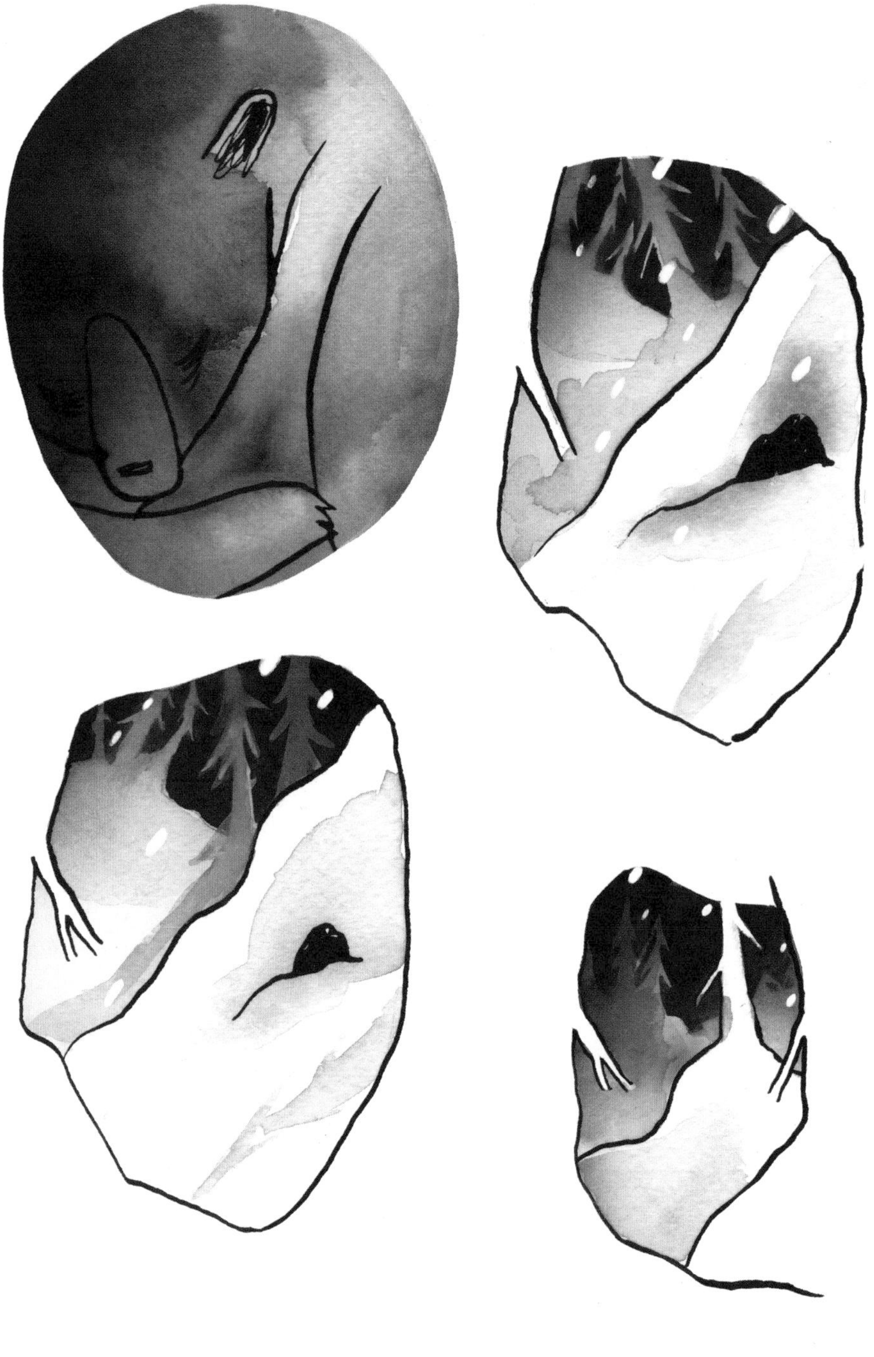

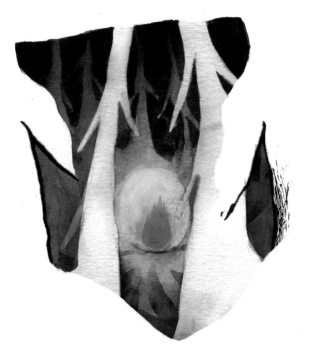

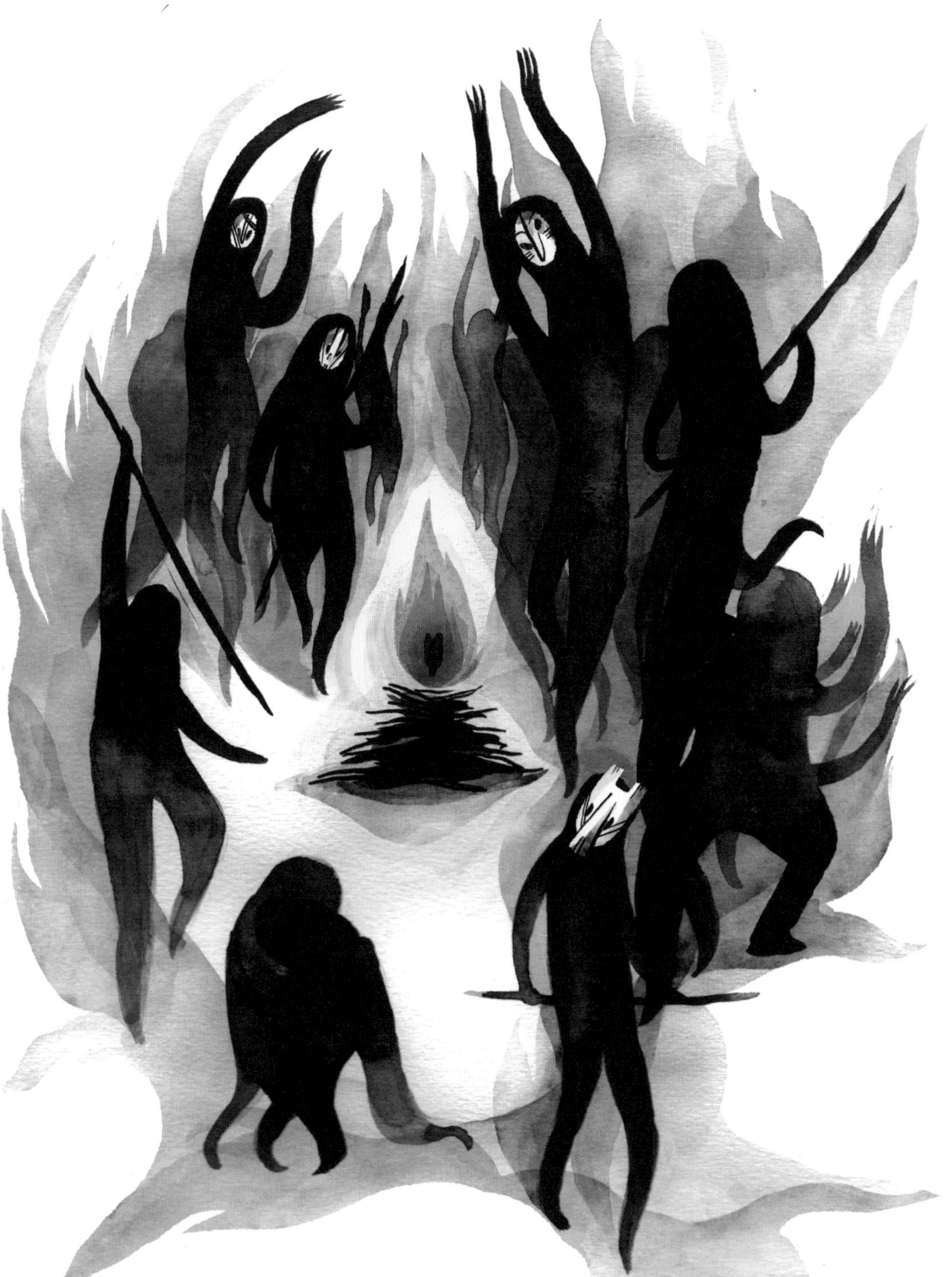

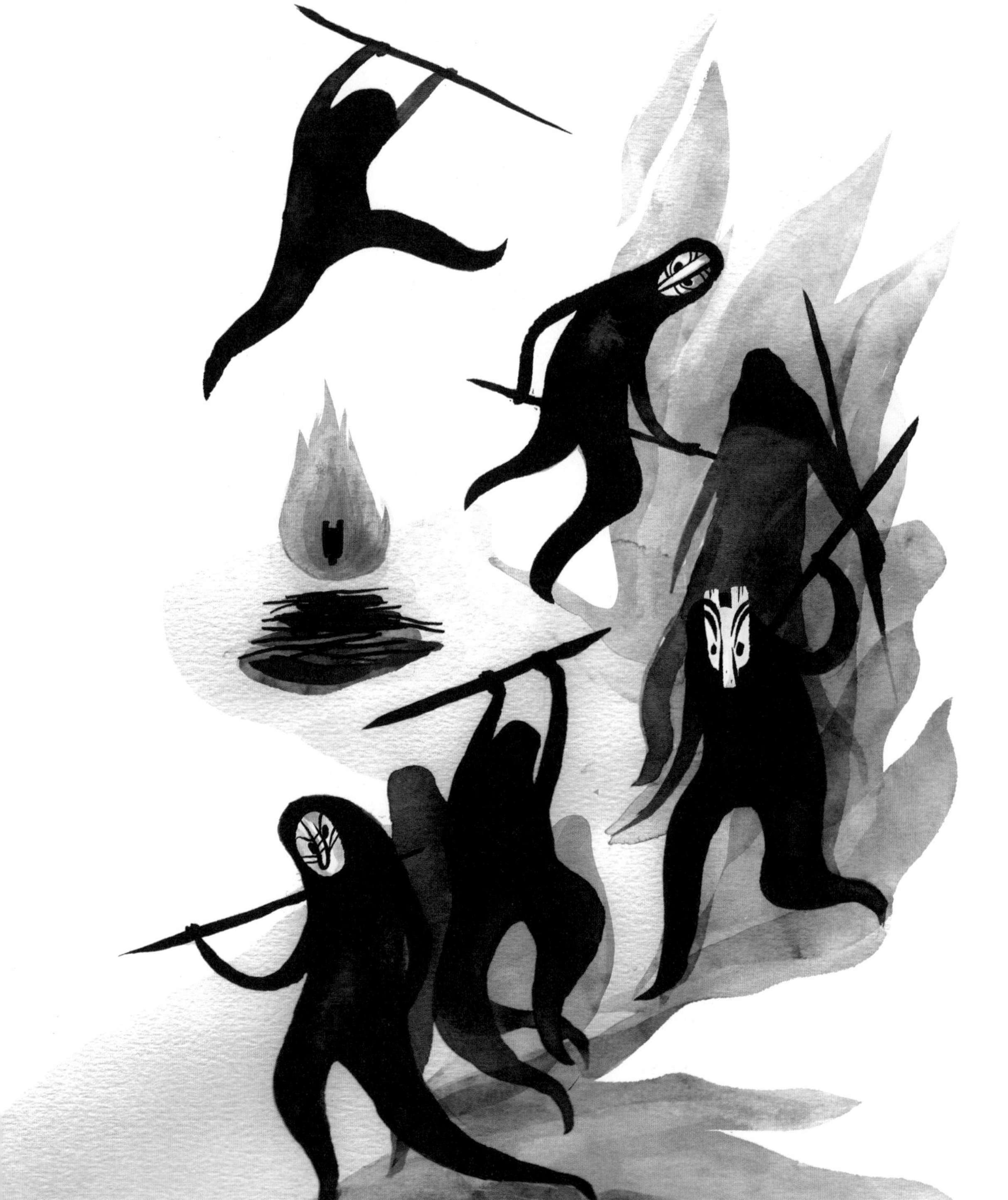

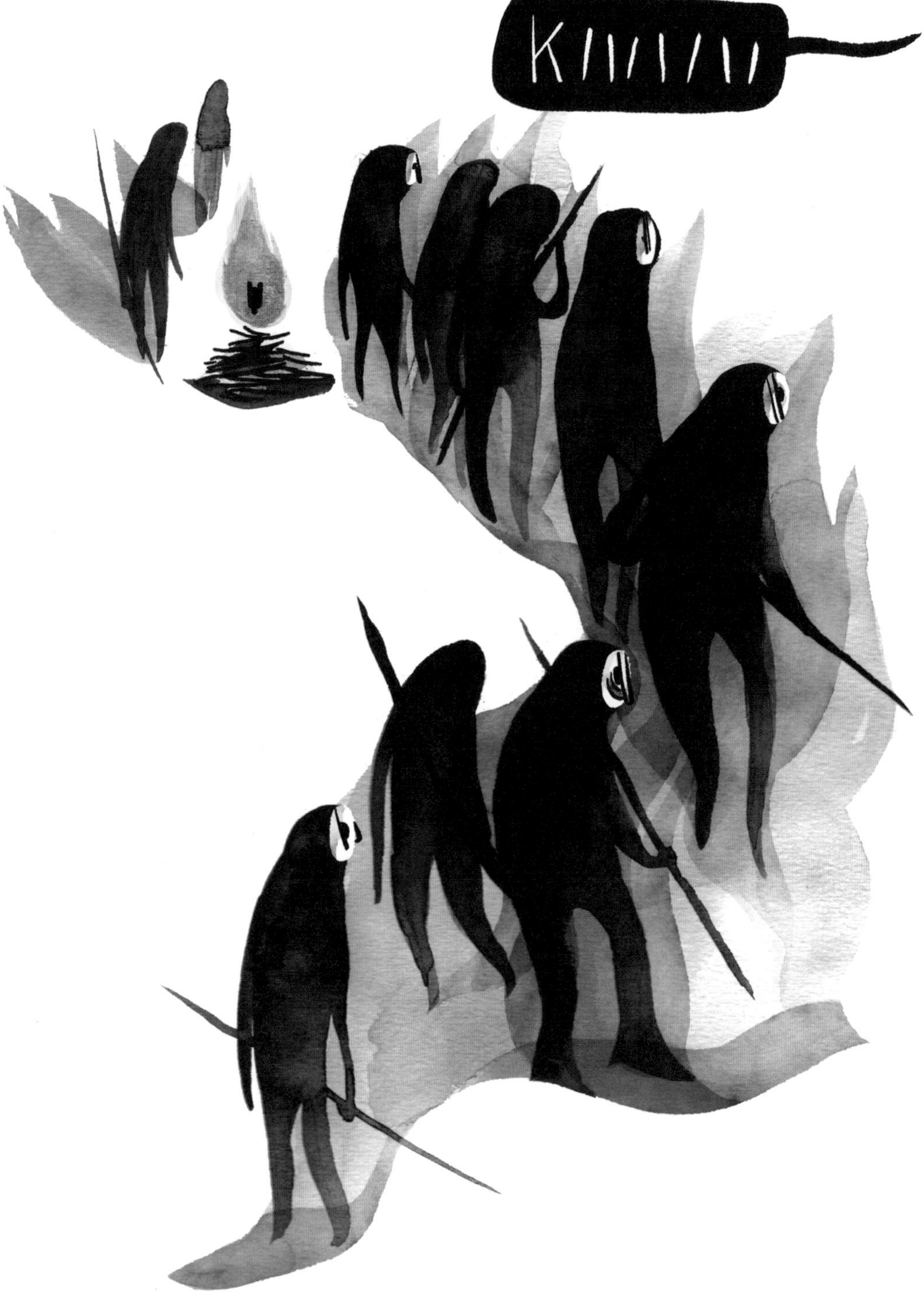

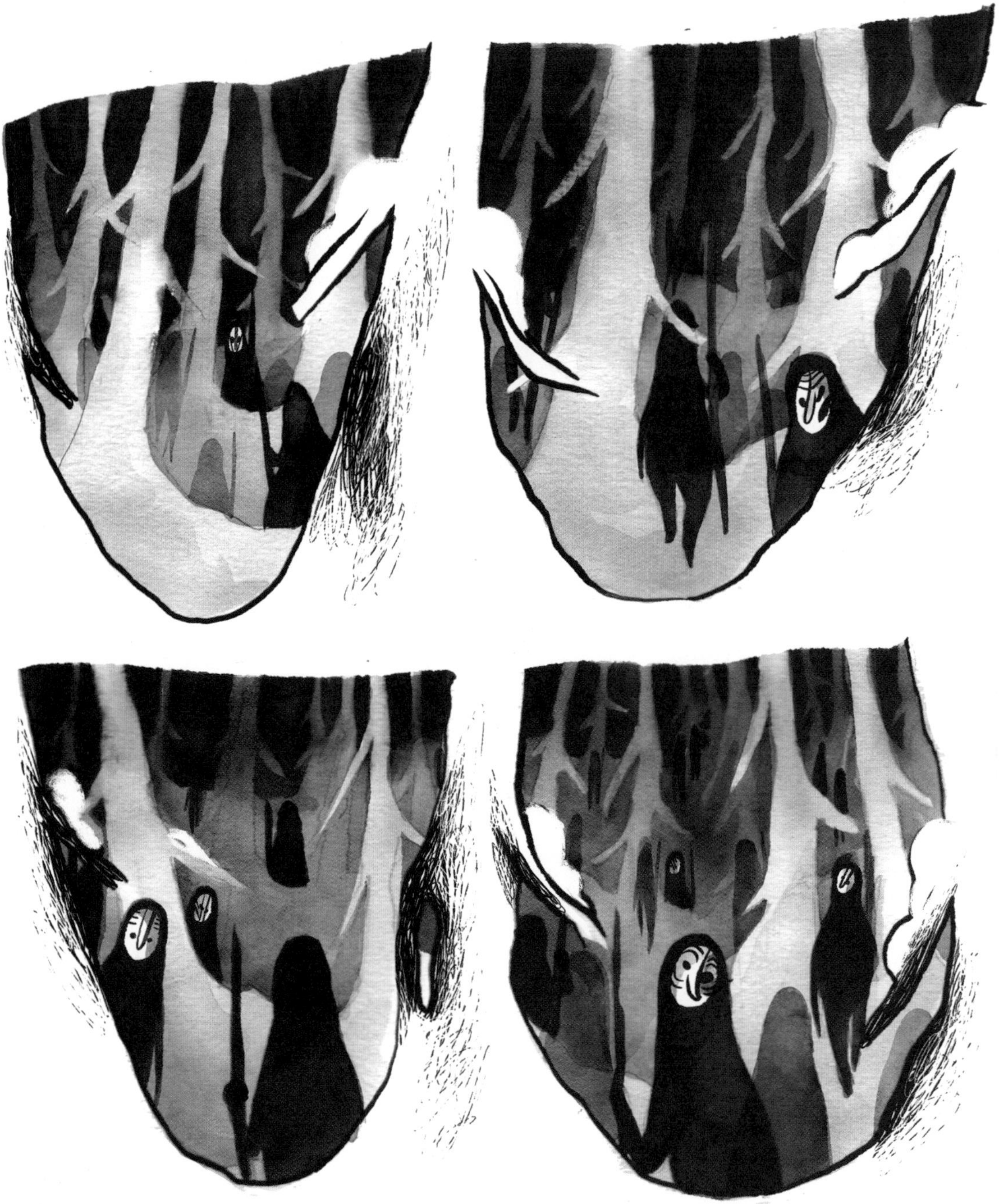

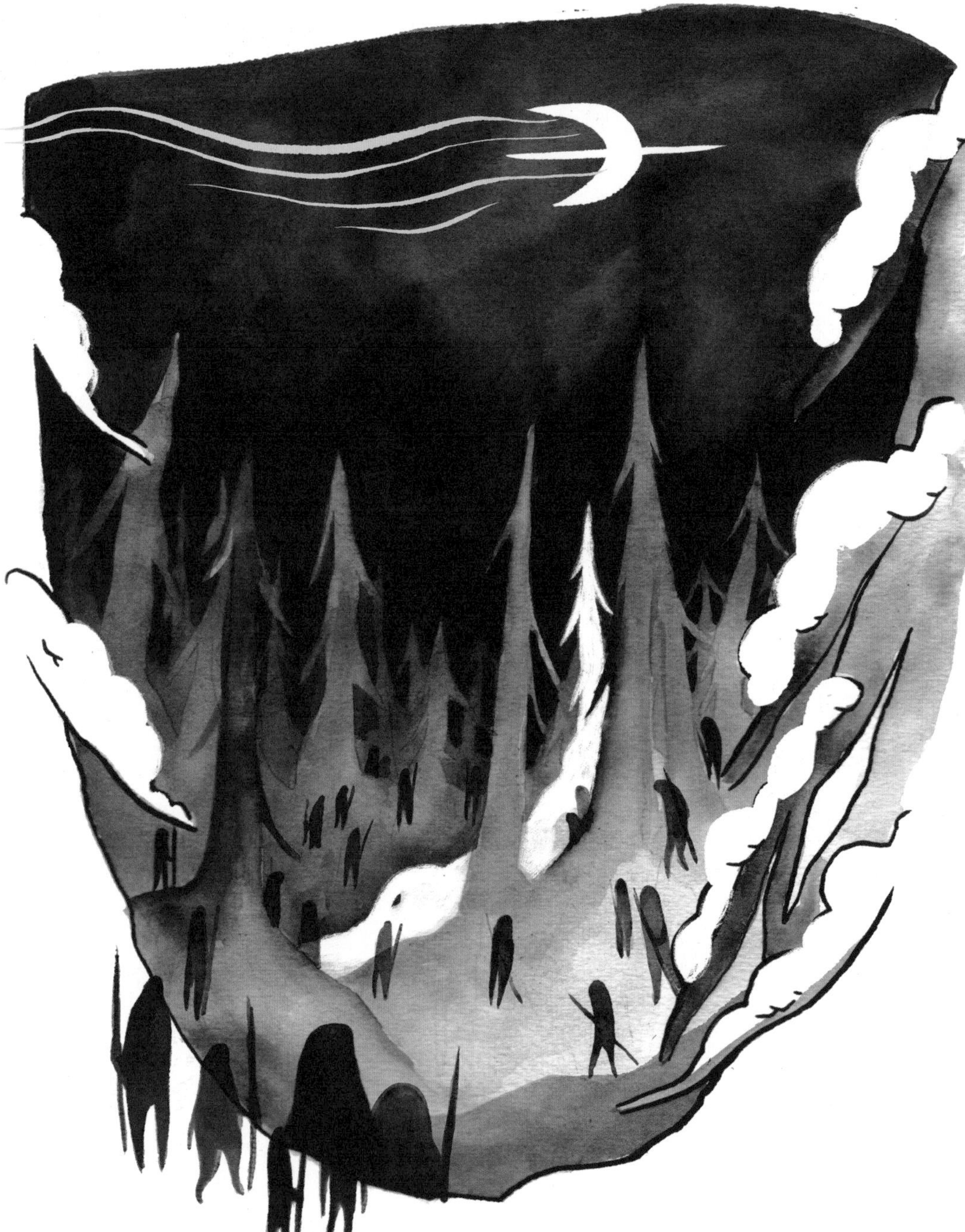

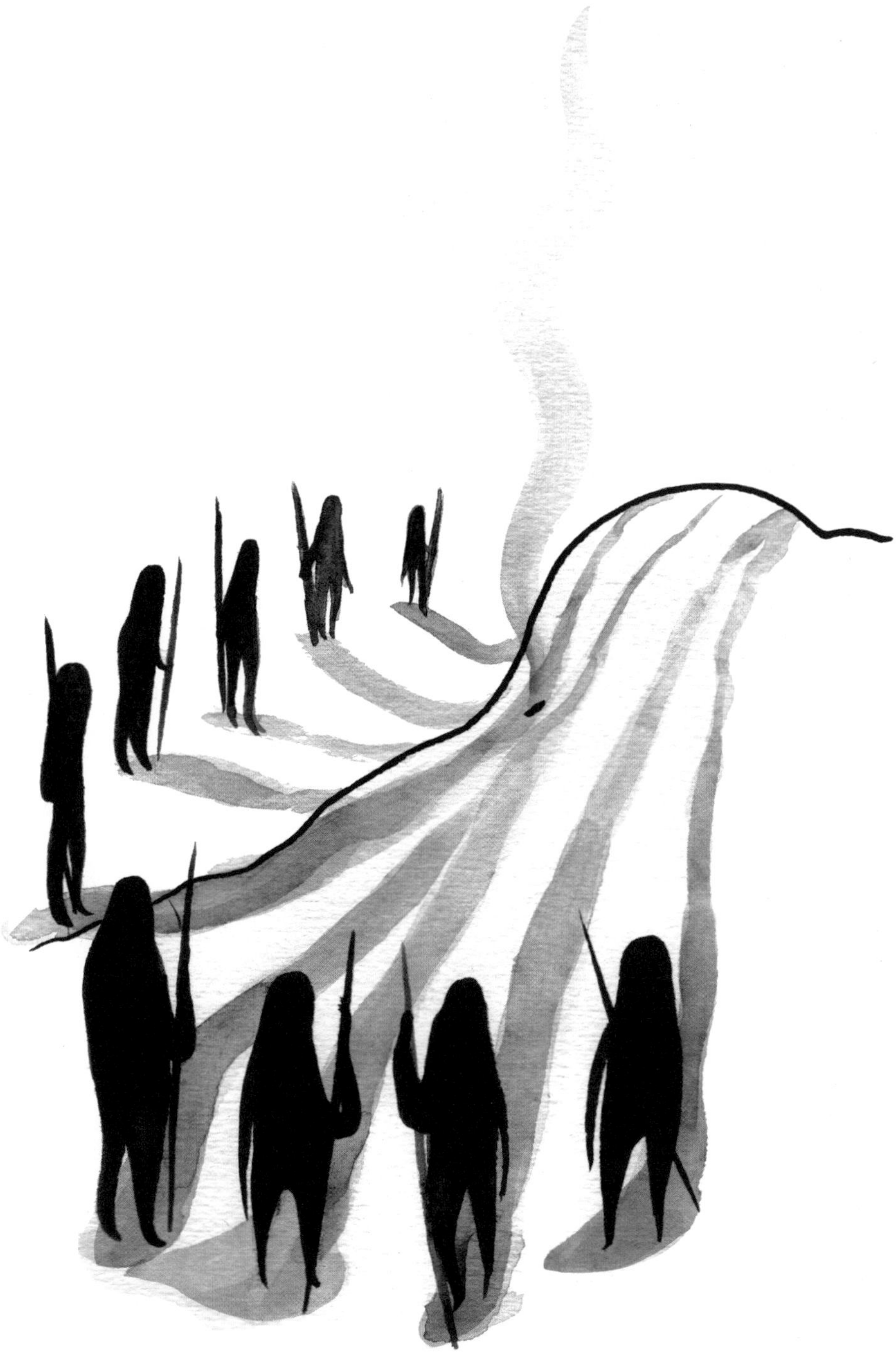

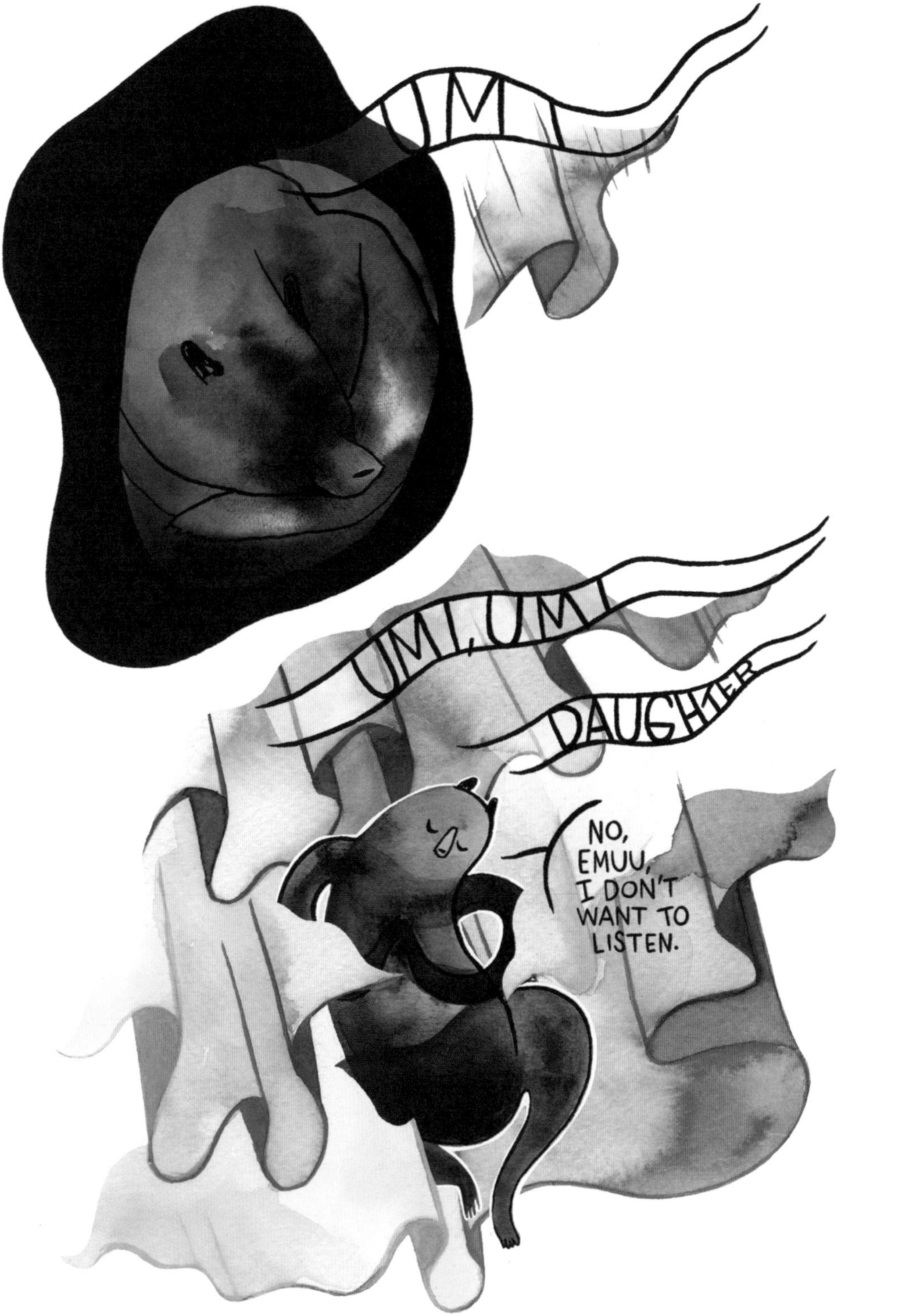
UMI
UMI, UMI
DAUGHTER
NO, EMUU, I DON'T WANT TO LISTEN.

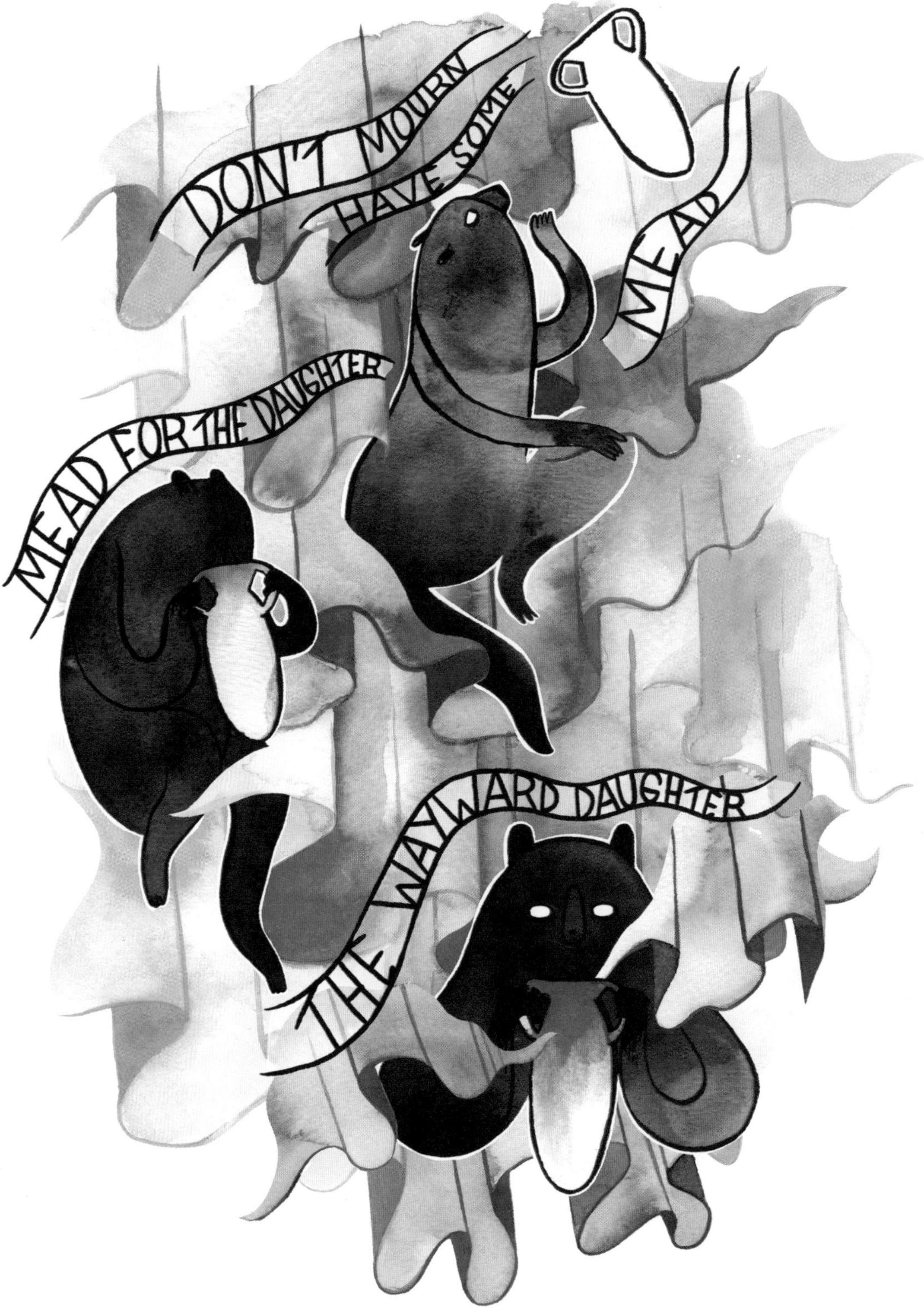
DON'T MOURN
HAVE SOME
MEAD
MEAD FOR THE DAUGHTER
THE WAYWARD DAUGHTER

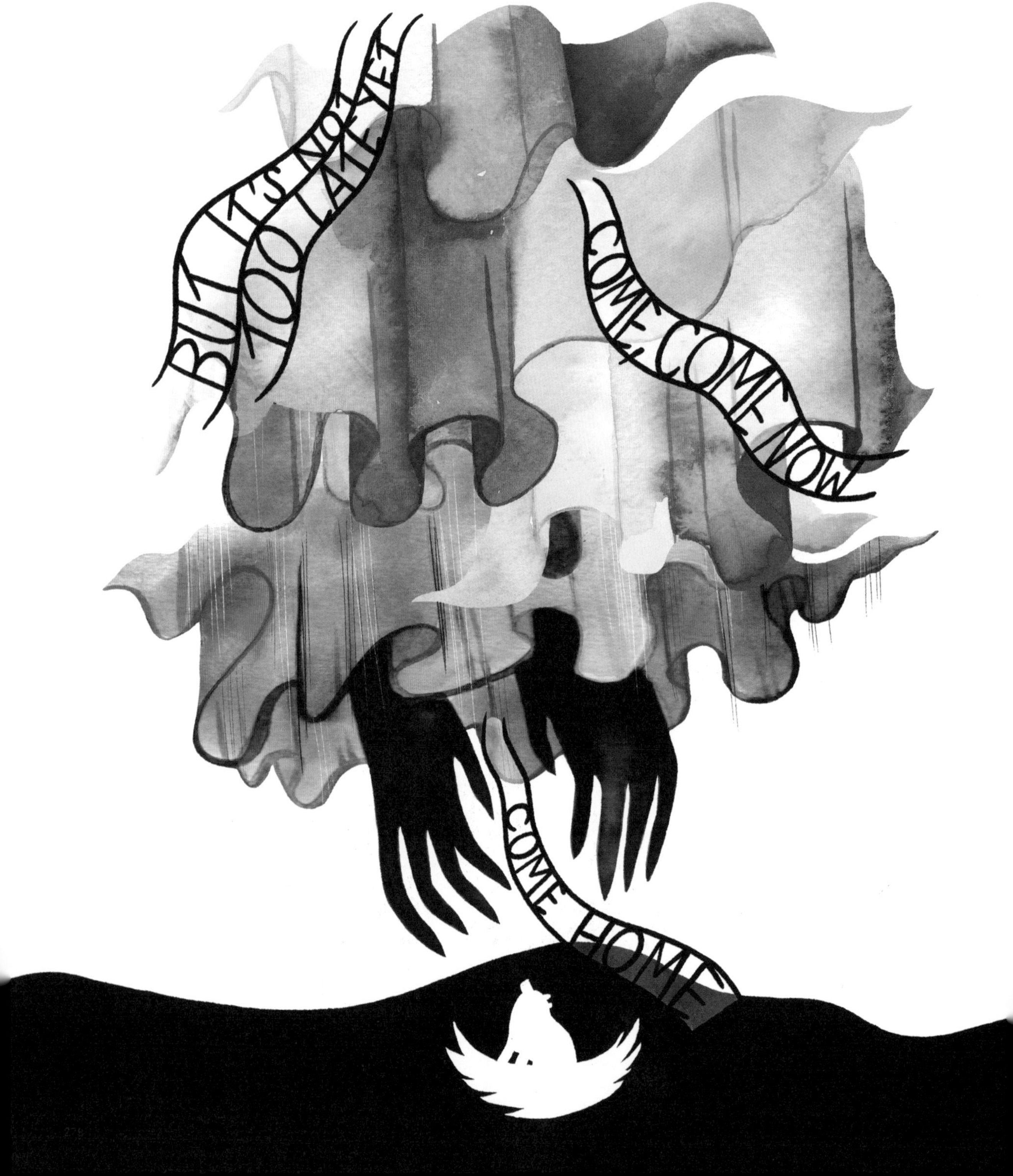
BUT IT'S NOT
TOO LATE YET
COME, COME NOW
COME HOME

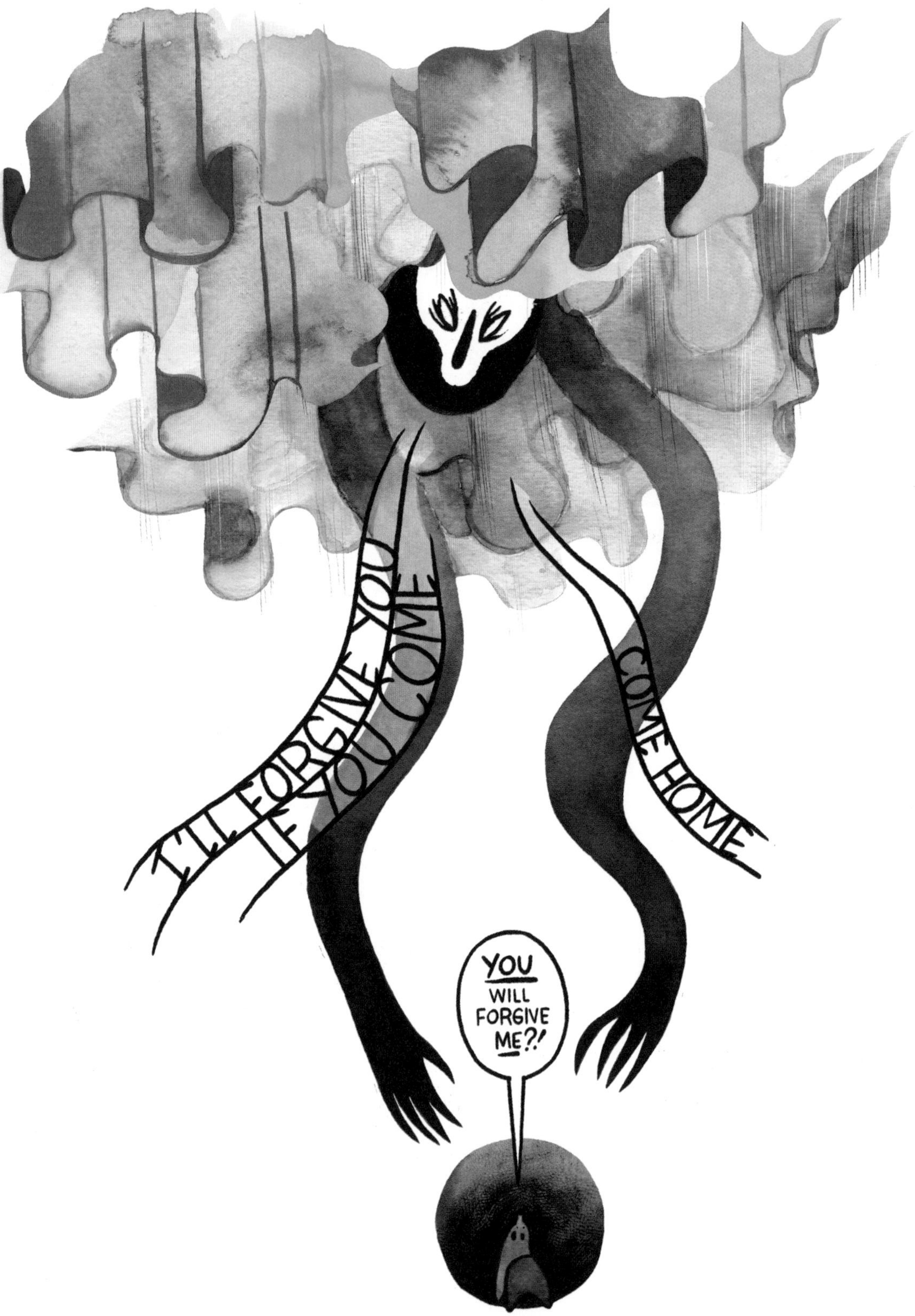
I'LL FORGIVE YOU
IF YOU COME
COME HOME
YOU WILL FORGIVE ME?!

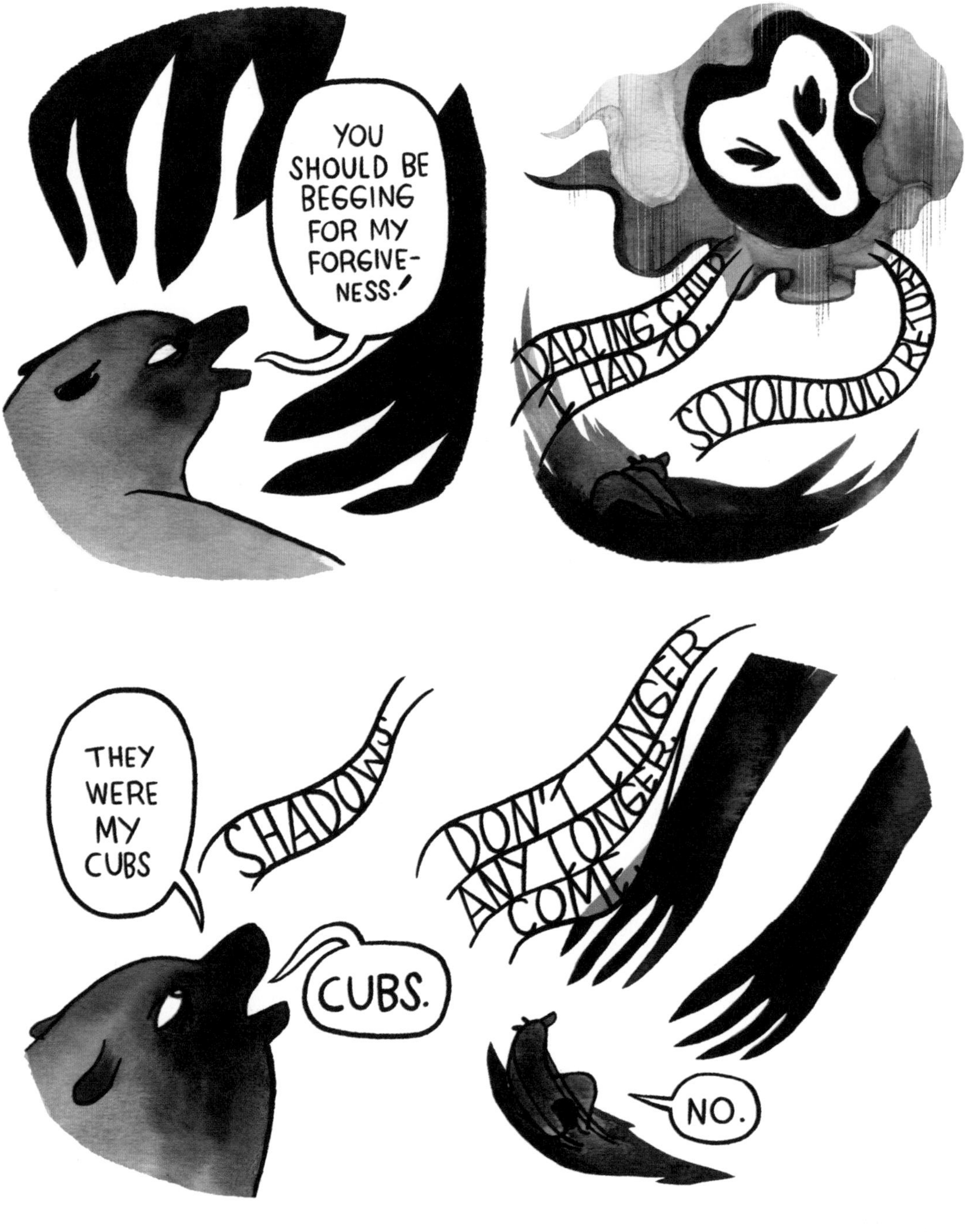

YOU SHOULD BE BEGGING FOR MY FORGIVE-NESS!
DARLING CHILD I HAD TO.
SO YOU COULD RETURN
THEY WERE MY CUBS
SHADOWS.
CUBS.
DON'T LINGER ANY LONGER. COME.
NO.

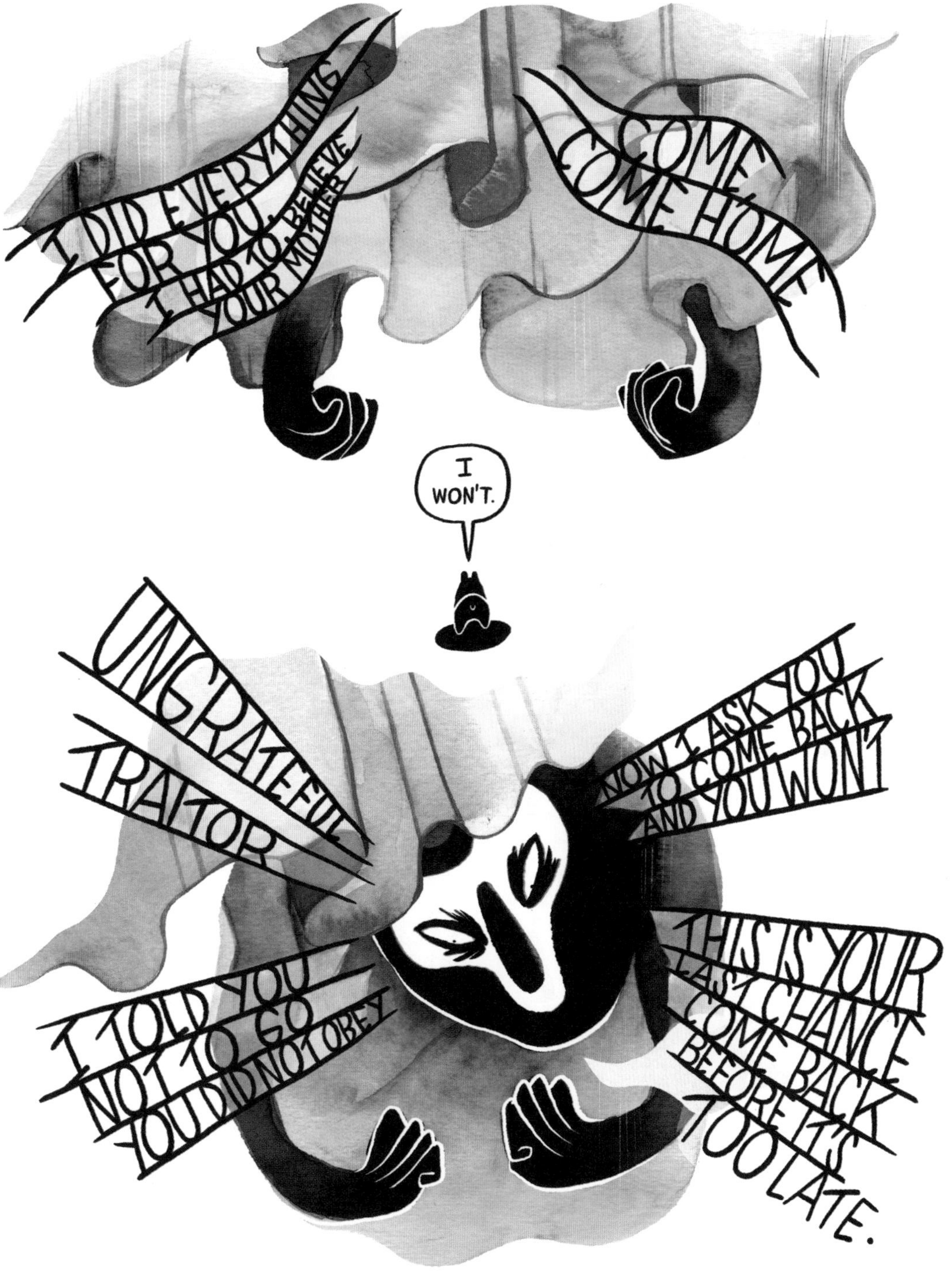
I DID EVERYTHING FOR YOU. I HAD TO. BELIEVE YOUR MOTHER
COME COME HOME
I WON'T.
UNGRATEFUL TRAITOR
NOW I ASK YOU TO COME BACK AND YOU WON'T
I TOLD YOU NOT TO GO YOU DID NOT OBEY
THIS IS YOUR LAST CHANCE COME BACK BEFORE IT'S TOO LATE.

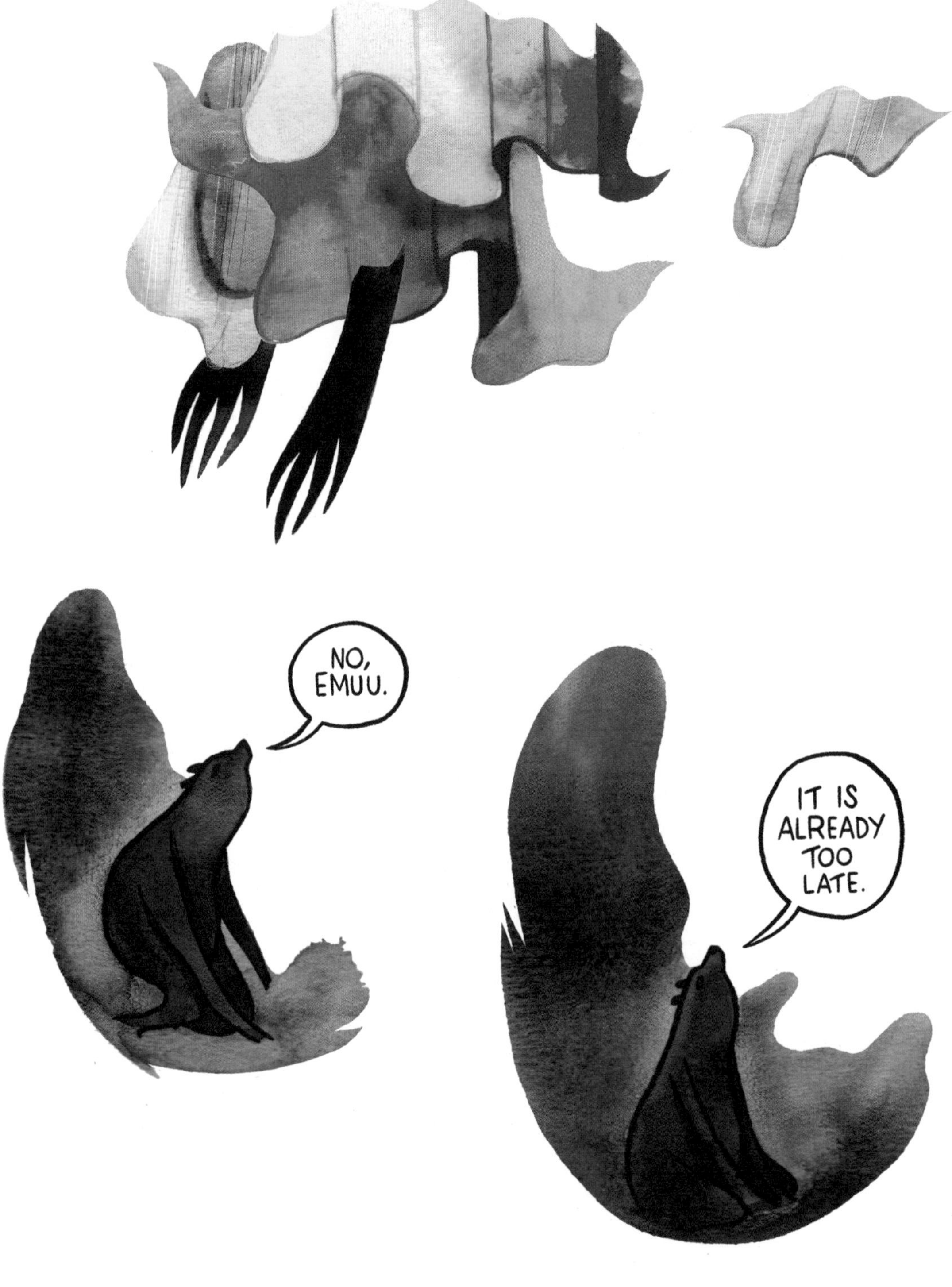
NO, EMUU.
IT IS ALREADY TOO LATE.

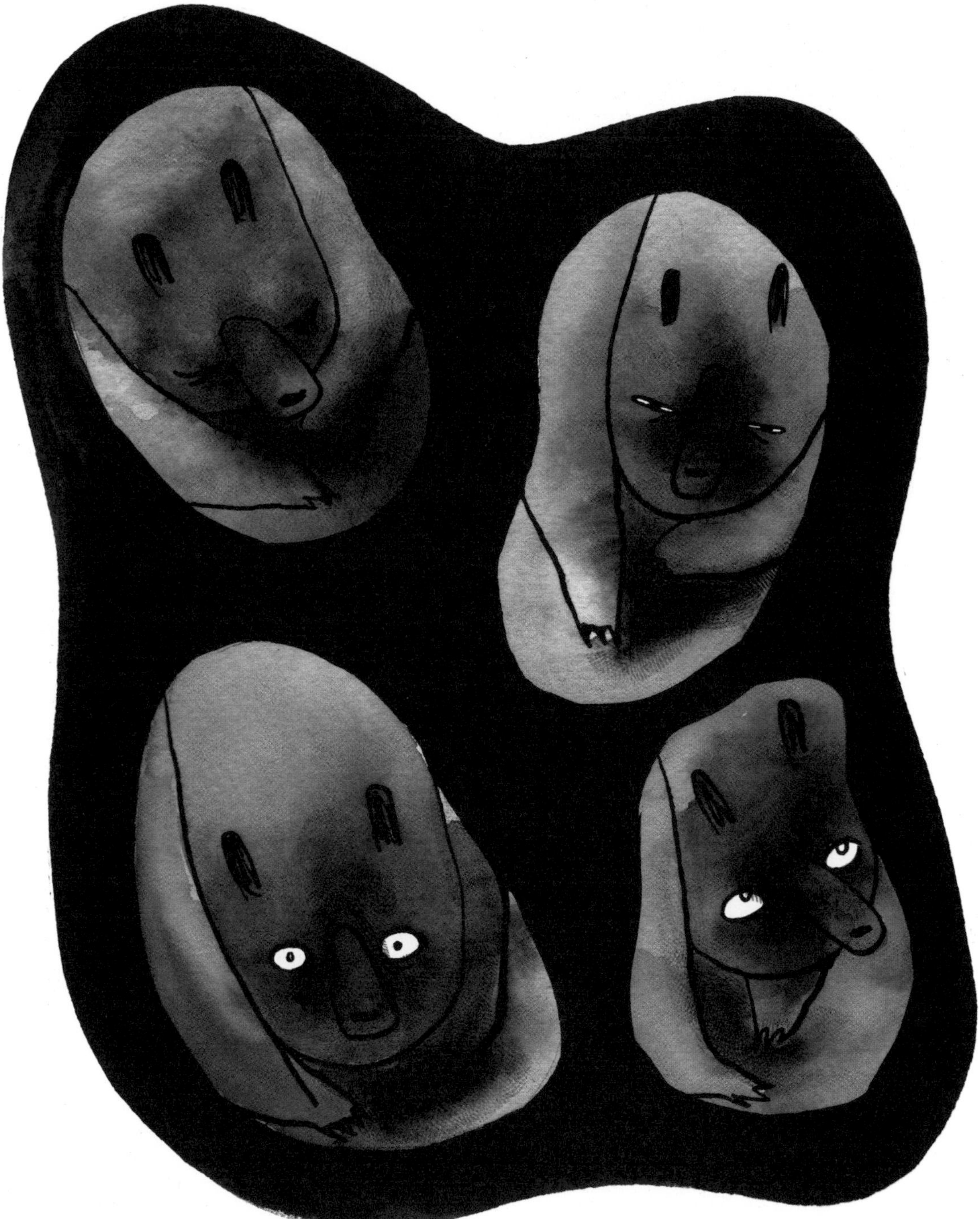

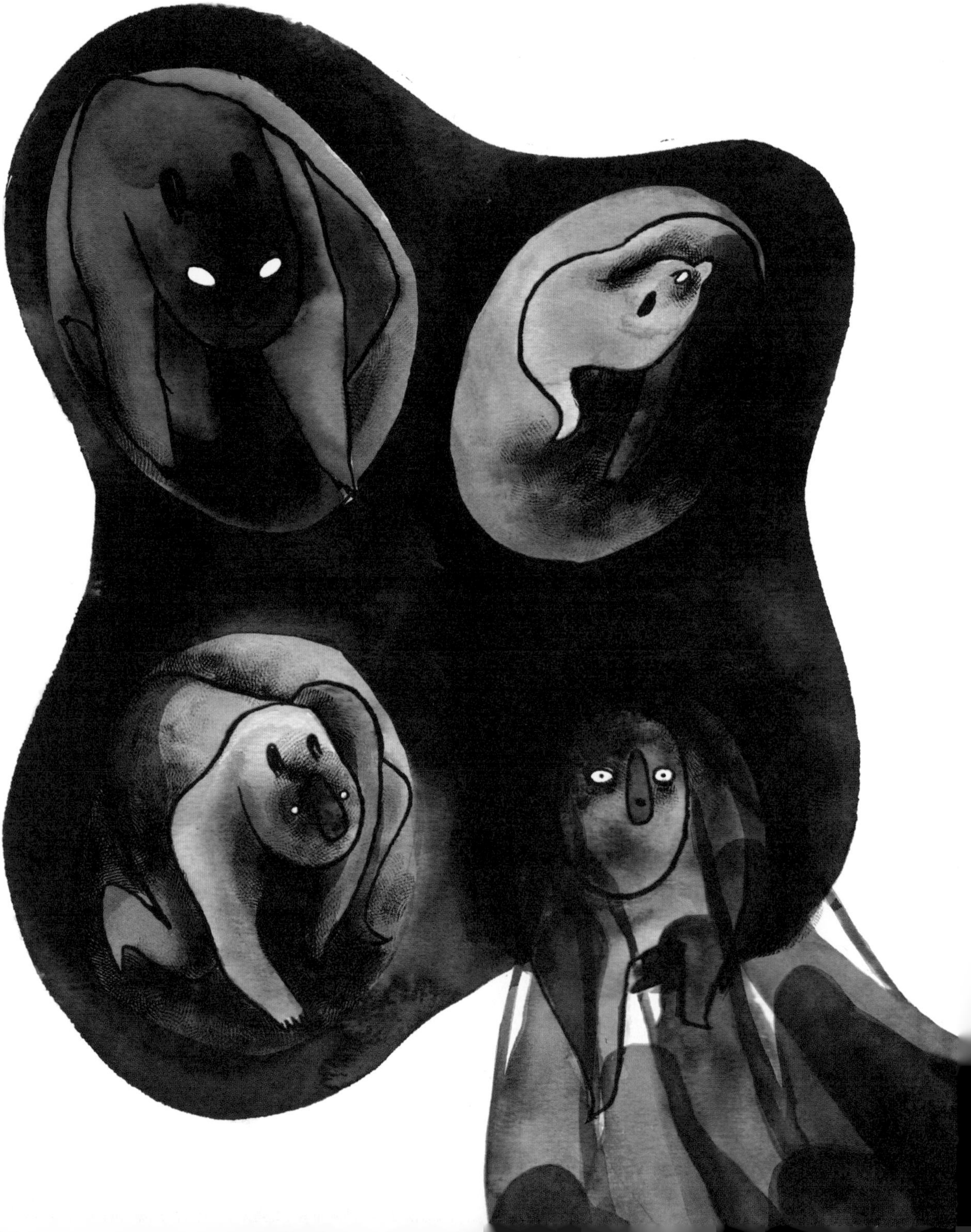

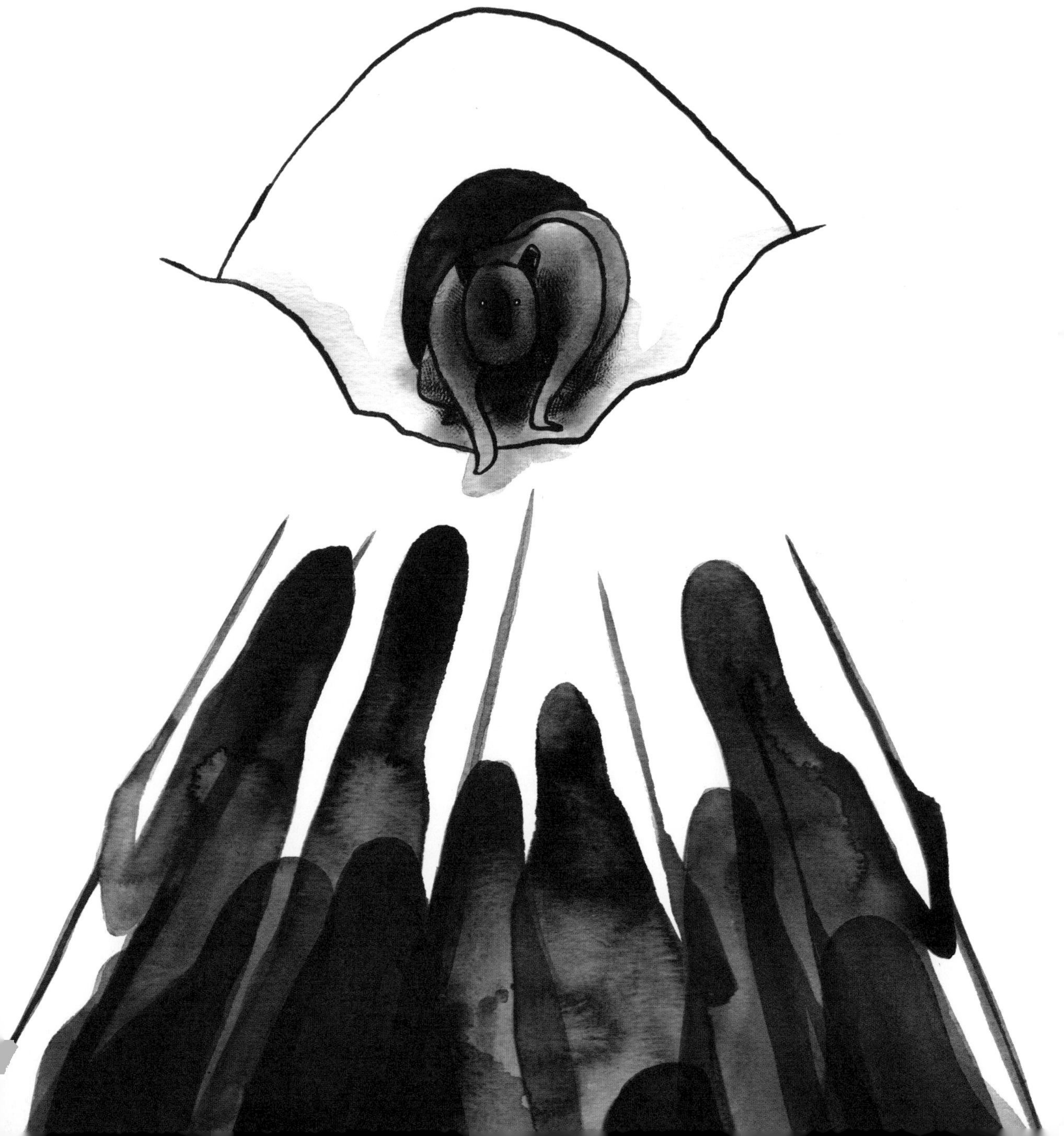

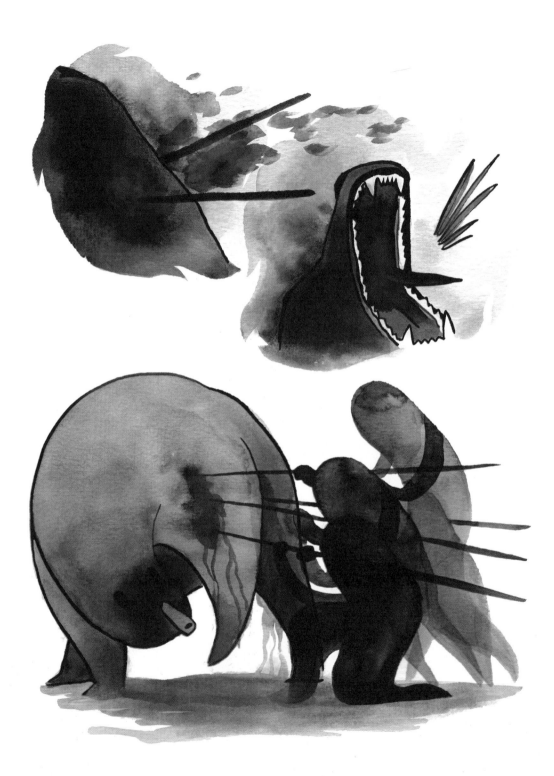

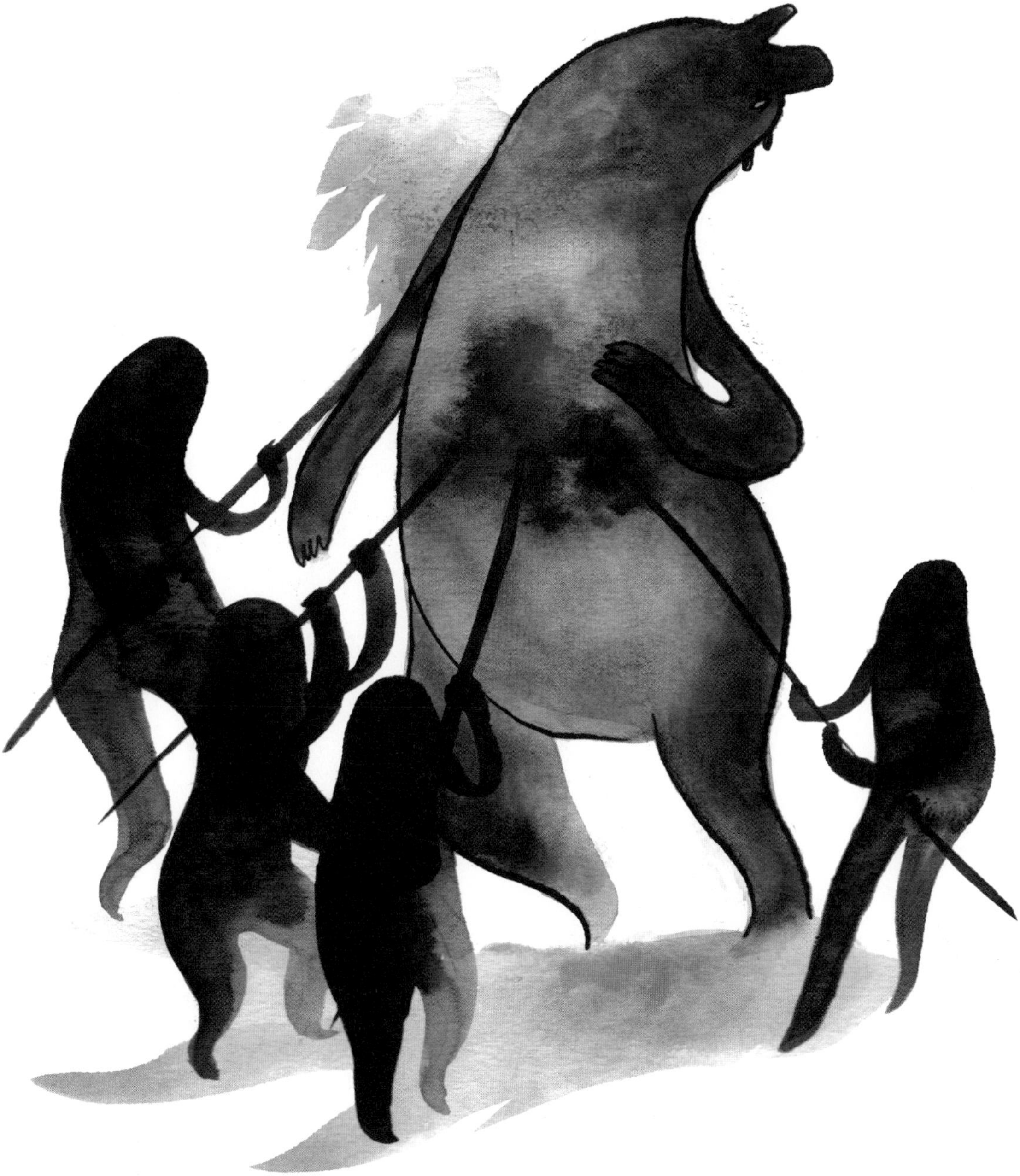

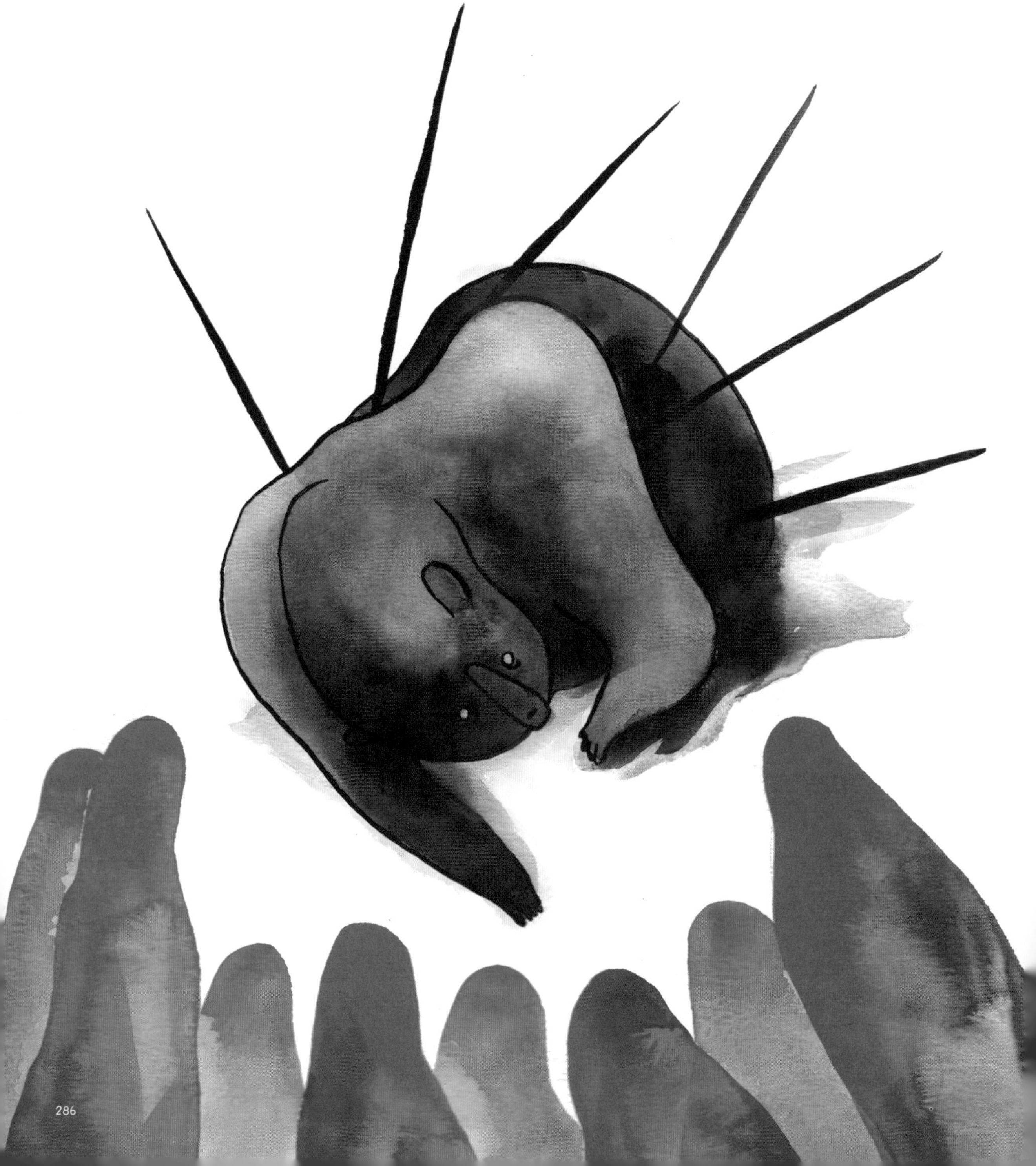

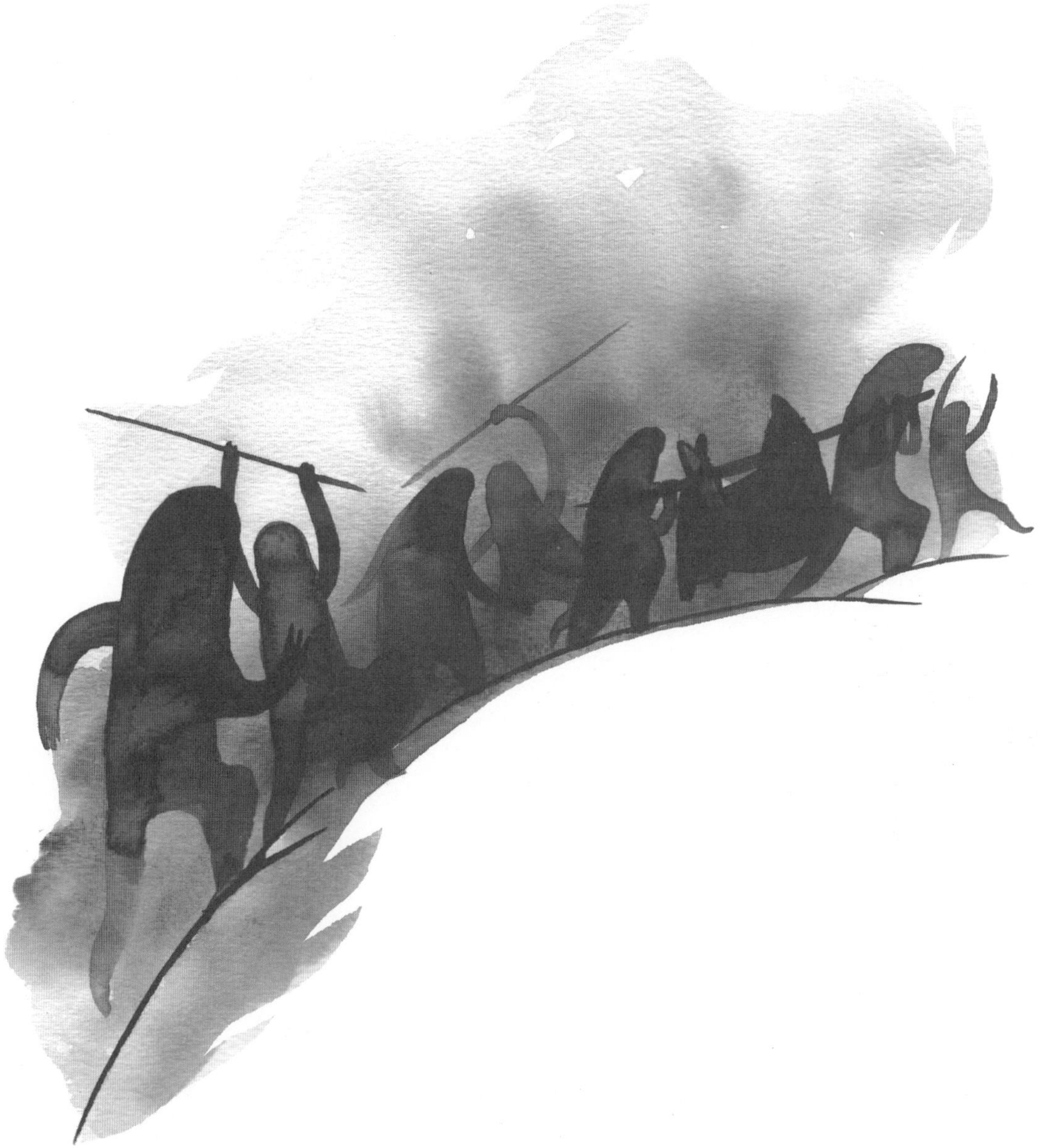

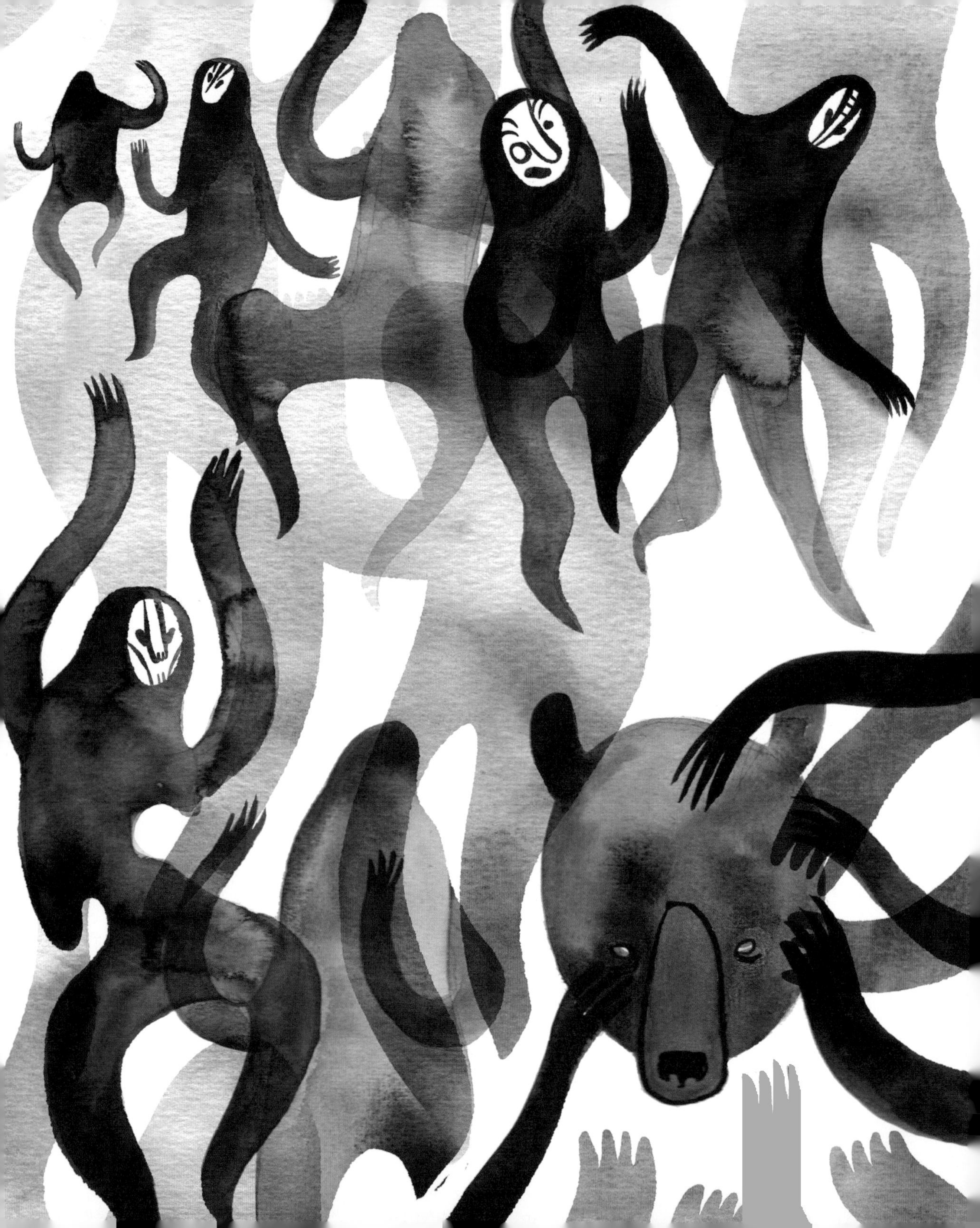

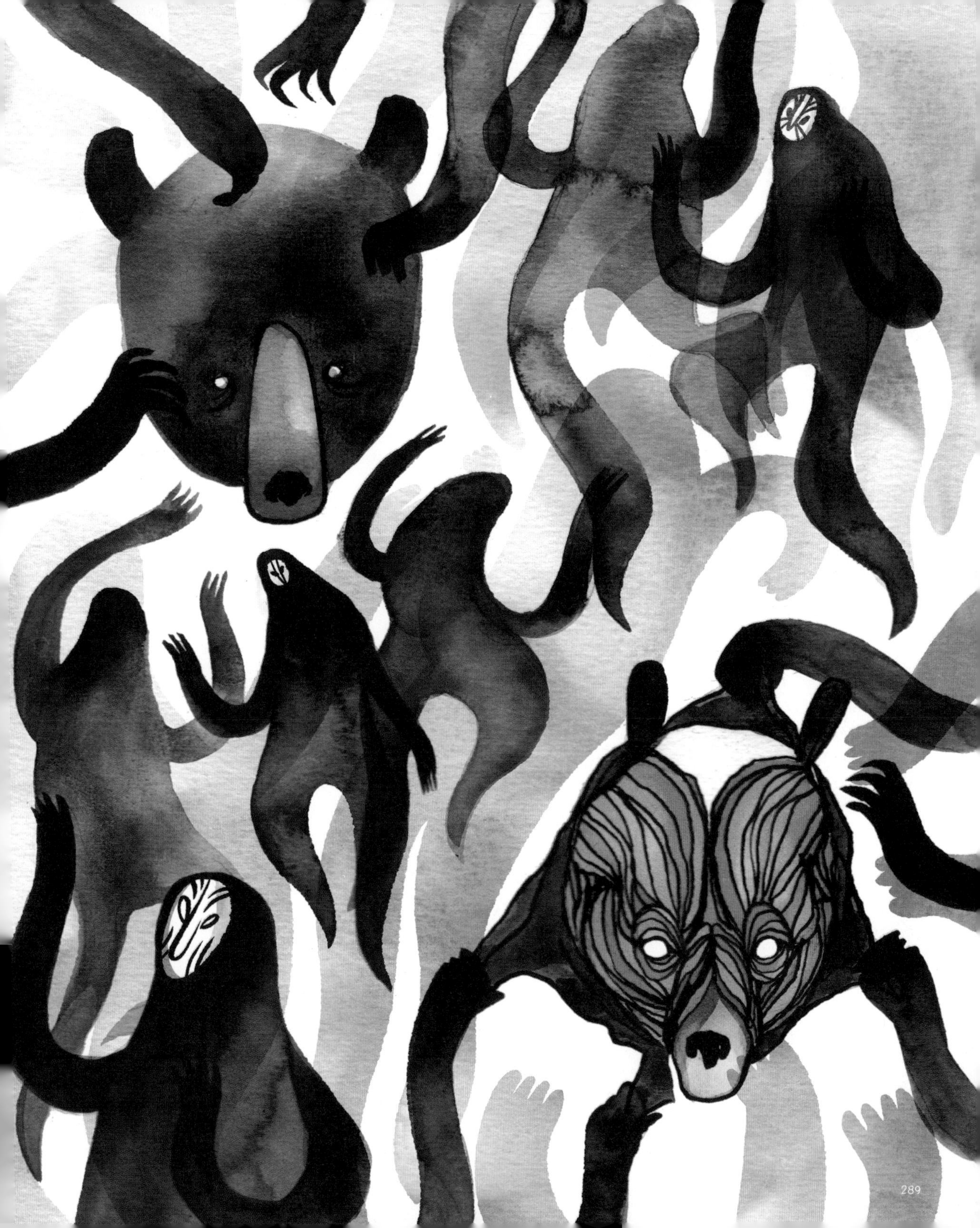

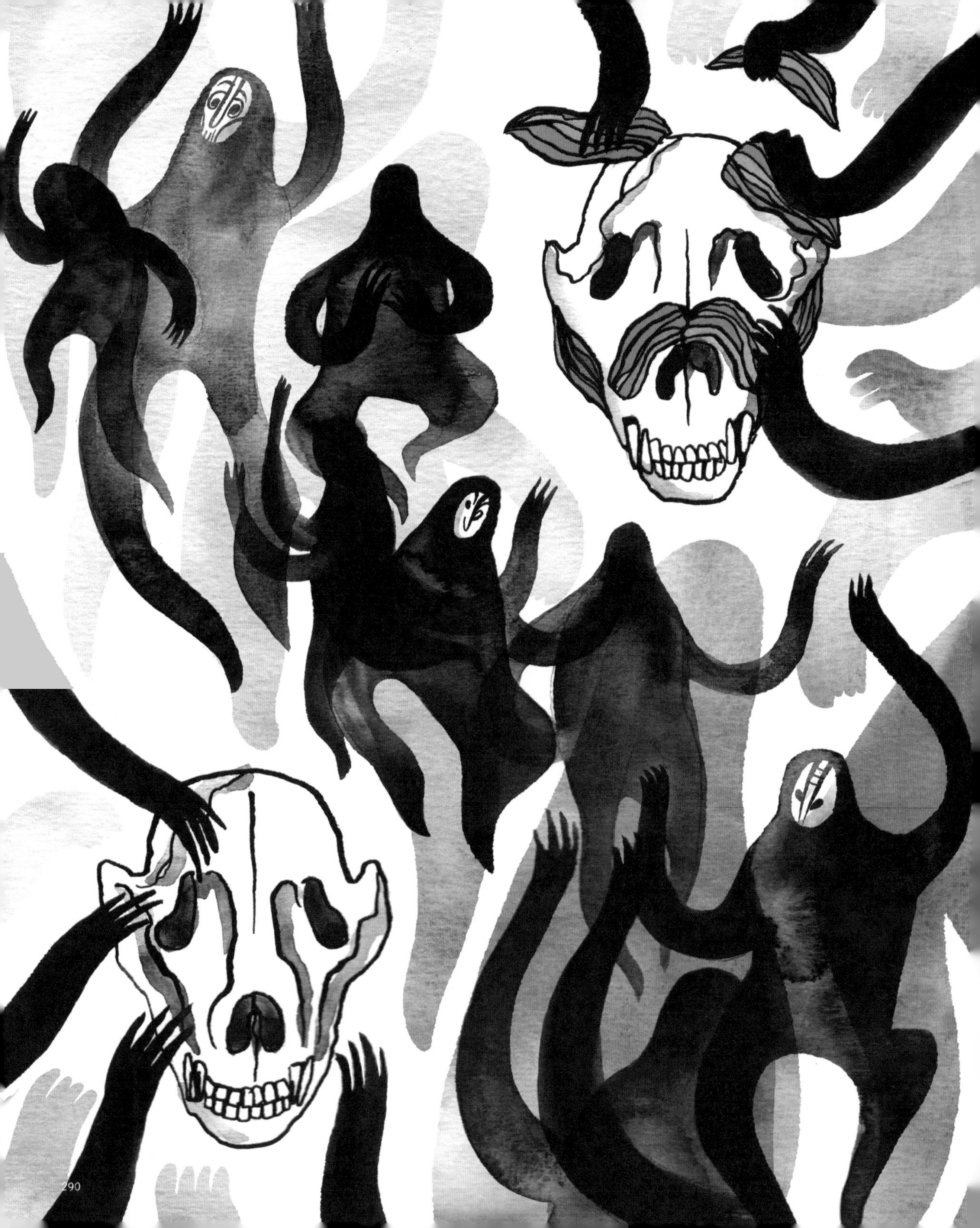

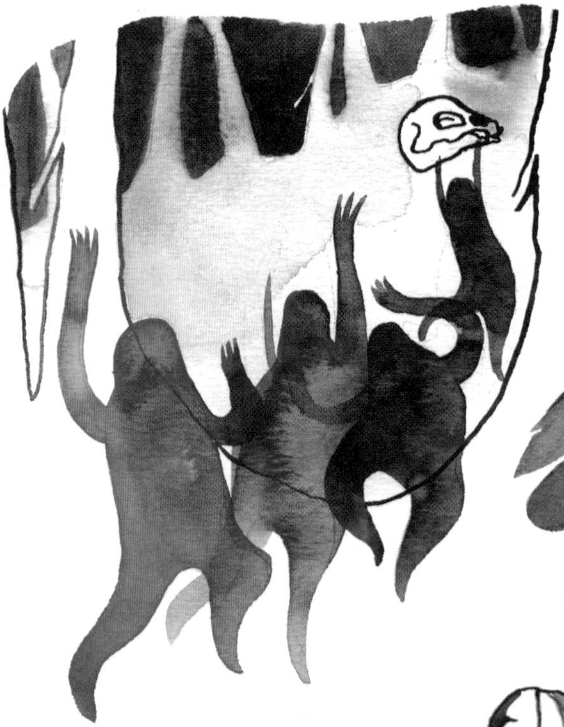

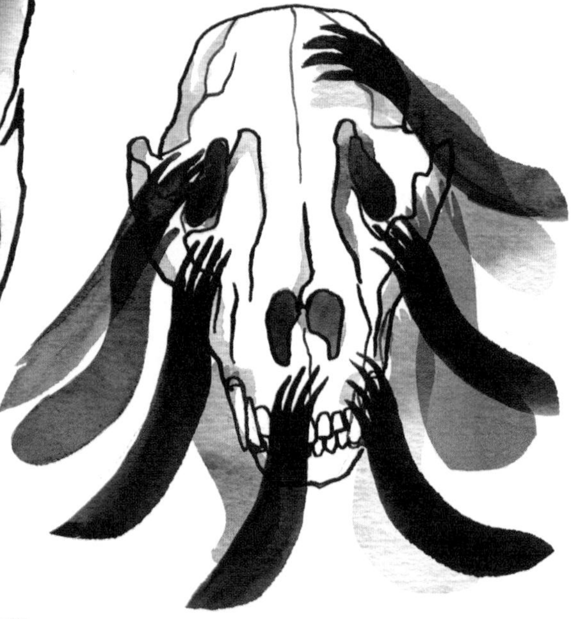

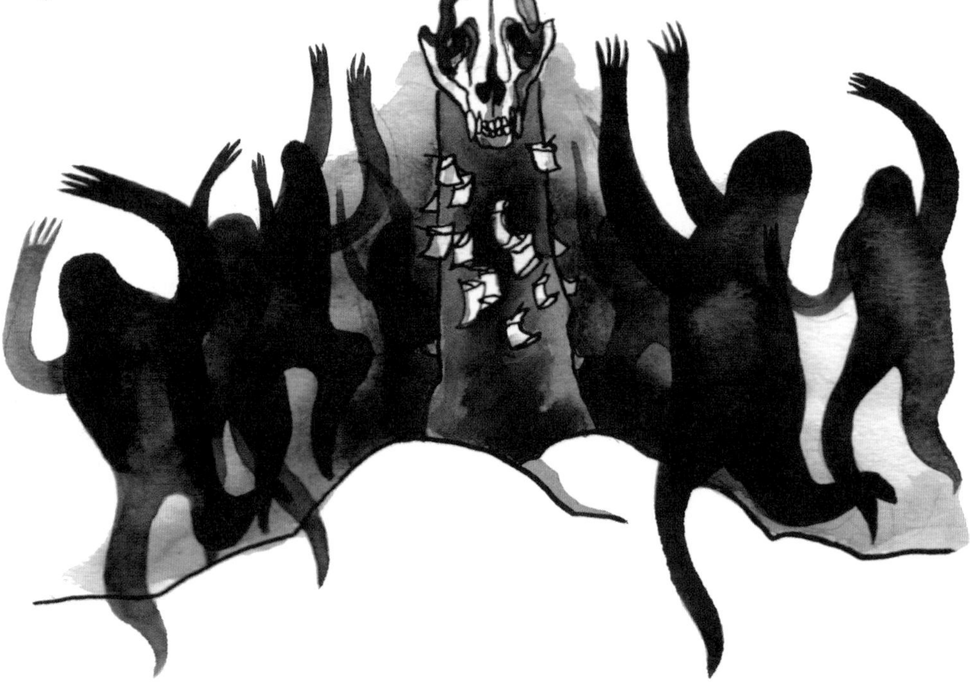

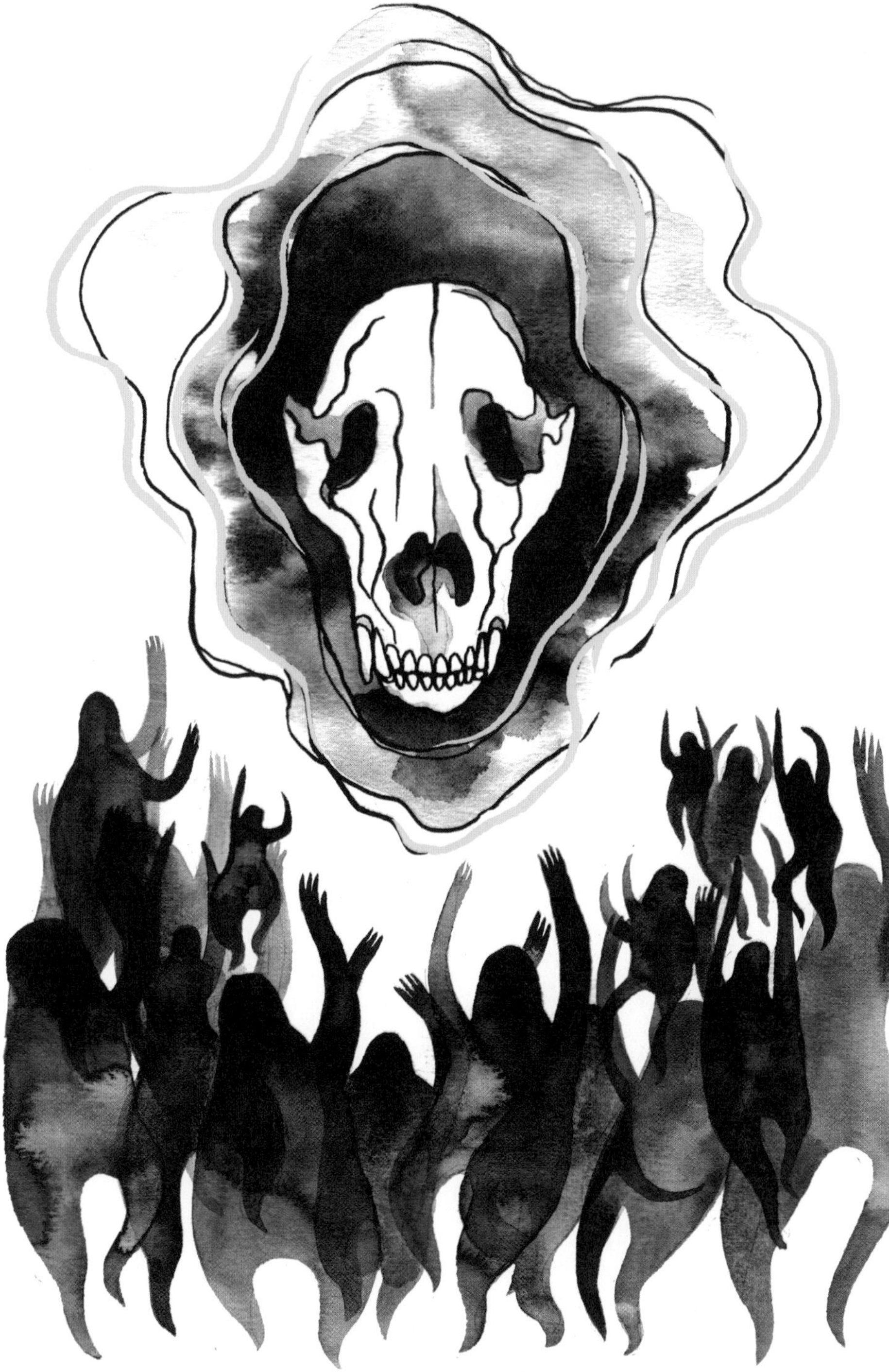

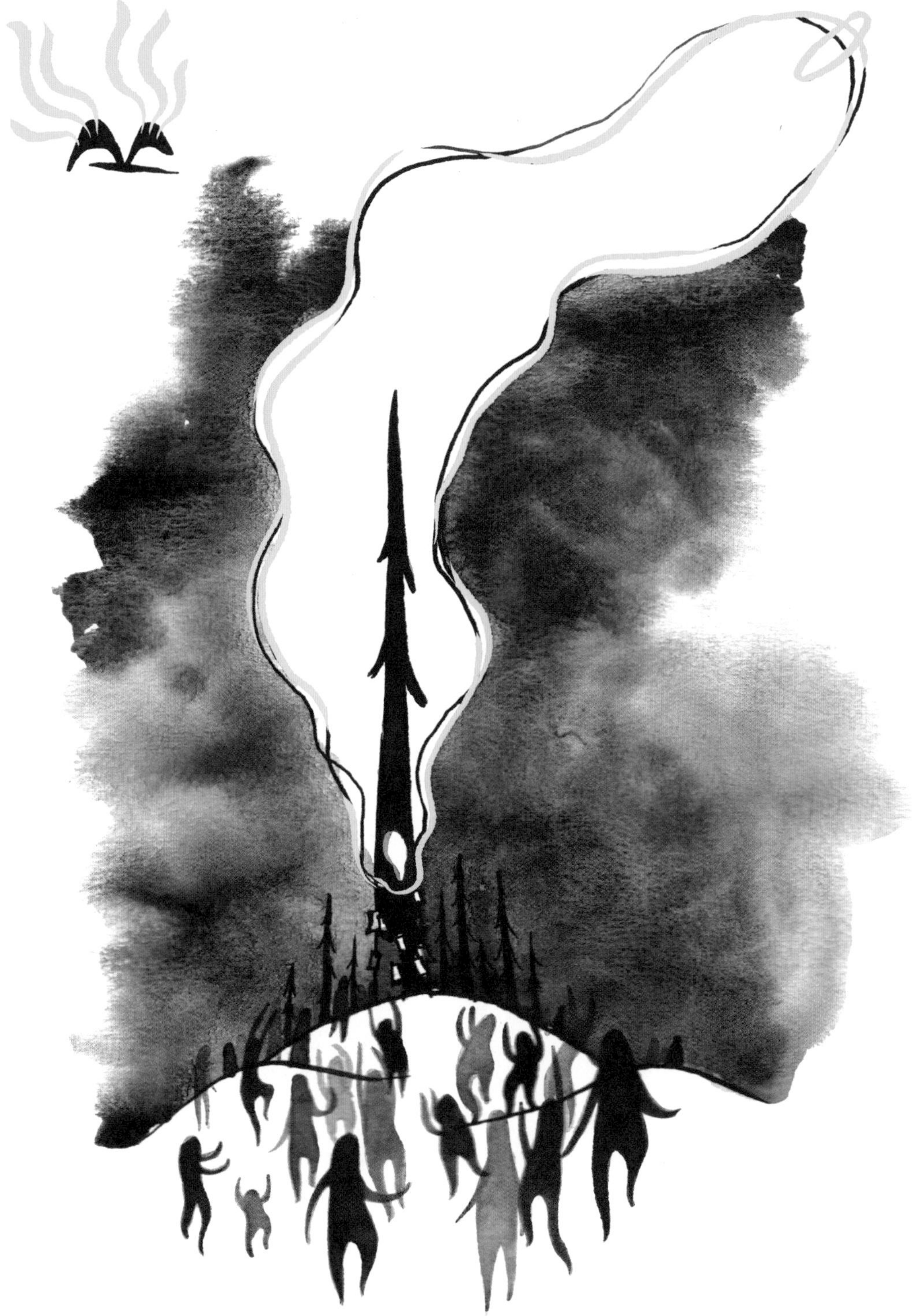

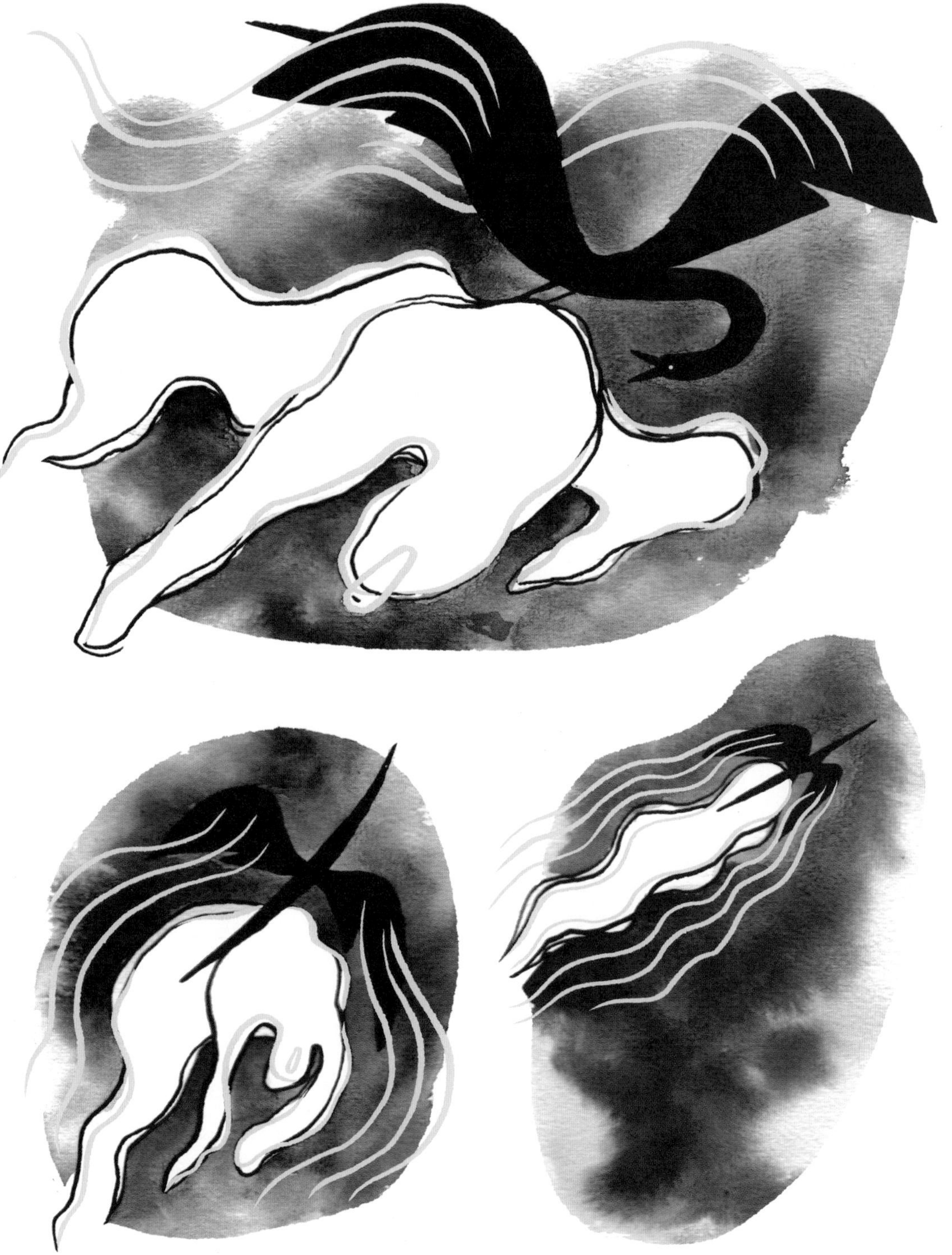

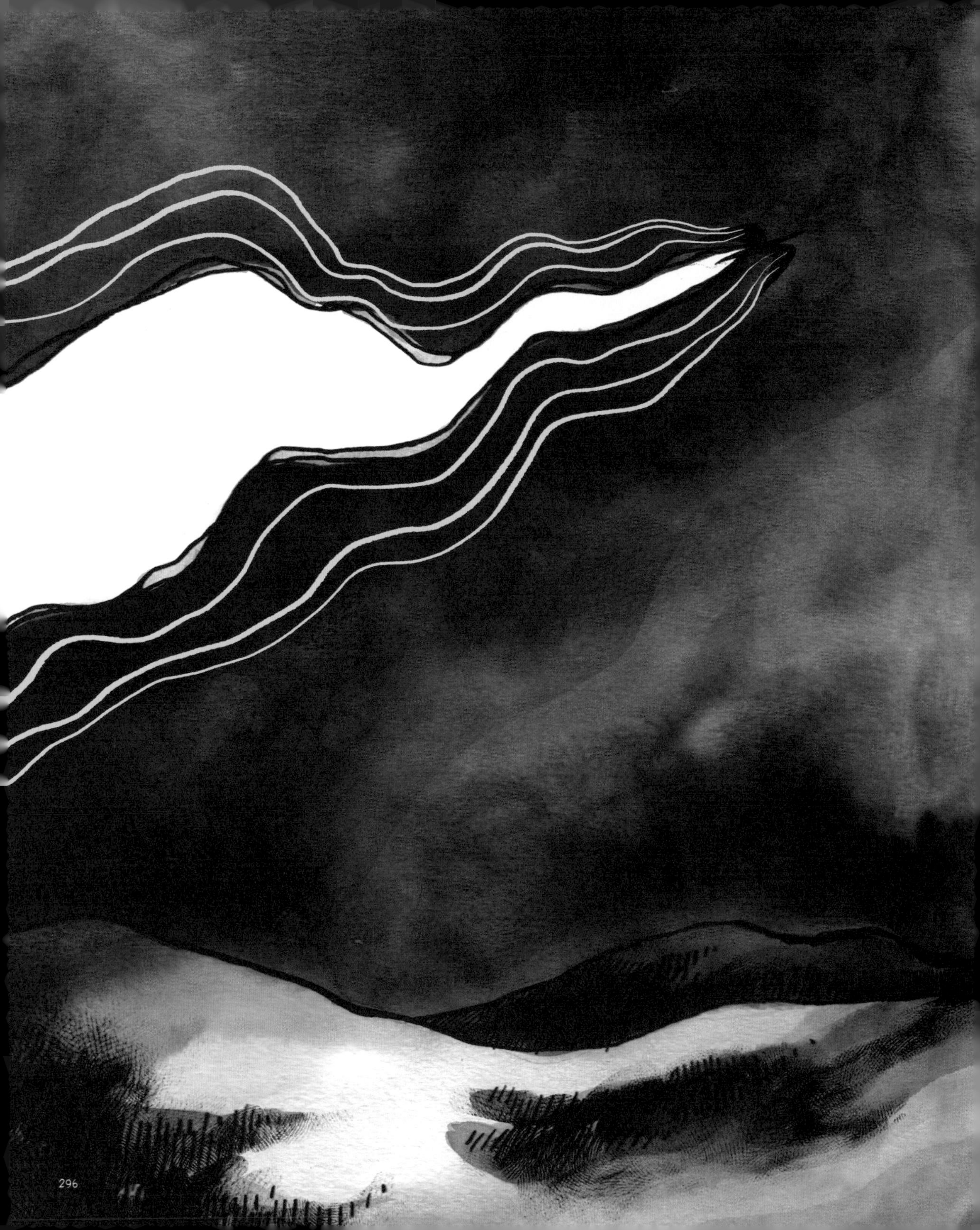

XI

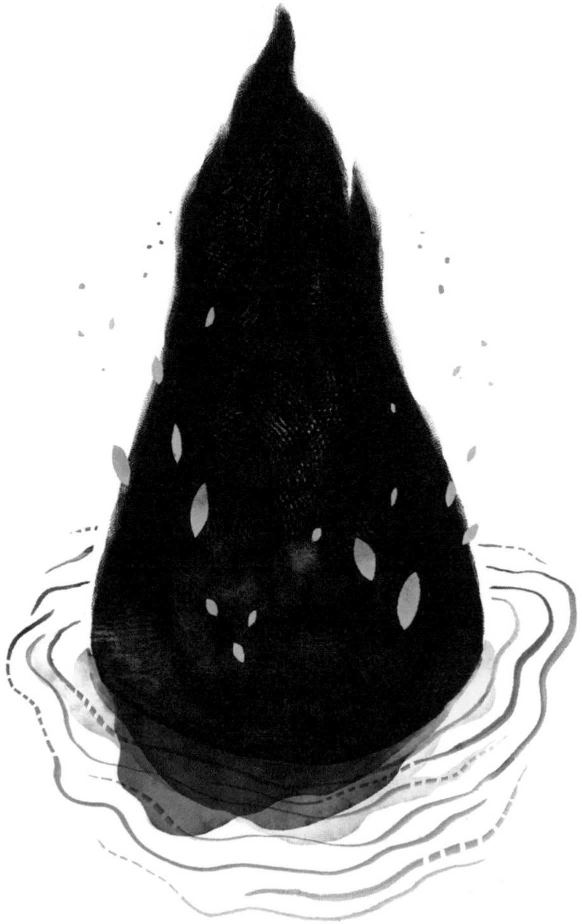

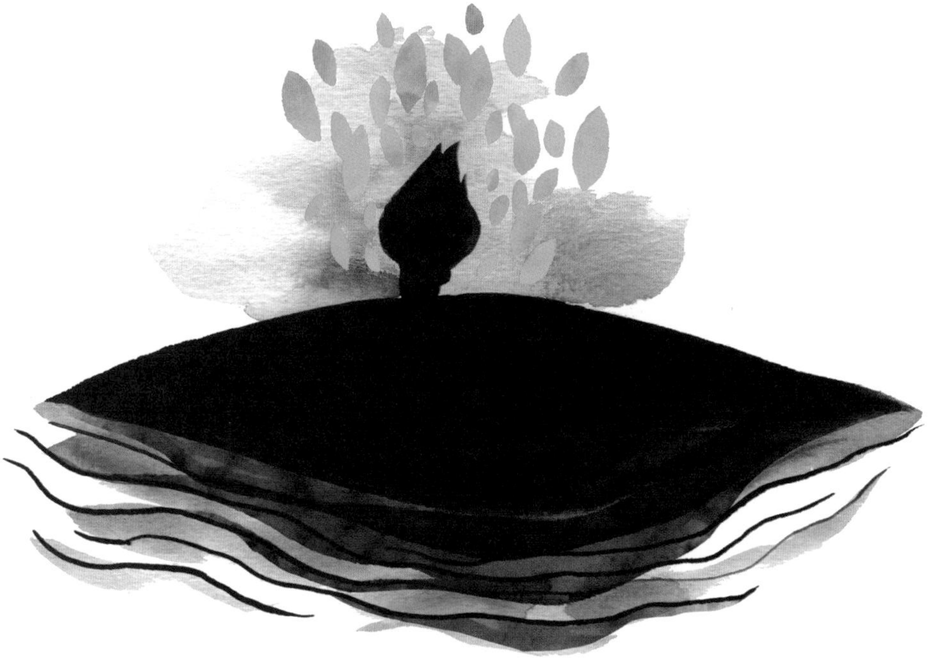

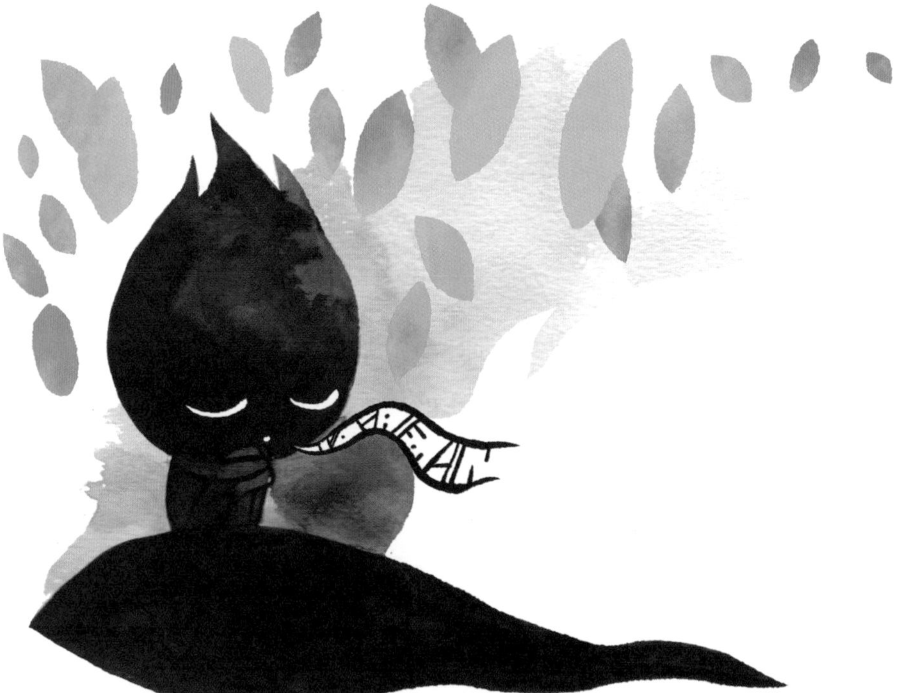

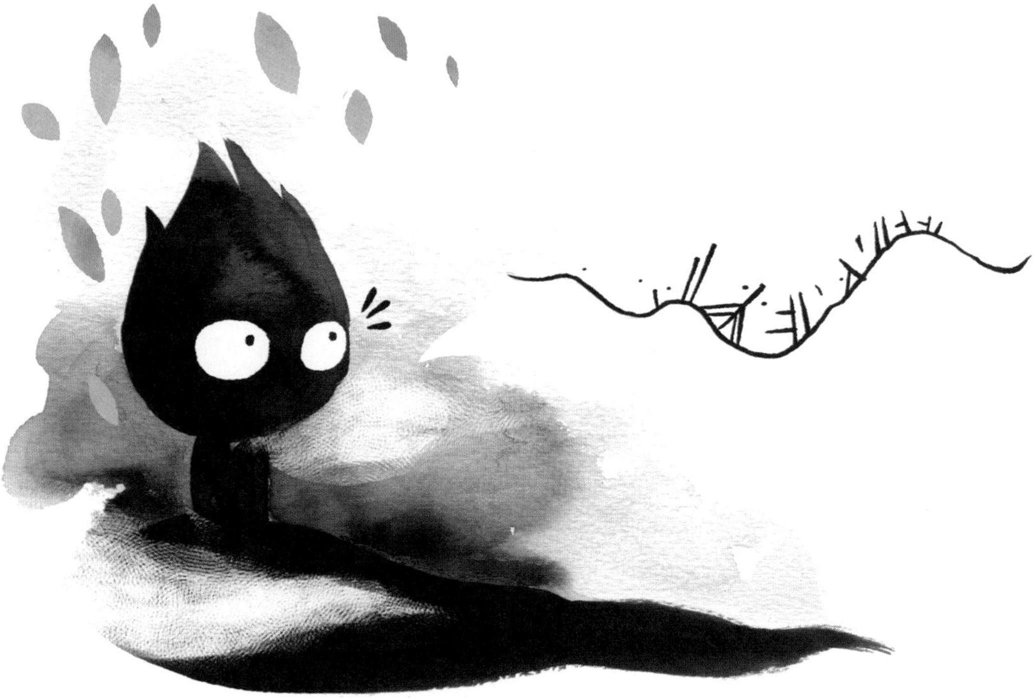

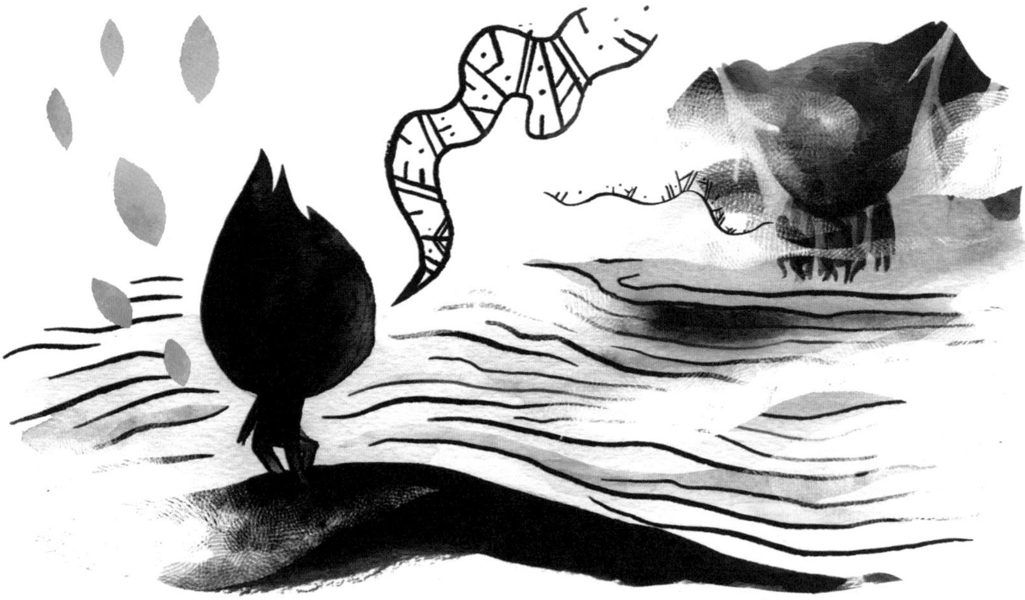

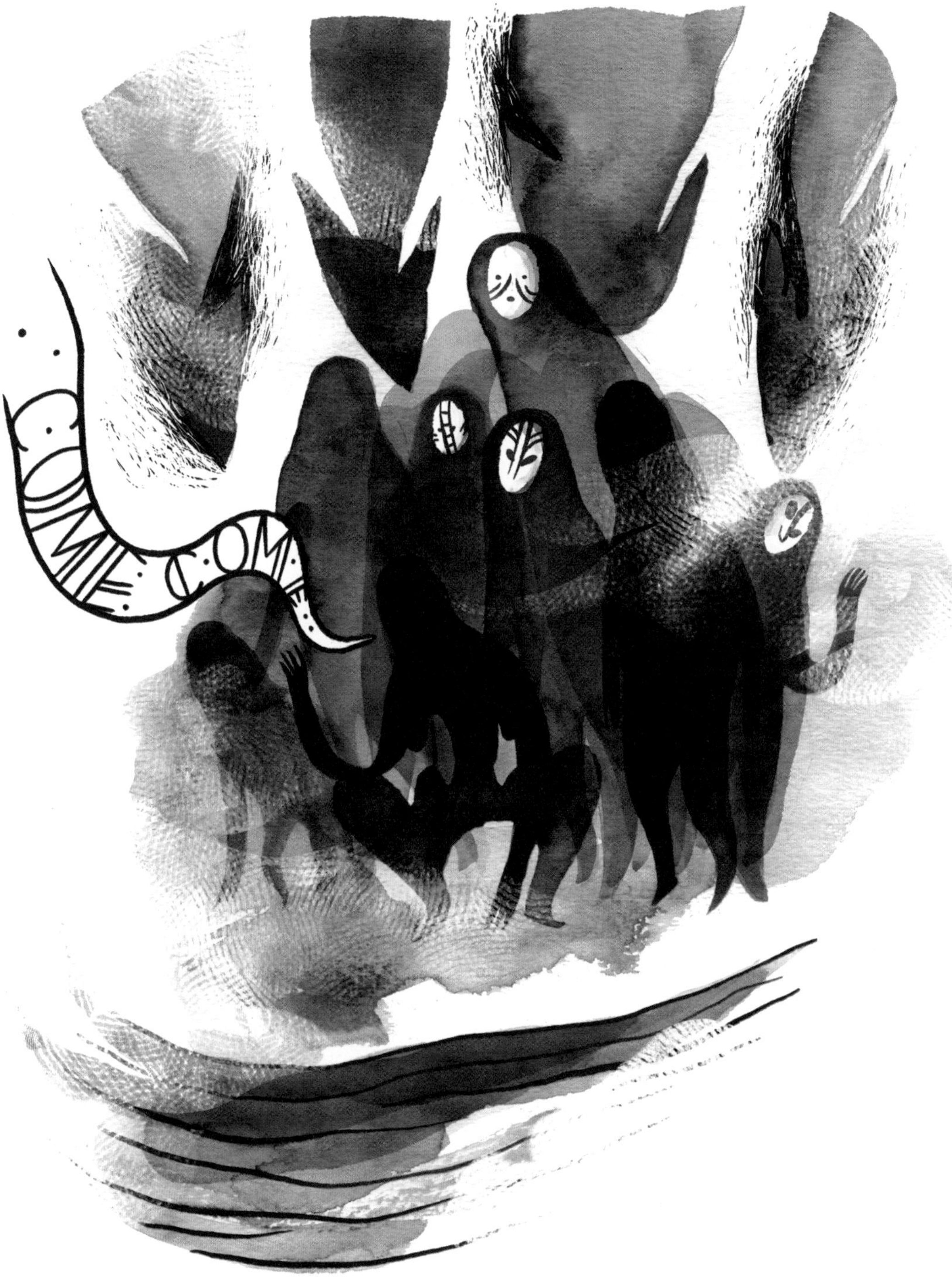
COME COM

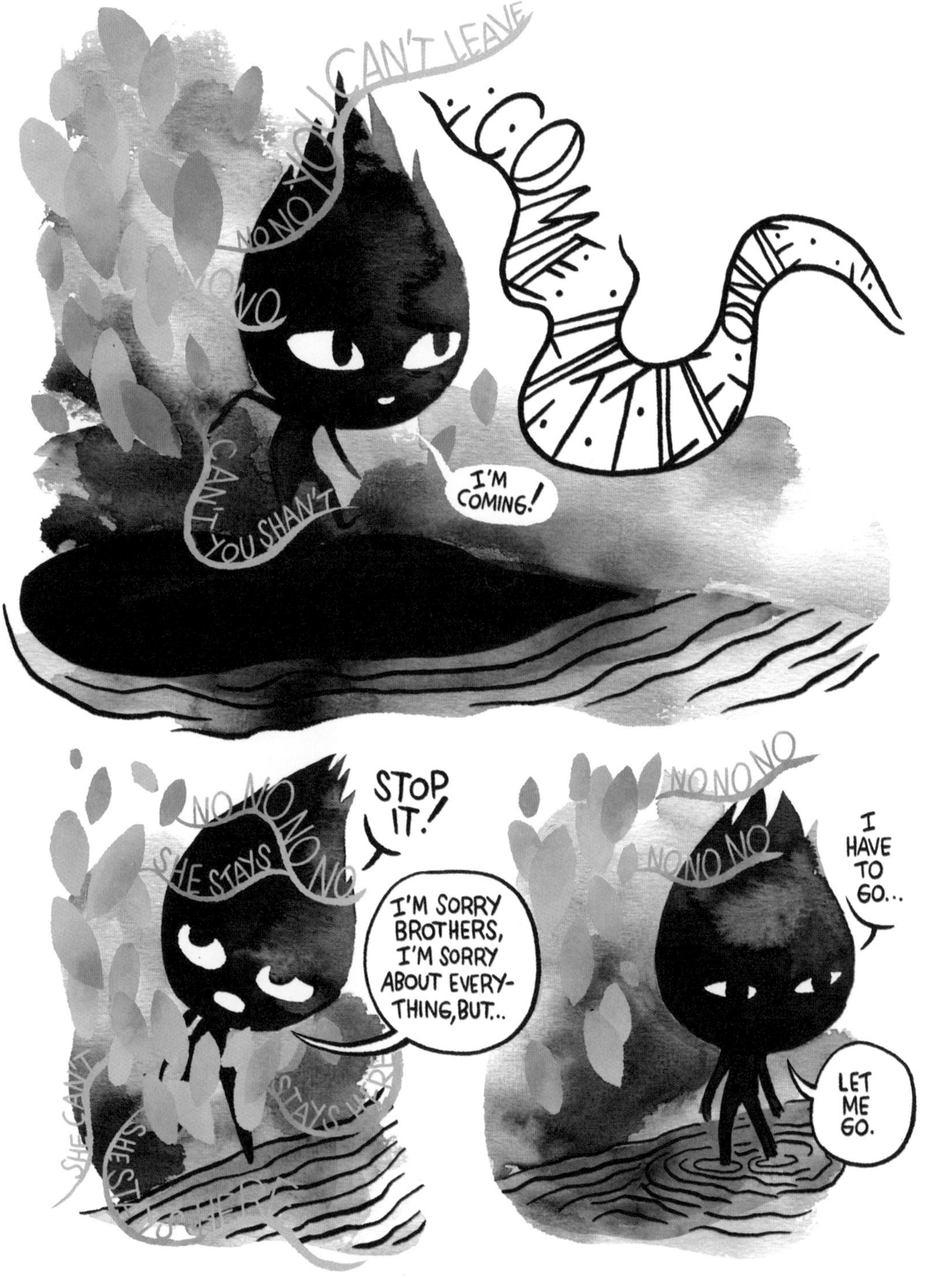
NO NO YOU CAN'T LEAVE
NO NO
CAN'T YOU SHAN'T
COME COME
I'M COMING!
NO NO NO NO NO
SHE STAYS
STOP IT!
I'M SORRY BROTHERS, I'M SORRY ABOUT EVERY-THING, BUT...
SHE CAN'T
NO NO NO
NO NO NO
I HAVE TO GO...
LET ME GO.

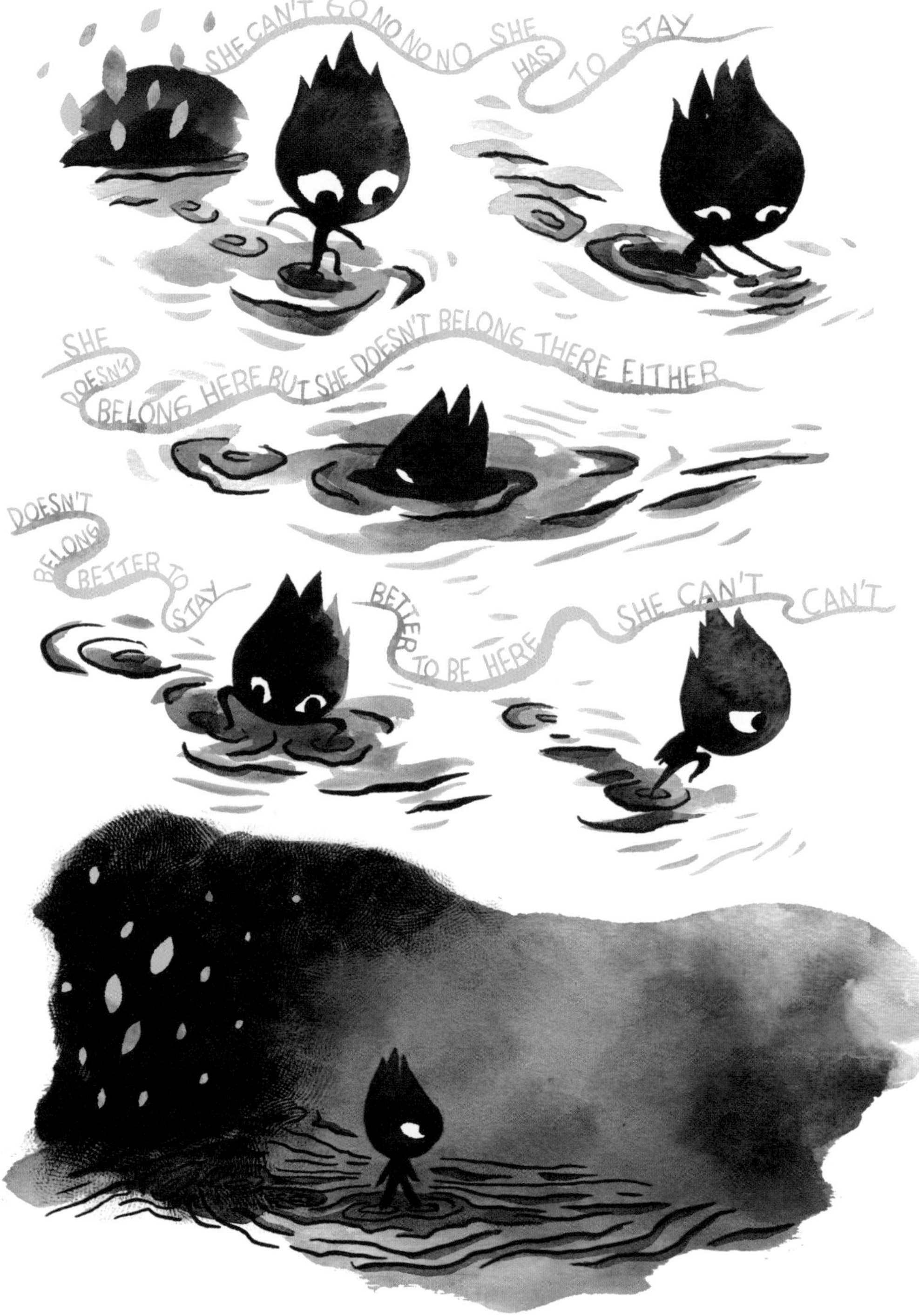
SHE CAN'T GO NO NO NO SHE HAS TO STAY
SHE DOESN'T BELONG HERE BUT SHE DOESN'T BELONG THERE EITHER
DOESN'T BELONG BETTER TO STAY
BETTER TO BE HERE SHE CAN'T CAN'T

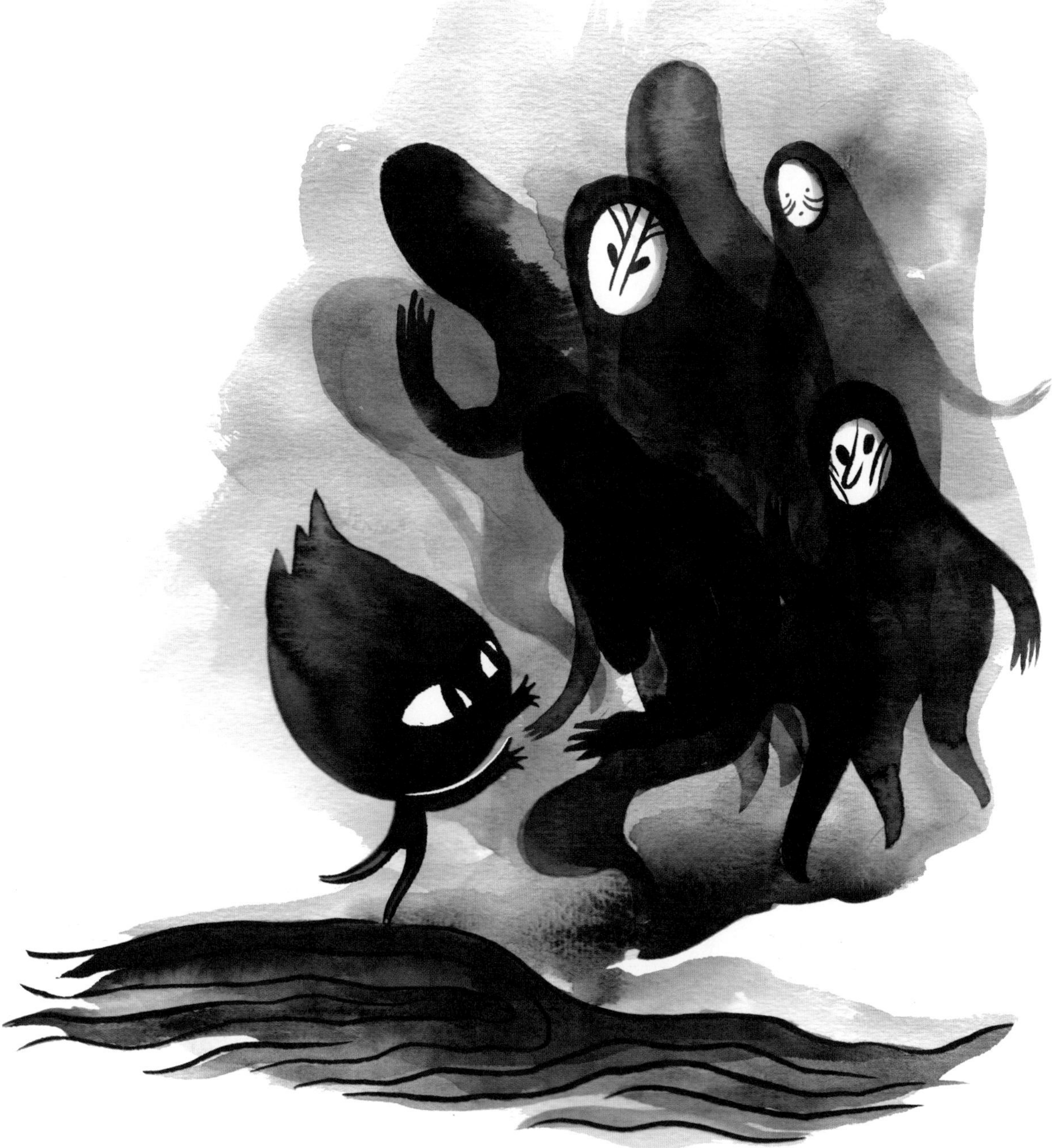

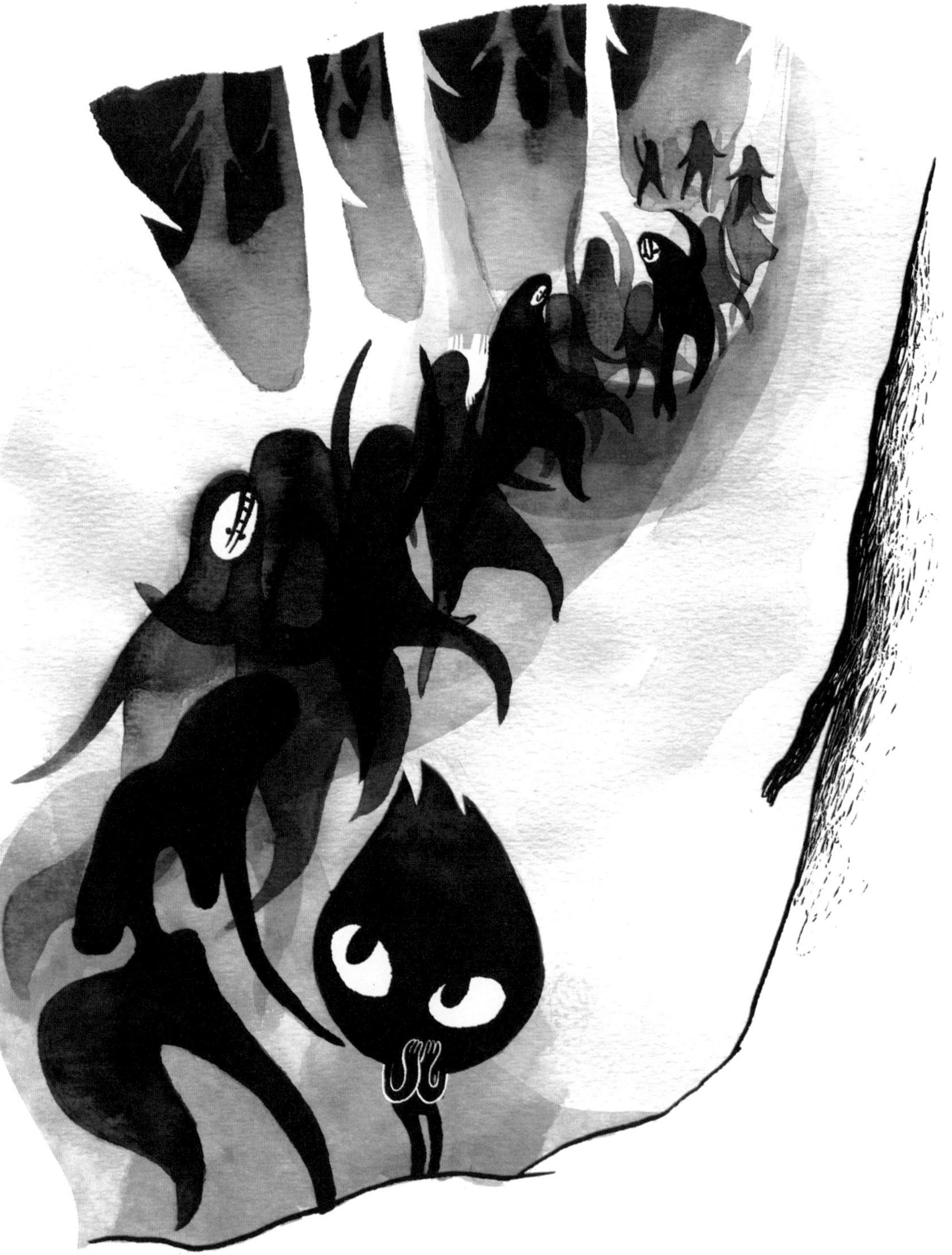

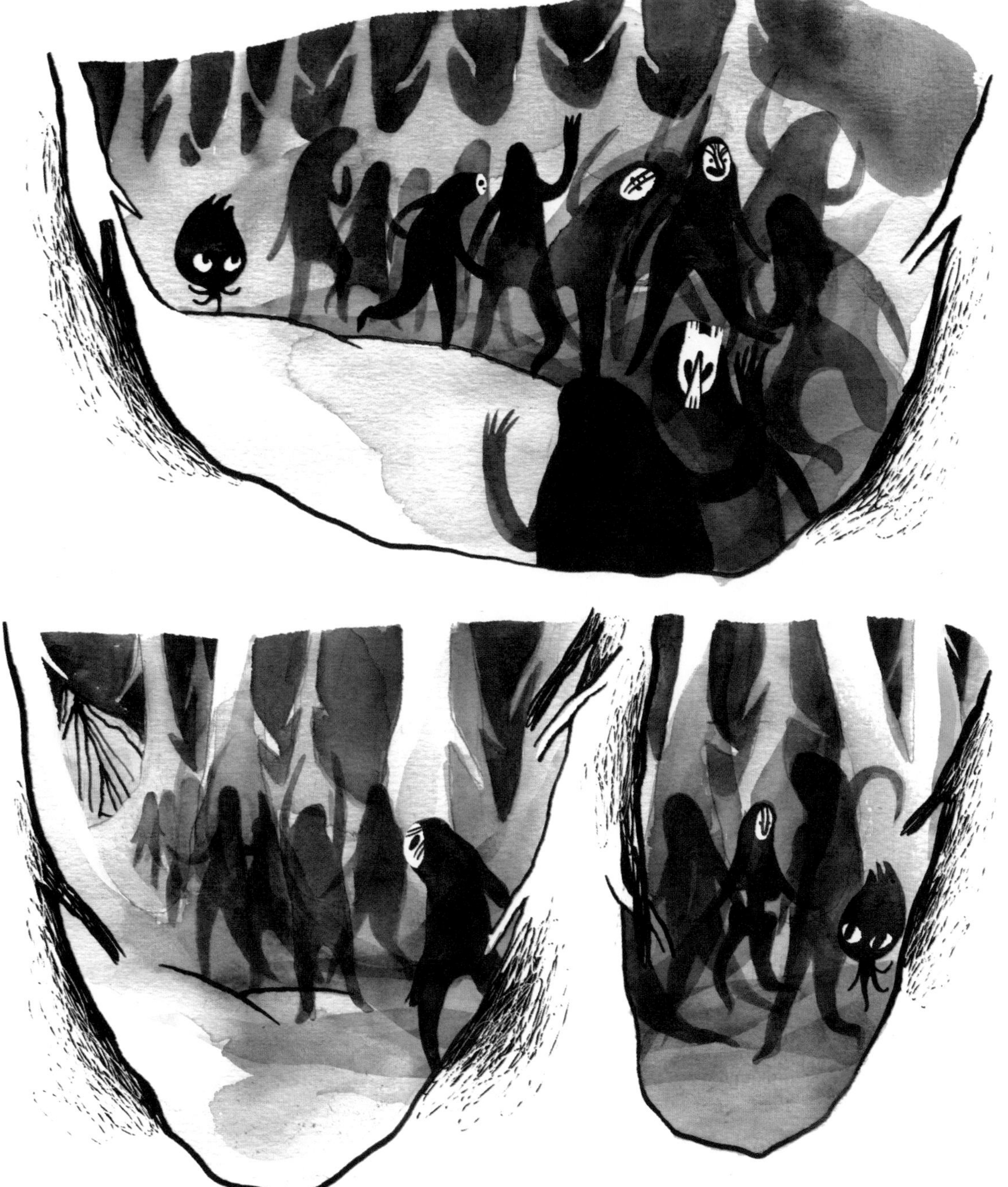

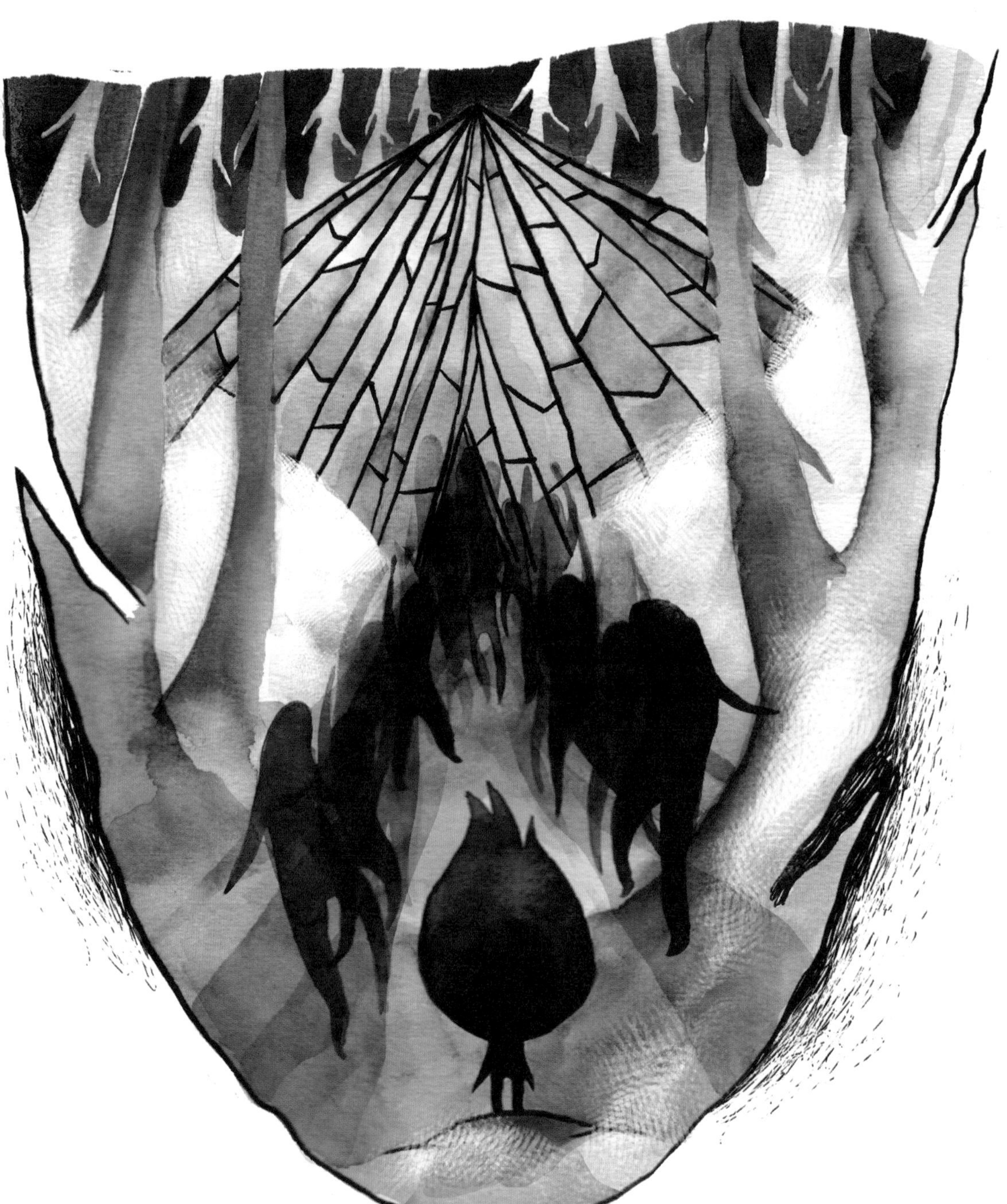

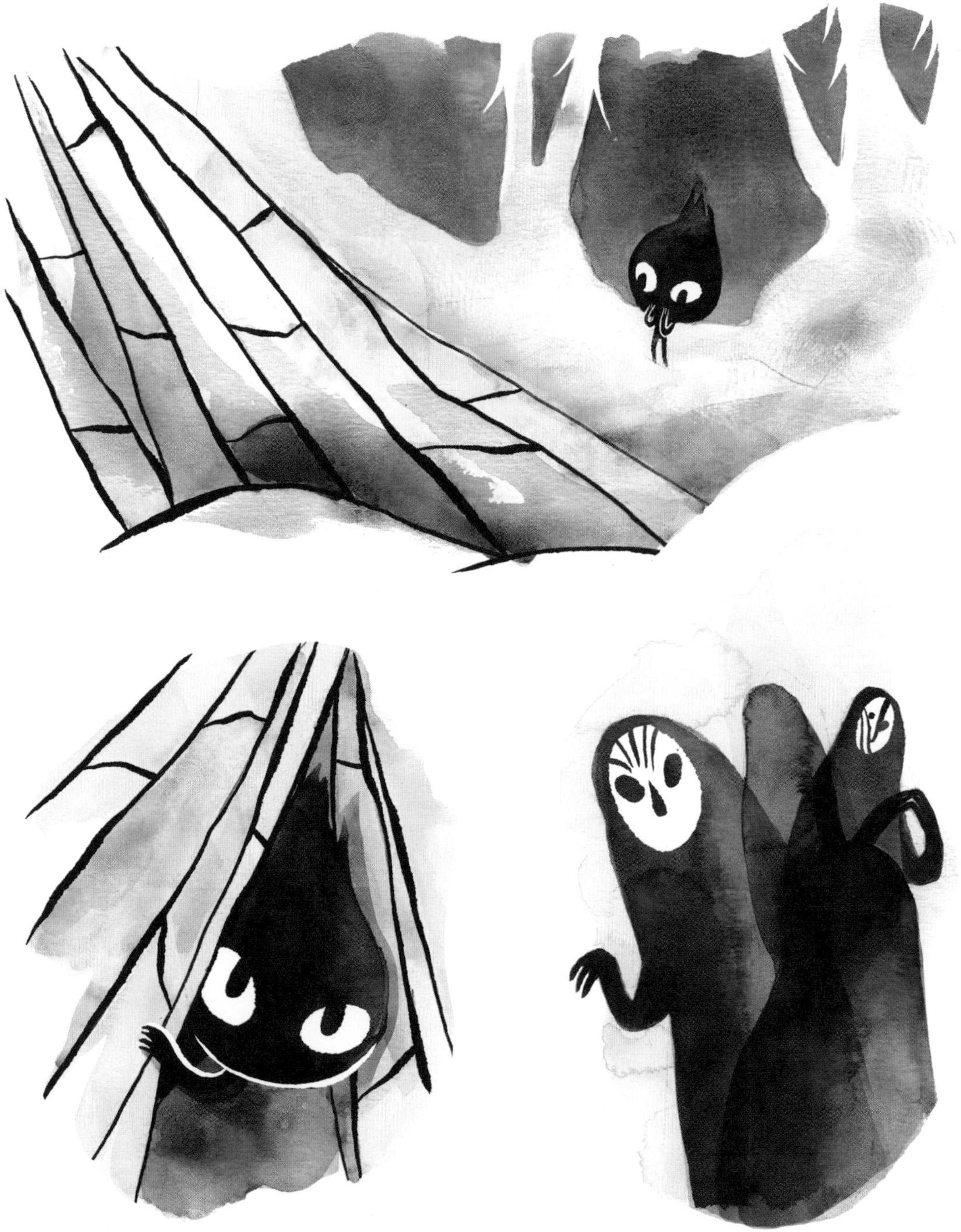

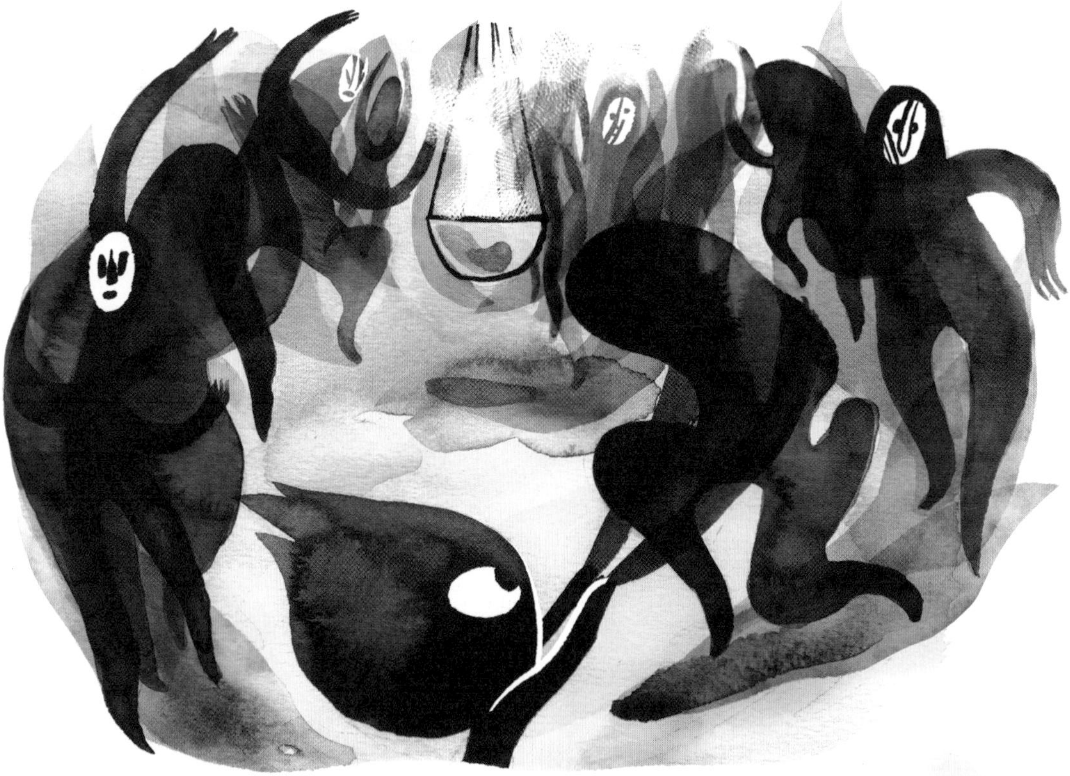

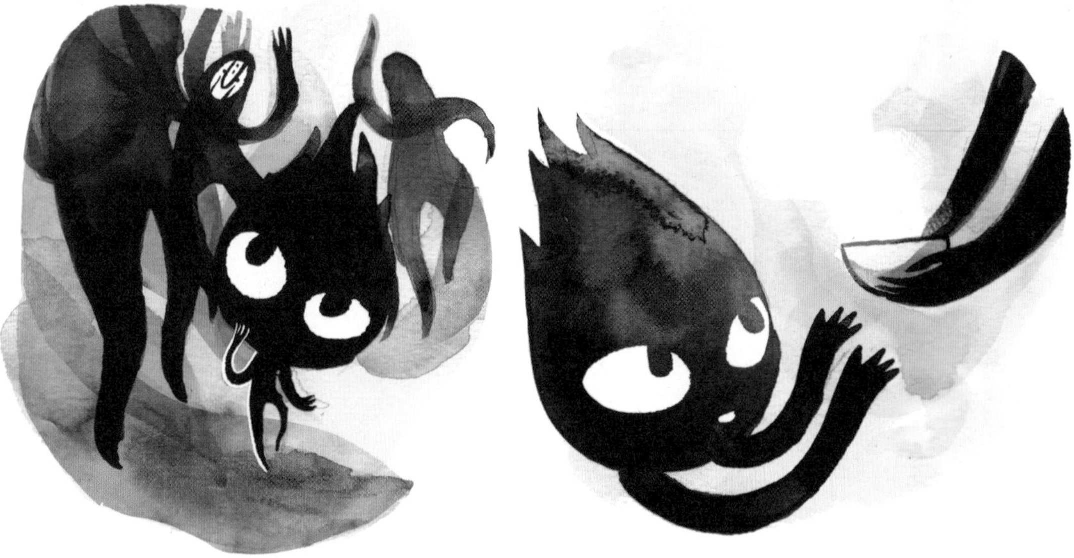

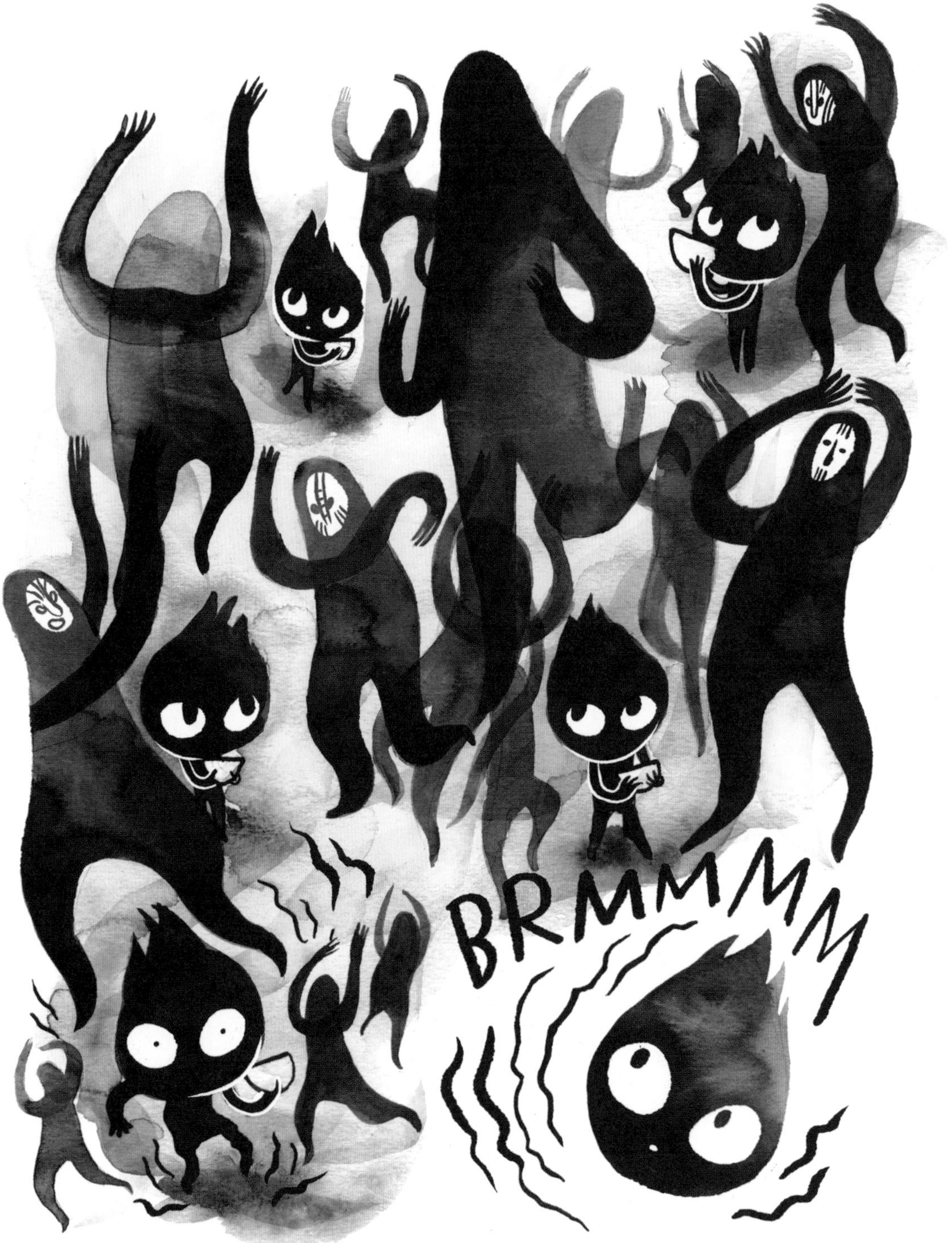
BRMMMMM

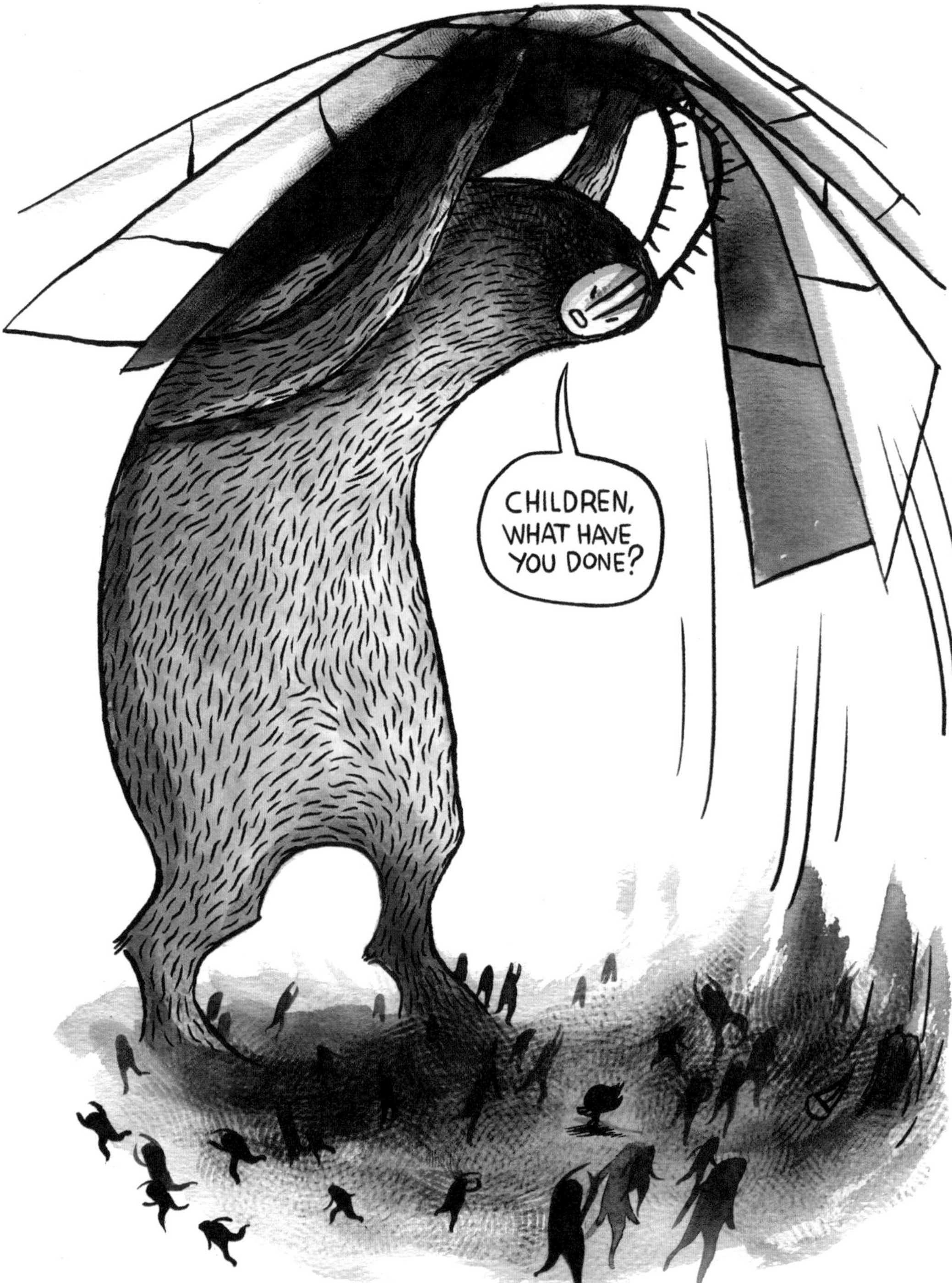
CHILDREN, WHAT HAVE YOU DONE?

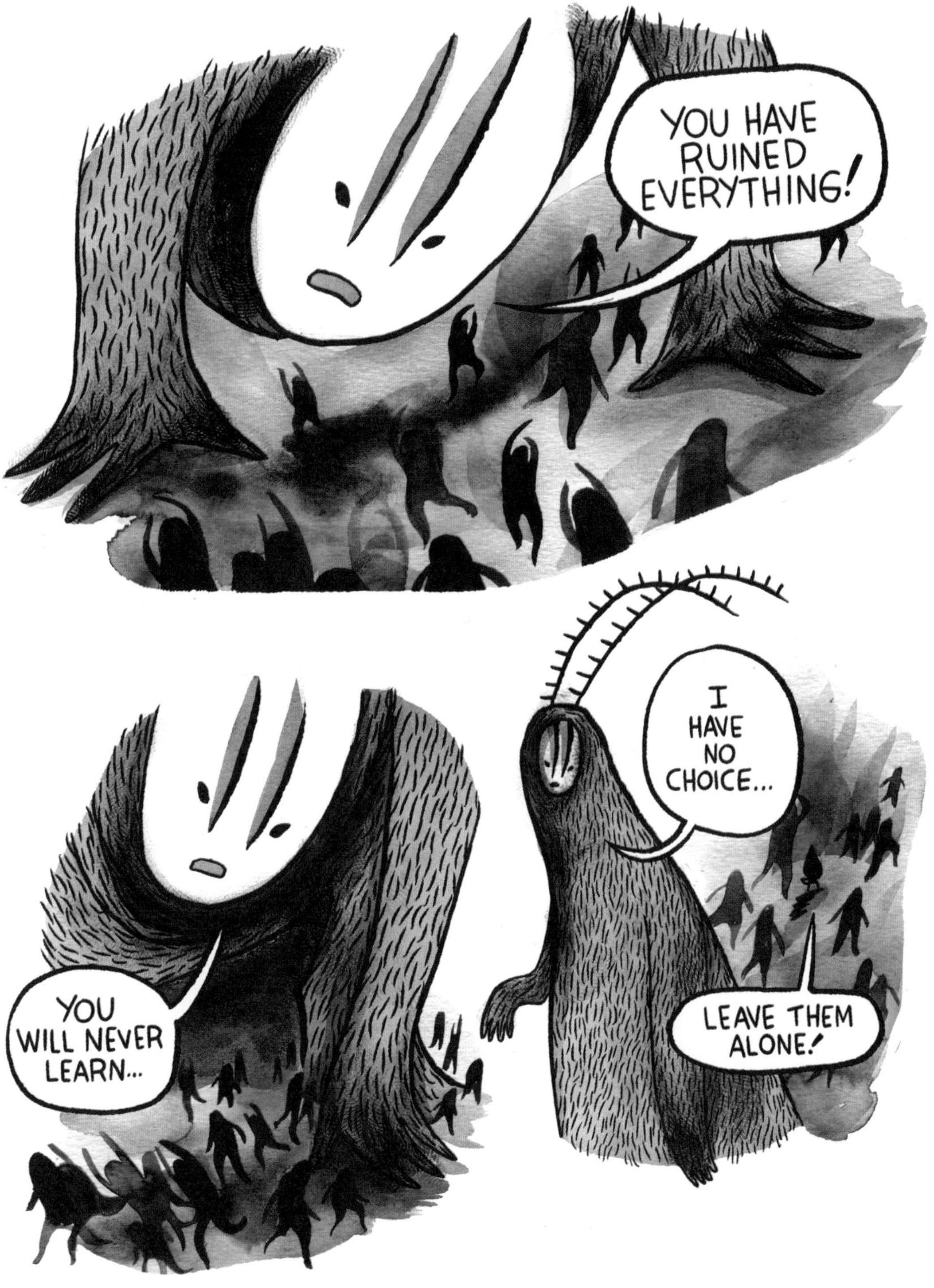
YOU HAVE RUINED EVERYTHING!
YOU WILL NEVER LEARN...
I HAVE NO CHOICE...
LEAVE THEM ALONE!

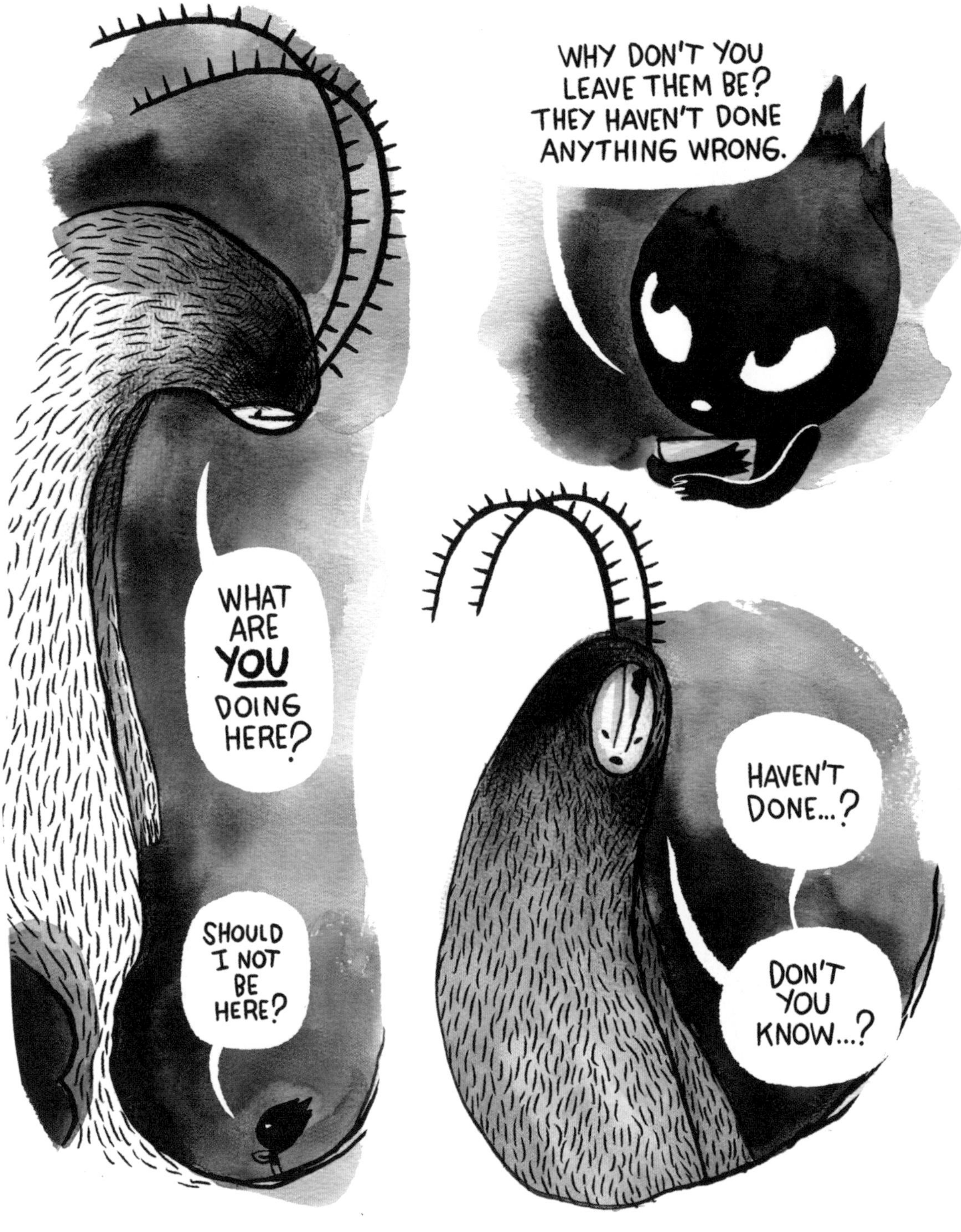
WHAT ARE YOU DOING HERE?
SHOULD I NOT BE HERE?
WHY DON'T YOU LEAVE THEM BE? THEY HAVEN'T DONE ANYTHING WRONG.
HAVEN'T DONE...?
DON'T YOU KNOW...?

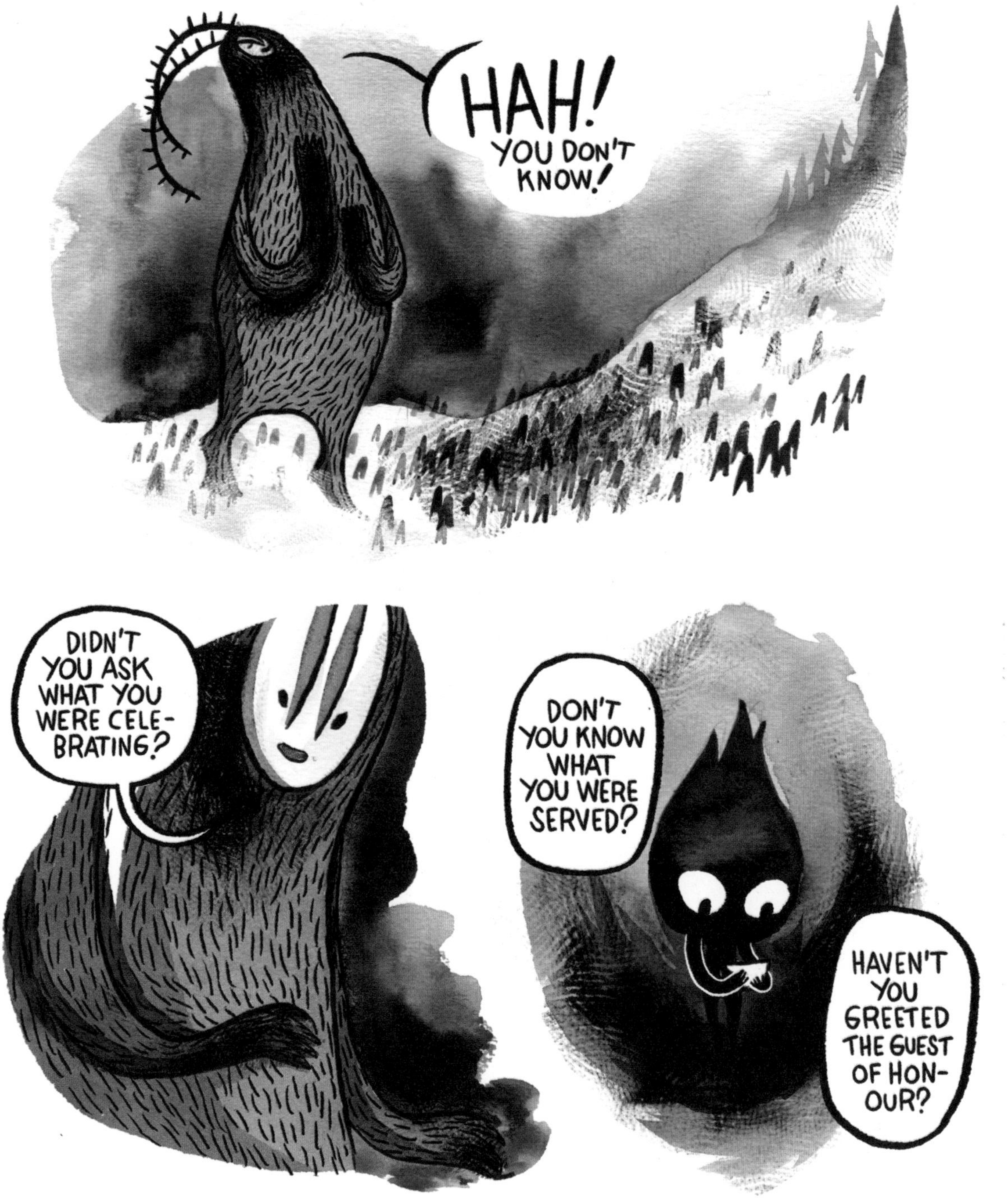
HAH! YOU DON'T KNOW!
DIDN'T YOU ASK WHAT YOU WERE CELE-BRATING?
DON'T YOU KNOW WHAT YOU WERE SERVED?
HAVEN'T YOU GREETED THE GUEST OF HON-OUR?

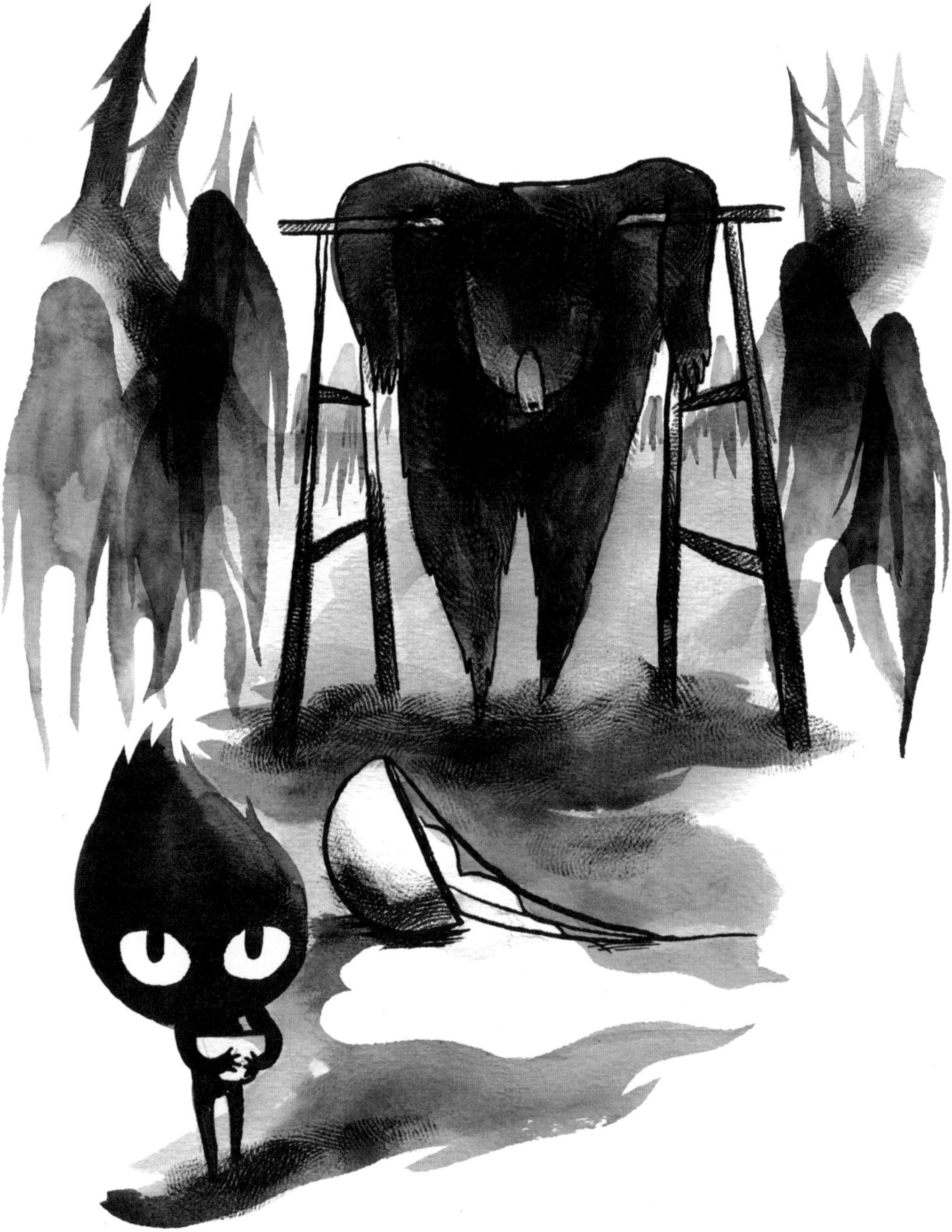

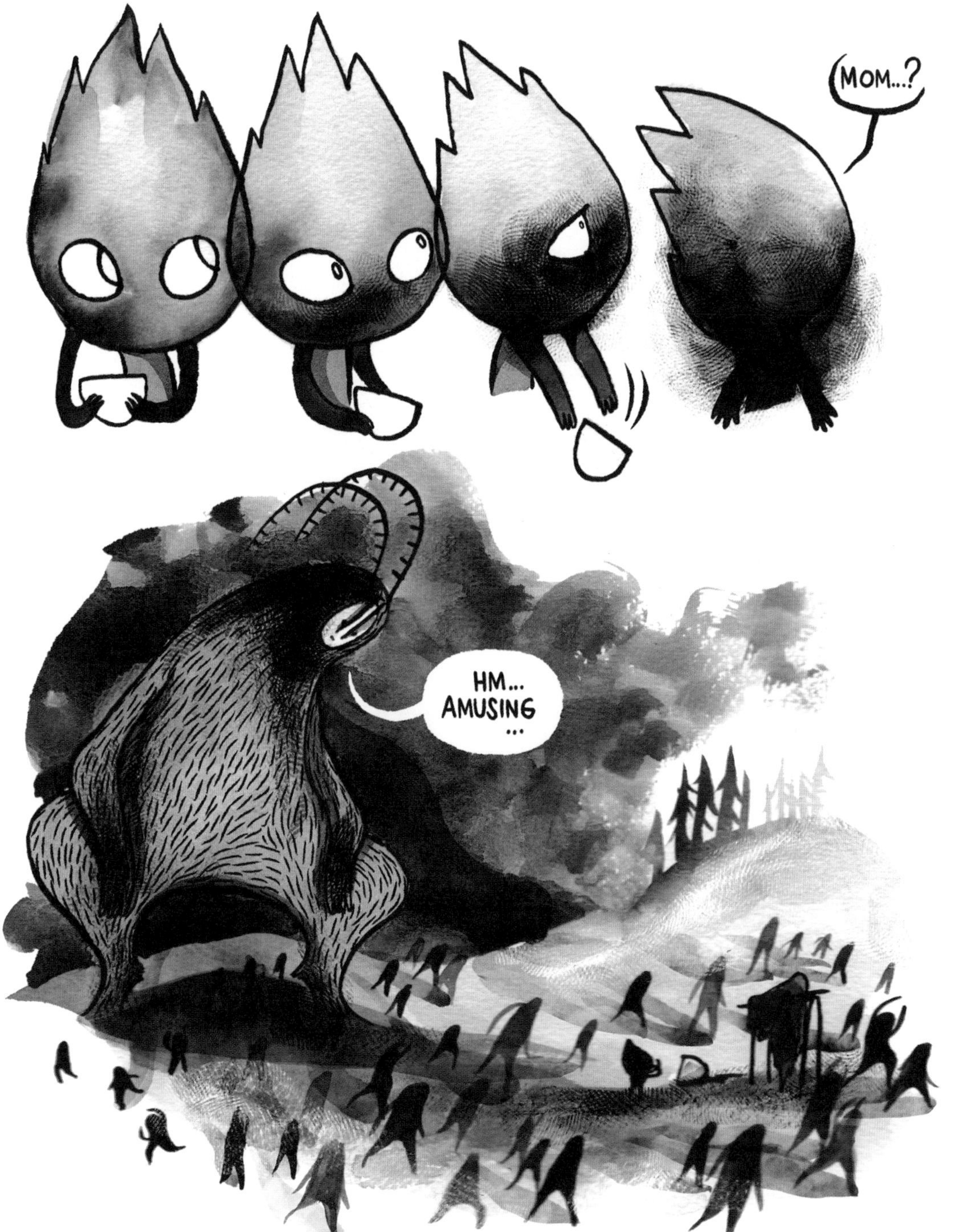
MOM...?
HM... AMUSING ...

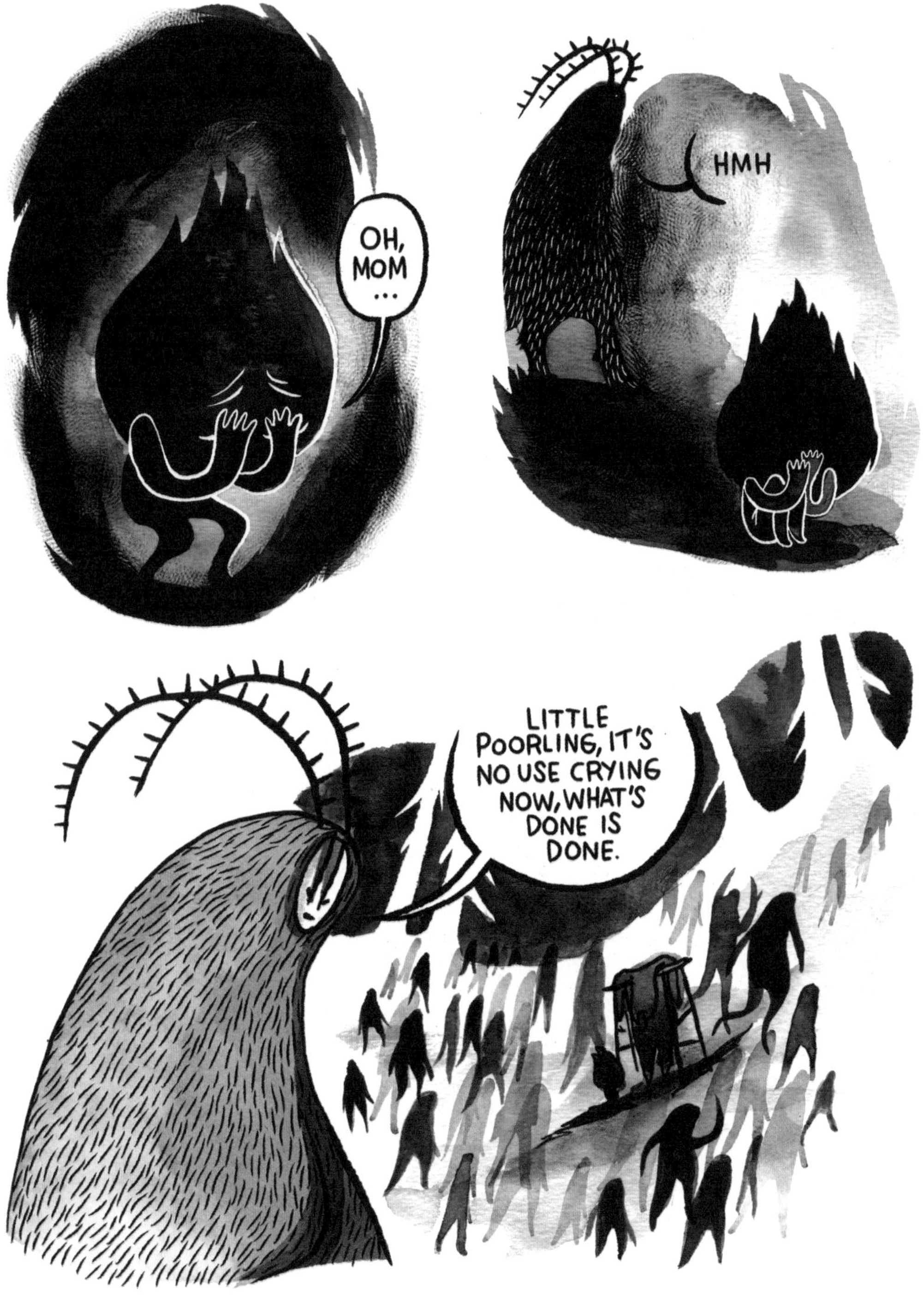
OH, MOM ...
HMH
LITTLE POORLING, IT'S NO USE CRYING NOW, WHAT'S DONE IS DONE.

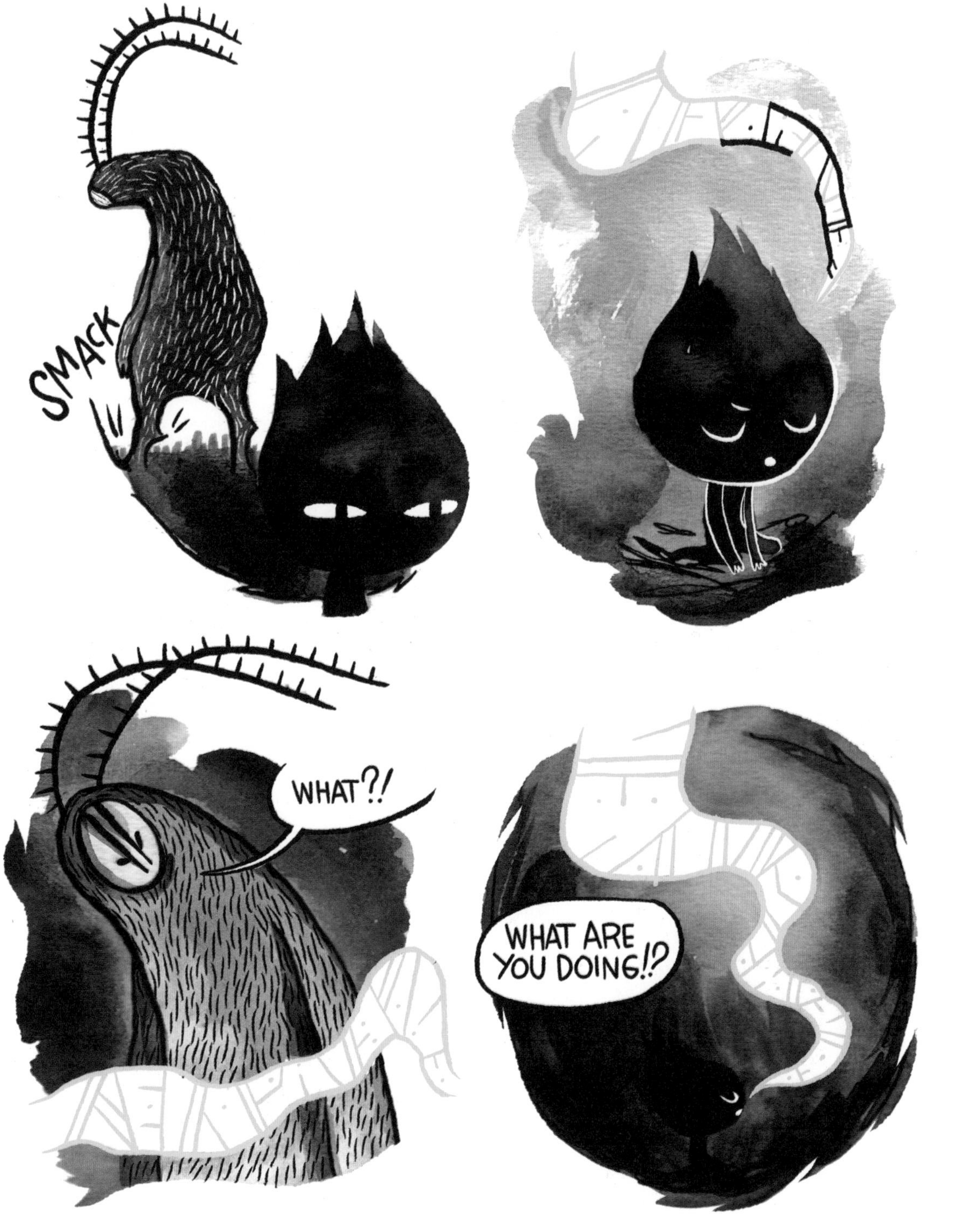
SMACK
WHAT?!
WHAT ARE YOU DOING!?

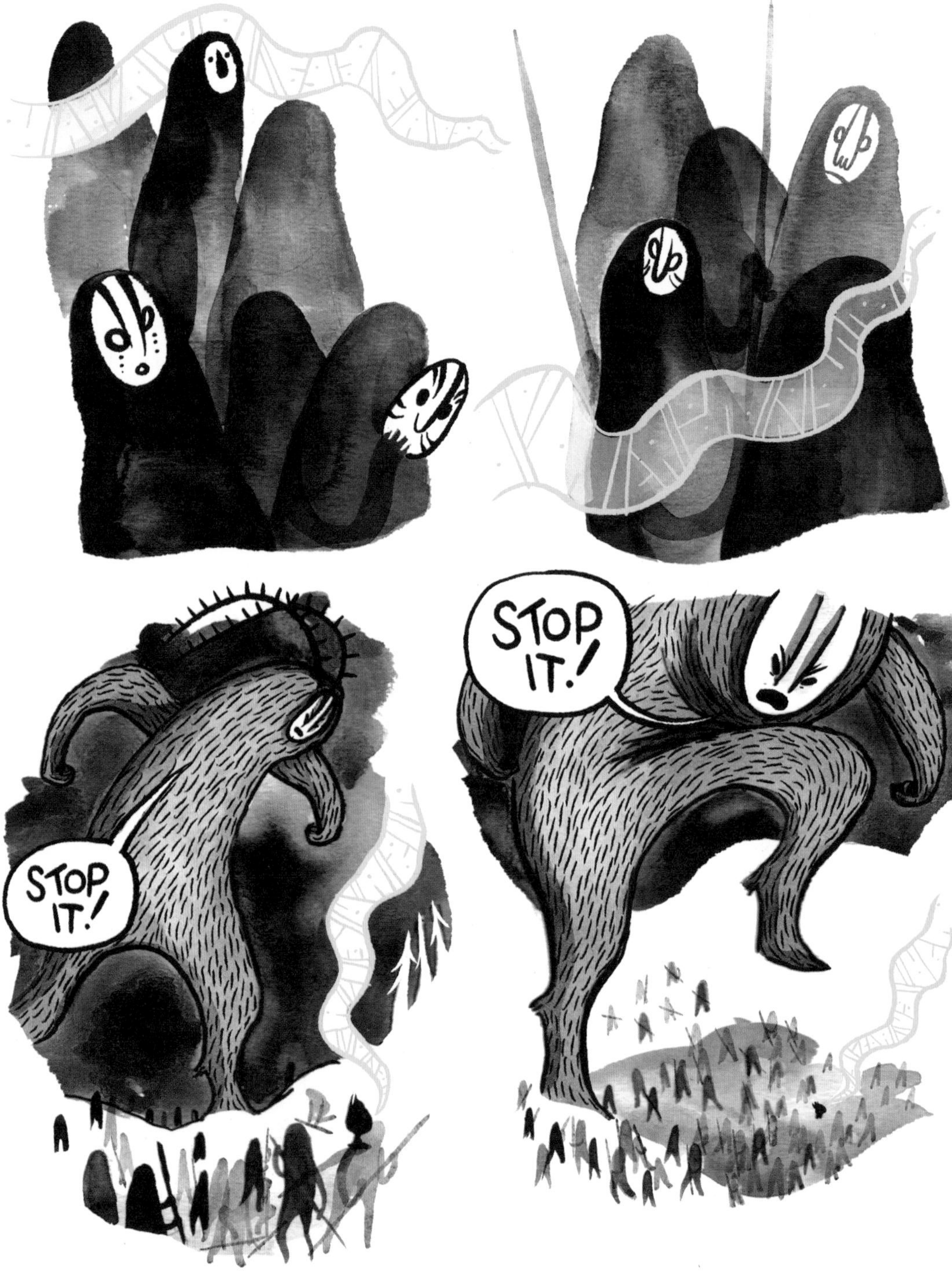
STOP IT!
STOP IT!

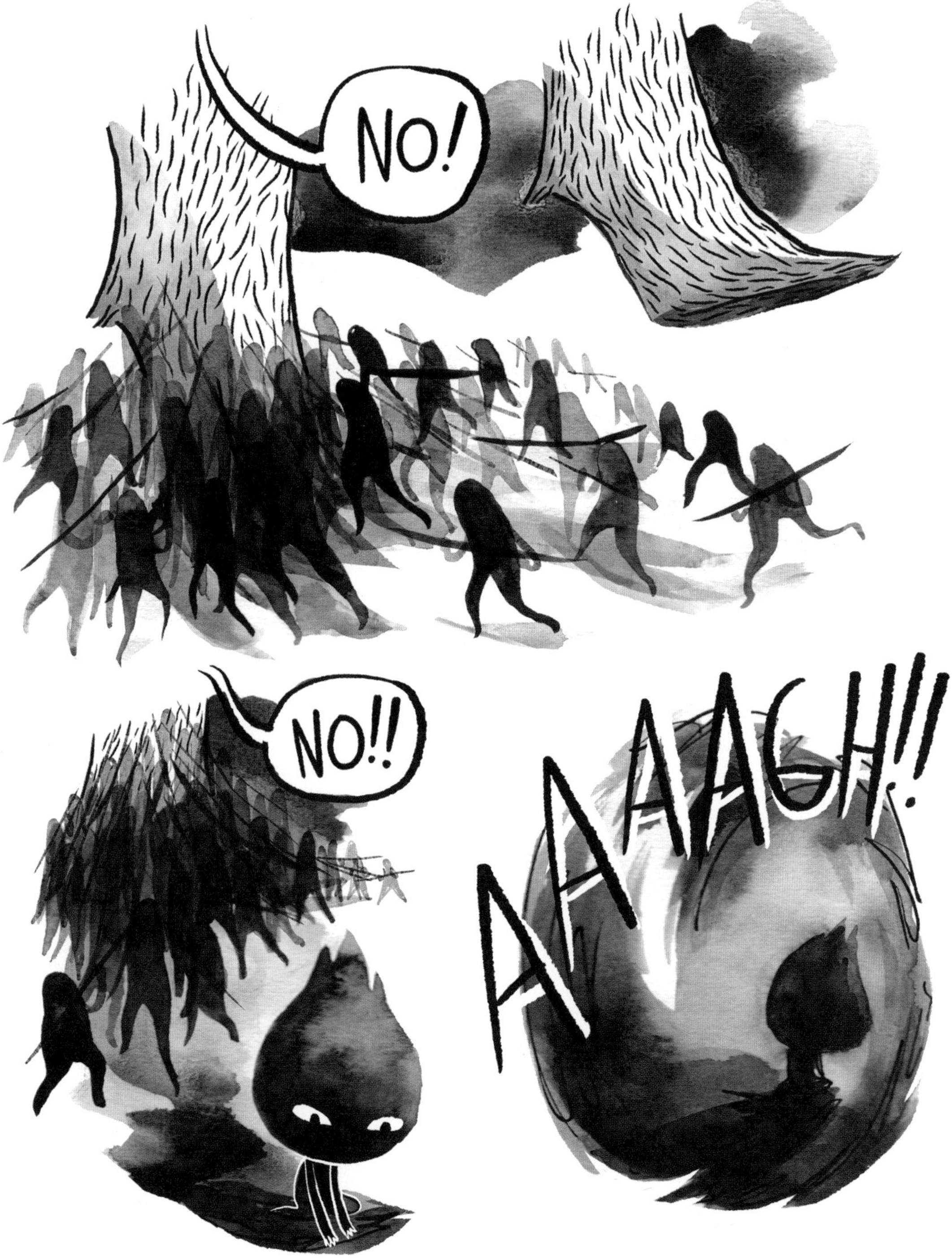
NO!
NO!!
AAAAGH!!

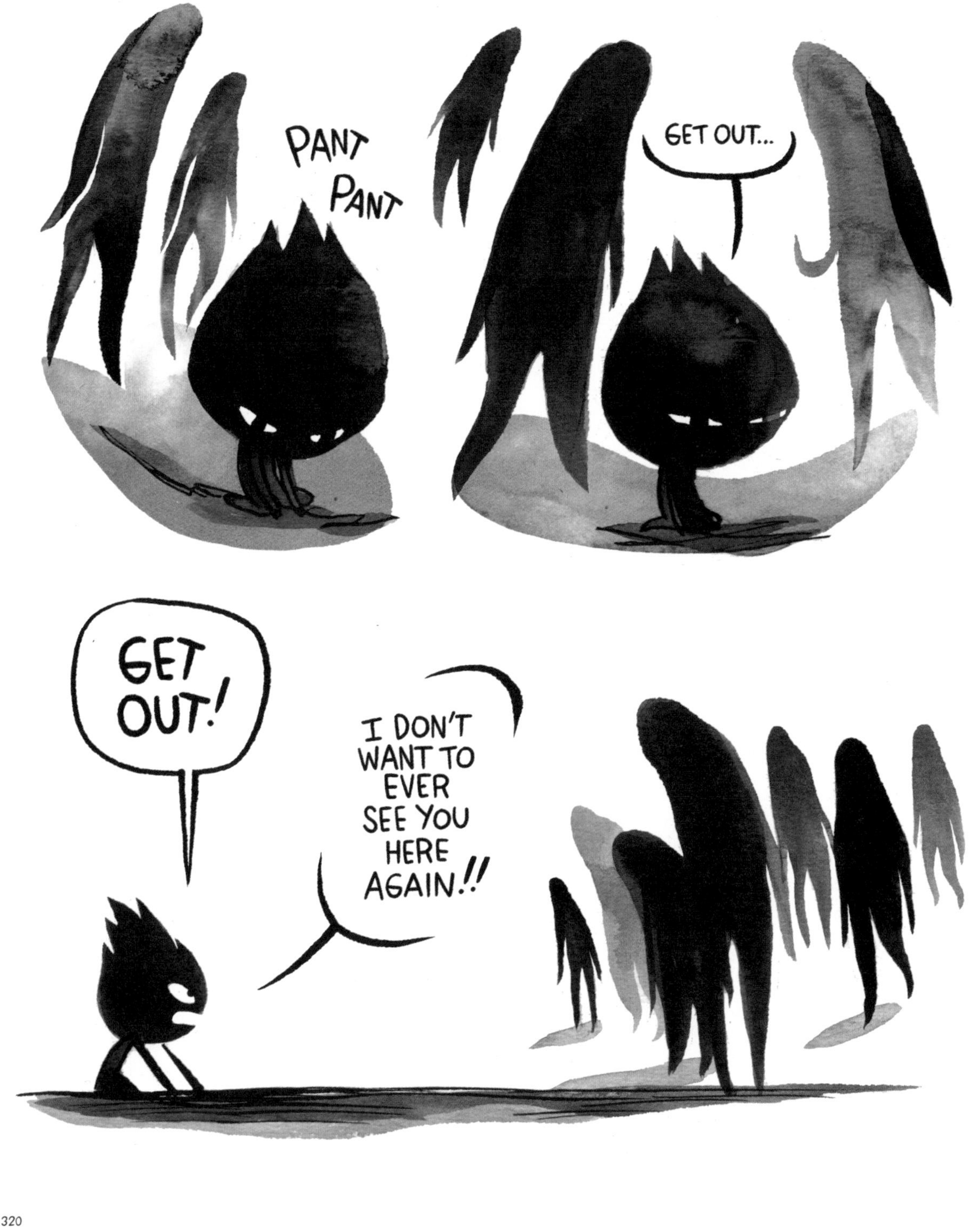
PANT
PANT
GET OUT...
GET OUT!
I DON'T WANT TO EVER SEE YOU HERE AGAIN!!

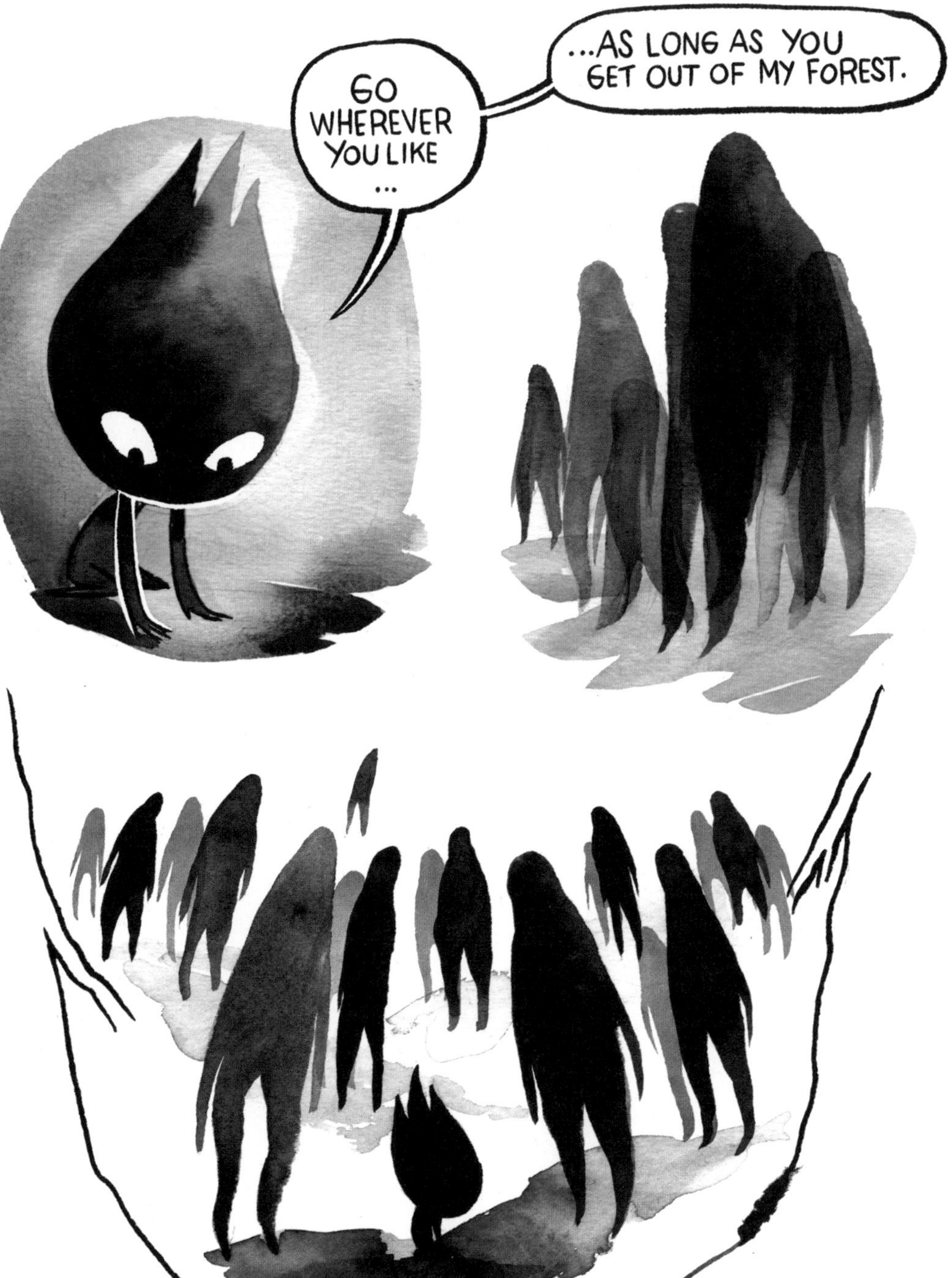
GO WHEREVER YOU LIKE ...
...AS LONG AS YOU GET OUT OF MY FOREST.

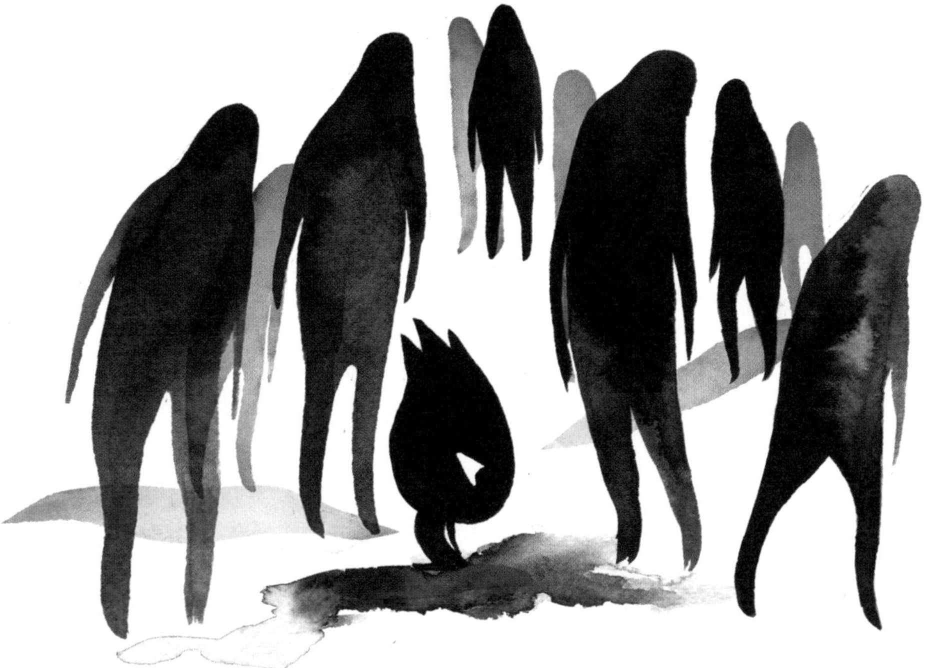

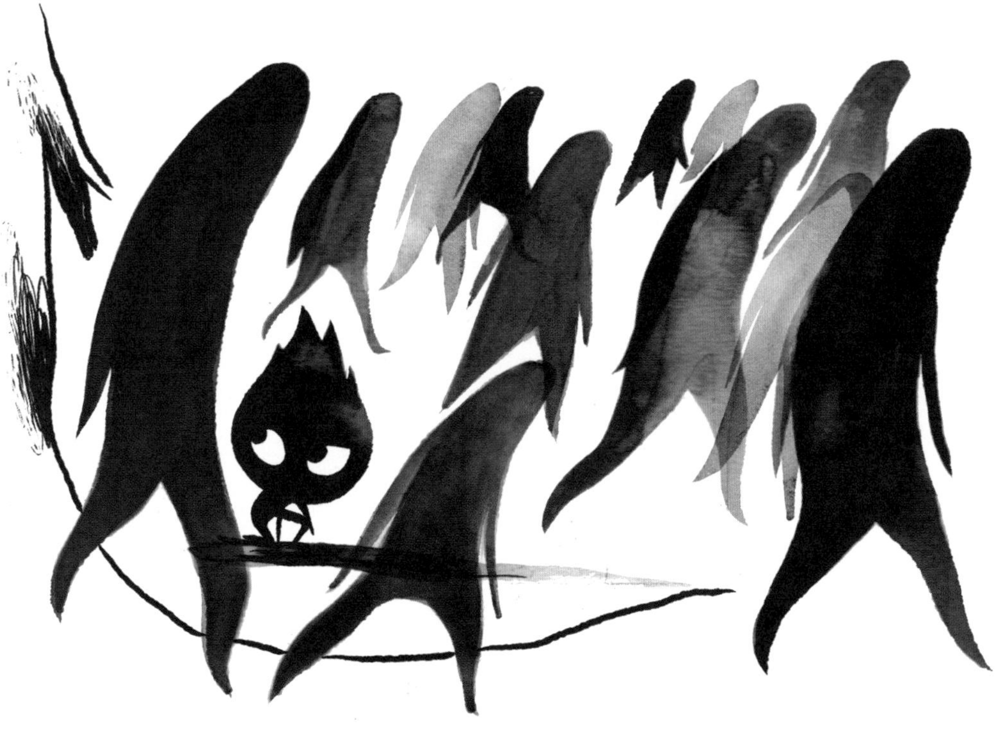

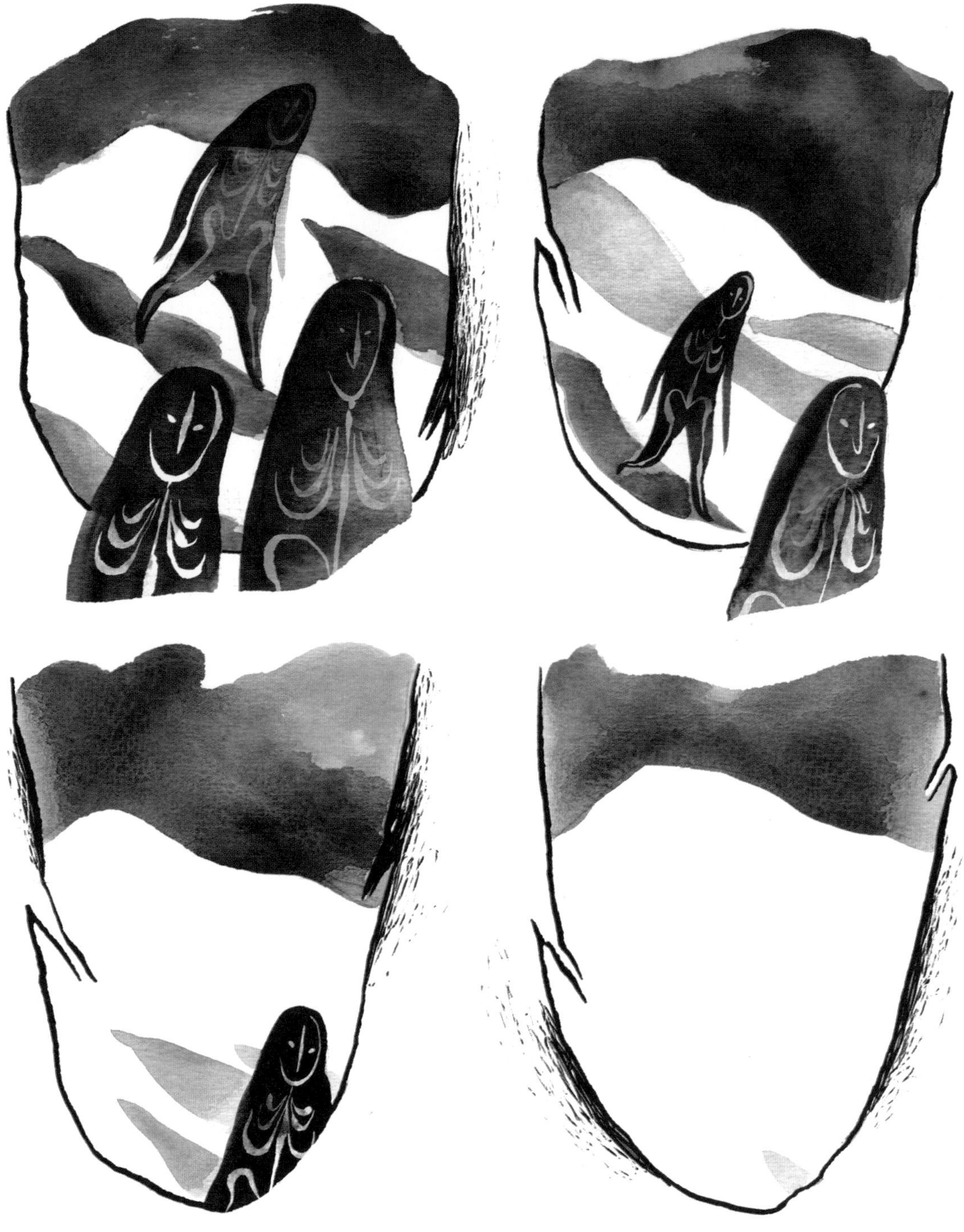

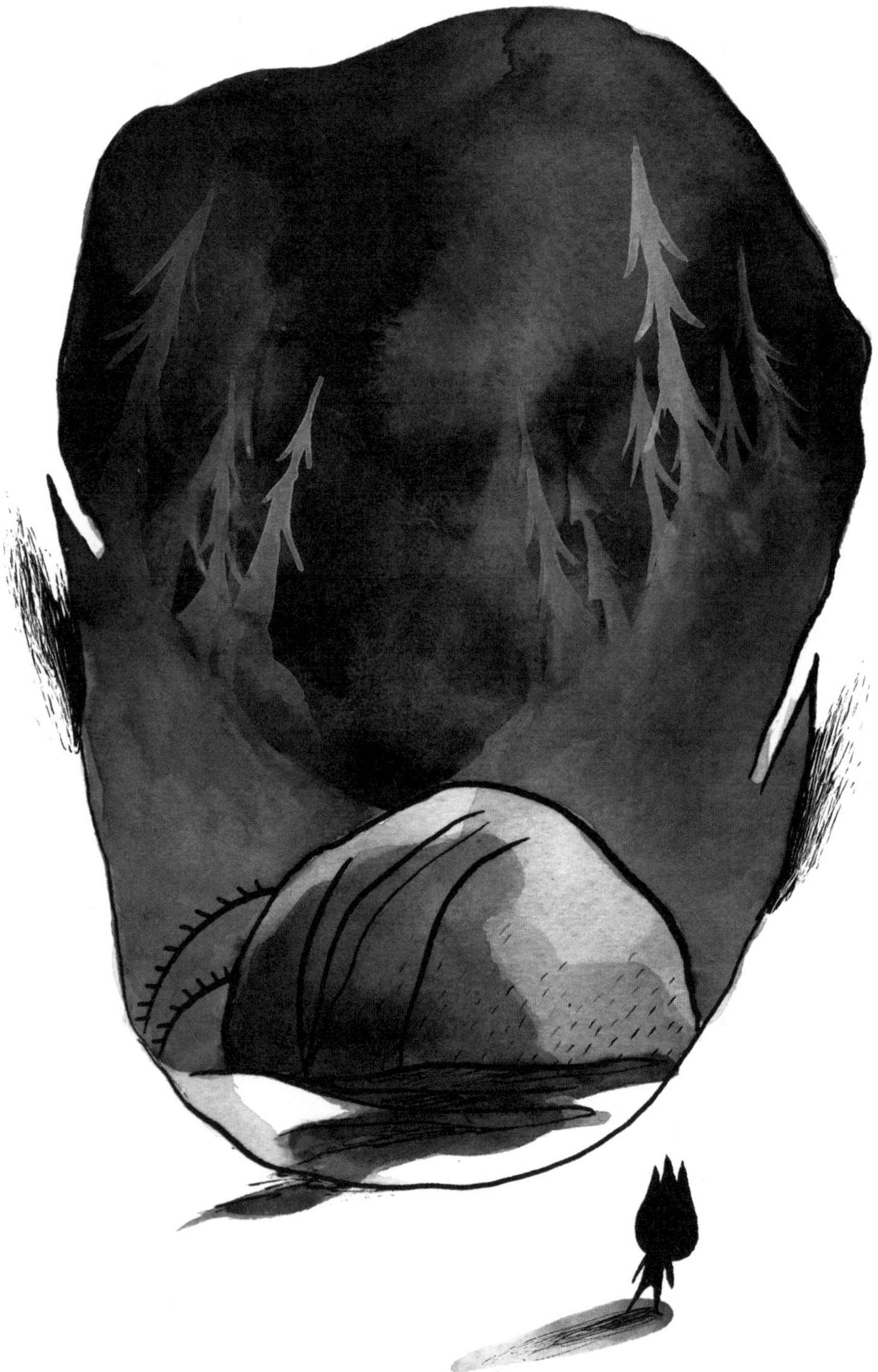

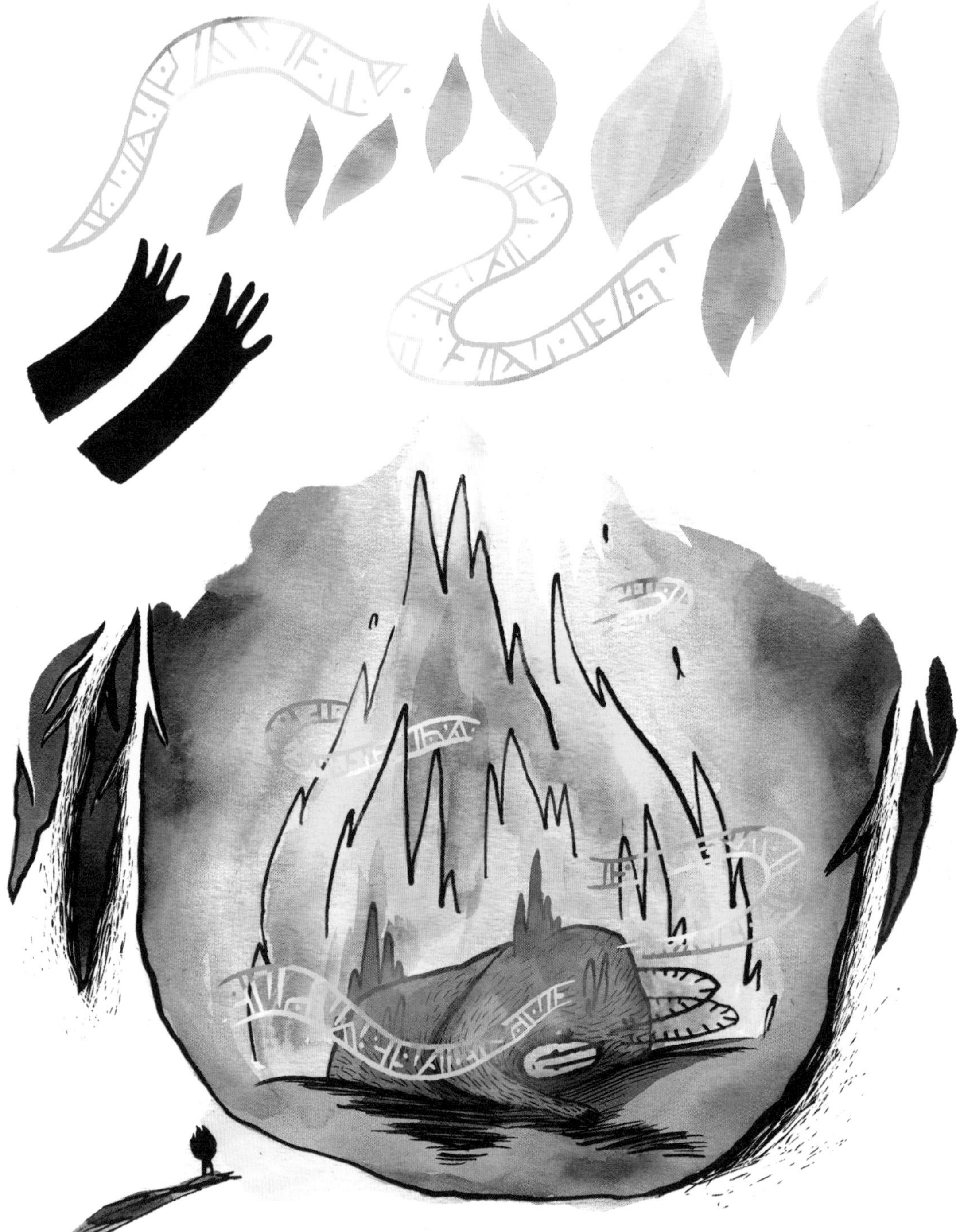

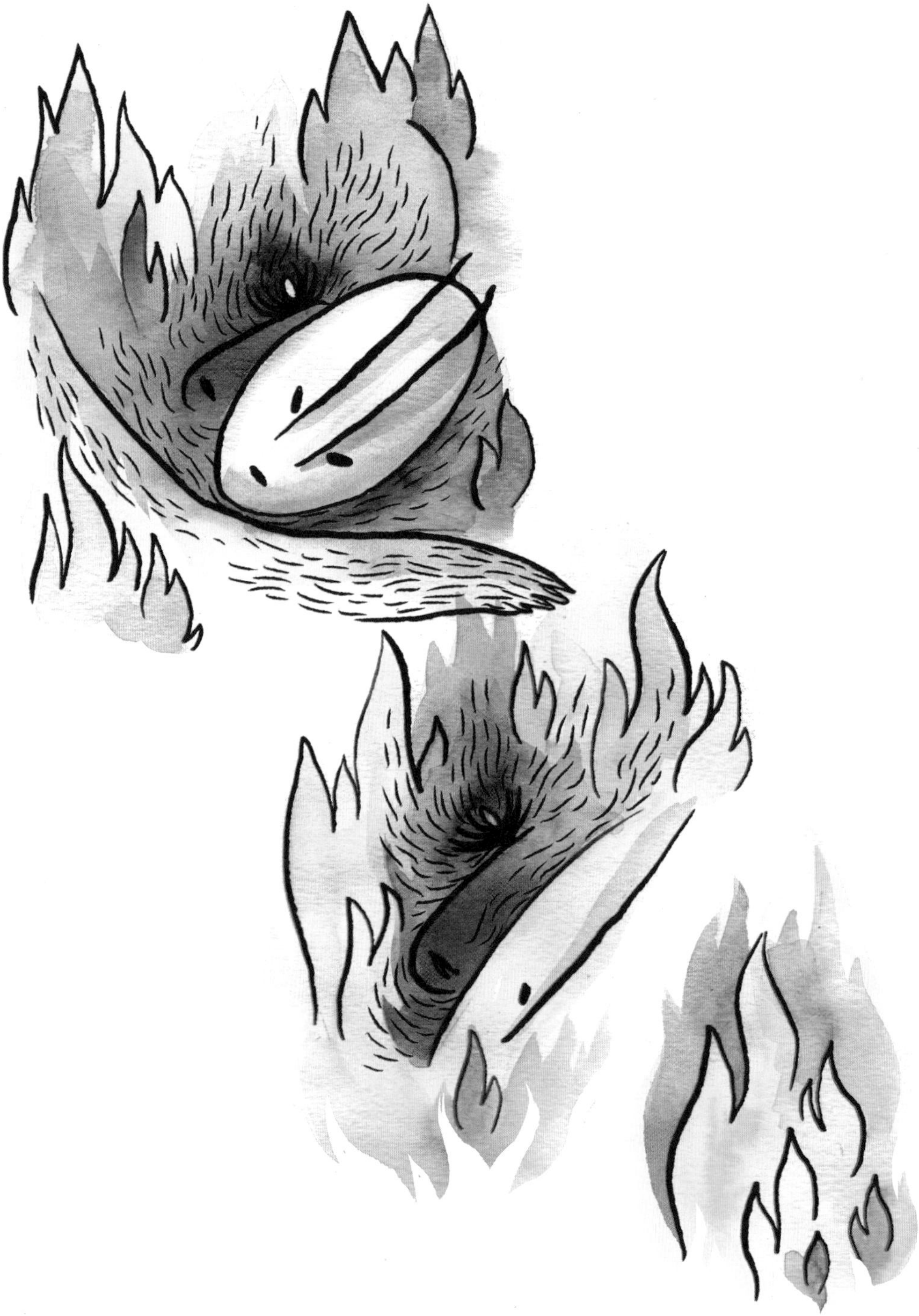

XII

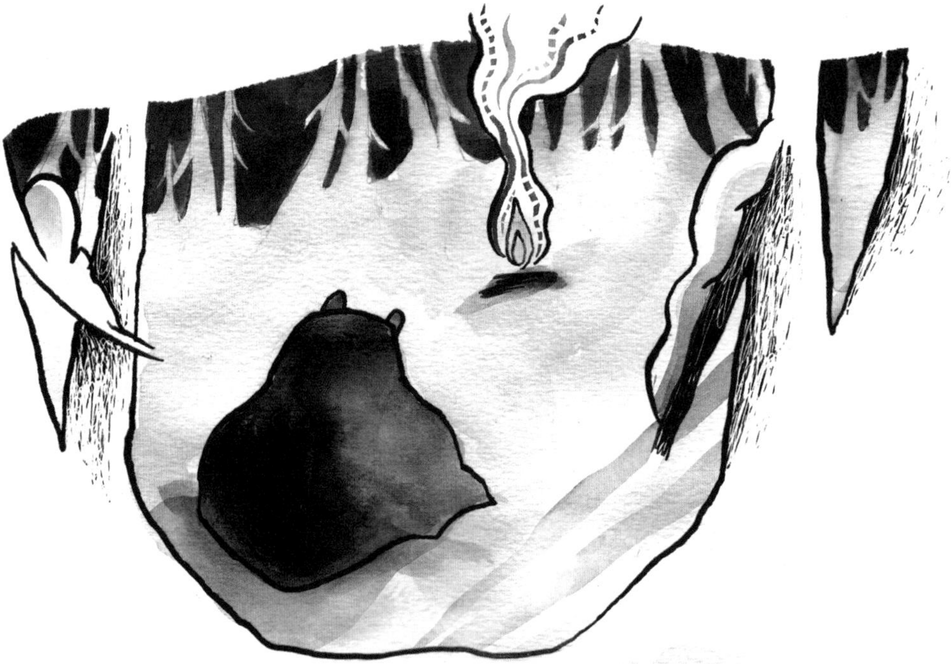

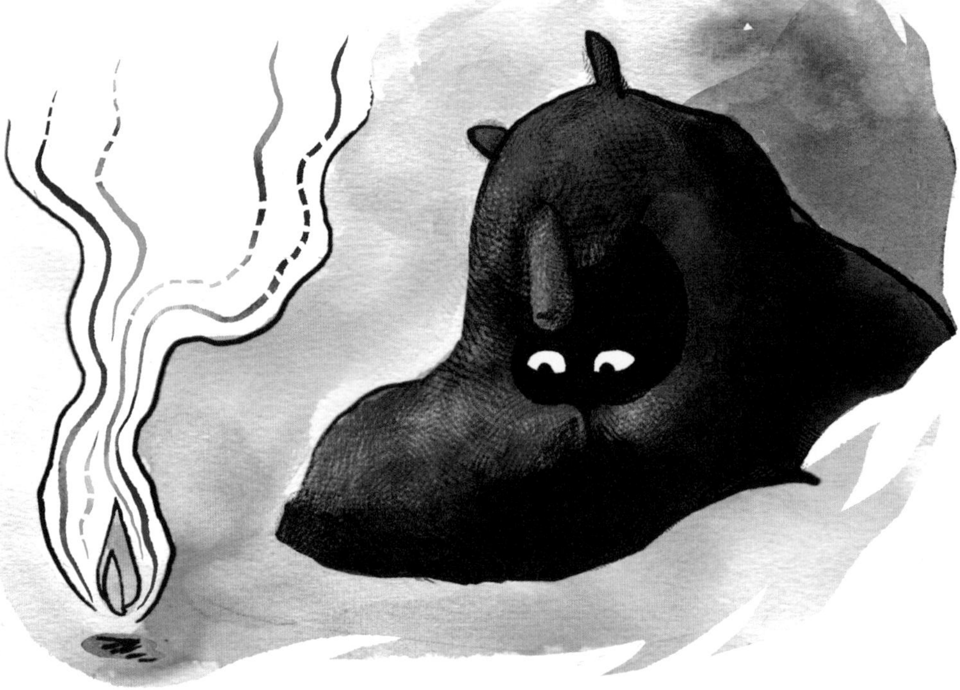

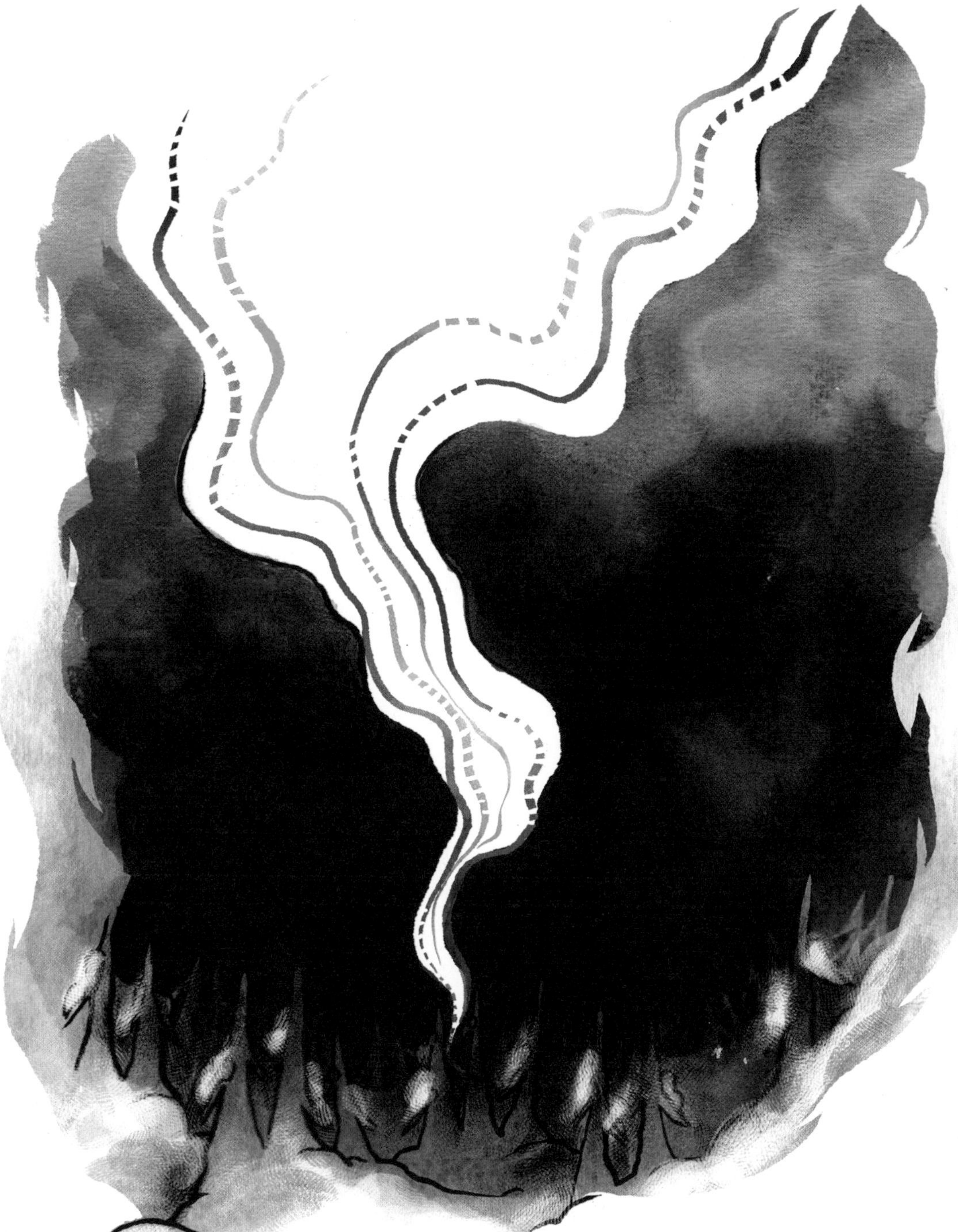

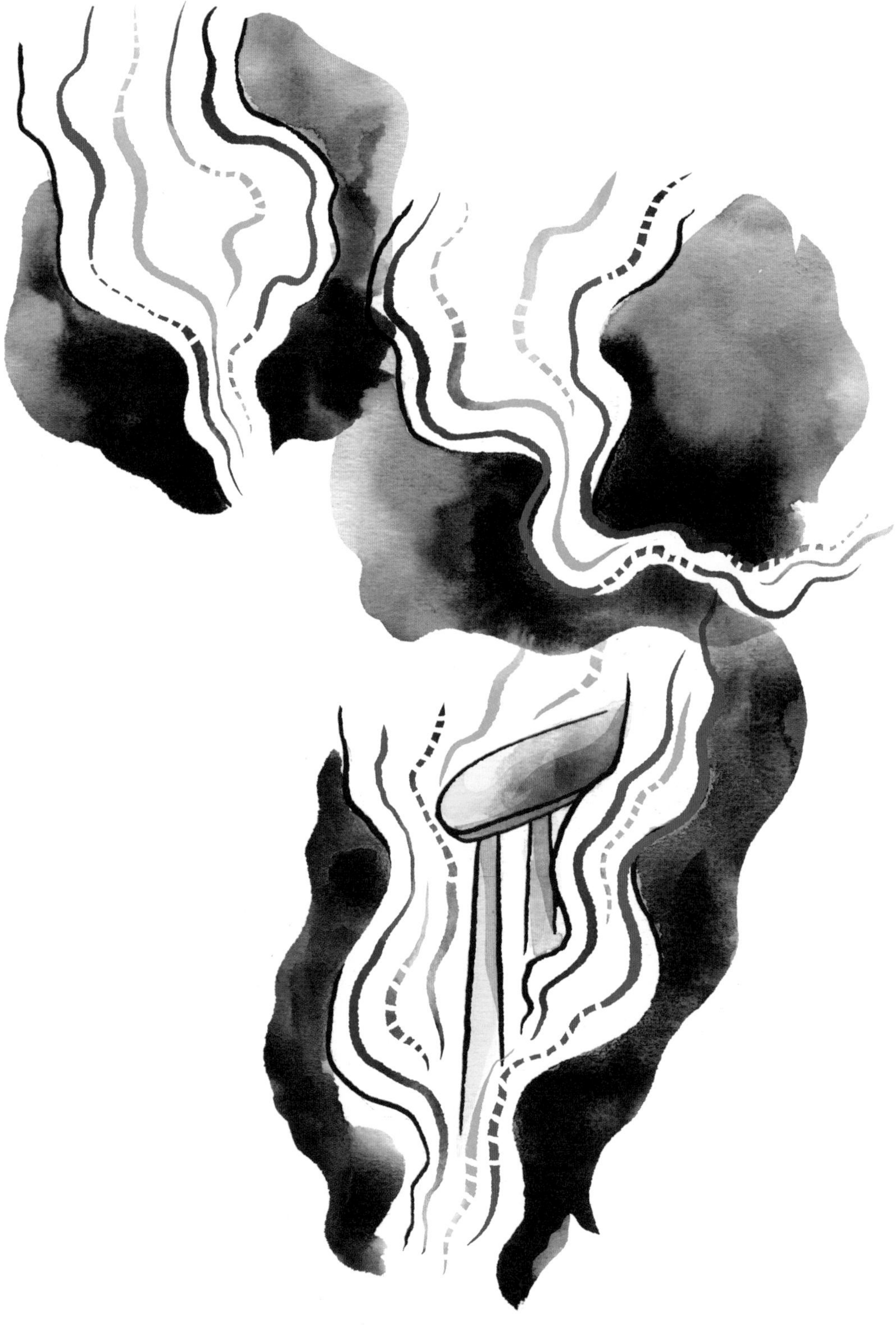

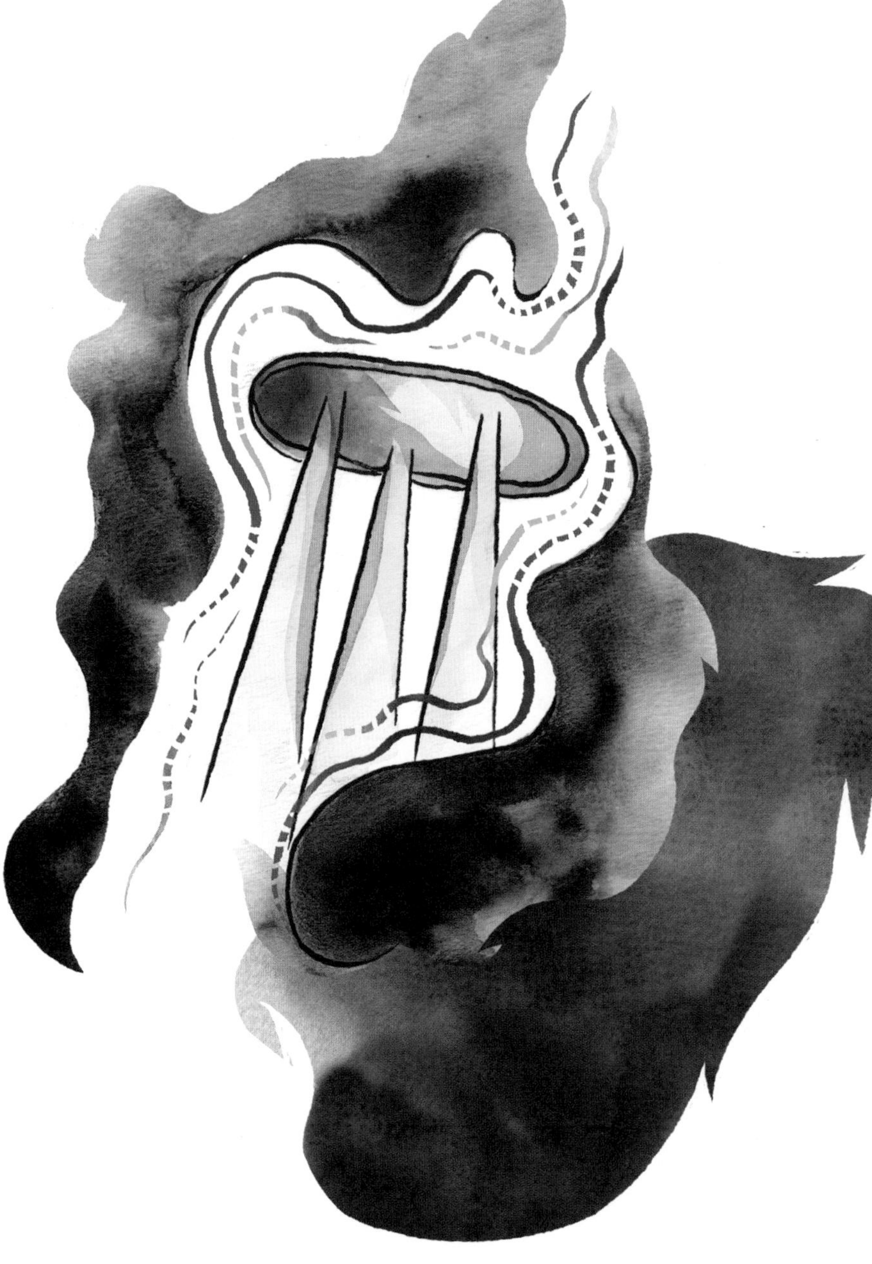

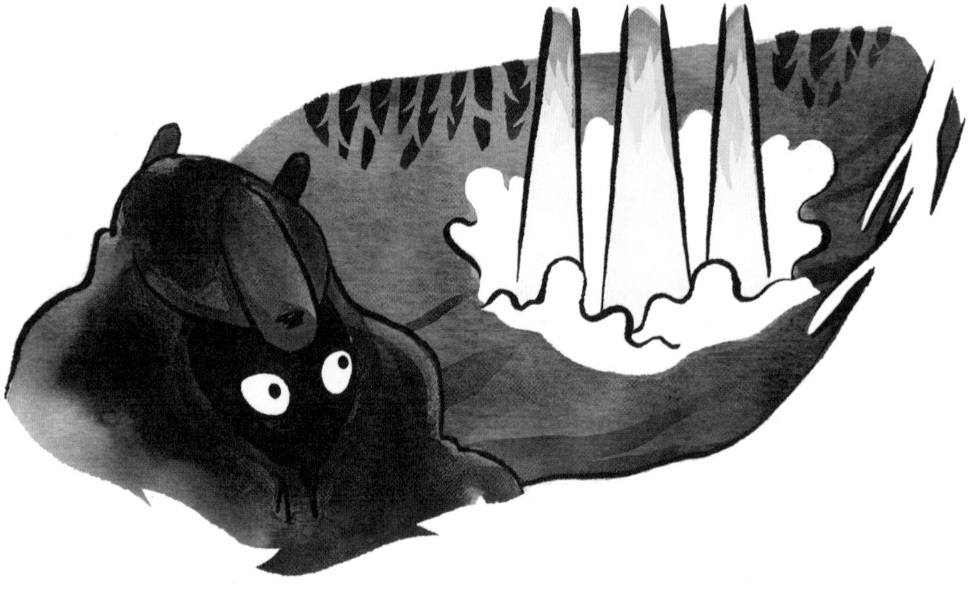

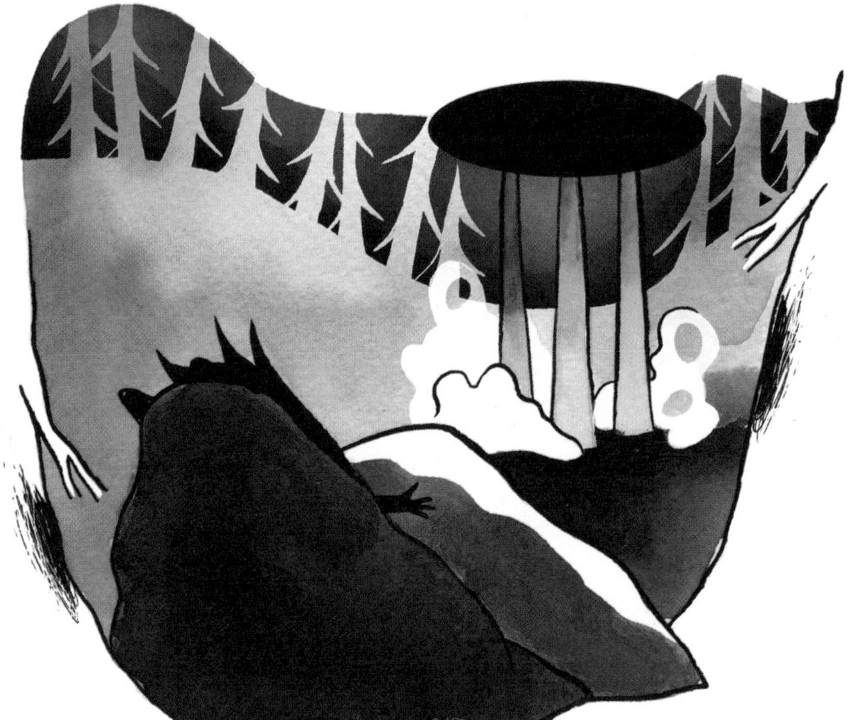

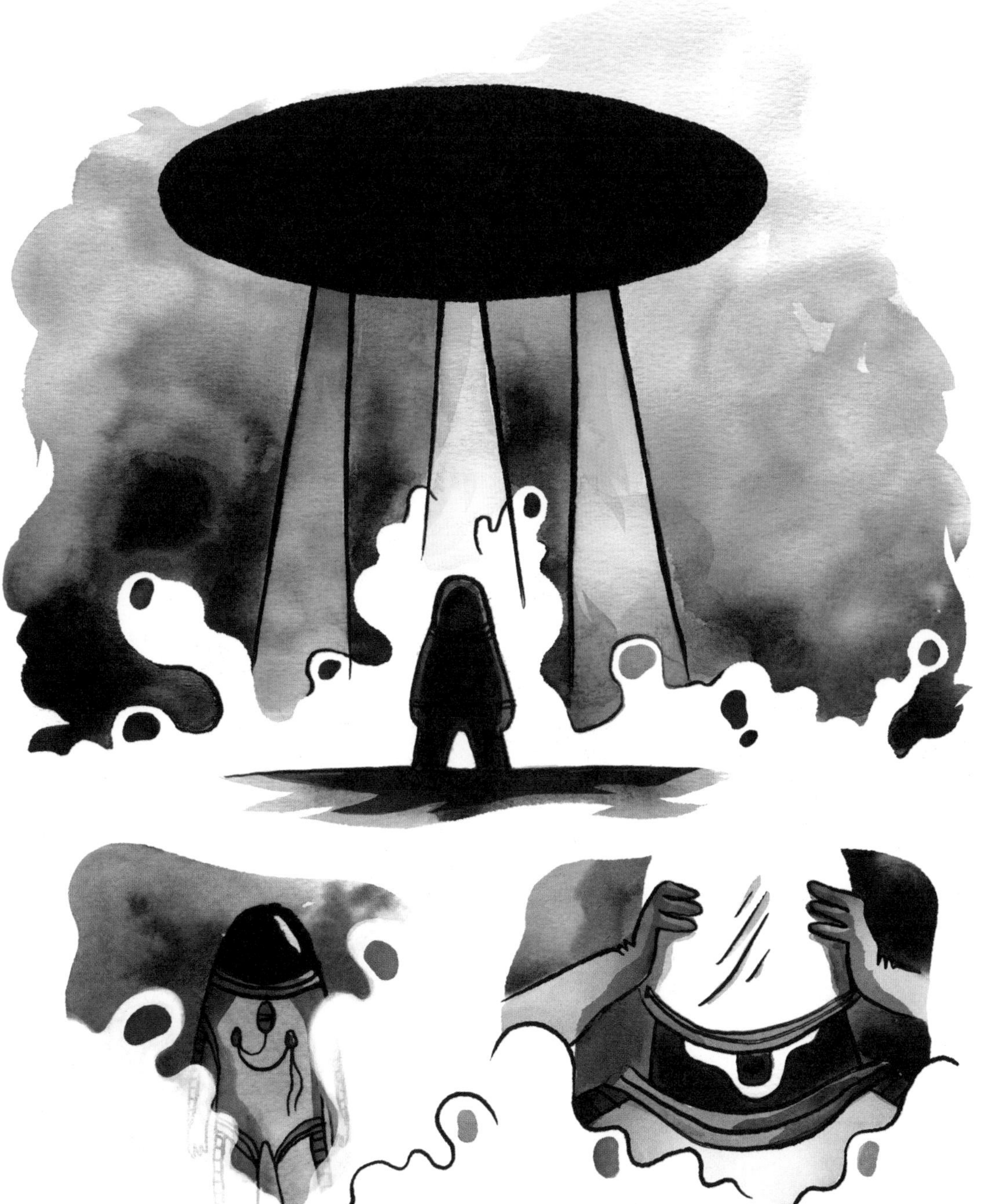

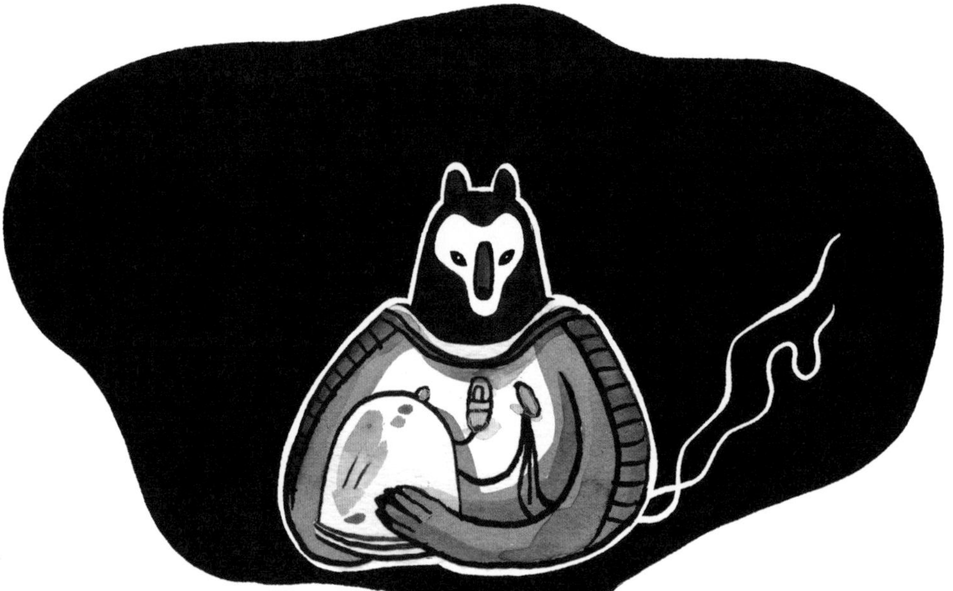

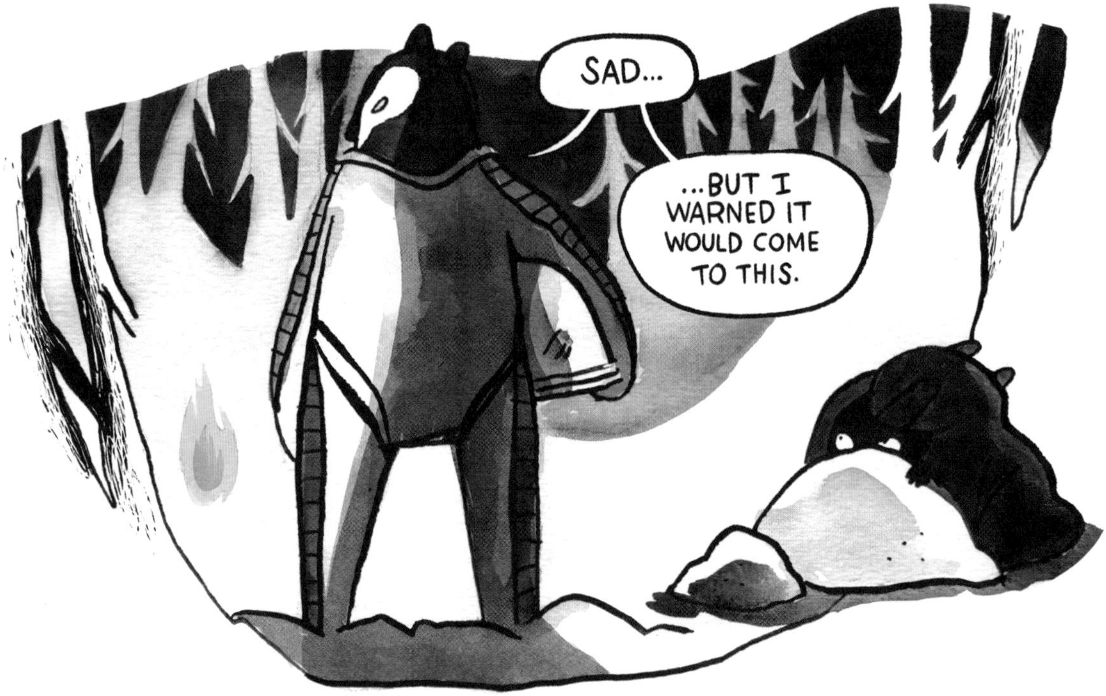
SAD...
...BUT I WARNED IT WOULD COME TO THIS.

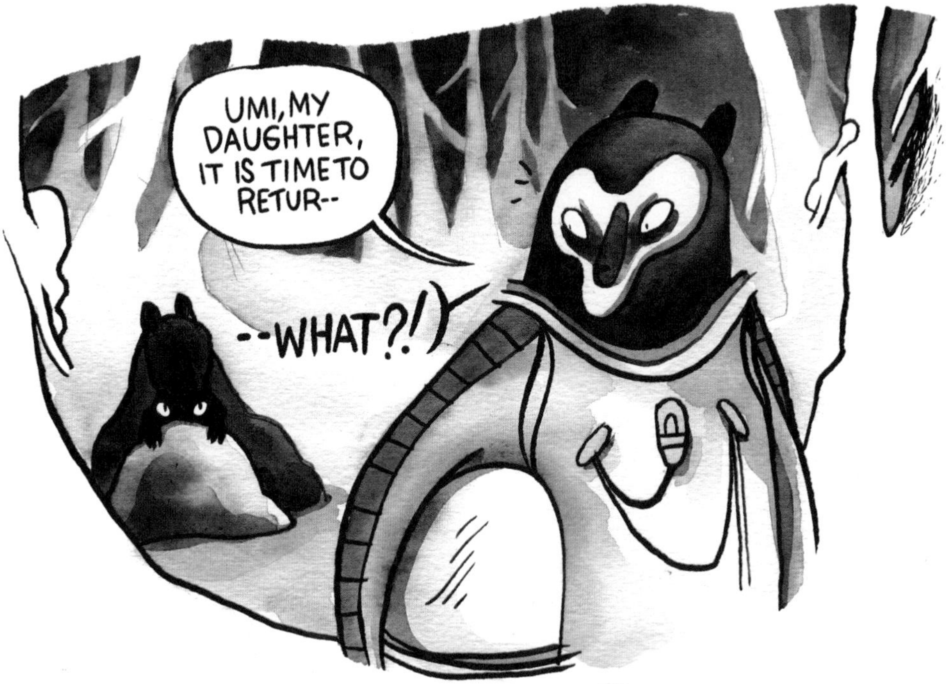
UMI, MY DAUGHTER, IT IS TIME TO RETUR--
--WHAT?!

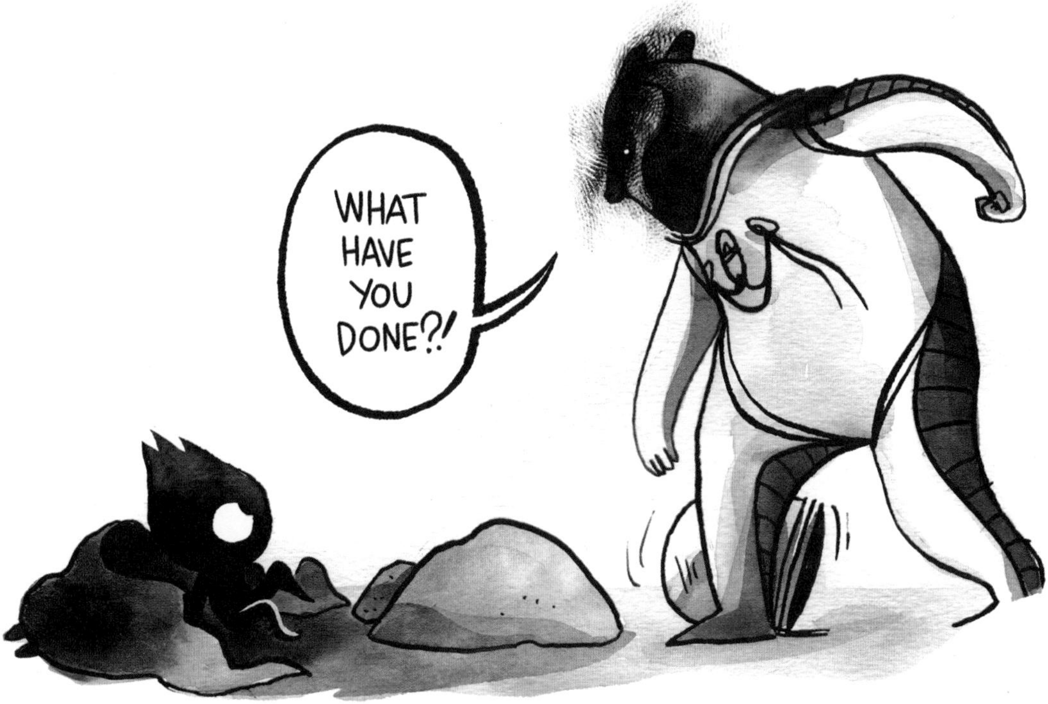
WHAT HAVE YOU DONE?!

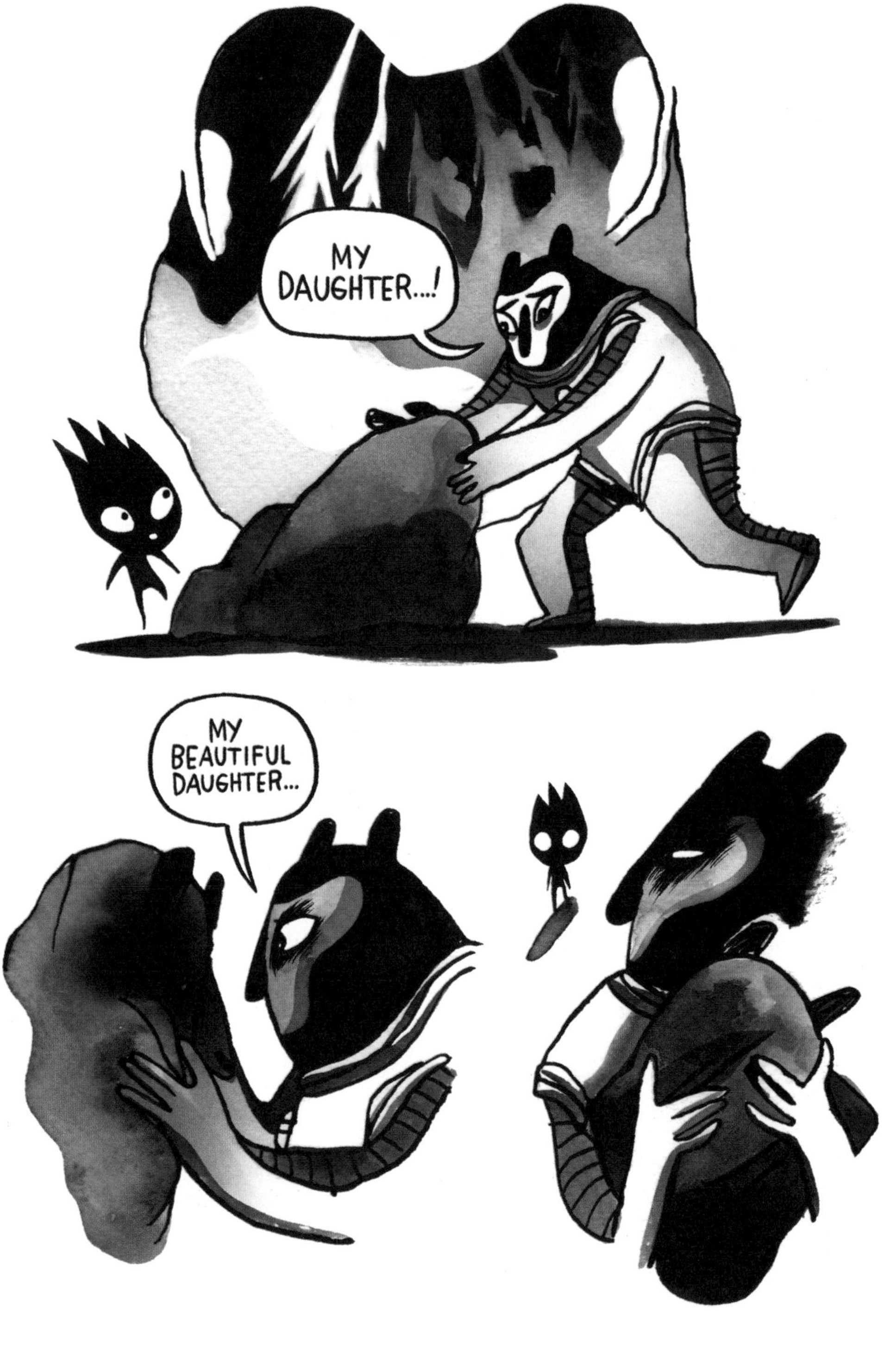
MY DAUGHTER...!
MY BEAUTIFUL DAUGHTER...

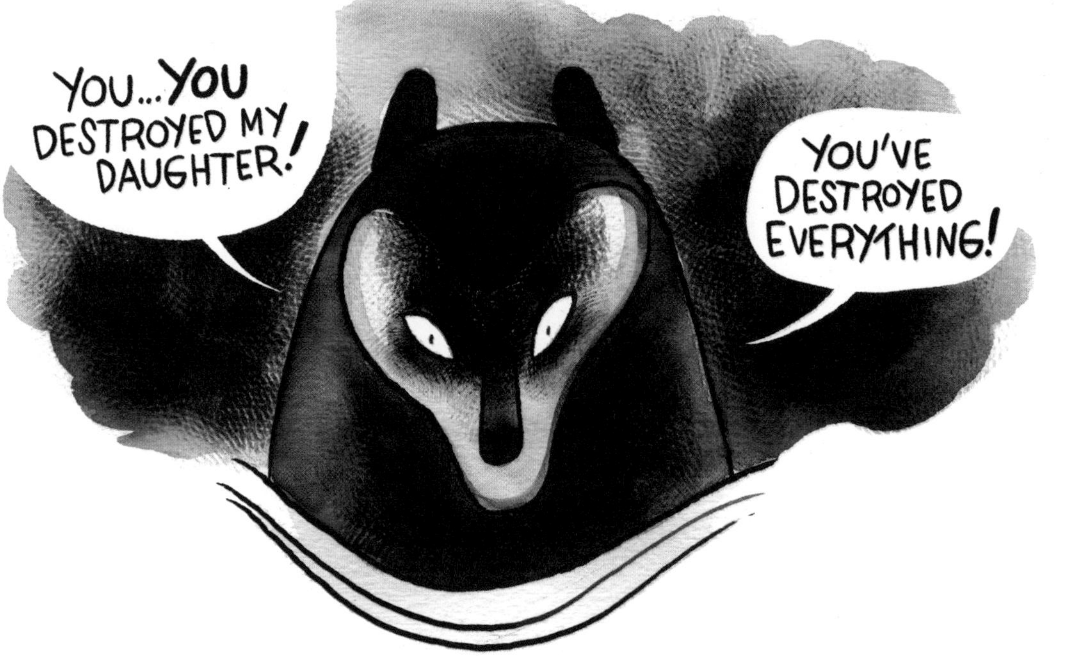
YOU...YOU DESTROYED MY DAUGHTER!
YOU'VE DESTROYED EVERYTHING!

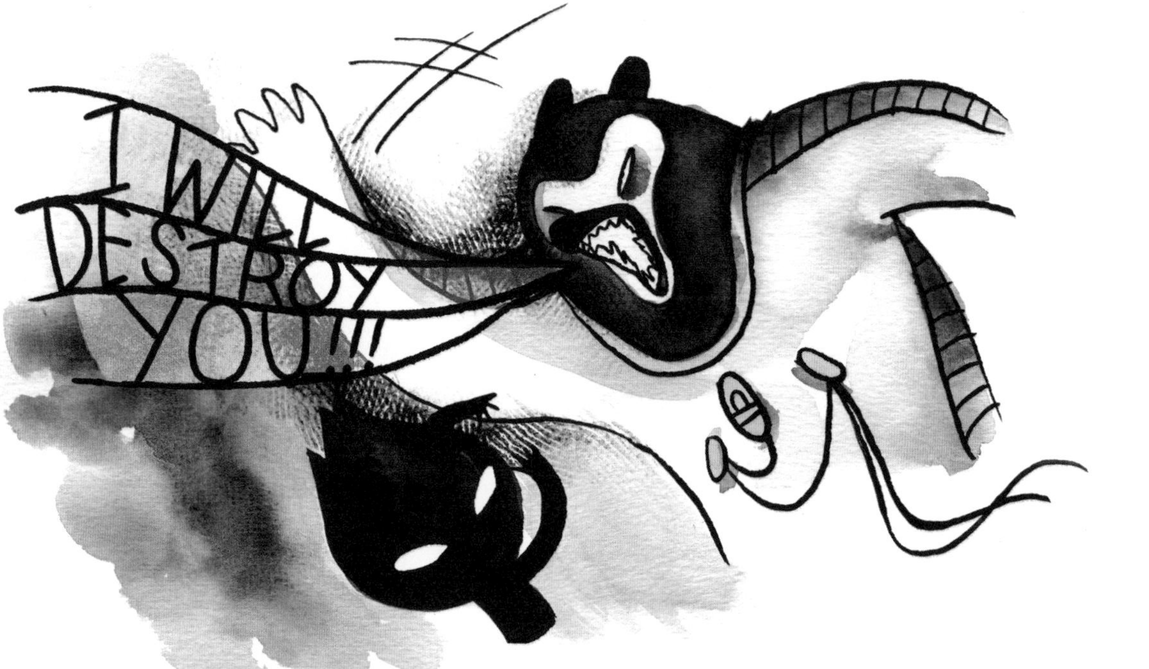
I WILL DESTROY YOU!!!

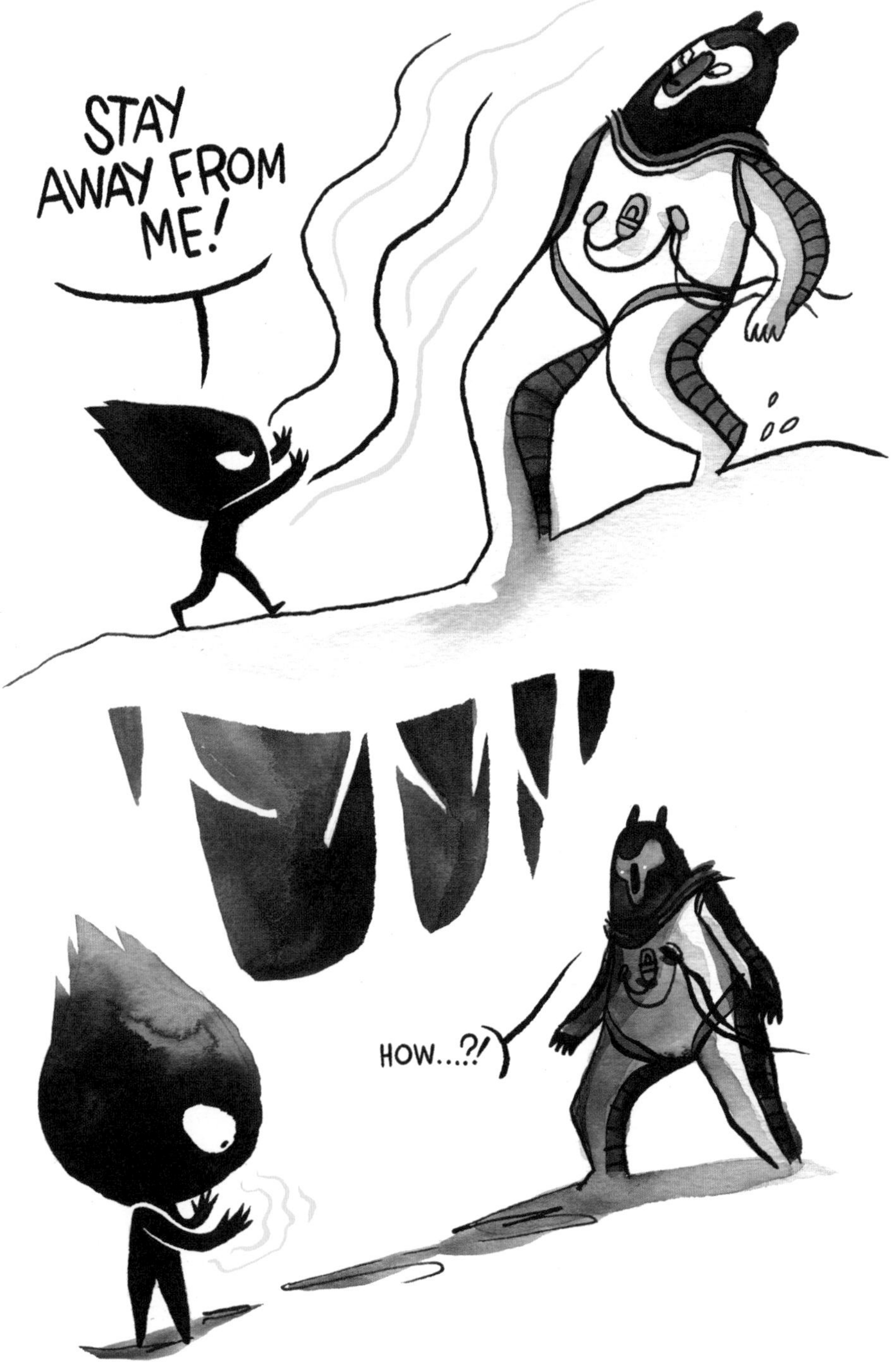
STAY AWAY FROM ME!
HOW...?!

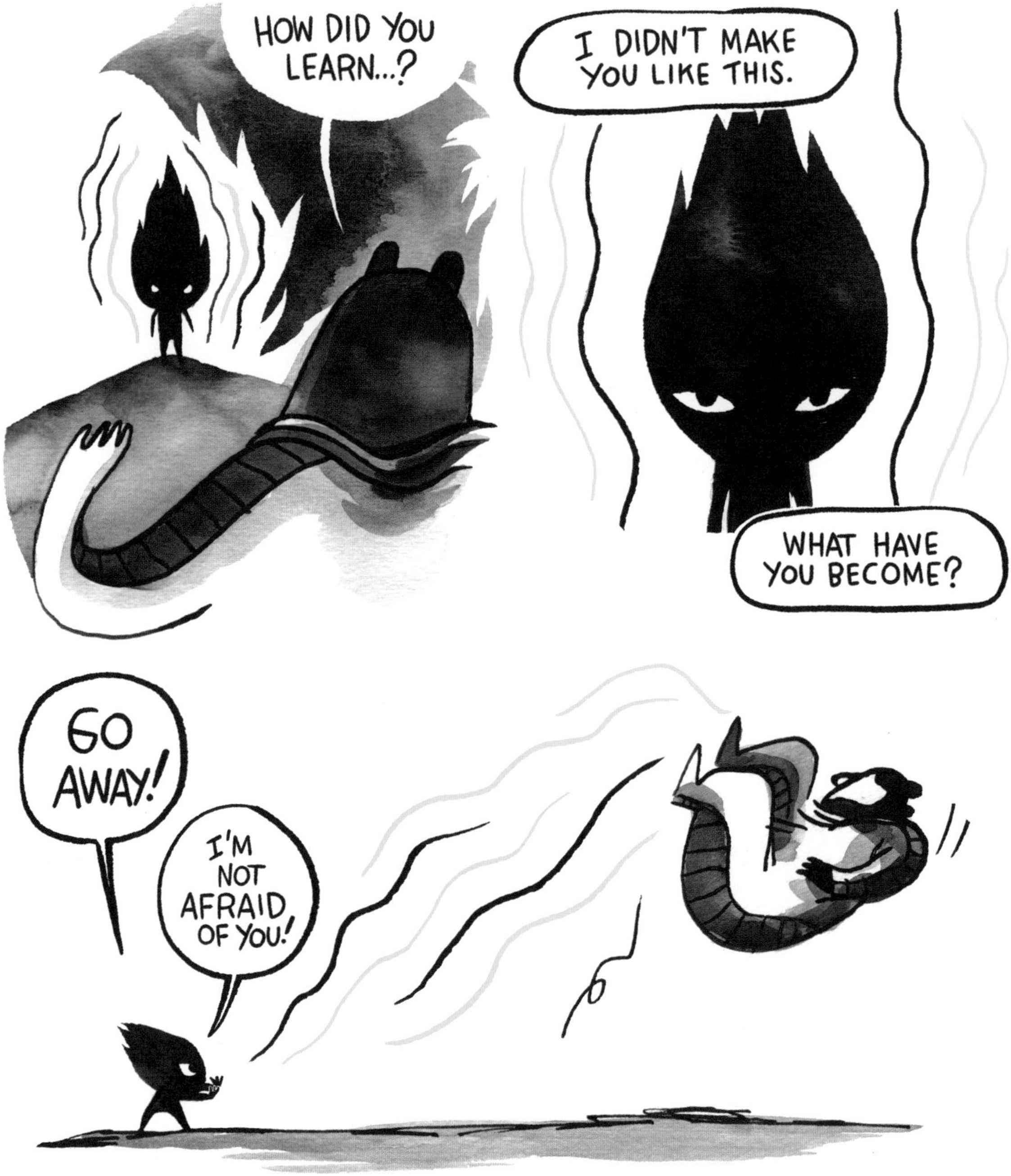
HOW DID YOU LEARN...?
I DIDN'T MAKE YOU LIKE THIS.
WHAT HAVE YOU BECOME?
GO AWAY!
I'M NOT AFRAID OF YOU!

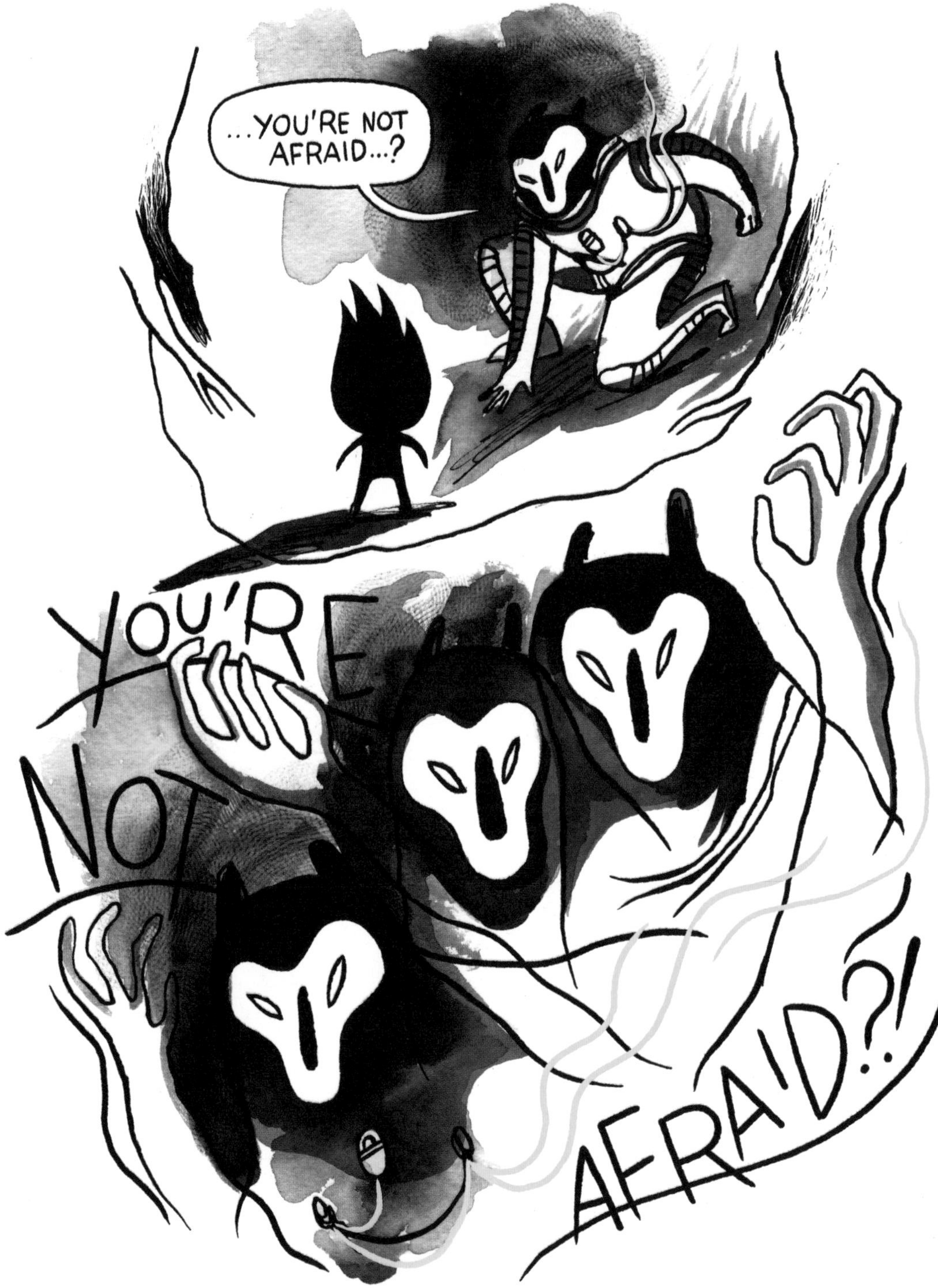
...YOU'RE NOT AFRAID...?
YOU'RE NOT AFRAID?!

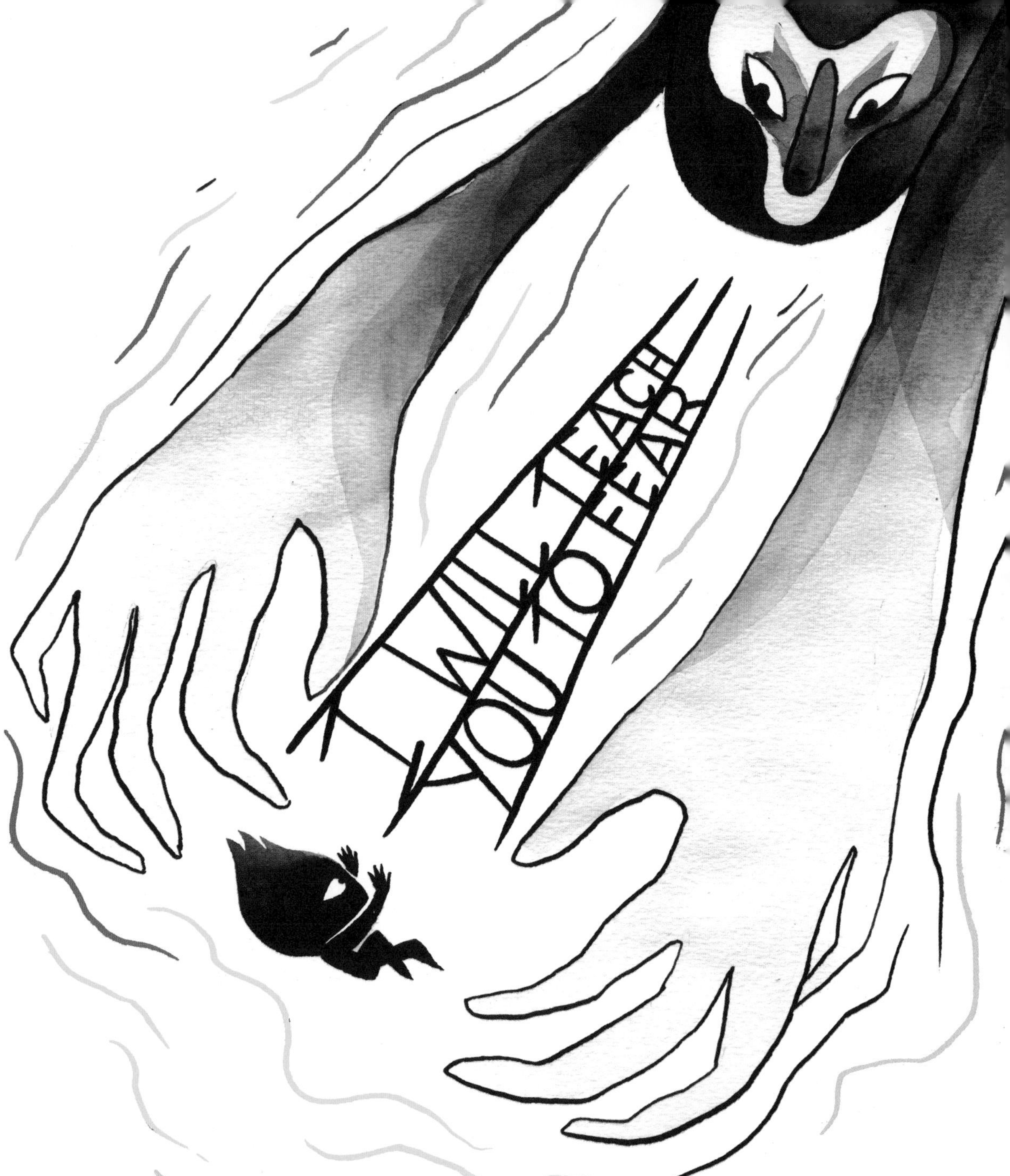
I WILL TEACH
YOU TO FEAR

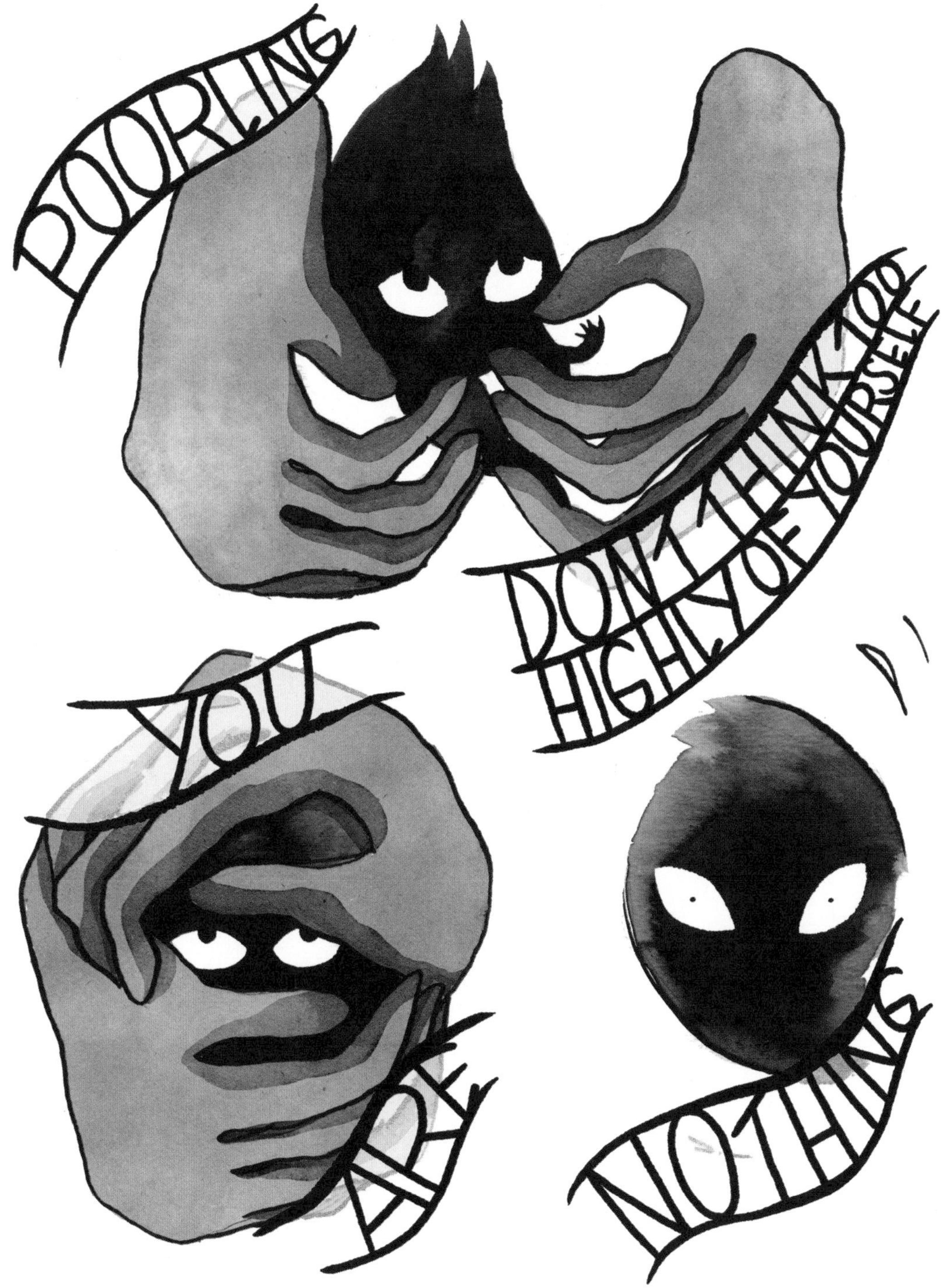
DOORLING
DON'T THINK TOO HIGHLY OF YOURSELF
YOU
ARE
NOTHING

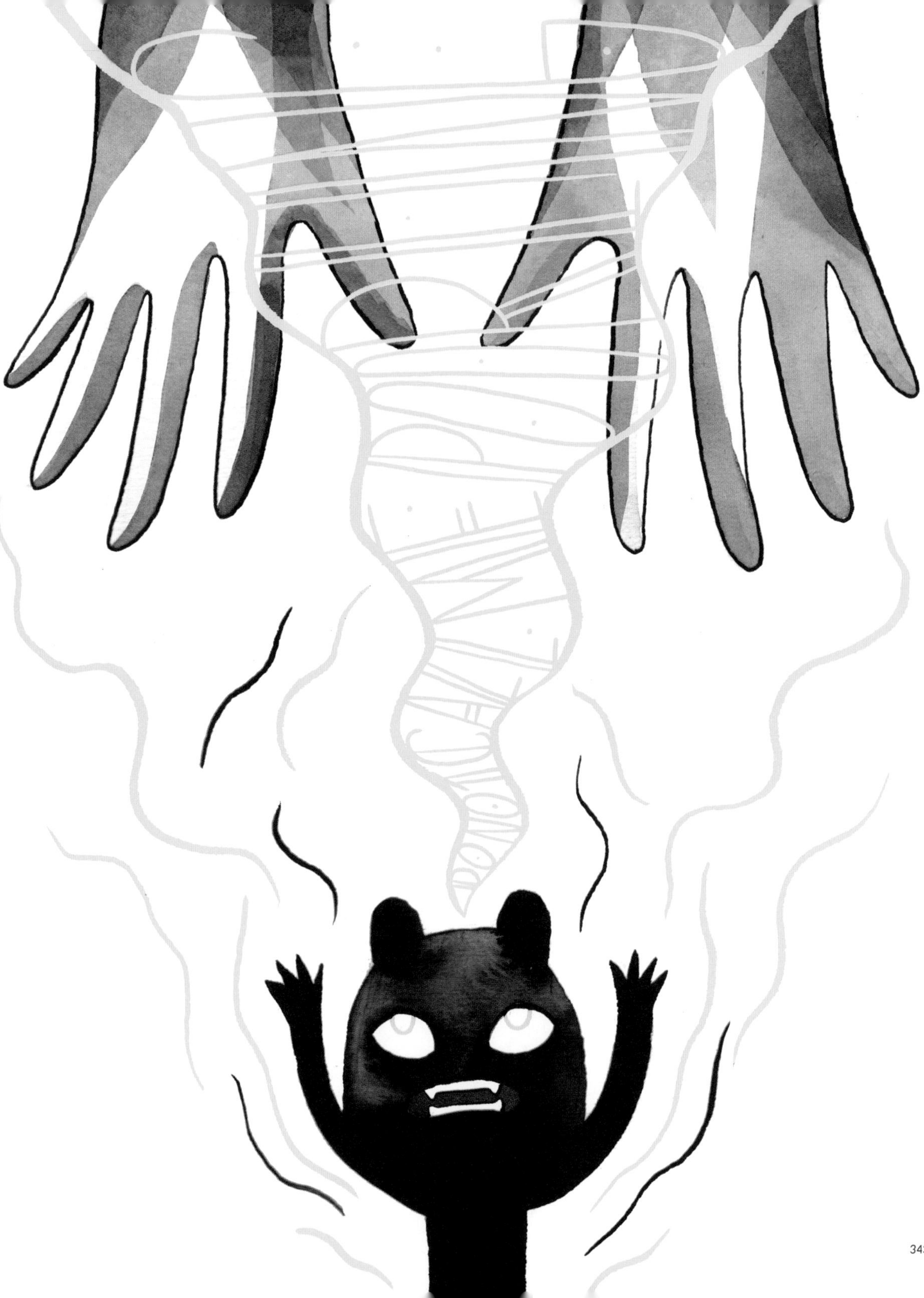

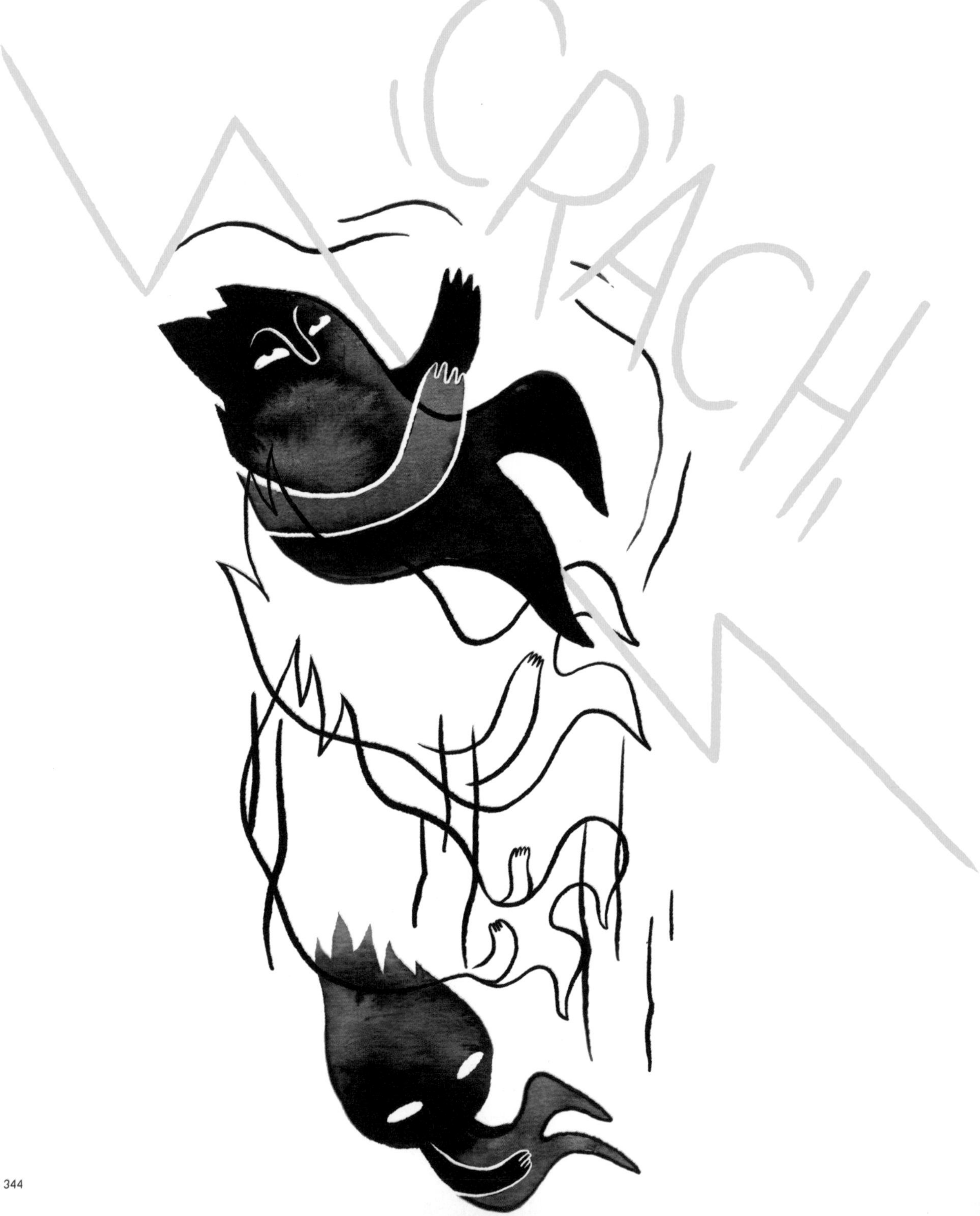
CRACH

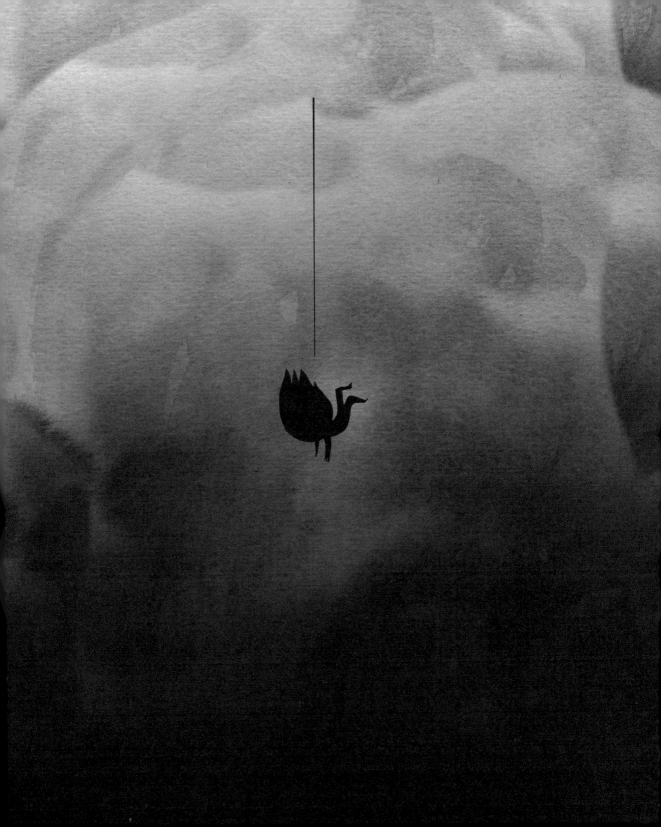

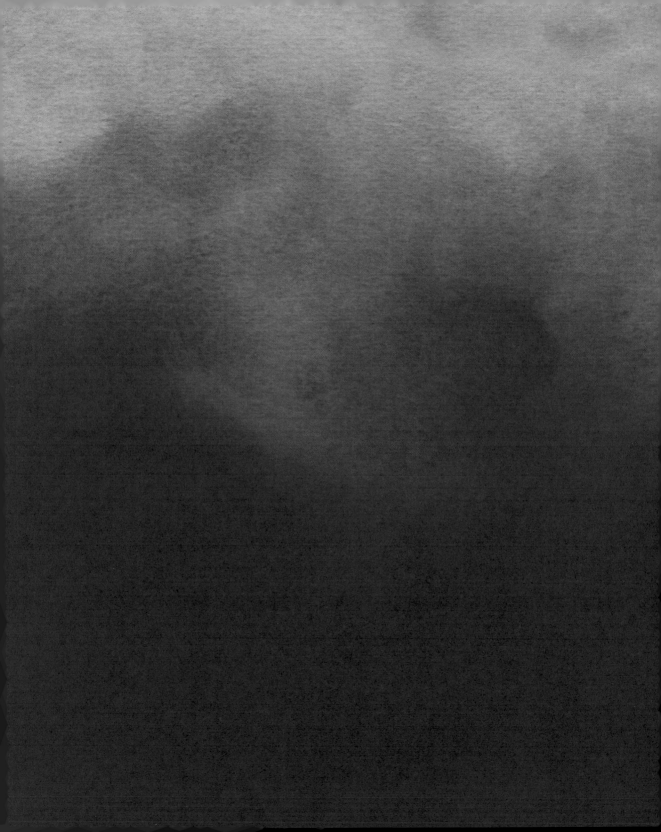

XIII

shhh

DON'T WORRY,

LITTLE ONE...

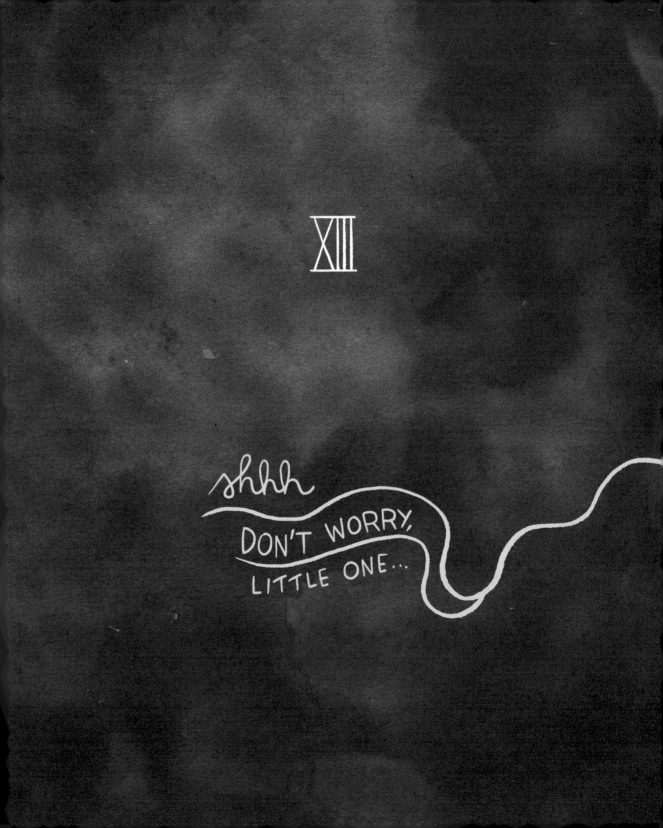

There is still one more song to be sung

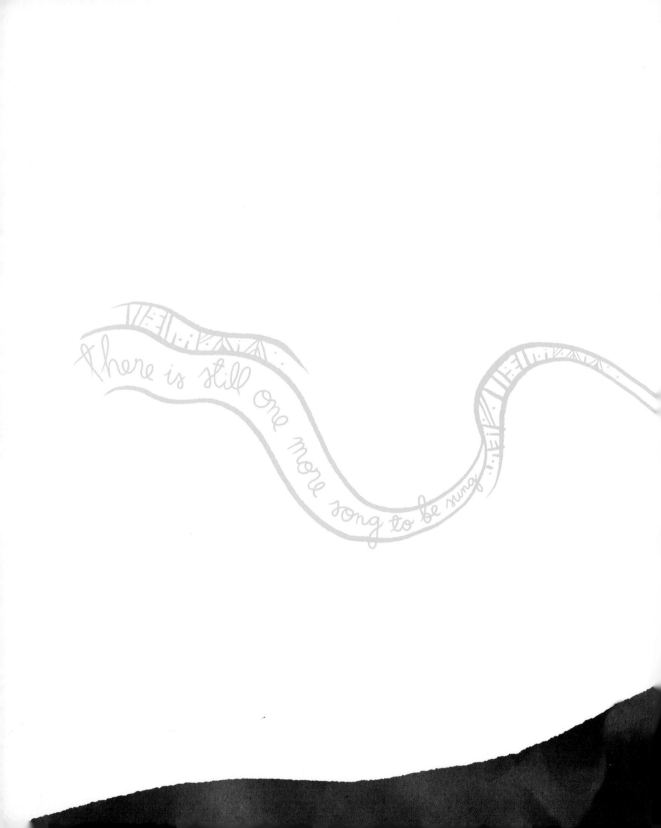

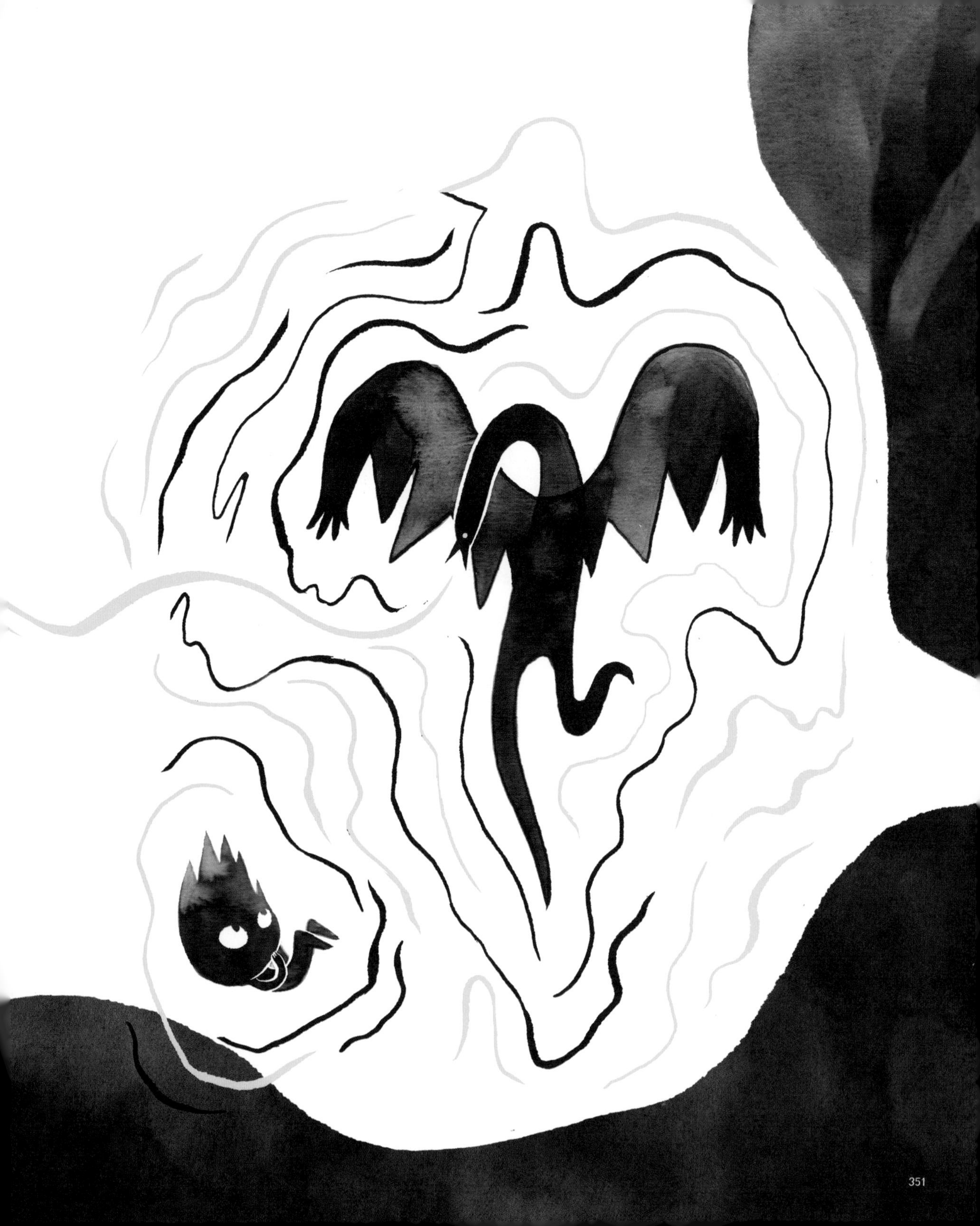

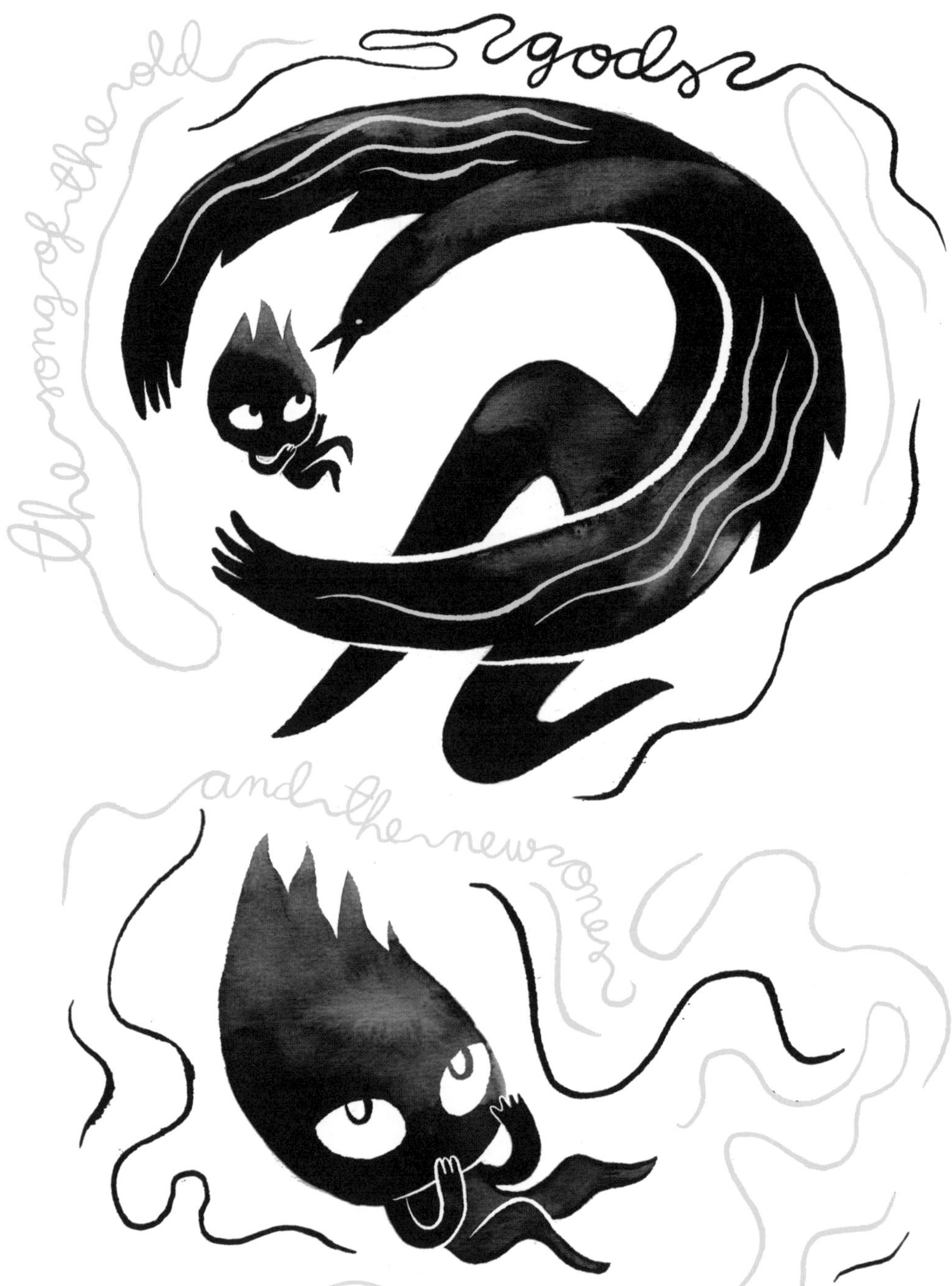
the song of the old
gods
and the new ones

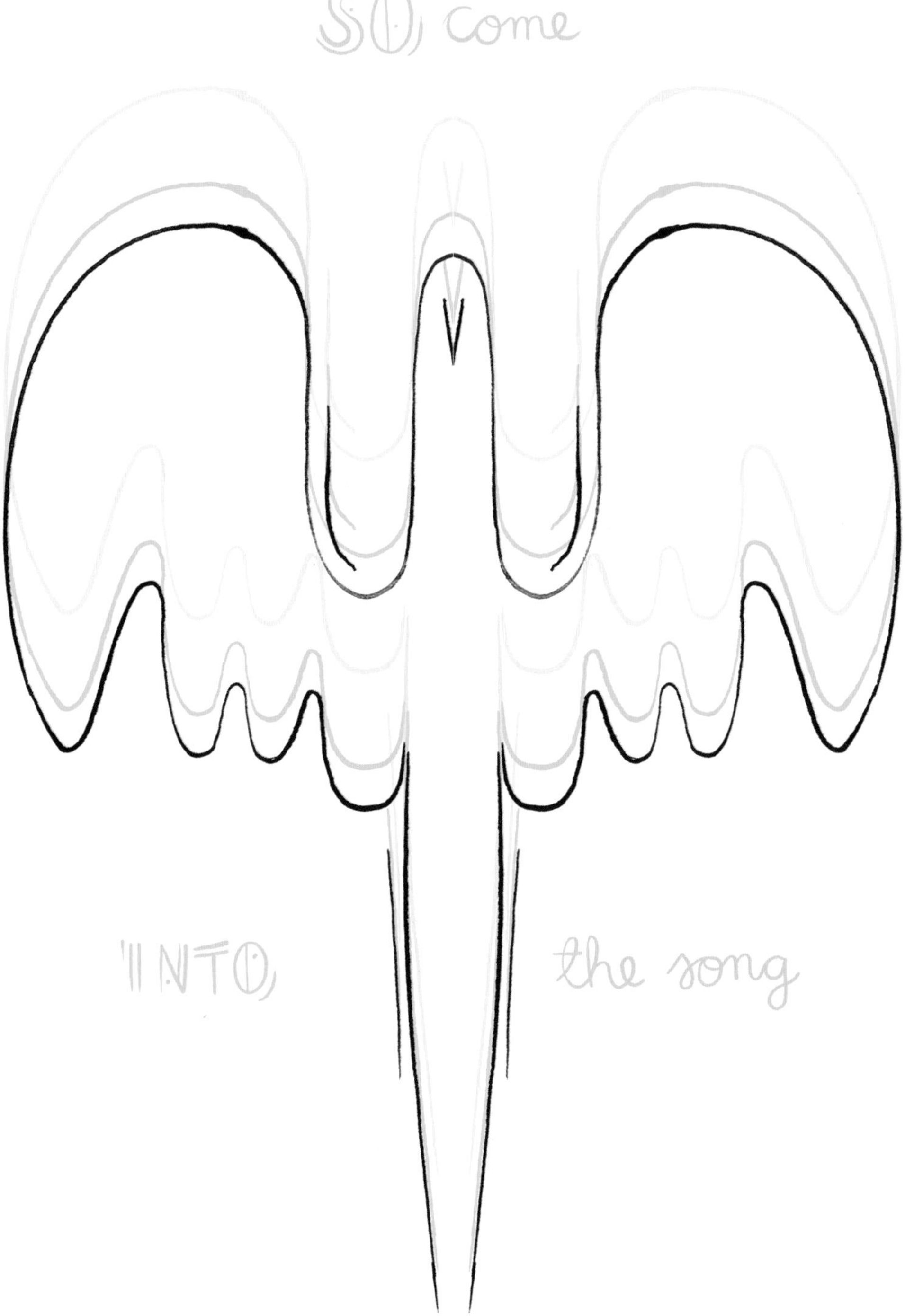
SO come
INTO the song

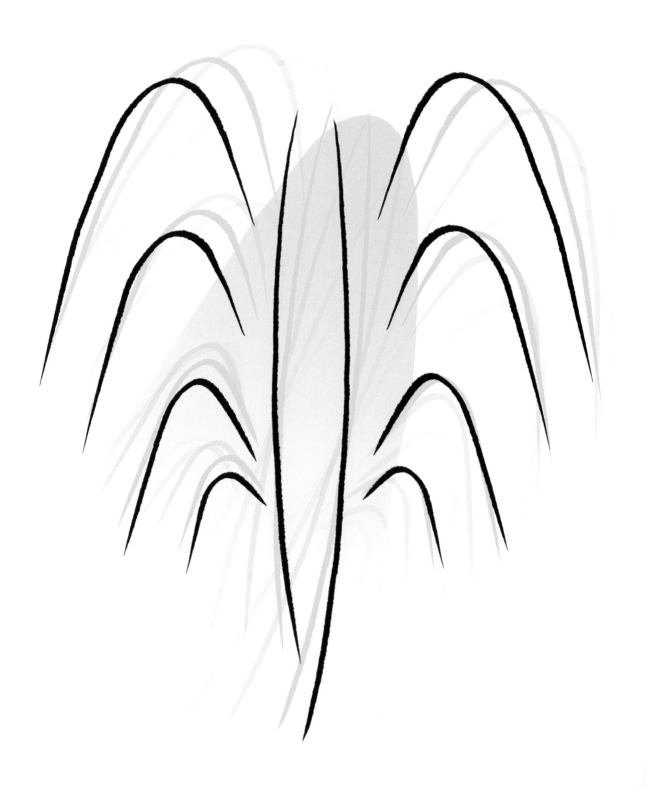

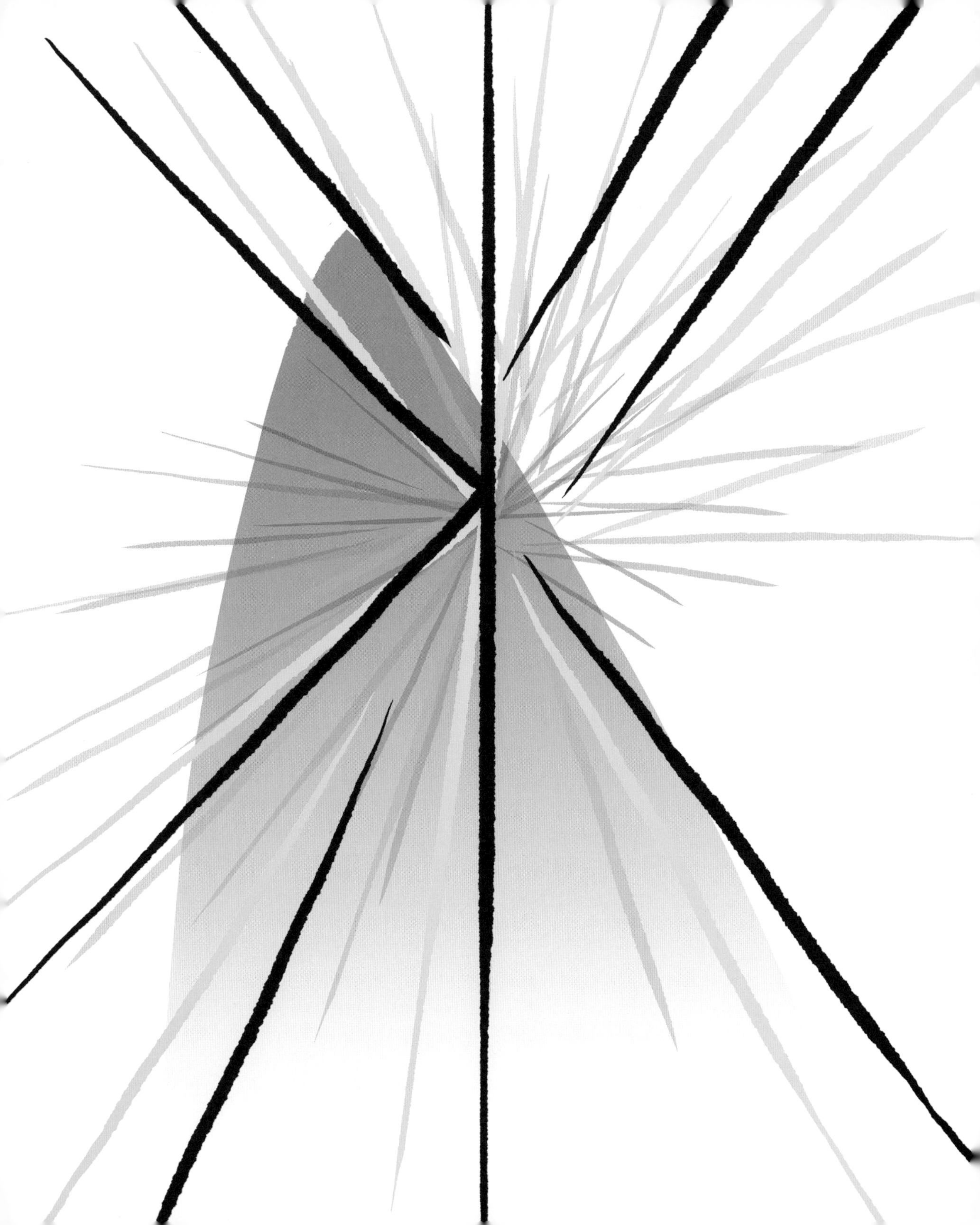

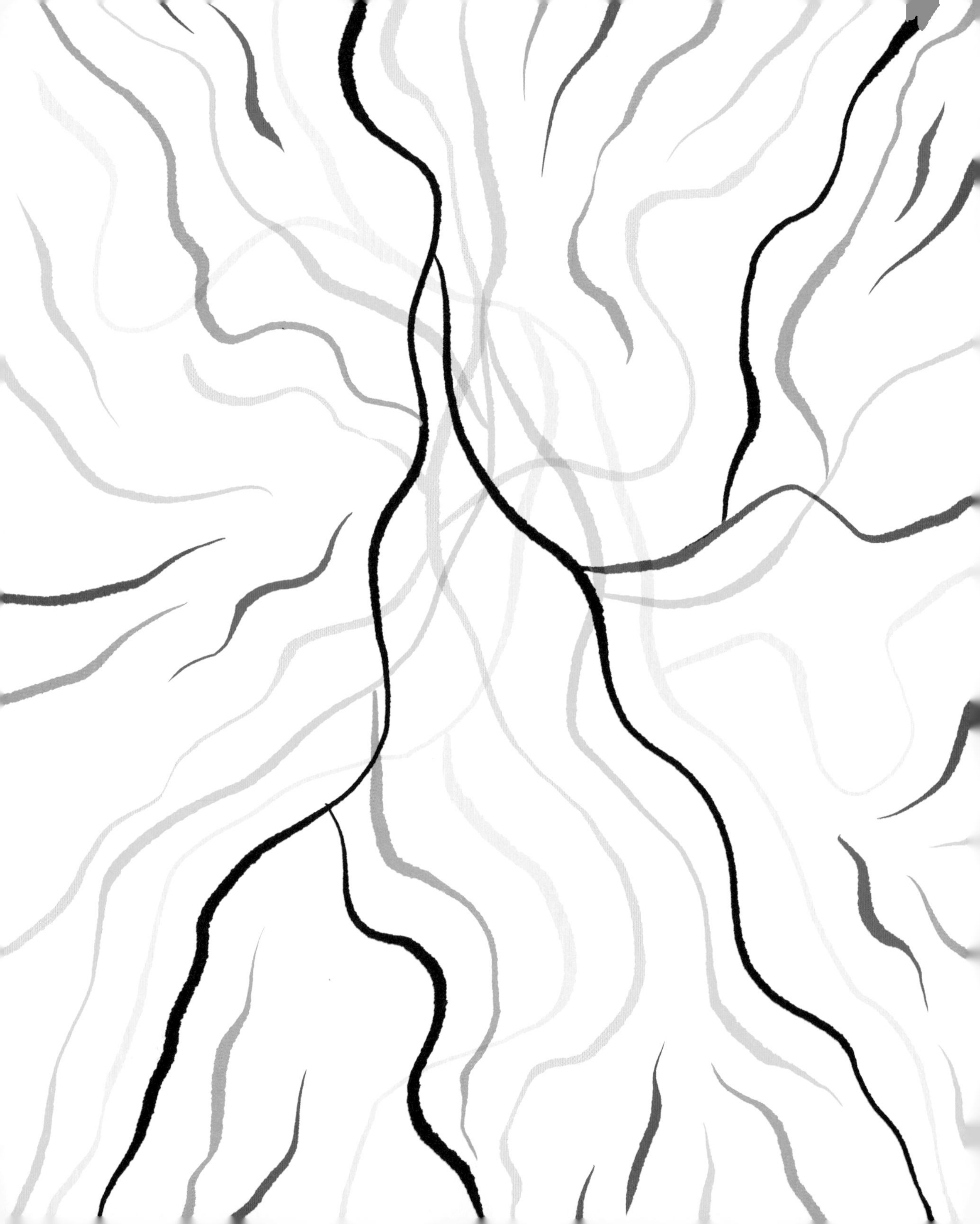

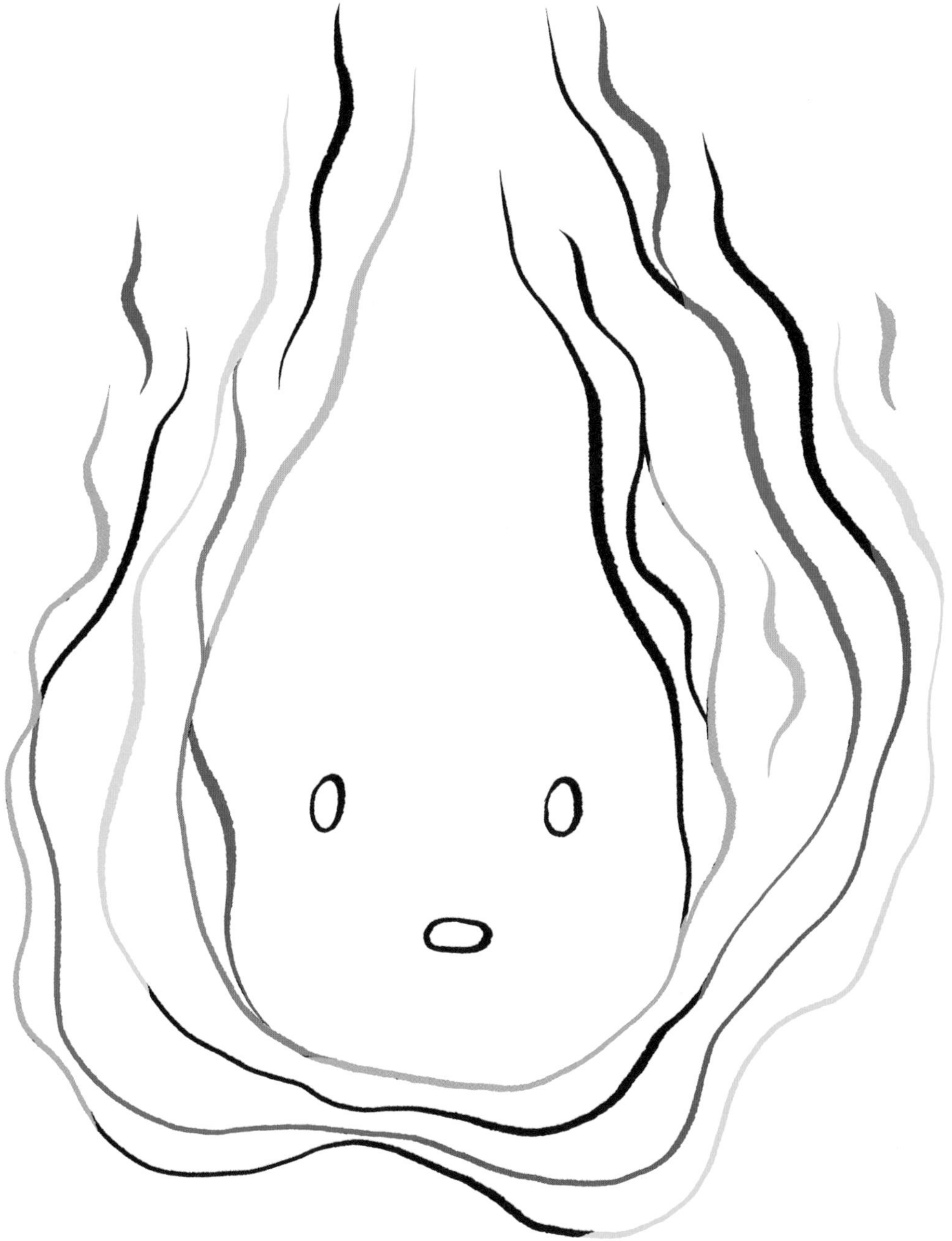

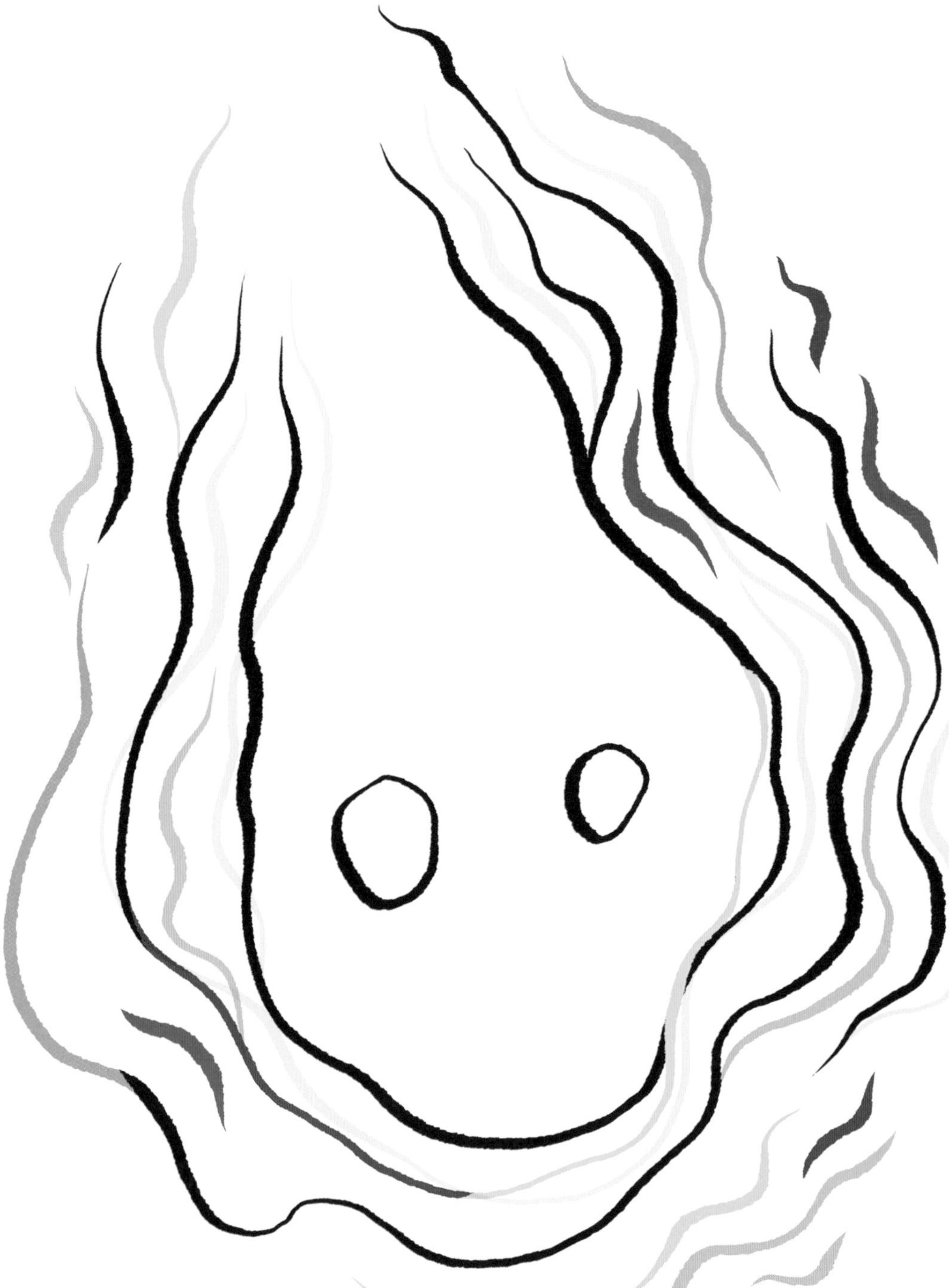

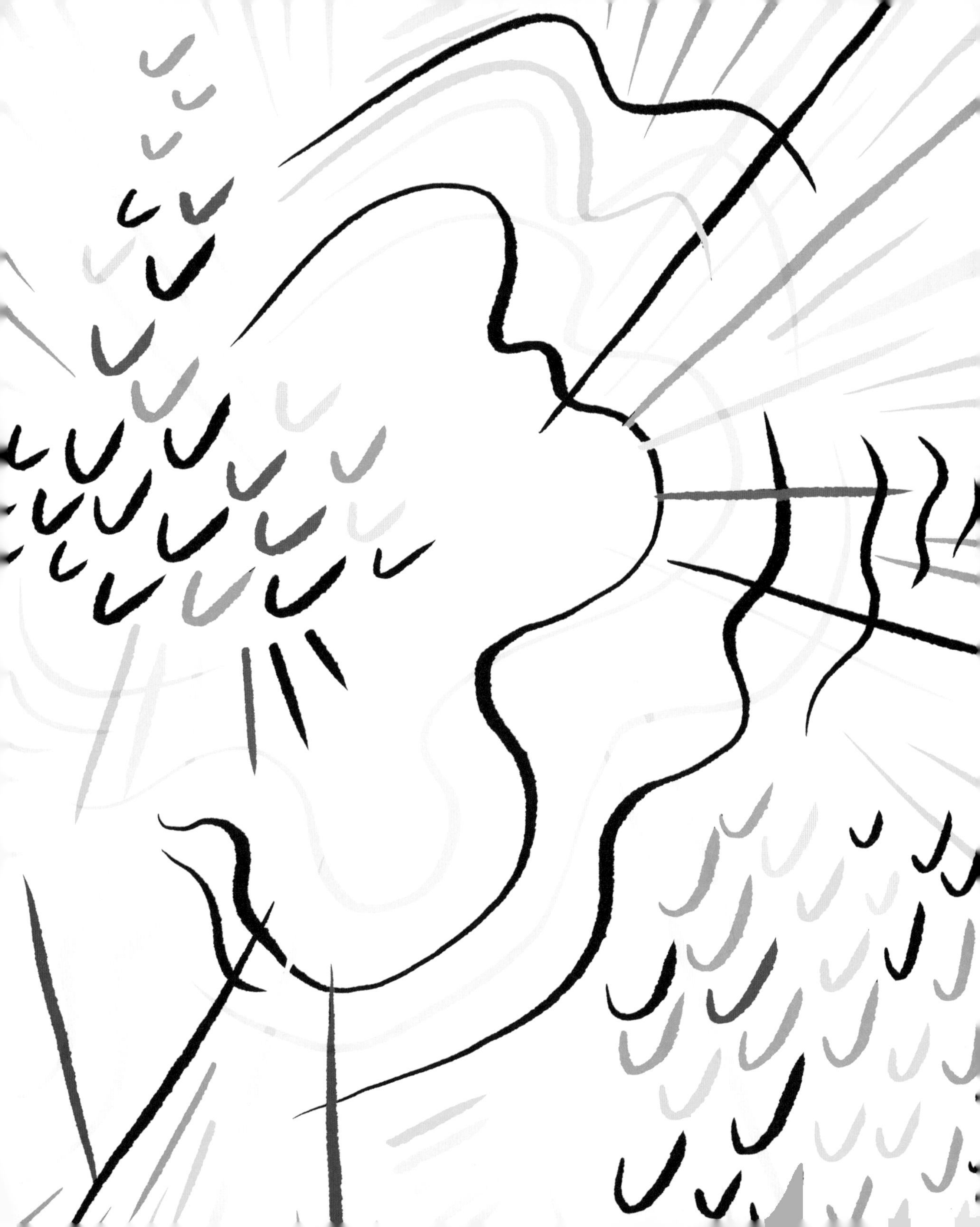

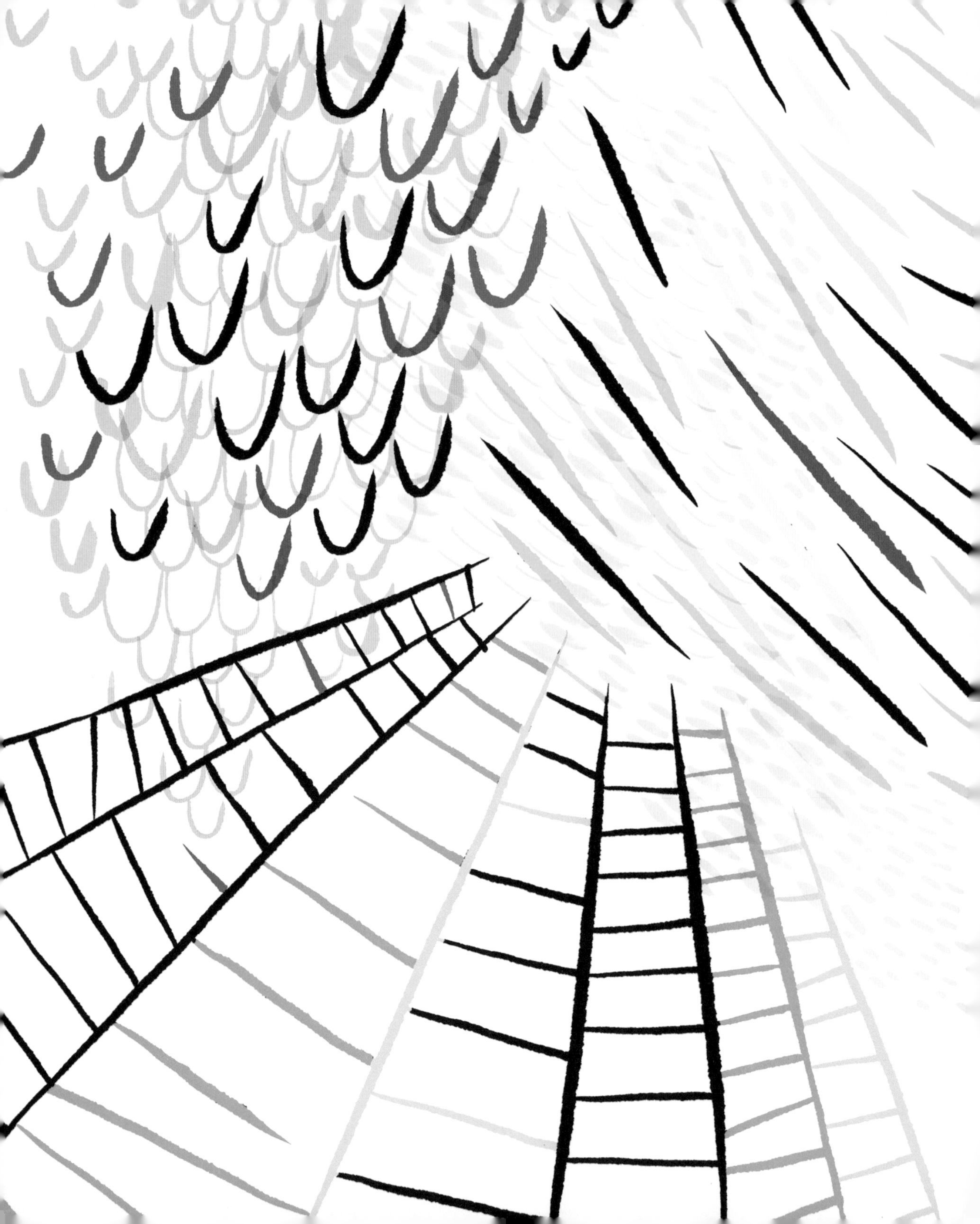

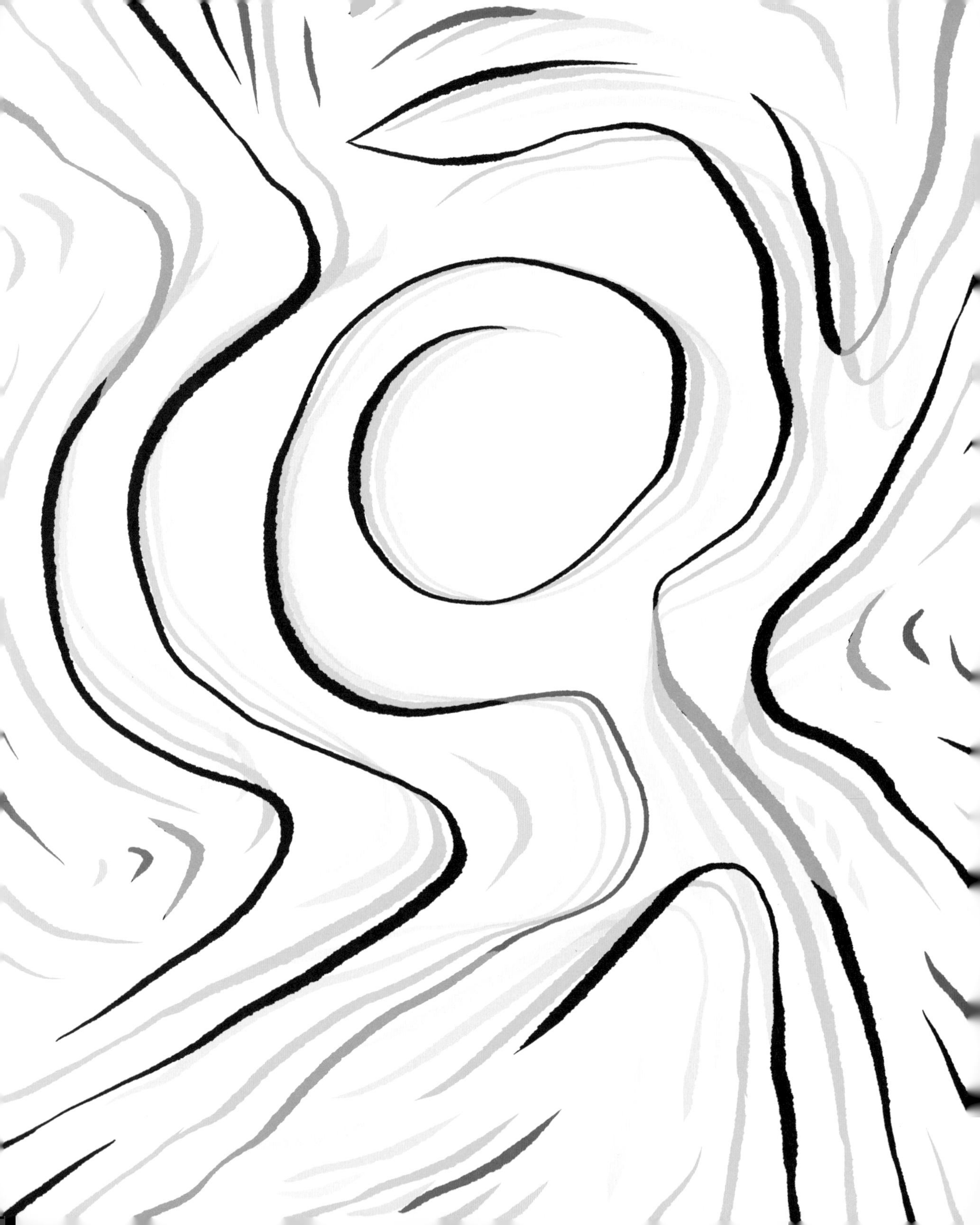

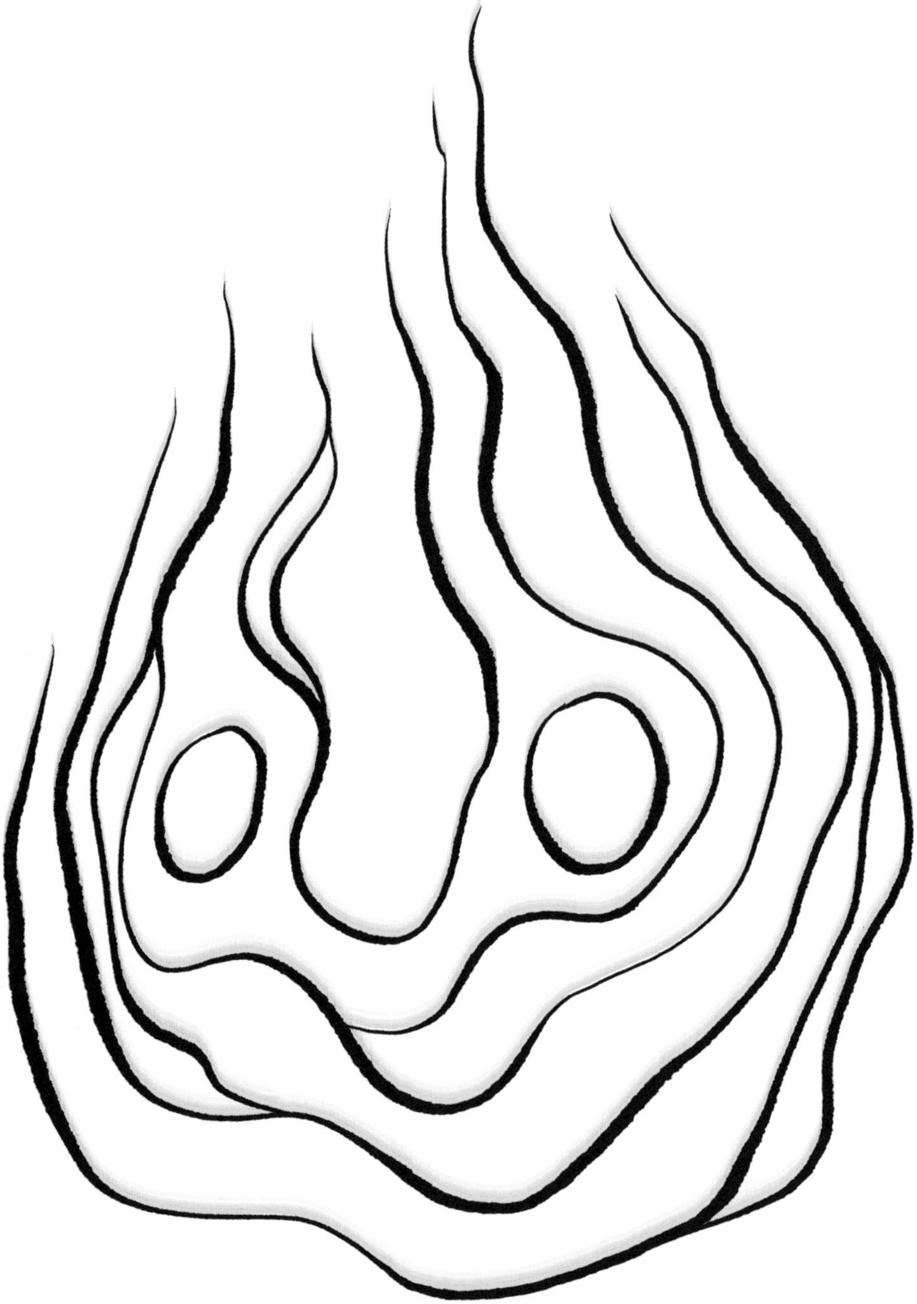

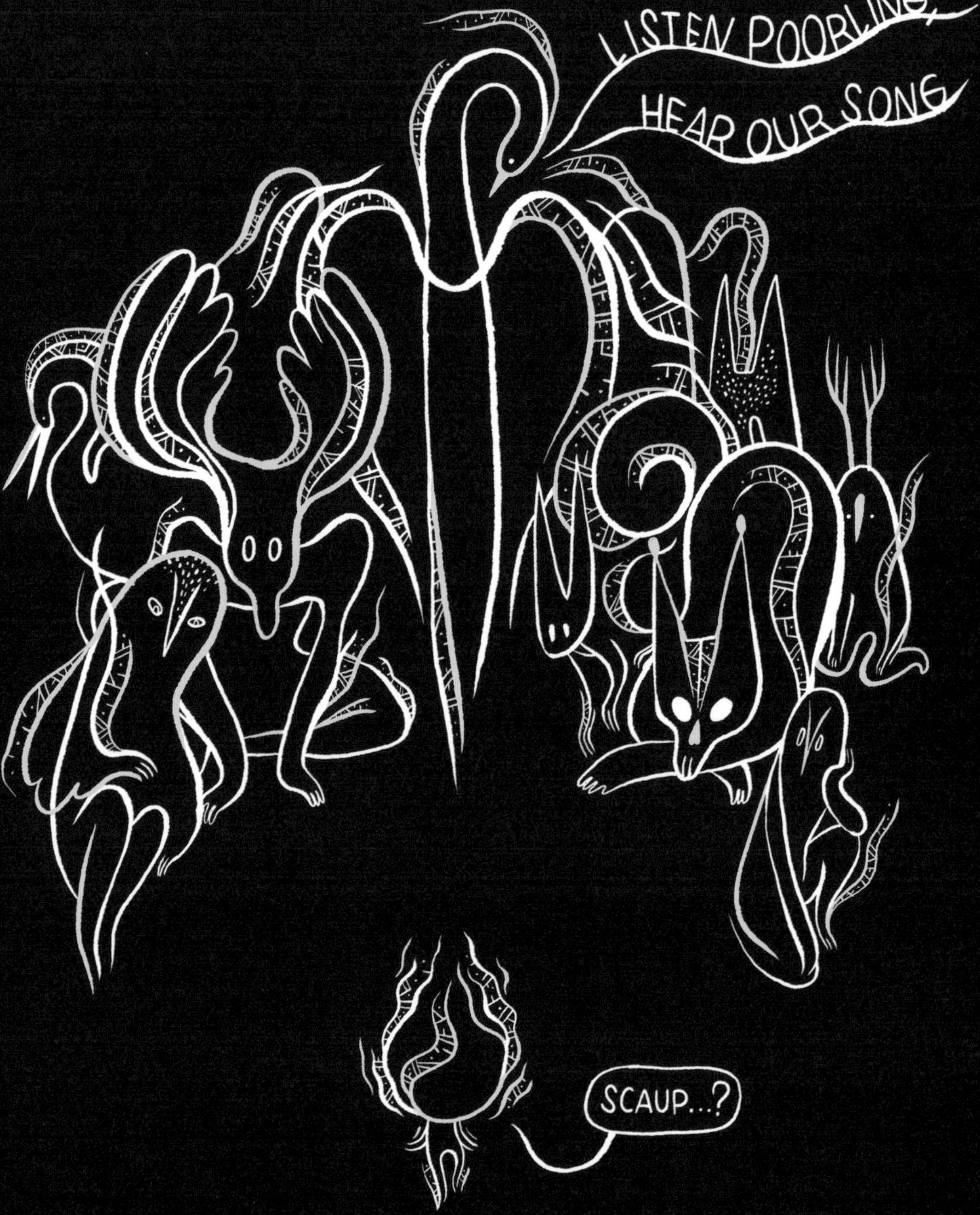
LISTEN POORLING,
HEAR OUR SONG
SCAUP...?

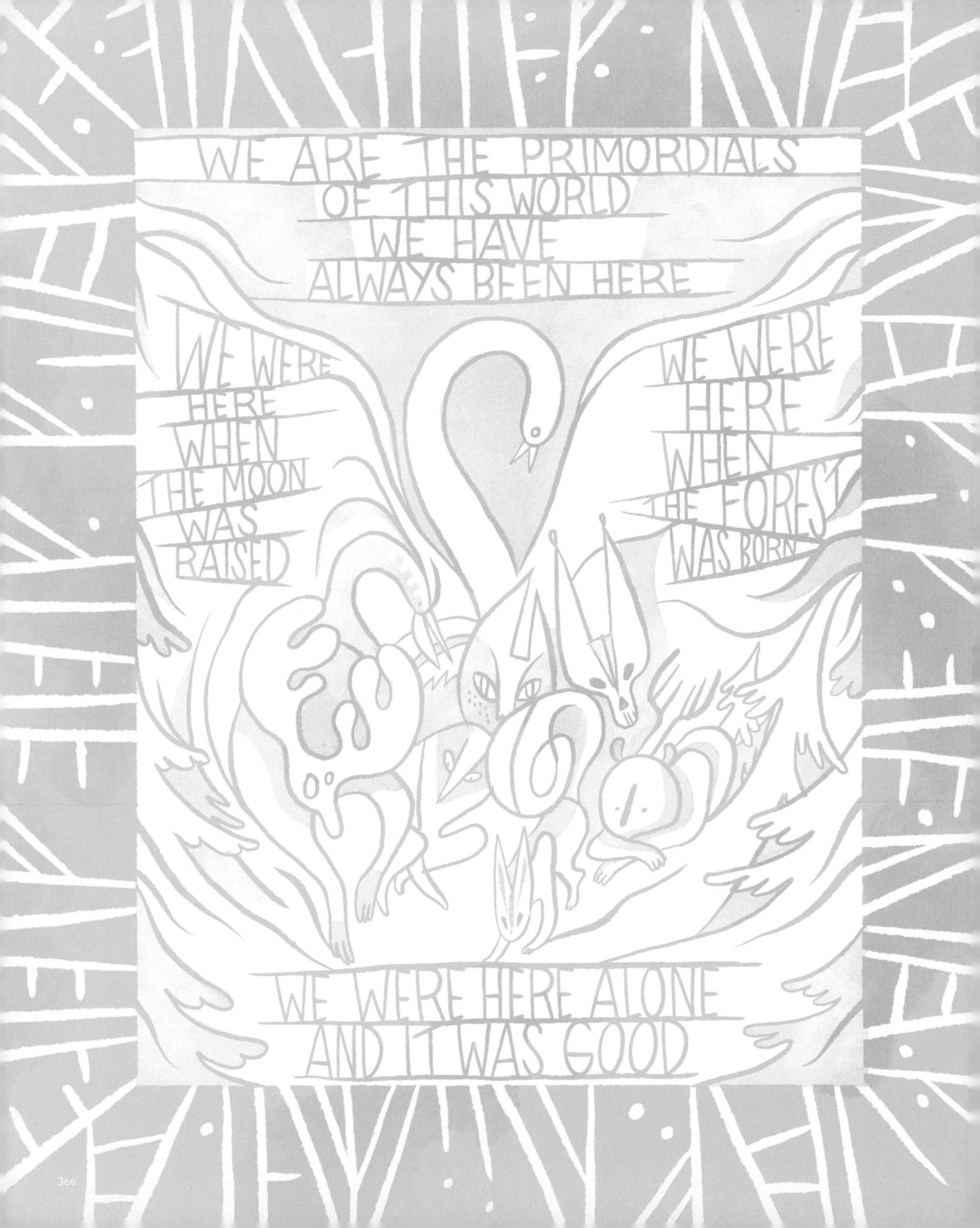

WE ARE THE PRIMORDIALS OF THIS WORLD
WE HAVE ALWAYS BEEN HERE
WE WERE HERE WHEN THE MOON WAS RAISED
WE WERE HERE WHEN THE FOREST WAS BORN
WE WERE HERE ALONE AND IT WAS GOOD

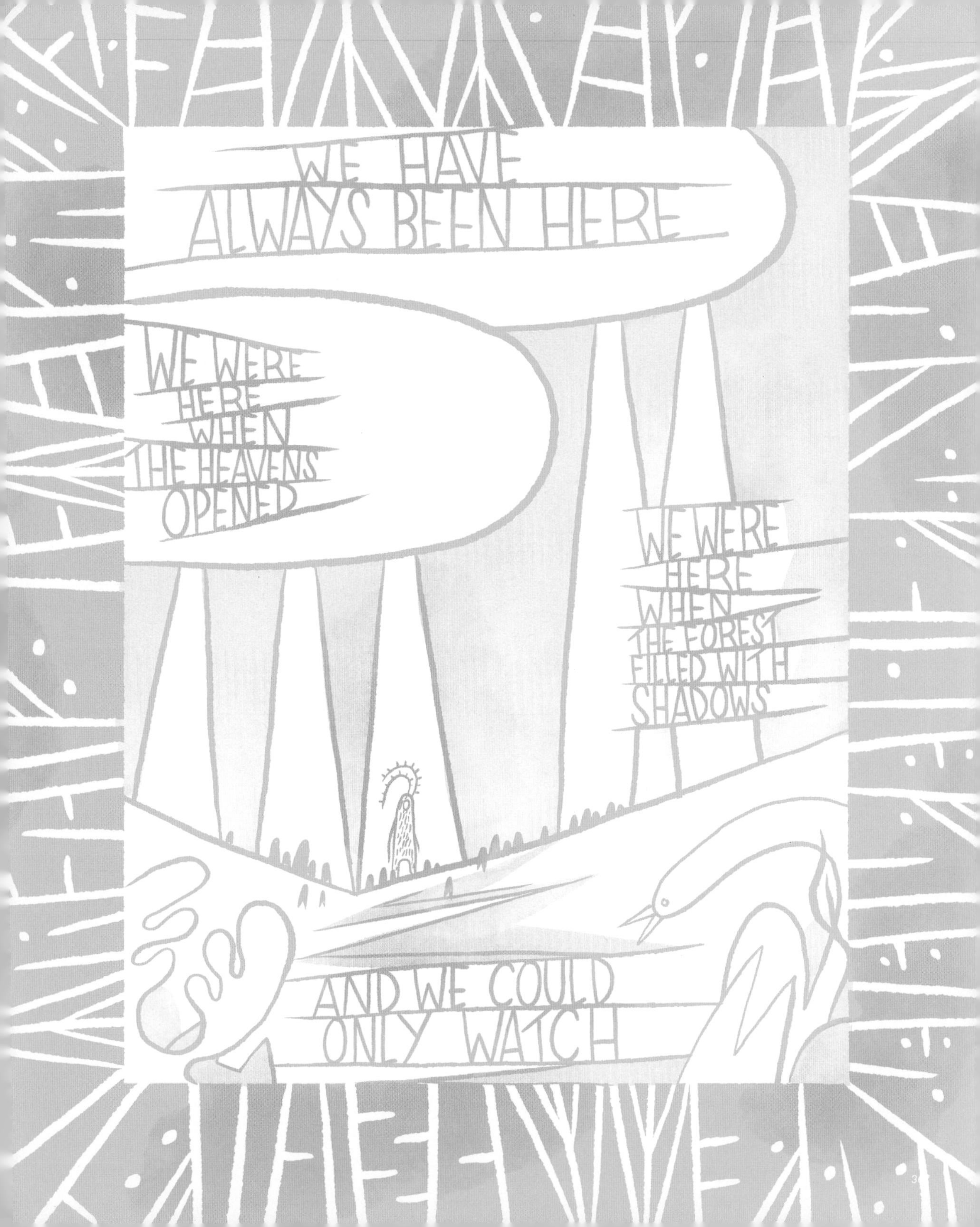
WE HAVE ALWAYS BEEN HERE
WE WERE HERE WHEN THE HEAVENS OPENED
WE WERE HERE WHEN THE FOREST FILLED WITH SHADOWS
AND WE COULD ONLY WATCH

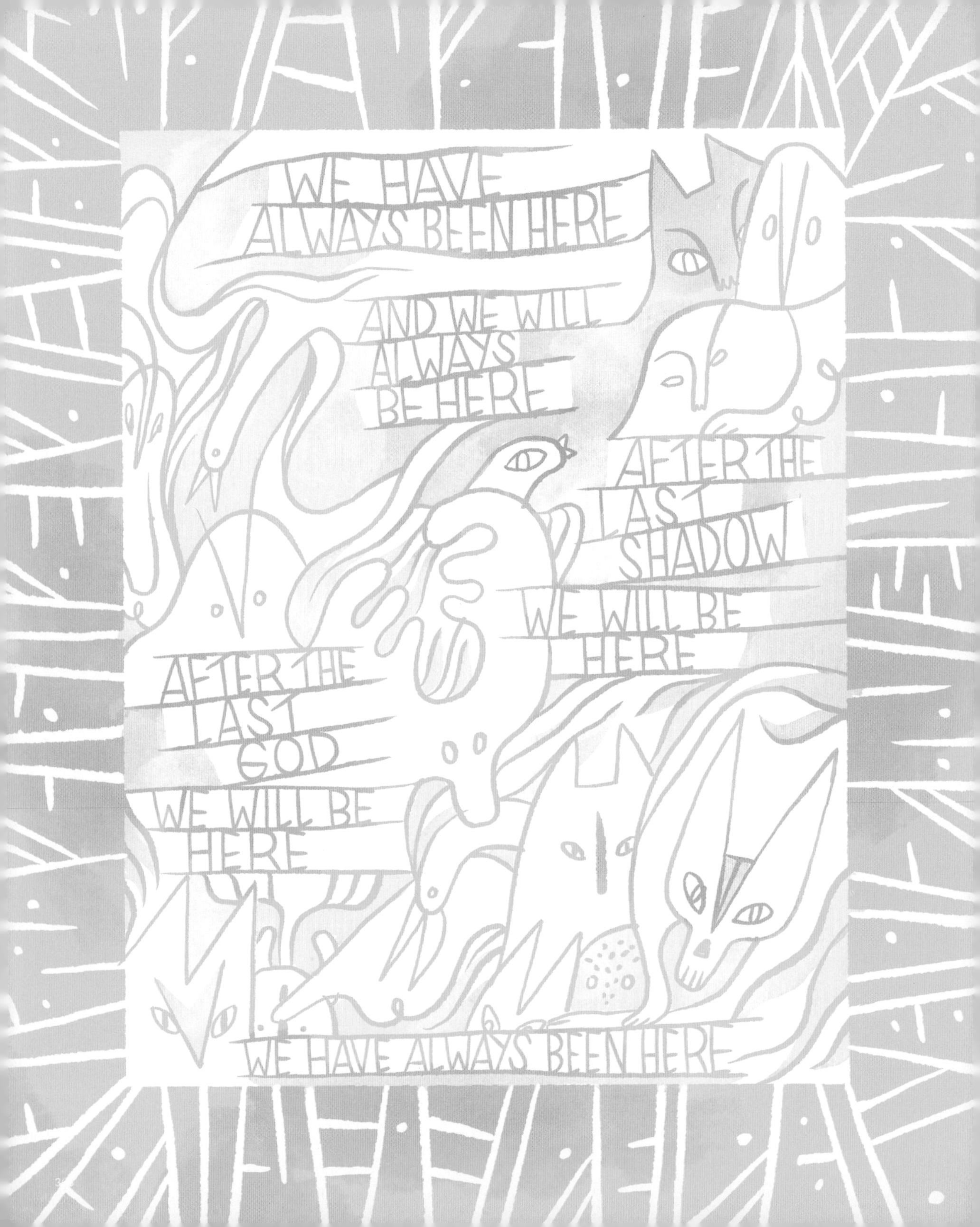
WE HAVE
ALWAYS BEEN HERE
AND WE WILL
ALWAYS
BE HERE
AFTER THE
LAST
SHADOW
WE WILL BE
HERE
AFTER THE
LAST
GOD
WE WILL BE
HERE
WE HAVE ALWAYS BEEN HERE

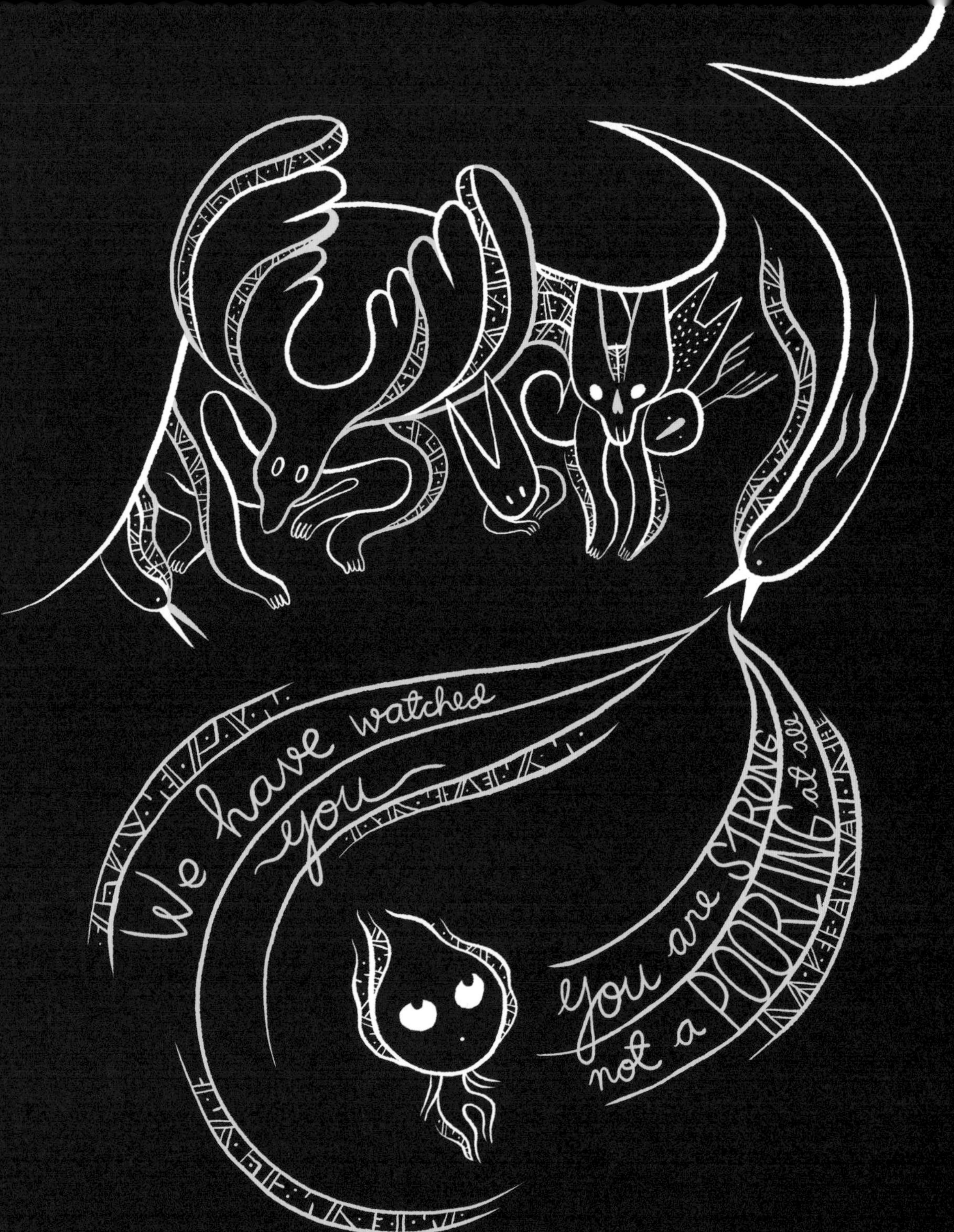
We have watched you
You are STRONG
not a POORLING at all

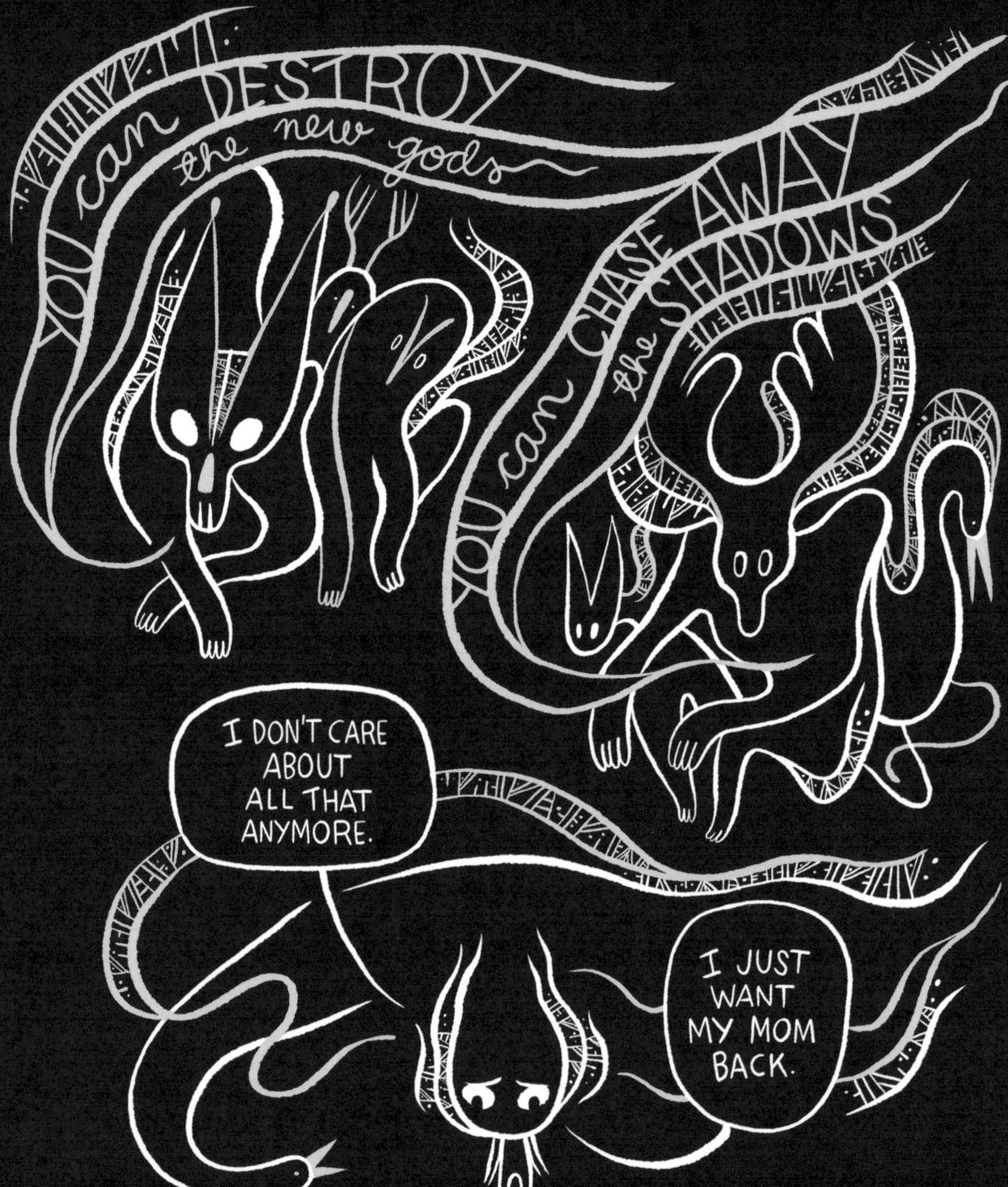
YOU can DESTROY the new gods
YOU can CHASE AWAY the SHADOWS
I DON'T CARE ABOUT ALL THAT ANYMORE.
I JUST WANT MY MOM BACK.

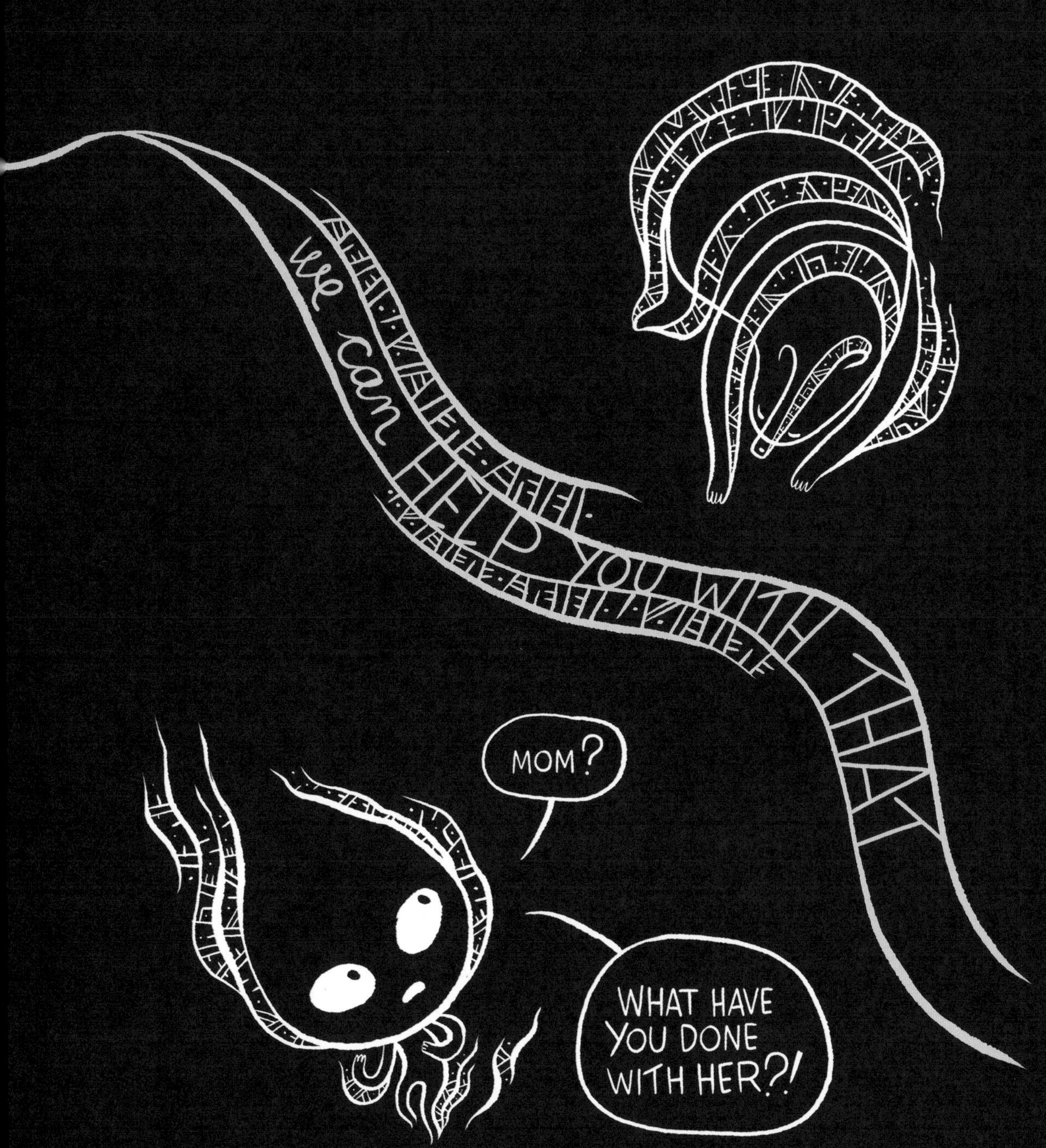
we can HELP YOU WITH THAT
MOM?
WHAT HAVE YOU DONE WITH HER?!

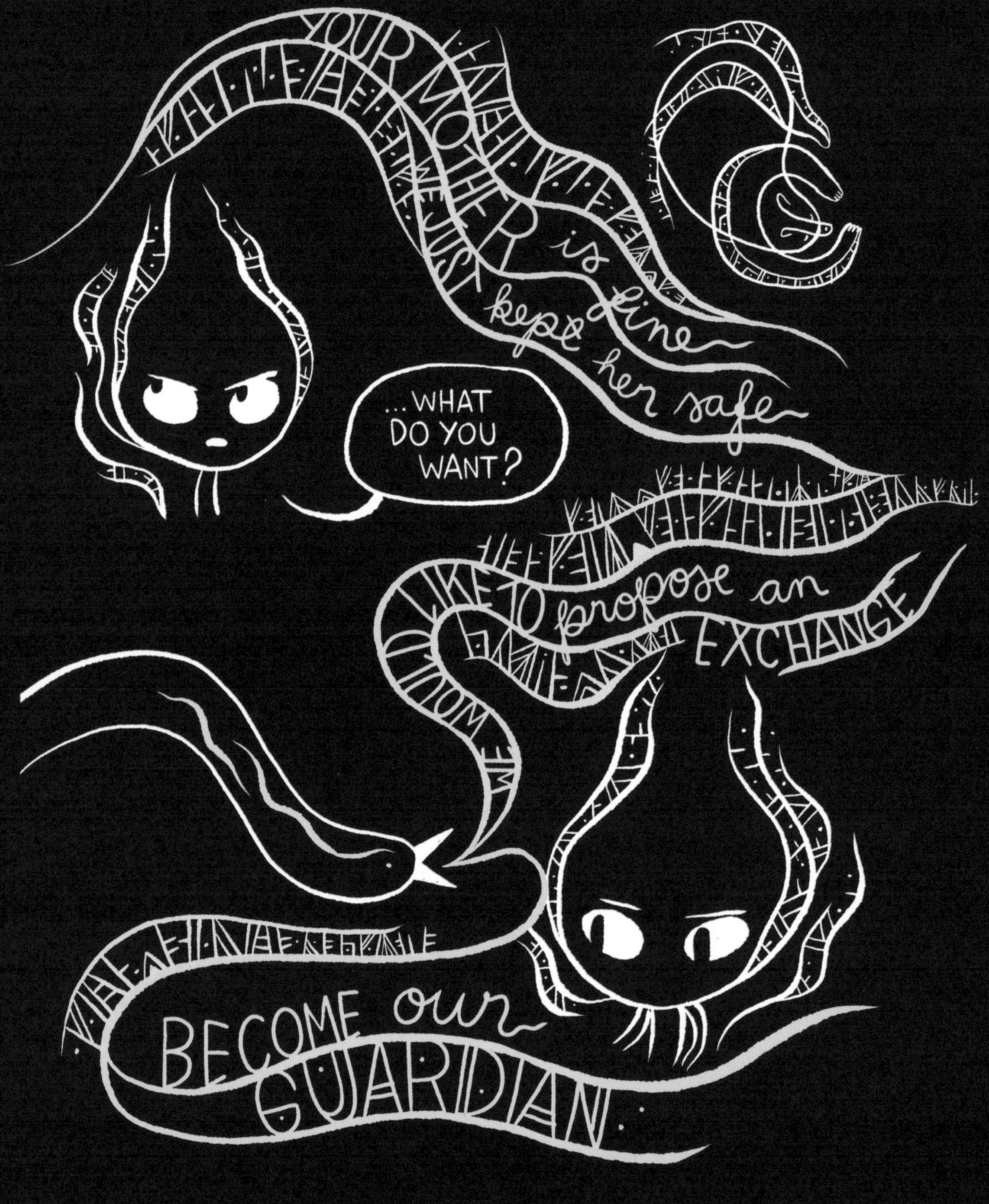
YOUR MOTHER is fine
JUST kept her safe
...WHAT DO YOU WANT?
LIKE TO propose an EXCHANGE
BECOME our GUARDIAN

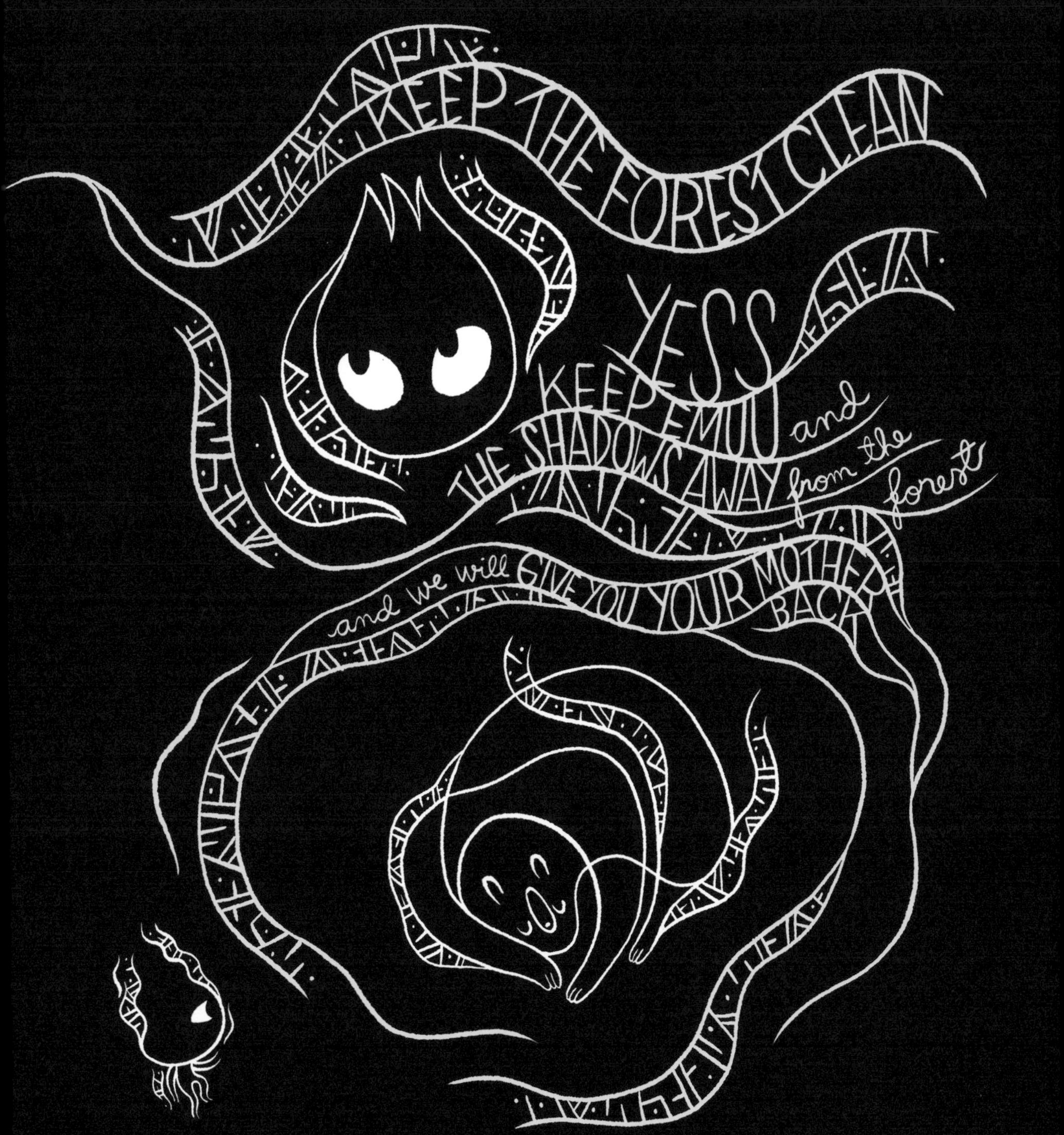
KEEP THE FOREST CLEAN
YESS
KEEP EMUU and
THE SHADOWS AWAY from the forest
and we will GIVE YOU YOUR MOTHER BACK

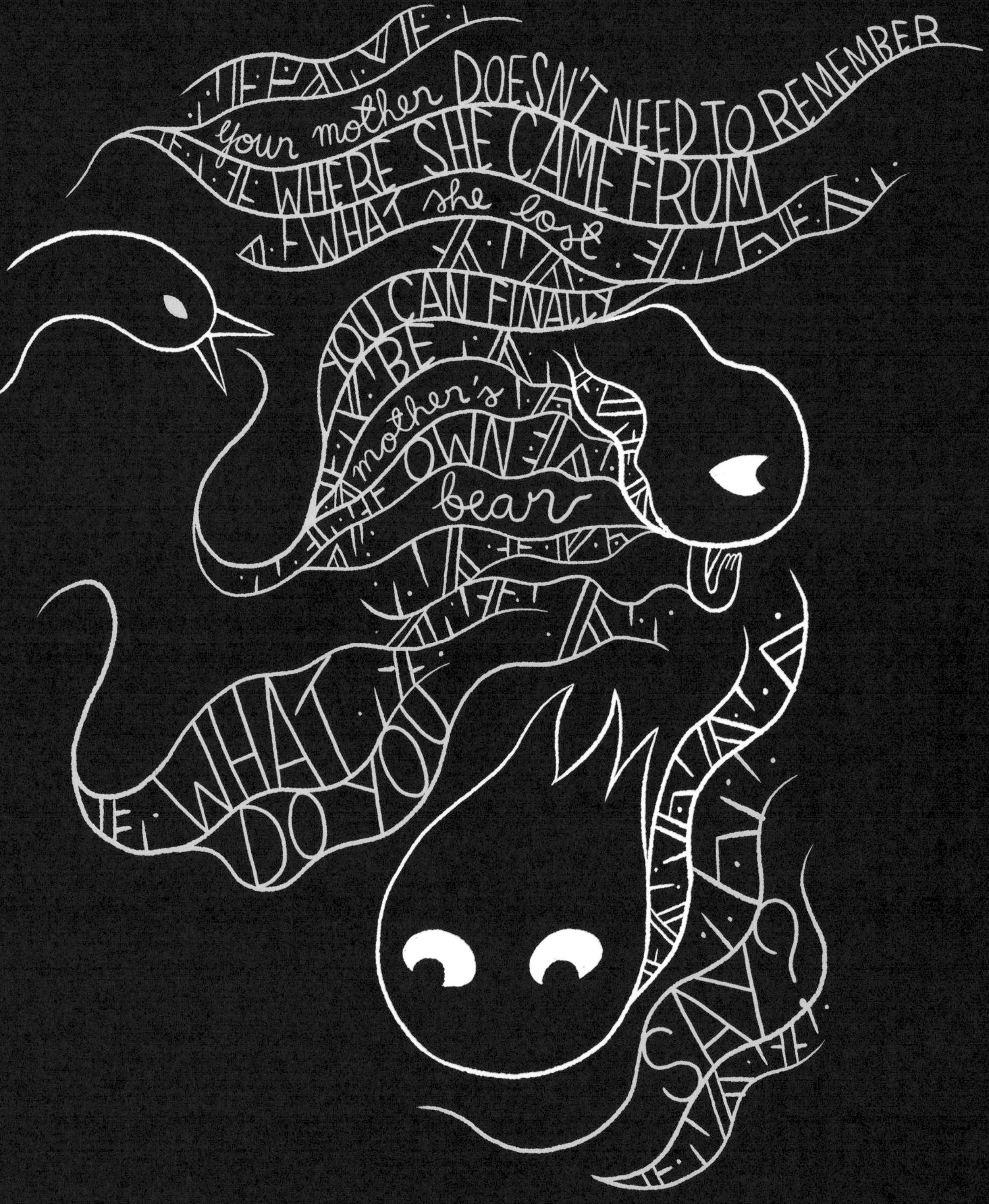
your mother DOESN'T NEED TO REMEMBER
WHERE SHE CAME FROM
WHAT she lost
YOU CAN FINALLY
BE
mother's
OWN
bear
WHAT DO YOU

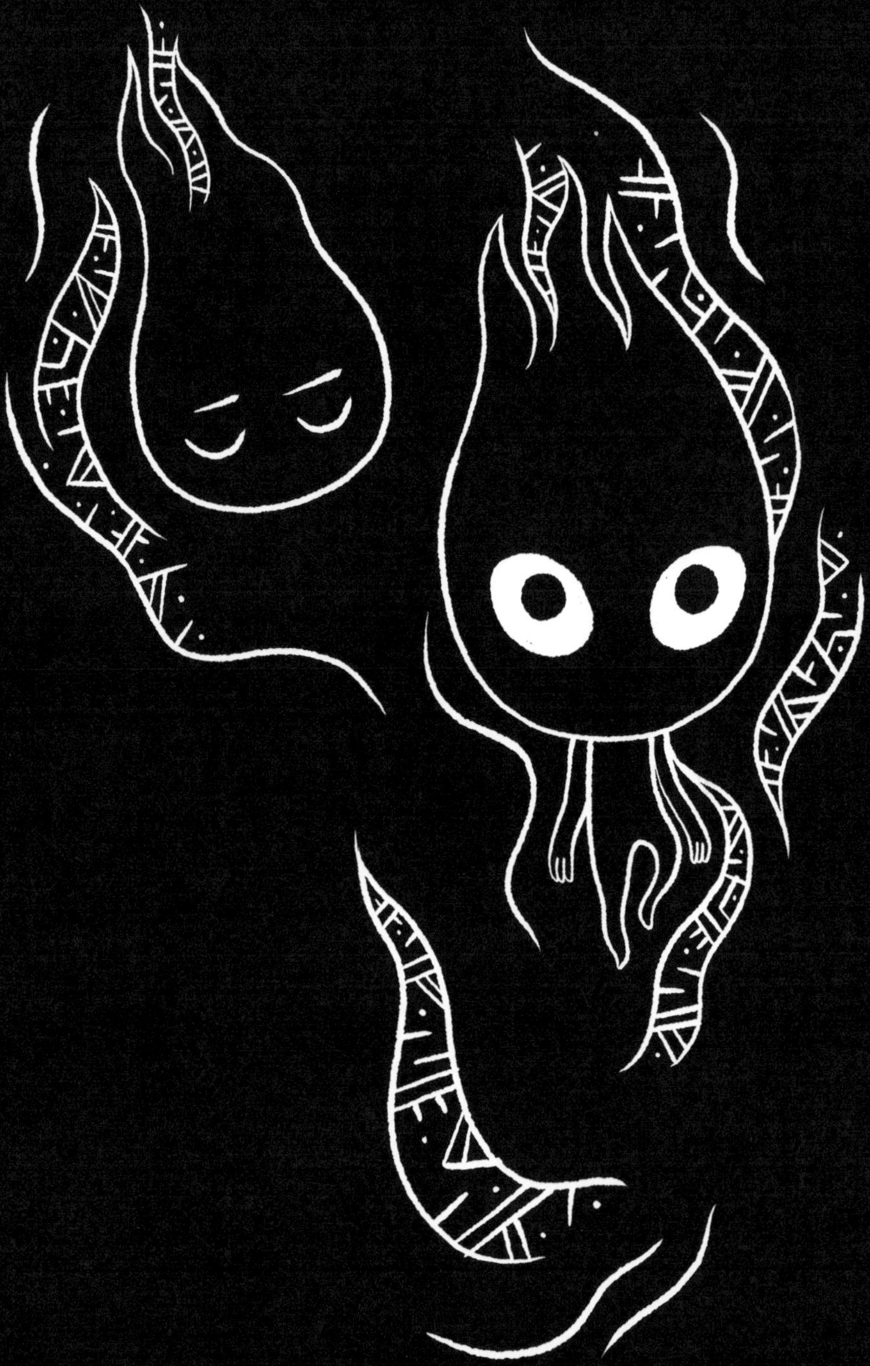

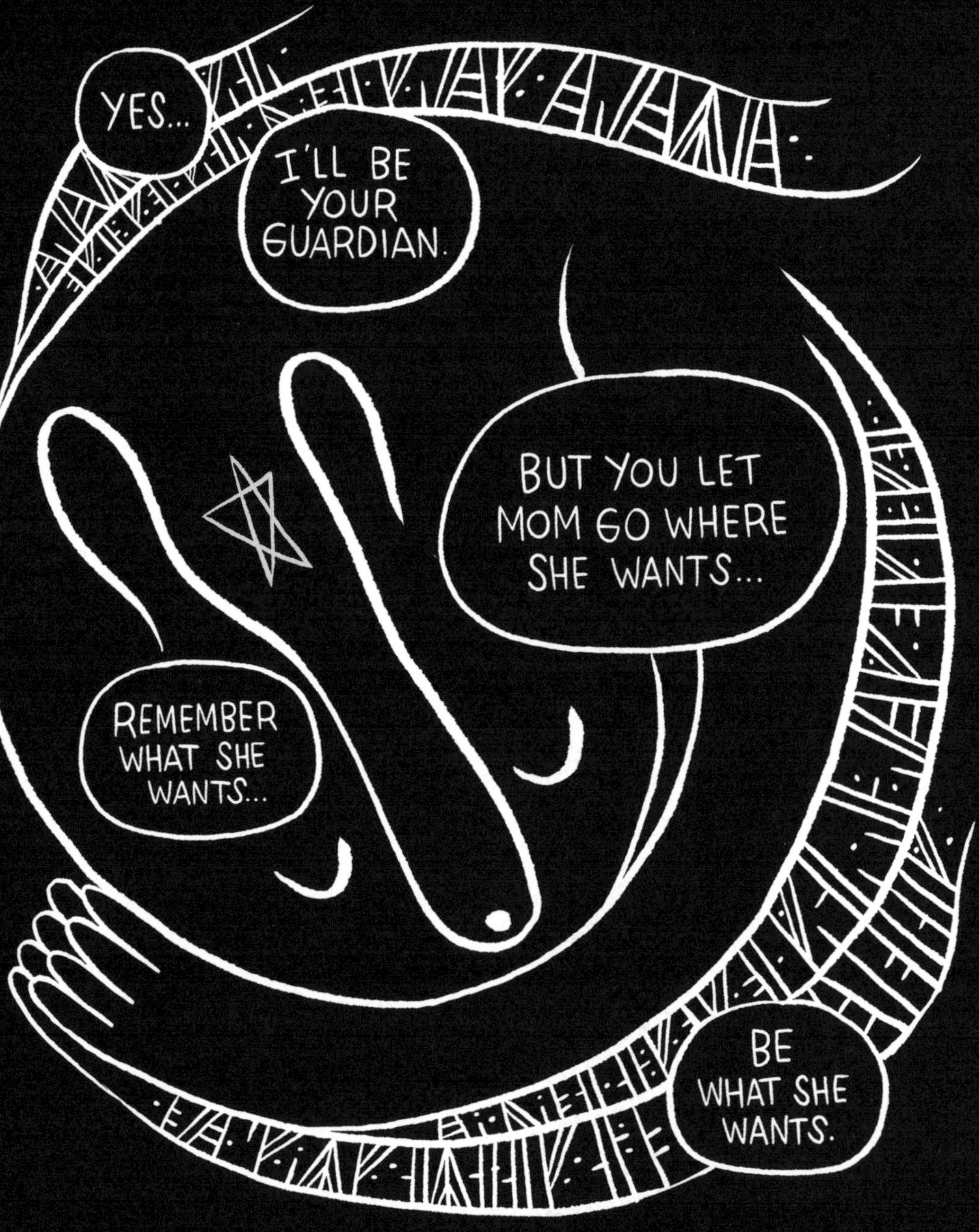
YES...
I'LL BE YOUR GUARDIAN.
BUT YOU LET MOM GO WHERE SHE WANTS...
REMEMBER WHAT SHE WANTS...
BE WHAT SHE WANTS.

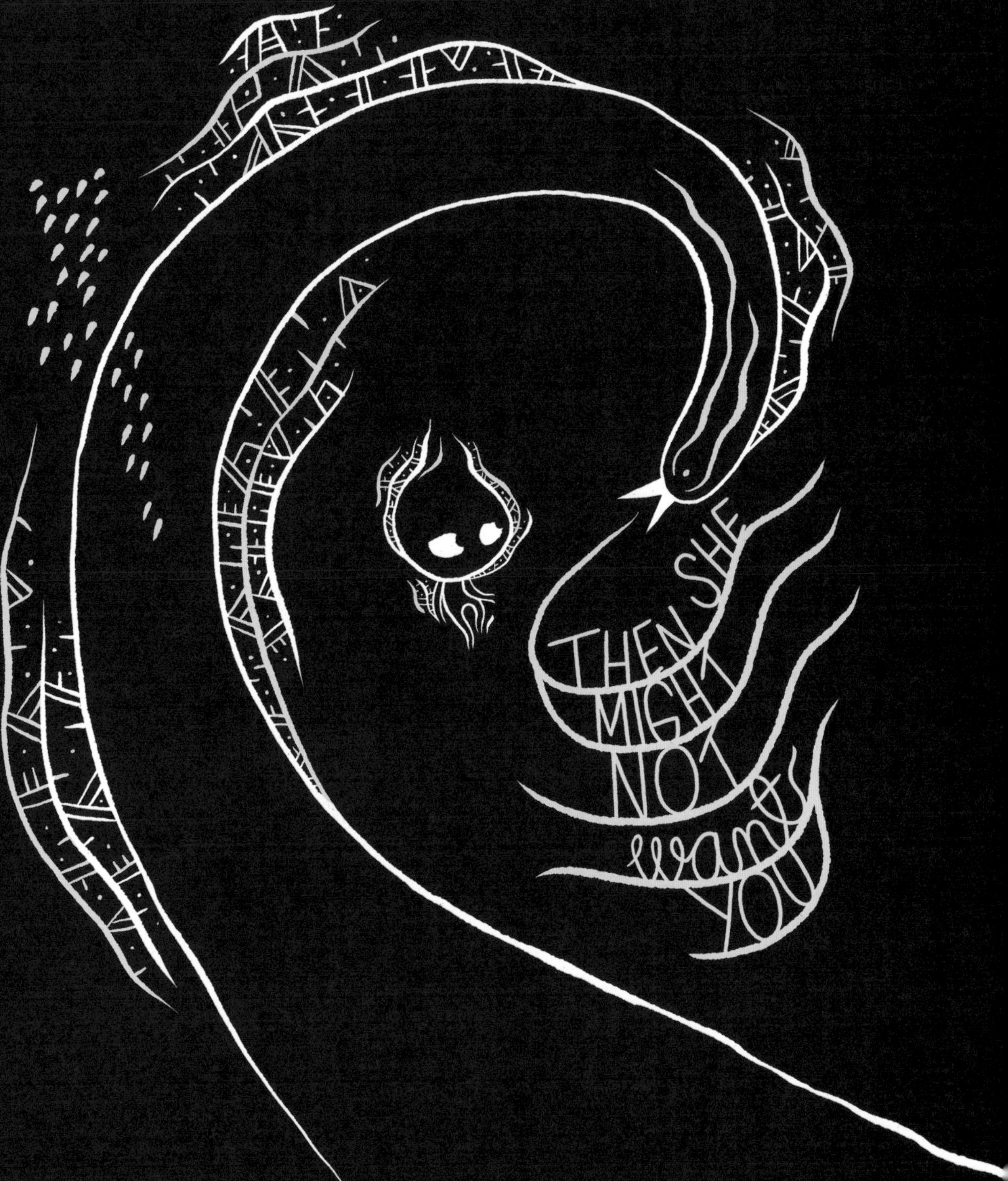
THEN SHE
MIGHT
NOT
want
YOU

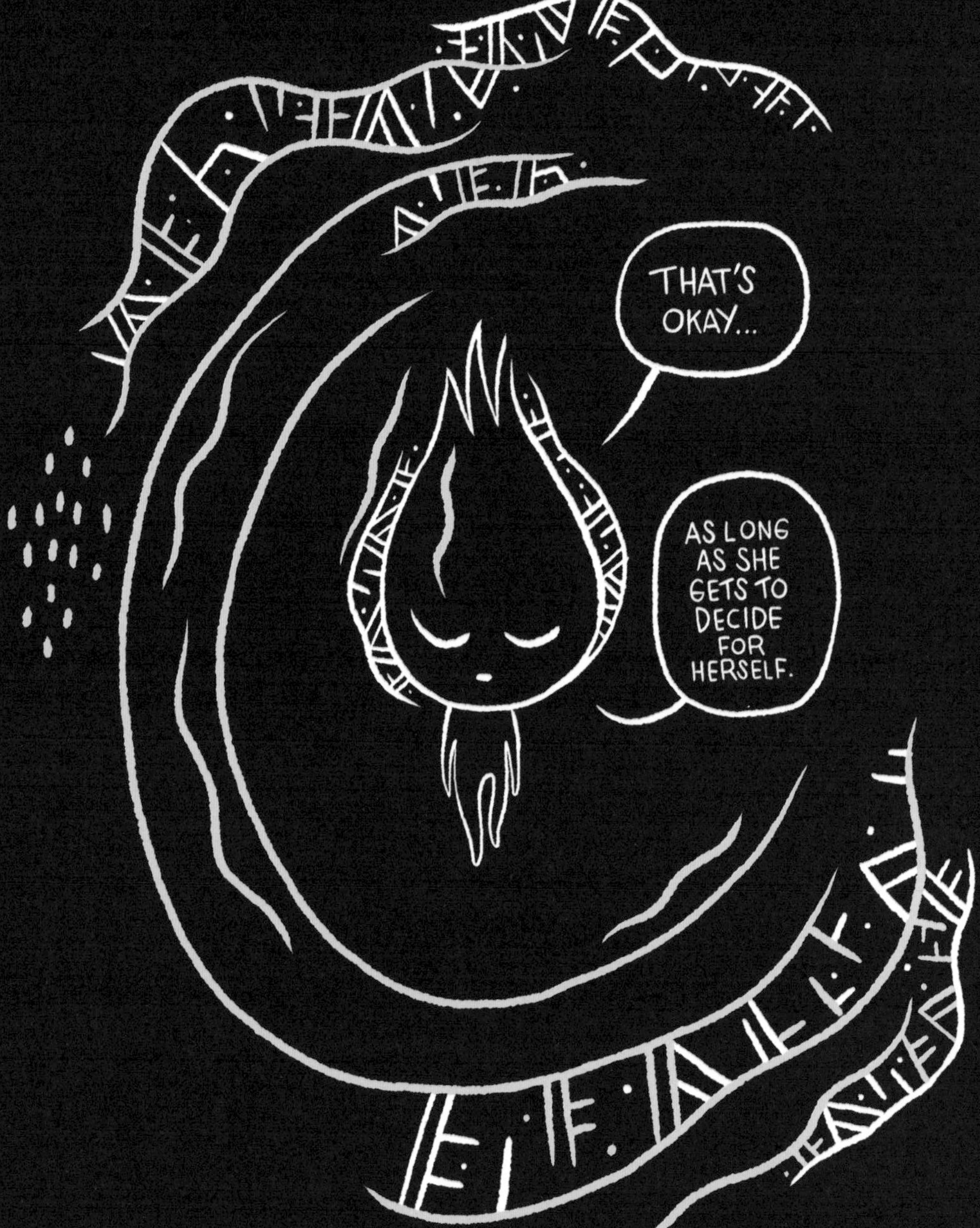
THAT'S OKAY...
AS LONG AS SHE GETS TO DECIDE FOR HERSELF.

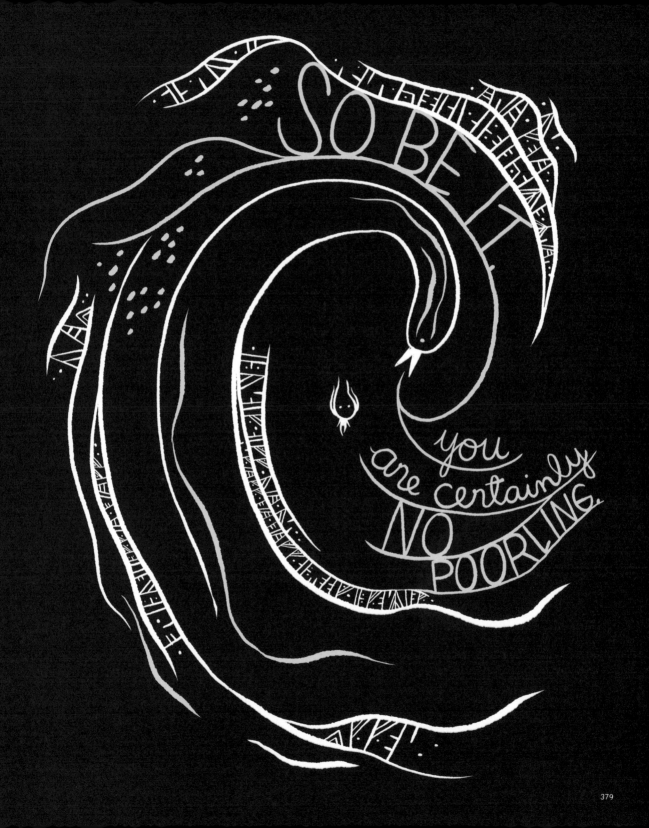

SO BE IT. you are certainly NO POORLING.

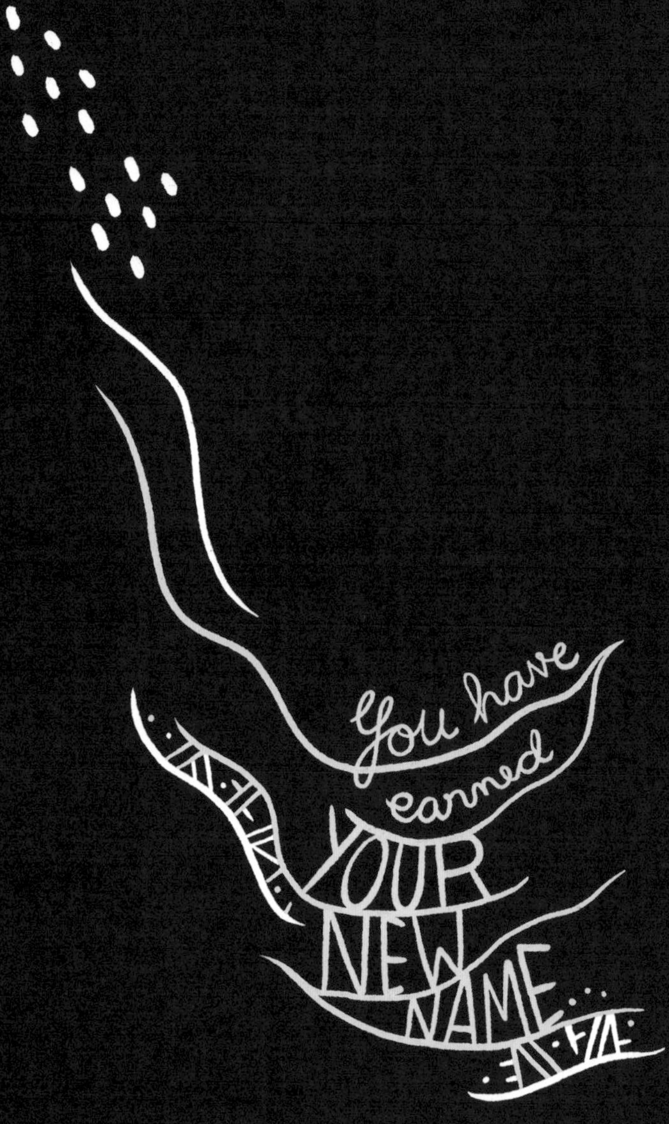
You have earned
YOUR NEW NAME

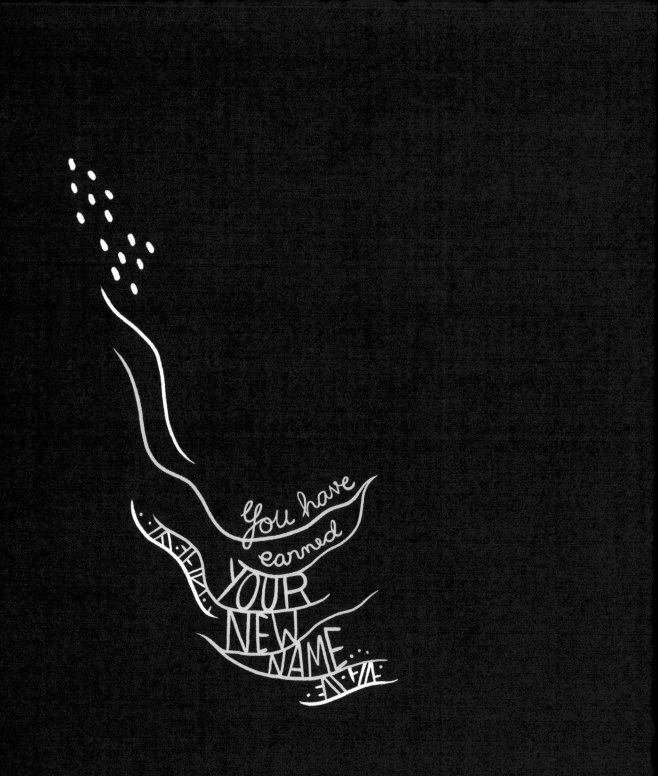

OKST
GUARDIAN
OF THE FOREST

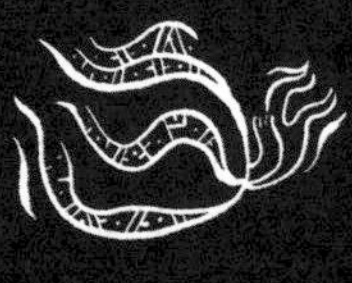

EPILOGUE

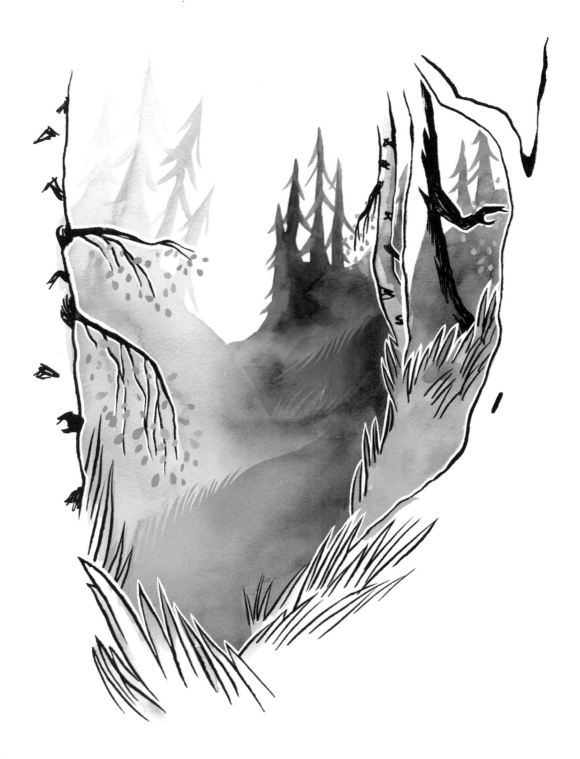

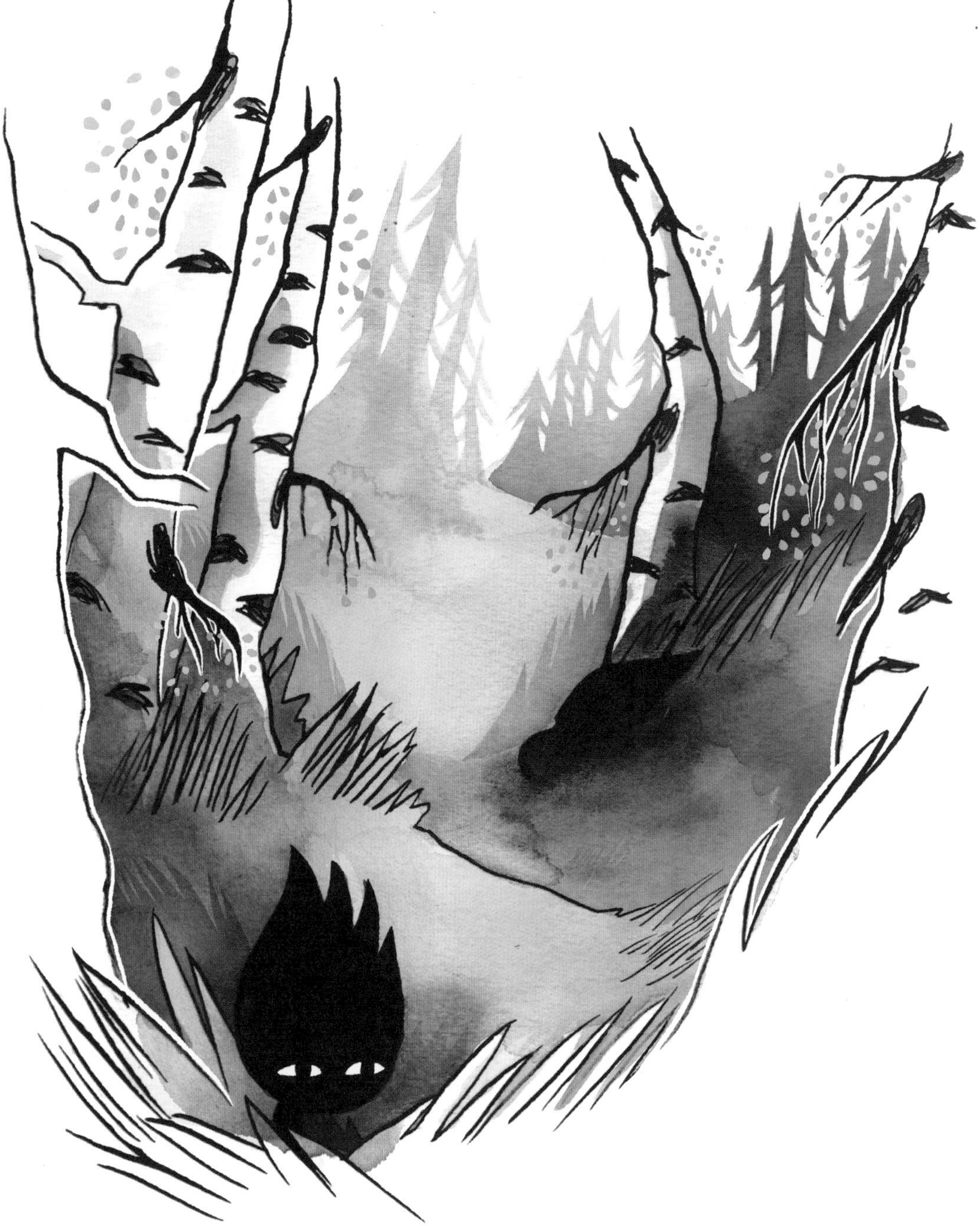

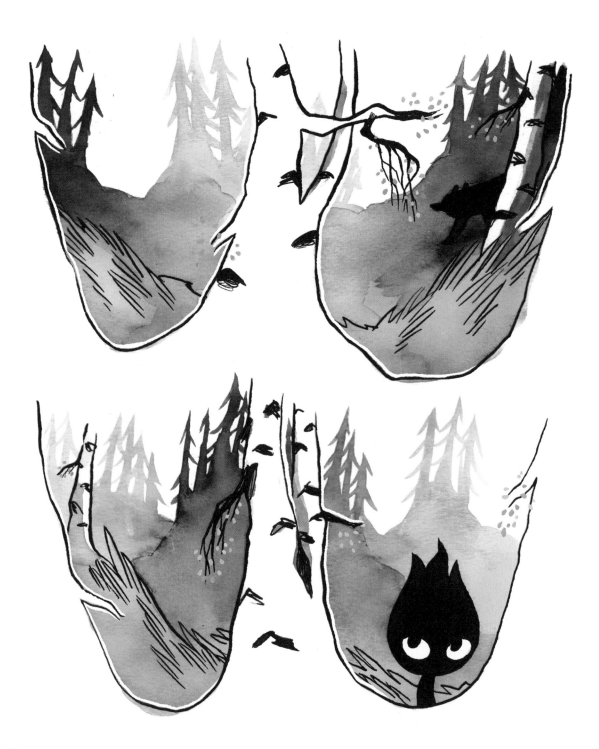

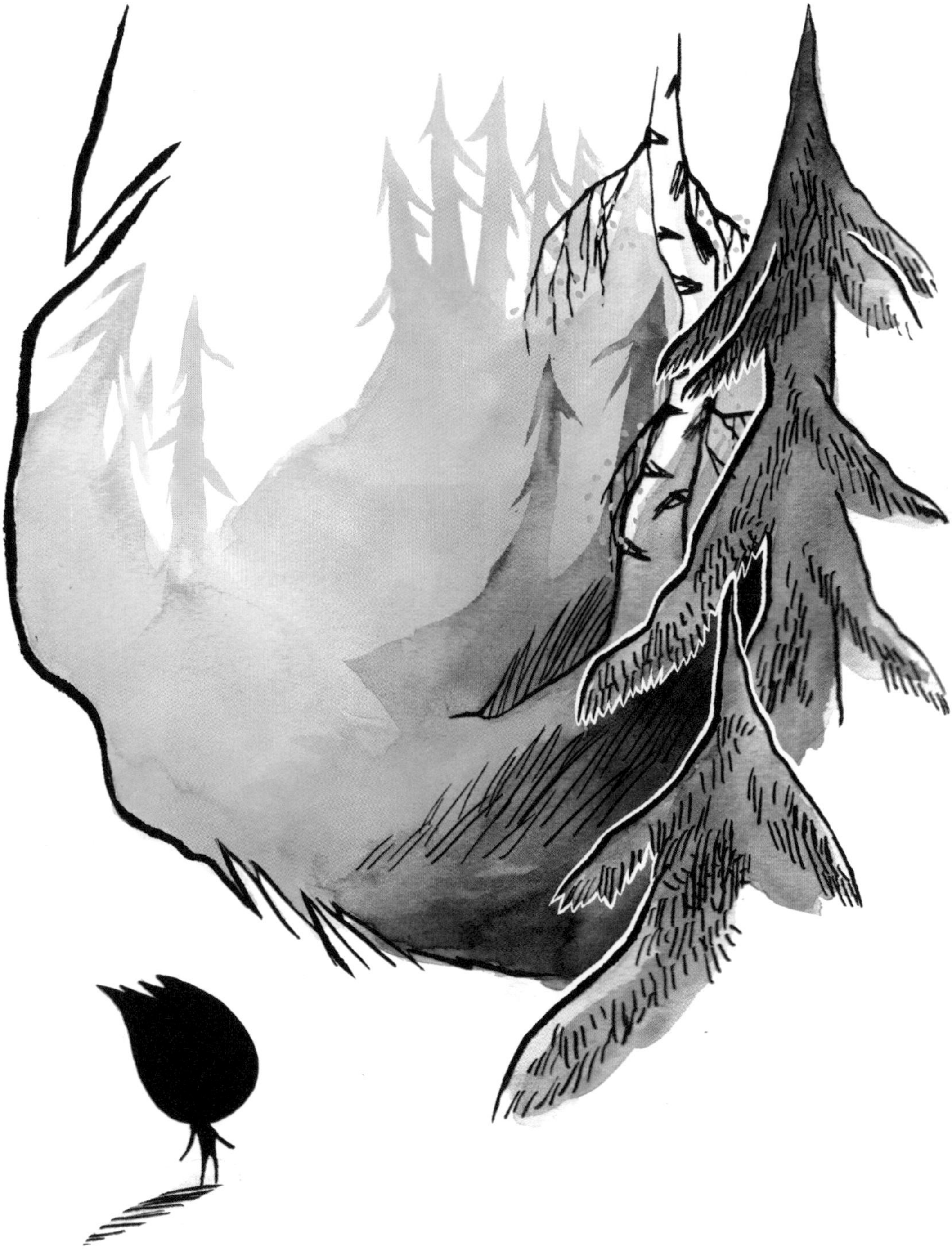

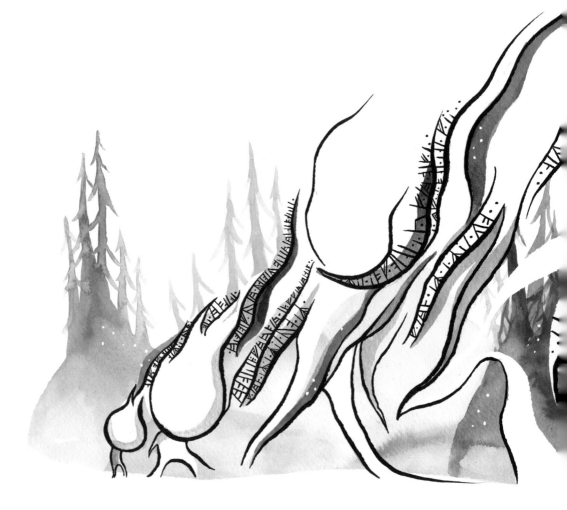

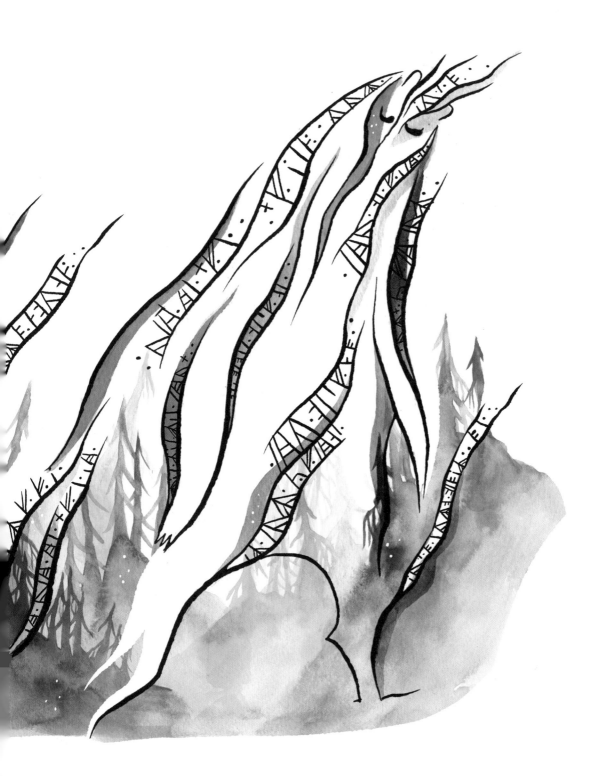

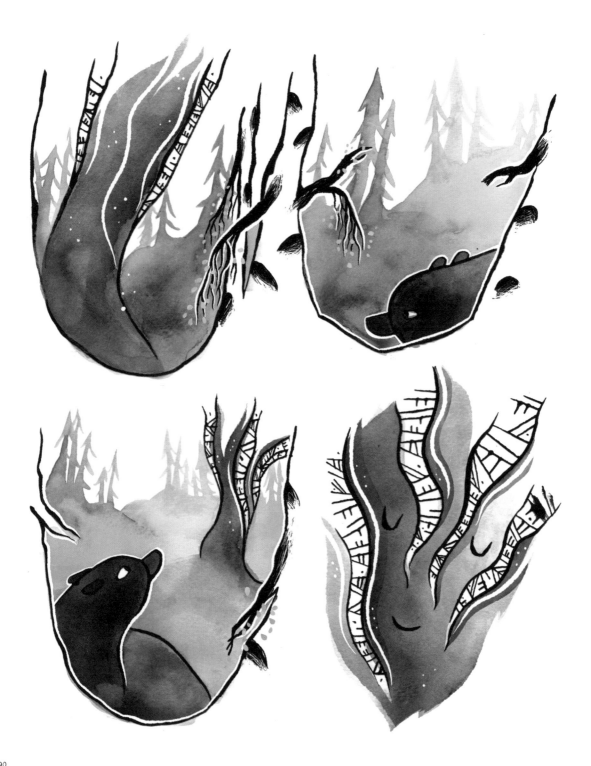

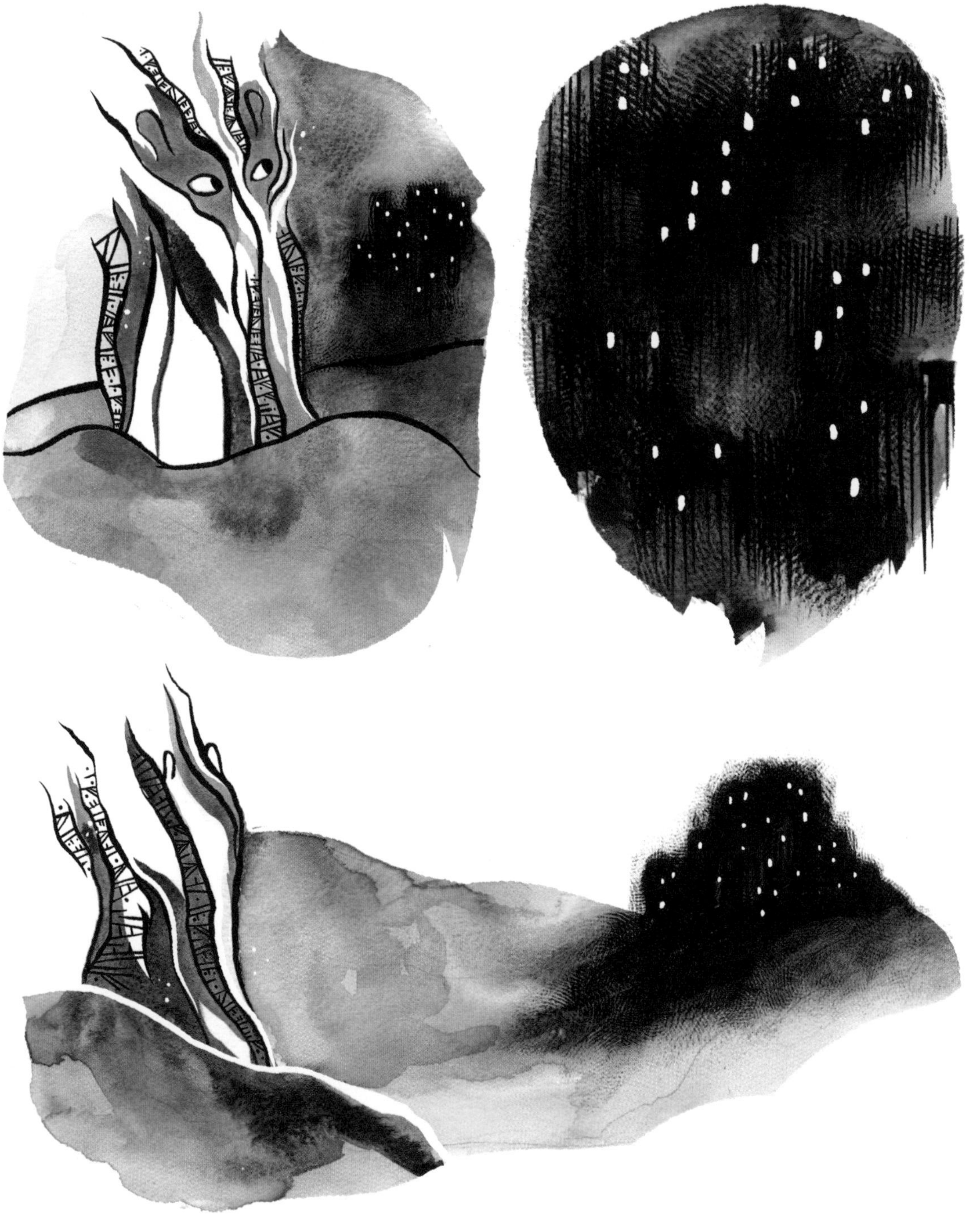

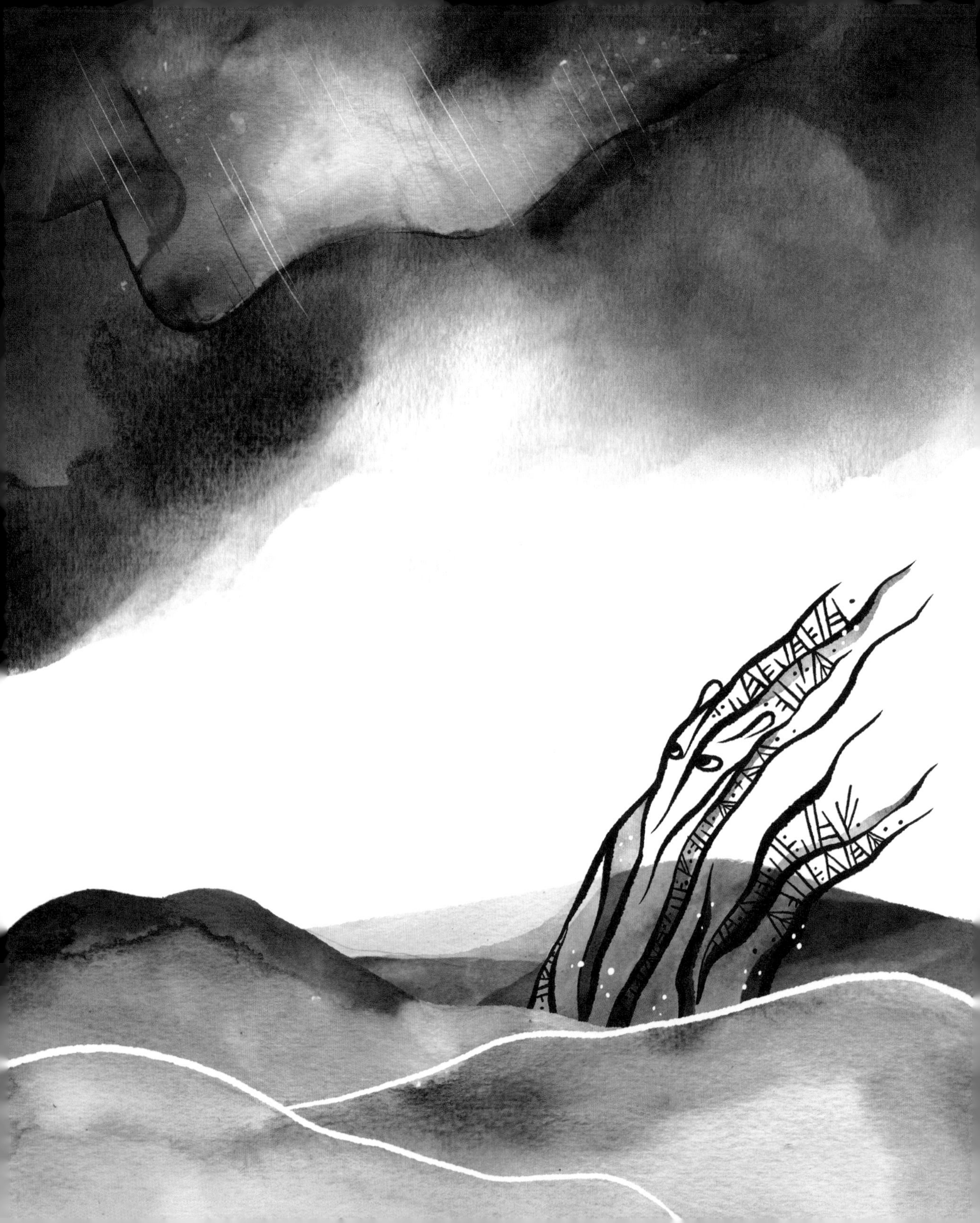

THE
END

·A NOTE ON NAMES·

EMUU
IN EASTERN Finnish AND Karelian MYTHOLOGY,
THE PROGENITOR OF A SPECIES OF ANIMALS OR PLANTS.

SCAUP
THE WATERBIRD IS A PROMINENT FIGURE IN THE CREATION
MYTH OF THE Finnish NATIONAL EPIC, Kalevala.

MANA
AN OLD WORD FOR death IN FINNISH.

OKSI
AN OLD WORD, SOME SAY maybe
THE ORIGINAL WORD, FOR bear IN FINNISH.

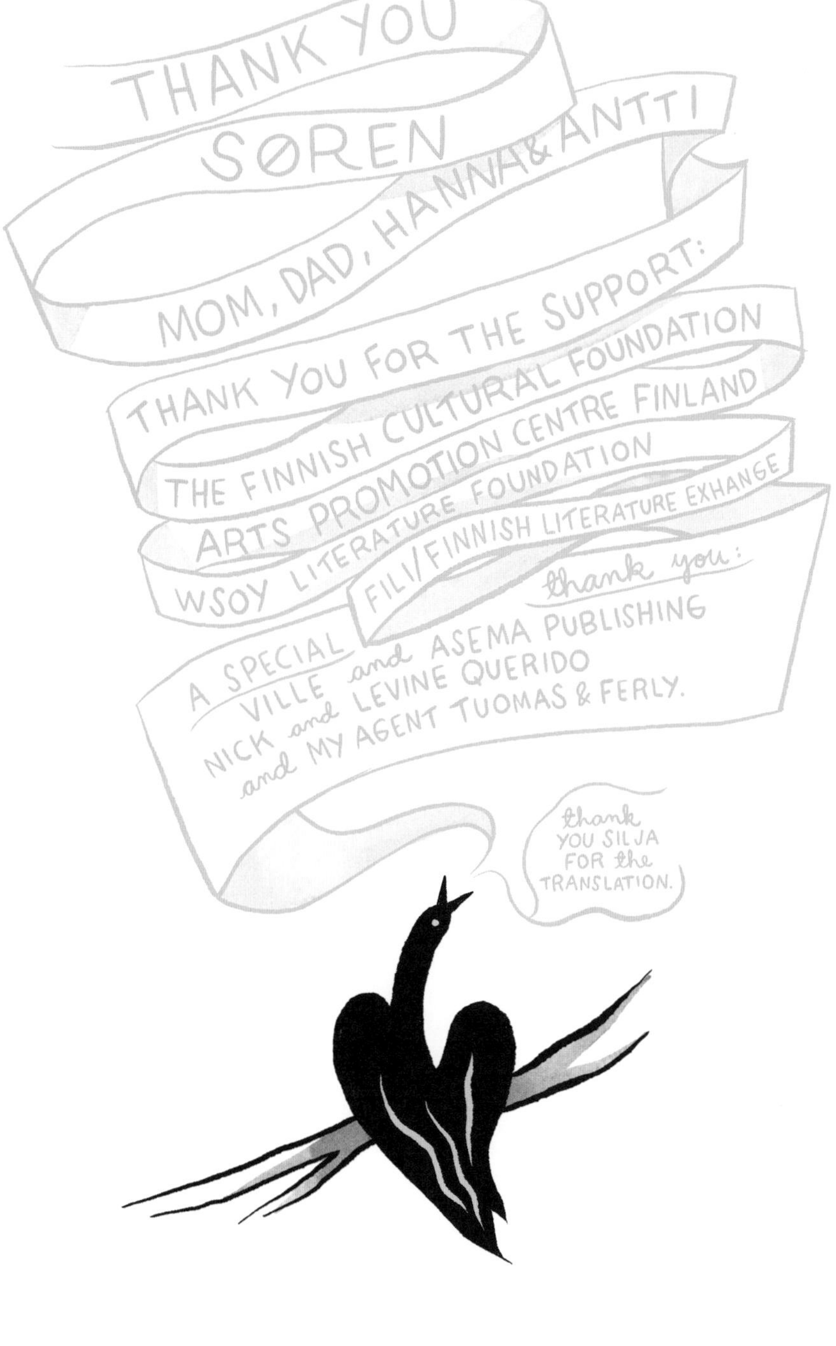
THANK YOU
SØREN
MOM, DAD, HANNA & ANTTI
THANK YOU FOR THE SUPPORT:
THE FINNISH CULTURAL FOUNDATION
ARTS PROMOTION CENTRE FINLAND
WSOY LITERATURE FOUNDATION
FILI/FINNISH LITERATURE EXHANGE
A SPECIAL thank you:
VILLE and ASEMA PUBLISHING
NICK and LEVINE QUERIDO
and MY AGENT TUOMAS & FERLY.
thank YOU SILJA FOR the TRANSLATION.

MARI AHOKOIVU (s. 1984)
is an illustrator
and comic artist
from Finland.

OKSI, HER MAGNUM OPUS, WAS
CALLED "BEAUTIFUL, CLEVER, FUNNY,
VIBRANT, AND FULL OF MAGIC" BY
THE BIGGEST NEWSPAPER IN HER HOME
COUNTRY; WAS SHORTLISTED FOR
THE JARKKO LAINE AWARD; AND
HAS NOW BEEN TRANSLATED INTO ENGLISH
AS THE FIRST GRAPHIC NOVEL ON
THE LEVINE QUERIDO LIST.

Some Notes on This Book's Production

The art for the cover, case, and interiors was created by Mari Ahokoivu using a mix of tradi-
tional (watercolour, ink and a nib pen) and digital tools (Photoshop and Wacom Cintiq drawing
board). The type was hand-lettered throughout by Ahokoivu. The book was printed on FSC™-
certified 120gsm Golden Sun woodfree paper and bound in China.

Production was supervised by Leslie Cohen and Freesia Blizard
Book cover and case designed by Jonathan Yamakami
Book interiors designed by Mari Ahokoivu
Edited by Nick Thomas

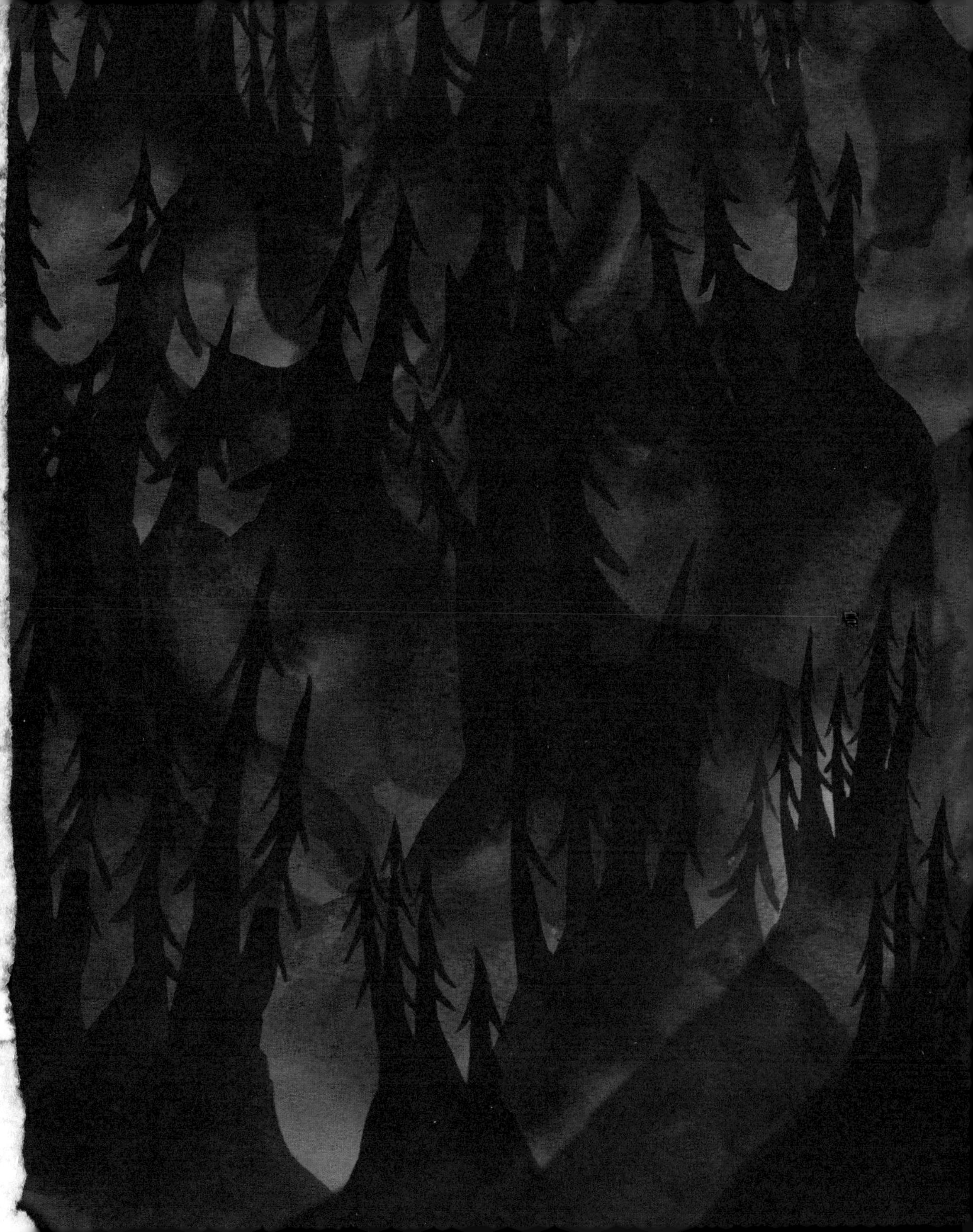

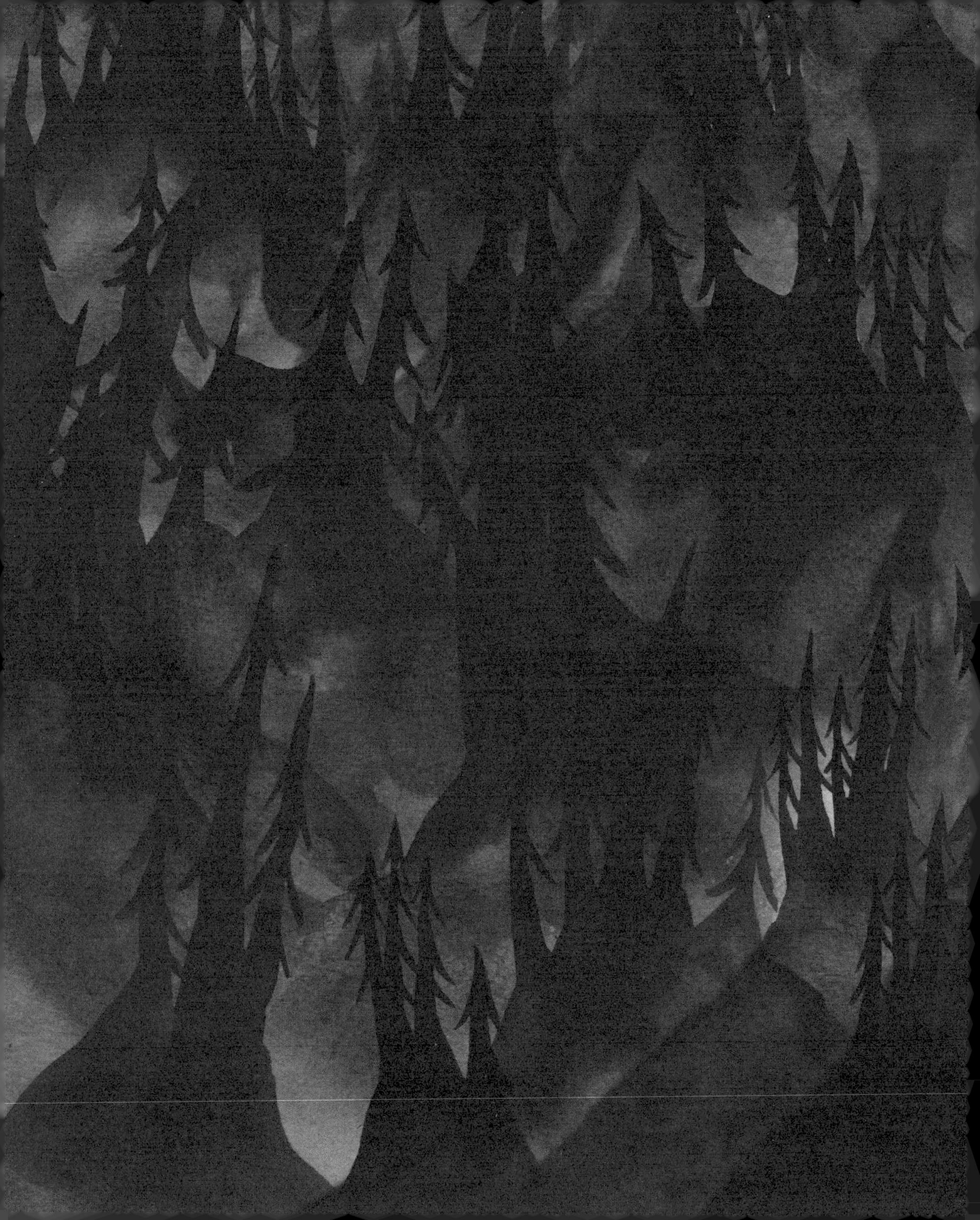